THE WIZARD AND THE WARRIOR

SERIES ONE

VIVIENNE LEE FRASER

The Wizard and The Warrior
Series One

Vivienne Lee Fraser
www.viviennelfraser.com.au

Formatting and cover design by KILA Designs
www.kiladesigns.com.au
Cover image: ©depositphotos.com

Illustrations provided by Anna Bazel
www.fiverr.com/annabazyl

Map illustrations: ©Jim Simpson

 Created with Vellum

Beginnings: For Harry Williamson, who always said I should be a writer. Finally, Granddad.

Trials: For Jim and Sam for supporting me as I follow my muse

Battle: For Heather.
This series would not have been the same without you.

Seamus' Map of Aria

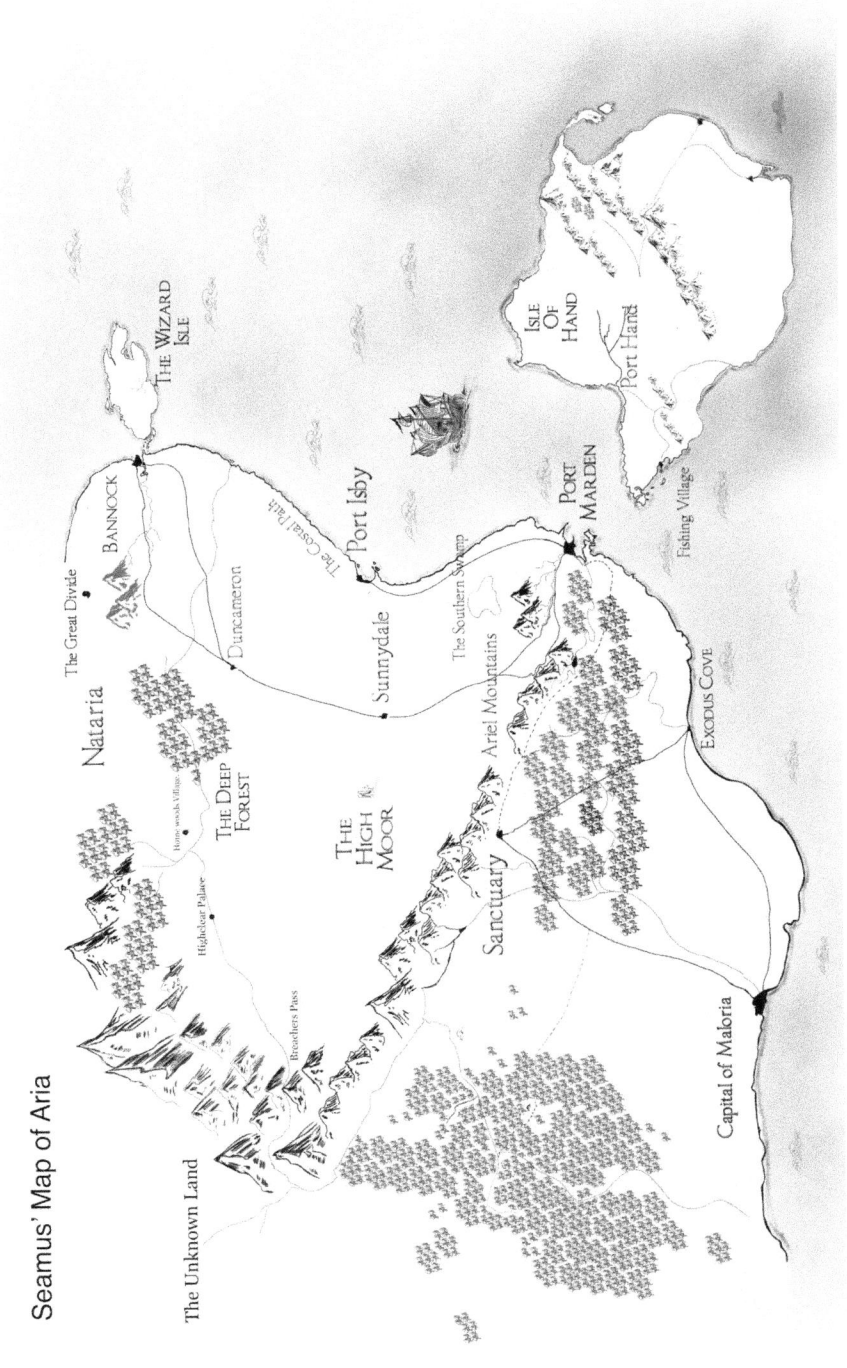

BEGINNINGS

THE WIZARD AND THE WARRIOR
Book One

PROLOGUE

*When the new power rises and the Wizard and Warrior meet,
old and new blood will combine to save one and all.*

The elderly man gazed into the fire, his eyes drawn to the ship he watched leaving Bannock Harbour. He continued to watch until it was well on its way out to sea, then rose slowly, rubbing his aching back. 'So it begins,' he thought to himself. 'And a good thing too, as there is none with the skill to follow me as High Seer. So none but I have the learning to pass on to the Wizard and Warrior that they will need to defeat their enemy. I just hope they make it here in good time.'

He looked up as his apprentice opened the door. 'Eon, please advise the Council I need to be heard.'

'The signs were correct? It is time?' his apprentice asked, his eyes gleaming with excitement.

'Yes,' the Seer said with less enthusiasm. 'It is time. Come now, we have much to do and little time in which to do it.'

CHAPTER I

ESCAPE

Aliah counted slowly to twenty before she slipped off the bed and tiptoed to the door, reluctantly passing the bread and cheese the boy had left on the wooden table in the middle of her cabin. Her hunger would have to wait. The ship rolled as she neared the door, throwing her off-balance and hip-first into the table. Biting back a yelp, she waited for another count of twenty to see if anyone heard the bang before trying the door handle.

The boy had been getting lazy and these last few days had not locked the door in between bringing her food and taking the empty plates away. Fortunately he had not changed his habits even though they were in port. Perhaps the excitement of being able to leave the ship after a six day at sea had prevented him from realising the opportunity he had presented to his captain's valuable cargo.

Looking down the corridor the only hint of other people on board was the hustle and bustle of sailors working on deck. She quickly grabbed her cloak off the sea chest and put it on. Then, without a moment to lose, continued her silent exit from the cabin that had been her prison for the last four days.

Hesitating for a moment at the end of the corridor, she peeked around the corner to see if there was anyone in the galley before darting quickly past the entrance. She halted again by some barrels near the foredeck stairs. Did she have a better chance of escape by heading up the stairs and hoping that everyone was too busy unloading cargo to notice her? Or was she best to try and stow away in the cargo hold and hope to be unloaded? No, too many sailors would be working there, she might be spotted. Best she take her chances in amongst the cargo on deck.

Aliah crept up the stairs on hands and knees. At the top, she stuck her head above the opening to get an idea of her next move. Ducking quickly back into the shadows at the side, she held her breath as footsteps approached hoping no one had seen her. The footsteps passed and she slowly let out her breath. Taking another look, she confirmed there was a stack of barrels about ten paces away, which were about another ten paces from the gangplank. If she could make it to the barrels she might be able to blend in with the sailors carrying cargo to the dock. She looked down at her blue gown and dainty white shoes; well, maybe if she weren't dressed for attending a state dinner.

Quickly, she crawled back down the stairs and moved aft towards the crew quarters. The ship boy was about her size. Surely she could find something to wear from his clothes. The sound of singing ahead halted her progress and she tried the door behind her.

Fortunately it was open and she slipped silently inside just before the cook passed on his way back to the galley. Luck must really have been on Aliah's side as she had stumbled into the first mate's cabin and he must have come in earlier to lay out clean clothes for shore leave. Even more fortunately he was not a tall man.

Aliah managed to change quickly, tucking in the rough shirt and rolling the trousers to fit.

There were no socks to wear with the boots under the bed so she tore her petticoats and wrapped bandages around her feet. With her make-do footwear the boots were considerably more snug on her feet. She then tucked her plait of blonde hair down the back collar of the shirt to ensure it would not get in the way, or immediately alert anyone to the fact she was a girl. She grabbed his spare cap and jammed it onto her head. Finally she laid out her own clothing on the bed as a bit of a joke, chuckling to herself as she imagined the first mate actually wearing her dress. 'Ready?' Taking a deep breath she moved to leave, then stopped.

There, behind the door, was her sword still in its scabbard with its blue jewelled hilt sticking out the top. She quickly grabbed one of her most prized possessions and tied its belt around her waist. Catching sight of her cloak she decided to take it with her, and swung it over her shoulders. Who knew what it might come in handy for?

Just as she was ready to leave, the door of the cabin began to open. Ducking in behind it she cursed herself for leaving her dress in full view on the bed. Well, it was too late now. The first mate started to enter the room then stopped. He must have spotted the dress.

'Sound the alarm!' The door crashed closed as he ran out yelling for all to hear. From her position behind the door she could hear footsteps run down the hall and then the door opened again. Aliah was crushed against the wall as the first mate showed his bed to someone.

'She's only gone and blimmin stolen my clothes,' He complained to whoever he was showing her dress to.

'Well, you had best tell the captain,' the cook told him. 'Rather you than me.' He chuckled as he walked away.

The door closed again and Aliah let her breath slowly out. What should she do now? They would surely be on the lookout for her. She had to try and get off the ship. She may not get another chance before they reached their final destination. Aliah made it back to the stairs with no further mishaps, and silently crawled back into position on the second to last tread listening to see what was now happening on deck.

'But, Captain, we should search for her.' Near the opening the first mate was pleading with the captain.

'The men are busy loading and unloading cargo, Jenkins. That is where our real money is. We are not being paid enough for delivering her to make me change that. Besides, she can only get off the ship down a gangplank and we can see it from here. We will have plenty of time to stop her if she tries anything, and if she doesn't, then we can search for her when we are back at sea.' Turning away, the captain watched as his men hauled another load of cargo up from the hold.

'And, Jenkins, get some men to move those.' He pointed to the barrels Aliah had been planning to use for cover. 'We need to have them off now. I don't care if the fellow what paid for them is not ready to pick them up yet. I want to be off at the turn of the tide regardless,' The captain blustered.

'But, sir, if we unload them onto the docks they are bound to go missing. And the chap what bought them, he only paid us half up front. Can't see him paying up what's owed if he can't get his wine,' argued the first mate.

'Well ... well send the boy to see if he can't find him hanging around the docks,' countered the captain.

'I've already sent him looking for that blasted girl, sir.'

'Of course you have. Can't wait 'til we be rid of her next stop. Well, you have your orders Jenkins, I've got to check in with the quartermaster. Only two candle-marks 'til the tide turns and I want to be off then. Cannot make any money waiting round here!'

The captain strode off, but the first mate did not move away. He stood there mumbling about stolen clothes and grumping about not getting shore leave. Holding her breath she willed him to go about his business. In spite of her mental urgings he stood there for what seemed like an eternity muttering under his breath until, finally, he shouted, 'Hey, boy,' and his boots made a clipping sound on the deck as he walked away to do as the captain bid.

Aliah popped her head above deck level. As luck would have it, apart from the first mate talking to the ship's boy there was no one else on deck. 'It's now or never.' She launched herself towards the gangplank, deciding at the last minute to throw away her previous plan and make a full break for it.

Running as fast as her legs would carry her Aliah dashed for the gangplank, and was halfway down it before an astonished Jenkins yelled, 'Hey. *Hey.* Stop her.'

Just at that very moment a sailor carrying a sack of flour over each shoulder stepped onto the gangplank right in front of Aliah. '*Stop,*' yelled the first mate. The sailor in front of Aliah hesitated for a moment, undecided whether to look after the flour sacks on his shoulder or grab her. Aliah took her chances, dodging left then right past the large man, and leaping the last few steps onto the wharf.

Another sailor following his fellow crewmate grabbed her cloak and threw her to the ground. He tried to hold her down, but Aliah kicked out hitting his arm and rolled away. Scrabbling to her feet she faced the two sailors. They walked towards her and as she backed away she looked for something, anything, to help her. There was nothing. She drew her sword and swung at the arm of the man on the right. He was not quick enough to move away and the blade made an angry red slash down his arm. He took a step back to examine the damage.

'You'll pay for that girl!' The other sailor growled as he went to grab her. But Aliah's training had been thorough and as he moved forward she swung back around and he had a matching slash on his arm. Using her momentum she dodged through the gap between the two injured men and began running towards the warehouses at the far end of the harbour.

Standing on her bed as they had entered the harbour, Aliah had seen the warehouses at the end of the docks through her cabin port-hole. Beyond that, she could just make out the buildings of the main town. It was towards those warehouses she headed now, hoping to make it to the town and get herself lost in the crowds. Weaving in and out of the hustle and bustle of the docks her captors struggled to catch up to her.

Three other ships were in port so there were plenty people

working and milling around. Some were loading and unloading cargo, others were chatting to sailors, and there were a few passengers with their luggage waiting to be helped aboard. With so many people it was easy for Aliah to evade her pursuers. Ducking behind one of the carts Aliah found herself face to face with the first mate.

'Thought you could get away from me you little sneak thief?' Snarling, he made a grab for her. There was no room for her to use her sword, so she went limp as he grabbed her cloak. Believing he had the best of her, Jenkins pulled the girl in close. That was what she had been waiting for. With all her force she brought her knee up and Jenkins fell to the ground, his face a picture of pain. But he still held her cloak.

A shout from behind told her they had been spotted, so she quickly undid the cloak and dropped it over the first mate. Sheathing her sword she took off again through the crowd. When she was sure her pursuers could no longer see her, she slipped into a doorway of a warehouse and hunkered down behind what looked like—and certainly smelt like—bales of wool. It was as good as any place to hide until her captors tired of looking and returned to the ship to catch the turning tide.

What seemed like more than two candle marks later she could still hear sailors questioning people whether they had seen a boy in too large clothing, might even look a bit girl-like? But no, no one had seen anyone of that description. If the docks were not so busy they could have found her hiding place by following the noise of her rumbling stomach. If only she had taken the time to eat some of the midday meal that she had so casually crept passed earlier. Aliah stayed in her uncomfortable hiding spot trying not to notice how hungry she was and wondered how long it would be before she could actually leave.

Finally the sun started to set, and the docks quietened down. She crept from her hiding place, needing to move before the warehouse was locked for the night. Surely the ship would have left port by now and she would be safe to leave. Poking her head around the door she drew back quickly. The ship was still there. And what's more they had posted lookouts on the deck. She would be an easy target walking along the deserted docks.

'Yep, they still be looking for you lad.' Aliah swung round, coming face to face with a white bearded man sitting on a stool in the shadows on the other side of the door. 'They must want you something bad to miss the tide like that.'

Dumbfounded, Aliah just stared at the man with her mouth open.

'Paid your parents for you did they? And you decided the sea not the life for you I s'pect.' The man nodded wisely at her, and Aliah nodded in return, too scared to actually tell him the truth. 'Ah, well.' The man rose from his stool, putting down the rope he was mending. 'You ain't the first and I s'pect you won't be the last, and it were many a long year ago I did the same.' He stretched out his back, then reached up and closed the warehouse door, leaving Aliah in the dark.

'Well, I best be heading home now. Out THE BACK DOOR, which is always open. Don't s'pose I would even notice if anyone went through it afore me.' He picked up his stool and rope, heading for the lean too beside the door.

Astonished, it was a moment before Aliah took the hint and headed to the opposite end of the warehouse. Fortunately most of the stock appeared to be wool bales as she caught her shins on them more than once in the half-light as she headed towards the back door. At the other end she began looking for a latch. Finally her fingers found what seemed to be a handle. She grabbed hold of it and pushed the door out, nearly falling into the alleyway.

A quick look both ways showed her it was deserted. Without further hesitation she ran up the paved street in the opposite direction from the docks hoping she was heading into the centre of town. It was glorious to be free after so long.

CHAPTER 2
PORT MARDEN

Seamus had been coming to Port Marden two or three times a year with his parents for as long as he could remember. So he knew the town well. Unfortunately that meant many people in the town knew him too. For this reason he kept to the back streets as he wandered, hoping he would not be easily recognised.

As he got closer to the markets the cobbled streets widened and the houses were larger and more prosperous looking. While many were still made of stone, some had second stories added made of wood and plaster. Many of these overhung the street, making a rough sort of cover.

Where the back streets had been quiet, those around the market were busier. The number of people increased. They were mainly traders carrying their unsold goods home to their waiting families. He kept his cap down but nodded to people he passed so as not to seem unfriendly. If people thought him unfriendly they may remember him later, then his parents might hear he was wandering around by himself.

As he walked his mind ticked over. He needed time to himself because he needed to think. He needed to decide what to do. And he needed to decide soon because things were getting out of control.

'Things.' He laughed to himself. 'Me. I am getting out of control.'

Seamus replayed the scene from that afternoon in his head. When his brother had barged into his room to hide, Seamus' fright sent the books on his desk flying towards the opening door. Fortunately he lunged to the desk before his brother realised it had not been possible for him to throw the books from where he had been standing. From his brother's reaction he had managed to hide what had really happened. This time.

For the last few years those incidents had been increasing. The type of incidents where he could move things without touching them. In some areas of the country, like the Southern Duchy, having magic would be cause for celebration. But on the Island of Hand magic was forbidden.

So far he had managed to hide his growing talent, but recently there were more incidents where things had just happened as he thought them into being. He knew he could not go on the way things were. But what to do?

If he stayed on Hand he would have to undergo the process of quietening. His magic would be silenced forever. He was not sure he really wanted that. Magic was part of him. If he decided not to be quietened then he needed to leave and find someone to help him control his magic. Of course he could go to the school in the Wizard Isles and be trained as a full wizard. But that would mean never returning to Hand. What he really would like to do is find someone who could help him control and hide his magic so he could return home and no one would be any the wiser.

His wandering had brought Seamus close to the market square. Many of the buildings he passed were shops. Most of them were closing as their owners headed upstairs to spend the evening with their families. He stopped on the edge of the square. Directly across from him was The West Way, the main road out of Port Marden. It joined the main road along the coast towards the capital, Bannock. If he decided to leave at this time on a market day he should be able to blend in with the farmers and landowners leaving town. That way he would not be noticed by the guards.

The stallholders in the market were packing up and chatting to passers-by, trying to make a last minute sale so as not to have to carry their goods home. He would have to be careful as he went through as many of them might remember having seen him with his parents and would remember his being there. Then they would be able to tell those who came looking for him later that he had passed through. He needed some sort of disguise to blend in.

He decided to take a turn round the square before returning home. Startled by shouting, he stopped by a half-dismantled stall. At the bread stall across the way it looked as though the baker had taken pity on a boy and was giving him one of the loaves he had not sold that day. But that was not the cause of the disturbance. On the other side of the square were three sailors running and yelling at the boy—or maybe the baker—it was hard to tell which.

The boy looked towards the sailors, his eyes were wide with fear. The baker held on to the loaf and turned towards the sailors, his mouth open as if he was about to speak.

Seamus moved fast. He focused on the crates in front of the sailors, pointing to where he wanted them to be. They wobbled, then toppled with a loud crash and scattered across their path. The unsuspecting sailors tripped over the crates and fell to the ground in a tangle of arms and legs.

Seamus ran into the square, grabbed the boy's hand, and the loaf of bread, and started running towards The West Way. Dodging around carts and people they came face to face with another group of sailors. Seamus spun around, but the first group had untangled themselves and where coming up behind them. Out of the corner of his eye the baker was talking to two guards and pointing their way. Looking around and spotting a gap, he dragged the boy between two stalls then down the alley behind.

'Wait,' the boy gasped. 'We'll be trapped.'

'Trust me.' Seamus pulled the boy through a line of washing, then ducked in behind a cart parked in the yard behind. He had often carried his mother's gowns here when she came to see the laundress.

Listening, he waited until the footsteps had passed, then pulled the boy back out the way they came and down the alley. As they entered the market, shouts from behind told him the sailors had spotted them and were back on the chase. He headed towards The West Way, running past the astonished guardsmen.

'Halt. Halt you there!'

Seamus had no intention of halting. He had used magic in public. He no longer had time to think about what to do in the future. The future was here, and it appeared it was time for him to leave Port Marden. He ran, pulling the boy behind him, until they joined the throng of farmers leaving the town after market day.

Now the best camouflage was to appear like everyone else, so he slowed down and took a quick look behind. He could not see anyone in pursuit. They ducked in behind a farmer's wagon for extra cover. Satisfied they now blended in with the crowd, he relaxed and started breathing normally.

'Can I have my hand back now?' A voice interrupted. 'I really am very hungry!'

Embarrassed, Seamus realised he still held the young boy's hand. He dropped it like a hot brick, and his face flushed red. Belatedly he also realised that he had no way of knowing whether the baker was indeed giving the bread to the boy, or taking it back because it had been stolen.

'Look here,' he said to the boy. 'I don't know what that was all about, but I hope you haven't gotten me into any trouble. All I want is to get out of town.'

The boy frowned at him, and hitched the long bundle he was carrying in a blanket a bit closer. 'I did not ask you to help me! Anyway, I don't know why, but those sailors have been following me all day. Something about a boy who skipped ship. All I want is to get out of here and head home as well. Now I don't know if I can because the sailors might make trouble for me, and if I don't get home my family will be worried.' Seamus could see the boy's blue eyes were brimming with tears in the shadow of his cap.

Seamus bit his lip, thinking. 'If you promise you are not in any trouble, then I might be able to help. Maybe it might be an idea to team up for a bit?' He took a breath and continued. 'The sailors are looking for a boy by himself, and not two boys together. Us leaving together may confuse them for a while.' In his head he added, *And it will help me at the same time because my parents will be asking questions about a boy leaving town by himself as well.*

The boy looked at him skeptically then his blue eyes twinkling almost in mischief. 'Fine. But can I have my bread back? I have not eaten since I broke fast this morning.'

Seamus had entirely forgotten that he still held the loaf and rather sheepishly handed it over. The boy broke it in half and offered half back to Seamus, who took it and began to eat. He did not know when he would get a chance to buy food on his journey so he had best eat when he could.

They shuffled with the crowd towards the gate in companionable silence, eating their bread and discretely looking about them for anyone following. Soon the traffic slowed almost to a halt as they approached the gate.

'What's going on?' Grumbled the woman behind them, trying to peer past. 'I have a long way to get home and these baskets aren't getting any lighter.'

'There's a hold-up at the gate,' came an answer from the farmer leading the cart in front of the boys. 'Guards must be checking for someone.'

Thinking fast Seamus shuffled so that he was beside the woman who had complained. She was carrying two baskets, one on top of the other, each half full of fruit or vegetables. Although her arms wrapped quite comfortably around the bottom basket, her head could barely see over the top.

'We sold all our goods today, perhaps we can help you carry

yours for a while?' He tried his best to look like he genuinely wanted to help.

'You'll not be tricking me that easily young man,' the woman snapped back, her head looking around the baskets to glare at Seamus and his companion.

'I meant only to offer help,' Seamus said. 'Anyway, we could not run away with a basket in this crowd even if that was what we had planned. We are squeezed way too tight, and the guards would spot us. We have had a good day and I only meant to share our good luck.'

The woman looked with questioning brown eyes at Seamus, obviously still not quite sure whether to trust him. 'I am not certain you are telling the whole truth, but I believe your kindness may be genuine. I am sorry I snapped young man, I am not used to people offering me help. If you and your brother would take the top basket for me, that would make my life a little easier.' Her back straightened a little as Seamus took the top basket down, then he and the boy took a handle each. Finally the other boy put his own strange bundle on top and they were ready to shuffle forward with the rest of the crowd.

Seamus adjusted his arm to account for the slightly shorter boy and they fell into pace beside the woman. She was dressed the same as many of the farm women at the market in a plain dark dress and her dark hair was caught beneath a scarf. At a guess Seamus thought she would be a little older than his own mother, and about the same height. Which meant she barely come up to his own shoulder. As she stared back at him, Seamus began talking as if he were with the woman.

'Your produce looks good,' he started. 'How come you are bringing so much home?'

'Mind your own business!' the woman snapped back. The look on Seamus' face must have softened her heart a little. 'Look, it's for reasons you best not know, young man. Carry that basket through the gates for me though, and you and your brother can fill your pocket's with whatever you can fit, for I do appreciate your help.'

'Thank you ma'am.' Seamus smiled his most charming smile. He only had the clothes on his back, his table knife, and a few coins in his pocket, so every penny he saved on food would make his journey a little easier.

'WHAT ARE YOUR NAMES?' the woman asked as they drew closer to the gate.

'Sean.' The boy who had saved her from the sailors said. 'Ali,' Aliah mumbled.

'I am Amelia.' The woman smiled for the first time. 'Now do you want to tell me why the guards up there are looking for one or both of you?' Amelia raised an eyebrow.

'Ah …' Sean started, but Aliah rushed in whispering, 'It's me ma'am. I skipped ship today and some sailors have been looking for me.' When the old man in the warehouse had believed she was a boy jumping ship she had decided then and there that he had provided her with a great cover story, one that people in a port town would understand. So she ignored Sean's shocked look as he reacted to the fact she had lied to him less than a half candle-mark ago.

She had already tried her story out when she sold her cloak, her necklace, and the first mate's clothes and boots for something more her size. The owner of the second hand clothes stall had been sympathetic, saying that his nephew had been in a similar situation once. He could not do enough to help her, and had even offered to buy her sword, assuming it was stolen like the rest of her goods.

'No, thank you,' Aliah said as gruffly as she could. 'I might need it on the road home.' The stall owner had agreed that might be wise, and even given her a length of old blanket to wrap it in until she was safely out of town. Her story gained her some sympathy with the towns folk, so she was a little surprised at Amelia's response.

'Sorry, lad, it is not that I doubt your story, but the duke's soldiers do not come out looking for a ship boy escaping his bond. You got a better tale young man? Best be quick as we are nearly at the gate.'

Aliah looked at Sean as he pulled his cap down lower on his head, almost hiding his nearly black eyes. She suddenly remembered the boxes that had moved seemingly by themselves in the market place. 'You,' she said. 'They're looking for you! Because of the boxes.'

'Boxes?' Amelia asked. 'What boxes?'

'He made the boxes move. In the marketplace,' Aliah blurted out and the boy on the other side of the basket turned red—not an easy task considering his dark complexion. It confirmed her suspicions, although he tried to pretend otherwise.

'Did not,' he mumbled.

Aliah did not know whether to be annoyed her escape might be thwarted by someone else running from the authorities, or relieved that the soldiers were not looking for her, or thankful he had saved her in the marketplace.

'Ah,' Amelia said. 'A budding wizard, that might be worth risking my hide for. Stay close by and let me do the talking. Then you can tell me the truth of the matter when we set camp for the night.'

Camp for the night? Aliah thought. *I shall be long gone by then.*

She and her companion fell in behind the woman as they approached the gate. 'Good evening to you,' Amelia said to the soldier who stopped them. 'We had little luck at the markets today and have a long walk home. Will you be keeping us much longer?'

'Have you seen a young man traveling by himself?' the soldier asked. 'He would be about the age of your eldest, but in better clothes and a might more refined looking?'

'Can't say that I have,' Amelia answered. 'Mind you, it would be hard to tell in this crowd!'

'That it is,' the soldier responded. 'But we have orders to look anyway. I will need your boys to stand aside until the captain gets here. He needs to check all boys around a certain age. You can go through and wait for them on the other side.'

Amelia relieved them of their basket as Aliah and the boy Sean were grabbed roughly by the arm and pulled to the right of the gate where two other boys awaited the captain's visit.

'Next waiting.' The guard had already moved on and their new friend Amelia had no choice but to go through the gate.

'We can't wait here,' Sean whispered to her. He was gnawing at his lip.

'I don't see we have any choice,' Aliah whispered back.

Sean suddenly stopped chewing his lip and half-smiled. 'I think I have an idea. Play along.'

'Oww,' he groaned and doubled over. 'Oww, me stomach. I think I need a privy. Fast.'

Aliah bent over him looking concerned, then looked at the guard. 'Oh, dear. We have had the flux in our village. Looks like Sean might have it. Is there a privy near?'

The two guards looked at each other. Reluctantly the younger one moved towards them. 'Right, come this way. There is a privy in the guardroom. But be quick.'

He took them under the gate arch and showed them the door to the guard's rooms. 'Go up one flight and the privy is on the first floor. Be quick.'

Sean groaned again. 'We will, sir. And thank you.' Aliah grabbed Sean's arm and helped him through the door. They headed up the stairs. On the first landing she went to take him through as the guard had directed, but he stopped her.

'Keep going up,' he whispered.

Up two more flights of steep stairs they came out along the top of the gates. Checking to make sure there were no guards up there watching, Sean started crawling along the ramparts to the left side gate tower. Aliah followed. He led her into the other tower, down the steps to the ground floor and into an empty room. The room had a barred door through the outer wall.

'Help me with this,' Seamus ordered, and began to lift the bar. He gestured to Aliah to open the door while he held the wooden bar up. He then had her squeeze through the opening. When she was done he propped the bar with the haft of a spear that was beside the door, before lying down on the floor and wiggling through the small opening. Once on the other side, Seamus jolted the spear haft out of place and the bar fell down, closing the door with a bang.

'How did you know about that?' she asked Sean in amazement.

'My cousin and I have used it a couple of times. Although I don't remember it being such a tight squeeze,' he told her.

'Come on,' she said, urging him forward towards the stream of people on the main road. 'We need to be well clear of here when they realise we are not coming back from the guard room.'

Watching the guards to make sure they were not spotted, Aliah and Sean joined the farmers leaving Port Marden for the night.

'Thought I might find you out here.'

Aliah jumped, startled to find Amelia standing behind them. 'But how ...?' Aliah frowned at the woman.

Amelia moved them through the crowd to the side of the road and she put down the baskets. Aliah realised the one she had been carrying still had her sword on top. It was a good thing Amelia had found them, as Aliah would not have liked to leave that behind.

'Do not worry. I will not tell them how you escaped. And I am as good as my word,' Amelia said to them. 'You can fill your pockets with fruit and vegetables and be on your way. But if you are smart you will help me with my baskets a little longer and we can plan your next moves. For as sure as I am standing here neither of you are prepared to journey far from here, and that is certainly what both of you intend to do.'

Aliah could tell Sean was considering the proposal, and she took some time to think it through herself. Given that it was nearly dark she really had nothing to lose by spending the night with these strangers, and it may turn out to her benefit.

'What exactly are you suggesting?' Sean asked.

'My place is on the edge of the Tangled Woods, which is a little under a half days walk from here. When I travel to market I leave some food in a spot not far off so I can stop for the night if it gets too late for traveling. If you carry my baskets that far, I can make you supper and we can sleep the night round a fire.'

'But I want to go north,' Aliah protested, thinking maybe staying with the rather strange woman was not such a good idea after all. 'The Tangled Woods are west of here, I would lose valuable time.'

'You will not be able to travel much farther tonight and I would not mind betting that your sailor friends know you will be heading north. They will be expecting you to go home. If you wait the night through and set off tomorrow you might actually be doing yourself a favour. If you were prepared to wait a day or two more I have no doubt your journey would be even safer.' Amelia grinned at her, her warm brown eyes crinkling at the corners.

Aliah pondered this for a moment, then nodded in agreement. There was a lot of sense in Amelia's words. If she took tonight to get some warm food in her stomach, she might just avoid her pursuers and start out fresh in the morning.

'And what about you young man?' Amelia looked at Sean.

'I might as well be on my way,' he answered curtly.

'I see you have not thought this through either.' Amelia stared intently at Sean. 'Your pursuers will know you are headed for the Wizard Isles and on the road north. Once they do not find you at the gate, they will head along the Great North Road looking for you. They will have horses and you will be walking. You will be easily found.

'Add to that the fact that you are not prepared for any sort of journey. No food. No bedroll. No idea, really. It may be best for you that those looking for you find you.'

'Why should you care?' Sean blurted, clearly not happy about the flaws in his plan being pointed out by a woman he had just met.

Amelia laughed. 'Fair question, and I have to say I am asking myself that very thing. Normally I would not bother, but it has been a while since anyone showed me any kindness, even if it was for their own ends. So I find I am quite well disposed towards the both of you at the moment.

'Maybe I am also thinking I may be able to talk you out of the roads you are following. I sense your journeys will bring you great troubles, and I would not wish those troubles on anyone, especially two as unprepared for travel as the both of you.

'However, the offer is not good for long as I am not generally a woman to take to strangers. Either you come with me now, or you don't. I won't press you either way.' Amelia picked up her basket, making it clear she wanted to be on her way.

Aliah did not need any more encouragement. She would like a good nights sleep and some warm food before starting her journey home. Picking up the handle of her basket she looked at Sean. He seemed to be having a harder time deciding what to do. Finally he bent down and grabbed the handle on his side and they followed Amelia on the path towards the Tangled Woods.

SEAMUS WALKED behind the strange woman in silence. He was still not sure he had made the right decision and, if he admitted it to himself, he was a little annoyed at Amelia for pointing out how ill prepared he was for his journey. His departure had been a last minute decision. So not only did he not have the basics he needed to survive travelling, he also had no real plan of where he was going.

He knew he was nowhere near as prepared as he needed to be, but he did not need anyone pointing that out to him. And on top of it all, that boy, Ali, had lied to him about who he was, and now he was stuck traveling with him. It was definitely not how he would have planned to leave home. Still, he was happy to let people think he was heading towards the Wizard Isles. Maybe he would go there. Now he had shown he had magic in public it was not like he would be able to go home again.

By the time Amelia reached the copse of trees where she had left her pack, the last of the days light was almost gone and the air was getting decidedly chilly. Seamus was feeling more than a little tired and grumpy, and really annoyed that he had lost his home because he tried to help a boy who ended up being a liar.

'Put the baskets down there boys, then rummage around and see what wood you can find for a fire. Looks like it will be a might cold tonight.' Amelia busied herself with pulling what she needed for an evening meal out of the pack she had stowed behind a tree.

Sean and Ali put their basket down beside Amelia's and they both went into the copse to find wood before it got too dark to see. By the time they had finished, Amelia had started a small fire and set up a cooking billy. She cut up some of the vegetables from her basket into it, and poured a little water from a water skin she retrieved from her pack. She used the last of the water then handed it to Seamus.

'Just on the other side of the copse is a stream, we will be needing more water.'

Seamus stopped himself from asking why he had to do it, appreciating it might seem odd for him to expect others to do the menial work. Taking the water skin, he hurried back into the copse and quickly found the stream. By the time he headed back to the fire it was almost pitch black and he was grateful for the light to guide him.

'Thank you young man.' Amelia took the water skin, poured some in the pot, and drank some from the skin. She then passed it to Ali, who passed it back to him so they could all drink something after their walk.

'The evening meal should be a few minutes more. Why don't you make yourself comfortable?'

Seamus sat down beside Ali. It seemed his task had been to find a suitable log for a back rest, which Seamus appreciated as he leaned back and relaxed, letting some of the tension go from his shoulders.

He took off his cap, placing it on the log beside him, then ran his hand through his unruly black hair. Closing his eyes while he warmed up and waited for dinner the rest of his grumpy mood disappeared. He was even feeling a little less grumpy with the boy Ali. After all, the boy had not actually asked for his help. It could not be easy being sold to work on a ship by your family.

He wondered what his family would be doing now. Had they returned to the Isle of Hand and left the search for him up to the soldiers? Or had they stayed in their house in Port Marden? Had they heard about him using magic? Were they disappointed? He had not realised he dozed off until he felt Ali's hand shaking him awake.

The stew of grains and vegetables Amelia had made was nourishing and surprisingly tasty as she had added some herbs from a pouch in her bag. Once they had eaten their fill she cleaned the billy out while Ali cleaned their plates. Amelia then started to brew a tea for them from a collection of herbs from yet another pouch she had stowed.

It seems like she is well prepared, Seamus thought to himself.

'Now my boys, time for some planning before you both fall asleep.' She spoke as she threw some herbs into the boiling water, took the billy off the fire, and left the tea to steep.

'Let's start with you my young wizard. You are headed for the Wizard Isles to see if they will train you, are you not?' Amelia asked. Seamus nodded, as it seemed it was now his plan. 'So you have your family's permission in writing?'

Seamus sat up, no longer sleepy. 'No, what do you mean?'

'You do know they will not take a wizard to train without the family's permission, don't you? They do not want trouble, and so to prevent any misunderstandings they make sure the family agrees to training before they take a boy on.'

Seamus had not known that. Training to be a wizard was not something very much discussed in his family. He thought about how that changed what he was doing, and concluded it didn't. If the wizards would not take him then he would find someone else to teach him. Besides, he rather suspected that, given who he was, the wizards would welcome him with open arms.

'My family are of the old blood,' he told Amelia. 'To them a person able to wield magic is an abomination. They will have me quietened if I stay, and if I do not agree they will kill me. Surely the wizards will take pity on me and agree to train me without my parent's consent?' He felt like he was almost pleading with Amelia to believe him.

Amelia's face had gone very still and he could not read what she was thinking. 'You are old enough to have your marque?' she asked almost in a whisper. Seamus pulled up his sleeve and showed her the tattoo on the inside of his right wrist all the old blood received on their thirteenth birthday to show their family affiliations. In two years, when he turned eighteen, it would have been altered to show his affiliation to his betrothed's family. He heard Amelia's quick intake of breath as she gazed at the marque.

'You walk a dangerous path Seamus of the Hand.'

Seamus froze. How had she known? She could not only read first blood marques, she also knew who he was!

'I don't know what you are talking about. I am Sean,' Seamus blustered.

Ali was looking at Amelia and Seamus, and then back again, clearly confused.

'Seamus, I know who you are, and your family history. I know as you do there are very few families of the old blood with the kind of magic you possess. Your family became entwined with magic— among other things—some generations back when your great-great-grandfather was married to the king of Nataria's granddaughter as part of a peace accord.

'Unknown to the old blood, the king's daughter was a witch. It was the final insult from the king to his new subjects. Ever since then, one child each generation has borne the stigmatism of magic. If it was a girl child, they had a choice. They could leave and live life quietly out of the family and bare no children, or be quietened. If a boy, they would have the magic removed by the rather brutal practice of quietening, or they would be put to death. In this way they had hoped to cleanse the family of the taint of magic blood. But still in each generation one child with magic has been born.

'And you are right that the wizards would more than welcome one of the old blood wishing to develop their magic skills, as they would be the first of their kind at the school. They have been waiting years for such a child to show at their doors. But this would be quite a blow to your family. Can you do that to your father? If you cannot bear to be without magic why not just leave and live a quiet life somewhere?'

All Seamus heard from Amelia was that the wizards would likely take him and his plan would not be thwarted. 'I will do as I planned,' he asserted, not thinking twice about how Amelia had known so much of old blood history. He settled back down thinking his time for questioning was over.

A frowning Amelia sighed. 'I wish you would reconsider, but I can see your mind is made up. If you insist on this journey then it is my duty to help you as best I can. I would suggest you come home with me tomorrow and we make sure you are kitted out for the long road you must travel.'

Seamus, used to having people organise things for him as the son of a duke, did not think to question why Amelia felt she had a duty to help him. However he thanked her for her offer and agreed to head home with her tomorrow. If he were better prepared for travelling he might actually have a chance of getting to the Wizard Isles. His ordeal over, he was pleased attention would now be focused on Ali. What would Amelia make of him?

ALIAH SQUIRMED UNCOMFORTABLY as attention moved to her. Amelia's face was kind but her deep brown eyes were strangely knowing. Would Aliah's story hold up under her scrutiny? She hoped so, as telling the truth might put all of them in danger and she did not want to endanger anyone who tried to help her.

'So, young man, you are heading back home? Which way is that?' Amelia asked.

An easy question, but Aliah could not afford to let down her guard. 'My family have a place not far from Bannock Town.' Well, it was close to the truth, 'So I will be heading north as well.'

'Mmm,' Amelia pondered, rubbing the side of her face as she thought. 'I suppose you have considered the fact that your parents let you go with the sailors, for the money they gained or for other reasons. They may not be as welcoming as you might be expecting when you return home.'

Aliah had not actually considered that. She had felt so sure the right thing to do was find her father and let him know she was all right, and had totally wiped from her mind the circumstances that led to her being on the ship in the first place.

Without knowing what had led to her adventure, Amelia had hit the nail right on the head. If she went home her father would be in serious trouble. Her best bet was to stay away from him and stay anonymous until she knew what had gone on in her absence. However, that did not prevent her from heading towards home, finding out what was going on, and making sure her family were all right.

'I understand what you are saying, and you might well be right.' Aliah looked bleakly at Amelia. 'But I need to at least try to get home and make sure everything is as it should be there. So I will be heading north tomorrow.'

Amelia stared at her for what seemed like an age before turning her attention to pouring the tea and passing round the mugs. Aliah wondered if Amelia always travelled with three bowls and cups, or if she had maybe had a strange feeling that she might need them on this journey.

With Amelia still staring at her, Aliah felt the need to tell her a little more of why her journey was so important.

'It is not just seeing my family that I need to return home for. While I was on board the ship I heard some things that were very worrying. The ship was sailing for Carsten, they had some important cargo for their king. The cargo was going to help the king stir up a war against Aria. I have to go north and warn our king.' Aliah stared Amelia directly in the eye, willing her to understand how important it was that she return home.

Amelia's eyes crinkled at the corners. 'And you will be able to talk to the king about this?'

'My family have served in Bannock Castle for generations. I feel I might have a chance of being listened to. Regardless, I have to try.'

'How very noble of you.' Amelia paused and continued to look at Aliah, then shook her head. 'I am not sure we have the full truth of you yet, young Ali, but I sense that you are at the centre of something not of your making and you will need all the help you can get before this thing is done. You had best come along with us tomorrow and we will see what we can do to kit you out as well. You will need more than that sword you are carrying to make your way that far north.'

A strange sense of dread fell over Aliah, almost as if she was picking up some of what the woman could sense. She also noticed that Sean's—no, Seamus'—interest had heightened at the mention of a sword and he looked at her a little differently, maybe with a little less superiority. Almost as if he were thinking a boy with a sword may not be quite his social equal, but he might not be far off it.

If only he knew. She smiled to herself, but then shook it off. *He can't know. No one can. It would be too dangerous.*

'Now you two clean up the plates and we'll get some sleep. I want to be off early tomorrow.' Amelia passed her cup to Aliah, and began unrolling her travel swag.

Although Aliah was warm enough with the blanket that had been around her sword she spent a restless night. It was not only that she was not used to sleeping on the ground, she also could not help thinking about her family. Had she caused them any harm by escaping her shipboard captors? How soon would they know she had escaped? It seemed as though she had just fallen asleep when Seamus was waking her with a cup of tea and some bread to break her fast. She was still half asleep when Amelia had them pack up camp and start on their journey to her home on the edge of the Tangled Wood.

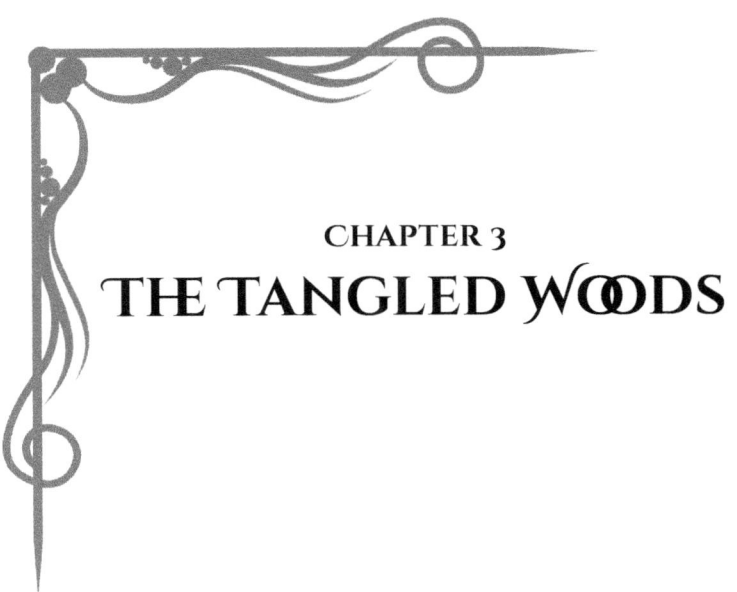

CHAPTER 3
THE TANGLED WOODS

A liah's feet hurt. Her arms hurt. Her back hurt. It was not even noon and her body was giving up. If this was how the short walk to the Tangled Woods affected her, how would she ever make it over the mountains? Let alone all the way back to Bannock? Spending a six-days on the boat had definitely left her out of condition.

Amelia had stopped them briefly for a water break and snack of some kind of oat and seed cakes not that long ago, saying that should keep them going until they reached her house. Once there, she would prepare a main meal for them all. Aliah's body had protested when they started out again and had been complaining ever since. As they walked through the wood she caught occasional glimpses of the rolling hills on the other side, but they never seemed to get any closer. Neither Amelia nor Seamus were inclined to talk as they walked, which left Aliah alone with her own thoughts.

She spent most of the morning trying to remember what she could about the Isle of Hand where Seamus must come from. If she remembered her history lessons correctly the island was mostly inhabited by what were now called the old blood, who had fled there as a result of the Natari Invasion. Their King had finally asked what the price for peace was and the Natari King leading the invasion had agreed terms with him.

It was at that time the Southern Duchy was created, which included The Isle of Hand and Port Marden. As a show of good faith, the Natari Emperor had married his granddaughter to the King—now Duke—of Hand's eldest son. Since that time, the Duke of Hand and his people had reluctantly paid homage to whoever ruled Aria.

As time progressed the new nation of Aria had pulled away from the constraints of the Natari Emperor, and the Archduke had become King in his own right. The king was supported by the five dukes, who were meant to be his closest advisors. In reality only four of the five dukes attended Court, or sent their representatives. The Southern Duchy of Hand had preferred to keep to itself.

She also remembered vaguely the old blood were formed into family units and affiliations and that the family of the Hand was the ruling clan. From the conversation last night, Aliah assumed Seamus was a son of the Duke of Hand, who was still known as King by his own people. Aliah tried to assess whether or not that made a difference to how she viewed Seamus. If she were honest, it did not really change anything. She was grateful he had saved her at the markets, and sad that he had to leave his family, but she had known him such a short time it did not really matter who he was. Although it did explain his arrogance, and the name Seamus suited him a little better than Sean had.

After their short break she had tried to fathom out Amelia, which was a little harder. Although she tried to act like a traditional farmer's wife, there was something about her that was a little different. She seemed to "know" or "feel" a lot about them, and it was odd she had come prepared on her journey to meet visitors with extra plates and mugs in her pack. Aliah was sure she also knew rather more about Seamus than she was letting on.

Bored with walking and her own thoughts Aliah decided maybe it was time to find out a little more about the person who seemed so keen to help them. Tucking a stray hair behind her ear, she shuffled up so she could walk beside Amelia, careful not to leave the track as it was now closely bordered by trees and under growth, and she did not want to twist an ankle.

'Ah. Amelia,' she started. 'I was wondering how you knew to bring three sets of eating utensils with you to market?'

Amelia raised an eyebrow. 'Were you just? You are the observant one, aren't you? Perhaps I just had an inkling I may have a need of them if I went to this market.'

'Do you not go to every market?' Aliah fished for more information.

'No, I do not. I only go if I have a need for something, or if I feel I need to go there.'

'So, this market trip was for a feeling?' Aliah prompted.

Amelia laughed. 'You are a sharp one, aren't you! Yes, I had a feeling. I often get them when someone needs to see me. Mostly they know to find me in the market as it is a long way to come out to the Tangled Woods. But this time there was no one there, so I am thinking maybe the feeling was for meeting the two of you. There you go, young one, that is enough for you to be getting on with? We are here and we need to get sorted for the evening.'

Without Aliah noticing they had arrived at a paved path leading to a cottage set behind a late-flowering herb garden. The cottage was thatched roofed, as she expected, but it was much larger than she had imagined the cottage of a market gardener to be. It was two storied, and had what looked like a stable behind although she could see no horse, and a paddock beside with a couple of sheep and a cow. On the far side there was a large garden patch, with fruit trees in behind, which ran nearly to the edge of the woods. In between the garden and the house was a water well and a chopping block. It was not the average cottage of a woman who was subsisting on what she grew and sold at market.

'Quit gawking! We have plenty to do before we eat our meal. There is a barn behind the house—beside the stable there—you can put both the baskets in it. I need to go and find Molly.' Amelia put her basket down and headed behind the stables towards the woods, alternating between whistling and calling out, 'Molly!'

Seamus and Aliah looked at each other, then Seamus took the handle from her. 'You take that one.' He pointed to Amelia's basket then took off with the one they had been carrying, her sword still perched on the top. Frowning, she picked up the other basket and followed. By the time she had reached the shed, Seamus had stowed his basket and had her sword out of its sheath, trying a few moves with it.

'Excuse me,' Aliah said in her iciest voice. 'Here I was thinking you were the son of a duke, not a common thief. I will have my sword back.'

'This is no mere sword. It is a work of art and belongs to nobility.' Seamus held the sword up showing its gleaming metal with scroll-work up the shaft and the jewel in the handle. On the blade were the runes her father's blacksmith had carved into it to make the blade strong. 'No common boy sold to work on a ship could have come by a sword like this honestly.' He hefted the sword and tried a couple of moves, getting the balance of it.

Furious, Aliah looked around. There was an old broom handle beside her. She grabbed it, felt its weight, and adjusted her stance. Then with three swipes of the broom, Seamus was on the floor rubbing his arm, the sword no longer in his grasp. Aliah picked up her sword and put it back in its leather scabbard. She placed the broom where she had found it.

'Some people have swords because they deserve them, others because they are given them.' Head held high she stalked out of the shed.

SEAMUS STOOD, dusting himself off. How had Ali done that? So he wasn't the best swordsman this side of the dividing mountains but he could handle himself if he had to. Ali had moved so fast he had been off his feet before he even knew he was going to be hit. He finished stowing his basket and left the shed nearly stumbling into a large black horse that was standing by the door. 'Not my day,' he muttered.

Amelia emerged from behind the barn. 'Oh good, you've found Molly. Can you take her to the stable and give her some fresh hay and a feed of grain?'

'You have a horse?' Seamus asked, quizzically. 'Why did you not ride her to market?'

'I just had a feeling that this time she would not be needed. Now off you go. I have to go and get started on the meal.' Amelia headed towards the house where she seemed intent on rounding up Ali, who was practising his sword work in the clear area in front of the house. Seamus paused long enough to see that Ali was putting away the sword in preparation for some task Amelia had given him.

Having stabled Molly, Seamus headed to the well. He drew a bucket of water and washed his face and hands as best he could before entering the cottage. The door opened into a single kitchen and living area. It was dominated by a large wooden table. On the left he could see two doors leading to other rooms, and some stairs that led to a loft room above. At the table Amelia took some bread dough out of a bowl and began kneading it. Ali followed him in with an armful of wood, which he deposited in the basket beside the open fire. He used one of the smaller logs to stir the banked fire before placing it, and a couple of others, on the now bright embers.

'Thank you, Ali, that will be perfect. The bread dough is nearly ready. Would you mind getting some vegetables from the baskets you put in the barn? We will need them for the stew. And you, Seamus, could get me the dried deer meat from the store room, over there on the left.' Amelia pointed vaguely then carried on, absorbed in her task.

Ali brushed passed Seamus without saying a word, and Seamus headed for the storeroom. He was surprised the room was nearly as large as the cook's pantry in his father's house, and nearly as well stocked. Whoever this woman was, she was not a peasant farmer. He found the dried deer meet hanging from a hook, and shut the door behind him before taking it over to the table. A few minutes later Ali came in with a basket of vegetables and took them over to a large bowl on the bench under the window. He poured water out of a jug and began cleaning off the dirt.

He may have the sword of a noble, but he cleans vegetables like a peasant boy. Seamus slumped down on the bench seat by the table.

'You are not finished yet, young man,' Amelia scolded. 'There are no free rides in this house. You can get yourself up those stairs. In the trunk under the window there should be bedding enough for you to make up two of the beds. Well, off you go then.'

Amelia did not notice Ali's look of dismay as she mentioned them sharing a room. *Well, if he is going to hold a grudge.* Seamus stomped up the stairs. *Two can play at that game!*

ALIAH'S HEART almost stopped when Amelia asked Seamus to make up two beds in the same room. How could she hide the fact she was a girl when they were sleeping in close quarters? Her hair alone would give it away. Even now she still had her cap on and collar up so no one could see her plait.

'It seems to me you have two choices, Ali.' Amelia's voice startled her. 'We can go into my room and cut your hair short before Seamus comes down and he will be none the wiser. Or you can let him know you are a girl. It won't make much difference to him, either way. But you must do what you feel comfortable with.'

'How ...? How did you know?' The surprise nearly caused her to slice her hand instead of the carrot she was holding, meaning she had to keep her eyes on the vegetables in front of her rather than turning around to face Amelia.

'Anyone with eyes can see your shirt is much too bulky for your size. Either you have a deformity, or that is long hair you have tucked in the back.'

'Oh.' Aliah was crestfallen. It would be much more difficult traveling if people knew she was female. People would think it was odd a girl being away from home without a family member. No parent would let their girl child wander the land unattended, no matter how poor they were.

'It does not matter to me whether you be a boy or girl, but if you wish to keep your hair you might as well be yourself here. We can devise something better to manage hiding who you are while you travel.' Aliah looked up saw Amelia was smiling encouragingly at her.

Somewhat relieved, Aliah took off her cap and jacket, and pulled her long blonde braid out from inside the shirt. It was somewhat of a relief not to have it tucked in there.

'Now we have that sorted, can you please cut the vegetables and meat and put them into that pot so we can begin making a stew for supper.'

Seamus was not the best at bed making as he was used to having servants do it for him. As his circumstances were somewhat altered he really should give this bed-making a good go, especially as this may not be the last time he had to do it. He doubted trainee wizards had servants.

He found sheets and blankets in the chest under the window as Amelia had said. There were three beds in the room, arranged against the walls. He made up the one closest to the chimney and put his jacket on it. At least he would be warm tonight. He then made up the bed furthest away by the opening of the stairs for Ali. If he wanted to be standoffish, Seamus would certainly help him. Job done, he climbed back down stairs.

Amelia was putting two bread tins in an alcove by the fire, and at the table Ali was chopping meat and putting it in a pot. Ali reached to take some vegetables off the workbench and Seamus' eyes widened in astonishment. Ali had a long plait of hair down his back.

It took a moment, then it hit him. Ali was a GIRL. Not only had she fooled him for nearly two days, SHE had knocked him off his feet as if he were no bigger than his younger brother. He was just about to say something when Amelia caught his eye. She shook her head and looked at Ali. The message was clear. Now was not the time to talk about this.

'If you have finished the beds you can go out and start work on the woodpile. You will find an axe inside the barn. We will call you when dinner is ready.' Amelia covered the pot for the stew and put it on the rack over the fire.

The sun was just about setting when Amelia finally called him in to dinner. He had managed to double the size of the woodpile before cleaning the axe and putting it back. He had to admit there was something satisfying in chopping wood. Maybe it was the manual labour, or maybe it was because he could put his worries to the back of his mind and do something that would actually benefit himself and others. Whatever it was, he was ready for a big meal.

He cleaned up in the small room off the pantry and sat down at the table just as Amelia placed three bowls of a thick meaty stew down beside three sets of cutlery. To accompany the meal was a fresh loaf of bread, rich creamy butter, and a white cheese. Amelia took the place at the head of the table and Ali sat down opposite him, still avoiding his eyes. Once they were seated, Amelia said a blessing to the goddess for their bounty and they all began to eat.

As Seamus stopped to butter some bread, Amelia put down her fork and looked at the two young people.

'Well we can all see now that Ali—'

'Aliah,' Ali interrupted.

'Aliah, is a girl. That is enough on that matter unless Aliah wants to add anything?'

Aliah shook her head.

'All right, then. I know we are all tired, but we need to make some plans. Summer has drawn to a close, and it looks like we will not have much of a fall before the snows this year, so you two cannot be dilly dallying for too long if you wish to head to Bannock before those on your tails catch you up. Agreed?'

Seamus lifted his head and nodded. He noticed Aliah continued to eat and said nothing. Amelia obviously took her silence as agreement as she continued to speak.

'Right then. Next step, as you are both heading the same way I propose that you travel together.' Anticipating both their objections she held up her hand and continued before they could interrupt her.

'Hear me out here. It is for both your benefits I am proposing this. Seamus, your family is looking for a boy traveling by himself, not a young man escorting his sister. And Aliah, you would only be able to keep up your appearance as a boy for so long, and you cannot travel by yourself as a girl. If you travel as siblings and have a purpose— taking Aliah to meet her intended husband—then you have a disguise that suits you both and puts your pursuers off your scent.'

Seamus looked up at Amelia in surprise, then turned to Aliah. She seemed to be seriously considering Amelia's words. Maybe it was a sensible thing to do? Aliah voiced her agreement and he reluctantly also agreed.

'Now that is settled, I propose we spend a six-day getting together the things you will need for your journey, and on the new first-day you shall set out. That does not give us much time to dry food and make the things you need, but any longer and you may not make it through the Ariel Mountains before the first snow.'

Again Seamus and Aliah looked at each other, both frowning a little. 'A whole six-day?' Seamus asked, facing Amelia and voicing both their concerns.

'It is a long journey you are undertaking, children, and most of it will be in the cold of fall, and maybe even in an early winter. You'll be needing warm clothing and plenty of dried food. And that will have to be gathered and made as I do not have that sort of stock here, nor do I have enough coin to provide for both of you. What we can do is make the most of the bounty here and that will take time.'

'I have a little money,' Seamus admitted, taking his coin purse from his pocket.

'And I also have a little. And we can work for food and coin on our journey.' Aliah broke in.

'That coin would not be nearly enough to see you to Bannock, Seamus. And, Aliah, yes you could work,' Amelia confirmed. 'But while that would save you time now it would add time onto your journey and you would definitely be traveling through winter. And you need to consider how it will look, a young girl heading off to a wedding not fully provisioned by her family. Your cover would be full of holes, ones that those following you would definitely see through.'

Seamus listened as Amelia spoke, respecting good planning when he heard it. He told her he thought it would work. He had been on many a hunting party and knew that preparation was essential for a good outcome. Aliah knew the battle was lost and concentrated on finishing her meal.

With the big decisions all made, they finished their dinner and cleaned up in silence. Amelia put the kettle on to make a soothing tea, which both Aliah and Seamus declined, their weary bodies needing a good night's sleep.

As they climbed the stairs Seamus cringed with embarrassment at Aliah's dismay when she discovered the bed he had made for her. Wishing to make amends he remembered there had been more blankets in the chest, and some old sheets cut into lengths of rag for cleaning. He made rope from some of the rags, and strung it up in the rafters between the beds and hung a blanket over top.

'It might make you feel more comfortable,' he smiled sheepishly at Aliah, and to his surprise she beamed a smile back.

'Thank you,' she said. 'That's the nicest thing anyone has done for me in a while.' Seamus ducked his head so she would not see the blush rising from below his collar.

The bed was warm and comfortable, especially after sleeping on the ground the night before. It was not long before Aliah's rhythmic breathing filled the room, and soon Seamus was sleeping the deep sleep of the exhausted.

CHAPTER 4
DAWN TIL DUSK

For the next two days Amelia worked her two young guests from dawn til dusk, and beyond. Realising Seamus was more proficient with the bow than a sword, Amelia sent him into the woods to hunt small animals. Aliah and Amelia then prepared the animals to dry in the smokehouse at the back of the barn. By the end of the second day the smokehouse was full of meat.

The following day Amelia started them on picking the last of the fruit from her trees and the last of the berries from the bushes in the woods. They also pulled the last of the herbs and vegetables from her garden. These were laid out on drying racks in the barn ready to pack. Day four was left for going through Amelia's own winter stores to see what she could spare for their journey. They packaged up flour, grains and pulses, and two thick yellow cheeses to add to their travel packs.

Amelia showed them how to cook their dried stores into a tasty meal in one of the billy pots she had included with their utensils. She also made up for them a small store of dried leaves for various tisanes to help with common ailments, and a larger portion of tea leaves for a restorative evening drink. There were also some herbs for flavouring their meals. With the food mostly sorted, the morning of day five, Amelia took them out to the barn. Standing at the bottom of the loft stairs she pointed upwards.

'Up there you will find trunks filled with all the things I have needed over the years. If I remember there should be a large traveling pack and a slightly smaller one that I have used for various journeys. Both have seen better days, but they should do this one last trip.'

'There should also be a bedroll or two, old water skins, and wet weather gear. Have a look through and see what is still usable. Also, Seamus, you may find a set of throwing knives in one of the trunks. If you are anything like the rest of your family, knives and bows will be your weapons of choice. I have chores to do, let me know if you need anything.' With that she departed, leaving them to their own devices.

It was dirty, dusty work but by the time they had gone through the first two trunks they had found travel packs and bedrolls. They took these downstairs and beat the dust from them, then hung them to air over a line they strung between the stable and the barn. They also found four water skins that would likely see them through the journey.

The third trunk was the largest, and they had left it until last. It proved to be the most interesting. On the top was the set of knives Amelia had mentioned to Seamus, and these he put over by the water skins to be cleaned and oiled. The rest of the trunk was full of clothing of various descriptions for both sexes. They took it all out to go through and were just closing the lid when voices drifted in from outside. They could not see anything out of the barn loft window, so they crept downstairs and went round the back of the house to sneak a peak at what was going on.

In front of the house, Amelia had been busy tidying up in the garden preparing it for a winter crop, but had been interrupted by a young squire. He had the same dark eyes and hair as Seamus, although it was cut and tamed into a bob, and he was gesturing wildly as they talked.

'They are saying he used magic to escape, Amelia.' The boy's voice drifted to them.

Amelia patted his arm in an effort to calm him down. 'You know people like to make up stories to make things seem more exciting.' Amelia then took his arm and walked him to the path that led back to Port Marden. To Seamus' surprise, the young squire bent and hugged Amelia before getting back on his horse and heading off.

He must have gasped out loud as Aliah turned to him, a look of surprise on her rather dirty face. 'What?' she asked.

'That is my father's head squire, my cousin, Liam. What was he doing here? And why was Amelia hugging him?' He frowned and bit his bottom lip.

'We won't find out squatting here.' Aliah stood and walked around to where Amelia watched the squire head back to Port Marden. When he was out of sight she motioned for Seamus to join them. Amelia reluctantly tore her gaze from the departing rider and wiped her hands on her apron. She looked at her two guests as if she were about to say something, then shook her head.

'I guess we can break for the midday meal early, we need to talk. Aliah if you can get the food ready, Seamus and I will tidy up.' And without another word she headed back to the garden.

Seamus and Aliah exchanged a quizzical look and, shrugging their shoulders, went to do as Amelia had asked. When they were seated at the table Amelia waited until after the blessing before she began her explanation.

'I take it you saw young Liam, Seamus?' Seamus nodded as he continued eating, not wanting to show how much his stomach had been churning since he had seen his childhood friend. 'Well, for some time he has shared a confidence with your father that perhaps it is time you knew of as well.'

At this Seamus did look up from his meal. Amelia was staring into her bowl and would not meet his eyes.

'When I was a little younger than you are now I started experiencing dreams. They were different to normal dreams in that a day or two after I had them they seemed to come true. I was frightened. I believed because I dreamt things I was the actual cause. I would dream that someone would fall over and break something, and then that would happen. It was like I was ill-wishing them. I started to not want to sleep.

'My mother noticed a change in me and after weeks of her coaxing I finally blurted out my secret. Far from being shocked and appalled, my mother took me in her arms and started crying. She explained to me I was not causing things to happen, I was merely seeing the future, and it was something others of my family had experienced. It made me feel a little better until she told me I must never tell another living soul what I could do. After she extracted my promise we never spoke of what she called my gift again.

'Just before my sixteenth birthday, I had a dream. My younger brother was going hunting and he was to have the honour of dealing the killing blow to the wild boar for the first time. I dreamt the boar would severely wound him and he would not be able to walk again. He was but a year younger than I and we were very close. I could not stand by and let that happen to him. So I crept into his room the night before the hunt and begged him not to go. He thought I was being a silly girl worrying needlessly about him. So I told him about my dreams, thinking it was the only way he would listen to me and stay safe. I thought he would understand and keep my secret.

'Rather than thank me he went straight to our father. I had not counted on my family's abhorrence of what they call mage-craft being stronger than his love for me. My father locked me in my room for being "hysterical", and the hunt went ahead as planned. My brother never dealt that first killing blow. The boar attacked him as I had predicted it would, and it was only because of his foreknowledge that my father was prepared and he was able to kill the boar before it did any lasting damage.

'Ironically, I had managed to save my brother, but the boar charging as in my dream sealed my fate. My father imposed the Rule of the Hand and told me that on my 18th birthday I could choose. I could leave the Isle of Hand, or I could take the honourable option of being quietened. I chose to leave the Isle and all my family. On my 18th birthday I was given my dowry and sent into the world to find my way on my own.

'I had planned to travel as far away as I possibly could from here, but the night before I was to leave my brother came to my room and begged for me not to go far. He felt guilty for the outcome of his actions, although he believed they were right and proper, but he said he could not bear for me to be completely estranged. He found this farm and agreed a price with the farmer that was only a small portion of my dowry. If I moved here we could visit and stay in contact, and maybe one day the Rule of Hand would change and I could come home.' Amelia stopped to take a drink.

Seamus stared incredulously at Amelia. He had realised she was telling a different version of a story he had grown up hearing. The story of how his father had been gashed by a boar during his first lead of the hunt. Seamus looked more closely at the woman sitting in front of him, noting especially the dark black eyes she shared with his father. And although her hair was a little lighter than his father's she definitely resembled him, perhaps more than Seamus did himself. But most of all, it was the wry smile she gave as she told her story that reminded him of the King of Hand.

'You are my father's sister. The one they call Amalie. We were told you died.'

'Yes, that was my name a long time ago. I will never go by that name again. I am now Amelia. And to all but a few of our family I am dead. And I am living proof that although your father upholds the Rule of Hand when it comes to those born with mage powers, he has a strong sense of family. He has never been able to completely let me go. He visits sometimes, and has taken Liam into his confidence so that I may have company when he cannot come. He does not know it, but your mother and our younger brother also visit from time to time. They stop by the markets when I attend, sometimes I am fore-warned that they need me and I will go especially to the markets to meet with them. It is through all of this contact that I know of you and your family. I know you almost as well as I would have had I lived with you.

'I only tell you this now Seamus because this is your last chance to reconsider your course of action. I told you before that your father would most likely not expect you to take your life, or live without using magic. I believe that because of how he has treated me, it is likely he would allow you to live a quiet life away from the Isle. Liam confirmed this today. He came to ask me to look out for you. Your father believes you have found out about me and you might come here. He sent Liam to ask if I would be prepared to let you live with me and carry on the farm after I am gone from this world to the next. I agreed that would be an option, should you come here. So, I ask you again Seamus, do you really want to go to the Wizard Isles to train?'

Seamus sat still for a while, his eyes not focusing on anything. In his mind he was going through all his options, but he really could see no other way forward. Soon the silence in the room became too much, even for him.

'So,' he broke the silence. 'The alternatives I face are death, having my magic removed possibly resulting in death, or following in your footsteps?'

'That is correct,' Amelia told him.

'Just so as I understand the full deal here, would I be permitted to marry and have children? Or have I guessed correctly that part of this arrangement would be I never have children so I do not pass on the taint of magic?'

Amelia nodded. 'Again, that is correct.'

'Do you believe that there is any chance I would be allowed to keep my magic and return home?' Seamus looked Amelia straight in the eyes.

Amelia shook her head. 'As the Rule of Hand now stands, that would never be an option.'

'If I don't have the protection of the School of Wizards then all my other options are about having a half-life, never being able to fully be who I am. No disrespect to you Amelia, but I cannot live that way.'

Tears came to Seamus' eyes as the full impact of the last few days hit him. Now that his family knew he had magic, there was no way they would let him learn how to control it and return home. There was only one future for him that allowed him to be himself.

Amelia frowned, 'As a woman my choices were even fewer than yours as there is no school for women with magical abilities. But knowing what I know now having lived my life, I wished I had half your courage when I made my choice.' Amelia took a deep breath. 'Right then, back to work. Liam is a smart boy and he will have seen the stripping of my gardens and the travel packs out the back. He may not have fully understood what they meant yet, but it will not be long before it dawns on him and he will be back. We had best plan for your journey to begin tomorrow.'

Seamus looked at Aliah and she returned his gaze, frowning a little. 'Are you sure this is what you really want to do?' she asked him.

He forced a smile. 'Not really, no. But at least it is a plan, and it is my plan.'

She smiled back and tucked a stray bit of hair behind her ear. 'Right, well we should get started then.'

For the rest of the afternoon Aliah and Seamus went through the clothing in the third trunk to ensure they had a set of clothes to travel in, a change of clothes, changes of under garments, a woollen cloak, and oilskins to keep off the rain. They hung them out in the barn to air overnight.

They then began wrapping the food for travel and putting them in the packs. Seamus sharpened his knives, made some arrows, restocked Amelia's woodpile for the winter and re-dug her garden making it ready for replanting in the spring.

After they ate a late dinner they packed their changes of clothes ready to leave early the next morning. While they were in the process of redistributing the food to even the weight, Amelia appeared from her bedroom with a sword belt and gave it, not to Aliah, but to Seamus.

'You will need this to carry Aliah's sword,' she said.

'I can carry my own sword,' Aliah protested, frowning.

'I know you can dear,' Amelia said wearily. 'But most girls going to meet her husband would not be gallivanting round the countryside with a sword at her side, would she? If she could defend herself, why would she need her brother to escort her?'

'But I am useless with a sword,' Seamus grumbled. 'As Aliah has already demonstrated. And if I carry this, how will I be able to get at a weapon I can use like my bow or knives?'

'If I am to do all your thinking for you, how will you get on when you leave here tomorrow?' Amelia smiled at them to take the sting out of her words. 'Firstly, Seamus, a bow will be of little use to you so that will be staying behind. Secondly, if you wear the sword on your left hand side, then your right hand is free to throw knives. If Aliah walks on your left she will be able to access the sword easily. Aliah, you may want to practice drawing your sword while you are walking *before* you get into any trouble.'

'Ah.' Seamus grinned. 'And if we do get into trouble it will create an element of surprise. They won't expect knives from my right hand, nor will they expect a sword-wielding woman. I like it.' His grin widened, then disappeared as he realised they would be leaving Amelia and the safety of her home tomorrow. He did not know how he could ever repay her kindness, and he regretted he had not had time to get to know his newfound Aunt better.

ALIAH SHRUGGED AS if not carrying her own sword did not matter. But it did. It frustrated her when people thought girls could not look after themselves. She also knew Amelia was right though, it was the best way to travel. For now.

Finishing her packing and doing up her pack she realised she was a little concerned about how they would fare without their host's help along the way. Especially her ability to smooth things over between her and Seamus when they could not agree. They would truly be on their own and would have to learn to give and take. She promised herself that once she was home she would find a way to repay Amelia for her generosity and all she had done to help them on their journey.

CHAPTER 5
THE JOURNEY BEGINS

Seamus' body was still in sleep mode when Amelia woke them. In fact, it was sure it had just laid down. Sleepily pulling himself out of bed he left Aliah to get dressed into her traveling clothes while he dressed before the fire downstairs. The tunic and hose he wore were of good quality, but the brown and cream woollen fabric was a bit more rustic than he was used to. Amelia had said his father stayed at the cottage sometimes and these were the clothes he wore when he was there. He pulled on his own boots and went out to the woodpile to get a days supply of wood in.

Amelia had started to prepare the porridge for breakfast when he brought the wood in. She was half-listening to Aliah with a decidedly unsympathetic ear. Instead of the tunic and hose Aliah had laid out last night, she was wearing a dress and tunic in similar fabrics and colours to his own. She had a cloak thrown over her shoulders, and bare feet.

'But it will be so uncomfortable to walk in, and I will not be able to wield my sword so easily.' She demonstrated for Amelia. 'Can I not have back my tunic and leggings? I can change back into these when we are in sight of any towns.'

'Your attire is entirely appropriate for a girl from a respectable family traveling to meet her husband. Boy's clothing is not. Trust me on this. You will get used to travelling in a dress, even though it seems cumbersome at the moment.' Amelia put the pot over the fire for the porridge to cook as Aliah looked daggers at her back.

'Now you have a change of clothes in your bag, and I have also put in a pair of indoor shoes. While you are travelling it is best to wear your boots. That will not be too uncommon a sight. However if you must stay at an inn you will need to change your footwear to something considered more suitable.'

Aliah stomped to the bench, flicked her skirts out of the way and sat to tie her boots, all the while throwing rebellious looks towards Amelia. Amelia, oblivious to the death stares, went into her bedroom and came back out with a money pouch.

'Seamus, you had best have this. It is not much, but it will be enough for you to sleep a few nights at an inn if needs be, and to replenish your supplies if you are careful.' This earned her another angry stare from Aliah, but surely she knew people would expect the male in the party to be carrying money.

Seamus was reluctant to take the purse for other reasons. 'You might need that money, Amelia, I cannot take it. Besides, I have a little money of my own.'

'Oh, my boy, my family have not abandoned me completely. I have only to ask and this money will be replaced. I will wait a while though, as I do not want them to become suspicious of my wanting coin so close to your visit.' She tucked the purse inside his tunic, and began serving the porridge. Seamus made a note to split the money with Aliah later just in case something happened to him.

It was a quiet meal. None of those sitting around the table wanted to think about the fact this would be the last time they would eat together. Lost in his thoughts, Seamus nearly knocked over his bowl when Amelia suddenly jumped to her feet.

'Someone is coming,' she said. 'We have but a few minutes. Your father, I think. And young Liam. And some of his men. If you are set on this course of action rather than fixing things with your father, you need to gather your belongings and go wait behind the barn. When they come inside, take to the woods alongside the track, not *on* the track. I will delay your father for as long as I can to give you a head start. Once your father and his men pass on the way back to Port Marden, you will be safe to come out of the woods.'

Amelia quickly gathered their plates and hid them under some logs in the wood basket. He and Aliah closed their travel packs and pulled the straps over their shoulders, then put on their capes so their packs were covered. They said only quick farewells as Amelia hurriedly bundled them outside.

'Goddess speed, my young friends,' she said as she shut the door behind them.

Seamus and Aliah hurried to crouch behind the barn before the company arrived. They had just settled when horses and riders burst into the clearing in front of the cottage. From their hiding place they could see four men on horseback wearing travelling clothes with their hoods pulled up, and swords strapped to their hips. They entered the clearing in front of the house and leapt from their saddles. Three of them handed their reins to the fourth and headed for the cottage. There was a knock at the door, some muted voices, and the sound of a door closing.

'What do we do now?' Aliah whispered. 'That man out front will surely see us if we head for the woods.'

'Just wait a minute,' Seamus whispered back. 'He will need to water the horses and when he heads to the well we will take our chance.'

Aliah voiced her agreement.

No sooner had Seamus finished speaking than the man tethered the horses to a tree branch, and headed over to the well. Seamus grabbed Aliah's hand and they made a break for the trees, running as fast and quietly as they could, packs bouncing uncomfortably on their backs. They managed to duck in behind the horses and hide in the brush, just as the man came back with his bucket of water.

As they crouched in the damp brush Seamus cursed himself as they now could not move to the track without disturbing the horses. He looked at Aliah, signalling for her to stay still. She nodded her understanding. Chewing his lip, he considered their options. Before he could think of any, Aliah half stood and threw something back towards the barn. The horses tugged at their reigns and the soldier stood to attention, looking where the noise had come from. Aliah grabbed his hand and jerked him towards the track.

When they reached the tree cover, they stopped and looked back. The soldier had just disappeared behind the barn.

'What did you think you were doing?' Seamus hissed angrily at Aliah.

'Getting us out of a tight situation.' She smiled infuriatingly back at him.

'We might have been seen.' He growled at her.

'But we weren't.' She answered through gritted teeth. 'Come on, if we don't move now they will definitely see us.' She stalked off through the trees. He reluctantly followed.

'That was just plain risky.' He muttered to himself as he walked. 'We so might have been seen.'

'You know I can hear you?' she whispered. 'At least we are on our way, not still waiting for you to have an idea.' She flicked her plait behind her and carried on walking.

What annoyed him most was she was right. He had had no idea how to get past the horses.

They walked in silence until they could no longer hear the horses snuffling behind them. The path they took was not an easy one. There was a lot of undergrowth grabbing at their ankles, and a couple of times they lost the track and had to double back, least they get even more lost.

'Phew!' Seamus said as he checked they could still see the track from where they were. 'This is not a great way to start.' That was as close as he was going to get to thanking her for getting them away.

'It was close,' Aliah agreed, ready to forget his earlier anger. 'And

I did not even get time to properly thank Amelia for all she has done.' She finished, sadly.

'I think she knows how much you appreciated it,' Seamus consoled her; it was the least he could do given his earlier behaviour. 'She has a knack for knowing a lot of things.'

'I guess so.'

'What she would really want is for us to be careful so all her hard work does not get wasted,' Seamus added. 'Come on! We need to keep moving as neither of us are safe this side of the Ariel Mountains.'

'Are you quite sure you know where we are going?' Aliah asked as they started towards Port Marden.

Seamus reached into his tunic and pulled out a piece of parchment. 'Amelia helped me draw this map last night and we worked out the best route through the mountains. Beyond that, she has little knowledge, so we will be on our own.' He put the map back inside his tunic. 'I can talk you through it when we stop for the night.'

'Yes, please.'

They walked in silence for a time, keeping their feet from the grasp of the undergrowth took all their concentration. Tree branches snatched at their packs and they had to make detours round trees and bits of scrub. Every now and then they stopped to ensure they had not gone too far into the woods and they could still see the track.

'Blast it!' Seamus exclaimed as his boot came off his foot for the third time.

'What was that?'

Seamus and Aliah both froze. Neither of them had said that.

Seamus motioned to Aliah. He could see a large fallen tree, and he directed her to it. Following, boot in hand, he slid in underneath beside her. Locked eyes, they both held their breath as footsteps drew closer.

'I was sure I heard something.' A voice was right above them. The tree slipped as it took the weight of someone.

'Careful. I am not carrying you out of here if you break something.' The other voice was to the front of them to the right. Seamus could just make out the colours of the Hand Guard. In fact, if the soldier turned now he would be able to see them both.

Aliah's eyes were wide with worry and he silently pleaded with her not to do anything hasty. The log shifted again as the soldier above them stepped down in front of their hiding place, effectively blocking his comrades' view of them.

'Can you see anything?' he asked.

'No.'

They both paused. Coming from the track was the sound of a horse.

'Come on. Let's go and see what the others have found.'

The man in front of them climbed back up on the log. Seamus held in a groan as the weight of the log pressed on his leg. When the weight released he heard the two men heading back for the track.

He put his finger to his lips, and they waited. They could hear three voices, but could not make out what they were saying. Finally the sound of horses leaving filled the woods, and they both let out a sigh of relief.

They pulled themselves out from under the tree and dusted themselves off. Considering the length of time they had been on the ground they were not too dirty. Just as they were about to move, the sound of more hoof beats stopped them, and they ducked behind a tree in time to see two horses head back towards Port Marden.

'By my count, that makes only three men returning from Amelia's, unless there are other people using this track.'

Seamus agreed. 'It is unlikely farmers out this way would be riding horses, they would most likely be pulling a cart.'

'What do you think happened to the other one?'

'Well,' Seamus said, thoughtfully. 'Either my father left him behind because he was not sure Amelia was telling the truth, or he left him to come slowly after, hoping to find us on the trail, *or* he is helping Amelia with something and will follow later. I really don't know.'

Aliah nodded her understanding. 'So do we risk the track?'

'I think it will be all right. We should hear the other horse coming. So long as we keep our ears open and be ready to duck into the undergrowth if we hear anything, we will be fine out of the woods.'

Aliah nodded again. 'And we should rest only in secluded places off the track,' she added.

Leaving the forest, they carried on their journey in silence, a bit fearful they might miss the sounds of a quieter rider if they talked. However the rest of the days journey was uneventful, if a little slower than their trip to Amelia's had been.

They stopped for the night on the edge of the woods near Port Marden, having found a quiet clearing just off the main track. Even though they still had at least a candle-mark more of light, they did not want to risk the open space the road took to the Ariel mountains, in case they were spotted by the man who had stayed behind.

After they had eaten and tided up, Seamus showed Aliah the map he and Amelia had made. 'She suggested we go the longer route through the High Pass towards Sunnydale.'

Pointing out the route, he added, 'It will take a little longer, but it is not the route we will be expected to take so we may be a little safer. We should be able to find a merchant train going through the mountains, and they might let us travel with them if we are lucky.'

'I would rather travel alone,' Aliah said. 'Less questions that way and we cannot be caught out in our lies.'

'But we would have more protection from bandits and we would be better hidden from those following us,' Seamus countered.

Aliah did not say anything.

Seamus sighed, 'Anyway, we do not need to decide now. What we do need is to get some sleep as I want to leave early tomorrow so we can pass Port Marden before the gates open and someone chances to see us.'

With that, he snuggled into his bedroll and pulled his cloak over him to keep off the night chill. Aliah sat frowning into the fire for a moment longer, then followed his lead.

THE NEXT MORNING they packed up camp quickly and filled their water skins. Eating some of the fruity travel bread Amelia and Aliah had made, they started at a brisk pace. As with the day before they spoke little as they walked so they could listen for the sounds of other travellers and leave the road if they needed. Aliah had difficulty keeping up with Seamus' long strides. Her legs were tired and sore from the walk yesterday, and they seemed very sluggish this morning.

After she had stumbled a couple of times she stopped them at the edge of the Tangled Woods. 'Seamus, I know you want to be past Port Marden early but I cannot keep up this pace!'

Seamus looked down at Aliah in surprise, as if he was just noticing for the first time that she was a good deal shorter than him. Aliah was tall for a girl, but Seamus himself was quite tall and she stood only as high as his shoulder. There was no way she could keep up with his long stride for any length of time. He looked ahead. 'We still need to walk quickly for this bit because we will be exposed as we leave the woods and head for the mountains. Once we are a little ways from the gate we can slow down.'

Aliah sighed deeply. 'All right, I will try and keep up.' Taking a deep breath she steeled herself to keep the fast pace, looking forward to the promise of slowing down once they passed the gates. By they time they reached the crossroads, where they had decided to follow Amelia's suggestion and take the high road, Aliah's legs were burning.

'Can we stop for a rest?' Aliah hated to ask, but she really needed a break.

Before Seamus could respond the sound of hoof beats filled the air. She looked around but could not see anywhere they could hide, so Aliah moved to Seamus' left hand side, ready to reach for her sword if she needed to.

'All we can do is walk and hope that they do not come close enough to recognise you,' she said. 'We'll put up our hoods to hide our faces. If they ask, you are Sean and I am your sister, Ali. Maybe the different names might put them off.'

They pulled up their hoods and continued on. The hoof beats got closer, then stopped. Aliah looked behind them to see a rider from the Isle of Hand at the crossroads. She waved and he glanced at her before turning his horse towards the Port, where the gates had already opened.

'Hopefully he will have thought we were early birds through the gate and will not give us another thought.' Aliah ran to catch Seamus up. Seamus merely grunted in return.

Excitement over, they carried on walking. The particular pass they were taking through the Ariel Mountains was not much used, but as the sun rose higher in the sky they heard the sounds of another horse and rider behind them. Fearing the worst, they moved to the side of the road and prepared to fight if need be. It was not long before the rider came into sight, and they sighed with relief as they realised it was only a Duke's Messenger, not someone sent by Seamus' father for them.

Still, the messenger slowed and stopped when he saw them. 'Good day. You are headed over the pass to Sunnydale?'

'Yes,' Seamus answered before she could. 'My sister's betrothed lives not far from there.'

'You might want to re-think your timing. Word is there is a big storm coming in from the sea and it will hit the coast within the next day or so. It will bring with it early snow I am told. I am sent to turn travellers back and advise others to take shelter. You have not yet gone too far so I advise you turn back.'

'Thank you for the warning,' Seamus called as the messenger rode on.

'We must turn back.' Aliah insisted. 'Maybe we can stay with Amelia until the storm passes.' Aliah looked at Seamus, who was frowning and chewing his lip.

'I have hunted in these mountains, and there are plenty of caves. If we push on today and make a good pace tomorrow, we can find a cave before the storm comes and hunker down there until it passes.' Seamus looked at her. 'I worry if we go back now my father will find us at Amelia's, and staying anywhere else is too risky. We also run the risk of being stuck at Amelia's until after winter if the mountains become un-passable. Not to mention the fact you want to let the king know about a potential invasion. That information would be too late if we got stuck for the winter.'

Aliah reviewed the arguments he presented. Although the risk of getting caught was not so great for her, she did not fancy making the journey home alone, and she did need to get news of the potential invasion to the king. She did not want to wait for winter to pass before she even started out for home. Shrugging her shoulders she carried on walking.

The going that day was quite flat and not too strenuous. Not long before they stopped for their evening meal the terrain started to get a little steeper and they entered the foothills of the Ariel Mountains.

Once again, they broke camp early the next morning as Seamus wanted to push on up into the mountains. They did, however, take the time to strap their left over firewood to their packs in case they could not find any further up. Before starting out, they agreed at noon they would stop and find shelter enough to see them through the storm.

It was a slow, tedious trek up through the foothills. Aliah's muscles were still sore from two days of walking and going up hill was making them even worse. From the strain on Seamus' face it was obvious he was also having difficulty, so she kept her complaints to herself.

After a candle-mark or so they had a brief rest beside a stream to refilled the water bags and have some trail bread. Aliah took the opportunity to search the sky behind them for signs of the storm. The sky looked clear enough, but without being able to see back towards the coast she could not judge how long they had before the storm hit. Seamus, noting her concern, hurried to tie the water bottles to their packs and start moving again.

'We had better get our wet weather gear out, just in case,' he advised. 'We are a long way from where I had hoped we would be by now and we may not reach the caves before the bad weather hits us.'

They found their waterproof capes, put them on and over their packs, and started out again. Aliah was not only tired, but also hot. The capes made it difficult to move and in the near midday heat they were stifling. However, as they trudged ever higher, the temperature began to drop and Aliah was grateful for the extra layer of clothing. Midday came and went without them breaking their journey as they were not high enough yet to find a cave for shelter. They trudged on, chewing some trail bread to ease their hunger as the first drops of rain began to fall.

The heavy rain started, each footstep treacherous as water began to run down the trail. The bottom of Aliah's dress was heavy with water and mud and she cursed Amelia for insisting she wear it.

'We have to keep going,' Seamus encouraged her. 'We are not far from some decent sized caves and we will need solid shelter once the storm fully hits us.'

Aliah grumbled under her breath, but carried on. There was sense in what Seamus said, but that did not mean she had to like it.

As if she were not uncomfortable enough, rain began dripping down inside her cape. By the time they reached the mountains proper they were soaked through, and the wind was starting to pick up speed. Aliah could see no further than Seamus' hunched figure in front of her. Still they kept going, with Seamus repeating, 'Not long now', every few minutes.

Not long now ended up being really too long when Seamus finally led them off the main path, down a narrow track, and into a clearing that miraculously contained a cave mouth sheltered from the storm.

Seamus had a grin on his face as if to say, 'See, I told you I would find shelter for us.'

There was little light outside the cave, and even less when they got inside. Seamus reached out and Aliah heard some shuffling, then with a 'snick' the darkness was brightened with light.

'My father's men have used this cave before. Each person replaces the torch before leaving so the next inhabitants have light.' He was still smiling as he pulled Aliah further inside the cave. He used the light from the torch to check they were the only life in there. Once he was satisfied, he put the torch up in a groove in the wall.

A shivering Aliah had already taken off her waterproof cloak and was beginning to open her pack for dry clothes when Seamus interrupted her. 'Fire first for survival.'

It was all she could do to stop herself from rolling her eyes.

'There should be some dry wood in the back. If you get that, I will have a look around for more wood out front to add to what we already have on our packs. It will need to dry out, but we do not know how long the storm will keep us here, and what we do not use we can leave for the next travellers.'

As he left to go back into the storm, Aliah cursed him under her breath even as she shivered her way to the back of the cave to find wood and some tinder. She dumped it into the depression in the floor in the middle of the cave, which had obviously been used for a fire pit in the past. Setting up the tinder, she stacked some of the wood to the side to be used later. Some of the longer sticks she leaned against the cave walls as makeshift drying racks for their clothes. As she waited for Seamus to return she kept warm by pacing out the cave. Ten steps from side to side, thirteen steps from back to front. She was nearly bowled over by Seamus returning with his arms full of wood.

'I have placed some more outside by the door in case we need it,' he grimaced. 'The storm is really coming in, if you need to go outside for umm ... er ... you know.' He blushed. 'I would do it now, the storm is coming in fast.'

Aliah blushed a little herself, realising she did need to go out and do exactly that. In her embarrassment she left without her waterproof and did not realise she would need it until the driving rain hit her. Too proud to go back in, she ducked behind a tree and tried to shelter as she relieved herself. Just as she stood to return to the cave the wind rose and the steady rain became hail and sleet. She fought her way back to the entrance against the elements, arriving even colder and wetter than she had been when she left.

Seamus had a small fire going and looked up at her as she came in, frowning at her bedraggled state. 'Best you get out of those clothes and into something dry fast,' he said as he moved so his back was to her, to allow her some privacy.

Feeling like a reprimanded child, Aliah fumbled out of her now drenched clothing. Her freezing fingers made it difficult to undo the fastenings and she got tangled in her heavy, wet skirt. She pulled on dry underclothes. Not wanting to get her spare clothes dirty she wrapped her sleeping blanket around herself. Satisfied she was respectable, she told Seamus he could turn around. Then, to allow him time to change, she moved from the fire and, still shivering, she hung her clothes over the makeshift rack. By the time she had finished hanging up her skirt and shirt Seamus was beside her hanging his wet clothes.

'I will make us some tea and something to eat while you get warm.' He handed her his blanket and went to their packs to get what he needed. Gratefully Aliah drew the extra blanket around herself, then dragged some of the rounder logs of dried wood over so they could use them as back rests. Having pulled out their bedrolls, she made two comfortable nests on either side of the fire. She curled up inside her blankets, and watched Seamus as he poured hot water into two mugs, then began making a stew from their stores.

Once he had dinner on the go, Seamus handed one cup of tea to her, and taking the other, he went to sit on his own bedroll nest. 'Are you feeling a little warmer?' he asked, and she nodded.

She had stopped shivering, and her hands and feet no longer felt like blocks of ice, but she was still a little cold. She hoped the tea would help warm her, and it did.

They were silent as they waited for the meal to cook. Seamus looked lost in his thoughts and Aliah was too tired to even think of a topic of conversation. Without Amelia to fill in the gaps they seemed to have little to talk about. The only sound in the cave came from the wind, rain, and hail outside the entrance.

When they had finished a passable meal and banked the fire for the night, the two weary travellers were happy to curl up in their bedrolls and sleep while the storm raged on outside. Aliah awoke the next morning expecting the storm to have passed over only to find it was raging as loud as the night before. She pulled on her waterproof coat and slipped out the door to relieve herself, and found a now white landscape. She hurriedly completed her task and slipped back inside, starting the fire going as much to get warm as to make some porridge for breakfast.

After they finished eating and cleaned up, Seamus went outside to gather some snow in one of their pots to melt. 'We do not know how long this storm will go on so we had best make our water last,' he said.

'Ever the practical one,' Aliah said under her breath as he left, but she was really quite pleased he seemed to know what he was doing. She had never had to survive in the outdoors before, and without his help she would have actually been lost. Even though she hated to admit she needed him.

With breakfast tasks done, they faced a long and boring day as the storm waged on around them. Aliah tried conversation.

'Do you have any brothers and sisters?' she asked.

'A younger brother and sister.' A long pause. 'You?'

'A sister. Younger.' Another long pause.

'Do you miss your sister?'

'No, Bela is not like me at all,' Aliah answered, although she did think to herself, *I miss my mother, even though she has been dead these last four years. And I worry about my father. He did not want to let me go, but he had no choice! If only he knew I was all right and on my way back to him.* But she said none of this to Seamus.

Instead she asked, 'Do you miss your family?'

'Yes.' Then after a pause, 'But it does not do to dwell on it as it is unlikely I will see any of them again.'

And on the day went. They found out more about each other in fits and starts. Seamus did not mind hunting, but would rather ride or read. He preferred eating with his friends in the kitchens rather than in the formal great hall where the heir was expected to show himself. How he had fought to be able to learn how to use knives and bows rather than a sword, which he had no flair for, even though it was known men in his family were quite handy with those forms of weapon.

In return Aliah admitted she was better at fighting and swordsmanship than she was at cooking and sewing. She did not mind reading, but wanted to be able to choose her own reading material. One of the things she and Seamus did have in common was a love of riding as they could both escape their daily chores and be who they wanted on the back of a horse. If Seamus found it odd that her pastimes were more in line with a lady than someone who had been sold to sailors, he did not comment.

During the day, Aliah developed a bit of a cough, which was made a little better by putting some dried sage leaves from Amelia's medicinal pack into her tea. That night the forced inactivity made it difficult to sleep and every time Aliah did doze off her coughing woke her. Eventually she drifted into a fitful slumber.

The next day was much the same as the day before, until some time after noon the wind died down and Seamus went to check what was going on outside. 'It looks as though the storm has passed,' he said on his return. 'But the sky is still very black. I suggest we wait until morning to move off, just to make sure the storm has really passed us by.'

'I suppose that is the sensible thing to do,' Aliah responded.

They spent another restless night. Aliah's cough was no better, but she took heart from the fact it was no worse either.

When they awoke the next morning they dressed for travel and while Aliah cleaned the cave, making it ready for the next travellers who needed it, Seamus went out to find the main track and make sure the snow had cleared enough over night. While she waited for Seamus to return, she stacked the unused wood at the back of the cave and bound some tinder round the torch pole, leaving it in the gap by the door next to the tinderbox.

Seamus returned with a smile on his face. 'The path to the pass has very little snow, it seems the wind has blown it away. Unfortunately, the wind is a little bracing, so we should put our waterproofs on. Other than that we are good to leave.'

CHAPTER 6
MOUNTAINS & MORE MOUNTAINS

Seamus was grateful to be out of the cave, but he had to admit the wind was a little more bracing on the exposed mountain pass than he would have liked. He estimated if they made good time they would be able to camp on this side of the pass that night, and by noon tomorrow they would be over the pass and walking in the shelter of the mountains the following day. If his map was right, he estimated they would have a further three to four days walk to Sunnydale, depending on their pace.

Anxious to get as close to the pass as possible that day, Seamus set a cracking pace. After the first candle-mark or so, he had to slow as Aliah was struggling to keep up and her breathing sounded a little shallow. The slower pace helped a little, but he did not like the look of sweat on her brow. It looked more like a fever sweat than sweat from walking. However Aliah insisted she was not ailing and urged him to keep going.

As the day drew on and they neared the pass, Seamus began to look out for some suitable shelter for the night. If he were alone he might just have slept in one of the small copse of trees by the road, but Aliah's cough had come back and he wanted to find something with a little more shelter so he could ensure she was not too exposed to the elements during the night.

Finally he found a rocky outcrop with a depression wide enough for the both of them to sleep. It was sheltered from the wind and there was even some scrubby wood close by for a fire. It was a little early to stop, but he decided that they needed to be cautious as neither of them could afford to get really sick.

They set the fire and made a hearty stew for supper. Seamus noticed their supplies were running a little low. They had hoped to be nearer to Sunnydale where they could top their supplies up. But they still had a way to go. They would have to start reducing what they ate, or looking for food on the way once they traversed the pass.

Aliah's cough seemed to settle with some sage tea, and he noticed she added a little dried garlic, so she must have been feeling worse. Monitoring her sleep long into the night, he was concerned she really was not well.

When they woke the next morning Aliah was not coughing as much. After checking she was up to it Seamus had them walking at a brisk pace. As they came closer to the top of the pass the air thinned and it was hard for him to breathe, so it must have been agony for Aliah.

Higher up, the wind grew stronger, and Aliah had to hold fast to Seamus' pack to keep from being blown off the path. He encouraged her to keep going as when they dipped below the pass the wind would not affect her so much. It would not be long now he said. But after the tenth time of him saying it, her eyes began to glaze over and she no longer looked as though she believed him.

It seemed like an eternity, but finally they crested the top of the mountain. Seamus took some time to look down on the rolling hills that finally flattened out towards a town he could just see in the distance. He would have loved more time to take in the view and get his bearings, but Aliah was fading fast. He took in just enough to feel relieved the passage down seemed shorter than the one up, then they started their descent.

As they moved down into the shelter of the mountain the biting wind lessened, but they still had to watch their footing on the patches of ice. It was not yet getting dark, but Seamus began scouting for a sheltered place to make camp, somewhere he might find something to scavenge to supplement their dwindling supplies.

He did not like the shallow sound of Aliah's breathing, and was relieved when he found a rocky outcrop with a half-cave. The floor was dry and there was plenty of wood around, which he quickly gathered. They used tinder from their packs to start the fire, and Seamus left Aliah to begin a stew and brew some tea while he went to see if he could find some additional food.

They were still quite high in the mountains and the weather had taken a turn for the worse. Winter was definitely in the air. That meant there would be little to hunt apart from the cross between lowland rabbits and rats that the locals called mountain rats. He looked around for what could be a likely burrow entrance, some- where without too much ice around. Just as he was about to give up, he spied a mountain rat darting back into a hole. Looking around, he found the back entrance. He placed the bag he had brought with him over it. At the front entrance he started a small fire, making sure the smoke went into the burrow, then went back to the bag and waited. Before too long he had two mountain rats in his bag. He prepared their meat, then buried the skins and debris before taking his catch back to camp.

Aliah had made tea and fallen asleep while he hunted. There was a pot on the edge of the fire with some dried vegetables and pulses mixed in, with a little of their precious water. Seamus added the meat to the pot and set it over the fire to simmer. He picked up the teapot and took it outside to gather some snow to melt for tomor- row. Finally he rolled out his bedding and leaned back to wait for dinner to finish cooking.

He would have dosed off himself had he not been concerned about the rattling he could hear in Aliah's chest. It was true she was not coughing as much but she was not breathing easily either, and her face had an unhealthy grey pallor. It was almost a shame to wake her so she could eat some stew.

After dinner he fed her some more tea, then let her go back to sleep while he tidied everything up and made ready for the next day. All the time he was thinking to himself thank goodness it is only four more days at most until Sunnydale.

That was what he kept repeating to himself for the next three days as they made slow progress due to Aliah's failing health. He repeated it when they took a turning and walked half a day in the wrong direction, then had to walk back. He repeated it when Aliah had to stop every few paces to get her breath. He repeated it when he put down both packs and eased his aching shoulders at night.

Each day they were covering less and less distance, and their food supplies were running perilously low. It took them more than the planned two days to get to the bottom of the pass, and by then, Seamus was exhausted. He had been carrying Aliah's pack and supporting most of her weight for the best part of the last three days.

On the fourth day they finally emerged from the foothills onto the flat. Seamus set up camp for the night by the side of the road under the shelter of a large Elm tree. Aliah had collapsed as soon as they stopped walking, so he unpacked her bedding and made sure she was warm so she could sleep. He then set up the fire and started a broth with left over meat from the day before, and made a medicinal tea for her. At least water was not a problem with all the ice still around. Food, however, was another matter. There was barely enough for breakfast, and at normal walking pace they still had about two days to Sunnydale. They would have to stop at a farm and see if they could buy some food.

While he fed Aliah the tea to bring down her fever and help her chest, he tried not to let on how worried he was about her condition, or how far they were from their first destination. 'We will be in Sunnydale soon,' he told her, but did not add he had no idea how they were going to make it that far. Seamus drank his broth, then forced Aliah to have some before banking up the fire and crawling into his own blankets. Although he was worried about how they were going to actually make it to the town, he was so exhausted he fell asleep almost before his head touched the ground.

He awoke before dawn the next morning unable to sleep any longer. Checking on Aliah he found her much worse. Her face was flushed, and she was breathing shallowly through half-parted lips. She would not wake when he shook her, and her fever was really high. Seamus knew if they continued walking for two days to Sunnydale, Aliah might not make it there.

Going through his options he busied himself with stoking up the fire and making tea. He waited for the sun to rise so he could have a look around and see if there was anywhere he could get help. In the distance he could just make out a farmhouse. He did not have much money, but maybe he could "borrow" a horse and take Aliah to town that way. He would return it later.

Making sure Aliah was well tucked in and the fire would burn for a while, he headed for the house at a slow jog. It seemed like candlemarks later, but really it was not even one, when he arrived at the farm just as the farmer was heading out of his cottage. He nearly scared the man half to death as he came up behind him. In fact, the farmer had scared him also, and Seamus realised he would not be able to borrow the horse as planned.

'Do not be scaring me like that, young sir,' the startled farmer grumbled. 'It is quiet in these parts, and normally somebody coming up that fast behind a soul does not have good intentions.'

Thinking on his feet Seamus said, 'I am sorry, sir, but I am in kind of a rush. I have been travelling with my sister who has fallen sick. I need to get her to a healer in Sunnydale. I was wondering if I could rent a horse and cart to take her?' Seamus managed to get his request out between panting breaths.

'I would be a trusting soul if I just let you take off with my horse and cart.' The man screwed up his face in thought. 'But the goddess would look poorly on me if you were indeed an honest soul with a sick friend and I did nothing.' Seamus looked at the man in what he hoped was a beseeching way, willing him to help.

'And I would never forgive you either.' The door opened and there stood a woman about the age of the farmer, although much shorter. 'Jon, why not take the boy back to his friend and you can decide whether or not he is honest then and there.' Her shrewd eyes bored through Seamus. 'I assume you have real coin to pay?'

It was like she was looking into Seamus' very soul, and it made him more than a little uncomfortable. Here was a woman you would not cross lightly. He put on his best "trust me I am honest" face, the one designed to get adults to agree to let him have something when he really should not, and pulled out his purse. Hearing the coins tinkle, the woman nodded to her husband, then spoke to Seamus.

'Go and help Jon hitch up the horse, then. Sooner he gets to your friend the better.'

Seamus followed the man to the barn where there was a rather fine looking horse and a beat up cart. He helped the farmer get the cart ready to go. When they were done he also helped the farmer load some baskets of potatoes and root vegetables onto the back. Jon included an old horse blanket.

'If I be going into town I may as well get the most out of the journey.' The man chuckled as he loaded the cart. 'I will need to make up for not working today.'

Guilt welled up, but then Seamus shook it off. His first thought had been he might steal a horse and return it later. At least this way the farmer would get paid for his time.

As they left the barn the farmer's wife came out. 'You seem true of heart young man, but just beware if anything happens to my Jon. I have seen your face and I will make sure you are hunted down.'

Seamus was sure she would hunt him to the grave, but Jon chuckled beside him. 'Her bark is worse than her bite,' he said. 'Heart of gold, my Maisie, but you would not want to cross her.' And with one last chuckle they were off.

Worrying all the way back about what he would find, Seamus

was even more concerned than he had been when he left. Aliah had not moved in his absence and her temperature seemed to be even higher, if that were even possible.

'She's not looking too well,' Jon offered helpfully.

'I have some herbs in my pack, I will make her some tea and it will ease her breathing a little.'

'I think she be needing a healer, not tea,' the farmer commented sagely. 'We best get her on the cart and get going as soon as possible.'

Seamus frowned and bit his lip, considering his best course of action. He voiced his agreement and began rolling up his bedding and packing their packs. All the while he explained to Aliah what was happening in the hopes she would be able to hear him. Jon helped him to place Aliah in the back of the cart and they both made sure she was warmly covered before Seamus put out their fire, buried their rubbish, stowed their packs and joined Jon on the wagon bench.

'Away ye go, Mabel.' Jon started them off, and some of the tension Seamus had felt for the last few days left his body.

CHAPTER 7
CASTLE DREAMS

A s she half-woke Aliah imagined a stranger was carrying her. An older man with a weathered face and a woollen hat pulled down on his head. But she forgot him as soon as she closed her eyes and started to drift off again. Her throat was so closed up she could barely breathe, her body was full of aches and pains, and her skin was on fire. There was a great pressure on her chest, like someone was sitting on her.

In some part of her mind she knew they would have to be on their way soon and she should be helping Seamus to break camp, but try as she might she could not will her body to move. She was not sure how she was going to walk at all today.

Drifting back off to sleep Aliah found herself back home. She was riding her horse, running and playing with her friends, and even doing her lessons with the court scribes. In some part of her mind she realised her body was being shifted from beside the fire, but she was too engrossed in living her life in the castle to take much notice. And soon she was being rocked back to sleep.

At some time during her ride Aliah began to feel cold and asked one of the grooms for a cloak. The rocking was encouraging her to sleep, but she was chilled to the bone even with the sun on her face. The rocking stopped and a voice penetrated her consciousness. She could not quite place it. The name Seamus popped into her head. He helped her drink water. There was some rummaging. Then she was a little warmer. The rocking started and she fell asleep again.

Her sleep was not as comfortable this time. She was back in the castle, but she was watching her father read a letter handed to him by the captain of a foreign ship. From the look on his face it was not good news. In fact, she would say it was extremely bad news. Then all hell broke loose. Her father ordered the guard to seize the ship's captain and his crew, and he stormed out of the throne room. The court broke for the day, and Aliah's governess grabbed her by the arm and escorted her back to her room and sternly told her, 'For once in your life, stay here as you are bid. I do not like the sound of what has been happening and your safety is paramount.'

During the session of her father's court Aliah had been deep in a conversation with her guard about the chance of a ride after the session was finished. As such, she missed the captain's entrance and the conversation that occurred before he handed over the sealed letter. It meant she had no idea why Mistress Narinda was so concerned about her safety, and she was not going to waste such a beautiful afternoon in her room. However, try as she might, she could not find anyone to escort her riding. No matter how much she wheedled they all turned her down, more worried about her father's wrath than normal.

In the end she had no choice but to obey her governess' command and return to her room. In the end it was a good thing no one had given in to her, as she was summoned to her father's rooms just as the dinner bell was due to ring. Dressing herself with special care, she allowed her governess to tie her hair back in a plait without complaint.

The guards admitted her immediately, and she was dismayed to see her father's mood did not appear any better than it had been earlier in the day. He curtly told her to take a seat by the fire while his squire finished dressing him. When her father was fully dressed in a brilliant blue doublet and dark blue hose the squire was dismissed and her father took the chair opposite her, on the other side of the fire.

'Aliah, I do not know where to start.' He brushed his hand through his curly, greying, dark hair. A frown creased his brow. 'I am going to have to ask you to be very grown up, more grown up than I have ever asked of you before.'

Aliah shifted uncomfortably in her seat as her father's grey eyes stared directly at her. She had only recently been included in court sessions and she found those boring. What more could her father ask of her? Still, she stared back at him, hoping her blue eyes conveyed an interest she did not really feel. 'Go ahead, father.'

'You will know from attending court that we have been approached by a nation across the sea, Carsten. Initially they were proposing a trade alliance. However, just recently their missives have been more strongly worded, and it has become apparent they did not want to partner with us, but want us to become a client state within a Carsten Empire. As our ties have always been with the Natari Emperor, we have been strongly resisting their advances.'

She knew that if she had been paying attention at sessions of the court, she would have noticed. But normally, when forced to attend, she found something else to occupy her time while her father was busy discussing matters of state. In her defence, the rules of state decreed she could never hold the Crown of Aria, that duty would fall to her husband, but she would have a seat at the Council table. That was why she was included in all important discussions. Aliah was beginning to wish she had taken her duties as potential heir a little more seriously. She nodded at her father to continue as if she knew exactly what he was talking about.

'We have appealed to the Natari Emperor for support should this state become hostile, but it appears our two nations have drifted so far apart we are no longer considered to be part of their national responsibility. Add to that a war on their eastern border which has gained their full attention and we are left on our own to deal with Carsten.' King Terion stood and began pacing the room. Aliah's brow creased as she realised the country could be in danger from a threat she had not even known about.

'Our nation is fragmented. Two of our five Duchies would be unlikely to support an all out war, and what intelligence our spies have gleaned, lead them to advise us not to antagonise the Carstenites as we may not like the results. They are a strong warrior nation and would take any opportunity to begin a war. That has placed us in a very weak position.'

Her father sat again and picked up a goblet of wine from the table between them. 'And this is what we are brought to.' He sighed. 'I don't like it, but I cannot see any way out of it.'

Terion leaned forward and took his daughter's hand, 'Their king, Spearon, has demanded the hand of my eldest daughter. If I refuse, there is no doubt in my mind he will invade our country.'

Aliah froze. 'Eldest daughter?'

'But surely you cannot give in to this man. You always told me if you give in once to a bully you are leaving yourself open to be bullied again,' Aliah spluttered as she tried to gather her thoughts.

'I am sorry, my darling, matters of state are a little different to courtyard politics. We, my advisors and I, can see no way around his request at this time. It is not as if you did not know that your marriage would be arranged to benefit the state.' He stroked her hand, but Aliah would not meet his eyes. She was frowning and it was like a dark cloud had crossed her face.

'Yes,' she ground out through clenched teeth. 'But mother always said that I was to marry someone who could help rule the Kingdom and consolidate the Duchies behind the throne. And that I would have some say in who that person was. It never meant marriage to a foreigner WHOM I HAVE NEVER MET!' She stood up and began pacing the room, her anger making it impossible to sit still.

Terion folded his daughter in his arms. 'I know, my love, and that was what we both wished for you. But I can see no other way around this, much as I dislike it on so many levels. As rulers of this land we hold a position of privilege, and in return, it is our responsibility to live our lives for our people. I hate that I am to ask this of you, but I am asking anyway. It will be of little consolation to you that Spearon thinks to unite our lands by marrying my heir. But he does not realise that you have not been formally named as Heir, and would not be until your eighteenth birthday. As he only asked for my eldest daughter's hand, not my heir, he will not be getting exactly what he bargained for.'

'I am glad you are so pleased with yourselves!' Aliah looked him in the eye, wanting him to see how hurt and angry she was at what he was asking. 'Such a small price to pay for you, but what will happen to me once he realises?'

'I do not know,' her father sadly acknowledged, and her heart melted a little as she could see the concern in his face. 'But I trust you will be able to look after yourself in any situation, and I am sending an advisor with you who is one of my best-trained wizards. He should be able to protect you in most situations. He will also enable you to communicate with us whenever you need. And it is no small price that I pay by letting you go. I appreciate that I am also asking much of you. If I could find another way ...'

Aliah tossed and turned in her sleep, alternating between shivering cold and a raging fever, not sure whether she was restless from her illness or from her tortured memories. In some part of her mind she noticed the rocking had stopped, and there were many people talking. Then she was back in the castle with so many people getting her ready to depart to her new life, trying to persuade her she was doing the right thing for her country. She gave herself over to their ministrations feeling dead inside. All too soon she was saying a tearful farewell to her father and sister and boarding the ship with her governess and advisor.

For the first part of her trip she was treated as a queen. Then at the first port Narinda and Servious were forced from the ship and left behind. After that Aliah was locked in her cabin. It seemed that women in Carsten were deemed little better than cattle, even those who were destined to become queen. The more Aliah learned, the more she realised her father had no idea what he was getting her in to. She overheard the captain saying, 'Once she meets her future king that little wench will get her comeuppance.' He would use her as a symbol of how weak the mainlanders were to rally his troops to war. If the comments of her captors were to be believed, rather than stopping a war, her marriage would be used to start one. Aliah realised she had to get away and inform her father, and she needed to do it quietly, before his advisors could talk him into returning her to her dreaded fate.

However, they had not only locked her in her cabin, they tied her up. She struggled, trying to get free from her bonds, sleeping when she could to get the strength to struggle again. She would break free. Whatever it took she must get home. It must be mealtime as she could smell meat cooking and, strangely, sunshine on her face.

Aliah forced her eyes opened and was surprised to see not a sailor, but Seamus smiling down at her.

'You were right, she was waking,' he said to someone over his shoulder.

She raised her head a little, surprised to see that they were in a simple, but clean house. She was in a bed and Seamus was sitting on a chair beside her. Behind him she could just make a figure by the fire. Struggling to get her mind around walking on the road, escaping ship, and being here—wherever it was—Aliah turned to the one person she recognised: Seamus.

'It's all right. We are in Sunnydale, Ali,' he said as he gently lifted her head and fed her some broth from a spoon. 'We have been here a six-day. Drink this and rest some more. I will catch you up on everything later.'

Exhausted after a few spoonfuls of broth, Aliah was pleased to lie back down and close her eyes. This time the sleep she drifted into was dreamless and healing.

CHAPTER 8

SUNNYDALE

Seamus sat by Aliah's bedside through the night. Each time she woke he fed her a little more broth. She would go back to sleep and he would doze in the chair for a while. He was so relieved she was no longer thrashing around the bed, nor did she appear to be running a fever. Healer Goodwyn had done a good job treating what she called a breathing sickness.

When they arrived at the Healer's house, Aliah's breathing was laboured and she had been flushed bright red with fever. Healer Goodwyn took them in, saying it would take time, but his sister, Ali, was young and strong and with rest and the right medication she would get better. She stressed the time element, saying these things could not be rushed. But time was not something they could spare, nor did they have enough money to pay for care and accommodation for any length of time.

Seamus was honest with the healer. He had very little coin left after paying for their transport, and they needed to be somewhere very soon. Having explained their situation he thanked her for her time and offered to pay her what little coin he had left for some herbs. The healer may have been elderly, but she was still strong of heart, and she showed him that it was the nature of most people to help those less well off. She shushed him.

'I have enough coin for my needs thanks to my late husband. What I do not have are a strong back and young legs. You can contribute to the household by preparing the garden for winter for me, and there are repairs I need around the house. Local gossip is that the blacksmith's apprentice has hurt his leg and he might need some extra help. So you might earn some coin for your and your sister's food.

'Bring that girl in here,' she commanded Jon.

Shrugging his shoulders Jon headed to the cart. 'You best mind a woman when they speak to yer like that,' he told Seamus as he helped bring Aliah into the house. When they were settled Jon exclaimed he best be off; he did not want to be back too late as his missus was a bit of a worrier. Seamus had thanked him for his help, feeling a little guilty that he had considered stealing from the man.

'You mind the healer, she will help you look after that sister of yours,' Jon yelled over his shoulder as he departed.

For two days, Seamus had stuck close to the healer's house, and Aliah. He repaired a broken shutter and a storage cupboard, then prepared her extensive garden for winter. In addition he tended to the herbs that were hardy enough to stand the early winter cold. That done, he chopped enough wood for at least two winters and stacked it in the lean-to beside the house. Finally, Healer Goodwin set him out in the direction of the Blacksmith's place, declaring his sister would not heal any faster for his moping around and he might as well make use of his time in Sunnydale to put some coin back in his purse.

The blacksmith was a large, hearty man with a ready grin and shock of wavy black hair. He had looked Seamus up and down, declaring him a little skinny, which made Seamus glower. Thankfully he was more than pleased to have whatever help was on offer. It seemed his apprentice had twisted his ankle a six-day before and still could only just bear weight. Many farmers had bought their equipment in for repair with the sudden change of weather and there was a pile of jobs backing up. He set Seamus to work straight away keeping the fire going, fetching and carrying and cleaning. The smith kept him pretty busy for the next few days, working long into the evening to try and clear the backlog of work.

The manual work in the blacksmith's shop tired him out as he was not used to constant physical labour, but still he kept vigil by Aliah's bedside during the night. Watching and waiting patiently for her to wake long enough so he could remind her of their cover story. While he was pleased she no longer breathed so heavily, and he trusted Healer Goodwin and Smith Brown, he did not want to take needless chances with Aliah blurting out the wrong thing as she awoke. Still, he could not stay awake forever, and not long before dawn he was started awake by a hand on his arm.

'Shh,' Aliah said, finger over her lips, 'I can see a woman asleep and I don't want to wake her.'

'Ali, you're awake. It's me, Sean,' he whispered back, nodding at her and then towards the figure sleeping in the room on the other side of the fire.

'I know who we are, numbskull! I have not lost my wits.' Aliah smiled to take the sting out of her words. 'Where are we? How long have we been here?' Aliah whispered.

'We're in Sunnydale,' Seamus whispered back. 'I paid a farmer to bring us here. We have been here for just over a six-day.'

'That long?' Aliah's face crumpled in dismay.

'And Healer Goodwin, who took us in, says it will be another six-day after you wake up before we can travel.'

'Twelve days?' she asked. 'We have lost so much time because of me!' Her brow creased in a frown.

Surprised, Seamus looked at Aliah. He knew she wanted to reach home as quickly as possible to tell the King of the potential war, but he had not realised it would bother her quite so much. 'Time?' he asked her, raising his eyebrows questioningly. Was she playing her part and appearing to worry about the delay in meeting her future husband? Or was there more to it?

'How can we have been here so long? We had so little money.' She ignored his question and asked her own. He noticed she had a tendency to do that when she was focused on something else.

'The healer has looked after us and I have done some work for her in return. I have also been working for the blacksmith,' Seamus said, rather proudly, for it was the first time he had ever actually been paid for his labour. But he could tell by Aliah's gaze she had moved on to something else. He tried to get her attention back. 'We now have a little more coin than when we started. We may even be able to afford to take a coach part of the way.'

There was a noise behind them, and it was Seamus' turn to put his finger to his lips. 'We'll talk more later,' he said. 'Go back to sleep. I have to get ready for work. Healer Goodwin will look after you.' He gestured to the elderly woman sleeping in the other bed. 'I will see you this evening.' If he noticed the frown on Aliah's face as he closed down any further discussion, he chose to ignore it.

SEAMUS HAD A QUICK BREAKFAST, checked Aliah was asleep, then headed to work. The day dragged on as if it would never end, and to make it worse, his mind was not on the job. When he let the fire go too low for the third time that day, Smith Brown told him to go as he was not much help anyway. Promising to do better tomorrow, Seamus ran like the wind back to the healer's house.

He rushed through the door expecting to see Aliah still in bed, but the house was empty. Nothing looked disturbed. Although he was worried, he decided not to panic. He stoked the fire and put the stew pot over the flames readying it for dinner before going outside to wash up. As he was changing into clean clothes, the cottage door opened. Aliah came in, fully dressed, leaning on Healer Goodwin, who was taking the strain well given she was a head shorter than her charge. Although she looked pale and drawn, Aliah seemed better than she had in many days.

'Sean, you are home already.' She seemed genuinely pleased to see him. 'Goodwin took me to the baths. She said a good soak would help me feel better, and it did. But I became tired on the way back.' Healer Goodwin helped her to the bed, and it was then that Seamus noticed the child standing by the door.

'I won't be a moment,' Healer Goodwin said to him. 'Just let me get my things and I will come with you.' To Seamus she said, 'Henry's mother is having her baby and needs my help. You see Ali back into bed, and make sure you and she have some supper. Keep some warm for me as I do not know when I will be back. Babies do not come to any plan.' She shuffled off to her back room, and emerged a few minutes later with a bag in one hand and a glass vial in the other.

'Give Ali half of this after she has eaten. It will help with her breathing, and also make her drowsy. She needs a good nights sleep to help the healing process along. If she wakes during the night she may have the other half.' And with that, Healer Goodwin followed Henry out the door and they were alone.

Seamus went to help Aliah into bed, but she waved him away. 'I shall be fine, if you would just turn your back.' He did, and a few minutes later she said, 'All right, I am presentable now.'

Aliah was propped up in her bed, wearing her tunic, her skirt was draped neatly over the end of the bed. 'So, what is for dinner?'

'Dinner will still be a little while, so we should take this opportunity to talk. We don't know how long Goodwin will be. As she said, babies can be unpredictable.' Seamus pulled over a chair and sat beside her. 'We need to make some plans, and I also think from some of the things you said while you were feverish, that you have not been very straight with me.' Seamus put on a stern face and looked her straight in the eye.

Aliah looked confused but met his stare straight on, giving nothing away. He pressed on. 'While you were in a fever you spoke of King Terion, and your father, and of Millard, who I know to be one of the king's advisors. You spoke the names of some of the Kingdom's most influential people and then said you must tell father. You kept repeating that phrase, *I must tell father there is danger coming.*' Seamus paused, waiting expectantly, but this time Aliah would not meet his eyes.

'And now you are very concerned that so much time passed while you were getting better. Is there something you would like to tell me? Or should I guess just what position your family has held in Castle Bannock, Princess Aliahanna?' He almost enjoyed seeing the shocked expression on her face, but it confirmed his worst fear. He had been travelling with the Heir to the Throne of Aria. Before they had only faced minor danger, but now he was caught up in something much larger and much scarier, an actual potential invasion of his home-land. And he might well be travelling with the very reason for it.

'I guess it is time I shared my burden with someone.' Aliah sighed, clearly wishing she did not have to tell him anything at all, which annoyed Seamus immensely. He had always been straight with her—well, at least since Amelia had outed him—but before he could say anything along those lines, Aliah carried on speaking.

'It is only fair you know what you are getting yourself into before we travel any further together.' She looked so serious and so worried that Seamus bit back his sarcastic comment and listened.

Some time later Aliah had told her story and they had eaten dinner. 'So you can see why I am worried about this delay.' She finished her recount. 'I need to get word to my father as soon as possible, and I need to do it without alerting his advisors.'

Seamus had been thinking things through as Aliah was talking, and he had a plan. He just had to see if he could convince Aliah it was the best course to take. And with her need for speed, it would not be an easy proposition.

'Firstly,' he said. 'Would you agree that you cannot just walk into the palace as Princess Aliahanna?'

'Yes,' Aliah confirmed.

'And secondly, there has been no sign of any invasion as we would have heard something in the days we have been in town.'

'That is true,' she answered. 'But that does not mean one is still not imminent.'

'Agreed, but it does mean we still have a little time. And, finally, one thing has not changed; we need to be careful as we travel as my family is looking for me. On top of that, there is nothing to say that your captors are not still looking for you.'

Aliah nodded.

'So, I have been doing some research while you have been sleeping.'

'Sleeping! A little bit of an understatement,' Aliah laughed and Seamus grinned at her attempt at humour.

'I have been asked to help drive one of the wagons on a trading trip to Duncameron. The smith's boy is travelling to meet his family there and will be well enough to drive the wagon back but they need someone to drive it there. That leaves in two days time. I do not think you will be well enough to travel by then.

'I had also thought to use some of our coin to take the coach to Port Isby and then maybe catch a ship from there. But the coach leaves tomorrow, and I think it is out of the question now for the same reason. We could take the one in six days, but I think my final option is better.

'If we stay here another six-day, I think I can earn enough for a small horse and still be able to top up our supplies. If you rode, we could start out within a next six-day, and head inland towards Duncameron. And from there, follow the inland road to Bannock. We still remain undetected and reach there quicker than going via Port Isby.'

Aliah's brow furrowed and her face clouded. 'Even if we move quickly, Duncameron is just under six-days walk away, and then it would be *another* six-day until we reached the Castle. In twelve days we could be facing a full-scale invasion, without the country being prepared.'

'I had a feeling you might say that, and I think you are wrong to believe your father does not at least have some idea of what is going on. After all, I understand he has quite a large spy network as he likes to keep his finger on the pulse of the nation. And at least this way, we have a chance of getting to see him before the invasion. If we get caught then we have no chance.' Seamus stood up and stretched. 'Anyway, we do not have to decide now. You will not be ready to travel for days yet.' He handed her the medicine Healer Goodwin had left. 'Let me carry on looking into all the possibilities, and we can decide what to do when the healer says you are fit to travel.'

'I know you are just putting me off, but I am too tired to bother arguing with you,' Aliah said tucking a stray piece of hair behind her ear as she snuggled into bed. 'Never fear, we WILL talk about it later, and I WILL be doing some looking myself.' She drifted off, still frowning her displeasure.

Seamus pulled his pallet out from under Aliah's bed and prepared to get some sleep himself. He knew things were now more tangled than they had been, more fraught with danger. But he was strangely calmer, not more stressed, for having his fears confirmed. At least now he knew what he was facing, and Aliah did not seem all that imperious for a royal princess. Well, not while she was still ill anyway. Although she did seem quite annoyed with him about something. Well, they could sort that out later. He fell asleep still going through a list of all the things he had to do to get them ready to leave for Duncameron.

THE FOLLOWING MORNING, Aliah waited for the sound of the door closing, signalling Seamus was heading off to work. Through half-opened eyes she could see the outline of Healer Goodwyn asleep in her bed through the open door to her room. Without the need to arise, she took the opportunity to snuggle beneath the covers and think through everything she and Seamus had discussed last night.

Seamus had seemed so certain of what they should do, but that was so like him. Aliah was not so sure they had the luxury of time, and she was going to do something about that. It had already been more than two six-days since she had escaped captivity. More than enough time for her captors to return to Carsten to recruit a small army. Soldiers could be leaving any day now and her father needed as much time as possible to prepare to meet them. Gathering a large army took time. This much she had learned from attending her father's council.

Although it pained her to agree with Seamus, he had been right that she was in no fit state to walk, or even to ride anywhere, if they left now. So that meant taking the coach, which left today, or joining the caravan leaving tomorrow. She did not know if she had enough for the coach trip, that meant the caravan was her best option. Would they take her even though she was unwell? Whatever she did, she knew she had to be on her way. She was not waiting another six-day.

Unable to find a solution, Aliah dozed off again. She was woken a little time later by the sound of Healer Goodwyn moving around. Drowsily she sat up, surprised that she was feeling quite a bit better than she had the day before.

'Oh, good,' her healer said. 'You are awake. Are you ready to try some of the morning out of bed?' She placed a pot of porridge over the fire.

'I think so,' Aliah responded. 'I am certainly keen to be moving.' She sat up and reached for her top and skirt, then tucked her feet into her indoor shoes.

'Not too much too fast though,' Healer Goodwyn admonished. 'I know you are probably very eager to be on your way to meet with your betrothed, but you have been quite ill. It will take some time for your body to repair. Maybe the morning up and about, then rest this afternoon.' She bustled about getting honey and dried fruit for breakfast and placed them on the table.

'Both Sean and I appreciate all your help, but we really would like to be on our way as soon as possible.' Aliah cleaned her face and hands in the basin of water Goodwyn left for her on the bench by the door.

'You cannot be walking and riding for some time, I fear,' Goodwyn told her as she brought the pot of oat porridge to the table and ladled some into the two waiting plates. 'I know you feel good now, but by the afternoon you will feel very tired. If you leave here too early you would undo all the good work I have done healing you, and you would not be a very welcome sight for your betrothed.' She placed the pan on the stove then sat at the table.

Aliah sat down, frowning. That was almost exactly what Seamus had said, and it was not what she really wanted to hear. 'My betrothed and his family will be worried. They will be expecting us any day now. I don't want to cause them any unnecessary concerns, or have them think I am not sturdy enough for their son.' She hoped that would be something a real betrothed country girl would worry about.

'I can understand that. If only you had been travelling by cart you could have left a mite earlier as it would not be such a strain on you. Especially as you are only travelling to the other side of Duncameron. It would only be two, probably three days at this time of year.' She pushed a bowl towards Aliah. 'No mind. Best eat your breakfast,' she finished as she added fruit and honey to her own bowl of porridge and began eating.

They ate in silence. Aliah helped clear the table and wash the dishes, then they spent some time preparing a simple meat stew for dinner. When they were done Goodwyn asked if she would like to help her bottle and store some of the herbs she had collected and dried hanging from the ceiling in her store-room. Aliah said she would and followed Goodwin into the small room where she prepared and stored her herbs and medicines.

'While you do that, I might just make up some more of your medicine.' The healer set Aliah at the main table and retired to her room to work.

The rest of the morning passed quickly as Aliah was kept busy, but she could not get her mind off the thought that it was only two or three days to Duncameron by cart. From there, only another three days to Bannock by cart. She could be home in a six-day. She was sure they could not afford a cart, but there was a caravan leaving and it would only take a little longer.

'Healer Goodwyn?'

'Mmm?'

'Is there any coach or the like to Duncameron?' she asked.

'No, my dear, most folk around here have no reason to go there, and they certainly would not want to come to a small village like this!'

'Oh.'

'But you can get a coach to Port Isby and then a coach to Duncameron. It takes about a six-day or so.'

'Oh, maybe I will talk to Sean about that.' Aliah made her best "I am going to do the right thing" face for Goodwin. Really she was thinking the opposite. *It was way too long going by coach, the caravan was still the best option.*

'Your betrothed is a lucky man to be getting such a smart wife.' Goodwin looked approvingly at her. 'I can enquire about the cost when I go out later to pick up some supplies if you like.'

'If you would not mind.'

'I tell you what, I will see you settled after the noon-time meal, then I will run my errands.'

Pleased with herself, Aliah continued to measure the herbs and bottle them as instructed. Just before noon, she complained of a tiredness she did not really feel. Healer Goodwyn insisted she take a nap before the midday meal. Explaining she would be out when Aliah awoke, she showed her where she kept the medicine she had made for her, and where there was some bread and cheese for her midday meal.

Crawling into bed Aliah feigned sleep. Healer Goodwin cleared away her workings, then made and ate her midday meal. A little later she checked Aliah was still sleeping, donned her cloak, and left her home to run errands.

Aliah made herself count to twenty slowly before leaping out of bed. She went into the storeroom and took enough of her medicine for four days. From the pantry, she took enough bread and cheese for the time it would take to get to Duncameron. Feeling guilty, she placed half of her coins down on the table, hoping if it did not cover what she had taken, Seamus would make up the difference. She did not like taking from someone who had been so good to her, but her duty to Aria had to come before any personal feelings.

She packed her travelling pack, dressed in clean clothes, and put on her walking boots. Finally she donned her sword and cloak. She was ready to begin her journey to Bannock, on her terms. Closing the door quietly behind her, she left the safety of Healer Goodwin's to find her own way home.

As a point of pride Seamus made sure he kept his mind on what he was doing all day, even though his thoughts wanted to race away and plan the next part of their journey. Smith Brown was pleased with his work and let him leave early as he needed to sort through what things he wanted to send with the caravan going to Duncameron.

Seamus rushed home, but stopped himself bursting through the door at speed because he did not want to scare Aliah with the noise. But it was he who received the surprise. He opened the door to find Aliah's bed empty and Healer Goodwin sitting in one of the chairs beside the fire looking decidedly angry.

'What has happened?' The question exploded out of Seamus' mouth before he could stop it. 'Where is Ali?'

'I have to say, Sean, I have enjoyed having you in my house, but I cannot say the same of your sister. I have never in my life met such a deceitful girl.' Healer Goodwin rose to her full height, which was not very high at all.

'I arrived home today to find your sister had packed up and left. Took some medicine from me and some bread and cheese. She left some coins, I assume to pay for things she took. No note. Nothing to say thank you. Nothing even for you to tell you where she has gone. Unless she left something in your belongings, I have not checked there. These are not the actions of a good girl going to her betrothed.'

The Healer's words took the wind right out of Seamus. He stood there in the open door not knowing what to do. So many things were going round in his mind he did not know where to start. Seeing he was not in a good way, Goodwin shut the door behind him, took his hand, and led him to the chair on the opposite side of the fire.

'You sit yourself down a minute. I can see this is a shock for you.' She busied herself then handed him a cup of warm tea. 'Here you go, drink that, boy. I let my anger get the better of me. This just does not seem normal.' The elderly woman sat down opposite Seamus, concern now creasing her face.

So many things were going through Seamus' mind. Where had Aliah gone? Why had she left without him? Had she gone mad? No, she had not gone mad. She had taken medicine and food, so she must have had a plan. He should have realised her worry over getting to her father in time meant she was not prepared to wait. Going over their conversation, he realised she had said as much. But to not even discuss it with him ... Then again, she had already shown a tendency to act first and think later. Should he try and follow her? He really did not know whether he even wanted to. He took a deep breath and found himself face to face with Healer Goodwin.

'Are you all right? You went blank for a while there. I was getting a little concerned.' She sat back down and sipped her tea.

'Sorry.' Seamus shook his head in an effort to clear it. 'I was just thinking. I am so sorry, Healer Goodwin. I have not been quite honest with you. It is true that we were heading to meet my sister's betrothed, what I had not told you is she had never met him before, and was not exactly happy about the arrangement.' Seamus should have been worried at how easily the lie rolled off his tongue. He told himself he was not trying to save Aliah, but was trying to make a stranger who had been kind to him not feel like she had been betrayed, and it was actually closer to the truth than their original story.

'Have you any idea when Ali left?' he asked, hoping to buy some time to decide what he should do.

Goodwin shook her head. 'I left around midday, and returned less than a candle-mark before you did. She was asking about carriage trips today, and I did tell her there was one to Port Isby. She may have taken that, although there is no way of knowing until it returns, unless someone saw her board.'

'If she took a carriage to Port Isby she could be heading home. She did have some coin on her, we split it in case we were robbed.' In his own head, he did think it likely she had taken the carriage. She could easily get to Bannock from Port Isby.

'So will you be following her?'

That was the big question. Seamus was so angry Aliah had not waited for him, after all he had done to help her get this far and get well. He had put his own plans on hold. Even so, he was drawn to follow her. Aria was in danger and as a duke's son he should be doing everything to help the people of the Southern Duchy and Hand. On the other hand, he could no longer return home and he needed to find someone to teach him how to control his magic. He should continue with his plan and head to The Wizard's Isle.

'I would like to follow her, she should not be travelling alone,' Seamus admitted. 'But if she is silly enough to run away then I think she can spend some time travelling by herself to see what it is like. Maybe that will teach her a lesson. I will need to go to Duncameron and let her future family know what has happened and see if I can repair the damage. I think that is what our parents would want.' Seamus tried to look like he imagined a worried brother should look.

'If you are sure. It is dangerous for a girl to travel alone. If you do not follow, you run the risk of never seeing your sister again.' In spite of Aliah's actions, the good-natured healer was still looking out for her best interests.

'I know. After I have been to Duncameron I will head to Isby and see if I can pick up her trail.'

The healer looked at him carefully for a moment, sighed, then stood up. 'If you are going to Duncameron you may as well take up the offer to drive one of the wagons. That way you can save your pennies for chasing after your sister. You had best be off, and see if you can catch them before they finish for the evening. They will be able to load another wagon now they have an extra driver, and that will take some organising.'

Seamus did not move for a minute, he chewed at his lip and then decided. 'Yes, you are right. I will head to the smithy, they have been loading the wagons in the stables there. Hopefully someone will still be around, if not Smith Brown will know where to find them. I can also tell Smith Brown that I am finishing today. Thank you for being so understanding.' He looked sadly at Healer Goodwin.

'Off with you. I will have supper ready when you return.'

It was not until much later that Seamus arrived back at Healer Goodwin's house. Although his ability to join the team had been treated as a gift from the goddess—even after he had explained he had never driven a team of horses before—there was a lot of work to do to load the third wagon and he had felt obliged to help.

By the time he ate his supper he was ready to drop. He managed to pack his belongings after having checked for, but not found, a message from Aliah. Then he crashed into bed to try and get some sleep before the long journey tomorrow.

CHAPTER 9

THE ROAD TO DUNCAMERON

The next morning Healer Goodwyn insisted on walking with Seamus to the blacksmith's stables to see him off. Seamus was genuinely quite sad to say good-bye to her and Smith Brown. Although he would never make a good blacksmith himself, he had enjoyed his first ever paying job and, if his pay was anything to go by, Smith Brown had appreciated his work. Healer Goodwin had opened her home to him and he took pride in helping her over the last six-day. It gave him hope to know he could find some sort of life outside of Hand. It was difficult saying good-bye to them both.

The rest of the travelling party was already outside the stables when they arrived. The head of the group was a seasoned caravan boss everyone simply called, "Boss". He was a large, heavily muscled man with a weathered face that was all stern until he smiled. Then it was like the sun had come out from behind a cloud.

He showed Seamus to his team and Seamus immediately started to get to know the horses. Checking they were tethered correctly, he fed them an apple each to try and make friends. Boss nodded in approval, and Seamus was pleased the tactic he used on new horses in his father's stables was appropriate for working horses.

He was introduced to Boss' daughter, Megan, and her husband, Able. They in turn introduced Seamus to the two guards who would be riding with them as Boss had other things to be getting on with. The guards were both retired soldiers. Grunt was the senior of the two, but it was his companion, Helen, who asked him what he was able to do in case of attack. She was satisfied with Seamus being able to use his knives, and that he was passable with a staff. She told him a bow generally would not be much use in the type of fighting they would likely encounter on the road. In any case, they did not have any with them for him to use.

Introductions done, Boss had them all get ready to roll out. Seamus hugged Goodwin and thanked her for taking such good care of him and Ali. She shushed him and told him to, 'Get away before I get too mushy'. He shook the blacksmith's hand then climbed up on his wagon ready to go.

Boss' cart took the lead with Seamus and Tom in the centre. The blacksmith's apprentice was returning home to Duncameron for a visit while his foot healed. Megan took the rear position. Abel rode at the front checking the route as he was working as a guard on this journey. He would take turns with the other guards riding the front and rear.

Seamus could not actually say much about the first day of travel. He could not describe the scenery, and he and Tom did not talk much except for Tom to pass on instructions. All his attention was taken up with keeping his team moving and making sure they did not leave the road, or run into the cart in front, or go so slow they were in danger of being run into from the cart behind. He was so relieved when they finally stopped for the evening.

Tom talked him through uncoupling the horses from the wagon and tying them to a lead line for the night. He helped Seamus brush, feed, and water them. Before settling down for their evening meal he and Tom put up their sleeping quarters, a tent that attached to the side of the cart. Their work done, they joined the others by the fire.

He managed to get through the meal, just, but was so weary he almost fell asleep sitting up. Tom finally told him to go to bed. 'The guards will take turns on watch, we should only have to take a turn if one of them falls sick. So make sure you get a good nights sleep. Goodnight.' Seamus left him to join the others by the fire.

'Goodnight.' Seamus yawned as he crawled into his bedroll and was soon fast asleep. The next thing he knew Megan was shaking him awake.

'It's sun-up sleepyhead.' She laughed at him. 'Come on, we have to take the tent down before breakfast as Dad likes to get moving pretty sharply.'

Seamus stumbled around trying to help Megan with the tent until she shooed him away. Able came over to help her stow it and their bedrolls in the trunk attached to the back of the cart. He went to see the horses were fed and watered and ready to continue their journey.

Once they were on their way the second day was pretty much the same as the first, with the exception that they passed through a couple of small villages. Seamus found he could not go straight to bed after dinner that night as it was his turn to help with washing the dishes. It seemed everyone took their turn at the camp jobs. As he started to doze, his thoughts drifted to Aliah, wondering if she was all right. He was still very annoyed with her, but he meant her no ill. She should have been at Port Isby, probably even on a ship heading for home. He hoped she was closer to her goal than he was.

AFTER TWO DAYS of constant movement Aliah appreciated the stillness of the night as she sat squashed between two crates of goods slowly nibbling some bread and cheese. Pulling her cloak around her to settle down to sleep in her cramped space she dreamed longingly of the bed at Healer Goodwin's, probably exaggerating how soft it had been. But she was warm, she had food in her stomach, and the healer's medicine meant she was on the mend.

It could have been worse, much worse in fact. She had found soon after starting her journey that the cost of travel was high, so she had to do some ducking and diving to get to where she was. She was lucky she had not had to go back to the healer's place and swallow her pride.

As Aliah started to doze, she guiltily wondered where Seamus was. She had kicked herself a number of times for not thinking to leave him a note in his pack to let him know what she was planning, and for him not to worry about her. That had always been her downfall, acting before totally thinking things through. On reflection, if she had spoken to Seamus he might have agreed with her plan and she would have had some company and maybe even been able to sleep in a bed.

Instead, she had repaid his kindness by running out on him without a word. Her only consolation was that she was putting Aria first. She vowed when she got home, she would contact the Wizards on the Isle and make sure he was going to be fine when he arrived. She owed him that at least. And she would send a note of thanks to Healer Goodwin when this was all over, explaining why she had to leave so suddenly. She was sure the healer would understand that matters of state came before any other considerations. She would send her a thank you gift just to be sure though. But before all of that she had to get home.

DAY THREE WAS to be their last full day on the road before reaching Duncameron. Seamus had expected it to be as uneventful as the other two days, but he was in for a surprise. At midday they stopped by a river to rest the horses and have something to eat.

Not long after they had pulled off the road a group of five riders galloped past heading towards Sunnydale. They had begun to see more people on the road as they drew closer to the larger town, so Seamus did not think this was anything unusual. That was until the guards ordered them to move their wagons into a triangle. Tom was asked to stay out of sight in the middle of the wagons, and the rest prepared to fight.

It was then Seamus noticed the dust coming back along the road as the five riders returned, escorting a sixth man dressed in black with a wizard's lightening bolt sigil clearly showing on his chest. It was coloured silver, showing he had nearly reached the top rank of wizards. There was no doubt they were heading straight for the group of carts and, by the look on their faces, their purpose was not friendly.

Boss stepped out to meet them, with Abel at his shoulder. Abel had his sword drawn, and Boss had his hand on the hilt of his.

'Whoa,' said Boss commandingly. 'Slow down! You will have our horses bolting, rushing by at that pace.'

'We do not,"rush by",' the wizard responded in an imperious tone. 'I have sensed one of your party is a person we are looking for. You will hand them over to us!'

'We don't want any trouble,' Boss answered. 'But all of our party are well known to me and I cannot for the life of me think why one of the king's wizards would be looking for any of them. Perhaps you could explain who it is you are looking for and why, and perhaps we can let you know if that person is amongst us.' Grunt and Helen moved up to stand on either side of Boss, hands on the hilts of their swords, signalling they would let their visitors no closer without an explanation. Seamus stayed back by the wagons with Megan.

The wizard visibly sighed, as if this was some troublesome intervention he did not need. 'You will introduce me to all your team and I will decide if they are who I am looking for.'

Megan moved closer to Seamus. 'Helen says you are good with knives?' she whispered.

Seamus nodded, without taking his eyes off the wizard and his men.

'Good enough to just miss someone?'

Seamus nodded.

'Ok, you take the two on the left, and I will take the three on the right. As soon as anyone moves forward or goes to get off their horse, you throw a knife in front of them as a warning. Yes?'

Seamus nodded once more, still not taking his eyes off the men in front of them.

'Well, I guess we will not be doing that,' Boss said. 'Although you wear the king's robes your men do not wear royal colours. So I am thinking you might be on the king's business, but it is just as likely you are not. And even if you were, you have no right to question honest folk without a warrant, and as you have not produced one, I am thinking you do not have one. So, with respect, I think you should be on your way and leave honest folk to get on with their work.'

The wizard looked directly at a man on his right, who started to get off his horse. Seamus resisted the urge to make the horse move as he was sure someone had told him once wizards could sense other wizards using magic. Besides he had never tried using it on an animal before. As the man's foot hit the ground one of his knives landed about a hand-span in front of it. The man halted where he stood, looking at the wizard for further instructions.

'As I said, I think you had best be on your way,' Boss told them, without even flinching. 'The next one will wound, the third will maim, and the fourth ...'

'You dare to challenge me? I am on the king's business,' the Wizard said through gritted teeth. 'And I sense the one I look for is here. You would do well to let me search.'

'And you would be best to have a warrant!' Boss did not waver.

An odd sensation like the wind rustling in his head caused Seamus to frown as the wizard's face took on a glazed expression.

'He is consulting with someone,' Megan whispered.

Seamus shook his head, unused to feeling magic being worked around him, and surprised Megan could feel what the Wizard was doing. He looked at her, shock clearly written on his face.

She merely met his gaze. 'I have a little skill, enough to know when magic is around, something you and I might talk about later.' They all held still until the wizard's gaze focused again on Boss.

'Very well. Johnson, you are to ride ahead to Duncameron. Talk to the magistrate, my mentor, one of the highest ranked Wizard of Gold, is arranging a warrant. You will bring it back to me. The rest of you, we will follow this group to make sure no one leaves.' The man on the ground remounted as one of their number took off for Duncameron.

Boss and Abel walked back to the carts, picking up Seamus' knife on the way. Helen and Grunt stayed between the wizard and their group, faces impassive, hands on their sword hilts. The four on the outside of the triangle watered the horses and passed about food. Boss whispered to Tom to stay under the cover of their wagon and try not to be seen. He did not want their *guests* to know they had an additional person who could not fight, as he could be targeted should things turn nasty.

Able took three horses to where Grunt and Helen stood, and the three guards mounted. Once they were in their saddles, Megan, Seamus, and Boss took their seats and moved the carts onto the road. Megan in front this time, Seamus in the middle, and Boss behind.

'We ride all the way through to Duncameron,' Boss ordered as they started moving.

They kept a steady pace throughout the afternoon. Every now and then the rustling sound disturbed Seamus, letting him know magic was being worked. A couple of times he turned around to see what the wizard was doing, and each time he caught the wizard looking at him curiously. It was a tense journey. At any moment he expected to see the rider return with the warrant.

As the sun continued its path through the sky, Seamus concentrated on keeping his team at a steady pace, and when he looked up he was surprised to see the wizard steering his horse towards his wagon.

'You, there?'

Seamus wearily watched the wizard come closer.

'Yes. You, boy. I can feel some magic in you. How about you help me find who I am looking for and I will offer you something someone of your station could never hope for: a place to train at the Wizard Isles.'

Until that precise moment it was what Seamus thought he wanted. As he looked into the cruel, hard eyes of the man riding beside him, he knew he did not want to be like this man, full of his own sense of entitlement. He had been brought up to serve the people of Hand and the Southern Duchy, and he had believed the wizards from the Isle were there to serve as well. But this man seemed to think his position put him above the law.

Without any intention of helping him, Seamus asked, 'Who is it you look for?'

The wizard's face curled into a snarl. 'An ungrateful wench. A blonde-haired, blue-eyed girl about your age who has decided her betters do not know what is right for her. She has run away from her betrothed and needs to be brought to heel.'

Seamus hoped the look he gave the wizard was one of wide-eyed astonishment. Inside he was sincerely pleased that Aliah was far away from this man. 'What makes you think she is with us? None of the women here meet that description.'

'I can smell her.'

The way the wizard said it made Seamus' stomach heave.

'If she is not here, then one of you has been near her in the last few days.'

'And why would a wizard be interested in a girl running from her wedding?' Helen pulled her horse up in between Seamus and the wizard.

'Because she is the king's daughter,' he snarled at her. 'She is to marry a king and cement our two nations. Such a great honour, but the ungrateful girl does not know what is good for her.'

'I cannot think why anyone would refuse the match when you put it in terms like that.'

Helen's irony was clearly lost on the wizard when he said, 'Exactly'.

'We think she has been travelling with a boy, an untrained magic user. Some foolish people are hailing them as the wizard and warrior from the old tales because she carries a sword. But do not let that romantic claptrap fool you. They are both very dangerous.'

'I am sure they are.' Helen raised an eyebrow that only Seamus could see, and he chuckled into his chest. 'Now, away with you. This boy is supposed to be concentrating on his job.'

'Don't forget my offer boy,' the Wizard said as he pulled at the reins and kicked his horse, then headed back to his own party.

'What did he mean, Helen, about boys like me not being allowed into the Wizard Isle to train?' Seamus asked before Helen rode off to keep an eye on the wizard.

'Megan sensed last night that you are leaking out magic, something untrained wizards do. She is a magic finder. In the past, parents would send boys like you to the Wizard Isles. But the last year or so many boys who are not of the "right heritage" have failed to gain entry. It seems people with no money for fees are no longer accepted on the Isle. This has many people grumbling.'

'How is that he has not sensed Megan's magic?' Seamus wondered out loud.

'She is a woman, and women with magic do not count as true magic users to those of his kind.' Helen answered disdainfully as she rode off to join Grunt at the back of the wagons.

'You have magic? How awesome.'

Seamus had forgotten that Tom was hiding in the wagon behind him until the other boy spoke. 'Just a little,' Seamus answered. 'Not even enough to light a flame.'

'Still ...' Tom's voice came from behind. Then, changing the subject he said, 'Funny that the princess ran away from her intended, and your sister did too. And they are both blonde with blue eyes.' If it were not for Tom's open and honest nature, Seamus would have believed he had actually put two and two together and come up with the truth.

'Maybe it is a sign people should stop arranging marriages for girls to suit their own ends, and let the girls choose,' Seamus responded.

'I agree,' Tom said. 'I am going to see my Maisie tomorrow, and I would not like it one bit if her father told her who to marry, even if it were me. Because I know Maisie would do the opposite just to spite him.' Tom then spent the next few candle-marks extolling the virtues of his fair Maisie.

As the afternoon rolled on to night, the pace slowed as both horses and their humans were getting weary. Just when he thought he would fall asleep at the reigns, Seamus swore he could see lights twinkling in the distance, and he sighed with relief. Still, it was another good candle length before they would come to the outskirts of Duncameron. Seamus was startled from his stupor by a voice close by.

'I know it is you, boy. You have been with the princess. I can smell it on you.'

Seamus could not see the wizard, but he could feel the waves of darkness rolling off him and his stomach churned in response.

'Tell me where she is,' he hissed.

Controlling his voice, he projected a calmness he did not feel. 'I really do not know what you are talking about. I have enough worries of my own without any trouble from you. Please, leave me alone.'

'You heard the boy.' Abel's voice came from the darkness. 'Leave him alone.'

Snorting his anger, the wizard turned his horse and headed towards the back of the caravan.

'You have really made a friend there.' Tom laughed from behind him.

'I don't wish to anger a wizard,' Seamus said. 'But I really have no idea what he is on about.' Although he said the words out loud, Seamus was sick to the stomach. How could the wizard know he had been with Aliah? Could he really smell her on him? And if he could, how was he going to get away from him?

When they finally reached Duncameron the gates to the main town were closed for the night. Megan led them through the streets that had spilled out from the old town to an inn with a large stable yard nestled in the shelter of the walls. Boss expertly backed the carts into the inn's courtyard. Seamus and Boss untethered the horses and took them into the stables to feed and tend them, while Megan went to speak with the innkeeper.

Under cover of moving the horses, Seamus smuggled Tom into the stables. Two of the wizard's men moved to the door to make sure no one left without their knowing. Helen and Grunt went and stood behind them to ensure they left the others alone to get on with their work.

'Right,' Boss whispered, as he bought a horse into the stall where Seamus was settling his horses in for the night. 'It is pretty clear for some reason the wizard wants you.' Seamus went to argue, but Boss held up his hand. 'I really do not want to know, because what I don't know, I can't tell. I know these men do not have a warrant for you, and lately there have been too many good men taken by wizards and their friends not to be seen again. I do not want to see that happen to you. So here's the plan.'

'Megan is arranging with the innkeeper to smuggle you out through the back and take you to a friend of mine. He will be able to help you control the magic Megan says is leaking out of you. He can also deal with the smell the wizard sniffer has found. Here is your pay.' He handed Seamus the three coins he was due. 'Now go wait at the back of the stables and be ready to go.'

'Thank you,' Seamus said. 'But won't you get into trouble when they find out I have left?'

'Well, doing the right thing can always get you in trouble, but I don't think they will notice for a bit. And if they do, I have a feeling we are better off saying you escaped than them finding you with us and confirming their suspicions. I plan to have Tom bed down in here to look after the horses, so they will likely assume he is you, unless they get a look at him walking, and we can prevent that for a little while.'

'Are you sure? What about the wizard saying he could smell me?' Seamus asked.

'Megan can work a small magic, make a distracting smell for a bit. Now grab your things and go wait in the back corner over there. Helen or someone will show you the way out.'

'Thank you,' Seamus said. 'For the work and the help.'

Boss looked abashed and mumbled, 'It's all right,' before turning back to the horse Seamus had been tending to finish his work. Seamus went over to the pile of bags that had been unloaded from the carts and grabbed his possessions.

He had not been there long when a head appeared at his feet.

'Oi,' the boy whispered. 'You are to follow me. Be quiet now as they have lookouts posted around the yard.' He then proceeded to push aside a couple of boards to make a hole big enough for Seamus to crawl through.

Once outside, they crouched down, and crawled along a narrow path between stacked barrels until they hit a fence. The boy pushed open a small gate and, crouching low, Seamus followed him through it. The boy reached back and re-fastened the gate.

'Shh.' He motioned with his fingers to his lips. 'This way and be fast! Old Earl at the gate will not hold it open for long. Stick to the shadows behind me and we will not be seen unless someone is truly looking for anyone trying to escape.'

Seamus struggled to keep up with the nimble young boy, weary as he was from a long day of travelling. They soon made it to the small gate beside the main gate into Duncameron.

'Slip him a coin.' The lad motioned to the guard standing by the partially open gate. As Seamus reached into his purse, the sound of running feet drifted from some distance behind him. 'Quick as you can,' the boy said. 'I think we may have been spotted. Better make it two coins, Earl will need to delay whoever is behind us.'

Seamus gave two of his small supply of coins to the gatekeeper, who ushered them through the opening and firmly shut the gate behind them.

'This way.' The boy motioned, and Seamus followed him through the maze of streets, completely reliant on the slippery figure as he moved further and further into the darkness of the town. They wove their way in and out of alleyways and streets until the boy finally stopped outside a door. Weary to the core, Seamus nearly stumbled over the boy as he stopped, but caught himself just in time.

Knocking twice, he paused, then knocked twice again. A few short moments later the door opened a crack, a head looked out, then up and down the street. An elderly looking man opened the door, and motioned them in. The boy handed the man a letter, which he immediately read.

'I had best get back, quick smart,' the boy said. 'Two coins is customary for guiding.'

'You young scallywag,' the elderly man said as he chuckled. 'It is only one if you are not stopped.'

'We was nearly stopped.' He looked hopefully at Seamus. 'Awright, one then.' He held out his hand and Seamus reached into his purse again and gave the last of his driving coins to his guide.

'Thank you,' he said as the boy took off.

'Well, don't dilly-dally in the street, else all our good work will be undone,' his host advised, and Seamus blindly followed him into the hallway of the darkened house, then into the front room.

It was a small, neat front room, sparsely furnished, but snug looking with tightly drawn curtains. There were books over every surface, and the small plate of food on the arm of a chair showed the man's evening meal had been interrupted by Seamus' arrival. The man peeked through the closed curtains to check the street, then he pulled his head back into the room, frowned at Seamus, and advised him to follow if he wanted to stay safe. Seamus trailed after him into the hallway, and through the door he opened.

'Down there.' He motioned. 'And be quick!'

'But it's a cellar,' Seamus said in a shocked voice.

'I know. But it is best you be there than here for the moment. Haven't time to explain.' And then he showed he was not as old and feeble as he appeared by pushing Seamus through the door and shutting it firmly behind him.

Exhausted, stunned and scared out of his wits, Seamus had reached a point where he simply did not know what to do next. Should he bang on the door and demand to be let out? Or should he go quietly down the stairs and wait? If he did the first he risked being found by his pursuers, if he did the second there was a chance he had just been kidnapped and would be aiding his assailants. So he stood there, undecided.

'I got this far,' he said to himself. 'Only to be locked in a cellar.' His face twisted into a smile. He could stand here all night, but he really needed to eat and sleep, so he may as well find himself somewhere more comfortable. He stumbled down the stairs in the dark then proceeded to set up his sleeping gear, which, fortunately, was on the top of his pack. When he was comfortable he rummaged around and found some dried fruit and travel bread. With his hunger quietened, it did not take long before the day caught up with him and he was sound asleep.

TRAVELLING in her cramped hiding space was uncomfortable, and it was boring. She had nothing to do for hours on end, and she could not even really hear the conversations of the people around her. At best she could hear muffled voices, at worst there was just the creaking and moving of the cargo around her. Perhaps the only good thing about it was that she was resting a lot and her strength was coming back to her. That and the fact Healer Goodwin's medicine made her sleep often.

The third day of travel was the worst though. The first two days had been relatively short, and by limiting her water intake she had been able to manage by sneaking out at night to take care of nature. But the third day for some reason was much longer. They did not stop until well into the night, and Aliah was bursting. A quick peak out of her hiding place showed her that there were too many people around for her to risk getting out.

She stifled a groan as she sat back down, wondering how long before her companions went to bed and she could sneak out? Then she realised that this was not like the other nights. There was no sound of camp being set up, and the horse hooves sounded like they were on cobblestones, not dirt.

Had they come to the end of the journey already? Aliah's mind began churning over. Would they unload tonight? If they did, would she be able to escape? And how far would she be able to run with an achingly full bladder?

Taking a deep breath she slowed her breathing the way her father's sword master had shown her when he taught her to fight. As she concentrated on her breathing she did not notice someone start to undo the canvas on the other side of her hiding place, she nearly jumped out of her skin when a voice came out of the darkness beside her.

'Crawl quietly towards me. Try not to make a noise or disturb anything. When you get to the side, slide out your bag. I will catch it. Then roll yourself out and follow me. Don't try to run away, you will be caught.'

A number of choice words her father would not approve of her uttering ran through her head. How had he known she was here? Did he mean her harm? Was there any way she could get out without following his directions?

'Quickly now. There is a king's wizard here. I suspect he is looking for you. He will find you easily enough if you don't follow my directions. And I am assuming you do not want that to happen.'

A wizard? Here? How did that happen? How could she not notice that? Should she trust this person, or should she give herself over to the wizard? Then she remembered her father's chief advisor, the wizard, Millard, and the way he looked as she boarded the ship when she left home. He was gleeful, almost as if he somehow gained something from her departure. She did not trust him. Her mind was made up. Slowly getting the circulation back into her limbs she began to move.

'Hurry up,' her rescuer whispered.

'I am going as fast as I can,' she whispered back. 'I would like to see you move fast after having been cramped like this all day,' she almost said, but bit her tongue. She managed to slide her bag and her cloak-wrapped sword through the hole.

'*Wait.*' Footsteps moved away from the canvas, there was some mumbling, then someone was back. 'Now it is your turn. Quietly, though. That wizard and his friends are a suspicious lot.'

Aliah began to slide her body round the crates she had been squashed between all day. It was not as easy as it seemed, and her skirt caught between two crates and the whole load began to topple.

'Hey, what's going on there?' someone shouted.

'It is just me,' the voice beside her said. 'I was trying to get my gear out for tonight, was not paying attention and just about brought some crates down.'

'Well, be more careful. Any breakages come out of your wages.'

'I will." He dropped his voice to a whisper. "And so will you.'

She had frozen during the exchange, but now worked her skirt free and made it to the opening in the canvas. With all her might she tried to roll herself over the side, but after her illness and sitting for three days, she was just not strong enough.

'Here. Let me help.' A strong arm snaked through the gap, grabbed her round the waist and rolled her up the side of the wagon, through the gap, then down the other side. The world looked topsy-turvy for a moment, then she was upright staring directly at a man who she guessed to be about five and twenty. He was carrying quite a number of knives, and there was as sword at his side. He looked her up and down. 'Can you walk?'

She nodded back at him. 'So long as it is not far.'

'Oh, it is not far at all. Boss wants a word with you.'

Aliah's stomach clenched, and she almost lost control of her bladder there and then. He grabbed her arm, picked up her gear, and pulled her to the front of the two wagons.

'Good, let's go while all their attention is on the barn.' He pulled her towards the back of the building.

'*Hey.*'

Instead of stopping, the man pulled her faster in behind the building, then popped his head around into the yard to see what was happening.

'Whew. Looks like they were calling someone else. In here.' He pushed her roughly through a door, which let to a hallway. On one side she could hear the hustle and bustle of a kitchen, the door on the other side was closed. He opened that door and pushed her through. 'Wait here.'

Before he could shut the door Aliah put her foot in it. 'My possessions?' she asked.

He flashed a smile, and she imagined she could see real humour in his eyes. 'Good try, but I know the feel of a sword.'

Aliah shrugged, it was worth a try. 'How about a trip to the privy before you lock me up? I have not been since last night.'

Was that genuine sympathy in his eyes? 'Sorry, cannot let you back out there. Too dangerous. For you and for us. I will get one of the girls to bring you a chamber pot.'

He locked the door behind him but, true to his word, he opened it for a girl a few moments later. A pot was passed through. He did not close the door, but he and the girl gave her privacy so she could take care of herself. Once the pot was removed the door was again closed and Aliah was left alone in the dark.

CHAPTER 10
NIGHTS IN A CELLAR

Seamus awoke as sunlight streamed down the stairs to the cellar. He blinked in the stark light as his eyes adjusted to the room, then groggily got to his feet. The morning light revealed two beds against the walls of the cellar, and he cursed himself for his stupidity at not lighting a match the night before. At the very least he could have slept in comfort.

'Apologies to you, I did not mean for you to stay here so long last night. There were patrols out on the street in larger numbers than normal all night, and there were definitely wizards with them.' The elderly man looked even older in the bright sunlight, after a sleepless night. 'I have coffee on the stove and breakfast cooking. No need to bring your bags up, we can sort them out later.'

Seamus stumbled up the stairs and followed his host into a room at the back of the house which, given the smells coming from there, was the kitchen.

'Please, sit down.' The man gestured to the table that was positioned in the middle of the room. When he was seated the man proceeded to dish up two plates loaded with bacon and mushrooms and tomatoes. Seamus immediately began devouring his as if he had not seen a meal in weeks, stopping only to drink some of the cool water that was already on the table. His host placed down cups of milky, steaming coffee, and then joined him at the table. He was about halfway through his meal when he placed down his knife and fork and looked at Seamus.

'That was a big ruckus last night and, if it was all to find you, someone wants you pretty badly. If that is the case then you are way more important than Boss Allum realised. He asked me to take care of you, to teach you how to shield your magic, and then get you home to your family. Before I commit to helping you, I need to make sure you are who you say you are, and that by helping you I will not be putting myself or others at risk

'I am going to finish my meal, and then I am going to tell you a bit about me. I do not do this lightly as even knowing a little bit about me may get you into trouble and compromise my security. I would appreciate it if you would give me enough of your story to let me know whether I should help you or not, and what I might actually be able to do to help you. If you choose not to tell me the truth—and believe me after you hear my story you will know I have the resources to tell whether or not you do—then I am happy for you to leave.' He looked steadily at Seamus, and then carried on eating.

Seamus kept his head down, no longer enjoying his food. The man knew there was more to his story than he had told Boss. He would help, but the cost was to tell him the truth. How much of the truth would he actually be able to share without compromising his family or Aliah? How much should he tell given the wizard from yesterday was clearly not going to give up searching for him? Finally, after what seemed an age, his host finished his last mouthful and refilled both their coffees.

'I am of a mind to start now, but you feel free to keep eating.' He smiled, but the smile did not really touch his eyes.

Seamus placed his knife and fork down on his plate and stared at the elderly man. Looking at him in this light, he did not seem quite as old as he had last night. His light blue eyes were clear, if a little weary from a night without sleep. His greying hair was a little unkempt, but there was still plenty of brown through it. The wrinkles Seamus remembered seeing on his face last night were no longer there. In fact, if he did not know better, the man might only be ten or so years older than his father.

'I will not be starting with my name, that you will have when I know the truth of you. This is to protect both of us, as knowing who I am could put you in danger. And if you tell the wrong people you know me, well, that would place me in serious danger as well. For the moment you can call me Walter, as many do, and I will continue to call you Sean. So we will start with what happened last night.'

'It seems a silver wizard was very interested in finding you so Boss Allum had you brought to me. Where you stayed last night, although not comfortable, was a warded room. That means only a very strong wizard would have been able to find you. A large number of people were searching for you for most of the night. They have stopped for the moment, possibly to regroup, so we have a small opportunity to decide our next step.' He paused to drink some of his coffee, and Seamus followed his every move.

'You want to know how I know they have stopped?' He looked at a surprised Seamus. 'I can feel they have stopped using magic to sense you, just as I can sense you through your magic. As an untrained wizard you are leaking magic almost continuously. This broadcasting will only get stronger unless you learn the most basic of techniques to control it.'

'And the only way you would know that is if you were a wizard yourself,' Seamus interrupted. 'And that would mean you are working for the same people as those who are following me.' Seamus moved as if to get up and leave.

'Settle down.' Walter calmly carried on drinking his coffee. 'While all those who call themselves wizards do report to the grand wizard, I do not call myself wizard and have not done so for a few years. In fact, there are many of us who no longer use the title, but that does not mean we are not strong in magic.

'There are many magic users out there from herb women to water diviners who use magic but are not wizards. It is true that men strong in magic are to be trained and regulated by the wizard council on the Wizard Isles, and for a while I was. In fact, I was a teacher of trainee wizards before I left.

'However, I became aware of some corruption and strange goings on there, and when I tried to investigate I was demoted from my position. I became a village healer and then, when I could no longer trust the actions of my fellow wizards, I left the order all together.

'After I left my post I wandered until I came into contact with a group of people who had heard of my issues with the wizards' council and knew of their corruption. Apparently it had been building for years. These people are allied with some other magic users, I am not at liberty to tell you anything about who these people are as it could place them in danger. What I can say is that we have been gathering information and watching events, waiting for our chance to thwart their grand scheme. The wizard who looked for you last night is known to be loyal to one of the inner-circle of plotters. Because of this, I was asked to look after you and get you away because we do not trust their intentions.

'Boss thought the Wizard was looking for you because your magic is very strong. I have to say I personally think it very unlikely that all those soldiers last night would have been mobilised for a mere magic user, no matter how potentially powerful a wizard they would make.'

'Is there not a danger that uncontrolled magic can be harmful?' Seamus asked, feeling a little sheepish because he knew so very little on the subject.

Walter laughed. 'That is a common myth. It has been rumoured that in the past people who could not control their magic have exploded, killing themselves and others around them. I have never seen this happen, in fact my experience leads me to believe that the body can only take in as much magic as it can safely hold, and it gets rid of anything it cannot cope with, hence the leaking of magic in untrained mages.'

'Oh,' Seamus tried not to feel foolish. 'So Boss and his crew are part of the group you talked about?'

'I really should not say anything more about them,' Walter responded. 'At least not until I know your story. I have told you much about myself, I hope you guard my secret as carefully as you guard your own.'

Seamus gnawed on his lip while he considered how much he should tell Walter about himself and about Aliah. Decision made, he took a deep breath and began.

'Up until Sunnydale I had been travelling with a girl. We told people she was my sister, but she was not. We were heading in the same direction and it suited us to travel together. We parted ways at Sunnydale. It seems the wizard last night could smell that I had been with her, and that is why he is looking for me.'

Walter raised his eyebrows and indicated that Seamus should continue.

'Her story is not mine to tell, and I will not betray her secrets. I will just say that what she was doing was important for all of Aria, and she was brave to be doing it, if a little foolish in her approach.'

Seamus could not be sure, but it looked like Walter was holding back a chuckle. 'And you, young man, what is your story?'

'I left home because I realised I had magic and I needed someone to teach me how to control and use it. I had thought to go to the Wizard Isle and ask to be trained there. Now I am not so sure. I did not like that wizard on the road. He really gave me the creeps and he seemed to be saying that a common boy would not be accepted there, but if I gave up my friend then he would make an exception.'

Walter agreed. 'Yes, it appears things have changed since I left. Now only the sons of the well to do who can pay fees are accepted. Listening to you though, I would be surprised if your parents were not wealthy enough to be able to pay the fees the school sets.'

Seamus ignored the lead to give him more information. 'Then

one of Boss' crew seemed to be saying that the wizards were responsible for the disappearance of certain people. That also made me uncomfortable.'

'It is true the wizards no longer have the confidence of many people, and that number becomes greater the closer you get to Bannock. So you will return home now and find someone close to home to train you?'

Seamus could feel himself going red under Walter's scrutiny. How much should he tell the man? He gnawed on his lip again. Walter had been a teacher of wizards, maybe if he told him everything he would take Seamus on as a kind of apprentice?

'I cannot do that.' Seamus admitted. 'Where I come from magic is not permitted. Now they know I have it I can never return home.'

Walter raised his eyebrows in surprise. 'You are from Hand? No ... wait ... you are. And if I remember rightly only the ruling family has magic running through it. So you are the duke's son? By your age ... You must be his oldest son. Well, I'll be ...'

It appeared Walter was speechless, so Seamus continued. 'I am Seamus, and I was heir to the Duchy before all this happened. I cannot go home and I need a teacher. I was hoping that maybe ...'

Walter suddenly found his voice again. 'Oh, no. Not me. Not in a million years. I am satisfied with what I have here, and I would be hard pressed to explain you away. No, do not look at me like that. It would be too dangerous for both of us if you stayed, especially since the wizards already know you are here in Duncameron. I can alter how I appear to others so I can hide in plain sight, but I could not do that for both of us.' As if he could not bear to look at Seamus' crestfallen face he immediately began clearing the dishes.

'I can teach you to manage your leaking and how to only draw magic when your stores are low. That I will do for you, because if I do not, then you will surely be caught. But that is all I can do.'

Seamus did not know what to say. He helped Walter with the dishes in silence. His gut was churning. He did not want to go to train with the wizards on their island. He could not stay here because

Walter was right, it was too dangerous to do so. What should he do? As his thoughts wandered through his options, a rustling brushed his head.

'Quick. Seamus, take that food and water from the bench and head to the basement. Quickly now! I feel the magic stirring.' Walter grabbed a candlestick holder and some candles and followed Seamus.

Feeling an odd prickling at the back of his neck, Seamus looked at Walter, who looked closely at him. 'You can feel it too, I see. We have not got much time.'

As they entered the basement Walter pulled the door closed behind him. Seamus noticed there was a handle on the inside, and laughed at how worried he had been last night about being locked in. He was soon settled in, and more comfortably than the night before now he could use a bed.

'Right,' Walter said. 'I have a plan of sorts, well for today at least. I need to go and talk with some friends of mine. We will need their support to leave Duncameron. In the meantime I need you to stay here in the basement. I know it is not great, but you cannot be detected here unless they send some stronger wizards from the Isle, which would take time.'

'How long will you be?' Seamus asked, not happy about spending any more time in the basement.

'As short a time as I need, but by supper time at the latest. That would be about two candles time. If I am not back by then you will need to assume something has happened to me. If I can, I will try and send someone to find you if it looks likely there will be any trouble.'

Walter looked Seamus straight in the eye. 'At the moment you are a big liability. A blood sensor, such as the one you met yesterday needs to be within sight of a person to get a full reading, but you are broadcasting your magical ability far and wide. While I am gone, I need you to practice shielding your magic.'

Seamus frowned. 'I don't know what you mean.'

'I know, but you need to trust me on this. I have taught many a young wizard to shield and control their talent. Admittedly, it can take weeks, but I need you to learn quicker than that. This will tire you, but you need to keep practicing all day for me.'

Seamus nodded. 'All right.' He settled and Walter asked him to closed his eyes and breathe deeply in and out, and relax his muscles. It was so much like the concentration techniques used before weapons practice that Seamus found it easy to follow.

'Now you are relaxed, I need you to keep your eyes closed and concentrate on your body. Can you feel around your heart a pulsating warmth?'

Seamus focussed. He felt the warmth, and as soon as he felt it he lost it in his excitement. He went through the relaxation techniques again, and after his third attempt, he managed to feel the pulse without losing it.

'Good,' Walter praised. 'Now I need you to concentrate on that warm pulse and push it to the ends of your fingers. You need to imagine it moving from your centre through your chest and down your arms until it reaches the end of your fingers.'

Seamus concentrated but could not move the pulse. He broke out in a sweat as he lost the pulse again.

'No one does it the first time,' Walter assured him. 'Do not think of the pulse as being separate from you, think of it as your lifeblood, and that it has channels to move along to the end of your fingers.'

Seamus began again. At first he managed to move the pulse to his arms, but was so surprised he lost his hold. He kept trying until he finally managed to get the pulse to his fingers. He could hear from Walter's voice that he was pleased with his progress.

'Now slowly bring the pulse back to the centre.' This process also took a number of tries before Seamus could send the pulse down to his fingers and back to the centre. When he achieved it he opened his eyes to find Walter smiling.

'Good. Very good. I am sure you have already found that you can move objects by willing it if you concentrate hard enough. Maybe even sometimes without meaning to. When doing this you have been using the magic that pulses inside of you. When you try to move an object you are pushing it out. What you have just learnt is the first step in beginning to control the magic, or the pulse. Now eat something then I will show you how to shield your pulse from others.'

Seamus was surprised to find he actually needed to eat, even though it was only a candle-mark since breakfast.

'Magic uses energy, as much as physical exercise does. If you have not used it for a while you will burn more energy, much like if you are unfit and you do physical activity,' Walter explained as Seamus ate some bread spread with a soft cheese. When he finished Walter restarted the lesson.

'Find your pulse again, push it to your fingers, bring it back to the centre. Good. Now in your mind make the pulse as small as you can, until you barely feel it.'

Seamus concentrated then looked up when he felt he could make the pulse no smaller. 'That is good,' said Walter. 'Already your broadcast is quieter. Now we have to hide it so no one can hear it.'

Seamus opened his eyes. 'Hide it? How?'

Walter patiently told him. 'Repeat the exercise.' He waited until Seamus confirmed he had done it, and he himself could feel the magical vibration quieten. 'Now, I need you to imagine that small pulse as a hard object, and I need you to imagine putting that object in a box and closing it.'

Seamus felt Walter watching him as he tried to hide his magic. Just when he thought he had it hidden, Walter's searching probe found the pulse and freed it from its bonds.

'*Goddess,*' Seamus exploded.

Walter laughed. 'No that is good! You managed to stop the vibrations, which is good for your first time. As you get stronger you will also be able to hide yourself from other lesser wizards when they probe. And that is how a teacher will test how strong your control is.'

'I think I understand.' Seamus told his teacher.

'Right, so today you need to practice these exercises, extending your pulse then hiding it, and we will work on this until you can hide your pulse without needing to feel the extension first. The step after that is to keep your power hidden until you need to use it. The final step I will teach you is to feel when your magic is low and how to draw more. Understand?'

'Yes,' Seamus mumbled, thinking it would be a slow process, given how long it had taken him to get this far.

'Fine,' Walter said. 'From the candle I can see if I do not leave soon it will be midday already. I need to meet with some friends at a tavern to find out what is happening, and await a message from some allies so we can plan. I will also ask around and find out if there are any magic users who might be prepared to take on an apprentice. You can keep practicing in my absence.'

With that Walter rose, climbed the stairs, and left Seamus alone. He finished eating his bread and cheese, drank some water, then continued with his exercises. While he was exercising his mind he also needed to exercise his body, but what could he do in such a confined space? An idea hit him. He started going through the main sword positions, both attack and defence, to keep his body moving.

As he did so he realised it was like a kind of dance. He wondered if one person attacked while another defended without swords, would that be a new type of fighting? Something stirred in his memories. It was not a new idea. He remembered seeing some visitors to the palace practice an unarmed combat similar to this. He wished he had someone to develop the idea further with. If only Liam was here. He stopped moving as a feeling of homesickness overwhelmed him. Sitting down on the bed he started his magic exercises again to take his mind off the loneliness he felt.

Halfway through the second candle he took another break. Half listening for the door, he tried to sleep. As soon as he heard a noise above him he jumped to his feet. The young boy from the previous night came through the basement door and stopped in his tracks, nearly dropping the bundle he had in his arms.

'I didn't mean to frighten you.' He blushed. 'Master Walter was worrying you might be fretting over his delay. Also that you might be hungry.' He tentatively came down the stairs, his blue eyes darting around from under his reddish-brown hair.

He placed the bundle gently on the floor and withdrew two covered pottery pots. Removing the lids from them he let loose a mouth watering aroma from the meat and vegetable stew and a stewed apple pudding. 'There be spoons in the bag, and another candle or two. Also some books to pass the time. I am to tell you it is not yet safe to come up, but Walter will speak with you tomorrow. If you wait a moment, I am also to bring you down some more bedding.' The boy backed away and ran up the stairs. Seamus covered his food and waited for the boy to return.

'I guess its another night underground,' he said to no one. 'I wonder why the boy seems afraid of me tonight ...'

The door above squeaked and the boy entered, burdened with a comforter and two pillows.

'It is not much.' He eyed Seamus warily. 'But it was all I could find on the beds upstairs.'

'That will do fine.' He smiled encouragingly at the boy, who blushed again. Seamus took the bedding from him and put it on one of the beds. The boy continued staring at him.

'Would you like to join me for supper?' Seamus asked. 'There is enough for two.'

The boy took a startled step back. 'Ah, uh, no thanks, I have my supper back at the tavern where I live.' He blushed again.

'Is there something you want to ask me then?' Seamus settled back on the floor beside his food. The boy looked, if anything, even more nervous. 'It is all right. I will not bite. Ask away.'

'Is it true you are a mighty wizard and have been travelling with a woman who is a fierce warrior? Like the two in the prophesy?' The words stumbled out of his mouth before he could stop them.

Seamus had to stop himself from laughing and causing the boy even more embarrassment.'Where did you hear that?' he asked.

122

'It be what the soldiers who are looking for you are saying. They say to keep away from the wizard and his warrior protector as you are mighty dangerous together. No approaching, just call the guards. Even if you are seen alone.'

Seamus found it harder to contain his laughter than he did to contain his magic. Finally it got the better of him and he burst out laughing. The young boy looked mortified.

'It's all right,' Seamus said to him. 'It is just that I am not much of a wizard. I have not even begun my training. And as you can see I am travelling alone. I am not sure why the soldiers are after me, but it is not for the reasons they are telling people. And if it were not for good people like you and Walter, I am not sure what would have happened to me. I really appreciate your help, and if there is anything I can do in return I will surely do it.'

The boy's face was a picture of confusion as he turned to go, then he looked back. 'I am not sure I should be telling you this, but I over-heard them all talking at the tavern and I think they may have a plan for you to do something dangerous to help us. Only I am thinking if you are not a wizard, it will be a mite dangerous for you, and you might have to ask them for some other way to pay them back.' And with that, he scooted up the stairs and was gone with the click of the door behind him.

'Whatever could he mean? They have a task for me?' Seamus took the lid off his stew and dug in. He was past hungry after the practice he had been doing that day. 'I wonder what the prophecy is that he spoke of?'

Seamus finished his meal then had a look at the books Walter had sent. There was one on the history of the Wizard Isles, and one on the theory of magic. He read for a while, then practiced some of the sword moves again, modifying them to work better without swords.

Not wanting to spend another night in darkness, Seamus lit a new candle then lay down on his bed, tired and ready for sleep that would not come. His mind kept wandering. Where was Aliah now?

Why were the wizards spreading rumours about them? To scare the public? Where would he go after Walter had taught him to control his magic? Finally his mind slowed down and he drifted off to sleep.

———

As with the previous morning Seamus woke to the sound of the door opening and the smell of breakfast cooking.

'It is all right to come up and eat,' Walter called down, and left the basement door open for him.

Seamus tidied up his bedding and stored his pack away, assuming he would have to return to the basement until he had his magic under control. Chores completed, he headed upstairs to the kitchen where he found Walter cooking bacon and sausages.

'You look a little worse off for your trials,' he said. 'That there is the washhouse.' He pointed to a door off to the side. 'I have heated water in a tub for you to wash, and there are some local clothes, kindly donated by some of our supporters. It would be good for us all if you cleaned up before breakfast.'

Inside the washhouse he topped up the tub with hot water and stripped off all his clothing. Washing himself and his clothes as quickly as he could, he had to admit it did feel better to clean the grime from his body. On the bench by the wall he spied clean under-garments beside a set of tight fitting trousers, and a linen over-shirt. He hung up his clothes, then dried himself on a rough piece of cloth. He put on his clean clothes before using his belt on the outside of his shirt like Walter, realising that was the only way to manage the extended length shirt. Boots back on his feet, he was finally ready to eat.

'While you are waiting you can make yourself useful.' Walter plonked a loaf of fresh bread and a crock of butter on the table as he emerged from the washhouse. Seamus took up a knife and cut the loaf into slices, and then buttered each one. He then sliced some of the cheese that was already on the table and used it to make sandwiches. He placed them on a plate ready to take downstairs.

'Well, you have made progress,' Walter stated as he continued cooking breakfast, 'Your magic is now a gentle hum, not a loud shout.'

'I do not understand how?' Seamus frowned. 'I did not consciously put up walls.'

Walter stopped what he was doing and looked at Seamus. 'The point of the exercise yesterday was to teach you how to reach your magic and how to quieten it. Your mind has done the rest. Subconsciously your mind has worked out you will call for the magic when you need it and keeps it contained until you do.' He went back to his cooking. 'A few more days practice and only the strongest of wizards will be able to tell you have any magic at all.'

Seamus felt inordinately pleased with himself. He had been worried about how to control his magic for so long it was a relief to know he could actually do it. Deep down inside, he had also wondered if he would ever be able to learn how to use his gift in a controlled way, and he now felt more like he had a fighting chance.

They ate breakfast in silence, although Seamus was bursting to be filled in on what Walter had found out the previous day. Frustratingly, Walter continued to eat steadily and silently.

Finally he placed his knife and fork on the plate and leaned back in his chair. 'We may not have much time before they begin searching for you today. Last night we were told there will be a street-by-street search today by the soldiers. Unfortunately that means you will need to spend most of the day in the basement again. But at least it is only soldiers. They will never even see the door, let alone suspect you are down there.

'From the information we gained it seems they are looking for you and the girl you talked about together. They appear to be putting the fear of the goddess into people by telling them you are the Wizard and Warrior of Prophecy.'

Seamus had to interrupt. 'I do not think that prophecy made it to Hand, or if it did, I have never heard it.'

Walter frowned. 'That is unusual as I am pretty sure the prophecy originated in Hand or there about. Anyway, the short version is a prophecy stated in a time of extreme danger a wizard and warrior will appear to protect the people from a great evil.'

It was Seamus' turn to frown. 'That does not even make sense. Firstly, it tells the people there is some great danger coming, and secondly I am no wizard.'

'True, but most people will not think that way. They are just scared of the people being looked for and so will be more likely to report them. I have a sympathetic ear in the local governor's office and he has been informed they are looking for a rogue wizard and a female warrior who may know where the Princess Aliahanna is. I am sure you have heard she is missing?' Walter looked rather strangely at Seamus as he said this. 'They are telling people that you are dangerous and should not be approached.'

'They do not know who I am?' Seamus asked to avoid the implied question about Aliah.

'That is what we believe,' responded Walter. 'There have been no rumours about your having left the Isle of Hand. However, that may be because of a much bigger thing on everyone's mind.'

'And that would be?'

'A merchant vessel called into Port Marden less than a six-day ago. It had passed by the Port at Ironhills in Carsten and saw a fleet of more than fifty warships loading and preparing for departure. They estimated they would be ready to sail within a short time, perhaps two or three six-days, which means they would be visible in the outer-Isles within maybe three six-days. The rumour is that this is in response to the princess refusing to marry the King of Carsten and running away. There will be a war unless the princess is found.'

Walter was silent to let the information sink in. Seamus was sure his cheeks were flushed and he was waiting for Walter to ask him a direct question about the princess. But he said nothing.

'Now you and I know, it takes more than a couple of six-days to gather that many soldiers and ships, and provision them for a sea journey of that length, while ensuring they are adequately armed. And that is how long the princess has been missing.' Walter continued when Seamus said nothing. 'To prepare a fleet for war takes many months, so this must have started before the princess even set sail. In fact we have information that tells us this was likely so.'

Seamus did not know what to say, so he said nothing. Walter was still giving him a strange look, and he was sure the man had guessed who his travelling companion had been, but he would not confirm anything out of respect for Aliah. Walter shook his head, and Seamus felt as if he had failed some sort of test.

'So, today you will practice and rest downstairs. Tonight, when it is safe, we will go down the sewers to a series of underground tunnels that lead out of the city. We have a friend that will meet on the other side of the walls, he will bring horses and will guide us through a safe passage in the mountains so we can avoid patrols. Questions?' He looked at Seamus.

'Yes. One. Where are you taking me exactly?'

'Out of Duncameron first and foremost. We will all be safer when you are gone. Our plan is to head to Bannock first. One more magic user will not be noticed there. From there we will use our network to send you to a teacher, either here or in Nataria.'

'Please do not think that I do not appreciate all that you and your friends have done for me, but maybe I would be better off on my own once outside of Duncameron.' Seamus did not like the feeling things were moving forward without his control. In the back of his mind he remembered what the boy said last night about him being asked to do something dangerous to help their cause.

'You can certainly do that,' Walter said to him. 'But I suggest you need to finish what I can teach you about the basics of controlling your magic before you head out alone. If you do not then you are more at risk of being caught by the wizard searching for you. It is three days ride to Bannock, and in that time you will be much more in control and can make your own decisions.'

Seamus agreed that was acceptable.

'However, I would appreciate it if you would at least come into Bannock town with me as I do need some help with an errand I have to run.'

Here we go, Seamus thought. *The scary errand the boy told me of.*

'We have something valuable we need to get into the castle and we may need someone to provide a bit of a distraction.' Walter looked keenly at him.

'Will it be dangerous?' Seamus asked.

Walter shrugged. 'Actually, we hope not to need you at all. But if we need a distraction it will just be talking to some guards to keep their attention in another direction.'

'Sounds easy,' Seamus said, skeptically.

'If all goes to plan it will be. But there is always a risk we will be caught out.'

Seamus nodded his understanding that there was potential danger. 'Can you assure me you intend no harm to anyone inside the castle?' Seamus asked.

'Most certainly not.' Walter seemed appalled at the very idea.

'All right. I will think on it.'

'That is all I can ask. Now, we should get set up downstairs as I will need to set the door ward before there are soldiers or wizards around who might feel what I am doing. Then I will sort out everything for tonight.'

FOR THE FIRST two candle-marks of the day Seamus concentrated on his magic techniques, then spent some time on his idea for unarmed combat. He broke for lunch and ate the sandwiches he had prepared that morning. After his midday meal he read some of the book on the history of magic and he soon felt sleepy. Aware he would be awake all night he made up his bed just after he lit the second candle and tried to get some rest.

As he started to doze, he wondered what Walter had been expecting him to say all morning. He also wondered how much he really knew about his having travelled with Aliah? Maybe he would find out on their journey to Bannock.

CHAPTER II
A NIGHT AT AN INN

The storeroom was dark and dank and there was nowhere to sit, which suited Aliah as she had sat down for almost the entire day. She walked around the room to loosen her muscles. Four paces across wise, six paces lengthwise. Not really enough room to walk around so she began to do some of the limbering exercises she did before weapons practice. Her body felt stiff and weak. That was what you got from illness and inactivity. She assessed it would be some time before she was up to full strength again. But at least now, she was ready to make a run for it if the opportunity arose.

She laughed to herself. What great progress she had made on her own since leaving Sunnydale. Trapped in a storeroom by strangers. She was a stow-away who could have charges brought against her. And she was only marginally closer to home. Suddenly her decision to take off on her own terms did not seem such a good one. Maybe she had been a little hasty?

Time dragged on. Still no one came for her. She sat for a while. She did some more stretches. She paced the room. She sat again. She put her ear to the door, but the corridor seemed quiet. She stood under the small window to see if she could hear anything from outside. But there was nothing. Too nervous to sleep, she sat and she paced and she sat again.

Finally the door opened and her captor entered. 'He will see you now.' He grabbed her by the arm and pulled her to her feet. He did not lose his grip on her as he marched her out of the storeroom and down the corridor to a room at the other end. She could hear the noise from the tavern through the door to her right, but he led her to the room on the left. His grip was so tight any thoughts of escape fled.

The soft lighting in the room was given from two oil lamps on the wall. The only furniture was a large square table surrounded by four sturdy wooden chairs, giving the idea this room was used for meetings.

Sitting in the chair across from the door she had entered was a large, muscle-bound man about her father's age. His face was stern as he watched her placed none to gently on the chair in front of him. Her captor went back to the door, shutting it and putting himself squarely in front of it, as if to deter any thoughts of escape.

'Now, Able, you should be a little more gentle. If that wizard is to be believed this is Princess Aliahanna. If Healer Goodwin's description is to be believed, this is Seamus' errant sister.'

'To me she is a stow-away,' the man replied from behind her. 'Anyone with an ounce of integrity pays their way in life. They do not hide away and steal.'

'I did not steal anything!' Aliah's temper flared, even though her better sense told her not to get upset.

'We in the wagon trade see stowing away as stealing. You stole space and you stole the coin we should have been paid for a lawful journey,' the man in front of her explained. To the man behind her he said, 'Able, I think this might go better if you guard the door from the other side.'

The door opened and Able grumbled under his breath as he went through. The door shut loudly behind him. Aliah was left alone with the stranger sitting in front of her. She stared at him, waiting for him to speak. He merely stared back, as if taking her measure.

Aliah could bear the silence no longer. 'What are you going to do with me? Hand me over to the authorities?'

He looked her directly in the eyes. 'That really depends on you. Or, more to the point, on what you tell me about you.'

Aliah was about to blurt out some sob story to cover her presence on the wagon, but before she could get a word out the man held up his hand. 'I do not want any lies or cover-ups. You may not realise what a dangerous situation we are in, or what we have all risked by even keeping you here.'

Aliah stopped and looked at him closely, noticing the strain around his eyes and the weariness in his posture.

'Outside the front and back doors are paid men, mercenaries. They have accompanied us most of today. They are here to see we do not leave before the wizard is satisfied we are not harbouring a runaway princess. A princess, I might add, who fits your description.

'On top of that they are now looking for a young boy who travelled with us. They say they can smell the princess on him. Yet he insists the only person he has travelled with is his sister. Strangely his sister's description also fits you.

'Normally, as a law abiding citizen, I would have handed you over to the wizard and he could work out who you are. But this wizard is with men who are not in the king's employ. And I would think the king himself would send his own men to find his daughter, not hire some mercenaries. So, I am giving you this one opportunity to tell me who you are.'

'Why not hand me over anyway if it is so much trouble?' Aliah asked somewhat defiantly.

'Because I have a daughter. And that daughter would make my life a misery if I handed a woman running away from an arranged marriage over to the authorities. She has a soft heart and strong opinions on women being treated as if they are a possessions.' A wry smile flitted across his face.

More than anything it was the last comment that decided Aliah on trusting this man. Well, at least trusting him partially. She would not land Seamus in more trouble by telling them about him. He did not deserve that after she ran out on him. But she would tell the man, who risked his life for her, everything else.

'I am Princess Aliahanna,' she told him. 'I have run away from my arranged marriage because I found out Carsten was preparing to go to war against us and they would use me as a point to rally their troops. I need to get home to my father and let him know what I have found out.'

'And I should believe you because ...?' He raised an eyebrow at her.

'There is no reason why you should believe me. And to be honest I do not really care whether you do or not. I am who I am and I have to do what I have to do regardless of what you think.' Aliah looked the man straight in the eye.

He laughed at her. 'Well, you are feisty, I will give you that. Why not just hand yourself over to the nearest garrison if you need to get back to your father?'

'Because I believe some of my father's advisors might be misleading him about the intentions of the King of Carsten. I need to speak to him before they do. That means I need to get home without being detected. So, if you will give me my things and let me go, I will be on my way.'

This time he let out a belly laugh. 'You are obviously an educated girl, I can tell by the way you speak. And you might very well be royalty. You are high handed enough for that. I have to say though, I thank the goddess that if you are the heir it will be your husband who rules, because I would not give Aria a candle-mark under your guidance.'

That was it. It was too much to take. She was tired, hungry, and a prisoner again. Then to be told she was not fit to rule her country— that was too much to bear.

'And what gives you the right to make that call? You hardly know me.'

'You know, I listen to my daughter tell me the tradition of a woman heir marrying and the crown going to her husband is outdated, and that women are capable of ruling a country. And then I think of you. I am here risking mine and my crew's lives to hide you, and you tell me to my face whether or not I believe you is not important. I am the only one at the moment who is able to get you away from those who are following you, and yet you still do not think my opinion is important. You think to walk out of here with wizards and armed men looking for you without a plan. You act on emotion, not on reasoning—'

'Father, we are not here to have a great debate on what traits a ruler should have.'

Aliah had been so engrossed in what the stranger was saying she had not realised the door opened or someone had entered.

'And as usual you have only stated half the case,' the woman continued. This girl has shown courage enough to escape her captors once before. She has demonstrated her love of country by trying to get home to warn her father of a potential war. She has shown ingenuity to get this far. She is young; patience and respect for others will come with age. I am Megan, pleased to meet you.'

Aliah smiled tentatively at the woman who had entered with a tray of food for two people. As she put the tray down, Aliah thanked her. 'But your father is right. I have this driving need to fix everything myself, and so I do sometimes act before I think. And especially before I think of others. I hope I get better at thinking through situations. I can only try.' She looked at the man in front of her. 'I am sorry, I have not even asked your name.'

'Toby Allum, but they call me Boss Allum, or Boss for short.'

'Well, Mister Allum, if I am to be entirely honest with you I do need to get home. It is urgent. I need to speak to my father, not just about the impending war, but to caution him about some of his advisors. I am tired. I am hungry and to be completely honest, I am scared. I left the one person who was helping me, thinking I could do this on my own. But the truth of the matter is I do not really believe I can. But I weigh that up against putting people in danger by asking them to help me, and I find I cannot ask them to risk their lives for me. So I must go on alone.'

'Now that is more like it.' Boss slapped his hand on the table, causing the soup in the bowl in front of him to spill over. 'Firstly, I should tell you that as a leader you often have to ask things of people that might put them at risk. A good leader is one who weighs the cost of that life before they decide.

'Secondly, I have to say I nearly believe you. Unfortunately for you though, I am not quite so easy to persuade. I have someone who can verify your story, but they will not be here until tomorrow. I believe we are safe for the moment as the search has moved to town to look for the boy.'

Aliah hoped she covered her concern for Seamus, but was doubtful as Boss Allum was sharper than he first appeared.

'Eat your food. Megan will make you a bed in the storeroom. It would be a bit obvious if we put you up in one of our rooms at the moment, especially with that wizard deciding to take rooms here to keep an eye on us. We will have to lock you in, in case anyone tries the door. But it should be all right for a night. Then we can think things through tomorrow.' Decision made, Boss Allum started eating the food on the table in front of him. Megan left them to it.

Aliah slowly ate her bread and soup, still not convinced she was not a captive. There was one way to find out. 'Boss, may I have my sword and pack back?'

Looking up at her over the rim of his bowl he searched her face, then shrugged. 'Can I have your solemn word you will not use your weapon on any of my people under any circumstances?'

'Yes,' Aliah confirmed.

'Swear it on the goddess.'

'I swear on the goddess I will not use my weapons on any of your people, except in defence.'

That brought a smile. 'Fair enough.'

THE BED WAS COMFORTABLE ENOUGH, and Megan left her a jug of water and a chamber pot. So Aliah had a reasonably comfortable night. Though try as she might, she could not rest once the sun shone through the small window above her. She took the last of Healer Goodwin's medicine, hoping it would relax her and let her fall back asleep. Today it seemed to have the opposite effect. Whether she liked it or not—and she did not—she was awake.

Rolling up her bed, she made a large cushion against the wall, then went through some stretching and sword exercises—the ones she could do in such a confined space. After a short time she was sweating and her body was tired. She took it as a good sign she wanted to exercise, but it was frustrating she was so weakened by her recent illness.

Then she had nothing to do but wait. For the first time in her life she wished she had a book handy. She wanted to read some more about Carsten and try and work out why it was suddenly so important for them to invade Aria. From her memory she knew they were not exactly a peaceful nation, but to try and invade a different continent seemed unusual to her. If only she had paid more attention to affairs of state when she had the opportunity.

Smiling wryly she thought, *I am learning a lot on this journey. For all that I used to argue with my father that I did not need a husband to rule for me, I find that I am really most unprepared to rule alone.* She frowned. *Or am I unprepared because I knew I was not likely to rule and so there was no point to all that knowledge?*

As she debated in her head, deciding no matter what, she was going to start behaving a bit more like she intended to rule Aria at some future point, the door opened and instead of Able, Megan entered. It was a welcome sight for Aliah as it meant she was earning Boss and his crew's trust.

'Come, be quick. We have breakfast for you in the side room.' Megan stepped aside to let her out.

Well, almost all of his crew. Abel was waiting for her on the other side of the door, hand on sword, just daring her to run. Instead, she inclined her head and said good morning to him as she walked demurely to the room she had been in last night. Able and Megan both followed her in, and Able took his position by the door.

'Don't mind him.' Megan glanced towards the door as she sat down to eat with Aliah. 'He takes a long time to trust. Besides, he is there mostly for our security. Eat Your Highness,' she said as she tucked into her own meal.

'Your Highness.' Able snorted. 'We don't even know if she is a high anything yet.'

Aliah chose to ignore him and sat in the chair she had used the night before, sitting at right angles to Megan. 'Please, just call me Aliah.'

'Oh, but I couldn't.' Megan blushed.

'But you must,' Aliah insisted. 'For your sake as well as mine, no one can know who I am. Also, my friends call me Aliah in private, and I believe I have you to thank for your father giving me a hearing last night, rather than turning me over to the authorities, so I am sure we count as friends.'

There was a snort from behind again. This time Aliah turned around and raised at questioning brow at Able. 'Boss would never have given you over to that miserable excuse for a wizard. He is up to something, and Boss would not have let him have his worst enemy.'

'Oh.' Aliah was a bit deflated. 'I am sorry, I must have misread the situation. I thought Boss believed me and was merely waiting to confirm my story.'

'Able.' Megan's voice came as a warning. Able glowered back at her but said nothing.

'What is going on?' she asked Megan.

Megan merely told her to eat her breakfast; things would be sorted later. Now the bread and cheese felt like sawdust in Aliah's mouth. She had thought she made friends last night, but now she was not so sure. Was she still in danger?

'How is your father going to prove my story? And what happens to me if he cannot?' Aliah asked Megan.

'Don't you be worrying about that. He has his ways.' Megan carried on eating as if there was nothing amiss.

Aliah took a sip of tea and looked around the room. Although it was morning the curtains were still drawn. She rose and went over to open them.

'Please, don't,' Megan said. 'If you want to look out, peak through the gap, but we don't want people looking in here.'

Suddenly Aliah did not want to see what was outside. Megan's tone of voice told her it was nothing good.

'Are they still looking for the boy?' Aliah asked as she paced round the room.

'They were out all last night,' Able said from the doorway. 'In the main town mostly. The wizard is sleeping in a room upstairs now. But the local soldiers and his hired help are doing a quick sweep outside the walls in the new town now.'

'Oh.' Aliah sat down again, her appetite mostly gone.

'He will be safe,' Megan assured her. 'He is with a friend of ours.'

There was a knock at the door and a young boy came in and whispered to Able. Able mumbled something in return, then said, 'You had best clear up in here then.'

The boy picked up a tray by the door and began clearing away the breakfast things, studiously not looking at Aliah. With the table cleared Able left the room and returned moments later with an extra chair, which he placed by the door. 'Looks like we are going to be here for some time,' Aliah said. 'Would it be possible for me to use the privy and wash up a little?'

'The privy is fine, but washing up will have to wait,' Megan told her. She led the way out of the room with Able following behind

Aliah. Megan checked the courtyard behind the inn before letting Aliah out to the privy. Able stayed by the door and Megan walked out with her, advising her not to lock the door as she would hold it to from the outside. It seemed they did not trust her enough to even have privacy.

Aliah was readjusting her clothing when the door opened and Megan rushed in through a small gap. 'Sorry, stomach. May be some time,' she said through the gap as she firmly shut the door and locked it. She put her finger too her lips, warning Aliah not to speak, then made gagging sounds that would have made most children proud.

Megan continued her mock gagging for some time, pausing in between to whisper that one of the mercenaries had been heading towards the privy. Finally there was a knock on the door. Two quick knocks, a gap then two more. Megan poked her head out, grabbed Aliah by the arm, and hauled her back across the yard and into the corridor behind Able.

As the door closed, Able pushed the two of them into the storeroom Aliah had stayed the night in, pulling the door to but not closing it completely behind him. After a short time Aliah could just see a figure emerge through the gap.

'Out of my way,' The man commanded, curling his lips at Able. Able moved to stand in front of the gap, blocking the man's view, and Aliah's as well. But she had seen enough.

'Have you changed your mind about telling me where the boy went? I will pay good gold for the information. Enough to set you and your wife up for life.'

Aliah could not be sure, but she thought Able shuddered as the wizard spoke to him.

'I was with your soldiers most of the night, as you well know. So how could I know where he has gone?'

'When I capture him, if I find out that you knew anything I will make what little life you have left very unpleasant,' the wizard spat at Able.

Megan squeezed Aliah's hand and it was then she realised Megan was the wife the wizard spoke of. Boss' crew were obviously his family and friends, so he had a lot to lose by keeping her hidden. Why would he risk so much? Aliah moved, intending to give herself up, not sure she could bear the responsibility of so many lives. But Megan pulled her back and shook her head, as if she had read her intentions.

Finally the wizard left, and Able spat on the floor after him as if clearing a bad taste from his mouth. He opened the door and the three of them continued back to the front room.

As Aliah entered her attention went immediately to the large pot of milky coffee on the table, a drink common to this area, and two men seated drinking. Boss was in the chair he had been in last night. The chair Megan had been sitting in was occupied by a bearded man who looked to be about sixty, except for his blue eyes, which seemed to look right through her. He seemed familiar, but she could not immediately place him.

'Come in. Sit down.' Boss indicated the chair in front of the window. 'Megan, you can go now.'

'I don't think so,' she said as she sat down in the chair Aliah had vacated. Able sat in the seat he had placed by the door, and Aliah had no choice but to stand, or sit in the remaining chair. She chose to sit.

'Megan,' Boss rumbled at his daughter, clearly displeased.

'I noticed her in the wagon. I covered for her when others noticed something amiss. I have aided you in keeping her a secret. I will not desert her to you now.' She folded her arms in front of her chest and stared her father down.

Boss chuckled and caught the other man's eye. 'You should be pleased you have never had children. I have a son who just wants to stay home with his mother and run the farm, and a daughter who would take on any man.'

'You have been truly blessed by the goddess.' The man smiled at Boss, seeing through his bluster at the pride he had in his children.

'And before you ask, she is probably who she says she is. I have one last test though.' His attention moved to Aliah. 'The royal family have a secret code they use to senior advisors and officers when they are in trouble but cannot say so openly. What is that code?'

Aliah looked around the room at the people she barely knew. From childhood it had been drilled into her that she should only use this code in extreme situations, and only with people in the king's employ who she could trust. Her first reaction was to say nothing, as she could compromise the whole royal family if this information fell into the wrong hands. Yet her natural instincts had not been so good lately. She needed help, and she needed to trust someone. Also the way the man asked the question it was as though he knew the answer already. She stared at him, trying to place his face, but could not. He merely raised an eyebrow back at her. She took a breath, tucked a stray strand of hair behind her ear, decision made.

'Black Swan,' Aliah said.

The man's face showed nothing, he merely nodded at Boss Allum. Boss focused his gaze on Aliah, 'So, Your Highness, we know what you have told us is the truth as you believe it to be. We also know from talk in the tavern last night that an invasion fleet is preparing to sail from Carsten. This reinforces your story. There is a missing piece of the puzzle that perhaps you do not know, and Walter here can provide that.' Boss indicated the other man.

Aliah also turned to him, and stopped. A moment ago she would have sworn the man in front of her was sixty—maybe even older. Now he looked somewhere in his forties. Something was tickling in the back of her brain now. She knew him, she had seen him round the castle. He had been clean-shaven. He had been in wizard robes. But he was not Walter. He was ... he was ... 'Walton,' she blurted out. 'You are Walton, the wizard who went a bit crazy and had to give up running the wizard school and was sent out to work in the towns and villages.'

The man in front of her shook his head. 'Crazy? That is a bit much.' He shrugged his shoulders. 'I am now Walter. I will never use that other name again and I would appreciate it if you do not, Highness. I changed my name when I left the wizard order. I am now an outcast, some would even believe a traitor. There is sure to be a price on my head. So if you would not mind, keep that name to yourself.'

Aliah was shocked. No wizard was allowed to leave the order and keep their magic. Especially if they were as gifted as Walton was. The wizard order regulated the use of magic, and made sure it was only used for the good of the people. Unregulated magic was an abomination. 'I am sorry.' Aliah rose. 'But I cannot work with a rogue wizard. I thank you for your help. But I must find my own way home now.'

'Reacting rather than thinking again.' Boss looked keenly at her. 'That is no way to make important decisions.'

Aliah stopped, then sat back down. Boss had a very annoying habit of speaking to her conscience. 'I am not sure what you can say that will change my mind. But I will hear you out.' She folded her hands on the table and stared at Walton ... Walter.

'I am not going to justify my actions to you. I had good reasons for what I did. What I will do is ask you to think on something, and this was something I did not think about myself until recently, so take your time. Magic is not limited to men only, yet there are no women attending school on the Wizard Isle, and there are no women on the wizard council. Recently the council started turning away all but wealthy students. There have always been mages outside the control of the Council of Wizards. Although it is said to be illegal, unless they use their gift to harm others, magic users are left alone. So you could say the regulation of magic, and the wizard council itself, are political constructs and have very little to do with the safety of the realm and managing all users of magic.'

Aliah looked at him, mouth open. Then shut her mouth because she was sure she looked like a half-wit. Why hadn't she thought about that before? Women were born with magic. What happened to them? Women like Amelia. And they were turning away boys from the wizard school?

'Is that why you left, because you thought all boys should be trained?' she asked him.

'No.' He shook his head. 'That happened after I left. But I was not surprised. I left because I realised that the wizard council in the hands of the wrong people was not merely a political construct but a tool that could be used to destabilise the country. At the moment it is in the hands of people who do not have Aria's best interests at heart and who are working for their own gain. They are involving themselves in things they should not. When I spoke out about this I was denounced and everyone was told I had a breakdown. I was forced to resign my post and take a position in the community. While I worked, I witnessed the impact the new council was having on people, and I could no longer be a part of it.'

Thoughts raced through Aliah's head and she closed her eyes, trying to put them in order. The Head of the Council had died, and a new head had been elected. Not long after, her father's chief advisor, a wizard, had a heart attack. The council had appointed a new advisor, Wizard Millard, and it had been he who had spoken most strongly in favour of Aliah being married to the King of Carsten. It was he who she most wished to avoid before seeing her father.

She opened her eyes and looked at Walter. 'I can see this from your point of view. I also have some concerns about the current wizard's council. I am happy to work with you if you are willing to help me. But what I do not understand is why you are all willing to risk so much to help me.'

Boss and Walter looked at each other. Boss broke away first.

'My reasoning is simple. Evil happens when good people stand by and do nothing. There is something evil going on in Aria. I cannot place my finger on it, but I know it is there. Me and mine will fight evil where we find it. And we fight along side others spread through Aria.' He sat back in his chair indicating he was finished.

'Thank you for your honesty.' Aliah now waited for Walter to answer.

'I have very specific reasons. I want to see the wizard council restored to what it was, and I believe what is happening to you may be part of the corruption that runs through it.'

'Is that it? Or are you going to tell me how you think this is all linked?' Aliah looked Walter in the eye.

'Will knowing help you?' he asked in return.

Aliah shrugged. 'Maybe not. But I like to know who my enemies are. And maybe it is something I can bring to the attention of my father when I get to see him.'

'Your father has already been told. He chose to believe the official version of the truth.'

Gritting her teeth in frustration, Aliah tried to keep her voice calm. 'Combined with what I have to tell him, he may change his mind. Even if he does not, maybe I will be able to do something about it when I am queen.'

'If you ever make it to be queen,' Walter retorted.

'If that is in question then I definitely need to know,' Aliah threw back.

'Just tell her already,' Boss interrupted. 'We do not have time for this arguing.'

Walter shrugged his shoulders and sat back in his chair. 'I went to the Wizard Isles when I was about ten, and spent many years there. For the most part I was happy to live there and serve my king and country. But a little over five years ago, my mentor, the Grand Wizard, died unexpectedly. It was said to be from a brain disorder, but I knew it could not be true as he had always been sound of health. So I did some digging. From the evidence I gathered I suspected he had been poisoned. I confirmed this when I over-heard two other council members planning what would happen next now they had rid themselves of their opposition.'

'It was an enlightening conversation, one that resulted in me learning there was a faction within the wizard's congress who had planned a different type of government for Aria. One where wizards took their rightful place as leaders of the people.'

'Their plan was simple but devious. They were to place a puppet as Grand Wizard, then begin moving the kingdom towards a war they could not win. When the royal family was removed and it looked like all was lost, the Council of Wizards would reluctantly overcome their restrictions on using battle magic and save the day, thus earning the support of the people to continue keeping them safe and ruling as wizards rightfully should.'

Aliah looked as though she was going to interrupt, but Walter held up his hand, 'Just a minute more, then you can ask questions. So, the new Grand Wizard was elected. Gregory is a noble man with more of an interest in magical research than the politics required to govern a diverse group of men. But he has a good heart and always puts the interests of the kingdom first, so he was confirmed in his position by the king.'

'When I took my fears about my mentor's death to Gregory, he listened to his advisors rather than me. I was quickly sidelined and told I was being foolish. That was the truth. I was foolish. I moved before I had concrete proof against those who plotted against the crown. My position became compromised. Against all advice I would not stop my investigations. Finally I was removed from my position as head teacher of the initiates least I subvert new wizard trainees, and I was exiled to work as a healer in a remote village.'

'I carried out my work diligently for a few months. Then I found out one of the men who was plotting the downfall of the king had been appointed as his chief advisor after the current advisor had had a heart attack. I realised I could no longer serve in an organisation that was so corrupt.'

Aliah was sitting there with her mouth open in disbelief. She quickly closed it. She went to say something to refute these preposterous claims, but held her tongue while her thoughts settled. She knew this timeline to be correct. She herself did not trust Millard. It was his lackey, Gaius, she had seen in the hallway before, and she knew no good reason to trust him as he had made his contempt of her obvious on numerous occasions.

'So ... I was to be sent away, my family was to be killed, and all so the wizards could run Aria?' Aliah asked, trying hard to keep the skepticism from her voice.

Walter seemed unconcerned with Aliah's lack of trust. 'It is the truth, but I did not expect you to believe me.'

'I don't disbelieve you,' Aliah said, thoughtfully. 'It is just a lot to take in.'

'If I may,' Boss interrupted. 'We have confirmed much of Walter's story through other sources. In fact, we believe the king's advisor, Millard, might actually be working with Carsten to set this war up. We are not sure of the exact details. But we are concerned.'

Aliah frowned. 'You know a lot for a farmer who dabbles in transporting goods.'

'Not all people are what they seem.' Boss smiled as if he had a secret to tell. 'I was a captain in the guard until I brought a farm and settled with my Ann. We had a family and I started running caravans on the side to make a bit of extra money. I began to pick up information as I travelled, and some of it was very worrying. Along with some like minded people, I helped form a bit of a network to share what we knew, and now we have a group of people ready to act in the defence of our country.'

It was Aliah's turn to smile. 'It seems like I was very lucky to pick your wagon to stow away on. What do we do now? I need to get to my father.'

'Leave it with us,' Boss said. 'There are further searches today for both you and the boy travelling with us. Guess you don't know any reason why they would want to find him?'

Aliah shook her head, Seamus was better off left out of all this.

Boss raised his eyebrows, but did not voice what was on his mind. 'We have had the storeroom cleared and when it is safe you will be taken up to Megan and Abel's room. You can tidy yourself up and change into some local clothes. We have some planning to do, but we have a way to smuggle you out of Duncameron, hopefully tomorrow evening. We need to get to work though and start shifting our goods before someone asks what we have been doing with our day. Tonight we will finalise our plans.'

Conversation time was clearly over. Megan and Able bundled

Aliah out of the room and up the stairs. Safe in a large, simple room Aliah was able to bathe and change into local clothing. Checking her pack and sword were safely stowed, she had nothing else to do. The boy brought a midday meal up, and he had thoughtfully included a book. Unfortunately it was a book of hero's tales and bedtime stories. Not really to Aliah's taste. She had grown out of childish tales like *The Wizard and Warrior* years ago. Based on a prophecy, she used to enjoy reading how the two young men saved the world from disaster after disaster using a mixture of magic and muscle. Still, she had nothing better to do, so she skimmed through some of the stories, only to be woken by the boy bringing her some supper and telling her to be ready to leave in about a candle-mark.

Walter came for her not long after. He led her through the back door of the inn to the town gates, then through the winding back streets of town to the industrial district. The streets were in utter darkness and there was no one about. Walter explained this was because the soldiers had imposed a curfew until she and the boy were found.

Quietly he led her through the door of a warehouse that was stuffed full with shanks of wool hanging from racks. Aliah smiled to herself, remembering how she had escaped ship into a warehouse full of bales of wool. Wool seemed to be a theme for her. Brushing through aisle after aisle of wool they came to a staircase and Walter led her upwards. There were two doors off the landing. He opened the one on the left, which was clearly used as a small office. The windows had been shuttered and a bed had been set up on the floor.

'There is food and water on the table, and I have left you some candles and books. There is to be a house-to-house search tomorrow. It is unlikely they will come around here, but it will be best to keep quiet during the day so no one suspects this room is in use. The manager who uses the office next door of course knows you are here, and should anything happen you are to look to him for help. He has not had an assistant for a while and no one will think it strange this door is locked.'

'I am to stay here tonight?' Aliah asked, looking around.

'Yes.' Walter confirmed. 'And all of tomorrow. After the search is over and the factory has closed for the day, someone will come and get you.' He busied himself lighting a candle for her so she would not have to spend the night in the dark.

The last thing Aliah wanted was to spend all that time alone, but she had little choice if she wanted help to escape Duncameron and get home to Bannock.

'Are you fine for me to lock you in?' Walter seemed a little concerned.

Aliah shrugged. 'I guess so.'

'Right. See you tomorrow evening then.'

The door shut behind him with the snick of the lock being activated. She was alone once again. She had never spent so much time by herself as she had since leaving the confines of Bannock Castle. It was something she was getting used to but she did miss Seamus' company.

ALIAH WAS ALREADY UP and doing some limbering exercises when she heard the first workers arrive the next day. She had packed her gear away and laid out her food earlier. When she heard noises downstairs all she had to do was retire to her bed and spend the rest of the day eating and reading. Not long after she heard the workers stop for the midday meal, she started to doze, but was woken by the noise of someone pulling at the door handle as if they were trying different keys in the lock. The sound was followed by voices.

Quietly, she pulled her bed and everything on it between the window and desk, out of view from the door. She crouched down and hoped everything was hidden from sight, then she spied her pack and sword behind the door where Walter had left them the night before.

But it was too late, the key was turning in the lock and the door was opening.

'As you can see, this room has not been in use for some time.' The door partway opened and someone entered the room.

'Fine,' a second voice said. 'No, wait, is that a story book on the desk? An odd thing to have in an office.'

'It is indeed a story book,' the first voice said. 'It belongs to my old assistant. He left it behind and he did not leave a forwarding address for me to send it to. I have not had the heart to be rid of it as it seemed to be special to him. Really, it was strange that he left it behind.'

'Mmm. Any more rooms up here?'

'Yes, on the next level up. This way.' The door closed and the lock clicked and there was a rattle as the key was removed.

Aliah let out her breath. No longer sleepy, she sat leaning against the window, willing the time to pass more quickly and marvelling at how much of her time on this adventure had been spent waiting around for something to happen. Boredom soon got the better of her and she eventually fell asleep.

CHAPTER 12
ESCAPE BELOW

Walter led Seamus out of the house and into the shadows of the darkened street. He stopped, muttered a few words in front of his door, then led him on through windy streets into what appeared to be the poorer section of town. Seamus followed silently, keeping to the shadows, until Walter signalled for him to stop. He waited while Walter crossed the street and disappeared into the courtyard behind a building. Hand on one of his knives, Seamus looked around for any movement that indicated they had been followed.

A few minutes later Walter signalled for him to cross the street. He did so as quickly as possible, nearly jumping out of his skin when a dog barked in a nearby building. Waiting, a few moments later the dog's owner yelled for it to stop jumping at shadows. Seamus carried on and Walter led him to the yard at the back of what looked to be a dye works. When they were inside he shut the gate and walked over to a large metal grate.

Walter motioned for Seamus to help him open it up, and as he did the stench released made him gag. Two figures emerged from the shadows and Seamus instinctively got ready to fight. Walter shook his head and motioned the figures over. It was the young boy who had been helping him over the last few days. He had a cloth wrapped around his mouth and nose. His companion was also similarly covered, but Seamus would know her anywhere. Aliah. He looked at Walter, who was clearly watching him to see what his reaction would be, so he feigned nonchalance.

The two figures approached and the boy offered Seamus and Walter coverings for their faces. As Seamus tied his he realised there was camphor and something else on the material to help deal with the smells of the sewer.

'Keep this tight,' Walter whispered. 'It not only helps with the smell but will help filter some of the sewer gases, which can be deadly if too much is inhaled.'

Aliah had kept her attention on the hole in the ground as she approached, and had not yet noticed Seamus. It gave him time to sort through his conflicting feelings over seeing Aliah again. Relieved that she was all right. But his overwhelming feeling was one of anger. He was angry at how she had treated him, and angry that she was again to be his travelling companion.

He tied on his mask and decided he would just ignore her.

ALIAH HAD BEEN surprised when the boy from the inn arrived at her door, but glad it was finally time to go. She could not believe such a young child was to get her out of Duncameron. When he said they would be meeting up with Walter she realised he was just a messenger and was happy to leave with him. They left the warehouse and went through a gate to the courtyard next door, which seemed to belong to some sort of dye works.

From the shadow of the buildings she could see two figures were already there, but her attention was focused on the drain they were to go through into the sewers. As they approached she could smell the odours waft up from below.

I cannot go down there. If the rats don't kill me the smell will. She kept her thoughts to herself though, merely wrinkling her nose under the cover of the wrapping round her face and looked up to greet Walter. Instead, she came face to face with Seamus.

She was so shocked she took a step back and nearly fell into the sewer. It looked like Walter was smiling knowingly under his mask as he watched her right herself. Seamus looked away, not even acknowledging her presence. It hurt, but what else could she expect after the way she had behaved? Once out of Duncameron, they could take their separate paths, and that would be that. Still, that loss of comradeship saddened her.

The boy nipped away and returned with four unlit torches. He handed one to each of them, and began the descent through the mouth of the grate into the sewer. Walter motioned for Seamus to follow, then Aliah, then he bought up the rear, pulling the metal grate over behind them as he climbed down. When they were all in the tunnel Walter spoke a word and his torch took light, another word and the one in the boy's hand was also giving off a smoky light.

'Right, we don't have much time, so I will keep it brief. Young Pauley here will lead; he knows these tunnels like the back of his hand. I will be rear guard. The flames will light our way but also, hopefully, keep the worst of the rats at bay.'

Aliah shuddered, she could already hear them scrabbling around and the thought of them anywhere near her made her want to scream in panic. But she kept her mouth firmly closed, muttering over and over to herself, 'I will get through this, it is only a short time.'

'You two, keep your torches dry as we might need them later. Right! Off we go.'

'Wait!' Seamus stopped them, 'Firstly, is it safe for me to be walking around, you know, broadcasting my magic?'

Walter chuckled. 'Your broadcast is now a mere trickle, and it is easy for me to deflect prying eyes from noticing it. Someone would have to be scrying specifically for magic users to notice us. And if they were doing that, we would be in trouble most definitely. And at the moment I can detect no such activity. So can we go now?'

'And what if we get split up?' Seamus asked.

'I would strongly recommend against that,' Walter answered. 'Pauley is the only one of us who knows these tunnels and if we lose him we could be lost down here for days.'

'Oh,' was all Seamus said in response, but Aliah noticed a frown crease his brow.

'Any more questions?' Walter looked at them. 'Right, no? Well, let us be going. The sooner we are out of the city the safer we will be.'

Aliah's heart lurched but she forced herself to put one foot in front of the other, keeping her eyes on Seamus' back directly in front of her, trying not to think about the smell or the creatures she could feel running over her feet. They followed Pauley through the tunnels for what seemed like a number of candle-marks. Aliah keeping her growing sense of panic from breaking out by chanting her mantra and ignoring the scratching and scrabbling. No one spoke until Walter quietly asked from the back, 'How much longer Pauley?'

'About half a candle-mark,' the young boy answered.

'We don't have that much time,' Walter said. 'We have a scryer working. They will find us within a few heartbeats if we keep this pace. We need to run.'

With that warning Pauley picked up the pace to a jog, and they all followed his lead. At the sound of voices ahead Walter dimmed the torches until they were just a small glow.

In the near darkness the slimy water splashed up Aliah's clothing. A rat squeaked as her foot landed on its body. She slipped and had to grasp Seamus to stop herself from falling into the sludge. The thought of joining the rat in the sewer water made her want to throw up. As she regained her footing and Seamus readied himself to lead them on, she realised they could no longer see the dim glow of Pauley's torch. Aliah moved to continue, but Seamus held her back.

'Just wait. Pauley will realise we are not with him and come back to find us.' It was the first time he had spoken to her since they entered the tunnels.

'But we are being followed, we need to keep moving.' She tugged at the arm that restrained her.

'Can you, just for once, take someone else's advice?' Seamus snapped back.

'He is right.' Aliah had forgotten Walter was still with them. 'Without Pauley we could be lost in the sewers for days.'

They waited for some time. They could hear footsteps echo in the sewers. Walter doused his light, then made a small mage flame so Pauley would know where they were. As footsteps came nearer, Walter doused the flame and Aliah's anxiety levels rose. She moved as if to start running. Seamus grabbed her arm and pulled her back.

'You will get us all caught,' he said through gritted teeth.

'I have shielded us while we are stationary,' Walter whispered. 'We should be all right unless someone walks right into us.'

As if his words had willed it a dark figured turned down the tunnel in front and headed straight towards them. Aliah held her breath and tried not to make a sound. The figure was getting closer. A body length away. Half a body length. If he reached out his hand he could touch Seamus. Then he stopped. Another figure appeared in front of them at the tunnel mouth.

'We heard something down this way. Come on.'

'I am sure there is something down here,' the man in front of them responded.

'It's nothing. *Come on.*'

The figure hesitated, then decided it was best to follow his mate. Aliah waited until they were out of sight before letting out her breath. It seemed like only a moment later there were more footsteps coming closer. This time from behind them. Aliah held still, but this time the feel of something scuttling over her foot broke her concentration. She bit back a scream, but a moan still escaped her mouth.

She froze, mortified that she had given away their position. She got ready to run.

'I have sent them through a maze of tunnels. Should be a while 'til they are back this way.'

Aliah let out a breath she had not even known she was holding. It was Pauley.

'Come on, this way.'

Walter sent a mage light after Pauley so they could follow him. They all ran as fast as they could for the next half a candle-mark. With her lungs burning they finally made it out the sewer entrance into a bubbling stream. Pauley led them up-steam back towards the city. He paused. 'You can wash off and change here. Just over there is the rendezvous.' He pointed to a group of trees. He went to turn back, but Walter grabbed his arm.

'I am sorry lad, but it is not safe in the sewers and the gates are long closed, even for those who know how to pay their way. It is not safe for you to go back home now. You will have to come with us.'

'But, Walter, my family will be worried. And I have to be at work in the morning.' Pauley looked distressed.

'I am sorry, son. Your family knew it was a possibility you would have to leave with us. We will get word back to them that you are all right as soon as we can. But for now, you need to clean your clothes, and hopefully they will dry by morning. I have a cape you can wrap yourself in until then.'

'I have a spare trousers and shirt for him, no sense in risking disease with keeping any of these,' Seamus interrupted. 'They are not local clothing, but should anyone ask, we can say we found him wandering dressed in strange clothes.'

'Most helpful, young man. And as we are unlikely to see anybody the way we are going, it will not matter too much that they are not local.'

Seamus paused to find the trousers, then returned to changing into his clean clothes and boots. When he had finished he grabbed his and Aliah's clothes and began digging a hole to bury them in.

Pauley look mutinous as he hitched up Seamus' too big trousers and put on the shirt he was passed. Still, he scrubbed his boots until there was no trace of the sewer mud on them and Seamus tied them onto his pack to dry. Walter found some cloth to bind his feet in to see them through to the meeting place. Seamus buried the last of their clothing and covered the hole he had dug. When they were ready to travel Walter hurried them to their rendezvous through the trees nearby.

'They are still in the sewers looking for us. I have placed a blocking spell at the exit we came through that will take a strong wizard to detect, so we have some time before they start looking outside the town. But we do need to be away as soon as possible.'

In the copse Walter led them to, there were four horses and a rather sun-dried looking man of an indeterminate age. He wore the leather clothing of the mountain people, with a broad hat that covered most of his face.

'You are late, and one too many,' he said, abruptly, to Walter.

'Slight change of plan with him,' Walter answered. 'Those who pursue us are already in the sewers. He has to come. This possibility was foreseen and accounted for.'

'He can ride with the girl.' The man pulled himself into his saddle and waited for the others to mount. All but Pauley had ridden before and there was a look of terror on his face as Walter lifted him up behind Aliah.

'Just hold on to me and we will be fine,' Aliah encouraged him, and immediately there was a vice-like grip around her waist. 'I need to breathe though,' she chided him and his grip loosened ever so slightly.

'We have one, maybe two candle-marks until it is too light to travel,' their guide told them as he looked at Walter. 'You know what to do?'

Walter nodded as their guide set off at a fast pace, Aliah following, with Seamus behind her, and Walter at the rear. They headed back towards the city to the base of the Highland Mountains and it was not long before they started their ascent. Aliah looked back to see Walter a little behind them, muttering and sweeping his arm. It took a minute, then she laughed to herself. 'Just removing the tracks.' She relaxed a little. One less way for their enemies to find them.

Tired and sore, they finally dismounted just as the sun was coming up. They took care of the horses first, removing their saddles, rubbing them down, then feeding them. Their guide said to let them wander, they did not like being tied up. As hill ponies they would not move too far from the stream running through their campsite. They set up their camp in the lee of a rock face, and their guide built a fire and started cooking porridge with dried fruit and nuts for their breakfast. Aliah went to fill a kettle with water for some tea, she was grateful she still had some of Amelia's leaves in her pack.

When their meal was ready they all sat down to eat, and Aliah expected introductions. When none were made she pointedly looked at their guide and said, 'We have not been introduced?' Before she could go any further their guide held up his hand.

'We do not do it that way.' He looked at Walter, expecting him to explain.

'We have contracted our friend to take us safely through the mountains. He is a member of a very old brotherhood who live as hermits in the remote mountain valleys. They take on special contracts from time to time to supplement their income in times of hardship. They know only the people who arrange their contracts and make payments. Our guide is honour bound to fulfil his contract and only that. We do not need to know him and he does not need or want to know us, or what we are doing. If you need to speak to him he goes by the name of Namate, which means guide in his language.'

Aliah knew her surprise must have been written on her face, as Walter spoke again. 'Not all who work with us are dedicated to our cause, but be aware we carefully consider any alliances we make. The Namate are an honourable group, and their agent has made sure we are not doing anything that would affect the karma of this Namate while he carries out his duties. This is a contract that benefits both groups and hurts neither.'

How strange the world outside the palace is, Aliah thought to herself. Although she was no stranger to political alliances they did not seem as odd as this agreement was to her.

'We must sleep now,' Namate explained. 'We move as soon as the sun goes down.' And with that, he took the blanket from his horse and went over to sleep by the stream, close to his horses.

Walter set up another horse blanket and made a bed by the fire for Pauley, who was just about dead on his feet. He, Aliah, and Seamus crawled into their swags. Aliah had to admit she was almost as tired as Pauley looked. Although she was now well over her illness she was by no means back to full strength. Still, as it appeared Seamus was to be travelling with them for a little while she knew she had something to do before she allowed herself to rest. Her stomach clenched as she sat up and leaned over to shake Seamus.

'What.'

'Seamus ...' she paused, unsure what to say next.

'Yes?' He still had not rolled over to look at her.

What could she say to make up for running out on him without a word, and leaving him to sort things with Healer Goodwin? No mere words could make that better.

'I am sorry. I acted on impulse without thinking about how it would affect you or others. I will try my best not to let it happen again.'

Seamus still did not move.

Aliah sighed. It was all that she could do. It was up to Seamus now. With a heavy heart, she laid back down in her sleeping bag and tried to sleep.

'It seems as if the fates keep throwing us together,' he said without rolling over. 'But we are travelling companions only now. I am not sure I can trust you more than that.'

'Fair enough.' What else could she say? It was up to her to make amends with actions. But she felt even more lonely knowing she had lost his friendship.

THE SMELL of meat cooking over a newly built fire awoke Aliah. Namate was cooking some kind of animal for the evening meal, so Aliah got up to see what she could do to help. She stowed her swag and went to the stream to freshen up and get water for everyone.

When she returned, Seamus was performing some sort of sword practice without a sword. She watched him for a while, finally plucking up the courage to go over and see whether travelling companions talked to each other.

'Do you want to borrow my sword to practice with?' she asked him.

'Not sword practice,' he said without breaking his stride.

She watched him some more. 'It amazes me how you can be so good on your feet, but the minute you put a sword in your hand it all goes wrong,' Aliah mused out loud. Seamus started to smile then stopped himself.

Aliah watched some more. It dawned on her what he was actually doing. He was using the formwork of sword practice for some sort of unarmed attack and defence. She continued to watch him and when he moved to defence she got up and faced him, starting with the attack forms to match what he was doing. Seamus faltered for a moment when she joined him, but continued a moment later.

'No, if you do that move like this it works better.'

Aliah followed him, then they repeated the moves with his change. It did indeed work much better. They switched, and with some more adjustments by Seamus, Aliah was able to pick up the defensive role. By the time they finished, Aliah was out of breath and ready for dinner. They had not spoken, but Aliah hoped the ice between them had melted a little.

They ate quickly and while Aliah and Pauley helped break camp, Walter spent some time with Seamus explaining to him some magic training he wanted him to do while they were riding. After his lesson, Seamus buried their rubbish and they were ready to leave. As they were riding away, Walter spoke some words and waved his arm around the area all trace of their having been at the campsite was removed.

For two nights they rode through the mountain trails. Seamus barely spoke to Aliah, but was happy to practice the unarmed combat he had developed with her when he was not having magic lessons with Walter. With no one following them, their journey became monotonous, so much so that Pauley fell asleep against her back for most of the night. They did not talk much as Walter seemed reluctant to discuss anything in front of Namate. As they rode closer to Castle Bannock Aliah's stomach begin to tighten. She knew she had to talk to her father, but she was unsure of what sort of reception she would get. Would he be angry with her, or would he be pleased she was safe? Would he believe her when she told him what had been happening?

When she left the Castle her father had been proud of her for taking on responsibilities for the kingdom. He would not know her escorts had become her captors, although he would have been concerned about her companions being asked to leave the ship. Would he be angry at her for disobeying him and placing the future of the kingdom at risk? And that was even if she could get in to see him. Walter said he had a way, but could he get passed the legion of advisors who surrounded her father whose express role was to keep others out. As princess, she could always get some time with her father, but she would not be able to play that role until after she had actually seen him. Having no one to discuss her fears with meant they began to take on mammoth proportions in her head.

Halfway through the fourth night Namate stopped them at a fork

THE WIZARD AND THE WARRIOR

in the path. 'That way is your way.' He pointed to the fork on his right. 'This way is mine. When you get outside Bannock let the horses go. They will find their way back. My part of the arrangement is met, your part will be met when the horses return to our home.'

'I agree your part of our contract is concluded,' Walter said formally, and with that their guide nudged his horse and headed off.

'How odd,' Aliah murmured.

'It is their way,' Walter said. 'For them, this is solely a contract. They want no thanks and no part of our lives. They have no care but for their own community. Come, we need to get to the foot of the mountains before daybreak if our plan is to work.'

CHAPTER 13
BANNOCK

The four weary travellers steered their horses down the path their guide had set them on. There was no more talking than there had been the previous nights as they were all so tired from the constant travel and having to sleep through the day. A little before sunrise, they reached the bottom of the mountain range. Aliah startled when Walter led them to two wagons and some goats being minded by an elderly man and woman who, from their dress, were farmers on their way to market.

'Hello.' Walter greeted them cheerfully.

'Come, we don't have much time before sun-up.' The other man was a little brisk in his manner. His careworn face seemed tense, and his eyes darted around as if worried someone might come upon them.

'We have ridden long friend, do we not have time to break our fast?' Walter asked.

'Mona has hotcakes with honey for you and fresh milk. You can eat as we travel. But we need to be back on that road by sun-up to avoid suspicion and arrive at the gates at our normal time. Also, I will feel better when we are travelling in the safety of market goers.

There have been a large number of wizards on the road this last six-day and I would not like to think what they would do should they find us here. It would be a little hard to explain.'

Walter sighed. 'All right. Seamus and Aliah feed and water the horses, then set them free. Pauley, come here, we have clothes for you to change into. You two can get changed into yours when you are done with the horses.'

They each went to their tasks, but Aliah had to say she was distracted by the smell of hotcakes. Mona quickly helped her change into a plain skirt and shirt similar to her own behind one of the wagons. When she emerged, she noticed Seamus wearing clothes similar to the man who had greeted them. Walter and Pauley too had been transformed into farm workers. She would hardly have recognised them and she knew them all. The large brimmed sunhats could be mostly responsible for that. Her sword and Seamus' knives were stowed beneath some turnips, and then the farmer climbed up on the seat of his cart. They were ready to go.

'I am Farmer Nobb and this is my wife, Mona. I will drive one wagon and Walter will drive the other.' Aliah wondered whether this man knew who Walter really was, or had he been kept in the dark about his real identity? Surely he would not order him about that way if he knew Walter was a powerful wizard.

'I come to the markets here once a week, and today is my day. Normally I have farm workers ride with me, but today I have my brother and his children helping me as a treat for his eldest children. We are Uncle and Aunt to you. Try not to speak and try to look as though you are amazed by your first trip to Castle Bannock.'

'That won't be hard.' Pauley laughed. 'It is.' Aliah smiled, Pauley's good mood was infectious.

'When we get through the city gates you must continue with me to market and help set up. Not to do so will be noticed. Then you will be free to wander. I will tell you when. It is then that you will meet your contact to get you into the castle.'

'This is your plan to get us in to Bannock? You expect us to just walk in?' Seamus looked shocked.

'There are no secret entrances to the city boy. You go in through the gates or not at all,' Farmer Nobb said disdainfully. 'You can try getting in without our help, safer for us all round, but being in plain sight and with someone the guard knows is your best bet.'

Walter merely shrugged his shoulders. 'The choice is yours Seamus. You can come with us and help us get into the castle, or you can go on alone. Though you need to make your mind up quickly. We need to be on the move.'

So Seamus had been aiming to help them get into Bannock Castle. She hoped he was still prepared to, even knowing she was there.

Trying not to let it show how much it mattered to her that Seamus came with them, she walked over to the farmer's wife. 'I guess Pauley and I are helping with the goats?' She smiled at Mona, who smiled in return and gave each of them a wooden switch and showed them how to move the goats.

SEAMUS STOOD there gnawing on his lip, watching Aliah learn how to herd goats. The princess doing a goatherd's work. It made him smile a little.

He had to say Aliah seemed prepared to do whatever it took to get back to see her father, and he had been rather surprised to find her following someone else's plan to the letter these last few days. After her apology, he was no longer angry with her, but he was still wary of trusting her too much.

When he had first seen her, he realised what the package was Walter needed to get into the castle. At first he had decided he would leave them at Bannock. He no longer had an urge to help Aliah. If only it were that easy for him. His desire to be rid of Aliah warred with his conscience which said he should be doing everything he could to help his people in the upcoming war.

Then Aliah had apologised. It did not change everything, but he knew what it took her to admit she was wrong. He also respected the fact she had not pushed him to accept her apology, but had instead worked with him as a travelling companion and showed that she was now listening to others.

'What am I to do?' Seamus asked himself, grumpily.

'Why, you can lead my ox.' Farmer Nobb laughed. 'He likes to wander a bit and does a little better with someone walking beside him.'

Unaware he had spoken out loud, Seamus had to laugh at the farmer's answer. Of course he was to lead an ox into Bannock. It was all so utterly ridiculous he could not stop himself from laughing. That did not mean he was committing to help Aliah get into the Castle though. He was still definitely undecided on that.

MONA HANDED out hotcakes and flasks of cool milk for the travellers to eat and drink as they walked. Aliah could see Seamus' ox ate most of his share of hotcakes when the boy was not looking. It did nothing to improve Seamus' mood as they joined other farmers heading towards Bannock. He still mumbled to himself and frowned under his hat.

As they walked towards Castle Bannock they each took a turn riding in the back of a wagon catching up on the sleep they had lost riding through the night. Just as the sun came up, the castle came into view, magnificent sitting atop its rock, and a lump caught in Aliah's throat as she got her first view of home.

Farmer Nobb called for all hands on deck as the town walls and castle loomed closer. The oxen became jittery, and the goats seem intent on losing themselves in the crowds heading for market. Aliah caught Seamus' eye. 'Does this seem familiar?' she asked as they joined the queue of farmers attending the day's market. Seamus beamed a genuine smile for the first time that day as he remembered the first time they met. After that, his mood seemed to lighten. The queue was relatively short when they joined it, and it was not long before it was their turn to have their wagon's searched by the guard.

'Good day for it, Farmer Nobb,' the guard said as he took the entrance fee to the city and noted it down in a ledger.

'It's always a good day to make a sale,' the farmer responded as he made his mark.

'Not bringing any of your regulars today?'

'They have the day at home working the fields. I brought my brother and his family to help, and to let his young ones see the town.'

'Hope they enjoy the sights. Bannock is always fun the first time, and today's market seems especially busy.' The soldier waved them through.

On the other side of the gate the farmer led them through the main road towards the large market square. 'That was too easy,' Seamus murmured to Aliah.

'Just hiding in plain sight,' she whispered back. But a glimpse of black wizard robes and a familiar face made her stop, heart in throat. Gaius was in the town.

'What?' Seamus asked her. She did not want to answer, they had been getting on so well this last candle-mark; actually talking. But she had promised herself she would deal with him honestly and so she would.

'There was a wizard in Duncameron. I remember him from my father's court. He was a nasty boy and he has grown into an even nastier man. I just saw him walk down that street. I am sure he is looking for me.'

'For us,' Seamus said. 'If he is who I think he is, then he was also

166

looking for me. He made my stomach curdle. He was spreading some tale about us being the wizard and warrior from some old prophecy to scare people from helping or approaching us.'

Aliah went to laugh, but the serious look on Seamus' face stopped her. 'Some people actually believed it. Ask Pauley?'

'Come on, you two, we cannot stand about here gawping.' Walter moved them along. More quietly he said, 'I saw him too. In all this bustle he will be unlikely to find us. But we need to be wary.'

The main square was busy with farmers and merchants setting up for the twice-weekly markets. Tents were everywhere and people were hurrying to get set up before customers arrived. The market manager waved them over towards the fresh produce area and, as they walked past, he took a special interest in Aliah. In the past he had shown her and her guards round the markets a few times so Aliah was sure he must have recognised her. Her heart was pounding in her chest, and her palms sweated so much she nearly let go of the goat she was leading.

'Maybe, miss, if you get some time later, you could perhaps do me the honour of breaking your fast with me.' He practically leered at Aliah, and she took a step back.

Fortunately Walter stepped between them. 'It would not be appropriate for my daughter to eat alone with a man not of our family, sir, as she is recently betrothed.' He grabbed Aliah's arm and pulled her forward before the market manager could respond.

Aliah let out a sigh of relief. 'I thought he recognised me,' she laughed.

'Nay, lass, that one is known for latching onto any new pretty face, and many have taken him up thinking they will get a better spot if they accept his affections. Many have been proved wrong.' Farmer Nobb frowned as he stopped his wagon in the assigned spot. 'It is a good thing you will be leaving after we set up today as he will no doubt not have been put off and we will see him later looking to get you alone. And I really would not like to offend him if I do not have to.'

They helped the farmer set up his stall and put out his vegetables, fruit, cheeses, and eggs for sale. Seamus and Aliah took the goats and oxen to the common to graze. Once they were done the oxen were left with a boy for a copper coin, and the goats taken back to a pen the farmer had set up in their absence.

'We are done now, you can be about your sight seeing,' Farmer Nobb told them. 'I would take some time to break fast at the Horse and Buckle before going too far,' he added, rather loudly.

With that, the farmer went to serve his first customer for the day. His wife shooed them away with her hands. Aliah could not go without saying good-bye, and impulsively hugged the older woman, whispering in her ear, 'Thank you, I shall not forget your help.'

The other woman looked startled, then blushed and said, 'Be away with you now!'

Walter set off at a purposeful pace, followed by Seamus then Aliah, who was dragging behind and looking back at the stall.

'What about Pauley?' she asked as she realised he was not following.

'It would not be fair to take him where we are going, it is too dangerous. He will go home with the farmer and his wife. They will get him safely back to his parents,' Walter muttered so he could not be over-heard.

Aliah half-turned to go back. 'But we did not get to say good-bye.'

Seamus grabbed her arm before she could head back to the farmer's stand. 'It would look too strange for people looking around Bannock for a few candle-marks to make too much of a farewell,' he said. 'Do not put us in more danger than we already face by doing something people will notice.'

Aliah paused, ready to fight, then realised he was right. She followed behind her two companions feeling a little sad inside that she had not properly thanked and farewelled the young boy, and worried that once again her instincts had nearly gotten them into trouble. If this was what adventuring was like she was not sure it was really the life for her. If she could take back all those times she had wished life had been more exciting when she had been tucked safely behind the castle walls, she would. Now she would be inclined to wish for something very different.

They arrived at the tavern and the smell of bacon cooking as she entered had Aliah's stomach grumbling, reminding her of just how hungry she was. The room was packed and there did not seem to be room for them to sit. Finally, a man made some room for them at a table by the bar. Seamus and Aliah sat while Walter went up to the counter to order them some weak ale and breakfast. Food ordered, he sat down by the man who had made space for them.

'Here for the market?' the man asked, conversationally.

'Helping out my brother,' Walter said. 'He does not need us until packing up time so we are having a look around. My children's first time in Bannock.' Walter looked at them and then took a swig of ale as he waited for their food to arrive.

In the following silence Aliah wondered why they were wasting time in the inn rather than heading straight for the castle. Yes, they were all hungry, but once inside the castle her father could have food bought for them. Her focus drifted as Walter and the townsman continued talking. Finally, a girl brought their food over and she began eating.

As she ate, she noticed a young man by the fire watching them. She went to say something to Walter, but held back because her gut had not been particularly helpful lately. What would it hurt to say something? She was just about to speak when the man who had made room for them at his table stood up. 'If you want to see that view of the castle I was talking about,' he said, 'I have a few errands to run but will be by the common in about half a candle.'

'Thank you. We will consider your offer,' Walter responded, shaking the man's hand.

As he departed the serving girl came over to refill their tankards with more watered ale. It was not until they continued eating that Aliah remembered the man who had taken an interest in their group.

However, when she looked back over by the fire he was gone. *Should I say anything? No, I will just keep and eye out for him.* She finished her meal as fast as she could, wanting to be on her way.

'I am ready to leave now,' she quietly announced when she had finished, dismayed to see that Seamus and Walter had barely touched their food.

'What's your rush?' Walter responded heartily. 'Bannock will still be there after breakfast.' More quietly so only she could hear he said, 'We do not have to be at the common for a while yet and I would rather mark the time here than in such an exposed place as the market where someone could easily recognise you.'

Aliah blinked, and then what was happening dawned on her. They had come to the tavern to meet their guide, and he would wait for them by the green. *I really must pay more attention to what is going on.* She slowly drank her watered-down ale to while away the time as Walter and Seamus finished eating.

'Now I am refreshed, we can look around the market and town,' Walter said, heartily, as he rose. Seamus and Aliah followed suit. Their place at the table was swiftly filled by waiting customers as they left the crowded tavern for the hustle and bustle of the market, which was now in full swing.

The three of them meandered through the stalls looking at goods, but buying nothing. As they neared the green Aliah could see the man from their table looking at some livestock and carrying some parcels. As she went to tell Walter her eye caught a figure casually leaning against a stall. As their friend moved, so did the man. 'So he was not watching us.' Aliah was relieved. At that moment Walter caught sight of their guide and raised his arm to call out. Aliah quickly grabbed his arm and spun him towards the stall. 'Father, look at this!' she gushed, and as they bent towards the cloth she had picked up she whispered, 'I spotted a man interested in our group in the tavern, he is following your friend, I think.' She moved so her back was to the man and said, 'That man behind me with the blue shirt and his hat pulled down low.'

'It is truly lovely, daughter, but I do not think we can afford the price. We will go and look at a stall more suited to us.' Seamus was frowning as he had seen their guide and did not understand why they were heading off in the opposite direction. They finally stopped by a pastry stall where Walter bought a pastry. He paid a little extra to have the baker's boy deliver it, with the message, 'Your companions will wait for you in the stable, but do not bring your friend.'

As they walked back to the tavern through the market, Aliah asked, 'Will he understand the message?'

'I understood it, and I am guessing I have not been at this as long as he has.' Seamus laughed. 'Good on you for spotting he was being followed. You have saved us from a bit of bother.'

'You are right, son, he has been doing this for some time. In fact, he and I met in the castle here. He helped me when I needed eyes and ears to get out of a difficult situation.'

They were heading through the back streets towards the tavern, mingling with the crowd, when Walter suddenly stopped. There was a figure dressed all in black standing outside the gate to the tavern's back yard. As he moved to talk to one of the men with him, Aliah glimpsed the flash of a gold lightening bolt. *Oh no. A Gold Wizard,* she thought. At that moment the wizard seemed to look over the crowd and stare straight at Walter.

'Carry on walking,' Walter whispered. 'Stay in the markets and meet me back here in a candle-mark.'

Then he was off, running back through the crowd. The wizard shouted and he began running towards them followed by two soldiers. Aliah grabbed Seamus' hand to steal her nerves and tried to do what everyone else was doing, watching the three running men chase after another. She let out her breath as they ran straight past her and Seamus without even a glance.

The ruckus over, people continued on with their business. Aliah let go of Seamus' hand and they walked past the tavern back into the market. Sick to the stomach, she tried to show interest in shopping. Seamus even used some of his hard earned coin to buy a knife and a leather sheath. 'Just in case,' he whispered to her. And it was then she realised that their weapons were still with the farmer.

'Should we go back and get ours?' she asked him.

'I am pretty sure that would not be a good idea. Would you like a knife? I could get you one too?' Aliah shook her head. She was not sure she could use one effectively in close combat.

'If we have trouble I will just have to try your new form of unarmed combat.' Her eyes were twinkling as she looked at him.

The candle-mark seemed to drag, but finally the church bell tolled and they headed back to the inn to meet with Walter. Aliah pulled Seamus to a stop. The man leaning against the wall of the alley beside the tavern was the same man who had been watching their guide earlier. 'Keep walking,' she told Seamus.

'What now?' he asked as she stopped by a stall to look.

'See that man over there?'

Seamus nodded.

'He is the one who was watching our guide.'

The man was carefully searching the crowd around him.

'What do you want to do? Do you want me to cause a diversion and you can go in?'

Aliah felt a rush of warmth that he was prepared to risk himself to get her into the castle. Although she knew it would be the simplest solution, it did not feel right. She walked around the stall picking up necklaces and putting them down, watching both the man by the inn and Seamus. She could not read from his face what he wanted her to do.

'I know another way into the castle grounds. It is similar to the one I think Walter wanted us to take from the inn. We could try that way. But it would mean we would have to go it alone. What do you think?' Aliah deliberately looked at the necklace she was holding rather than his face, as she did not want to see his reaction. She could tell he was watching her, and probably chewing his lip while he decided what to answer.

'I think that may be a better option,' he finally said. He reached over to pay the stallholder for the necklace Aliah held. 'To divert suspicion,' he whispered. 'That will do nicely for our mother.'

'I am sure she will love it,' the woman said as she passed his parcel over to him.

They slowly wandered through the market again, making sure that the man from outside the tavern was not following them. Seamus added a leather bag to his purchases for the day, and swiftly stowed his two parcels in it. When they were satisfied they were not being followed, Aliah led them through the streets near the wall to another tavern.

'I am beginning to see a pattern here.' Seamus laughed.

'It seems one of my ancestors liked to nip out for a drink or two.' Aliah shared the family joke with him, relieving a bit of the tension she felt.

There was no one hanging round outside this tavern, so Aliah decided it was quite safe going down the alleyway to the door leading to the back yard. Her hand stopped on the door handle as the sound of feet running towards them reached her ears. She hardly knew what was happening as a weight bowled into her. She and Seamus fell through the door with a stranger on top of them.

Seamus was up first, knife drawn, and hauling the other person to their feet.

'Shut the gate, you fool. They will know where I have gone.'

Seamus did not move. His knife was held at the man's throat. The man shook his head and managed to wiggle his foot and lift it to shut the gate. He stared at Seamus, who glared back at him. A few moments later there were running feet in the alleyway and the man visibly relaxed.

'That was lucky finding you here.' His dark blue eyes twinkled as he smiled at Seamus and Aliah.

Seamus glowered back as Aliah picked herself up off the ground, brushing herself off and checking for wounds. She noticed a bundle on the ground and looked at the man Seamus held. They had helped a common thief. She shook her head in disgust.

'Let him go, Seamus. No doubt the people he stole this from will find him soon enough. If they don't, the city guard will.'

'You think I stole that.' The man burst out laughing. Not really the response Aliah was expecting. Even Seamus looked perplexed.

'You do not recognise me? My disguises must be getting better.' The man was almost doubled over in laughter.

'Your Highness.' The man bowed to Aliah. 'I am at your service.'

'And you are also sometimes called your Highness, but as we are in Aria, I will stick to sir.' He bowed to Seamus as much as he could with a knife held to his throat, giving Aliah an even bigger surprise. 'I have been at your father's court a number of times and I never forget a face, even when it is such a long way from home.'

'I am Dominic Du Bray, son of the Count of Du Bray, or the Eastern Duchy as it is now called, and your father's top information gatherer.' He looked down at the knife. 'Now that we have been introduced we can dispense with that.'

Aliah shook her head and Seamus did not move. If this man worked for her father then his first allegiance was to him. If he left orders for his daughter to be brought back to the court then he would do just that, publicly, and their plan would be for nothing.

Dominic watched Aliah's face and knew that his situation had not changed. 'You look worried, my princess.'

'I think I know what it is,' Seamus answered for her. 'You work for her father, and we are trying to sneak in to see her father. So you do not exactly fit in with our plans.'

'And if you do work for my father surely you are meant to pick me up and carry me publicly back to court. If you do not do this, then you are not working for my father but another group and then, sir, I am not sure I trust you.'

Dominic laughed. 'You definitely have your father's brains and your mother's beauty. An interesting mix! Let me quickly explain. I am a spy, and as such I get a very broad interpretation of what is in the best interests of the kingdom, being as I cannot always get word to your father or my master to clarify every detail.

'In this instance, I have been working with Walter to return you to your father, which is exactly what he commanded me do should I come across you. I am just choosing to do that in a very secret way.

'In addition, I have become aware there are some men close to your father who do not have his or the kingdom's best interests at heart. I have been investigating them and that is why I am followed, and we had trouble today. Does that explain this rather strange situation to your satisfaction?'

Aliah frowned, and looked at Seamus. He shrugged his shoulders, seeming to say it was her call.

Dominic interrupted. 'We need to move. The king has a council until noon, and the easiest way for me to get his attention without others being present is when he is with them. He can leave the room as required and those others we want to avoid can be asked to remain and continue with state business.'

'Don't we need to wait for Walter?' Seamus asked.

'Walter is otherwise detained at the moment. We can do nothing for him until we get to the king.'

Aliah looked at Seamus and he nodded. 'I cannot say I trust you,' Aliah said, 'But at this moment I cannot let you go either. I think it best if we all travel together until I make up my mind.'

'Well isn't that just a vote of confidence!' Dominic laughed. 'We had best be moving then,' he said as he picked up the packages off the ground and led them into the kitchen of the inn.

The room bustled with activity. The cook and her boy were still making breakfast for the crowded tavern, and serving girls were coming in and out. They did not appear to even see Dominic leading them through their domain and into the storeroom. Noticing Seamus and Aliah's curious glances, Dominic advised them that the tavern was paid handsomely by the crown not to see such things as strange people passing through. Dominic closed the storeroom door behind them and in the gloomy light of the room's one window he handed Aliah one of the bundles he had picked up off the ground, the other he gave to Seamus.

'You will probably be needing these,' he told them. They unwrapped the parcels to find they contained the weapons they had left with the farmer and his wife. 'The way we are going is quite safe, but it is always better to be sure than dead.' And with that, he pulled a dresser out from beneath the window, revealing a door. He opened the door and gestured for them to go through.

Aliah went first with Seamus following. Coming last, Dominic closed the door then pulled a cord that ran through the door, bringing the chest back into place. He squeezed past Aliah and Seamus until he had the lead. They waited a moment until their eyes adjusted to the darkness, then began moving.

'Right then, we head down first, walk for about half a candle-mark, then we go up. In the downwards and upwards sections it will be best not to talk as going down we are near the tavern and could be over-heard, and the same applies when going up as we are in the castle grounds. The rest of the way is under the streets of the city, and you would have to be very loud for anyone to hear us.'

He led them down some stairs, and as they walked they could hear the noise from the tavern. When it was silent, and they had been walking on the flat for some time, Aliah chanced conversation. 'You seem to know these tunnels well.'

'Although they were designed as escape routes for the royal family, there are others of us who need to come and go in secret who also use them,' Dominic answered.

'So these are considered spy-ways?' Aliah asked.

'Spy is such and ugly word, don't you think? Let us just say that a king needs information and sometimes that information needs to be gathered in secret. There are those of us with certain skills who find this occupation the best way to serve our king and the kingdom. We are merely soldiers with different skills. And sometimes we need to come and go without others knowing, so we use these secret passages.' Aliah could hear the smile in his answer.

'But I find this an unusual occupation for you. Surely your father, the duke, does not think this is a suitable way for you to spend your time. He is not a strong supporter of the crown. Some would perhaps say he is even an enemy.'

'And you would be right, my princess. As one of the few surviving Duchies from pre-Natari times my family considers your father to be a foreign king imposed on us as our liege lord.'

'And you do not?' Seamus asked.

'No. But maybe that is because I am a second son and will not inherit my father's title. I also have not inherited his commitment to our historic past. I am more interested in maintaining a prosperous Aria, and I also admire the king's stance on men being rewarded on merit, rather than title. And while the nation continues to thrive under his stewardship he will have my full support.'

'Besides, my father thinks I am spending my time at court looking for a suitably rich bride to marry. For him, that is exactly the thing a second son should do.'

'Oh.' Aliah could not think of anything to say to that. This man was not what she had expected. Neither when she had first met him, nor when she found out he was a spy in her father's employ. For some reason she had always believed spies were a little unscrupulous, without honour, little better than thieves. But Dominic did not seem to fit easily into the image she had. That was if he was to be trusted, and only time would tell that.

They walked in silence and it seemed like no time at all before they found themselves walking up hill. *The castle already,* Aliah thought, and immediately butterflies invaded her stomach. She was a little scared about seeing her father again, and also about being caught in the castle. The butterflies flew faster as they reached the stairs and began their ascent.

DOMINIC PUSHED OPEN A DOOR, and they found themselves in the castle laundry. The women did not stop their work as Dominic led his companions through the laundry to a locked room at the end. Producing a key, he opened the door and hustled them in. Inside the room was an array of clothes and a screened off section.

'I think you will find a tub of water behind that screen,' Dominic said to Aliah. 'Wash up quickly and put up your hair. There is a servant's uniform and scarf for your head. Change as quickly as you can.'

'You seem well prepared,' Aliah said.

'Different tunnel, same plan as I had with Walter,' Dominic replied. 'Now hurry, we have not got much time before the noon bell.' It was only then Aliah realised he was the same man they had eaten breakfast with.

Aliah washed as quickly as she could, wishing she had time to actually soak in the bath rather than just rinse the grime of travel off herself. And oh, to have the time to wash her hair! That would be a luxury.

She emerged to find her companions dressed in palace livery, taking turns in front of a mirror to shave off their travel growth so they would not stand out amongst the clean-shaven staff. As he stopped what he was doing to see she was fit to be presented, Aliah realised Dominic was not as old as she first thought. Clean-shaven and freshly washed with his hair tied back in the customary ponytail of courtiers, he looked to be only a little older than Seamus.

He handed Aliah an apron to put over her skirts and she realised he was laughing at her, 'Ah, now you can see me as the son of a duke rather than a slimy spy.' His blue eyes twinkled for a moment, then his face changed and he was all business again.

'Right, Seamus, you can carry that sword as the princess cannot be carrying that as a servant. Hold it as though you are going to present it to the king. Put your knives in that bag you have and carry it over your shoulder. All of them! We will need to leave them all at the door though, as to go into the presence of the king armed invites certain death.'

'They are all in there. It is the same custom in my father's court. I know the penalty of baring arms in the king's presence,' Seamus told him looking very serious.

'Ah, we are ready then. Come!' Dominic put his hands on his hips, faced them and gave them a good once over to ensure they would fit in. 'You cannot take those packs with you, though. Place them under the bench there and we will come back and get them later.' They placed their travelling packs under the bench and followed Dominic out through the laundry, across the courtyard, and into the kitchens. There he found a tray with a pitcher of water and a bowl of fruit, which had conveniently been prepared for someone. The under-cook, who was about to add some flowers to the tray, was about to complain when he realised it was Dominic doing the stealing. He stopped mid-word and reached for a new tray as if that had been his intention all along. Dominic waved and led his team to the back stairway used by the palace servants.

They followed him up three flights of winding stairs barely two people wide. Her jaunts around the castle using the servants' staircases told Aliah they were going to her father's personal suite. As they entered the corridor she nearly bumped into Dominic, who had stopped short. Aliah just caught a glimpse of a black robe as she ducked her head, hoping not to be seen. She need not have feared because Gaius would never take a second look at an actual servant.

'Dominic.' He sneered. 'Still playing at spies. Haven't you found a real job yet?'

'Gaius. Such a pleasure to see you, as always. I would have thought guarding prisoners was beneath you now you have been raised to The Silver.'

Aliah could hear the sneer in Gaius' voice. 'This is a criminal we have been looking for for some time. As the only wizard with enough power to contain him should he attack, I have the responsibility of taking him to Millard for questioning.'

'Mmm, I was under the impression the king had asked to see this particular criminal immediately on his capture.' Dominic casually leaned against the wall and Aliah caught a glimpse of Walter behind Gaius. She could not be sure, but it looked as though he winked. 'I am heading to the king now, why don't you let me take him off your hands? Save you the trouble.'

Trapped, Gaius faltered before he answered. 'I will take him. I could not trust him in your care.' He stopped and sniffed. 'I can smell her. The princess.' He sniffed again. 'She was on Walton, and I smell her stronger now.'

Aliah tensed, and almost ran. It curdled her stomach when Gaius used his sensing ability.

'Gaius, I feel you are really losing it. Perhaps it is the pressure of being elevated to the silver so early. The princess? On Walton? Really? You imagine her everywhere. And of course you can smell her here. How many times has she been in these halls? Maybe I should talk to Millard about giving you a break. We cannot have you cracking up completely.'

Gaius stiffened at the veiled insult to his skills. 'Let us get this prisoner to the king. Then I can be rid of your loathsome presence.'

Dominic followed Gaius and Walter back to the door of the king's personal chambers. They were stopped outside by one of his personal guard.

'Your business?' the older of the two guards barked.

'I have fresh water and fruit for the king's rooms, as he requested. His new sword has arrived, and I have an urgent message to be delivered to him,' Dominic responded. 'Oh,' he said as if he only just remembered. 'And after I am done I believe Gaius would like to see him. He has a rather important prisoner I believe the king is most keen to see before anyone else.'

'The king is in council.' The guard stood stony faced.

'The message cannot wait,' Dominic persisted. 'It is an urgent matter from the Fox.'

The guard's face barely changed. 'Broad,' he said to the younger guard. 'Tell the king he has a message from the Fox. Discretely, mind you. You can take the refreshments into the king's room and wait there, but the sword stays out here.'

'Surely you cannot expect me to wait while he goes first.' Gaius spluttered.

Stoney faced the Guard responded, 'The Fox always takes precedence.'

Dominic indicated the bench against the far wall and Seamus placed the sword and his bag of knives there, taking care not to let Gaius get a good look at his face. Aliah then followed him and Dominic into her father's personal sitting room. The guard closed the door firmly behind them. Seamus and Aliah stood together by the window while Dominic made himself comfortable in a chair by the fire. The very chair Aliah had sat in when her father told her she was to leave home.

It was odd being back in her father's outer-chamber under such different circumstances. She was not the trusting girl who had left this room more than two moon turns ago. Then, she had thought her father was infallible. She now knew he was just as able to fall prey to bad advice as any other man. There was a noise outside and her stomach clenched. Seamus took her hand, sensing her unease, and gave it a quick squeeze before dropping it as the door opened.

CHAPTER 14

AN AUDIENCE WITH THE KING

'Dominic, please tell me that is not who I think it is standing out there with Gaius. I was under the impression we had agreed he was to be left in peace until we uncovered what is really going on with the wizard council?' The tall, lean, dark haired man scolded as he took the gold coronet off his head and placed it on a stand on the chest beside the door. 'And please, if you can, be quick with your report. I have a squabbling council who cannot decide what they want me to do about a rather large fleet of ships heading our way. They not only need guidance to make the right decision, but also to stop them throttling each other. Actually, I need someone to stop me from throttling all of them.'

'Your Majesty, it *is* who you think outside the door, and all will become clear soon,' Dominic said as he bowed to his king, and at the same time glanced towards the window.

The king stopped mid-stride, frowning. 'Do you not bow in the presence of your monarch?' His haughty blue eyes glared at Aliah and Seamus. Seamus inclined his head, a suitable greeting for the son of one monarch to his superior. This earned him a frown and there were obviously some harsh words on the way, which Aliah forestalled by stepping forward.

'Do you not recognise me, father?' she asked as she removed the cloth covering her hair. Seamus was sure it was not often King Terion was lost for words, but the sudden appearance of his daughter stopped him mid-sentence, mouth wide open.

'Aliahanna?' he stepped forward opening his arms. 'You are safe? Thank the goddess!'

Aliah ran to her father and entered his warm embrace. Seamus knew the moment the king took over from the father by the change in expression on the face over Aliah's shoulder. The king pushed his daughter away to arms length. 'Where have you been? Do you know how much trouble you have caused? We are on the brink of war and your behaviour may or may not have had a little something to do with that, depending on who I speak to. Do you know how worried I have been?'

'If I may, sire?' Dominic stepped forward. 'Time is of the essence here. Perhaps you should hear the princesses' story, then maybe ask questions after?' There was a long pause before the king nodded his assent, and led Aliah over to the fire. Dominic gave up his chair for the princess, coming to stand by the window beside Seamus.

The king and his daughter talked in low voices for some time with Seamus and Dominic watching on. By the time they finished Seamus was stiff and tired and grumpy.

'So, young man, it seems I have you, among others, to thank for looking after my daughter.' The king finally turned and looked at Seamus. 'While I appreciate what you have done for my family I cannot abide bad manners. I will ask you again to bow in the presence of your king. Did your family not teach you manners?'

Seamus raised an eyebrow at Aliah, and she smiled back at him. Obviously she had told her story, but not all of his. It was up to him to tell the king who he was if he chose. 'Apologies, sir, I did not mean to offend, but as my father is my king, I bow to none but him. And while I do not wish to appear rude, well, it is awkward.'

The king laughed. 'Well, I thought I could be shocked no more today, but it looks like I was wrong. No one would have bet my daughter would stumble on the errant son of the Duke of Hand. Need I remind you, young Seamus, in this court you are considered one of my subjects not the son of a Monarch, but I understand your sentiments and will forego formalities today only.'

Seamus bowed his head in acknowledgment of the courtesy the king had just granted him. This was not an issue to push at the moment, they all had far more to worry about than the strained relations between Hand and the crown.

'And you, lad, what do you make of my daughter's tale? That Spearon never intended to wed her and bind our countries, but always intended to invade us?' King Terion asked his spy.

'Sire.' Dominic stepped forward. 'It does tie in with what I have been hearing on my travels. There is a captain in Port Marden who saw a fleet massing before the princess could even make land there. I heard talk in the taverns there that the sailors on the princesses' ship were not that concerned about losing their lord's prospective bride as it seems he was not in a mood to marry her anyway. There were many hints about how the princess would be used, though. And none of them sounded like fun.'

The king's brow furrowed. 'And I guess you have your friend out there because you give some credence to his ramblings about a plot to de-stabilise my rule and for the wizard's council to take over running Aria?'

'I may not agree with all he says as I have not been able to verify it all. I have, however, spoken to enough people to know the captain on your daughter's boat was working with some people high up in your government here, and it was they who were pushing for the princess to be found, not the captain himself. There have also been wizards around the countryside stirring unrest, trying to find the princess. They have been working independently of your guard, hand in hand with mercenaries. You have to ask why?'

'So you believe there is a plot?' The king asked point blank.

'I believe something is going on. I also know that Walton has been working on uncovering this for a lot longer than I, and it might benefit you to talk with him and find out what he knows.'

The king pondered for a time. 'He has been discredited by both my council and the Council of Wizards. I would lose a lot of support if it were found I had met with him behind their backs, and it is something Gaius would not keep to himself.'

Aliah placed her hand on her father's arm. 'Perhaps you could have one of your guards take Walter ... Walton to the dungeons, thank Gaius and dismiss him, then have Walton brought back. He did risk his life to bring me home, and I believe he deserves a hearing.'

There was a further silence, and the king sighed. 'Dominic, you and I will speak with him. Aliah, put your head covering back on and I will have the guards take you to my private study. They will have some food brought for you and the young man. We will meet there after we have talked.'

'But ... this has nothing to do with me anymore.' Seamus stepped forward, 'I would like to leave.' He had had enough of all this intrigue. His part was done and all he wanted now was to find out who Walter would have him go to for training and be on his way.

The king held up his hand. 'I am sorry, young man, but this is the business of my realm we discuss, and I make the decisions on what is important and what can wait. This meeting is the most important thing at the moment, your future can wait. We will not decide anything about you without your presence. Rest assured. In the meantime, please enjoy my hospitality.'

Seamus looked at Aliah, she shrugged her shoulders. Reluctantly, Seamus agreed and followed the guard down the corridor to the king's study.

'I have done my bit, I just want to be away from here.' Seamus paced around the study once the door was closed.

'Be fair, Seamus.' Aliah leaned against her father's desk. 'We have done our job but we may still be needed to help Aria survive this war.

We may still have important information they need. We may even have a role to play. We should wait and hear what comes out of this meeting. Walter and Dominic know way more than they told us, and it is only right my father hears their council. This could be their only chance to get their point across without my father's advisors being present.'

'I know all that, but I do not know what I can contribute now. All I want is for Walter to keep his end of the bargain and send me on to someone who can help me manage my magic.' Seamus slumped in a chair in front of the desk.

'I know that is what you want.' Aliah frowned at him, 'But can you really desert Aria in her time of need? This will affect the people of the Southern Duchies as well.'

Seamus frowned and reluctantly had to admit he probably would not. Then, before he could find something else to grumble about, the soldier who had escorted them brought in a tray of bread and cheese and a pitcher of fresh, cold milk. There were also a few small honey cakes. Aliah thanked him, and the two fell on the food like they had not eaten in days. As they ate, Seamus realised some of his bad mood was due to hunger. He was so much happier once his stomach was full.

When they finished, Aliah challenged him to a game of Last Man using the board and pieces her father had set up in the corner. The strategy of the war game had him enthralled for a time, but after he won one game and Aliah another, he began to get bored and started pacing the room again.

'Aliah? Do you think your father has a book on the prophecy we have been hearing so much about? I do not believe I have ever seen it. We have time we may as well have a look at it.' Seamus did not know why the idea popped into his head.

'I think so.' Aliah went to a shelf over the other side of the room, and after a few minutes she took down a book. Taking it over to her father's desk she opened it up and began flipping through it. 'Here it is!' She pointed to a page and Seamus went over to read.

'It is from a seer who made the prophecy during the Natari expansion, apparently. She was in Hand at the time.'

Seamus looked where her finger pointed.

'When the new power rises
And the Wizard and Warrior meet,
Old and new blood will combine
To save one and all.'

'That is really vague!' Seamus was a little disappointed. 'It could mean anyone or in any time. Is there anything else?'

'Not here, although there might be in the main castle library. This could be real or it could just be propaganda to try and unite the two nations,' Aliah suggested as she put the book back. 'This was written just after the Natari invasion after all.'

Seamus nodded thoughtfully. 'It did not do a very good job if that was the intention. I wonder if my people have a similar prophecy? If we did, then maybe it might actually mean something.'

Seamus continued his pacing and Aliah went back to the game of Last Man she was playing against herself. Sunset was near when the door finally opened and the king entered along with Dominic, Walter, and another man about the age of Aliah's father dressed in guard's livery. Seamus started at the sight of a military man, but Aliah beamed. 'Uncle Tomas. Seamus, this is father's oldest friend and captain of his personal guard.'

'Aliah, you have led us on a fine chase. My boys have had bets on how long it would take me to find you, but young Shane won. He said I wouldn't. You would find us when you were ready.' He returned Aliah's smile.

'I am sorry to cut this short,' King Terion interrupted. 'But, Tomas, you cannot tell Shane or anyone that Aliah came back. All must think her still lost for our plans to work.'

'Yes, yes, of course,' Tomas looked abashed.

'Plans?' Seamus stepped forward. 'I hope they do not include me?'

'Yes, they do include you, in so far as you want to be included.' The king firmly held is gaze. 'I make no apologies about that. Aria faces a war and there are things to take into consideration that you are not party to. However, we have not set anything in stone with regards to your participation. What you do from here is up to you. Of course we hope you take a certain path but I will not force you. Look what happened when I did that with Aliah. I will not make that same mistake again.'

Aliah stepped forward. 'Does that mean I can come home father?'

King Terion hugged his daughter. 'No, my sweet, I am sorry. If there is one thing I am convinced of it is you are not safe around me and you must remain lost. How you remain lost though will be up to you.'

The king released his daughter and went and sat behind his desk. He gestured for the others to sit in the various chairs around the room, with Aliah and Seamus taking the two seats in front of him.

'After much discussion I have become open to the possibility that not all of my council—or those on the wizards' council—have our people's best interests at heart. The depth of this, I have no way of knowing, but I feel the only way to find out is to carry on as if this visit never occurred, at least in the open. I plan to have a few select people closely watched by some of Dominic's friends, and we will wait and see if they slip up.'

'In the meantime I need to get ready for a war that we are ill prepared to fight. One of the things we were discussing today was sending an envoy to the Isle of Hand and suggesting we join forces to defend the South. Many in my council, some of whom I now suspect to be sabotaging plans for our defence, talked the council out of that idea. I would like to do that anyway, sending you as secret envoys.' King Terion looked directly at Seamus.

'But, I cannot go back,' Seamus said. 'Even if I wanted to.'

'Ah, yes. Your reason for leaving. Walter told me you could

become a wizard of great strength one day with the proper training. I can only imagine what that means within your family. By now they must have guessed the reason you ran away, and this will make it difficult when you see them again.'

'They may have guessed,' Seamus admitted. 'If they have, then I will not be welcomed back into the family.' Seamus hung his head, there was no point in wishing for something that would never happen.

'You might be surprised.' The king reached into a drawer in his desk and pulled out a letter, which he handed to Seamus. 'Go ahead, read it.'

Seamus looked at the letter. The writing seemed familiar. As he read he realised it was from his mother to the king. She wrote she had reason to believe her son was travelling to the Wizard Isles and she would appreciate the king letting her know when he arrived. If he could also pass on whether he was in good health, and let him know his mother would not be against receiving an occasional letter.

A great wave of homesickness rolled through Seamus, then he realised the reality. 'My father will never accept me back.'

'No. Perhaps not. But you will be going to the Isle of Hand as my representative and therefore under my protection. I just wanted you to know that should you return, you would have at least one supporter in your father's court. Think on it.'

'And if I choose not to return?'

'You could be admitted to the school on the Isle of Wizards to learn magic. Or if you choose not to learn magic there, then Walter says he found a mage in Nataria who would consider taking you on as an apprentice.'

'He is a good person and a good teacher.' Walter said encouragingly. Seamus frowned, unsure of what to do.

'Of course, if you decide to become my envoy then Walter could travel with you as an advisor and you could continue your magic training under his care. Walter has agreed to this.' The king's eyebrows raised questioningly.

Seamus frowned and gnawed his lip. Unsure what to do, he was saved from answering by Aliah.

'And what about me? What are my options?'

'There are two I can see to keep you safe.' Her father's attention swung to her. 'Tomas has offered to escort you to his estates and there you will be protected by his wife and his son, Angus, who you know runs the estate in his father's absence.'

'No offence, Tomas, but your home is in the Highlands, surrounded by forests and mountains on all sides. And Angus and I have never gotten on. We would drive Alyssa mad with our fighting.'

Tomas laughed. 'But you would be safe, and Alyssa would enjoy some female company after raising four boys.'

'And the other option?' Aliah dismissed this one immediately and looked at her father to see if he could do better with his alternative.

'The other option would be to spend some time with my cousin in the Natari Capital. He is a minor noble as things go in the Empire, but he could introduce you to court and you could perhaps find a suitable match there.'

Seamus held his breath for the explosion, and was not disappointed by its magnitude even if Aliah's voice was controlled and low.

'So, you failed to marry me off to some barbarian who really did not want to marry me, and then you tell me my only other options to stay safe are to hide in the middle of nowhere, or to marry some foreigner. Meanwhile Seamus gets to be an envoy or learn magic, or both. That is the only role you see for me in your narrow view?' The room was quiet, as if no one was sure how to treat this outburst. Before anyone could speak Aliah continued. 'Well, I am just as capable of being an envoy to the Isle of Hand as Seamus! I am as educated and as able to hold my own in a court. Once more, I would be out of sight of the court here while you ferreted out your enemies.' She sat back and folded her arms.

Dominic burst out laughing, which served to anger Aliah even more. 'Sire, she has you there. And in this instance two envoys may be better than one!'

'I don't need your support,' Aliah flung at him.

Dominic's face remained impassive as the king responded. 'Well, I see nothing wrong with both of you going as my envoys. And you, Dominic, can accompany them to ensure my needs are met, as a guard of course, so you are not noticed. Walter you can be their trusted advisor and tutor. Tomas, you can send your son, Daniel, and a couple of men as honour guards. I am sure your second son can keep these two in line.'

And with that, it was all organised, much to Seamus' annoyance. He was of course, going to choose to be the king's envoy as he wanted to be a part of the fight to save his country, and the fact Walter would continue to teach him was a big bonus. But to have the decision taken away was most frustrating.

While Seamus fumed and went over what he wanted to say in his head, the king began drawing up requisitions, orders, and formal letters of introduction. The others chatted quietly. As Seamus went to speak there was a knock on the door.

'Sire. Chief Advisor Millard is requesting an audience,' the guard announced.

'Where is he?' the king asked.

'He is standing outside, sire. He knows you have Captain Tomas and someone else in here.'

The king was silent for a moment. 'Dominic, take Walter and my daughter the back way to the docks. The Golden Hawk is ready to sail on my order. Seamus and his guard will join you soon.' He handed Dominic some papers. 'You can get suitable supplies at Port Isby. Seamus will have the official letters of introduction when he boards.' The king's voice was low so it would not carry.

Dominic did not delay. Leading the others to the chest by the Last Man table, he fiddled around for something and the chest moved into the room revealing a hidden passage. When they were safely inside and the chest had swung silently back in place, the king nodded to the guard. A man in wizard's robes barged into the room seconds after the guard had opened the door.

'Forgive my intrusion, sire.' He bowed. 'You had not returned and the council has disbanded, then Gaius informed me we had captured Walton and that you were in private meetings. I thought you might need my services, so I stayed behind.'

'Ahh, Millard, how helpful you are. However, this is nothing you can assist with.'

'You look to be writing, sire, may I at least scribe for you?'

'That will not be necessary, it is only a short personal note. Wizard Millard, meet Seamus, Heir to the Duke of Hand. He has been missing for some time on a personal journey of discovery. One of Tomas' men found him in the city today and brought him here knowing his mother had asked me to look out for his safety. He is about to depart for home on the Golden Hawk, which should be passing by the Isle in its reconnaissance mission.' The king handed Seamus the letter he had just added his seal to, plus two others. 'This is for your mother, the other two are for your father. Tomas, see to it that trunk waiting in my room is sent with him. It contains gifts for the duke and duchess. And, if you could spare Daniel and a couple of guards to go with Seamus to ensure he makes it to the Golden Hawk, I would appreciate it, as would his mother I think.'

'Your Highness.' Tomas bowed and left the room.

'So this is the young man who has been leading his family on a merry dance?' Wizard Millard's smile seemed overly friendly and Seamus felt a whisper as the other wizard tried to sense his magic. 'And the rumours he is a magic user are untrue?'

Seamus froze, surely a wizard of the gold could feel his magic even if it were shielded.

'I guess they were not true if you cannot detect any magic in him,' the king responded. 'Now, young man, I hope you have a pleasant journey, and perhaps next time you will think a little about how your mother will feel when you try to adventure off!' He shook Seamus' hand and called for the guard. 'Please take this young man to my chambers where he is to wait until Guard Daniel arrives to take him to his ship. 'God speed, young man.'

'Now, Millard, perhaps you can inform me of what the council decided in my absence ...' And with that the king moved on to other matters, dismissing Seamus.

IN THE KING'S chamber Seamus waited, with the guard firmly on the inside of the door this time as if he did not trust him. A large trunk had been added to the furnishings, and Seamus resisted the urge to open it and see what was inside. Instead, he sat down in a chair and quietly waited for his escort. He used the time to mull over his encounter with Wizard Millard.

He knew his shielding was perfect now. Walter had had him work on it every morning before they slept until he could perform small magics such as creating a light without leaking. That said, Walter told him a stronger wizard could always tell a lesser wizard, even when they were shielded. So that meant one of two things. Either Millard was not truly strong enough to be a gold, or Seamus was stronger in magic than one of the strongest wizards on the wizard council. Then a third option occurred to him. Was Millard playing some sort of twisted game by not admitting to his magic?

It seemed an age before there was a knock at the door and a young guardsman entered. He was obviously Tomas' son, with the same blond wavy hair and laughing brown eyes.

'Your Lordship.' He made a rather sketchy bow. 'I trust you are ready to travel.'

'According to the king, I am.' Seamus grinned, instantly liking the young man. 'Please, call me Seamus. We have a long voyage and to stand on ceremony would be a shame.'

'Yes, that is true. Come now. The captain is rather grumpy at being delayed for so long. Afraid he might miss the tide or something. Then again, he is normally grumpy so it is hard to tell. Boys, I have Lord Seamus, so I guess the trunk is yours,' he said to the two guardsmen standing behind him.'

Protesting, they picked up the trunk between them and carried it out of the castle to the waiting carriage. All four young men jumped aboard and they were soon off to the harbour.

The ship was a large clipper and a hive of activity. The young men left the carriage, and one of the guards called a sailor to take the trunk to Seamus' cabin. They then led Seamus on board, one in front and two behind, just to make sure he did not escape.

The captain stopped them as they boarded. 'Guardsman Cameron, and our final guest for the Isle of Hand, I presume.'

'All present and correct, captain.'

CHAPTER 15

A NEW JOURNEY

'About blimmin time! We nearly missed the tide because of your tardiness. You share a cabin with Dominic and Walter,' he said to Seamus. 'You gentlemen are across the way. The boy'll show you!'

'Yes, sir!' Daniel performed a mock salute for the captain, who had already moved away as soon as he had spoken to them. After all, he had no time for pleasantries, he had a ship to get underway. As they walked towards the stairs to the cabins Daniel said under his breath, 'And I can see by the fact they are still loading it was only us they were waiting on.' His companions laughed as they followed the boy below deck.

Seamus' cabin door was opened first and he could see a room larger than expected. There were three beds around the walls, and a table bolted to the floor in the middle. Beside the table was the trunk the king had sent, and on top were his and Aliah's packs and the bag with his knives. Through the other door he could see the room for the guards was a mirror image. Daniel and the guards went to settle themselves in and Seamus entered his room to find Dominic had been hidden by the door.

'Here at last,' he said to Seamus. 'Make yourself comfortable. We will not be allowed out until the ship is well underway. Captain Hanks does not like anyone under his feet while he leaves the harbour. A boy will bring us supper, and then I think we should all get a good night's sleep.'

Seamus was about to ask after Walter when the door opened and he entered. He was dressed in smart simple clothes and looked younger than he had before. Seamus guessed this must be what he really looked like and was surprised to see he was around his father's age, maybe a little older. Walter was carrying some reading materials. 'Princess Aliah's trunk is a bit of a mish-mash of things. Some for her and some for us, I suspect this is the same.' He pointed to the trunk that came with Seamus.

'Where is Aliah?' Seamus asked, realising no one had mentioned her since she left the king's study.

Walter shut the door behind him before answering Seamus' question. 'She is in the cabin down the end of the hall. It is usually used for the maids of travelling ladies. It is best no one know who she is until we have left Port Isby. By then no one will be able to tell anyone else she is on board.'

'The captain knows, of course. But he has worked solely under the king's orders since the king gave him his first ship. He is more than trustworthy,' Dominic added.

'Oh.' Seamus answered the same time there was a knock on the door. The ship boy who led them to the cabins entered carrying hot stew and bread for their evening meal. A slightly older boy carrying a pitcher of ale followed him.

After finishing their meal a quick look out the window showed the ship slowly leaving a darkening harbour. Almost as one they decided it was time for sleep and rolled into their beds. Seamus was asleep almost before his head hit the pillow. He had been going for over a day and a half without much rest and even the hard bed could not prevent his body from getting the sleep it craved.

The rocking boat kept Seamus asleep until a knock on the door brought the ships' boy back with food to break their fast. After they had eaten, the three took turns in the confined space at washing and changing into the clothes provided for them by the king. Dominic looked resplendent in his guard's uniform, and Walter very dignified in his black advisor robes. Seamus nearly choked when he saw the splendour the king expected him to prance about in.

'I'm not wearing that! I'll look like one of those court toadies.' He spluttered holding up some sky blue silk trousers and a white ruffled shirt. It did not help that Walter and Dominic were rolling on their beds laughing at his discomfort.

'The king could hardly send you home in what you are wearing, it would have been a sign of contempt for the duke to see you so. Also, you are entering your father's court as the king's representative, so he would like you to dress appropriately. Your clothes need to display his wealth and power,' Dominic solemnly advised him when he finally calmed down.

Seamus had to admit there was some sense in all that. No one would listen to him in servant's clothes. 'Well, I am wearing what I have on until we get to the port on Hand. Then maybe we can ask my mother for some of my clothes.'

'You would be a might smelly by then, and I really do not fancy sharing a cabin with you under those conditions. In fact, I have to say you are a little smelly already. The captain holds some clothes for me in times of need, he may have something that would fit you until you need to become a peacock on display.'

'Thank you,' Seamus said gratefully.

'And while I am finding out, you could perhaps take that frippery to Aliah.' He pointed to the pile of women's items on the table.

Pleased to be doing something, Seamus picked up the clothes along with a couple of books from their chest and took them down the hall to where Aliah's cabin was said to be. As he drew close, he heard laughter from within. He knocked on the door and was surprised to see it opened by Guard Daniel.

'Come in, come in ... Oops, maybe not. It is a little tight for space in here with the mess Aliah has created.' He shuffled around to try and make room for Seamus. 'Perhaps it is best if I come out so you may come in.'

'No, it is all right,' Seamus mumbled. 'I just came to drop these off for Aliah.'

'And no doubt pick up some of what she has just pulled from her chest. We were just discussing what would happen if she arrived at your father's court wearing some of this. It was obviously meant for you.' Daniel smiled. 'I have to check in with the captain, then have a talk with a new recruit I seem to have acquired. I can only imagine how Dominic feels his new position in my guard will work, and I need to talk to him before some of those ideas take hold. So you can keep Aliah company in my absence. Maybe persuade her to actually clean up after herself because there is no one else to do it.' Daniel moved out of the room to make space for Seamus then shut the door behind him.

'I did not mean to cut his visit short,' Seamus said, a little confused at the scene he had witnessed, and still not really comfortable being in Aliah's company.

Aliah looked up from her place on the floor beside the trunk. Clothes were strewn throughout the room, every surface covered in something.

'Daniel has work to do but it was nice to spend a little time with him. It was hard being at home like that and not getting to see all of my family. Daniel and I grew up together so he is like a big brother. We used to practice sword work until he joined the guards and it embarrassed him if I beat him.' Aliah's face softened fondly at the memory.

'I am sorry, it must have been hard for you yesterday. To finally arrive home and then to leave so quickly, not seeing your sister or even really getting to say good-bye to your father.'

'Mmm,' Aliah answered, her head in the trunk rummaging. When it popped out she said, 'But there is an improvement. This time, I am leaving as my father's representative to talk with a Head of State. Last time, I was being sent off to marry a barbarian. It is nice to be good for something other than getting married.' Her head ducked back into the trunk.

'Are you looking for something in particular?' he asked.

'I most certainly am. If I am to be stuck in this room until Port Isby they could have at least given me something to pass the time.'

'You mean some embroidery perhaps?' Seamus said, then ducked the shoe Aliah threw at him. 'Or maybe these?' He held up the three books he had in his hand, bound with a note from Aliah's father. The note read, 'If you are going to represent me it is about time you read some of our history written by earlier statesmen.'

'Ahh, he is so frustrating!' Aliah exclaimed.

'What do you mean?'

'Well, take these trunks with clothing that just happen to fit the both of us. I think it is likely he had them packed while he was talking with Dominic and Walter. And the fact that there are books on the history between Hand and Aria? I thought when he was presenting our options that he was doing it in a way that led us to choose what he wanted us to do. I believe he never had any intention of sending me away, in fact he planned for you and I to both represent him all along. This note just proves it.'

Aliah flopped down on the one chair ignoring the clothing it was covered with.

'He knew you would come rather than be married off to some stranger, but he cannot have known I would agree to his plan,' Seamus said.

'Really? Walter knew you were no longer keen on studying at the Wizard Isles. Could you really have gone to some foreign land while a war raged through Aria? I think not, and Walter would have known that too. This option gives you an opportunity to spend time with your family again, even if you do not get to stay. I would have bet on your going ... so did he.'

'The crafty old ...'

'Careful. That is the king and my father you are talking about.' Aliah laughed, and he joined her.

'Are you happy to be going home?' Aliah finally asked him.

'It will be good to see my mother, my father too I guess. But I really have no idea how my father will react to my having magic. He could just as soon banish me or have me held in the dungeons as welcome me home.'

'Maybe it is as your aunt said, he is not as strict about the old ways as he seems. You should trust him to find a solution.'

'Maybe. But at least it will be out in the open. And I have a little protection being on your father's business, so my father with think twice about doing anything rash when he sees me. I guess the king thought of that as well.' Seamus surprised himself at how relieved he was to have the opportunity to see his parents again. Being away from them made him realise how much he missed them, and to not have them in his life at all would be hard.

'And it is kind of nice to be travelling home in luxury feeling safe again, even if it is only for a while.'

Aliah found a small area not covered in clothing and indicated he should sit. 'My last experience was not so different to this though. I will still be stuck in a cabin unable to see what all the fuss over sailing the seas is about.' Clearly she did not have fond memories of her first trip.

As if suddenly struck by a thought Aliah looked at him. 'Are you all right with this. I mean working with me really. You know ... after ...'

'After you left me without a word and headed out on your own,' he finished for her.

Aliah wriggled in discomfort. 'Well, yes.'

Seamus looked her in the eye. 'I really am all right with it. It seems the fates want us to be together for the moment, and you have shown me you are not so likely to act without consideration again. And if you do decide to go off on a tangent, I am at least prepared for it this time.' Seamus was almost as surprised as she was at the words that came out of his mouth. As he uttered them he realised he really was no longer angry with her.

'Shall we sort through these things and see what needs to go in my trunk. Then maybe I can find some cards or a set of Last Man Standing. There is nothing to say that you have to be stuck here alone. And there is always your father's books.' He smiled. 'Then after we leave Port Isby you will be allowed on deck and maybe we could continue with developing our hand to hand combat techniques. I would love to try actually using them to fight.''

Aliah returned his smile. 'This trip will definitely be better than the last! We will make it so because we have seen that together, there is nothing we cannot do.'

'Aliah?'

'Mmm.'

'I spoke with Walter last night. Wizard Millard could not find a trace of magic in me. He thinks this means I am either a really strong wizard, or that Millard was playing games.'

'Now that is interesting.' Aliah looked closely at him. 'Which do you think it is?'

Seamus paused and watched her put away some of her clothing into the trunk. 'I don't really know. You don't suppose that what Pauley said about us being The Wizard and The Warrior from the prophecy could be true do you?'

Aliah spluttered in a very unladylike way. 'No, silly. Those old men would not have written a prophecy about a woman warrior, and though you can fight I would not describe you as a warrior. And although you can make a tiny flame no one in their right mind would call you a wizard.'

'I guess you are right.' Seamus agreed, but in his head he wondered if maybe he and Aliah had less control over the events that had brought them to this point than they imagined. He shrugged his shoulders, only time would tell. For now he had best help Aliah sort out the mess that was her room.

TRIALS

THE WIZARD AND THE WARRIOR
Book Two

PROLOGUE

"After the decimation and the fall,
When the new power rises
And the Wizard and Warrior meet,
Old and new blood will combine
With the two who are not what they seem
To save one and all."

'Eon,' the elderly seer called. 'Eon.'

'I am right here, master.'

Caraig jumped as the voice came from behind him. He had not heard his apprentice come into the room and for some reason that thought made him uneasy. He frowned and tugged his beard. *What was he thinking? Eon had been with him for years, he had no reason to feel wary in his presence.* He shook his head to clear his thoughts.

'Eon, they are moving closer. If all goes to plan, they will soon be on our doorstep. I would like you to call a Prophecy Council meeting on my behalf. It is time we have this out once and for all.'

'But, master, at the last meeting they asked you bring more proof that the omens foretold in the prophecy were actually happening now. We have not been able to find anything new.'

'I know.' Caraig wearily ran his hand through his snow white hair. 'Regardless, the ones we wait for are on their way here. At the very least, we need to know what we are going to do with them when they arrive.'

'As you wish, master.' Eon turned to leave the room, but Caraig called him back.

'Can you bring Emer with you when you return? I need to start preparations, and I will need you both to assist.'

'Are you sure we need to involve Emer? I think she is out on patrol.'

'Yes, I need you both. I fear we will not have much support from the others in this matter.'

Caraig caught the sound of Eon's sigh as he closed the door behind himself. In the silence that followed Eon's departure, Caraig mentally reviewed the signs he had seen and tried to decided which would convince the Council he was right—the time of the Wizard and Warrior had arrived.

CHAPTER 16

AT SEA

'What the...' Aliah picked herself up off the ground, then held out her hand to help Daniel. She had been practicing her sword fighting with the guardsman in the makeshift arena he and his men built in the ship's store-rooms, when a blast had blown them off their feet.

'Stay here,' Daniel commanded. 'Remember the crew do not know you are aboard, and we are not yet ready to change that.'

He rushed through the door to the stairs that would take him to the upper deck. Aliah watched him disappear then, unable to stop herself, followed him into the corridor and crept slowly up the stairs. Staying hidden in the shadows, she observed the scene on the deck above, reminded of her escape from a ship a few moon turns ago.

Her initial worry the ship was under attack by someone who had found out she was aboard proved to be unfounded. It seemed the explosion had been caused by Seamus, heir to the Duke of Hand. During their journey Walter, a renegade wizard, had been teaching Seamus to control and use his magical powers. Today Seamus' magic flared out of control when trying to move a barrel from one place to another on the deck. He had obviously used too much force and the barrel, which happened to contain tar for caulking the ship, had exploded. Fortunately, no one was hurt. But there was a large hole in the deck over a cargo hold, and the tar was nowhere to be seen. From the look on his face, the captain was less than impressed. He was yelling at Seamus and gesticulating wildly.

Resisting the urge to go above deck and make fun of her travel companion, Aliah quietly returned to the cargo hold and began practicing the moves she and Seamus had been working on for unarmed combat. Based loosely on the sword forms used to teach attack and defence, it looked rather like a dance. Seamus had started developing the new way of fighting, and lately she had been helping him. Her concentration was interrupted by the sound of slow clapping hands.

'A very pretty dance for a princess.'

Daniel had returned and was clearly amused by what he had seen. 'What is that meant to be? Some girlish form of sword practice without a sword?'

Annoyed, Aliah took a ready stance and faced the son of her father's oldest friend. 'We will see how girly it is, Daniel. Attack me,' she commanded him.

Daniel stopped laughing. 'You have no sword, it would not be fair.'

'I will not always have a sword to hand when attacked. Princesses do not carry swords to balls or state functions. *Attack me.*'

'As you command, Your Highness.'

Daniel readied himself, then thrust his sword towards Aliah. Moving to her right, she allowed the attack to pass her, took a step back, and pushed Daniel's outstretched arm, tipping him off balance. With a kick to his bottom, Aliah almost knocked him over. She laughed gleefully as Daniel rounded on her again.

'I will be more prepared this time, little princess.'

Daniel attacked again and Aliah just managed to move out of the way, feeling the swish of the sword as it went past her head. Maintaining his balance this time, Daniel pushed her back against the hull of the ship.

'Admit defeat,' Daniel commanded, his sword a finger-width from her chest.

Daniel relaxed now he had her cornered, and Aliah ducked below the sword point, turned, and came up on Daniel's left hand side, jabbing her elbow into his stomach. As his balance changed, she swivelled and pushed all her strength behind the flat of her foot, sending him to the ground.

Standing over her felled opponent, Aliah smiled at the figure in the doorway. 'You were right, Seamus. Not having a sword does allow you to use your feet more effectively, and that is very useful in certain situations.'

Seamus walked over to help Daniel up. 'I am pleased it worked so well, but I suspect poor Daniel is not.'

'You caught me by surprise, that is all.' Daniel rubbed his bruised bottom. 'Anyway, what was that?'

'I am so pleased you asked,' Seamus said. 'When I was hiding out in Walter's cellar while making my way to Bannock, I had time on my hands. One evening I came up with this form of fighting. It is based loosely on sword moves, but also on something I remember seeing used by some visitors to my father's palace.

'It allows you to fight when you do not have weapons, and also benefits from using what you have already learnt training as a soldier. Aliah began practicing with me when we travelled from Duncameron to Bannock, and we have continued to work on it aboard the ship. We added feet yesterday, something you cannot do as easily when weighed down with weapons. It seems to work quite well.'

'How long have you been doing this?' Daniel asked Aliah.

'As Seamus said, I have not been doing this very long,' Aliah answered. 'If you have learnt sword work then you can pick it up quite quickly.'

'Impressive.' Daniel nodded.

'Yes, she is,' Seamus admitted. 'I am better at this than I am at using a sword, but I am still not at her level. She has better natural instincts when it comes to combat.'

'No. I mean, yes, Aliah is a good fighter, always has been. I meant the idea is impressive. It uses sword forms, but also uses your opponent's momentum and balance against them. The applications... the ability to fight when you have lost your sword, or are in a situation where you do not have one... very interesting.' Daniel's eyes gleamed as he silently contemplated this new form of fighting.

'You will have to excuse Daniel,' Aliah told Seamus. 'Even as a child he would follow his father around, trying to learn as much as he could about being a soldier. It was all he ever wanted to be. And we have just handed him a very special gift, something new to learn about fighting.'

'Could I join you? Next time you practice, I mean,' Daniel asked.

Aliah looked at Seamus, who nodded. 'Sure. Besides I may need you, Seamus may not get much time to practice over the next two days before we make port. Did I overhear the captain say something about you fixing that hole you made single-handedly?'

'He may have,' Seamus mumbled.

Daniel laughed and clapped the younger boy on the back. 'Never fear, the captain would not let such a rank amateur touch his prized possession. We will be in Port Isby tomorrow. One of the shipwrights in port will be set to fix the deck. We had planned a day there to get supplies anyway.'

Seamus still looked sheepish. 'I really do not seem to be able to get this magic thing. Some days I can do exactly as Walter asks, other days I cannot control anything. Maybe it would be better for every one if I had my magic removed.'

'I am sure you are doing fine.' Aliah put her hand on his arm. 'It is just like learning anything new, we all have off days. You must also remember, you really have only been learning for a short time. Walter said some of the boys he taught on the Wizard Isle took years to get full control of their power.'

'I guess that is true. Anyway, I actually came down here to tell you the captain wants us all in his cabin.'

'We will just tidy up down here and join you.' Aliah turned to pack up her weapons, and Seamus left to meet up with the others.

Aliah oiled then sheathed her sword. While Daniel was finishing up, she gathered her cloak and put it on so the hood covered her face, grimacing as she did. It annoyed her that she had to travel hidden away, even if it was for her own protection. Daniel picked up the two swords, then pulled the hood of the cloak down even further, almost covering her eyes.

'It would not do for anyone to recognise you.' He winked at her.

Aliah frowned and tugged the hood back off her face a little, mentally cursing the traitors on the Wizard Council who wanted to send her to Carsten to marry a king she did not know. It was to ensure when something happened to her father she would not be there to take the crown. Those very same wizards had been working with the King of Carsten to set up an invasion of Aria, causing her father to be in danger, which made her even more annoyed.

'Curse them all,' Aliah mumbled as she followed Daniel out of the hold. He promptly stopped and looked under her hood.

'Curse who?' he asked, obviously bewildered.

'Wizards. If they were not plotting, there would be no invasion. If there were no invasion, I would not be on a secret mission to nego-tiate military support from the Duke of Hand. Then I would not have to hide myself away.'

Daniel laughed out loud. 'I may only be a mere soldier, not able to fully grasp matters of state, but it seems to me if it were not for those wizards you would not have been on your way to Carsten. You would not have found out what they were planning, and you would not have escaped and travelled home in time to warn your father.'

'But...'

'... What is more, you would not have met Walter and found out about the wizard's plot in the first place,' Daniel continued as if she had not interrupted him.

'Humph,' Aliah commented.

'And, if I remember correctly, you did not have to come with Seamus to meet with his father. You were given the option of hiding with my mother, or your uncle in Nataria. But you got what you wanted—a chance to prove to your father that you are ready to take on the responsibilities of heir to the throne.'

Aliah swirled her cloak around her as she stalked past Daniel, now more annoyed with him than the wizards. 'Mere soldier indeed,' she muttered under her breath as she made her way to the captain's cabin.

THE OTHERS WERE all assembled when Aliah and Daniel finally made it to the captain's cabin. The captain sat behind a large desk covered almost entirely by a sea chart. He was a burly man with a sea weathered face that often wore a frown, and had the air of someone used to barking out orders and having others jump to follow them. Aliah had known him all her life, and knew his bark was definitely worse than his bite.

'Highness.' He nodded. 'Young Pup.' He acknowledged Daniel using the name he had called the guard since first meeting him as a child, when Daniel had followed the Captain round the ship like a puppy dog. 'As we are all here, let us make this quick. Barring any further internal attacks on my ship,' he said, glowering at an embarrassed Seamus. 'We should make Port Isby in the early hours of tomorrow morning. We will be there for one night, taking the tide on the following morning. I have to give my men shore leave as it will be expected. They will talk as they do. I am concerned as there are already mumblings on deck about the mysterious woman travelling with us. Dominic, perhaps you can take it from here?'

A tall, brown haired man with a trim goatee and shoulder

length hair tied back tidily, moved from his position behind the captain to stand in front of the desk. Even though his guard's uniform suggested a lower rank than Daniel, in this room he was clearly the one in charge. 'What do your men know, Daniel?' he asked.

'My guards were told the princess travels with us. But I have known each and every one of them since boyhood, and all of them would go to the grave rather than tell a soul she was here.' Daniel looked at all of them one by one to make sure they understood they could trust his men as thoroughly as he did.

'I wish I could say the same for all of my crew, young Dominic.' Captain Hank shook his head. 'We took on some new men in Bannock and, while each was vouched for by an existing crewman, many are only known as workmates. They have all been told we have a lady travelling with us who is of a nervous disposition and prefers privacy. I am sure there are some on board questioning this. My first mate has already caught a couple of them trying to sneak into the cabin area.'

'Can we continue without having that hole in the deck fixed?' Dominic asked the captain, who thought for a moment before answering.

'If young Seamus, along with Daniel's men, could help fashion a makeshift cover we should be fine so long as we do not hit any rough seas.'

'And this time of year would we be able to make it directly to Hand without encountering any bad weather, and without running out of supplies?'

Again, the captain weighed his thoughts before answering. 'If I put us all on rations from today, and we dip into some of the cargo we are carrying, I believe we could.'

Dominic looked at Daniel, who nodded his head. Walter also nodded when Dominic met his gaze.

'All right then, we head straight for The Isle of Hand.' Dominic turned to leave the room.

'Good of them to let us listen in on their Council,' Seamus whispered to Aliah as they entered the hallway.

Before she could reply, Aliah lost her footing as the ship lurched and she stumbled into Seamus. He steadied her before holding up both hands and exclaiming, 'That was not me.'

They rushed for the deck, Aliah included, unwilling to wait in her cabin until someone remembered to tell her what was going on. She wanted to see the cause of the second explosion of the day, first hand.

THE CAPTAIN, Dominic, and Daniel headed straight for the bridge, while Walter led Aliah and Seamus slowly after them.

'Pirates?' the captain asked his first mate as they arrived.

'No, sir, but I do not recognise the flag they sail under either.'

Captain Hanks picked up a spyglass as another missile hit the water beside them, rocking the ship and spraying the deck with water.

'They are in range and nearly have their eye in, sir. Orders?'

This time the captain did not hesitate. 'All hands on deck, full sail. We will have to try and out-run them.' He turned to Walter. 'Wizard, is there anything you can do to speed us, or slow them?'

Walter nodded his head. 'I certainly can, Captain. Just let me know when you are ready to go.' Walter headed to the stern of the ship and Seamus followed to see what he was going to do. Aliah drifted behind them, also interested to see what a wizard could do in battle without actually attacking a person, which they were forbidden to do by law on pain of being quietened. This process prevented them from ever using their magic again.

Walter stood silently, waiting for the sails to be raised, and when the first mate confirmed the sails were full, he started a complex series of hand movements as he wove his spell. Beside her, Seamus exclaimed in wonder, 'He is making an air bubble around the other ship so it will have no wind.'

She sensed rather than heard a presence to her left, and turned in time to see a sailor lunge at her, sword in hand. Instinct set in and she ducked away from the blade, kicking the sailor off balance, only to find another set of arms around her and a knife at her throat.

'What...' she started to say, before realising her life was actually in danger. While her mind whirred around, trying to make sense of what was happening, instinct honed from years of training took over. She went limp and, as her assailant relaxed, she simultaneously bit into his hand and elbowed into the soft flesh of his stomach. He dropped the knife and stumbled backwards.

'Who are you? What do you want?' Aliah gasped, still trying to understand what was going on, but her attention was drawn back to the first sailor. He was again coming at her, sword at the ready. Before she could react, he dropped the sword and began screaming and shaking his hand.

Her view was blocked by Daniel's body as he stepped between her and her assailant and pushed her back towards the stern. Two of his men appeared beside him and disarmed the two sailors. With hands held behind their backs by the guardsmen, her attackers struggled, desperately trying to break free as they were marched towards the lockable storeroom below the bridge. The ship lurched in the water and the first sailor escaped his guard while they were all off balance. He grabbed hold of a sword and turned to face them all, daring them to come closer.

'We will not be taken alive, there are some fates worse than death.' Still being held by a guardsman, the second sailor's voice was defiant, but his face was sad, as if he were resigned to his fate.

Then, surprising them all, the first sailor plunged the sword into his companion's heart and, before anyone could react, he withdrew the weapon and fell on it, taking his own life. Aliah froze, staring at the bloody scene on the deck.

'Why?' she started. 'Why would he do that?' Shaking her head, Aliah tried to comprehend what she had witnessed.

'Sometimes the punishment for not fulfilling a contract is worse than death,' Daniel told her as he took her by the arm and swung her round to face him, forcing her to look at his face rather than watch his guards clear away the bodies. 'Are you alright?'

'Yes,' she answered shakily, then took a breath to steady her nerves. Although her father's sword master had often trained her on how to handle herself under attack, this was the first genuine attempt on her life and she was a little shaken, as much from the fight as having seen men die in front of her.

Still trembling, Aliah focused on the captain, who walked up to Walter and tapped him on the shoulder. As Walter turned to the captain, the spell he had been holding to slow the other ship fell apart as his concentration wavered.

'Can you make wind as well as take it away?' he asked Walter, who nodded.

'It is a little harder, but it can be done.'

'Good, we need to make it to Hand with all speed now, even if it is a little risky. If you could give us some help, we will head out from the coast and catch the main trade wind to speed our journey.' He turned to Aliah and Seamus. 'I need you two confined to your cabins under watch until we dock. The most important thing now is to deliver you both safely with all speed.' With that, he was off to make sure his crew were ready for the impending race to Hand.

Before they could even speak to each other, Dominic had Aliah by the arm and Daniel took hold of Seamus. They were marched down below to their respective cabins before they could even voice a word of protest.

'Great,' Aliah forced through gritted teeth to Dominic. 'I am now to be treated like more of a prisoner, even though I have demonstrated I am perfectly capable of looking after myself.'

Dominic flashed her a smile in return. 'Not a prisoner, princess, just precious cargo. Your father will have our heads if we do not deliver you safely,' he said as he opened the door to her cabin and steered her through.

Jerking her arm free, she turned to find him planted firmly in the doorway, an amused look on his face as if he was daring her to try and leave. Balling her hands into fists, she resisted the urge to punch him.

'Thank you for escorting me to my cabin, I think I will be able to look after myself from here.' She forced her voice to an even pitch, disguising her anger. If she wanted to be treated like an adult, acting like a spoilt child would not help her cause.

Maintaining her calm until Dominic closed the door behind him was all she could manage. As soon as she was alone, she plonked herself down on the bed and punched the pillow, letting out her frustration at not being able to control her own life. Sinking back on the bed, suddenly weary now the adrenaline from the fight had left her body, she had to admit, if only to herself, it was comforting to be safe and secure in her cabin.

CHAPTER 17

HOMECOMING

'Seamus, I am really not sure that is what the king had in mind for you to wear as his representative.' Walter shook his head and looked to Dominic for support. Dominic was busy doing up the buttons on his dress uniform, but paused for a moment when Walter spoke to him.

'Do not look at me. I am with Seamus on this. The clothes King Terion sent for him to wear would outshine any princess. They would not be my choice either. I say let him wear what he feels comfortable in. After all, this is just an initial meeting. The real fun will not begin until tomorrow.'

Seamus finished doing up the silver buttons on the midnight blue coat he found in the stash of clothes Dominic left on board for emergencies. The final button at the neck was low enough to show a little white of the dress shirt he wore underneath. It was straight cut and came down to the middle of his thigh. Black fitting dress pants and plain black dress shoes with a slight heel finished the outfit.

'At least wear the shoes with the silver buckles.' Walter pointed to the pair on the bed that sat beside the sky blue coat and blue

218

brocade trousers he had set out earlier for Seamus to wear. 'You are representing a king today, you really should dress for the part.'

Angrily, Seamus turned to take his wardrobe frustrations out on Walter, however the expression on the older man's face showed his genuine concern. He sighed, allowing the tension to leave his body, and his voice as he responded to the wizard was calm.

'Walter, this finery may be suitable for court attire in Castle Bannock.' He gestured to the clothing Walter had laid out on the bed. 'But it would make me stand out like a sore toe here in Hand. I appreciate I am indeed representing the king today, but at my father's court a person is judged by the quality of their contribution, not their clothes. If I enter the court dressed in that at best I would be seen to be showing off, at worst I would be seen to be hiding something or setting myself up to be something more than I am. Believe me, today will be difficult enough without people drawing unfounded conclusions from my clothes.'

He took a deep breath, walked to the table, and picked up the leather bag that contained his and Aliah's letters of introduction as ambassadors for King Terion to the Duke of Hand. The pouch shook as he rechecked he had everything, then buckled it closed, fumbling a little with the clasp. He passed the bag to Dominic, who was acting as his aid today, and asked him to make sure Aliah was ready to depart.

When he left his home a little over two moons ago, he had not thought he would ever be able to return. Magic was outlawed on Hand, and practitioners had their magic removed, or had to leave forever. Seamus had chosen to leave, knowing he could never return if it was found out that he had magical abilities. Now he was going back into his father's court not knowing how he would be received. As an ambassador from the king he would not be dismissed or harmed, but that did not make him feel any safer. Nor did it loosen the knot that had been growing in his stomach since they sighted the island.

He took another deep breath. 'We can go up on deck now,' he said as they were interrupted by a knock on the cabin door.

Walter opened it to admit Daniel, who also wore his dress uniform to mark the occasion. 'I am heading up on deck,' he informed them. 'Aliah is already up there with the others. She is very excited.'

Seamus smiled wryly. 'I am pleased she is enjoying this.' Clasping his hands nervously in front, he walked passed Daniel on his way to meet his fate.

Aliah was resplendent in a sky blue gown over a cream under-dress. Her honey blonde hair was in a single plait down her back, and she wore a circlet of gold to denote her royal heritage. 'Will you be able to find out who sent those ships after us?' she was asking Dominic. 'I know they gave up the chase when we were in sight of Hand, but we need to know if they are going to continue to be a problem.' She frowned as Seamus walked into her line of sight, and he steeled himself for her scolding.

'Sky blue, I told you,' she growled at him. 'I even gave Walter a specific set of clothes for you to wear.'

'Now, now, princess.' Dominic draped his arm over Seamus' shoulders. 'Blue is the royal colour, no matter the shade. Give Seamus a break. If he is to build a bridge between the Arian Court and the palace of Hand, then you have to let him do it his own way.'

Aliah's azure eyes looked from Dominic to Seamus. Seamus was about to speak in his own defence when she smiled. 'You know what? I am too excited to let this ruin my day. We have out-run those pirates and are about to embark on an important mission. I am not going to let anything spoil that. Seamus, you do look very formal, and I am sure you know what you are doing. Shall we go watch the ship dock? I cannot wait to meet your family.'

Seamus grimaced at Dominic who winked back in sympathy. 'It is going to be a long day for you, I fear.'

'Any tips?' Seamus asked. As a spy for King Terion, Dominic had been in many difficult situations, and he understood this was the first time Seamus would be entering his father's court as an adult, let alone as a representative of the man the duke owed his position to.

Dominic turned to answer. 'The reception today will be short. We sail under the King's banner, but they have no official word of who is coming because we travelled in secrecy. Today we will be introduced, and the letters will be handed over. It will be a full court, so nothing personal is likely to be said. My advice? Just stick to the formalities. Say as little as possible. Be polite. No doubt Aliah will do most of the talking anyway because of her more senior rank.'

'You make it sound so simple.' Seamus looked out over the port of his hometown as the ropes were thrown down to tie the ship to the wharf. 'If it is that easy, why do I feel like I want to be sick?'

Dominic laughed. 'It is anything but simple. There is a likelihood your father's spies will be watching the docks for our arrival, and will report back that you are on board before we get to the palace. Knowing you are coming will create gossip from everyone as you meet with the duke. They will all be speculating on how a runaway returns as the king's representative. Were you sent away to meet with him? Or were you just lucky?

'And I am sure they have all discussed whether or not you were seen to use magic in the Market Square in Port Marden. Many will be hoping your father banishes you to the dungeon—do you *have* a dungeon? But we can worry about all of that later. Today all we have to do is get the formalities over and done with. The rest will come tomorrow.'

Seamus continued to watch the sailors carry out the docking process like a well oiled machine, and thought about what Dominic had said. He could manage the people of The Court, he had been doing it for years—what he was not sure he could do was look his father in the eye and see his disappointment. It had been his inability to face his parents that led to his running away when he had been forced to use his magic in public. Yet he needed to do just that if he was to play a part in helping Aria fight off the impending Carsten invasion.

As the gangplank was set in place, he drank in the familiar dock-side scene, stopping in surprise as the Ducal carriage pulled up in front of him. Then he shook his head and grinned. Of course the carriage would never be sent for him, Seamus, Heir to the Duke of Hand, but it would be sent for an ambassador from the king. That was who he had to be now, for the sake of Aria and The Southern Duchy.

Walking over to Aliah, he formally held out his arm. She smiled up at him and placed her hand on it, then said through gritted teeth, 'I hate this courtly "a woman cannot walk anywhere without a male escort" stuff. But I guess we have to look the part for the sake of convention.'

'Just think of it as play-acting, you are Princess Aliahanna now. You can go back to being plain Aliah when we are all alone,' Seamus said as they walked down the gangplank towards the carriage. He smiled and nodded to the dock workers, who had stopped to stare at the royal envoys.

That is strange. For a moment he thought he saw an eagle on the roof of a warehouse, but when he turned to take a closer look, there was nothing there. He must have been dreaming; an eagle would not be this close to the water.

The footman opened the door of the gleaming black carriage with the Hand insignia on the door. Seamus allowed Aliah to enter first, as convention dictated, then followed her inside and sat on the ruby, velvet seat beside her. Dominic and Walter both sat opposite, and Daniel took his position outside, beside the driver. After closing the door, the footman took his seat at the back of the coach and they were off through the streets of the Port of Hand.

Seamus looked out at the familiar buildings as they passed, and his stomach churned with fear and excitement over the upcoming meeting with his parents. The warehouses around the dock gave way to the single story buildings of the lower town. Then, as they began to climb the hill towards the palace, these dwellings gave way to the double storied houses set in their own fenced and gated gardens. As they drew closer to their destination, the dwellings and gardens grew larger as the more wealthy citizens of the Southern Duchy had gravitated here to be close to the seat of power in Hand.

FINALLY THE CARRIAGE entered a gate in a defensive wall that surrounded the palace precinct. Following the main road through the outbuildings, it swept around in a circle to draw up by the grey stone steps, leading to the main entrance. A blue carpet had been rolled down the steps to stop where the carriage door would open. This meant someone knew one of the ambassadors was royalty, as this carpet was only used when a member of the royal family visited.

Dominic left the carriage first to ensure their safety. When he was joined by Daniel, Aliah was assisted out first as befitted her rank. Seamus followed her, with Walter acting as rear guard. As they walked up the steps, Aliah with her hand on his arm, looking every bit the princess she was, Seamus had to steady his other hand from shaking. He snuck a look at his parents, but their eyes were fixed firmly on their royal guest.

'Welcome to Hand, Princess Aliahanna.' His father bowed and his mother curtseyed, but only just enough to meet required convention for visiting royalty, not low enough to show true deference.

'Thank you, Duke Damon, we are pleased to be here,' Aliah responded.

'We have arranged a formal reception and exchanging of papers for this evening to allow you and your party time to rest from your long journey, if that is convenient for you?' Again the duke looked only at Aliah.

'That will suit us very well. Thank you.' Aliah inclined her head.

'My head of household will show you to your rooms.' The duke motioned to the woman standing behind him. Martha could not help but risk a quick smile of welcome to Seamus before saying, 'This way, Your Highness, sir.'

Seamus was not quite sure, but he thought his father smiled and winked at him as he walked up the stairs and past his parents, but when he turned to confirm it, the duke already had his back to him, deep in conversation with the duchess and his chamberlain. Seamus shook his head—he must have imagined it. His father would be too angry with him for such a private gesture of welcome.

As their party walked through the main entrance hall and up the main staircase, before turning down the corridor to the left, Seamus was vaguely aware Martha was telling Aliah she should let her know if anyone in their party needed anything. His body was tugging him to the right, to the familiar quarters his family occupied in the palace. He was unsure he would be welcomed there, so he followed Martha to the more ornate staterooms, reserved for high ranking guests.

In fact, Martha led them to the suite reserved for only the most distinguished of visitors. As she opened the double doors to the sitting room that separated the two bedrooms, Seamus remembered the first time he had come in here. He had been hiding from his tutor to avoid a particularly boring session going over the Duchy's accounts. Thinking these rooms were empty because there were no visitors at court, he had been surprised to find a rather elderly man sitting by the fire reading. Seamus had stopped just inside the door, and was about to apologise for the interruption when he felt a presence behind him. His mother looked as surprised to see him there, as he had been to see the rooms occupied. The surprise had not lasted long. He left in a hurry, with his mother's scolding voice following him as he hurried back to the school room on the other side of the palace.

With a smile on his lips, he waited as Martha led Aliah to the bedroom on the right, all the while explaining her things would be brought up for her as soon as they arrived from the ship and if she needed anything before then she just needed to say. Aliah stood in the doorway as Martha bundled Seamus to the other room.

'And did you not create a merry dance for us all?' she scolded Seamus, but her smile and the warmth in her eyes took the sting out of her words. 'We are glad to have you back, you little scallywag.'

'Martha, I am surely too big and too old to be called a scallywag.' Seamus smiled down on the short, plump woman who had been like a second mother to him while he was growing up.

'To me, you will always be that boy sneaking into the kitchen to steal hot biscuits from the cook.' Martha laughed. Seamus was sure if she had not had to reach up to do it, she would actually have ruffled his hair.

'Anyway, my Lord Ambassador, this is your room. There are a few of your clothes in the closet, and if you need anything else, you just have to ask. I better go and settle the others in their quarters, but Tom says to tell you there is a horse in the stables needing some attention.' With that she was gone, and Seamus was left looking around the bedroom he was to occupy while he was "home".

The bed was twice the size of the one in his room, and was draped in heavy brocade covers. It all looked very formal and he wished for his own room with the soft, woollen blankets that covered his bed. He sighed and returned to the sitting room to find their trunks arriving, and Sarah, his mother's own maid, taking Aliah into her room to unpack.

The servant carrying in his trunk was followed by Liam, his cousin. 'Would you like me to unpack for you, My Lord?' he asked formally, avoiding Seamus' eyes.

'*My Lord?* Liam, You do not need to treat me like a guest.' Seamus smiled and shook his head.

'My Lord, you are ambassador for the king.' Liam motioned the servant to take the trunk he carried into the bedroom.

'I am also your cousin, and your friend.' Seamus stood in the doorway of the bedroom after the servant had departed. He was angry and hurt by his cousin's manner. He knew Liam had good reason to be annoyed with him for leaving home without a word to the boy he had grown up with, but he had not thought his childhood companion would be so upset with him. Until then, he had not realised how much he had been counting on at least having Liam on his side while he was on Hand.

'*Friend?*' Liam turned to face him, his anger clearly showing on his face. 'Friends share things. They do not run off without any explanation.'

Seamus' own anger died as he also saw the hurt in his friend's eyes. 'I am sorry, Liam. I really am. It all happened so quickly. I did not plan it. I was scared and did not think everything through clearly.'

'I know why you left,' Liam spat out. 'The fact you did not trust me enough to tell me about it is what hurt the most. You could have talked with me about it any time before you left, but you chose not to. I have no problem with magic. You know that.'

'Was I supposed to guess?' Seamus asked. 'We never talk about magic at all on Hand because it is forbidden. On top of that, if my father knew about me, he would have had to act. And you are sworn to serve my father. How could I have put you in a position to lie to him? Or, even worse, to not lie to him?

'And no one told me about Amelia. No one told me my father was allowing contact with his sister, even though she uses magic. So how was I to know things were changing here? I really believed I was alone in this.'

Liam stared at him, searching for the truth of his words in Seamus' eyes.

'I guess everyone is talking about how I used magic?' Seamus asked.

'No. Your father told me what the town guards thought they saw in the Market Square. Amelia confirmed it when I visited her after you left. I told your mother about where you were going, and she sent a note to the king. Your father always knew—guessed it, I think —before this even happened. He was sure you would end up with

Amelia. But everyone else has been told that the rumours are not true, and you ran off after an argument, as boys apparently will.' Liam's shoulders sagged as his anger drained away. 'What a mess this all is. Do you want me to unpack?'

Seamus laughed. 'Are you kidding? If my father chanced to hear I had not unpacked for myself, that would be the first thing we discuss when I see him later, regardless of who else was in the room.'

Liam's own smile warmed his eyes, 'I have a little time before I am expected back, the least you could do is spend it telling me how you got to be here.'

Relieved the ice was thawing, Seamus turned to answer as the door to the suite was thrown open and some arms wrapped around his legs.

'Seamus! You came back. I told mother you would.'

Seamus turned and picked up his younger sister, and she snuggled into his neck, happy to be back in his embrace. 'I missed you, Cara,' Seamus whispered into her hair. Over her shoulder, he caught the eyes of his younger brother. 'I hope you have not been annoying Jonas too much?'

'I never annoy anyone.' Cara leaned back and Seamus looked into a pair of eyes as dark as his own. 'He is not as fun to play with as you, Seamus. And since you have been gone, father made him do extra lessons, and so Jonas has been far more grumpy than normal.'

Seamus looked at his eleven-year-old brother. 'It has not been so bad. You know Cara, she exaggerates.' The boy shrugged his shoulders, and Cara poked her tongue out at them then snuggled into Seamus' shoulder. Jonas held out the bundle he carried. 'I thought you might like these.'

Seamus moved out of the way so Jonas could put two of the blankets from his room on top of the bed. It reminded him of how he and his brother used to curl up together, and Seamus would teach Jonas everything he had learnt that day, saying maybe one day he would need that knowledge as much as Seamus did, because you could never predict the future. Perhaps even then, he had realised it was unlikely he would be the next Duke of Hand. He carried his sister over to the bed and pulled his brother into a family hug. 'I have missed you both too.'

Tears welled in Jonas' eyes, but he pushed them away with the back of his hand. 'Are you back for good? I mean will you be staying after you have finished with this king's representative thing?'

Seamus gnawed on his lip, unsure what to say to his brother. Taking a deep breath, he started, 'It is complicated, Jonas. I do not think I will be allowed to stay.'

His brother frowned and looked sad. 'I understand. For what it is worth, I think it is all very silly. Come on, Cara. We must get back before mother notices we are gone. She will not be with the other guests very long.'

'Other guests?' This news superseded Seamus' concern for his brother. He raised a questioning eyebrow, and Liam looked away.

'I am not to talk about them with you. Sorry.' Liam looked sheepish. 'I will say that one of the guests here is someone who will be happy to see you safe and sound.' With those parting words, he ducked past Seamus and left to resume his normal duties.

'We had better go too.' Jonas smiled at his brother. 'You have to get ready for the big banquet tonight. That will be such fun for you.' One of the things Jonas and Seamus had in common was their distaste of state functions.

Seamus placed Cara back on the floor. Jonas reached down taking her hand, and half-led-half-pulled her out of the room.

'Maybe I can sneak away early, and come and see you before bed?' Seamus asked as they reached the outer door.

Jonas looked up at him, his face very serious. 'No, you will not have time. You are one of the grown-ups now, Seamus, and you have a job to do. We can wait until tomorrow. I have been exercising Satin for you. Maybe you could find time for a ride after the formal meetings are over?'

Smiling fondly at his younger brother, Seamus marvelled at how grown up he had become in the few moons since he left home. Jonas really would make a much better duke than he ever would have. For some reason though, the thought saddened him, perhaps because the role he had been trained for since birth was not so easy to give up. Especially as he had not yet found anything else he could do with his life.

'I will see you tomorrow then.' His eyes followed them until the closed door meant he could no longer see his brother and sister. Until he had spent time with his cousin and his siblings just now, he had not realised how much he had missed them.

LEFT ALONE IN HIS ROOM, with nothing better to do, Seamus set about unpacking his trunk. He left the totally unsuitable clothes the king had sent in the bottom, and hung up a few linen shirts and another dark blue jacket in the closet. He was pleased to see a collection of his hunting and court clothes already there, along with another pair of indoor boots, and an old pair he used for riding and hunting. He pulled the brocade blanket off the bed and stuffed it in the trunk, shut the lid, then stowed it at the end of the bed. Aliah's voice startled him just as he finished laying out the blankets his brother had brought.

'How did you manage that?' she asked, pointing at the blankets. 'The cover on my bed looks like it might suffocate me in my sleep.'

'A perk for a local you might say.' Seamus shrugged his shoulders. 'I am sure you can ask Martha for some. We have plenty spare in the family quarters.'

'Will she be offended I am complaining about the decor?' Aliah asked skeptically, and Seamus laughed.

'She will probably dine off the story about the princess who prefers wool for quite a while, but secretly she will think all the better of you for not putting on airs. And even if she did think it odd, would you not rather be comfortable than pay mind to gossip?'

'I will just ask Sarah then.' And with that, she hurried back to her room, her door clicking as it closed a moment later.

As the formal dinner was some time away Seamus decided he needed a snack to keep him going. He hung up his coat and went into the sitting room where he had spied refreshments on a table by the fire when they entered. He filled a plate and went to sit, only to be startled by a voice behind him. Turning, he found an amused Dominic already sitting in the chair he had chosen.

Covering his embarrassment at having nearly sat in his lap, Seamus spluttered, 'How did you get in here?'

Dominic smiled serenely back. 'Seamus, I would not be a very good spy if I could not go about undetected,' was all he said as he continued to eat food from the plate in his hand.

Seamus took the seat opposite, and silently ate, glancing occasionally at Dominic and wondering how he had not seen the other boy was seated in the chair. Aliah joined them not long after, but before she sat, there was a knock at the door. Aliah went to open it herself, admitting Walter and Daniel.

'Ah good,' Dominic said. 'I asked you all to come so we could have a quick strategy meeting before tonight's formalities.' He waited until they had chosen something to eat from the buffet and taken their seats before continuing.

'First thing, there are other guests here. I have not seen them. They seem to be keeping to themselves and I cannot get any of my contacts to tell me anything about them. There is an order from high that instant dismissal will occur should anyone talk to us about them, or to them about us. I do not know what the duke is playing at. I would not be happy to find he was meeting with an envoy from Carsten.' Dominic glanced at Seamus, who shifted uncomfortably in his seat.

'I found out that there were other guests too. My brother and cousin would not talk to me about them, except to say I might know one.' Seamus shrugged, unable to help any further.

Dominic frowned but said nothing, as if hoping Seamus would elaborate, but when there was no response he continued. 'I also overheard one of the servants chatting about your father meeting in the library daily with a strange woman. The woman also meets with your mother and your father's squire. Any ideas?'

Seamus shook his head. 'No, no one is talking to me.' As the words left his lips, a thought flitted across his mind. *Amelia? No, surely not.* As a magic user, his aunt would not be welcome on Hand. Still, part of him wished it to be her as he had not seen her since she helped him and Aliah get away from Port Marden to begin their journey to Bannock.

'This is all a bit worrying, especially after having been chased here by a ship of unknown origin.' Dominic's gaze swept the semicircle of people around the fire. 'We may need a slight change of plan until we know who the other guests are. Normally we would announce the intent of our visit at the banquet tonight while presenting our papers. I suggest we hold off until we know who these other guests are. Agreed?' The last was more of a statement than a question, as if they would all follow like sheep.

'No,' Seamus said. 'I do not agree. We do not have time to play games. We need to talk with my father as soon as possible about getting help from Hand to fight off the Carsten invasion.' He silently willed Aliah to come to his support.

Aliah closed her eyes, then opened them as she tucked a stray hair behind her ear. 'It is true we only have a few days, maybe not even a full six-day, to get this sorted.' She looked directly at Seamus. 'However, we do need to be careful what we say and do when we know nothing about the other guests. Perhaps there is a compromise. We could say we have come to talk about the Carsten ships heading this way, and request an audience on that matter as soon as the duke is able to fit us in. We might be able to glean something from the way he responds to the request.'

Seamus studied at the princess in front of him, so sensible and regal, and tried to remember the girl he had travelled the length of Aria with. It was almost like with her change of clothes, she had changed her personality. On that trip, when she had not agreed with his plan, she took off on her own without saying a word. Now as her father's representative, she was listening to all sides, taking everything into consideration, and coming up with a reasoned solution.

'You look surprised, Seamus,' Aliah laughed. 'Although I have fought against it, my father has been training me for just this sort of situation all my life.'

Seamus nodded in response. 'I think that might just be the best course of action. Do you want me to take the lead on this, or shall you?' Compared to Aliah, he had little experience with formal court life. Yet another reason why his more studious younger brother would make a better duke than he ever would have. Jonas would have been watching and learning so he was prepared for just this sort of occasion.

Dominic interrupted. 'If my experience would be of help here?' His blue eyes sparkled with merriment, as if he somehow found Aliah taking control of this situation amusing. Aliah tensed, then seemed to get herself under control, causing Seamus to wonder whether it was the interruption, or the person, that annoyed her most.

'Of course, Dominic, I am sure you have learnt much as you secretly spied on many courts.' Aliah's tone dripped syrupy sweetness.

Dominic appeared to ignore the barb, but having spent time in a cabin with him, Seamus found the spy was not as hard as he appeared on the outside. He could tell from a tensing around his lips how much Aliah's words hurt him. Unlike other younger sons of the nobility, Dominic had a certain pride in the fact he was able to provide a service to his king. He wanted to do something for his country, and he did not consider marrying a wealthy woman to be the limit of his contribution. For some reason though, Aliah seemed disturbed by the fact Dominic spied for her father.

A firm knock on the door saved Dominic from having to respond to the question. Daniel opened it to Martha, who had a jacket in Hand Green over her arm, along with a pair of formal dark brown trousers, and some shiny new indoor boots. 'Your mother asked I deliver these for tonight.' She entered Seamus' bedroom and laid the clothes out on the bed.

On her return, she spoke to Aliah. 'One of the maids will change your bed for some Hand woollen blankets while you are at the reception this evening, Your Highness.' Martha curtseyed and then left.

'We are very proud of the wool produced on the island,' Seamus said as the others stared at him with raised eyebrows.

'I asked for them,' Aliah helped him out. 'Everything else is so formal, I thought it would be nice to have something comforting in my room.'

Ah, Seamus thought to himself. *There is the girl I travelled with.*

'I think your Martha may have a few more requests for those blankets,' Walter surmised.

'Back to the problem at hand.' Aliah gestured to Dominic to continue.

'Well,' Dominic resumed. 'In terms of seniority, the princess should take the lead, but I know what the king put in the documents and Seamus' name is first, in an effort to win favour with the duke.'

'Ha.' Seamus snorted. 'I am unsure how much favour I can bring, when my father will not even look at me.'

'Obviously court intrigue is not your strong suit.' Dominic's tone was measured to ensure Seamus did not take offence. 'Your mother has sent you formal Hand court attire hoping you will wear it tonight.' He met Seamus' eyes, as if willing him to make the connection. The sound of the fire crackling filled the silence as the others waited for Seamus to catch up with them.

'Ah.' Seamus could not help grinning as understanding dawned. 'So I will be petitioning on behalf of the king in the colours of Hand, showing there is already a strong relationship. My mother sending the clothes shows my father is not against our approaching him for support, and that I am not totally out on a limb as she would not have made so public a statement without first discussing it with him?' He looked to Dominic for approval.

'You will never be a natural at this, but there is hope for you yet.' Dominic winked, taking the sting out of his words. 'Princess, after the introductions you will request the audience as it will hold more weight coming from you.'

Tugging at her braid, Aliah appeared to be mulling over the plan in her head, when really, Seamus could tell by the little smile playing at the edge of her lips she had already agreed to it. 'I have one small change.'

'Of course, princess.' Holding back his own smile, Dominic played her game, knowing she would not be able to accept his plan without tweaking it a little.

'Seamus, you must wear some blue as you are a royal representative.' She thought for a moment. 'I have a blue scarf you can wear as a cravat.'

Seamus wrinkled his nose. 'Really? Are you sure it will not be too much?'

Dominic and Daniel laughed at his discomfort. 'Just go along with it, or she may think of something worse.' Daniel wiped the tears from his eyes.

Walter, who had been silent for most of the meeting, stood. 'I suppose we must all dress now or we will make a bad impression by being late.' His movement signalled the meeting was over and they should retire to their rooms to get ready.

Seamus walked slowly to his bedroom, wishing he could put off the evening for as long as possible. Even though he now believed his parents were happy he was there, his nerves still caused flutters in his stomach.

As he began to undress, two servants brought in a bath and a procession of servants began to fill it. *Private bathing, what a pleasure.* He had always had to bathe in the room by the kitchen as the duke took pride in his children not having to be waited upon. As he stepped in the water, he tried to relax and prepare mentally to meet with his father in front of the assembled nobility of the Southern Duchy, who would be hovering ready to pounce at any mistake he made.

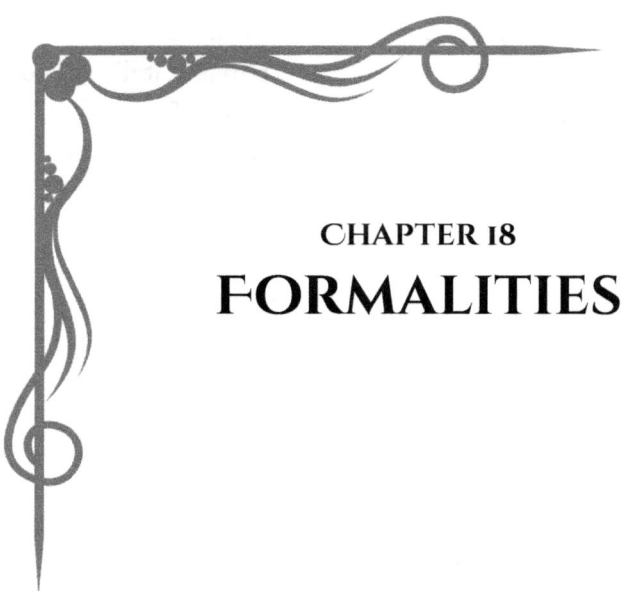

CHAPTER 18
FORMALITIES

'If Seamus fiddles with that collar one more time, I may just have to cut off his hands,' Aliah whispered furiously to Walter as they walked through the halls of the duke's palace to the formal reception room.

'He is a little nervous,' Walter whispered back, trying to show some support for his young friend.

'So am I. But it really will not do to let other people know we are new to this. They might not take us seriously, and we cannot do our job if they do not think we are capable.' Aliah frowned and tugged at a loose strand of hair.

'You know I can hear you.' Seamus turned and stared at them. 'It is this scarf you made me wear. It will not sit properly with this shirt.' He tugged at his collar again, then sighed and gave up.

Aliah had to admit that he did look the part of an ambassador, dressed in his thigh length, green coat, buttoned up with just a hint of white and blue at the collar. She herself had dressed in a simple blue gown that was fitted and fell gracefully from her hips. The only jewellery she wore was the royal gold circlet.

'I will pull myself together before we reach the hall,' Seamus assured her. 'But no one can see us here, so I do not see how it matters.'

'I should hope you will be on your best behaviour at the reception.' Aliah was surprised at how much she sounded like her mother when she scolded Seamus.

Their small procession stopped at the sound of a new voice. It came from a petite, dark-haired woman, sitting on a sofa facing the windows overlooking the castle's inner-courtyard. The woman rose and walked straight to Seamus, her beautiful face lit with a smile as she took his hands.

'Welcome home, my son. I have missed you.'

As Seamus wrapped his arms around his mother, some of the tension he had displayed since leaving Bannock left his body as he once again connected with his family. Aliah understood just how much this meant to Seamus as he had feared those closest to him might be forced to reject him because of his magic.

'Mother, it is so good to see you.'

'I would so love to hear of your adventures and how you managed to worm your way into Terion's graces and become one of his ambassadors, but I have to get to your reception. We can talk of family things later. I just wanted you to know that even though your father may not show it tonight, you are welcome here. Tonight is not the night for family issues, it is all about the threats facing Hand and Aria.' Duchess Elise pulled her son's head downwards and kissed him on the cheek. 'Do us proud, son.' Then, with a swish of her green skirt, she left them all standing there.

Seamus brushed a tear from his eye and turned to continue their journey. Dominic put a restraining hand on his arm. 'We should wait here for a bit.'

Aliah's eyes widened as a sign of her surprise. 'But we cannot be late to a dinner held in our honour.'

'They will not start the proceedings until the duchess is ready to welcome us, and Seamus needs to take a breath and steady himself for the reception to come.'

They all looked at Seamus, who had clearly been affected by his mother's sudden appearance. He was still wiping tears from his cheeks. 'I am all right,' he told them. 'I just want to get this public bit over and done with so we can get on to the real work and start preparing for the coming war.'

Aliah sighed. 'You know this public bit is as much a part of the real work as the private meetings?' she asked. 'Tension between Hand and the other Duchies has always been high. What happens tonight will go a long way towards making people's minds up about whether they should support the rest of Aria in this war.'

It was Seamus' turn to raise an eyebrow. 'Really? I had not thought of that.'

Aliah smiled. 'Sorry, Seamus, I did not mean to preach. I am nervous too. I want to make my father proud, and I am worried if I muck this up, he will never let me do anything like this again. Then I will be relegated to sitting at home and doing needlework with the other ladies.'

They all laughed, as if the idea of Aliah sitting sewing with other court ladies was something they could never imagine.

'I think that would frustrate the other women, as much as you. I really cannot see needlepoint being something you are good at.' Dominic smiled.

'Actually, I am disgustingly good at it, mores the pity.' Aliah grimaced. 'Well, we have dawdled enough. Shall we proceed?'

Aliah nodded at Seamus, who held out his arm. Aliah placed her hand just above his elbow, squeezing his arm lightly in a show of support. Dominic and Walter moved in behind as Seamus nodded at Daniel, and he led them forward, round the corner into the main hall. There they were met by a rather tall, gaunt looking man, in the formal robes of the Duke's Court.

'Princess Aliahanna, Lord Seamus, if you would follow me.'

'Thank you, Robin.' Seamus smiled at his father's chancellor and right hand man.

The small group followed him to the double wooden doors of the formal hall. Before they reached the doors, two guards opened them wide to admit their group. Just inside the doorway, Robin stopped and stepped to the side.

'Princess Aliahanna, Heir to the Throne of Aria, Lord Seamus, Heir to the Duchy of Hand, and their party, request permission to enter the court and petition the duke on behalf of Terion, King of Aria.'

The hall was packed with well dressed people who had made an isle down the middle of the room between the main doorway, and the dais at the other end, where the duke and duchess stood on a raised platform. Below them stood the duke's squire, a boy Aliah had first seen at Seamus' aunt's house, when she was helping them get ready for their journey from Port Marden to Bannock, and who had been in Seamus' room earlier on.

'The Court of Hand recognises the envoy from King Terion, and asks them to approach.' The squire stepped forward to say the formal words that confirmed their status in the duke's court.

Seamus and Aliah walked towards the dais. As they walked, the people on either side curtseyed, not as low as they would have else-where in Aria, but the mark of respect for the crown was there. At least she supposed it was for the crown and not because Seamus was the duke's heir.

They stopped in front of the duke and duchess. Aliah stole a quick glance at Seamus and then at his father as Dominic came forward and handed their formal papers of introduction to the squire. The squire handed the papers to the duke, who opened them and read them through quickly. 'You are welcome in my court, Princess Aliahanna, Lord Seamus. And you are also welcome, young sir.' Duke Damon looked pointedly at Dominic. 'I am sure you have been here before, in some other capacity perhaps?' There was a smile playing around the duke's mouth as he let Dominic know he was aware of exactly who and what Dominic was. 'But you, sire, I do not know.' He glanced at Walter questioningly.

Aliah stepped forward. 'This is Walter Ivanson, my advisor, and tutor to Lord Seamus.' She then nodded to Seamus, who also took a step forward.

'Thank you for your kind welcome, we hope our visit will be fruitful for both Hand and Aria.' Seamus spoke the formal words they had agreed upon. That was her queue. Aliah took a deep breath and looked Duke Damon in the eye.

'As you know, we come here on behalf of the king to discuss a grave danger all the people of Aria will face not long from now, and we request a meeting with you, and your advisors, at your earliest convenience.'

Aliah swore the duke's eyes were twinkling, as if he had known how much courage it had taken for the two of them to walk through the hall to face him. There appeared to be pride mingled there as well. As she looked at him, Aliah realised this was a glimpse of what Seamus would look like as he grew older, so alike were he and his father.

'Ah, the impatience of youth.' The duke beamed at his court as if sharing a private joke with them. 'I will need to fully read the letters sent from your father, and discuss them with my advisors before there is any meeting. I will let you know when we can arrange such a discussion. I promise the wait will be short. In the meantime, we have prepared a welcome dinner for you, if you would be good enough to join us.'

Aliah quickly glanced at Dominic, who inclined his head slightly, acknowledging this was the best they could do tonight. Thanking the duke, she confirmed the formalities were over, and allowed Seamus to lead her into the formal dining room to their left. They followed the duke and duchess, and were in turn followed by the other people present.

There were two long tables down each side of the dining room, and at the top was a table set crossways between them, where the duke and duchess were seated. Aliah and Walter sat to one side of the duke, and Seamus and Dominic to the other side of the duchess. Aliah relaxed when Daniel took a place beside the duke's squire behind the main table. From there, Daniel would be able to keep an eye on everything that happened during the meal.

As with all state occasions, it was a long meal with many courses, and filled with small talk about nothing of consequence. After they had discussed their journey, and the weather, and the state of the Hand economy, there was a lull in the conversation. Aliah took a quick look to the other end of the table where Dominic and the duchess seemed to be having a lively conversation.

Just my luck to get the dull end of the stick, I wish things were more lively down here, Aliah thought to herself, and was immediately reminded why you should always be careful what you wish for.

'So, you have been tutoring my son?' The duke leant forward to look at Walter. 'I thought his formal education long since finished. I would be interested to learn what you have felt the need to tutor him in?'

Oh no, just the topic of conversation we wished to avoid. Aliah's brow creased with a frown. She need not have worried though. Walter had spent many years around her father's court, and was more than capable of answering the trickiest of questions.

'Well, sir, I would not like to bore you with the details on such an important occasion as this. Suffice to say, I have a unique set of skills that allow me to teach your son some things that will enable him to better survive in life.'

The duke stared at Walter, almost as if he was looking into the wizard's very soul. Then he smiled, the same slow smile Seamus had when it had taken him a while to realise something. Quickly he looked around, aware that others were listening in on their conversation. 'There is always something to learn in life, and I would be a fool to think Seamus learnt all that he needed here on Hand. I am sure there are many things an envoy needs that we would not have been able to teach him.'

With disaster deftly averted, Aliah was able to relax again. Walter, taking the duke's lead, continued the conversation. 'With that thought in mind, sire, during our studies, Seamus told me about the extensive library here in the palace, part of which date back to before your people came to Hand. With your permission, I would like to take a look through it while we are here?'

The Duke stopped for a moment and frowned, putting Aliah immediately on alert. A common request such as Walter's should not have raised any issues. Then, as if he realised this himself, the frown disappeared from his face and the duke was once again a disarming host. 'Of course. It is in heavy use at the moment by another guest, but I am sure I could talk with them and find some time when you would not be disturbing their study.'

'I would appreciate that.' Walter bowed his head in thanks.

At a gentle touch on his arm, the duke turned to the duchess, bending slightly towards her as she whispered in his ear. While he was distracted, Aliah lowered her own voice to speak to her other dinner companion. 'Surely we will not have time for you to be losing yourself in a library, Walter?'

Walter smiled as if he found her conversation amusing. 'No we do not,' he quietly confirmed. 'Before dinner Dominic told me one of the other guests is spending all their time there and he asked me to request use of the library to see what response I got. An interesting answer, was it not?'

Aliah was saved from adding her thoughts as the duke rose from his seat. While Walter and Aliah had been distracted, the squire had brought him a message and it seemed Duke Damon was being called away.

'I am most sorry, I must apologise to you all, and our distinguished guests, but something has arisen that requires my immediate attention. Please carry on with your meal and enjoy.'

The duke looked regretfully at Aliah. 'Please accept my apologies, Your Highness, but I really must deal with this now.'

Aliah inclined her head, granting her host leave to go.

After the duke's departure, the rest of the meal continued without anything of note happening. Many of the nobility of Hand were either in awe of the princess, or refused to talk to her because of the long-held belief her family had no right to rule over them. That left her with only Walter to talk to, as she watched the people around them sneak glances at Seamus and his mother.

Finally the duchess looked at Aliah for permission to leave, then stood, signalling the end of the meal. Using this as an excuse to depart as well, she and Seamus gratefully followed the duchess, with Dominic, Walter, and Daniel falling in behind. As there were people still milling around the halls, they held off talking about what they had learnt at the dinner until they were back in the privacy of the state room.

'WHAT WAS THAT ALL ABOUT?' Aliah asked them when they were back in their rooms and seated comfortably. 'Did anyone hear the reason the duke was suddenly called away?'

'All I know is that Robin gave Liam a message, which he then delivered to my mother. She interrupted my father and he decided to leave. I could not hear what they were saying,' Seamus offered.

Aliah looked pointedly at Dominic, who laughed. 'I have no idea. I am not sure you fully understand what a spy is. It is not someone with very good hearing, or who reads minds. What I do is blend into the background and pick up on gossip. Sometimes I cultivate friends. Normally I start up conversations and hope I can read people's responses, or they might slip up and tell me something they should not have. All I can tell you is the duke was surprised, but in a good way.'

'Well, you have done ever so well at your job given the duke recognised you,' Aliah spat back at Dominic, tired and somewhat irritated by his glib answer.

'Aliah,' Seamus said sharply. 'Do you have a problem with Dominic we should know about?'

'Sorry, Dominic. I should not have taken my frustration out on you,' Aliah apologised quickly, hoping it would be enough for Seamus to drop the subject.

'It is all right,' Dominic answered, although his eyes betrayed he had been hurt by Aliah's outburst. Shame she had lashed out so quickly washed over her.

'No, it is not,' Seamus told him angrily. 'That is the second time today Aliah has sniped at you because of the work you do. We all have to rely on and trust each other, and Aliah seems to have a problem. I am not sure if it is with you, or with what you do. But we really need to get it out in the open.'

'It is with what I do, I am afraid.' Dominic kept his eyes on Aliah as he spoke, but she could not meet his gaze. 'Will you tell them, or shall I?'

Aliah dropped her head, her new-found poise deserting her for the moment. She could feel everyone's eyes upon her, waiting for her answer, but she was not sure she was ready to share the reasons for her unease around her father's spy.

'When Aliah was little, her mother happened on what we believe was a Natari spy in her rooms. She called the guards and there was a fight. During the melee, the queen was stabbed. We are unsure whether it was intentional, or an accident.

'Although she was injured badly she seemed to recover, but the wound continued to trouble her. A little over a year later, she died from heart strain caused by an infection in the wound.' Dominic spoke as if he were reciting a history lesson.

'How could this have happened without everyone knowing about it?' Seamus asked, his face displaying his shock.

'The king commanded it be kept quiet. He did not want anyone to know his court had been infiltrated so easily. Also, if it were known that someone from Nataria had caused the death of the queen, it would have strained relations with a rather strong neighbour on our borders. So the king ordered the whole thing hushed up.'

'And that is why you have a problem with Dominic?' Seamus asked Aliah directly.

'Yes,' she responded slowly, still not able to meet anyone's eyes. 'It is not Dominic himself, you understand, it is what he does. The logical part of me knows spies are necessary, and I also know my father would not employ anyone as unscrupulous as my mother's killer, but still...' In spite of all her best intentions to be more stately and grown up, Aliah could not deal with this one thing unemotionally.

'I imagine it is very hard to get over something like that,' Dominic consoled her, but still she would not raise her head and meet his eyes.

'I can not even imagine how any decent person can live their life being someone they are not,' she admitted, looking into the fire.

'It is not easy,' Dominic's voice came from behind. 'And sometimes I really want to give it up and go back to being just me. But I have a brain that is able to piece together bits of information and see how it fits into the big picture of what is going on in the world. I also have the ability to get people talking, which helps with gathering information. And it is information your father needs if he is to make good decisions. Also, your father asked me to do this work for him when he recognised my particular talents, and I could not refuse.

'I am good at this, and I can contribute to Aria by doing it,' he told her proudly. 'The alternative for me is to be sold on the marriage market to the highest bidder so I can further my father's ambitions. I am capable of so much more than that. I want to make a worthwhile contribution.'

Aliah sensed for some reason it was important to Dominic that she accepted what he did. Also, some of what he said struck a chord with her. Something she could not quite place her finger on. Then a light blinked on in her head, and she turned to Dominic. 'Funny, for a moment there, you sounded just like me. Trying to escape being a pawn in someone else's game.' She marvelled at how alike they were in that way. Wishing to make some amends, she continued. 'If I am honest, and ignore my feelings about spies in general, I have to admit we could not be doing any of this without your input and advice. I promise I will try harder to see you as a person, and not a spy.'

The room fell silent after Aliah's words. Before anyone else could speak there was a knock on the door. Daniel opened it to admit Liam. 'Excuse me, Your Highness, sorry for the intrusion, but the duke would like a private word with his son if you are finished with him.'

Dominic raised a questioning eyebrow as Aliah tried to hide her annoyance at being interrupted.

'He did say I should tell you it is a family matter, not a matter of state,' Liam assured the company.

Seamus rose to leave, ready to go whether they had finished talking or not.

'Ah... he did also say that if Tutor Walter wanted to accompany us, now would be a convenient time to visit the library.'

Keeping up the ruse about his interest in Hand's book collection, Walter joined Seamus as Aliah attempted to quieten her annoyance at being left out.

CHAPTER 19

THE PAST RETURNS

S eamus followed Liam down the dimly lit corridor into the public reception area of the palace, past the doors to the room they had dined in that evening. As they passed the large wooden doors of the reception room, Seamus thought there was a noise on the stairs behind them. He glanced back over his shoulder, but could see no one there.

'Did you hear that?' he asked Liam.

'What? I did not hear a thing. You will be jumping at your own shadow next.' Liam laughed.

That was the longest sentence he managed to get from his cousin as they turned down another corridor, which led to the library and some other rooms, housed in the oldest part of the building. All attempts to find out why his father summoned him late at night were frustratingly rebuffed with, 'You know I am here as duke's squire now, I cannot tell you anything except what I have been told to say. So stop asking.'

The candle-lit corridor wound deep into the old part of the palace. The walls were dark with age, and years of soot from the candles housed in the sconces placed every few paces. They finally arrived at the large, wooden library door. There was a guard standing outside. Recognising Liam, he opened the door to admit them.

'A guard outside the library? That is a little unusual,' Seamus whispered to Liam as they passed into the room. Liam ignored him. As they entered, Seamus' eyes were drawn to the two figures standing by the large wooden table that dominated the centre of the room.

'Amelia.' Seamus grinned as the woman standing with his father walked towards him and drew him into a hug. 'So this is the secret guest you have been hiding?'

Duke Damon frowned, seemingly confused, but the expression was so fleeting Seamus thought he must have been mistaken.

'Seamus, you have no idea how glad I am to see you again. To know that you are safe and well at home warms my heart.' Amelia stood back and studied at her nephew. She had taken Aliah and Seamus in when they had escaped from Port Marden three moons ago, then helped them prepare for their journey north.

'Amelia, I did not expect to see you in Hand of all places. You know, because of your...' Seamus looked over her shoulder to his father, who stood by the table looking at a large scroll.

'...magic?' Duke Damon turned. 'Well, desperate times call for desperate measures.' He walked towards Seamus and caught his son in a hug. 'I am also pleased to see you are safe and alive,' the duke said gruffly. 'You had your mother and me worried out of our skins.'

'I am sorry, father, I truly am. But surely you know why I left. Amelia...'

'Yes, yes. Amelia told us you wanted to go to the Wizard Isle to train, rather than stay here and take your rightful place as Heir to the Duchy.'

'How could I stay?' Seamus asked angrily. 'If I stayed, I would have faced having all trace of magic removed. That would have been denying who I am.' He pulled away from his father. 'I have magic and that is part of who I am.' Saying the words out loud felt strange, but also liberating.

'Whoa, slow down Seamus.' His father placed a restraining hand on his arm. 'I know why you left, and I sympathise. You have no idea how much I have regretted what happened to my own sister because of her magic. I am most annoyed because you did not come and talk to your mother and me about this. Did you not even consider that we may have been able to help you through? Even after that dust up in Port Marden where you moved some crates. We could have worked to cover that up while we decided what to do.

'Instead, you placed yourself in danger by running away. Your mother and I had to put on a brave face and deal with all manner of rumours, all the while not really knowing where you were, or what you were doing. Your mother was distraught...'

As if on cue, the library door squeaked. They turned to see Duchess Elise, who had been standing listening. 'Yes, Seamus that really was very thoughtless of you. We worried so much, even after we found out you had been with Amelia. You undertook a perilous journey, travelling to the Wizard Isle with only a strange girl for company.'

'I am sorry you and father worried about me.' Seamus had the grace to look a little embarrassed. 'But as you can see, I am perfectly able to take care of myself.'

'Yes, I can see that. In fact you seemed to have done more than that, given you have turned up here with a princess who is supposed to be missing somewhere in Aria. And on a mission from the king, no less.' His mother's eyes searched his face. 'That must be quite a story you have to tell.'

'I may be able to help with that.' A voice came from the opening door. 'Sorry to interrupt,' Aliah said as she let herself into the library, not looking very sorry at all. She smiled at the guard, and handed him back his sword. 'Your guard thought to stop me from entering, but when Dominic told me he believed the stranger in the library was a female relation of the duke or duchess I had to come and see for myself.' She walked over to Amelia and hugged her. 'I am so glad to see you again Amelia, and to have the chance to thank you for all your help in getting me home.'

The duke and duchess turned to Amelia questioningly, and she smiled as she responded. 'Well, who would have thought... So that is how young Seamus managed to join forces with a princess.' Amelia put her arm through Aliah's and turned to her brother. 'The young girl I sent off travelling with Seamus turns out to be Princess Aliahanna, not Ali as she first introduced herself.' Amelia chuckled. 'Although I can see much of the future, I did not see that coming. But once you know, it all fits together.'

'What are you doing here?' Seamus asked Amelia. 'I thought you were banished from Hand because of, well, you know...'

'Magic?' Amelia helped him, and he nodded.

'She was, and still is,' Duke Damon interrupted. 'That is why her presence here has been kept a secret, and why we will not openly discuss what your tutor Walter has been teaching you.

'By the way we have been treating your disappearance as a youthful indiscretion. Remind me later I will have to devise a punishment for you, maybe one that involves you moving to Port Marden for a while until we decide what to do for the long term.'

'So things have not changed then.' Seamus had to admit there was disappointment tinged with resignation at the news he would unlikely return to Hand. Seeing Amelia had led him to believe maybe there was a chance, however small, for him to return home.

'I did not say that Seamus.' The duke gestured to the table. 'Come, sit down, all of you. By now, Liam is fetching Lord Dominic. Best he hears this directly from us rather than his usual sources. Do not worry,' he said to Aliah. 'We will only use his true name in this room.

'We have found something, but it would be easiest to explain it to all of you at once. Our original plan had been to ask Walter for his help tonight, and talk to the rest of you tomorrow, but we may as well take advantage of the fact you are all here now.'

'Then why did you need Seamus?' Aliah promptly asked.

'For what we are to talk about tonight we did not, I just wanted to see my son.' The duke gestured for Aliah to be seated and, once she sat down, the others found seats around the table and waited for Dominic to return with Liam.

Liam only seemed to have been gone a moment when he and Dominic came through the library door. 'I did not have to go far,' Liam informed them. 'I found him lurking in the main entranceway.'

As Dominic and Liam took a spare seat each, Seamus had to admit that never in his wildest dreams had he thought to see this group of people sitting down together in his home.

DUKE DAMON STOOD and looked down the table at the people assembled in front of him. 'Before we start, I want assurances from all of you what we discuss now will stay in this room.' They mumbled their agreement, except Aliah and Dominic.

'I am not sure we are able to do that, sir,' Aliah said. 'Our first allegiance is to Aria and the king, and we might feel it our duty to pass on something we discuss here.'

Duke Damon nodded. 'Good. Forgive my little ploy, but I wanted to test your mettle. I need to know those of you I am not familiar with will speak honestly. How about we agree that before you pass on any information, you let me know what you intend to do first.'

Aliah and Dominic exchanged a glance before answering. 'That we can agree to do,' Aliah answered for them both.

'I have one more request. While we are in this room, we dispense with titles and politics. I believe we all need to work together to help save Aria from the forces that threaten our peace. I think that can best be achieved if we feel we can speak openly.'

'So you will join forces with my father?' Aliah was quick to ask.

That was too easy, Seamus thought to himself, and he was proven correct when his father responded to the princess' question.

'That is a matter for myself, and my council, and we will discuss that at a later time. Tonight, I want to talk about something a little less... um, tangible. Something I am not really comfortable with, something I am not sure I even fully understand. I believe it affects all of the people in this room, so maybe together we can work this out.'

Seamus had not seen his father so lost for words before. He normally assessed a situation and acted with full authority. Then Duke Damon did something else Seamus had never seen his father do. 'I will pass over to my wife. I believe she and Amelia have a much better understanding of what might be going on here.' And with that, he sat down.

Although his mother was no mere figurehead, sitting as an advisor on his father's council, Seamus had never seen her lead a meeting. Pride welled up inside as his mother stood to address the room.

'All this started when Seamus ran away. Before he could walk, we were sure he was pulling things he wanted to himself, so we were aware he was likely the child of his generation to have a magical talent. Lately, his father and I had been sure his magical abilities were growing stronger, and we perhaps waited too long to talk to him about them,' Elise's sad gaze turned to Seamus. 'Largely, because we were not sure what to say to him. Magic is outlawed in Hand, and we knew it would be hard to change so many years of prejudice against magic users. We waited, because we did not want to lose our son.'

Seamus blushed and suddenly found the grain on the wooden table very interesting, attempting to hide his embarrassment. He could not believe his mother was speaking so openly of such private matters.

'Then we lost Seamus anyway. Damon thought Amelia was hiding something, so he spent time at the cottage to see if he could wheedle the truth out of her. Eventually, she admitted Seamus had been there, and where he was heading. Damon led a small group over the Ariel Mountains, following Seamus' trail. In Sunnydale, they found he had already left for Duncameron. In Duncameron, the trail went cold, he seemed to disappear into thin air. Damon had no option but to return home. In the meantime, I sent a letter to the king asking him to look out for Seamus, and to let him know we would like to hear from him.

'However, I could not sit at home and wait for my son to be returned. I needed to do more. I wanted to find a way to bring Seamus home, if not to take his place as Heir, then at least to be with our family. So I started looking through the histories and records of our people. I wanted to know more about why magic had been banished in the first place. That is the problem with not talking about a subject, we soon forget why we stopped talking about it in the first place.

'We all believe magic was outlawed completely when the Natari Princess Damon's forefather was forced to marry, turned out to be a witch. The people of Hand were so disgusted they sent her to live in Port Marden. It was then the practice of not using magic on Hand was formalised into law. Before that, magic users had been frowned upon. After that, anyone showing magical abilities suffered the fate of banishment or quietening.

'I found some ancient scrolls in the old library below that told a different story. These scrolls suggested our distrust of magic began long ago.

'The people of Hand migrated here from what is known in Aria as The Unknown Lands. This was already a part of our historic knowledge. The Ariel Mountain range has prevented the people of Aria from interacting and trading with their western neighbours, but on Hand, we occasionally trade with the tribes through their main settlement on the coast. Sometimes we receive visits from their dignitaries. Seamus used to love watching some of their soldiers train in the courtyard when he was younger. These people call themselves the Malorians, and they are distant kin to the people of Hand.'

Seamus interrupted his mother. 'So let me get this straight. The people of Hand migrated here and we were originally from Maloria?' He was getting a little lost in the story, and a little bored as well.

'Yes, son, but Amelia and I found out more than that. Sorry, this is beginning to sound like a history lesson, but it is important you fully understand the background before we get to the really interesting things Amelia and I found.

'Before moving to the coast, the Malorians were an inland tribe, part of the Talagra nation. From what we can make out, they broke away from the other tribes due to some conflict over using magic. At first I could not understand much of what the scrolls said, I have very little knowledge of the branches of magic so I asked Amelia to come and help me.'

Seamus shook his head. 'How could Amelia help? She has been living away from everyone on her farm for years, not even using her magic.'

His mother smiled at him. 'Your aunt may have given that impression to others, but I have always known she is part of a network of magic users who use their gifts to benefit others. She knows more about magic than anyone here, except maybe you, Walter.' Elise acknowledged the wizard sitting at the table. 'Amelia, will you tell them all what we found out?'

As the duchess sat, Amelia stood to take over. 'Not much more to go, and this is the interesting stuff. I will summarise. The Talagra were heavy magic users, but some tribes began to rely on magic too much, to the extent they began using battle magic to expand their tribal holdings. The Maloria tribe were known to have great seers and they foretold this would lead to the destruction of the Talagra Nation. When the other tribes would not listen to them, they walked away from the Tribal Council and Talagra, leaving their traditional lands and family ties behind.

'When they had established themselves near the coast they

began setting up a new community. As they debated new laws, they found themselves divided over the issue of magic. Some thought banning the use of battle magic as had been done in other countries would be enough to ensure they did not suffer the same fate as Talagra. This way they could still use magic defensively to keep themselves safe should they need too. Magic had become so much a part of their culture they could not see how they could live without it.

'Others believed magic should be outlawed to ensure no one would be tempted to use it against other people. The latter group were in the minority, but many of them strongly supported the ideal of giving up magic and living by the work of their hands alone. They could not agree a way forward together, so the smaller group broke away and moved to an island off the coast. Naming their new home Hand, they enshrined their commitment to living without magic.'

'So based on our history,' Seamus interjected. 'A hatred of magic has been part of our culture for generations. You and I will never be able to come home.' Seamus' eyes sadly found Amelia's.

'Maybe not anytime soon.' Amelia placed a hand on his shoulder. 'But there is hope for the future, as you will soon see. We found that the marques we have always given our children to identify their families, and to celebrate different stages on their journey to adulthood, have a very different origin.'

'Really?' Seamus sat up straighter in his chair. Now they were reaching the really interesting ideas, they had his full focus. Beside him Aliah fidgeted in her chair, her attention wavering, and he worriedly hoped her new found need to be more statesmanlike would stop her from interrupting Amelia long enough for him to find out more of his history.

'Yes, originally the marque placed on each child showed their family bloodline or clan. The marque was not finished until a child had reached adulthood and had demonstrated a magical skill, and that skill had been tested and confirmed. It appears our family were strong in reading the future, and the marque that we get when we reach adulthood identifies us as being minor seers. We have found many of the other clans within Hand show other types of magic, such as healing, or growth.'

Seamus laughed. 'So you are suggesting there may actually be other magic users on Hand, we just do not know about them? Like the Paster family generally become healers, and the Agrit clan are known for their ability to grow the best produce? That might be magic at play?'

His father smiled at him. 'We suspect so, but we still need to do a little delving into family histories and have some discreet words with a few people before we can say for sure. Then we need to consider what this means for us as a people. Our ancestors abhorred magic, and many in the tribe of Hand still do. We need to decide if we want to change, and then if we do, what that change will mean in practice.'

'This is all very interesting, and I can see for your family it could be life-changing. But I do not understand why you needed Dominic and me here for this. Or even Walter, for that matter.' Aliah shuffled in her chair as if getting ready to stand.

'Please bear with us a moment longer, Aliahanna,' the duke requested. 'We have only a little more of our tale to go.'

Aliah fidgeted some more, then sat still with her hands folded on the table in front of her. In contrast, Seamus continued to sit rigidly in his seat. Although this was his family history, he could not escape the feeling this meeting was very important to everyone here, but he could not place his finger on exactly why.

'I know it is late, but what Amelia and Elise discovered when they were looking through the old records surprised even me. While my men and I were in Duncameron, rumours circulated that the Wizard and Warrior have risen, and would champion Aria in the coming battle. We have the story here in our archives. I had always thought this prophecy came from one of my ancestors at the time of the Natari invasion. I understand there is a similar version in the histories of Aria. When I returned, I searched through the library to find a copy, wanting to refresh my memory.

'I found it in one of the books here and Amelia happened to glance over my shoulder as I read. She said she had come across a similar prophecy, but worded slightly differently.

"After the decimation and the fall,
  When the new power rises
And the Wizard and Warrior meet,
Old and new blood will combine
With the two who are not what they seem
To save one and all."

'That is all very interesting, father, but I still do not see where we fit into all of this,' Seamus interrupted before Aliah could.

'No, you probably do not. And I am not really sure either. That is why you are all here. At this moment we have visitors in the castle from Maloria. They also have this prophecy. Their belief is the decimation refers to the fall of the Talagra Nation. They also believe the time the prophecy spoke of has arrived, and they will find the Wizard and the Warrior here on Hand. Representatives came a few days ago to await their arrival, and to take them back to Maloria for some sort of testing. For some reason they have convinced themselves the Wizard and the Warrior are amongst your group.' Duke Damon ignored the rest of the group and stared directly at Aliah, as if he were making sure she fully understood the importance of his words. 'I do not know whether all this is true or not. I mean ,we here on Hand do not deal with magic, let alone the High Magic that is prophecy. I fear we do not have long before they insist on meeting you all and discussing this with you directly.'

'And that would be bad?' Seamus asked.

'Maybe, maybe not. But we need to consider them seriously in light of the fact they have offered to provide assistance with the invasion should the Wizard and Warrior agree to return with them to their Sanctuary. Their warriors could be the tipping point in our favour, should we have to fight a force larger than ours.'

'I can see why this is important,' Aliah now spoke. 'Although I do not fully understand what is going on here either.'

'That is why before we meet with the Malorian Ambassador we should have completed our study of the ancient documents my wife and sister have found, to see if they shed any more light. In the interest of saving time, Walter, I was wondering if you would work with Amelia tonight and see if there is anything else you can find out from our documents? Or perhaps you can contribute something from your extensive knowledge?'

'It would be my pleasure,' Walter responded. 'Although I must admit there is a reason why Maloria is called the Unknown Lands in Aria—it is because we know so very little about them.'

Seamus wondered why Walter was almost glowing with pleasure? Was it because he loved working with ancient documents? Or did it have something to do with the way he had been looking at Amelia since they entered the library?

'That is not very comforting. Well, do the best you can. In the meantime, the rest of us should get some rest. We have a formal meeting with the council tomorrow morning, and I think we will need to have all our wits about us when we face them.' Duke Damon called the meeting to an end.

ALIAH, Dominic, and Seamus rose and headed towards the door. Duke Damon hung back and halted Seamus as he went passed. 'I am truly sorry we could not welcome you home as I would have wished,' the duke said to Seamus, as he embraced him. 'But it is fortunate you arrive as the king's emissary as it means we will not have to answer any suspicious gossip at this point.'

'I understand father.' Seamus started to leave, then turned back at the door, 'I am truly sorry I did not trust you and mother enough to talk things through before I left.'

'We know you are, son, but everything happens for a reason. I truly believe that.' The duke turned to go back to Amelia and Walter, who were bringing armfuls of new scrolls to the main worktable. Seamus shut the door quietly behind him.

Liam and his mother had disappeared, but Dominic and Aliah were waiting for him the corridor. Seamus took the lead, heading back towards their state rooms.

'Well, that was all a bit unexpected,' Aliah stated the obvious. 'I wonder if all diplomatic missions are this exciting?'

'They most certainly are not.' Dominic started laughing. 'We have an errant son returning home, a battle on our doorstep, and a prophecy enacted. That is enough for a bard to write an epic song about.'

Once inside their suite, Seamus left the other two with a curt goodnight, and retired to his bedroom. Totally drained after the meeting with his family, and worried about the coming war, he flopped down on his bed, not even bothering to remove his clothes. To find out someone believed one of their group was part of a prophecy written hundreds of years ago, was all a bit too much to take in. Were he and Aliah destined to be plagued by that silly prophecy all their lives? It was not long ago a wizard named Gaius was using it in Duncameron to scare the locals out of helping them.

Mentally exhausted, he just wanted to sleep, hoping that when he woke in the morning he would find it had all been a bad dream.

CHAPTER 20

AN AGREEMENT IS REACHED

Aliah awoke the next morning to the scraping of a chair across the floor, and realised it was probably Seamus moving about in their shared living room. There had been a lot to take in last night and with Seamus heading straight to bed, they had not had a chance to discuss the implications. Arising quickly, she grabbed the dressing gown from the end of her bed and pulled it over her nightgown as she headed for the door.

Seamus was seated at the table to the left of the fireplace, looking out the windows into the back courtyard. He jumped in his seat at her *good morning*. She joined him at the table as a polite knock on the door was followed by servants bringing in their breakfast.

'Your Highness. Milord.' The girl leading the procession placed a basket of hot rolls on the table. She was followed by another servant with hot tea, and another with butter and a range of honeys and preserves. 'Please accept our apologies for the meagre meal, but the duke would like to see you both as soon as possible,' the first serving girl primly informed them and then led her tail of servants out.

They had no sooner shut the door than it opened again, this time admitting Dominic. 'Ah, I see I am in time for second breakfast,' he said as he joined them at the table.

'Second breakfast?' Aliah raised an eyebrow.

'Yes, I have been up since the crack of dawn trying to find out anything else I can about the other guests.'

'And?' Aliah asked as she buttered a steaming roll.

'Not a thing!' Dominic admitted as he helped himself to the food.

Seamus had not stopped looking out the window for the entire conversation, and had made no effort to eat breakfast. Aliah was worried about him.

'Seamus. *Seamus?* Are you all right?' she asked, and Seamus' gaze slowly focused back into the room.

'What? Umm... Yes, I guess so.' His eyes glazed back over as he returned to whatever he had been thinking.

'Do you want to talk about what went on last night?' she asked him, trying to draw his attention back to the things they needed to discuss.

'There is not really much to talk about,' Seamus answered without looking at her.

'There is *a lot* to talk about,' Aliah corrected him. 'There is the history of non-magic and Hand. There is the prophecy. There is what we will do if the Malorian's want to take someone from our group away in return for their help with the war...'

Seamus looked thoughtful as he turned his gaze on her. 'Yes, there is all of that. But really, what can we do prior to going before the council? You heard the maid, my father wants us there as soon as possible. Besides, we do not know anything more than we did last night. So let us focus on the job at hand: getting my father to agree to working with the Arian Army to stop the invasion.' Seamus calmly reached for a roll.

Remembering her resolve to act more statesman-like, Aliah forced herself not to bang her cutlery on the table in frustration. Yes, their mission was important, but this was a whole new thing. They could bring additional forces into the upcoming battle, and it may just be the difference between winning and losing the war. It was important they agreed a strategy. She turned to Dominic.

'What do you think?' she asked.

Dominic stopped eating the roll he was biting into and looked at her. 'You're asking me for input?' He looked shocked, and she could not tell if he was laughing at her or being serious.

'Yes, I am asking for your opinion,' she said in as level a voice as she could manage when dealing with two frustrating friends.

'Oh, well I agree with Seamus, actually. Your father wants us to secure Hand's support when Carsten invades. That is our main goal, but if we can get agreement to their navy and guard units working alongside ours under a united command, that would be a real bonus. We need to concentrate on that, rather than some pie-in-the-sky support based on an old prophecy. It would all be supposition anyway, and we cannot plan to cross a bridge when we do not even know where it is.' He calmly carried on eating.

Before she could vent her frustration, there was a knock at the door and Liam opened it from the other side to admit the duke and duchess. Seamus and Dominic rose, and the duke waved his hand. 'Carry on, we have little time for formalities. I have to be in the Council Chambers in a quarter candle-mark.' The duke and duchess were followed in by Amelia and Walter, with Daniel and Liam bringing up the rear.

'Why are you not dressed yet?' Daniel looked appalled at Aliah, sitting there in her nightclothes, hosting the duke and duchess of Hand. 'You have to be in the Council Chambers in a half-candle-mark, you cannot simply throw something on for that. And you have company...'

'Not to worry,' the duke said to the flustered guard. 'We are running a bit late ourselves. Walter and Amelia asked to talk to us all before going to the Council Chambers, so this is a bit rushed. It seems they found out something last night. Is it all right to speak in front of your guard?' the duke asked Aliah.

Aliah briefly considered paying Daniel back for his rude remark by asking him to leave the room, but thought better of it. 'Daniel is head of my personal guard,' Aliah told the duke. 'He knows most of my secrets as we grew up together. He is more than trustworthy, and our word last night extends to him.'

'What word?' Daniel asked quizzically, but the look Aliah sent him stopped his questions short. It also made her take a good look at her friend, and she had to say he did not look at his best this morning. *Too much time spent in a tavern, no doubt.* She had to stop herself from smiling. It was good to see her normally focused and duty-conscious friend taking some time out for himself.

'Fine. Amelia, you may begin.' The duke brought her attention back to the room.

Amelia stepped forward. 'We read a lot of the history of Talagra last night. In summary, there was a major war and the nation descended into a number of warrior groups, who then banded together into a single tribe, located not far from the Malorian boarder. The Malorians and Talagrans have been trading together for some time now. Since their countries have settled down, it seems neither used battle magic again,' Amelia summarised.

'Nothing about the war and the prophecy?' the duke asked impatiently.

'Not exactly.' It was Walter who answered. 'What we did find is the Malorian's had a great seer who is protector of the history and the prophecy. From what we read, we believe it is likely that the Malorians want to take the supposed Wizard and Warrior to be confirmed as such by their Seer.'

'Not exactly comforting,' the duke said. 'In truth, we really know no more than we did before.'

'Do we need to know any more?' Aliah asked. 'We face a great enemy. An enemy that outnumber us and are better prepared than us, if reports are to be believed. If we are being offered a fighting force from a warrior nation for the small cost of allowing two of our number to be taken to meet with a seer, then surely we must do that. At the least, we will lose two people, at the most, we might gain a

Wizard and Warrior on top of another army. That could turn the tide of the upcoming battle.'

'Now is not the time.' It was the duke's turn to interrupt Aliah, and she frowned while furiously tucking her hair behind her ear. Before she could say anything, Seamus stood up.

'I agree with Aliah,' he said. 'We must explore every avenue we can to ensure we win this war. The consequences should we lose could be even more devastating than you can imagine. Some of the wizards on the Wizards Isles have been working with the people of Carsten. They plan to seize as much power as they can through this conflict and they must be stopped at all costs.'

Aliah was touched Seamus had come to her defence, but it also dawned on her the duke's face showed Seamus' revelation was not news to him.

'We have known this to be true for some time.' The duke confirmed her suspicions. 'But talking to the Malorians could be risky. We do not know who they are going to take. It could be the two of you.' The duke looked directly at Seamus and Aliah.

'I appreciate your concern.' Aliah stood between Seamus and his father. 'However, as the people in question are part of the Arian Embassy it will be up to us to make the decision whether or not those chosen will go to Maloria. We will of course take your wishes into account, but the final decision will be ours.'

With that, Aliah left the room to dress appropriately for the council meeting. As a maid helped her into her formal clothes, raised voices penetrated the door, but by the time she finished dressing and returned to the sitting room, Seamus was alone, staring into the fire and chewing his bottom lip.

'Aliah, do you think that was wise, cutting my father off like that? We will need him on side today if we are to get Hand to agree to the Arian and Hand armies working together.' Seamus rose from his chair to stand in front of her.

'It was a little risky,' she admitted to Seamus. In fact, she had been cursing herself about that very thing as she dressed. She worried that in asserting her control, she would alienate the duke, but she felt it important he understood that in spite of her age she was not his subordinate. 'I only spoke the truth. The duke cannot order any one of us not to go with the Malorians. But perhaps I could have considered my words a little more carefully.'

'What about me?' Seamus asked. 'What if I turn out to be the warrior they talked of. What master would decide whether I go or stay?'

'You are surely not the warrior.' Aliah burst out laughing. 'I have seen you fight. You can defend yourself, but no one would call you a warrior. Anyway, you are a part of my father's mission and remain so until the king releases you, therefore you are under my power. And I would let you make up your own mind.'

Seamus laughed with her. 'Well, I am definitely not the wizard. I can make a strong flame, and sometimes I can make things move, but that is the extent of my skills. If we are relying on me to be the great wizard to save Aria from certain doom we may as well surrender.'

Aliah wrapped her arms around her stomach, she was now laughing so much it hurt. 'I am sure one day you will make a perfectly adequate wizard, Seamus, but I am thinking they mean Walter. He always was one of the strongest in magic on the Isle. And Daniel has the best military mind of his generation, I am sure if there is a warrior in our party it is him. Anyway, we should go. They will be waiting for us.'

Seamus shrugged his shoulders and held out his arm so he could formally escort Aliah to the Council Chambers.

—⁂—

ALIAH WAS surprised at how little time it took to persuade The Council of Hand that their interests would be best served by fighting along side the Arian Army in the upcoming invasion. Apart from two aged lords who swore never to work with enemy forces—as they thought of Aria—the rest realised they could not hope to stand alone against a fleet the size of the one sailing from Carsten. After some too-ing and fro-ing, they all agreed Daniel and Captain Hanks would liaise with the army and navy of Hand, helping them integrate with the Arian forces when they arrived.

Many of the council members closely watched Seamus and his role in negotiating the agreement, and Aliah was sure they were all wondering how he had come to be in the position of King's Ambassador. One had even gone as far to suggest how smart the duke had been to send his son to Bannock to make first contact with the king. Lord Damon neither confirmed nor denied this comment, and Aliah had followed his lead. If it helped with their cause, for people to think the agreement to fight together had been initiated by the Duke, then Aliah was happy to oblige.

Back in her bedroom, Aliah asked the maid to help her change out of her state clothes. Aware Seamus was spending some much needed time with his brother and sister, she wondered what she would do with her afternoon. Her thoughts were cut short by a knock at the door. She sent the maid to answer it.

'It is one of your guards, Your Highness. He says there is a man waiting to see you in the other room, and he strongly suggests you meet with him.'

Frowning, Aliah began pulling back on the dress she was half out of. The maid finished doing up the buttons she had just undone, then checked to make sure Aliah looked presentable.

On entering the living room, Aliah acknowledged Dominic standing to attention inside the door in his formal guard pose, but immediately turned her focus to the elderly gentleman standing by the fireplace.

'Lord Ambury, of Maloria, Your Highness.' The man bowed low from the waist. 'I have come on a special mission from The Great Council of Maloria and beg an audience with you.'

'Lord Ambury, this is most unusual, all requests to speak with the king's representatives should come via his staff. And none of my advisors are here.' Aliah paused as if she were considering his request. 'But maybe I can spare you a moment of my time. Please, take a seat.' The elderly man waited until she was comfortably seated before taking the chair directly across from her.

'The Duke of Hand has already told me something of your mission here. He mentioned a prophecy, and that you thought the people from this prophecy were numbered amongst my company?' Aliah started.

'How very direct you are, Your Highness, but you are only partially correct.' Although the man in front of her had to be in his sixties, his brown eyes sparkled with appreciation at her taking control of the situation. 'Let me fully brief you. There is some debate in our council as to whether or not recent events mean this particular prophecy has been activated. This is a very important matter for our people, as we have been entrusted for generations with ensuring the Wizard and Warrior are equipped for their tasks when the world needs them. This is something we all take very seriously.

'So I have been sent here to retrieve the Wizard and Warrior of the prophecy to bring them to the council. This is so the members can make an informed decision about whether or not the prophecy has begun.'

'And if I release them to go to Maloria, you will ensure your army supports Aria in the upcoming fight against the invasion from Carsten?' Aliah asked.

'Again, partially correct. We have no army as such. Each tribal group has their own warriors, and they have pledged half of their men to come fight with Duke Damon's forces.'

Aliah appreciated he was reaffirming their alliance was to the duke and they would follow his orders. This made her doubly pleased they had already agreed with the duke the forces under him would be working in concert with the Arian Army, as she would have hated to lose these additional troops if they had not been able to reach an agreement.

'So, if I release these people to accompany you, then what exactly will that mean for them?' Although Aliah would agree to almost anything to have the Malorian forces join them, she believed it part of her duty to make sure they knew exactly what Walter and Daniel were getting themselves into before she agreed they could go. Out of the corner of her eye, she caught Dominic nodding his head in approval, and a surprising warmth spread through her belly.

'The Wizard and Warrior will have to travel with all speed to the sacred meeting place of our council, The Sanctuary. The Prophecy Council will then judge whether they are in truth the ones foretold in the prophecy. More than that, I cannot tell you. The workings of the Prophecy Council and the High Seer are a mystery to me.' Lord Ambury folded his hands in his lap, waiting for her response.

'What if it turns out my people are not the Wizard and Warrior you believe them to be? How quickly will they be returned to us?'

'I cannot answer that, Your Highness. They will be entering our sacred grounds and it is up to the High Seer and the council to decide what will happen.'

'So just to clarify, you want me to send people with you, to go through some unknown test they may not return from...at all?' Aliah did not know if she could ask this of anyone, even for a fighting force of the size Lord Ambury was promising.

'It is perhaps even worse than you fear, Your Highness, for the people we want to take with us are yourself and the young Lord Seamus.'

If the aged Lord Ambury had pulled a knife and tried to kill her, she could not have been more shocked. In fact, she was speechless. Looking hopefully at Dominic to help her out, she was disappointed as he simply raised his eyebrows and shrugged his shoulders. This was something he had obviously not been expecting either.

As if he sensed her discomfort, Lord Ambury spoke. 'Surely you have heard the rumours about the two of you being the Wizard and

Warrior. They have been circulating since the Wizard's Council sensed you were travelling with someone with magical powers.'

'There were rumours, but we were sure they did not apply to us, and that did not seem unreasonable given the circumstances. We thought it just a ploy to keep people wary of us, as I have only ever raised my sword in a fight once, on the boat on the way here. And to call Seamus a wizard is a little premature, he has only just started his training.'

'Still, many a truth has been said in jest. Our High Seer has been following your progress these last few moon turns. He feels sure you are the ones.' Lord Ambury seemed unmoved by Aliah's protestations. 'And you are the ones the seer wishes to have brought to him. That is why he sent me here to meet you.'

'I understand you arrived here a few days before us. Only a select few people were aware of our last minute plans. So how did you know we would come here?' Aliah voiced her surprise.

'I did mention we have a High Seer who has been tracking you, did I not?' Lord Ambury smiled serenely at her.

'I. Um, I...' Aliah was simply lost for words.

'I can see you were not expecting this, and you will need time to think. I should leave you and perhaps return before the dinner bell?' the lord asked, and Aliah nodded her head, allowing him to retire.

The Malorian lord rose and, after bowing, left the room. Aliah stared at the fire, stunned.

Me, the warrior? Really? Frowning, she ran the idea through her head. *It must be some mad sort of joke.*

'That certainly puts the cat amongst the pigeons.' Aliah was so lost in her own thoughts she actually jumped. She had not realised Dominic had come to take the seat beside her. 'I cannot think what your father would say if we let you traipse off into Maloria. He would not he happy at all, not even if you did raise a considerable fighting force by going.'

Aliah wanted to tell him it was not his, or anyone else's, place to "let" her do anything. But somehow she could not find the energy.

She merely rose from the chair and went back to her room to finish changing. Stopping at the door, she turned. 'Can you please go find Seamus and Daniel. I think we really need to talk about this.'

'Not Walter?'

'No, not at the moment. I think he is of more use working with Amelia.' And with that, she closed the door behind her, not able to think through what had happened with Dominic in the room.

Seamus, the wizard? The seer must be out of his wits. The thought popped into her head as she sat on the edge of the bed. Still, even though she tried to dismiss the idea as foolish, she could not help thinking what if she really was the warrior?

SATIN NUZZLED HIS NOSE INTO SEAMUS' hand. Reluctant to leave the comfort of his old friend, the boy buried his face into the horse's neck, breathing in his familiar scent.

His ride with Jonas had been liberating because for a time he could forget about the coming war and the fact he would unlikely ever call Hand home again. Unfortunately, all good things come to an end, and soon Jonas had to return for his afternoon lessons.

Waving the groom away, Seamus took care of Satin himself. The rhythmic movement of the brush as he brought Satin's coat up to a brilliant shine had allowed him to forget the rest of the world for a few moments longer.

A prickling between his shoulder blades forced him to raise his head and look around the stable yard. Throughout the ride with his brother, he had had a similar sensation of being watched. However, every time he checked, there was no one around, just forest animals and birds. He did think he saw the same wolf a few times, but dismissed that thought as improbable. Now, as he glimpsed a familiar grey tail disappear around the side of the stable block, he wondered if he had not been right.

Acting on instinct, he trailed after the wolf. When he turned the corner into the yard in front of the kitchen, all he found was one of the maids sitting in the sun churning milk into butter, and a hooded figure heading towards the guard's barracks to the other side of the main palace building. The long grass was standing tall, no flat patches suggesting a wolf had snuck through to hide in the surrounding trees.

Wondering if the stress of the last few days had caused him to see things that were not there, he shook his head and decided it would not hurt to have a look behind the stables, just to make sure. Rounding the corner he found not a wolf, but Daniel, leaning against the wall looking decidedly unwell.

'Are you all right?' he asked worriedly, as Daniel really did look quite ill.

'No, not really,' the guard answered. 'Must have had some bad seafood to eat last night.'

'But the seafood course was left out of the dinner last night.' Seamus frowned, remembering his mother had commented on how cook had complained he did not have enough to serve all the guests, so no one was getting any.

'I was on duty last night, so I did not eat at the formal dinner. I had something later.' Daniel winced in pain.

Unusual, Seamus thought. *The kitchen does not have time to make two meals when we have a formal function, so staff generally eat a plainer version of what is served at the main table.* Then he shook his head. Of course Daniel did not have to eat at the palace, he could have gone out to a tavern for dinner.

'Come with me. Cook has a great remedy for upset stomachs.' Seamus took hold of the guard-man's arm, and led him towards the kitchen.

As Daniel swallowed the last of the tonic cook had prepared,

Dominic joined them at the large wooden table that dominated the centre of the kitchen.

'Finally found you. I have been looking everywhere. Aliah wants to see you both. Something rather unusual has happened.'

'What?' Daniel asked, clearly not happy about having to move, although he did look a little less green.

'I will let her do the honours.' Dominic smirked, and they had no choice but to follow him back to the state rooms.

WHEN ALIAH RETURNED to the living room, she found Seamus and Daniel sitting with Dominic, engrossed in the details of Seamus' ride through the forest and a stray wolf. Part of her wished she had gone out riding today, then she would have missed the meeting with Lord Ambury, and she would not feel as confused as she did now.

They stopped talking as she took her seat. Instead of beginning, she turned to Dominic and asked him to tell the others what had happened.

Dominic's eyebrows raised in surprise, but he quickly went through wha the Malorian Ambassador had said. Hearing the lord's words a second time did not give her any more clarity, and she was still trying to sort out her jumbled thoughts when Dominic finished.

On the one hand, as Heir to the Throne she could not simply run off on a whim, on the other, it was her responsibility to do what she could for Aria's safety. And what about Seamus? Theoretically she could order him to go, but she really could not ask him to place his life in danger for Aria, and that was if his father did not object to his leaving.

There was a lull in the conversation and her guard, her spy, and her friend all looked towards her as if waiting for her to answer a question. She did not have a clue what they had asked, so she just stared blankly back.

Should she and Seamus go? Looking at Seamus, she realised she did not want to discuss it with everyone and come to a group consensus. If they were to go, it would be Seamus and her making that choice.

'So will we journey to Maloria?' she asked him, wanting to hear him say out loud what he thought on the matter.

'Do we really have a choice?' he asked in response, and she could see from his eyes he was as unsure what to do as she was.

She closed her eyes, unable to bear his gaze, and said quietly, 'Yes we do, and we are the only ones who can decide.'

She opened her eyes in time to see Seamus take a deep breath, as if he had just made up his mind, and he looked her directly in the eye, nodding once. She knew then he was going. And if he was, then so was she.

Then reality struck. They actually had to see this through because they needed to find out for themselves if they were part of the prophecy. Even if there was only a slim chance they were, then they might be the sole hope of saving their homes, and the lives of the people they loved.

CHAPTER 21

STEALING AWAY

Once Aliah and Seamus had made the decision to go, they calmly sat back and watched the uproar it created. Daniel and Dominic talked over each other, each coming up with new reasons as to why they should not leave. It seemed they were being thoughtless, putting their lives on the line for something so vague, even if it did mean they gained a substantial armed force in return. But Seamus knew deep down in his soul this was what he and Aliah had to do. While the other two argued, he turned to Aliah.

'We have to stand strong, I am sure no one is going to be in favour of us going to Maloria.'

Aliah twirled the end of her plait. 'I know, but we have achieved what we came here to do. Hand has agreed to work together with Aria against the invasion. There is no real reason for us to stay.'

When Dominic and Daniel finally realised they would not change their minds, things moved swiftly. The duke and duchess were told and, although to say they were not happy was an understatement, they agreed to arrange transport across the straight to the Malorian coast.

Then Lord Ambury was called and told of their decision. After informing them they would need to travel light and in secrecy, he advised he had brought a guide with him who would be able to show them the way. It seemed The Sanctuary was hidden and would be difficult to find on their own. He suggested they chose a small party to accompany them. That had caused even more arguments. Sick and tired of everyone trying to talk over each other, Seamus closed his eyes and tried to block out the noise. If anything, the sound was louder, as if making up for the loss of one of his senses. He opened his eyes and sighed.

If Seamus had to go, Duke Damon insisted Liam went as his body guard. Daniel and Dominic disagreed over which of them should go as Aliah's protector. When Aliah maintained she could do well without either of them, as the warrior of prophecy did not need protection, they ignored her and carried on arguing. Finally Duke Damon stepped in and said Daniel needed to remain behind to liaise between the Hand and Arian forces, therefore Dominic would go with them.

Then there was Walter, who argued he had to go because Seamus would need to continue his magic lessons, especially if he was supposed to be some sort of wizard saviour. His expertise and knowledge of magic would come in useful when dealing with the Malorians, he added.

Then Amelia took a stand. If Walter travelled with them, why should she not go? She had done most of the research and knew about Malorian customs. She wanted to meet the Great Seer and discuss her gift of foretelling with him.

Once the expanded travelling party was agreed, transport became the next issue. Duke Damon wanted them to take one of his navy ships. Concerned about them being attacked at sea again, he wanted them to have extra protection. Dominic assured him his sources in Port Marden confirmed the ships they met on the journey to Hand had been pirate vessels from further north. Bad weather had forced them south and they thought to chance their arm at some booty before returning to the Natarian coast.

Even after he agreed the attack on their ship had been pure coincidence, the duke still would not put aside his concerns and insisted on a full naval escort.

Dominic pointed out they could not really maintain their need for secrecy if they left on a naval ship. Someone was bound to see them. The duke had stood firm. It was only when Lord Ambury impressed on them the need to move quickly given the Carsten forces were close by, did the duke reluctantly offer the use of a fishing boat from a village close to the port to take them to the mainland.

The details were all agreed, and everyone went to get themselves ready. On the duchess' suggestion, Aliah sought Martha to find out what travelling clothes they might have in storage. Seamus decided although he still had the travelling pack given to him by Amelia for his journey to Bannock, this time he would leave with his own possessions.

Opening the door from the state room he nearly fell over Robin. 'Erh, sorry Robin,' he mumbled, wondering what the man had been doing outside his door. As his father's chancellor, he should have been busy dealing with matters affecting the Duchy, not lurking in corridors.

Surprise flitted across the older man's face, before he composed himself and half-bowed to Seamus. 'I was coming to see if you or your party needed anything. I saw them all rushing out and thought maybe you might require assistance.'

Seamus raised his eyebrows, not sure if it was common practice for a chancellor to personally help state guests, then shrugged his shoulders. He had far more important things on his mind. 'Thank you, Robin, but we are all fine. I think the princess wants to talk to Martha about getting some of our woollen blankets shipped to Bannock, and the others, well I am sure they have things they are meant to be doing. I am going to my room to gather some personal items. I think I can manage that myself.'

The Chancellor gave the briefest of nods required when dealing with a superior, and Seamus smiled in return. He had always had a prickly relationship with the man his father trusted with so many of the tasks required to run a Duchy. For some reason he had taken a dislike to Seamus at an early age, and barely tolerated his presence. Never rude, he was not quite polite either.

Turning, Robin led him down the corridor and left him at the stairs without another word. Seamus carried on through the door that led to the family quarters—a suite with a large sitting room and three bedrooms branching off it. His parents occupied the main bedroom across from the doorway he stood in, the room to the left of the door was his, and his brother had been moved into the room on the right on his tenth birthday. In the far corner there were stairs leading up to a nursery, school room, and bedrooms for a nanny and a tutor.

He had expected to feel at home walking into these rooms, but instead he felt more of a stranger than ever. Perhaps because he did not believe he would never come back here to live, or perhaps because he had out-grown the need for the security blanket the palace family rooms represented. After all, he was nearly at the age when he could have been moved to his own suite as the Heir anyway.

Sighing, he opened his bedroom door, surprised to see the contents almost as he had left them. A little tidier perhaps, but everything still pretty much in the same place. He ran his fingers over some of his prized possessions; his books, his bow, his set of throwing knives. *Mmm, those are definitely coming,* he thought as he picked them up.

Heading over to his wardrobe, he found his hunting pack at the bottom where he had left it, picked up a favourite pair of sturdy boots, then chose three changes of clothes. Finally, he took his warm, woollen hunting jacket out. Shutting the wardrobe door, he took one last look around before leaving his childhood room.

———

DANIEL CARRIED THE CLOTHES, boots, and travel pack Martha had found for Aliah between two blankets to hide them from prying eyes. They were taking the servant's stairs back up to their rooms to ensure they did not come across anyone who might ask questions about what they were doing. Aliah glanced over her shoulder at her childhood friend, who was not doing a very good job of hiding his annoyance at being left behind.

'Daniel,' she started. 'I know you are upset, but I think you are looking at this the wrong way. What guard of your age gets the opportunity to play such a senior role in a war? This is a great opportunity for you.'

'If you disregard the fact I will be failing at my duty to protect you and Seamus, then I guess you could see it that way,' Daniel answered, his words sharp and surly.

'You did what you were asked to do.' Aliah was exasperated. 'You got Seamus and me here safely so we could agree terms with the Council of Hand. Now you are going to work with the people of Hand to thwart the invasion, and we are all starting on a new journey. So your role is different. But better different. Come on,' she tried to jolly him out of his bad mood. 'This is what you have been studying for all your life, to lead an army into battle.'

Daniel did not respond, and so intently was she watching his reactions that she did not hear the duke's chancellor come down the servant's stairs behind her.

'Can I help you with anything?' he asked, and Aliah nearly jumped out of her skin.

'Um, ah...' Aliah started.

Dominic had appeared behind Daniel. 'It is fine, thank you, Robin. Sorry, Aliah, Martha delayed me with some story or other about woollen blankets. Daniel, I can take some of that from you if it is too much for you to carry upstairs.' His voice as he spoke was polite, but Aliah could see a hardness in his eyes as he almost glared at the chancellor.

Moving to the side, Aliah and Daniel allowed Robin to sweep past them down the stairs.

'What was that about?' Aliah whispered to Dominic.

'There is just something... I cannot place my finger on it, but something about him makes me uneasy. Come on, we have not got much time if we are to be ready for this evening.'

Dominic passed them both, and Daniel followed behind. Aliah paused, frowning at Daniel as he passed. *Speaking of things being not quite right, something is bothering him, and I aim to find out what it is...* she thought as she began to climb after them.

SEAMUS CLOSED his travelling pack and made sure his bedroll was securely attached to the side. Even with all the arguing and planning, they had managed to get some sleep before their pre-dawn departure time to catch the morning tide. His parents had come and gone, saying one last farewell before the group departed. They were to hold to the story that Seamus and Aliah had been taken ill with a strange sickness and the doctor had quarantined most of their group to prevent spreading the illness. Only Martha would be admitted to their rooms to bring food and medicines. They hoped that would give them a six-day before anyone raised serious questions about their whereabouts.

More relaxed about leaving this time, perhaps because he had an opportunity to say goodbye to everyone, but also because he left for a specific purpose, Seamus whistled a tune under his breath. This new journey allowed him to put thoughts of the future from his mind for a while. However, there was still a sadness surrounding his leaving.

The previous night Jonas had hugged him gruffly. Seamus told him to keep up his studies and he would make a great duke someday. His brother merely nodded in response, saying Seamus would be proud of him when he returned. His younger sister had given him a chain with a round metal disc showing the sign of The Lady, shyly saying if he wore it, The Lady would protect him.

He touched under the neck of his linen shirt to feel the round metal with the three lines of waves on it; one each for birth, life, and death. He let it fall back in place. His mother had simply hugged him tightly. His father had told him how proud they were of him as he held him close. Seamus had fought to hold back his tears.

Still a little reluctant to say goodbye to his home again, he stared out the window into the courtyard below. Only the outlines of buildings were visible as it would be a candle-mark or so before the sun rose, but he filled in each and every window and doorway from memory. Although he knew duty called him, it would be so easy to stay here where he felt comfortable, and try to rebuild his life.

'It is time to go.' Standing in the doorway, Aliah was dressed similarly to him in a loose linen shirt, fitting trousers, and a woollen coat, all in various shades of green. They both wore travelling boots with thick soles that laced up well over their ankles to support the long walk they anticipated.

'Yes it is,' he said slowly, turning back to face the room, holding out the small package he held in his hand.

'I have something for you.' He handed her the gift. She opened it to find it contained a necklace with a charm of the ancient sign for good luck, an open hand.

'Oh, Seamus, it is lovely. Is it the necklace you bought in the market in Bannock?'

'It is. It brought good luck to us then, and I hope it will bring luck to you now. I have a feeling we will need all the good fortune we can find on this journey.

'I have to say I am not happy at having to leave home again so soon. Lately I feel like a great wind is pushing me down a path I am not sure I want to be travelling on. Maybe that is what being part of a prophecy feels like, but I cannot in any way believe I am the wizard they talk about. Every time I think I might actually be the wizard, I look around for someone to jump out and say *tricked you*. Funny thing is, I would feel more relieved that it is not me, rather than embarrassed someone had caught me thinking I might be.'

Aliah put on the necklace and adjusted it under her shirt as she answered him. 'I know what you mean. I keep saying to myself, if I am the warrior who is to save us all in battle, then the Goddess help Aria.'

'Remind me again why we are doing this then?' he asked.

'Because we need to know the truth, otherwise we will always have this hanging over us.' Aliah flung her plait over her shoulder as she picked up her travel pack. 'And because the Malorians will send warriors to help fight the Carstenites.'

'Well, if you put it that way, I guess we had best be off and see if we are destined to save the world.' Seamus sighed wearily as he picked up his own pack and slung it over his shoulder. He knew better than to offer to carry Aliah's. At best, that would earn him a cold stare from those icy blue eyes, at worst, a tongue lashing.

Shrugging her pack on more securely, Aliah followed him out the door. 'I have not even thought as far as saving anything. I am getting through this by taking it one step at a time. At the moment I am concentrating on just getting to meet this seer. Everything else can wait until after that.'

There was some comfort in knowing Aliah had her doubts as well. With her uncertainty mirroring his, he felt less alone on this unusual journey.

As they entered the hallway, they were joined by Dominic who had retrieved his own travel clothes and pack from the ship. Instinctively the older boy reached for Aliah's pack to carry it for her, and Seamus had to laugh at the look of outrage she threw.

'I am quite capable of carrying my own things, thank you,' she forced the words out through gritted teeth. Sticking her nose in the air, she stalked off down the corridor, long blonde plait swinging behind her as if to emphasise her words.

Seamus laughed again at Dominic's perplexed face. 'She travelled the length of Aria pulling her own weight. I can imagine she finds it insulting you think she needs help now,' Seamus explained to his travelling companion.

'Everything I do is wrong. I will never understand her.' Dominic sighed.

'Why do you need to?' Seamus asked as they followed the princess downstairs.

'I do not need to understand her,' said Dominic somewhat defensively, in a way that made Seamus realise for some reason it was very important to Dominic that he did. Smirking, he had to stop himself from chanting *Dominic likes Aliah* in the most childish of ways. He hoped the spy could win over the princess, but he would have to get her to see past the work he did for her father first. Well, it would make for an interesting journey.

They quickly followed Aliah through the courtyard to the stables, where saddled horses were waiting for them. Mounting quickly in the pre-dawn darkness, they rode through the city and out towards a fishing village not far from Port Hand.

ON ARRIVING AT THE VILLAGE, they found Liam, Walter, and Amelia waiting for them. Standing alongside them was a smaller cloaked figure who barely came up to Liam's shoulder. As they rode closer, Seamus realised Liam was arguing strenuously with Walter.

'This pack weighs a ton? What have you filled it with? Books?'

'Well, yes, of course books.' Walter stared benignly back at the irate squire, who groaned in frustration.

'What part of "we are to be travelling light and fast on foot" did you not understand?' Liam lectured. 'No one else will be carrying these for you when they get too heavy, you know.'

'I would not expect them to,' Walter calmly informed him. 'These volumes have information we may need and I did not have time to read them before we left, so I brought them along with me. Anyway, I have a spell that will ensure they weigh little more than a feather, so I do not see the problem.' Walter smiled and Liam groaned again, unsure what to make of the first wizard he had ever met.

Amelia put a comforting hand on Liam's arm. 'It will be all right, you'll see.'

Before Liam could say anything else, there was a loud crash, and they all turned to see the small figure who had been standing behind the squire, wrestling someone to the ground, a knife held to the intruder's throat. In the process, the small person's hood slipped back, and Seamus was surprised to see a girl of about his own age with short, spiky brown hair and large dark eyes too big for her elfin face. At the moment, those eyes were focused on the person below her and, before Seamus could stop himself, laughter bubbled up inside and forced its way out.

'Fine bodyguard you turn out to be.' When he managed to control himself he spoke to a wide-eyed Daniel, who was clearly surprised to find himself with a knife at his throat. 'Whoever you are, you can let him up. He is one of us.'

There was more laughter all around as Daniel scrambled to his feet and dusted himself off. He turned to his captor. 'Captain Daniel of the Arian Guard at your service.' He bowed to the girl who moments ago had him pinned to the ground.

'You are lucky to be alive,' the girl responded tartly.

'What were you doing, Daniel?' Aliah ignored the girl's rude response and glared at her friend.

'Joining you on your trip,' Daniel answered, as he picked his travel pack up off the ground.

'That was not your assigned duty.' Aliah used her princess voice as she berated the royal guard.

Daniel lifted his chin. 'I was ordered by your father to see to your safety and, as my king, his order trumps yours. I have left military liaison in the capable hands of Captain Hanks who, incidentally, will be of more use than me over-seeing Hand's contributions to the battle ahead, as the initial attacks will be at sea. Besides, I cannot let you all go off on a great adventure without me. Life is too short to be left behind.' He stood there waiting to see what Aliah would do, a confident grin on his face, and determination in his eyes.

Seamus knew Aliah could never stay angry at her childhood friend for long, especially when he happened to be right. The king's order would always take priority over anything Aliah said.

'All right,' Aliah conceded, dismounting. Shrugging her shoulders as if it made no difference to her whether Daniel came or not. She told him, 'You may join us if you wish.' Stalking over to the fishing boat moored nearby, her posture showed how closely she was holding in her anger.

The others followed in her wake and, when they were all assembled ready to board, Liam introduced them to their guide.

'This is Emer. She has been sent by the seer who has called us to Maloria, and has been tasked with taking us to meet the Prophecy Council. Once we reach land, she will guide us to Sanctuary, which, by all accounts is quite well hidden.'

'Are we destined to be led by women on this journey?' Daniel cried dramatically, and Seamus was surprised to see their guide's eyes crinkle with laughter, which she quickly smothered.

'Maybe when you can beat a woman in a fight, you will get a chance to lead,' Emer told him, her face a study of seriousness. 'Come now, we must be away or we will miss the tide,' she commanded, before Daniel could think of a suitable comeback.

They boarded the small vessel and took a position near the bow, where a canvas shelter had been erected for them. The trip would take them well into the morning, so they settled out of the crew's way, and tried to get some sleep.

THE CROSSING WAS uneventful and the gentle rocking had them all asleep in minutes. Before drifting off, Seamus mused this time yesterday morning he had been in full court attire attending a meeting of his father's council. Now he was more humbly dressed, travelling on a fishing boat on another adventure. How quickly things could change. How odd his life had become.

Just as dawn was breaking, Seamus awoke to shouting. The captain had caught sight of a ship heading directly towards them at full speed.

'I cannot make out the insignia,' he informed them. 'And in these times, I cannot take the risk it is friendly. I will not be able to set you down on the beach at Exodus Cove as planned. The coast is a short swim away. If you slip over the side, I can head back out to sea and lead them away from you.'

'That would be perfect if we could all swim,' Aliah muttered, and the rest of her group gasped in astonishment.

'What? Am I the only one?' Aliah frowned, annoyed to have her short-coming made so obvious.

'Daniel, you take Aliah's pack. I will make sure the princess gets to shore.' Dominic took charge. 'Just for this once, princess, could you please do exactly as I ask, when I ask, because if you do not, both our lives could be in danger.'

Seamus could see Aliah holding in her frustration. She did not like to be vulnerable at the best of times, but she was in no position to argue. Walter offered to spell their packs so they could use them as floats. This done, with an additional spell to keep the contents dry, they all slipped overboard and kicked off for shore. Seamus looked behind to see Aliah lying on her back, Dominic had her chin cupped in his hand and was hauling her side-stroke towards the beach.

The captain kept the fishing boat between the swimmers and the approaching ship to shield them for as long as it was safe for him to do so. Occasionally Seamus glanced back over his shoulder to see how much time they had before the other ship realised there were swimmers in the water. Each time he looked, he saw Dominic and Aliah falling further behind the others, and he worried that when the boat moved, the two of them would be vulnerable to attack.

When he was three-quarters of the way to the beach, the captain was finally forced to move the fishing boat to avoid an imminent collision. A yell from the deck of the other ship warned him the swimmers had been seen. Instead of following the fishing vessel as a pirate ship would have done, the ship lowered anchor and the crew began readying a row boat for launch.

'Faster,' he yelled to the others between breaths. 'They are coming for us.'

They sped up and, with lungs bursting, finally made it to the expanse of sandy beach they had been aiming for. Seamus waited impatiently for Dominic to bring Aliah to shore. When they reached the beach, Aliah primly thanked Dominic for his help before releasing his grasp and moving to pick up her pack.

'This way. There is no time to lose,' Emer called. 'We have no time to dry off. We have to get into the forest before they land.' She turned and started jogging towards the cliff face.

Seamus looked up at the steep cliff looming over them. *How are we going to climb that?* he wondered as he shouldered his pack and headed after her.

Running on the sand was hard going even for someone as young and fit as he was. Seamus worried about Amelia and Walter, and turned to help them.

'Do not worry,' Walter shooed him onwards. 'I have a few tricks to make things easier for us that will not tire me as they use little magical energy.'

At the base of the cliff, Emer stopped and waited for everyone to catch up.

'Walter, can you create illusions?' she asked. The wizard nodded, too breathless to answer.

'It will only seem real from a distance, the closer they get the easier they will be able to see through it.' Walter finally managed to get his words out.

'It is the same with our mages,' Emer said. 'Can you create an image of us climbing up a pathway?' She waited until Walter nodded before continuing. 'Good, I know a secret passage to the top. If we can avoid them finding it, they will be forced to take the longer path at the end of the cove. It will buy us quite a bit of time.'

'If you can create an illusion, why did you not do that to hide us from the ship? Then we could have been set ashore as planned.' Aliah angrily rounded on Walter.

'Well, um, no one asked, and I did not think of it. Now you mention it, that would have been a perfect situation for an illusion spell. You have to understand I am foremost a scholar. I have rarely had to use magic in stressful situations. I normally have more notice to think through potential danger and which spells might be useful, like when we escaped through the sewers in Duncameron,' the wizard admitted, and he turned towards the rock face, ready to cast his spell. His answer seemed to quench the flames of Aliah's anger.

Intrigued, Seamus watched intently as Walter wove his spell, wondering if he would ever be able to do magic as easily as his teacher. At the end of his spell, Walter moved his hands as if he were pushing something up the cliff.

'I cannot see anything.' Seamus said.

'We are too close to the spell,' Emer told him. 'Come on now.'

She walked down the beach about ten paces, and they all followed. Emer seemed to disappear into a rock before their very eyes. As he drew closer, Seamus saw there was a gap between two rocks that was just wide enough for a person to slip between. Once they were inside, Emer led them to the top of the cliff via a subterranean tunnel. They were not in complete darkness as enough light diffused from the opening at the top for them to see, but there were a few stumbles from tired feet as they climbed.

At the top, Emer walked to the edge and looked over. Seamus joined her, seeing about twenty men searching the bottom of the cliff. Fooled by the illusion, they were looking for the path that would supposedly take them to the top. Dominic joined the two of them, staring out to sea.

'That is an Arian ship,' he said almost as if to himself.

'What do you mean?' Seamus frowned. 'Are those not pirates? We have been chased by one of our own ships?'

'Yes, I mean exactly that. You would find a merchant ship like that in any Arian harbour.'

'Which means someone is specifically chasing us?' Emer asked, frowning.

At a shout, the men below looked up as one. Seeing their quarry looking down at them, bows raised and the group at the edge of the cliff were forced to move back to avoid the arrows sent their way.

'We really must not delay, if that is the case. They will not likely give up pursuit while we are easy to find,' Emer warned them. 'Look, they have found the path at the end of the cove. It will not take them long to climb up here, and I would like to be well into the woods when they arrive so they will not know exactly which path we are travelling.'

Weary, wet, and cold from their swim, they picked up their belongings and trudged after Emer, over the scrubby grass towards the woods they could make out in the distance.

CHAPTER 22

FULL MOON

Before following her companions, Aliah turned and could just make out the Isle of Hand on the horizon. If she turned the other way, she could see a strip of coastal scrub that changed to woodland some way in the distance. After her humiliating swimming experience, she wished herself back in the comfort of the palace on Hand. Sighing, she trudged towards the relative safety of the forest.

As they entered the shade of the woodland, Emer asked, 'I know we are all tired, but we have no time to stop for refreshments as I have just seen the first of our pursuers come over the top of the cliff. We must hurry.' She led them off on a fast walk through the woods, on what could not even be described as an animal trail.

Dominic told them all to use some of their travel rations to keep their energy up as they walked, and he passed some to their guide. They kept up a brisk pace until well into the afternoon. A couple of times Emer had them pause, and she asked Walter to use magic to sense if there were pursuers close by. Both times he confirmed they were definitely near, but he could not tell exactly where. When they camped for the night, Emer instructed only cold food and no fire. Tired, cold, and hungry, they huddled together for warmth.

While they ate, Emer said she was going to scout around to see if she could find out exactly which course their pursuers were taking. Daniel and Seamus both offered to go with her, but she said she knew these woods like the back of her hand and she would be better off alone.

Aliah was tired to the bone, but she could not relax. Every noise had her jumping, wondering if the people pursuing had finally found them. Finally, her eyelids began to flutter closed, but they opened wide to when she spied a grey wolf looking through the bushes at them. Shaking herself awake, she went to reach out for Daniel, but before she could wake him the wolf disappeared. Her hand dropped and she gazed around the group to see if anyone else saw the intruder.

Dominic was on sentry duty, but his back was to her and he did not seem alarmed. Just as Aliah went to speak out, Emer emerged from the darkness. She spoke briefly to Dominic, then sat beside him. If they were not worried, then she may as well go back to sleep.

Stretching the kinks out of her body the next morning reminded her of why she did not like travelling rough. Before she could voice her complaints Emer beckoned them all over.

'We need to be quiet today. There is a group of about five military looking men about half a candle-mark to our left. As best I could tell, they have been tracking in the same direction as us, sometimes ranging out to see if they can find us. Fortunately if we veer to the right, we will distance ourselves from them, and will still be able to reach our destination. It will take a little longer so we will have to make better time than we did yesterday. I suggest we start off at a slow jog.'

Aliah bit back a groan. She was already tired and sore, but she was young and relatively fit. She glanced towards Walter and Amelia to see how they were taking the news and was surprised they did not look worried at all.

They broke camp quickly and followed after Emer, who had asked Walter to use his magic to cover their path through the forest. Aliah had seen Walter do this after their escape from Duncameron, and so was not surprised to see him drop to the back of the group where he could erase any sign they had been travelling through the trees.

Emer spoke little during their journey, except to give directions. When they took a break, she would politely answer direct questions about the land around them, the trail they were following, or about Maloria. She would tell them nothing about the Prophecy Council, or of what might happen when they reached their destination. They did find out that at this pace, it would take them almost two days to reach the Sanctuary, and even then she suggested they would be cutting it close.

'Close to what?' Aliah asked, but Emer acted as if she had not spoken.

All of their party were quite fit, but they dropped exhausted when Emer allowed them to rest that evening well after the sun had gone down. After checking the general area, she asked Walter if he could sense those following them. He told her they were now at the very edge of his range, so she allowed them to build a small fire and cook some rabbits Seamus and Liam caught while walking, so long as they kept the smoke from rising too high. After a warm dinner, they curled up to sleep.

Daniel took the first watch and, not long after he took his position by the fire, Emer went and spoke to him before slipping into the forest; no doubt to check they were safe.

Aliah could not settle that night again, fitfully dozing off and on. Not sure whether she was dreaming or not, a grey wolf wandered in and out of her vision. Finally she drifted off, and next thing she knew Emer was shaking her shoulder, telling her she needed to be up and on the move when the sun rose.

Their pace was brisk, but a little slower that day. As they walked, Walter took the time to train Seamus, explaining to him the steps he went through when erasing their path. He had Seamus practice by moving branches and debris on the forest floor. Aliah could see the concentration it took for her friend to move a branch out of some-one's way and hold it there. When the strain got too much, the magic disappeared. At one stage, the branch swung back and hit Liam squarely in the face. He swore Seamus did it on purpose, in a good natured way that showed he was trying to make light of the whole thing.

Seamus dropped to the back behind the group, clearly upset Liam would suggest he had done such a thing on purpose. Appar-ently lessons were over for the day. It seemed Seamus did not have much of a sense of humour when it came to his magic.

While they were walking, Walter occasionally left Amelia's side and dropped a little behind to try and sense how close the people following them were. On one of these occasions, Daniel took his place beside Amelia. They were deep in conversation for a short while. It appeared to be something serious, but when Daniel rejoined her, he would not tell her anything. Frowning, Aliah decided to ask Amelia when she had a chance.

All was quiet until part-way through the afternoon when they were walking through a clearing in the woods and were suddenly surrounded by a group of men armed with spears and dressed in the colours of the forest. They had blended in so well, no one had known they were there until they suddenly appeared.

Stomach clenched in fear, Aliah joined her friends in a defensive circle, adrenaline pumping through her as she prepared to fight the pursuers who had finally caught them up. Looking around, she noticed Emer had remained where she stopped, clearly amused.

'Stand down,' she said in her lilting accent. 'They are our guides, not our enemies.'

'If they are friendly why did they appear like that? Why not announce their presence in a non-threatening way?' From the looks on her friends' faces, Aliah surmised she was not the only one annoyed by the way their guides had behaved.

Emer turned to a man who stood back a little from the main circle of warriors. 'I thought we planned for you to meet us at the boundary Eon. If you had stuck to the plan you would not have frightened our guests and nearly caused bloodshed.'

The elder man stepped forward. If Aliah had to describe him, she would have said he reminded her of a rat who had sucked a lemon. He was thin and balding, with wispy grey hair and grey eyes, and he had the air of a man who had been constantly disappointed in life.

'You are late. We came to see what happened to you,' he said in a petulant voice, indicating he did not like being challenged by Emer.

'We were followed so we could not take the main path. We have been avoiding pursuit for the last two days, which has put everyone on edge,' Emer responded. 'We still would have made it to the meeting place in good time. You had no need to change the plan.'

'There is not as much time as you think. The full moon is tomorrow and we must have time to vet and prepare the initiates. Your delay means we must rush.' Eon dismissed Emer's words and motioned for them all to leave.

Before she left, Emer turned to two of the men accompanying Eon. 'There are strangers in our forests. Make sure they do not find our home,' she ordered them, before following after Eon.

Aliah moved so she could join Amelia on this stretch of the journey, fully intending to ask her about Daniel. Forced into a jog to keep up with their guides, she did not get a chance, however. Finding it difficult to maintain the pace, she worried about Amelia.

When asked how she was doing, Amelia responded, 'I know how to feed my body additional energy to ease the aches and pains. Besides, I do not think we will be travelling much longer. Someone in the group we met has the ability to fold the trail.'

'Fold the trail?' Aliah was confused.

'Yes,' Amelia responded. 'It is a specific form of earth magic that shortens the distance you are travelling. The path we follow is flat, but if I use my magic I can see in between each step I take, the ground is raised a little, so the distance each step covers is almost doubled. They must be strong in magic to be able to fold the trail for this many people for this length of time.'

No matter how hard Aliah concentrated, she could not see the ground folding under her feet. She could tell landmarks they passed became distant more quickly than their slow jog would suggest, but if she tried too hard to see how it was done, she became dizzy.

Finally their guides halted and while they were all taking some refreshments, Aliah remembered she meant to talk to Amelia about Daniel.

'Amelia, what were you and Daniel talking about earlier?' she asked discreetly.

Amelia fixed her with a hard stare, then frowned. 'That is something for Daniel to tell, or not, as he chooses.' The older woman abruptly left to refill her water cup, leaving Aliah feeling she had just been told off.

When rest time was over, Emer approached them with some strips of cloth. 'From here, we need you to be blind-folded,' Emer explained. 'None but the initiated may see the pathway into the Sanctuary.'

When no one moved she said, 'Do not fear. You are under the protection of the Great Seer. No harm will come to you. These men will lead you and protect you with their lives.' She signalled to the men, and each of them stood in front of one of the group of Arians, ready with blindfolds.

Although she did not entirely trust these men, especially the one called Eon, and she was concerned about what needed to happen with the full moon, Aliah nodded her head and allowed them all to have their eyes covered.

It was truly disorienting not being able to see where she was going. Her guide did a good job of stopping her from stumbling while allowing them to keep their fast pace. After what seemed like an age, but was probably less than a candle-mark, the group stopped and were told they could take off their blindfolds.

Aliah stood at the edge of the forest, in a clearing in front of a rock face. Carved into the cliff were magnificent dwellings, some of which had openings two or more stories high. The rock face curved to either side of them, meeting with the edges of the forest. The number of entrances to dwellings made her head spin. The carvings around the entrances were even more astonishing, and she realised the work could only have been carried out by magic. The Sanctuary was an amazing city carved into a mountain.

Standing open-mouthed, Aliah slowly pulled her gaze from the marvel in front of her. When she did, she was relieved to find the rest of her group were in much the same state of awe. It seemed none of them had ever seen anything like this rock city before either. It was a magnificent sight in the light of the setting sun.

DIRECTLY IN FRONT of them stood a large opening with ornate pillars on either side. A group of men dressed in the same manner as the men who had led them through the forest were exiting from the opening, their leader an elderly man leaning on a staff. He had the most piercing blue eyes Aliah had ever seen—or perhaps they only appeared that way because his beard and shoulder length hair were snow white. He seemed to be looking right at her except, she thought for a moment, he could not be as he was walking like someone who had lost their sight. When he was right in front of them, he stopped and inclined his head to one side. As he did, she was able to confirm the man was in fact blind.

'Welcome to the Sanctuary.' He smiled with a warmth that softened his eyes. 'I am Caraig, sometimes called the Great Seer, but you may call me Caraig. I know who you all are, but for the sake of formalities, would you like to introduce your group?'

Aliah called each of them forward one by one, and Caraig formally welcomed them all.

'You must be tired after your journey. Emer will take you to the guest quarters so you may refresh yourselves, and I will visit with you soon.'

Aliah looked at the others, and they all seemed as bewildered as her. They had rushed here because of some supposed deadline and now were being sent to rest. It was all very odd.

'This way.' Emer turned.

They were so used to following their guide's directions they immediately fell in behind her, walking towards an opening on the left side of the cliff. They entered a doorway into what initially appeared to be a natural cave with a high roof, except the roof was smooth. There were no marks of the rock being formed naturally, or even chiselled out. Clearly a communal area with doors leading off it, the room contained tables and chairs arranged around a blazing fire, which made the room glow with a welcoming light.

'Each guest room will sleep three people, and in there is an ablution pool.' Emer pointed to the door on the far right. 'Someone is bringing refreshments, and Caraig will be here soon.' Her mission completed, she slipped out the door without another word.

'I get the feeling she does not like us much,' Amelia said.

Secretly thinking Emer's face was usually unreadable so it was actually hard to tell what she was thinking, Aliah said nothing, instead she diverted Amelia by asking, 'Shall we take the room on the end? If we hurry, we should have time for a quick clean before Caraig arrives.'

She could not wait to get out of her salt-laden clothes and wash her hair. At least then she might feel up to dealing with this rather strange place and its even stranger people.

Not waiting to see what arrangements the boys made, they opened the door to their room. There were brightly woven woollen rugs on the floor and walls, which helped soften the fact they were essentially in a cave. Gas lamps on a table between the beds had been lit to provide a warm light.

Aliah sank onto one of the beds, surprised to find it was lovely and soft. Covered in a warm, snug, brightly woven woollen blanket, it was almost irresistible. Fighting the temptation to curl up and sleep, she decided after two days in the same clothes and a dip in salt water, the need to be clean outweighed the need for sleep.

After unpacking a change of clothes, she and Amelia went next door to see what the bathing arrangements were like. They were pleasantly surprised to find a deep natural pool in the room beside them. Aliah put a hand in the water, sighing as its warmth spread up her arm. There were toiletries and towels in a basket by the door. She and Amelia wasted no time in shedding their clothes and submerging themselves in the water. Both of them could have stayed there all evening, soaking away their aches and pains, but they were aware others needed the room. Quickly they dried and dressed, then searched around to see how they emptied the pool. It was Amelia who eventually found two trap doors. One emptied the pool, and the other refilled it.

'I really want this system installed in the palace,' Aliah told Amelia.

'I am afraid this all relies on a natural spring.' Amelia smiled. 'Quite a smart design really, but it cannot be transported elsewhere.'

The main cave was empty when they left the bathing room, so they returned to their bedroom and stowed their belongings in the trunks provided. After plaiting each other's hair to keep it out of the way while it dried, they returned to the communal area to await Caraig. Walter, freshly washed and dressed, sat in the chair closest to the fire. In front of him stood a tray with a steaming pot full of some strange liquid. Aliah smelled it. It was not like any tea she had ever had, but it did smell a little like the coffee drink favoured by people around Duncameron.

'They call it caffe,' Walter said. 'It is like our coffee, only stronger. The woman who brought it suggested we might like to put a stick of sugar cane in it. If you do that, it is quite refreshing, if a little strong.'

Aliah fixed herself and Amelia a cup, smiling at the noise coming from the bathing area. Clearly someone was enjoying themselves in there. She was sipping her caffe and enjoying the unusual flavour when Liam and Seamus emerged from the room on the far right. So Dominic and Daniel were the ones making the ruckus in the bathing area. The five of them were happily drinking their cups of caffe when Caraig entered a few moments later, followed by Eon and Emer.

'I am sorry to barge in so quickly,' Caraig apologised. 'It is our custom to let guests bathe and have refreshments before any formal meetings occur. In this instance though, we have met the spirit of the tradition, if not the substance, and for that I apologise.'

Aliah found it disconcerting the way the seer stared directly at the people he spoke to, even when they had not spoken first, as if the sightless man could somehow see them. As she watched Caraig speak, she attempted to determine his age. His white hair made him appear ancient, as did his reliance on his staff to move around, but on closer inspection she decided he must only be in his sixth decade. Realising she was staring, Aliah averted her eyes as the seer finished speaking.

'It is getting late in the day and we have so very little time to get everything done.'

'Everyone keeps saying we have very little time, but no one has explained why timing is so important.' Seamus frowned. 'In fact, no one has explained anything much at all.' Aliah could not have said it better herself.

'Please accept my apologies again.' Caraig took the seat Eon had dragged over for him, before taking his place with Emer behind the seer. 'I forget you have not grown up with the prophecy and its traditions as we have, but we must wait a moment before continuing as you are not all here.'

At that very moment, the door to the bathing room opened and Dominic led Daniel out. Seeing they had company, they dropped their dirty clothes back on the floor, shut the door, and went to stand guard behind Aliah's seat.

'I shall begin. Please enjoy your caffe while I speak. It has great ability to keep a person awake.' Caraig spoke their language in the same sing-song tones as Emer, and Aliah found it quite pleasant to sit back and listen to the elderly man.

'You know we believe that The Heir of Hand is the wizard of a great prophecy, and that the Heir of Aria is the warrior. How did we arrive at that conclusion? Where do I start?' He paused, and it was hard to tell whether it was to think or for dramatic effect. 'All seers are able to see the future. Sometimes it is minor things such as a queen will have a daughter. These minor prophecies occur frequently, and are quite specific. Many people have the gift of this type of seeing.

'Every now and then, gifted seers will be able to see into the distant future and get a sense of crucial turning points in history. They see possible futures and the events that might affect the outcome. These prophecies are called Great Prophecies, and they are of such great importance they are recorded, studied, and passed down through history. Sometimes others seers add to them. Sometimes, even after many generations, they still remain unclear.

'Hundreds and hundreds of years ago, seers banded together to codify the Great Prophecies and to monitor their progress. The prophecy of the Wizard and the Warrior is one of the Great Prophecies. In fact, it may be the most important prophecy as we believe the futures of not just Aria and Maloria hinge on its outcome, but the future of all the known lands in our part of the world.'

'Because of this, we have done a lot of research and know a considerable amount about this particular prophecy. Our studies have led us to believe certain ceremonies must be completed before we are able to confirm the prophecy is active.'

'This all sounds a little airy-fairy to me,' Daniel interrupted. 'A group of people have seen into the future and have prepared themselves for something to happen sometime, yet there is a ceremony that must be followed exactly?' He raised an eyebrow.

'I agree completely.' Caraig smiled. 'It sounds like something someone would make up for a bit of a joke. But I can assure you, this is most serious. I have been watching events unfold, and I am sure we are now in the time of that Great Prophecy. There is more I could tell you about why things must be done in a particular order, however, until the Wizard and the Warrior have met the Prophecy Council and been approved, I have promised I will say no more than I have here.'

'All right,' Seamus pondered. 'Let us assume we believe all of this, what would happen now?'

Caraig turned to Seamus. Although he clearly could not see, it was as though he looked Seamus directly in the eye. 'You and Princess Aliahanna will meet the council this evening. You will answer some questions, and they will decide if we proceed.'

'Sounds simple enough.' Seamus checked with Aliah, who bowed her head in agreement.

'They go alone?' Dominic stiffened. 'You want us to let the heirs of two of Aria's most important families go somewhere and meet with unknown people without protection?'

Caraig laughed, and Dominic stiffened even more. 'They have nothing to fear from us. We have been waiting to welcome them for many hundreds of years.'

'We only have your word for that,' Daniel said. 'And nice though you may seem, we have only just met you.'

Walter pulled his attention away from the book on his lap. 'If we have not come here for this, what have we come for? And if this is our reason for being here, we need to trust these people to see us through something they clearly understand more than we do.'

'That does not mean we should just blindly do everything that is asked of us,' Daniel persisted.

'I agree with Walter,' said Aliah, and Daniel scowled at her. 'If these people had meant us harm they have had opportunities aplenty to so. Goddess, they could even have left us behind for those men from the ship.'

'Let me cut this debate short,' Caraig said. 'We must go to the chamber now as timing is everything. How about if I leave you Emer and Eon as surety? If Seamus and Aliahanna do not return, their lives are forfeit to you. I do not do this lightly as Emer is my daughter and Eon is my oldest apprentice.'

Hiding her shock at finding their guide was the daughter of the seer, Aliah glanced from under lowered lids at the two people standing behind Caraig. Emer's face was as impassive as always, but Eon screwed his face up in disgust, turning red with anger.

'I should be there with you, master. After all, I have been working with you towards this moment for decades, and I am your second on the council,' he complained in his whiny, nasally voice.

'I am sure you agree after all our hard work the most important thing is to get these two in front of the Prophecy Council. And I am sure you would want to do everything in your power to see that happen.' Caraig did not look at Eon as he spoke, and he definitely could not see the man's scowl showing he still strongly disagreed, even though he had been outmanoeuvred.

'You have your hostages. They will stay here until Seamus and Aliahanna return safely.' Caraig took a breath to continue, but Daniel cut him short.

'I will be making sure of that.' Daniel glared at the two who would be in his charge for the foreseeable future.

'As it should be.' Caraig smiled benignly. 'The rest of you, please feel free to make yourself at home here. If you need anything, or want to go anywhere, just ask. Our people are friendly.'

'I will certainly be making use of that.' Aliah just caught the words Dominic said under his breath before she looked at Seamus. He nodded his agreement to leave, and they both stood. She dared not look behind her at Dominic and Daniel as they left the Sanctuary with Caraig leading the way, lest she see how truly annoyed they were.

CHAPTER 23
PROPHECY COUNCIL

F ollowing Caraig from the guest rooms through to the main cave was almost like being in a dream. The entrance on the inside was just as ornate as the one outside, framing a picture of the setting sun. There was a walkway running around each of the three stories, enabling access to the numerous doorways they could see.

Caraig explained each opening took you to an area called a commune, which usually housed an extended family from a number of generations. They would look similar to their guest commune, but the larger, main room would have also cooking facilities and a lounging area. Most families cooked and ate together, but had separate areas for sleeping and privacy. The rooms branching from the main area would often contain a single family and were large enough to be broken into smaller room using curtains.

Each door on the walkways led to a family commune that would extend back into the mountain. Caraig proudly informed them the Sanctuary was fully self-contained. With a surprising amount of natural light from the openings into the main courtyard area and the skylights, a person need never go outside.

Although they were called communes, to Seamus they were still caves. Very large caves, but still caves. He wondered if he might be claustrophobic, even though he had not been here for very long, he already found it difficult to breathe normally. His brain could not comprehend there was air enough for all who lived in this closed off cavern.

At last they came to a communal area very similar to the guest one. There was a seating area and behind the seats were five doors. Caraig motioned for them to sit. He walked over to one of the doors, then turned.

'I think I can tell you this much before you enter. The Prophecy Council is a subgroup of our main ruling council. It is made up of people who have a specific interest in prophecy. They are not as sure as I am about who you are, but I am sure we can convince them.' Turning back, he knocked firmly on the middle door. The door was opened from the inside and Caraig entered.

'Funny,' Aliah said. 'But I feel like I am about to sit one of the tests my tutors used to set for me so they could report progress to my father. My tummy is fluttery, and my palms are sweaty.'

'I do not think that is funny at all. I feel a little the same way, although I do not know why.' Seamus fidgeted in his seat, unable to get comfortable. 'Either we are the Wizard and Warrior, or we are not. There is little we can do to change that. Mind you, this does have all the elements of some sort of test.'

They sat in silence until the door opened and Caraig invited them to enter. Seamus took Aliah's hand, and for once she did not pull away from him and insist she could walk perfectly well by herself. It was as though she was agreeing with him that they would face this together.

The room they entered was twice the size of the area outside, but seemed smaller because most of the space was taken up by a large, round table, which was drenched in a flickering light from candles set into alcoves around the room, each about a hand span from its neighbour. Seated around the curve of the table facing them were two men who made Caraig look young, and a third, much younger man. Behind the two older men, stood two other men, around about the age of Seamus' parents.

Caraig walked around to take a vacant seat. When he was seated comfortably, the space behind his chair was conspicuously bare. Seamus wondered briefly if Eon was supposed to take that empty spot—if so, why Caraig had been so quick to leave his assistant behind? Before he had time to mull that question over, the man beside Caraig spoke.

'I welcome you to Maloria, and to the Sanctuary. Let me introduce you to our Prophecy Council. You know Caraig.' He gestured to his left, then turned to his right. 'Mikel is our representative from the Writer's Guild.' He indicated the man to his right who had no one standing behind his chair. 'He sits for Brianna. She is ill and unable to attend today. Beside him is Angus, Head of our Guild of Scholars.' The last man smiled mischievously as he was introduced. Seamus liked him immediately. 'I am Vira, and I sit as the peoples' elected representative. The others are seconds, and will only be a part of the proceedings should something happen to one of us. And you are Lord Seamus and Princess Aliahanna.'

'We are happy to be called Seamus and Aliah,' Aliah informed them.

Acknowledging this concession, Vira continued, 'I believe it is your wish to be tested as the Wizard and the Warrior from the End of Days prophecy.' He gazed expectantly at them.

Seamus glanced at Aliah, hoping she would take the reins and answer. Aliah merely shrugged her shoulders and his stomach sank as he realised she was leaving it up to him.

'We were asked to come here as potential candidates. It would be a stretch to say we believe ourselves to be the Wizard and the Warrior. In fact, I would say it was quite the opposite.' Out of the corner of his eye he glimpsed Aliah nodding her head in agreement as she gently squeezed his hand.

Angus grinned at Seamus. 'The prophecy states the true Wizard and Warrior will not believe they are the ones until after they pass the test.'

'Well, that is just stupid,' Aliah spluttered. 'Who would actually believe themselves to be a part of a prophecy? Certainly not someone you would want to be your hero in a crisis. So anyone and everyone coming here to be considered for the roles would feel the same way.'

'I like her,' Angus told the group, and he actually winked at Caraig. 'She is feisty.'

Aliah squeezed Seamus' hand even harder, he assumed in an effort to control any further outbursts at the councillor's comments.

'So,' the council leader continued. 'You do not ask for this, but it is asked of you. Why did you come?'

Aliah nodded for Seamus to continue. *She probably did not want to risk saying what is on her mind after that outburst,* he thought briefly, before responding. 'Firstly, to be honest, for the warriors you promised to Hand in the war against Carsten.

'Secondly, because from what we understand of the prophecy, these two will save Aria from disaster, and if there is even the slightest chance it may be true, we owe it to our people to do what we can to identify them and help win this war.'

Seamus could tell nothing from the faces in front of him. Caraig dropped his head to one side as if in thought, but the other three men were looking intently at them and not saying anything. It was unsettling.

Finally, the man who had so far been silent, Mikel, turned to Caraig. 'It could be a deep sense of duty, or it could be seen as self-interest.' Was all he said.

'Or it could be both,' Aliah's fan Angus interjected.

'I fail to see how you could think it was in *our* interests to traipse through forests to the middle of nowhere on a slim chance we could help our people in the upcoming war.' Aliah forced out through gritted teeth. Angus seemed to be needling her in a way that made her lose her self-control. Wondering if this was deliberate, Seamus tried not to get lost in his thoughts as he needed to concentrate on what was happening in the room.

'At the very least you show your knowledge of the prophecy to be limited,' the council leader said to Aliah. 'The End of Days Prophecy is not about Aria, it is about the known world and the future of all who live here. If the conditions of the prophecy are not met, then all that we know will be destroyed, and humankind will be sunk into misery and despair'

'Well, that all sounds very dramatic,' Aliah said scathingly. 'How exactly is that supposed to happen?'

'If I may?' Caraig asked the leader, who nodded. 'The prophecy recounted in Arian histories is part of a larger prophecy that has built up over a number of years. The first part tells of the fall of the Talagran nation due to the unrestricted use of battle magic. They call that the decimation. This already came to pass when the Malorian nation formed. The second part tells of the loss of battle magic, and the spread of the Northerners. We believe that refers to the Natari invasion of what is now Aria.

'The final phase of the prophecy, and the least clear section, tells of the rise of a great evil and what will be required to stop it.'

'May we see the full prophecy?' Seamus asked, interested to see how it differed from what they had read.

'You may, but not until you have been confirmed as the wizard. One of the requirements I spoke of is the Wizard and Warrior cannot know the full prophecy until they have undergone their testing,' Caraig informed them.

'Does it actually say that in the prophecy?' Aliah queried.

'No,' Caraig admitted. 'But in my younger years I had a true seeing from the gods. It told me the Wizard and Warrior will arrive not knowing who they are, but will have a deep sense of duty. The seeing said the council will know them for who they are and will send them to the cave of trials where the gods will test them. I had this seeing because the time of the Great Prophecy was drawing close, and we needed to know how to identify those who could save the world.'

'I am not so sure about the saving the world bit,' Aliah said. 'In fact, I am not sure I believe in the prophecy at all. But why not just take us to the cave of trials and get this over and done with?'

Seamus could not have agreed more.

'She truly is feisty, but my dear you should err on the side of caution a little more.' Aliah's fan smiled at the other council members. 'We are not just old men trying to feel important by deciding whether or not you should go to trial, we are looking out for you. For Caraig's true seeing told him anyone who attempted these particular trials and failed, would not likely return from the caves.'

Again, Aliah's grip on Seamus' arm tightened, almost unbearably. Wanting to calm the situation down a little he asked, 'Why was there such a rush to get us here?'

'Before entering the trial caves, all candidates must spend the night before in prayer and contemplation to rid the mind of all but the coming ordeal. As all but special trials are traditionally held on the day of a full moon, which is tomorrow, the reflection period needs to occur tonight. If we miss this, we would have to wait another moon turn before we could test you. By then, the Carsten invasion would be well and truly over and we may have missed the opportunity to fight off a great evil.'

'But you said this is about more than the Carsten invasion.' By the tone of her voice, Seamus could sense Aliah becoming more frustrated.

'It is, and it is not,' Caraig said.

'Let me guess, you cannot tell us until we have passed the trial?' Seamus asked dryly.

'No, we can tell you this now.' Clearly the council had no sense of humour as they did not even smile at Seamus' attempt at a joke. 'The Carsten invasion is not the great evil, but from what our seers tell us, the great evil is driving it. The people of Carsten have already been infected, and they will spread that evil should they succeed in invading Aria.'

'What do you mean "infected"? And what is the great evil?' Now it was Seamus' turn to be annoyed. He did not want to be a part of a prophecy if it meant everything was so vague.

'I do not mean infected like an illness,' the council leader told them. 'I mean the people of Carsten have changed over recent years. The country has become focused on war, and has conquered all the neighbouring lands. Then instead of concentrating on building a more prosperous, united country by repairing the damage after years of war, it is as though war has become an end in itself.

The people live in poverty, barely able to feed themselves. The weak and the sick are left at home, and everyone else is conscripted into the army. There is no one to till the fields, or tend the orchards, or to take out the fishing boats. This is what we fear will happen to Aria and Maloria should their invasion be successful.'

'So it is merely that the leaders want to continue with war.' Relief washed through Seamus. He had imagined they would have to face something far more scary than a king bent on conquering. Human leaders could be defeated in battle. Destroy the leaders, the war goes away.

'You could say that,' Caraig responded. 'Except, as best we can tell, one of the minor gods somehow has control of one or many of the leaders of Carsten.'

'So we merely kill those leaders?' Seamus asked hopefully.

'If only it were that easy.' Angus grinned wickedly. 'The god would merely seek to control the next leader in line.'

'And to make it worse, we also believe the god may be working in concert with, or have control of, some people high up in Aria. Maybe even magic users,' Vira, the council leader added.

'The Wizard Council,' Seamus and Aliah said together. Pieces fell into place to make some sort of confusing sense. Although Seamus had no idea how they would fight a god, he could glimpse the bigger picture, and this gave him some reassurance.

'So, in your opinion, are we the Wizard and Warrior?' How like Aliah cut straight to the heart of the matter.

'The fact is,' the leader said, after looking around the table. 'We really cannot be sure. We think there is a good chance you might be, we even *hope* you might be, but we could not say that definitely you are.'

'So where does that leave us?' Seamus asked them, confused again.

'If I may?' Caraig asked for permission to speak. 'It may be that this is exactly what is supposed to happen. You are ideal candidates, and you are the most likely we can find. But maybe you do not need to believe you are likely to be those spoken of in the prophecy before you enter the trials. Maybe the test will reveal to you personally, whether or not you are the Wizard and the Warrior.'

Seamus turned to look directly at Aliah. 'What do you think?' he asked. 'This is no longer the simple test we thought it would be when we left Hand. Now we are told we might not actually leave the trial if we are found not to be the Wizard and Warrior.'

'I do not know...' she started to say more, then paused. 'You?'

'I find all this prophecy stuff a bit like air. It seems to be all around us, but I cannot really see it clearly.'

Aliah closed her eyes as she considered what he had said.

'In saying that,' he continued. 'You could look back over the last few moon-turns and see a lot of things have conspired to get us to this particular point together. Two people, who otherwise would not have met. It is just as likely I am the wizard as I am not.'

'But would you bet your life on it?' Aliah asked him, frowning as she tucked a stray strand of hair back behind her ear.

Seamus chewed his lip and frowned. 'If I think rationally, no. But something in my gut is telling me I have to do this, even though I am scared,' he admitted, surprised at how openly he shared his thoughts in front of total strangers.

'Funny. Me too.' Aliah frowned. 'I need to know one way or another.'

They turned back to the four men around the table. 'We will take the test,' they said together.

'Tests,' Caraig corrected them. 'You will both be tested individually.'

Seamus shook his head, of course it would not be that easy.

'Are you sure you want to do this?' the council leader asked them again.

No, not really, and especially not alone, he thought. Out loud, Seamus found himself saying, 'Yes.'

Aliah twirled her plait thoughtfully, and had not yet answered. *Oh no, please do not pull out now.*, Seamus worried.

'We will do these tests you talk of once you confirm your warriors are on their way to Hand.'

Confusion spread over the faces of the men in front of them. They had not expected this. 'I believe they are mustering already?' Caraig asked them.

'We will send someone to the guest commune tonight to liaise with your guards.' Vira confirmed.

'We will go ahead then.' Aliah let go of Seamus' hand, ready to leave.

***

ONCE THE DECISION had been made, a strange calm washed over Seamus. Which was odd for someone preparing for their potential demise, he admitted to himself. He could not really get his head around being the wizard, yet he did not really believe in his heart of hearts that he and Aliah would not come out of their individual trials alive either.

As he followed Caraig back to the guest commune so they could eat dinner with their companions, he likened his journey to the time he had been washed out of a boat caught in some rapids. While in the rapids, he could not control where he was pushed, he could only control how he reacted, and how he kept his head above water. He had to let go of his worries, and wait and see where their journey took him next.

Emer and a relieved Eon followed Caraig out, and soon after their departure, a sumptuous evening meal arrive. Seamus had never eaten anything as spicy as the meal they were presented with, and concentrated on the rich and varied taste of the food, rather than the various attempts to talk Aliah and him out of their decision.

Everyone seemed so worried about what would happen if they failed. How would they ever be able to tell Aliah's and Seamus' parents they had let them go to their deaths? But no one thought of what they might be able to achieve if they actually passed, Seamus mused as he tried a dish topped with some kind of nut he had never tasted before.

All the while Seamus felt as if he were enclosed in a bubble; a part of, but separate to everything happening around him. He was calm and centred in the midst of all their noise. He did not even bother defending his position, and he noticed Aliah did not speak either.

When the time came to leave for the contemplation rooms they were both hugged and cried over. Seamus did not know what to say, so said nothing at all. Caraig led them back to the commune outside the Council Chamber. After informing them all they needed for the night would be in their rooms, he bid them goodnight.

Seamus let go of Aliah's hand and she walked to her door, entering without turning around.

'Good night, see you in the morning,' Seamus said as she closed the door without looking back. Shrugging his shoulders, Seamus was saddened Aliah was so caught up in her own thoughts she had not even wished him a good night.

Taking one last look around the room, he thought he saw a flickering outside in the corridor. Shaking his head, he walked over to look out. Nothing there. *I must be dreaming.* He reached for the door to his room, entered, and closed it firmly behind.

The contemplation room was the most cave-like area he had been in so far. There had been nothing done to make it less like a cave at all. A single candle smelling of jasmine sent a flickering light around the walls. That, and a comfortable bed, completed the furnishing. Seamus lay down on the bed, and found his hand going to the chain he wore round his neck. His fingers worried the sign of the lady his sister had given him. It was hard to believe he might not ever see his family again after tomorrow. It was even harder to believe he was a person someone hundreds of years ago had written a prophecy about. He fully expected to spend a wakeful night worrying, but was asleep not long after his head touched the pillow.

CHAPTER 24
ALIAH'S QUEST

'Wake up.'

Aliah grunted. She had only just gone to sleep, why would she want to wake up now?

More shaking and a more insistent, 'Wake up, Aliah.'

Slowly she opened her eyes and Emer's face came into view. Sitting up, Aliah's gaze focused on the cup of steaming caffe the other girl had in her hand, and the change of clothes she laid out on the end of the bed.

'You may not eat before the trial, but many prefer to have some caffe before they enter the cave. Also, I brought you some leather trousers and waistcoat. In the caves you will need something a bit more sturdy than the fabric your clothes are made of. I will wait outside while you change.'

When she had gone to bed last night, Aliah had been strangely calm. She expected the nerves to come this morning though, especially with the possibility she might actually die during the trial. But the strange sense of peace and rightness from the previous night was still with her.

Slowly she changed her trousers and did the waistcoat up over her shirt, having first made sure the necklace Seamus had given her was safely tucked away. She plaited her hair and tied her boots securely. Finally, she placed her sword belt around her waist. After a few quick gulps of caffe, she had prepared as best she could for anything they might throw at her.

She emerged and Emer checked her over, shaking her head. 'I am sorry, but you cannot take any weapons of your own into the trial.'

Aliah did not move. 'You expect me to go into potential danger unarmed?'

Emer shrugged. 'Everything you need will be provided for you. It is the way. I am not sure why, but I believe it is some sign of trust. No matter the reason, you cannot take that in with you.'

Those few words were the most the other girl had ever said to Aliah outside of a command, making Aliah more inclined to listen, just this once. After placing her sword back in the contemplation room, she followed Emer out through the door.

'Where is Seamus?' She looked around quizzically.

'This is your trial,' Emer said as she led them from the commune.

'Oh,' she replied out loud. *But I did not even say goodnight to him, or wish him good luck for today,* she thought to herself, worried Seamus may think she did not care.

Although Emer led them through the main part of this strange city, hardly anyone was about so Aliah guessed it must have been early in the morning. Their route took them deeper into the mountain, through many large caverns with walkways running around them. Just when she thought they could not possibly go any further, Aliah glimpsed a pinprick of light in the distance. Growing larger as they walked, she saw the source was sunlight shining through another entrance to the Malorian Sanctuary.

'Why is this place called the Sanctuary?' Aliah asked Emer as they emerged into the sunlight.

'Because when the magic wars were being fought, many Talagrians came here to get away from the carnage. After the fighting finished, we made contact with the Malorians, joining to become one nation. This place became a centre of learning and retreat for the new Malorian nation. However, we still call it *Sanctuary* in recognition of its past role as a shelter from the war.' Aliah marvelled how in Emer's natural habitat, she did not seem nearly as forbidding as she had on the journey there.

The doorway they had come through opened into a natural amphitheatre. *This place is easy to defend as it would be hard to enter from the back. I can see why people escaping the war chose to stay here,* Aliah thought as she looked around.

Caraig waited for her in the shade nearby. He carried a knife, and a water bag slung over his back, both of which he handed to her as soon as she came alongside him. She settled them on her person as Caraig gave her instructions for her trial.

'The rules are strict and have been passed down over hundreds of years. This is all you may take in with you.'

'How long will it take?' Aliah asked him.

'Each trial is different. It depends on the person, what they are questing for, and how the gods decide to test them. However, each quest must be completed within twelve candle-marks. A bell will sound at six candle-marks, then at nine candle-marks and then at every candle-mark after that. At the last bell of the twelfth candle-mark the cave will be closed off and will not open again until the full moon, when we can hold other trials. That is all I am allowed to tell you. There are three caves. You choose one and enter. I will wait here for your return.'

'Why did Seamus not start his trial with me?' Aliah asked Caraig.

'This is your quest. He has his own. Which cave?'

'Has his quest started?'

Caraig shook his head. 'You have been told all I am permitted to tell you. Each person is to have their own quest. Concentrate on yours.'

Realising she would get no more information from Caraig, she turned her attention to the three cave entrances directly opposite where they stood. How to choose? Did it matter? She brushed a strand of hair behind her ear and stilled her mind. This was a quest of the heart for her and so the heart side it must be. 'The cave on the left,' she told Caraig.

He led her to the cave entrance. She checked the knife was securely tucked into the belt at her side, and that the water bag would not slip from her back. With a deep breath, she entered the cave.

'Goddess be with you.' The blessing came from behind as the darkness engulfed her.

AFTER THE BRIGHTNESS OUTSIDE, it took a moment for her eyes to adjust to the lack of light. The narrow entrance way meant she had no option but to go straight ahead. Her path started sloping upwards, and very soon came to an abrupt end. In front of her was a sheer rock-face. Her only choices were to go back or climb.

Fortunately some natural light came from somewhere above, helping her make out hand and foot holds in the rock face. The climb did not look too difficult. Although there were plenty of places for her hands, nerves caused them to shake. She was physically fit, but climbing was not something she had ever been good at.

Beginning her assent, it seemed only moments later her arms and legs started cramping. As she climbed, she glanced up, then down. *Not even half way up,* she thought wearily. At that stage, she was high enough that a fall to the ground would badly injure her. A little higher, and it could result in death. She searched and found a ledge where she could sit and drink some water, allowing her weary limbs to rest.

After too short a time, she started off again. The actual climb was no harder this high up, but her arms and legs were already tired, so she moved much more slowly. The cramps in her arms started again, and a strand of hair kept falling in her eyes, no matter how often she shook it out. As the sweat slithered down her back, her legs began to shake. As she wiped the sweat of her brow with her arm, she searched for another ledge to rest upon.

There was nothing close, so she forced her protesting limbs to carry on until she found a small crevice where she could wedge herself and look for the best place to rest. There, just to the right, was a a small ridge jutting out from the rock face. One last push and she reached the small shelf. As Aliah flopped down her arms and legs were shaking, relief flooded through her as she thought how close she had been to falling to the ground.

Taking a sip of water, she glanced down. The ledge where she sat was higher than the highest tower in her father's castle. If she fell from there, she would not survive. Exhausted, she could not believe she still had a quarter of the climb to go. Closing her eyes, she contemplated the enormity of what she had left to do. Her ears picked up a rustling sound and her eyes flew open as the sound grew louder.

As her eyes adjusted, she spied a colony of bats heading straight for her. Angry at having their territory invaded they swooped, trying to knock her off her perch. While swinging her knife in front, she slowly stood up, and shuffled until the rock face pressed into her back. There was less chance of falling from this position, but the knife was not very effective against so many bats determined to see her out of their cave. They left her covered in cuts and scratches. She could not go on like this. Something had to change, and soon.

Quickly, she grabbed the water skin off her back and, holding it by the strap, she swung it around. The water bag cut through the swarm of bats, knocking many of their number to the ground. Another sweep and more bats fell to their doom. At first this made the bats attack harder, but they were quickly becoming fewer in number, so she kept it up. Suddenly, as one, they realised the cost of this battle was too high and flew away in a squawking flurry.

Aliah's body shook with exhaustion, but if she sat now, she

would not have the energy to get back up. Taking a quick drink of water, she cleaned her wounds as best she could, slung her water skin over her back, and started on the final ascent. Using the adrenaline produced during the fight, and before her body could protest that it could go no further, she started climbing, determined to reach the top before the bats regrouped.

That last quarter of the climb took her twice as long as the rest put together. Tiredness caused her to loose her footing a couple of times, but fortunately she managed to keep a hold, and quickly found new places for her feet.

At long last, she pulled her weary body over the edge and flopped flat on the cold ground. For a moment, she stayed on her back, panting and staring up at the light coming through the roof of the cavern, enjoying the feel of the cool earth on her tired muscles. A bell tolled six. It had taken her half her allotted time just to climb up here. Forcing herself to sit up as her stomach clenched in worry, as this was unlikely to be the sum total of her quest.

Aliah looked around. At the far end of the cave stood an altar, and on that alter sat a sword. Something in her gut told her to complete the quest she needed to take possession of that sword. Taking a deep breath, she tensed to stand. Before Aliah could move though, a low growl rumbled from the shadows, close enough for it to vibrate through her body. Moments later a mountain lion stalked into view. Crouching low, the lion slunk towards her.

Great, I only have a knife. If only the sword was not over the other side of the room.

As the lion approached, she slowly shuffled backwards on her bottom. Her hand knocked against something... something wooden. She did not know how big the object was, but it was all she had. She stopped moving and so did the lion. It tensed, ready to pounce.

The lion's muscles released and it flew through the air towards her. Aliah rolled to the left, away from the edge of the cliff face and, picking up the wooden object with her right hand, rolled onto her knees. With all her might, she swung whatever was in her hand at the lion's head. It fell to the ground, stunned, and shook its head groggily. It started to rise, but before it could recover and attack again, Aliah stood on shaky legs and ran at the lion, took a swing with her leg, and kicked it over the cliff. A twang shot through her thigh and Aliah dropped to her knees, heart racing. That was all she needed, a pulled muscle. Still, she was alive, and that was all that mattered.

Slowly standing, she bent over, hands on knees, and gulped in lungs-full of air, trying to calm her nerves. Her body trembled with fatigue, but her mind was alert to what might advance from the shadows to stop her from achieving her goal.

Surveying the altar, she searched for any obvious traps to prevent her from taking the sword. It sat on a wooden pedestal with nothing apparently securing it there. That meant the threat would come from somewhere else.

Warily, she crept forward. As she did, the darkness at the back of the altar began to shimmer, and a serpent larger than any she had seen before slithered out from behind.

'Nooo...' She groaned. 'It is not fair. I have nothing left. I cannot fight you.'

To her surprise, the serpent responded. 'Life is not fair. It sometimes asks more of us than we think we can give. But if something is worthwhile, the truly worthy will find they have a little more inside, if they just dig deep.'

The serpent reared up, standing a head taller than Aliah. 'You can end your quest here and the world will face its threat without the Wizard and the Warrior. Or you can find a way to defeat me.'

Once again, Aliah gulped in great lungs-full of air, while searching around for any way to evade or defeat the serpent. Whatever she did, it needed to be done quickly. Not only because time was running out, but also because she did not have the energy for a prolonged fight. She stared the serpent in the eyes and then, without giving anything away, she formulated a plan.

Drawing her knife, she moved to the left of the serpent, away from the altar. Slithering, with its head raised, the serpent followed her, slowly closing the distance between them. Aliah kept moving steadily to the left. As it moved, the serpent lowered its head due to the slope of the cavern ceiling. When Aliah finally reached the wall on the left hand side, about half-way between the altar and the ledge, her adversary's head was level with hers and she could almost see it smile, believing it had her trapped.

Now. Aliah moved as if she was rushing forward and the serpent rose to strike, hitting its head on the ceiling. At that exact moment, Aliah hit the ground in a roll to the left, landing on her feet. Still, the serpent only missed her by a hair's breadth. As the serpent rose ready to strike again, Aliah ran to the altar, grabbed the sword, and swung as her enemy struck. Ducking back just in time, the serpent surveyed her with dark eyes.

Although backing away, the serpent blocked her exit down the cliff. However, Aliah had gained a surprising new advantage. As she gripped the sword in both hands her fatigue disappeared. In addition, she could clearly see the serpent's moves, anticipating them, almost as though she read its mind. No, it was more like she was seeing moments into the future, which allowed her to assess what the serpent would do.

While she got used to this new insight, she practiced moving the serpent around, all the while looking for another exit. The serpent and the lion must have come from somewhere. Moving behind the back of the altar, she could not find where they had entered the cave. She checked the whole cavern and found the only way out for her was the way she had come in.

Sighing with fatigue, a plan began forming in her head, to kill the serpent so she could begin her descent. As she moved into position to strike, her newfound skill showed her that to complete this trial she did not need to kill her enemy, just get away without getting hurt. Changing her tactics, she began moving towards a place where she could easily start her descent.

Almost as soon as she made her decision, the serpent changed its form. The scales melted away, revealing a rather tall, see-through woman. Aliah would not have described her as beautiful, her face and bearing were too haughty for that. But she was certainly striking, and it hurt to look too closely at her. Tensing, Aliah began to reassess the situation. Would she now have to fight this woman?

'Stand down, princess, you are in no danger from me.'

Unable to fully believe that, Aliah stayed tense, ready to strike if need be.

'It takes a special kind of warrior to choose not to kill, even when it may be the easiest course to take. You have shown you have the courage, the ingenuity, and the pure heart required of the warrior. You have passed your trial.'

Aliah let out a sigh of relief, but the woman held up her hand. 'This trial will seem as nothing when you face the truly great evil that walks the world. Though you have little time, you need to learn to master your sword and to work hand in hand with the wizard. You also need to understand that although the wizard may strike the final blow, he cannot defeat your enemy without the warrior.'

'How do I master the sword? What can it do?' Aliah asked.

'That is for you to learn yourself. Go now! Your quest is nearly over, but you must hurry or you will be trapped by the closing door and all your good work will have been for nothing.' With that, she disappeared as the ninth bell chimed.

Aliah put the sword down the back of her shirt, muttering under her breath some words no royal child should know. As she lost direct contact with the sword, her renewed energy left her. She cursed again. There was no way she could climb down while holding the sword, she would just have to do the best she could without its help.

Knowing she only had three candle-marks to get back to the cave entrance, she quickly lowered herself over the ledge and reached for footholds. Descending as fast as she could, she did not even stop for water, though her mouth was dry and her lips cracked. The tenth bell tolled and she still could not clearly see the bottom. The eleventh bell chimed, just as she lost her footing again in her exhaustion.

About three body lengths from the bottom, the first of the twelfth bells filled the cave. Turning around, she slid all the way to the end and started running to the opening. Ten paces. Five. Two paces from the opening the twelfth bell finished tolling and the door began to slide shut. Launching herself towards the door, her hands grasped at the edge of the rock as it slid shut to no effect.

Pounding the rock in frustration, Aliah collapsed on the floor. Lying on her back panting, she stared into the blackness. Her head spun as her hand reached to the neck of her shirt to grab the necklace Seamus had given her. *I am sorry, Seamus, I let you down.* A tear slipped from her eye, and she imagined she saw Dominic's face just before she lost consciousness.

CHAPTER 25
SEAMUS' QUEST

Seamus was riding through the woods in Hand, heading towards the high plateau. He could hear nothing but the sound of his horse crashing through the undergrowth. This was his favourite place in the world, and he was more relaxed than he had been in a long time.

'Seamus. Seamus!'

Who would be calling him this far from the palace? He ignored the voice and carried on riding.

'SEAMUS.'

He was roughly shaken and his perfect morning slipped away. Back in the cave he had fallen asleep in, Emer stood over him with a cup of caffe in her hand.

'Glad you decided to join us.' She looked down at him. 'Here, drink this and dress in the clothes I brought you.' She indicated some clothes she had draped over the end of the bed. 'I will meet you outside when you are done.'

He dressed quickly in the leather trousers and vest Emer had provided, all the while taking sips of his caffe. He was a little hungry, but his stomach churned so much he could not eat a bite, which turned out to be a good thing as when he emerged from his room, Emer informed him he was not allowed to eat anything before the trial.

'Are you ready then?' she asked. He shrugged his shoulders, nodding. She turned and led the way out of the council commune.

'What about Aliah? Is she not coming with us?'

'This is your quest,' was Emer's response, and Seamus looked closely at the girl who had been their guide. Although her face was normally inscrutable, he imagined a touch of sadness there.

Seamus' stomach shrunk even more. For some reason, he had thought although they had separate trials, he and Aliah would at least set out together. Alone, without Aliah, his confidence was deserting him. As if sensing his sadness, Emer touched his arm, gently leading him through the door.

Following Emer through the tunnels further into the Sanctuary he took note of the people moving about. Most ignored them as they went about their daily business, some greeted Emer, and a few stood and watched as they passed. It was strange to see people doing the ordinary things people did in any town, but underground. It was not dark and cavelike exactly, as natural light was flooding in from some where, it was just that it seemed so... well... confined.

'Does living inside a mountain not bother you?' Seamus asked Emer.

'I was born and grew up here, this is my home so I know no different,' she answered. 'But, truth be told, I do prefer to be outside. I am fortunate that as a protector I spend most of my days roaming through the forests.'

'A protector?' Seamus asked, intently watching Emer's face. If you looked closely enough you could see small changes of expression, tell tale signs of what Emer was feeling, like the way her eyes softened when she spoke of Sanctuary.

'One sworn to protect the Sanctuary from harm and ensure all live in peace,' Emer explained.

'Ah.' Seamus understood. 'We would call you a guard. Daniel is a guard in Aria.'

Emer actually chuckled as she remembered when she met Daniel. 'That explains his eagerness to join you all on your journey. A true protector never deserts their post.'

They left the Sanctuary by a back entrance. As they exited the cavern into a natural amphitheatre, they stepped into mid-morning sun. Seamus was surprised he had been allowed to sleep for so long. Waiting for him by the back entrance was the High Seer.

'It is time for your trial,' Caraig said formally. He handed Seamus a knife and a water skin he could sling over his shoulder.

'You must choose one of the three caves to enter, you then have twelve candle-marks to complete your quest. A bell will toll at the sixth candle-mark, and the ninth candle-mark, then every candle-mark after that until the twelfth. At the twelfth bell of the twelfth candle-mark, the cave will be closed off, and you will remain inside until the gods open the cave for the next trial.'

Great. Shut in a cave for goodness knows how long. What more could I wish for? He studied the openings in front of him, chewing thoughtfully on his lip. *The left cave looks as good as any.* To Caraig he said, 'I choose the cave on the left.'

'You may proceed.'

'Is that it? No ceremony or wise words?' Seamus raised an eyebrow in surprise. He thought he detected a little bit of a smile from Caraig as he voiced his thoughts.

'If it helps, I hope the grace of the gods is with you.'

Seamus shrugged his shoulders, not sure if it was any help at all. He could put the moment off no longer. Walking towards the cave on the left, he entered its cool interior. He found himself in an enormous cavern. It was so tall he could not see the ceiling. It was so round he could not see the far side. It was bathed in natural light and in front of him were seven figures, three male and four female.

The figures were taller than most people he knew and, it may have been a trick of the light, it seemed as though he was looking right through them. He could not be certain as he could not look directly at any one long enough to really see them. For some reason, his gaze shifted away just as the one he looked at came into focus. It was much more comfortable looking at all seven as a group.

'Come forward,' one—or was it all of them?—commanded.

Reluctant to move, Seamus turned around to find the cave mouth he had entered through was longer there. His only options were to step forward, or stay still. He took a tentative step forward.

'You wish to be tried as the Wizard of Prophecy?'

Maybe it was not the time to go into the fact he was not sure he wanted the position and all it might entail. After all, he had made the decision to come here. 'I do,' he found himself responding.

'You do this knowing the threat facing the world is bigger than anything faced by humankind before?'

What do they mean by "humankind"? Are they not human? He wondered. *Are these... Gods?*

'So I have been told,' Seamus answered, a little more wary now he thought he had guessed who these seven were.

'You know that one of our own has decided to conquer your world?' they asked him.

'I do. I also do not understand why the other gods cannot stop him.' Seamus responded, taking a chance he had guessed their identities correctly.

'If only it were that simple,' they answered. 'If a god were to interfere directly with the working of another god, there would be all out war. A war of the gods would destroy more than your land, it would destroy all the known worlds and time itself.'

'So you can do nothing?' Seamus was flabbergasted, but also quite pleased with himself that he had realised he faced the gods before they had told him.

'We did not say that. We have been helping your kind for millennia to prepare for this moment. We have warned you and we have made it possible for the Wizard and the Warrior to be born to combat this evil.'

'So you tell me how to defeat this god, and Aliah and I go forth and fight him?'

'No, that is beyond what we are able to do.'

'Can you even tell me which god we are facing?' They must surely be able to give him this simple piece of information, Seamus decided.

Silence fell as the gods looked at each other. Then one stepped forward, a woman, who was vaguely familiar. She had the same face as the statues of the goddess he had grown up with.

'I am sorry we cannot tell you even this. We will give it some thought and see if there is any way we are able to help you find out using resources you already have. If we have any ideas, we will find a way to get them through to you.

'The time for questioning is now over. Do you confirm that you take this test willingly, knowing you could die during it, and also knowing should you pass the trial, you will have committed to doing all you can to fight the evil plaguing your land?' The goddess spoke in a strong, compelling voice.

He took a deep breath and decided to say exactly what was on his mind. 'I do this willingly, but I think you have chosen the wrong person. I am no mage. I can light fires, and I can sometimes move things. Any attempts to do more have ended in disaster.'

The goddess smiled benignly at him. 'We have been watching your progress, and we believe it is as we expected. You are perhaps the most gifted mage of your time, but your gift is not something often seen in your lands, so no one has the experience to help you master it.'

'Well, that is useful,' Seamus said sarcastically. 'I have a great gift but will never be able to use it.'

'You are perhaps too quick to judge, young mage. Your gift has come from all of us. From me, you have been given the ability to nurture and heal, from the others, you have been given foresight, control of the air, water, fire, and land, and the ability to kill with a thought. Although you have been given these gifts you have only a small amount of magic in each. You can use each gift individually, which is how you have been approaching your training to date, but your true power comes from combining your magic and using them together.'

'That goes against everything Walter has been teaching me. He said many people have two, maybe three, forms of magic, but all mages are usually strongest in one. We have been trying to find my one.'

'That is the usual way gods bestow gifts. However, your gifts are special, forged in response to specific circumstances. Because of this, should you pass your trials, we have taken it on ourselves to train you in how to best use your magic. You will earn a wand made from the elder tree at the heart of the known worlds. This is the only tool that will allow you to channel such diverse, melded magic. We will not leave you to face your foe without being as prepared as we can make you.'

'It sounds like you have chosen me to be the Wizard from birth, ensuring I had the right mix of magic. If that is so, why do I need to go through a trial?'

The goddess moved back in line with her fellow gods, and Seamus found once again he could no longer look directly at her. The gods answered his question together.

'It is a great power you have potential to wield, but you do not have the key to unlock its full potential, only we can help with that. However, while you have been born with the power, we need to assess whether or not you are the right type of person to use it. We need to test your resolve, and test you personally to see whether or not you are capable of using the power wisely. So, we ask once again, do you agree to this trial knowing it may end in your death, and knowing you will then be committing your life to defending your world against great evil?'

Again, Seamus took a deep breath, but did not answer immediately. He did not really want to die, but he did not want to see his world overrun by war, and see the people ground into the ground by uncaring rulers. In the end, he did not really have a choice. 'I agree.'

'Then let the trial commence.'

As Seamus was thinking that this was more like the introduction to the trial he had expected, the seven gods melted away, and he found himself in the palace on Hand.

Seamus stood in the doorway of the family quarters in the palace on Hand. The noises of battle surrounded him. Two guards were fighting what looked to be outlanders. Behind them stood his sister, clutching the hand of her nanny, fear written on her face. The guards were tiring, there were too many attackers. Behind him, there was a full blown battle as more barbarians fought to get past the guards at the top of the stairs. For the moment, the guards managed to keep them at bay.

Fear and anger rushed through him. How dare these people threaten his family and his people? He could help them, but first he needed to get Cara to safety. Closing his eyes, he reached out for his magic. Grasping hold of it, he pushed out a small flame. Instead, a rush of fire leapt from his hands, burning all in its path. Trying to call it back, Seamus cried out as the magical flames burned uncontrolled, killing those from Hand and Carsten indiscriminately. Through the flames, he could just see Cara's nanny pulling her up the stairs, away from the fire.

Dropping to his knees in despair, Seamus cried uncontrollably as he was whisked back to the cavern of the gods.

'I cannot do it,' he cried as he relived the destruction he had caused in his mind. 'I am not strong enough.'

A figure stepped to his side, and he peered up to see the goddess. 'What you did was unforgivable, using magic to kill. You need to take a deep breath and calm yourself.'

Slowly getting his emotions under control, Seamus thought his was probably the shortest trial ever.

'We had not understood how much not being trained how to use your magic would affect your ability to wield it under pressure,' the goddess said once he stopped crying. 'It is especially susceptible to influence by emotions, more so than the usual gifts, but we had not fully understood how much. What were you thinking when you released you magic?'

Seamus thought for a moment. 'I was scared, and angry, but I was thinking to call fire to try and help my family. I have never been able to call forth that much fire before, and I panicked. I could not control it.'

'Think back,' the goddess commanded. 'Has anything like this happened before?'

'On the ship,' Seamus answered. 'Walter was teaching me to move things and I could not make anything move. I got frustrated and blew up a barrel of tar.'

The goddess leaned her head to the side as if examining him. 'What have you learnt from this?'

I am a bad wizard, he thought to himself.

'I am a god, I can hear your thoughts. You are an untrained wizard. Think again.'

This time when Seamus thought hard about the two incidents, understanding finally hit him. 'If I act without a plan, with emotion and no thought, then my magic flares out of control.'

The goddess disappeared, then reappeared with the other gods. They seemed to be conversing. While he head learnt something today, he wondered why they had not ended his trial and sent him home.

'We have been unwise.' Seamus' attention was jolted back to the cavern. 'We thought you could learn to control your magic without help. We have set you up to fail.'

Shaking his head disbelievingly, Seamus stood up. 'I have failed then?' The silence that followed his question was total.

'You did something wrong for the right reason, but you did it because you did not know any better. Had we trained you, you may have acted differently. We need to confirm this before we decide.'

There was more silence as the gods looked to each other, then the goddess moved closer to him again.

'Your magic is different to others. You do not need spells, hand gestures, or chants for it to work. You need to clearly envision in your mind what you want to happen, then your magic will follow. Do you understand?'

Seamus turned this over in his mind, thinking what he might have done differently had he known this, then answered, 'I think so.'

'We will try you again. The battle in the family quarters is lost, but there are others who need your help.'

SICK TO THE stomach with worry, Seamus found himself at the back of a very crowded formal reception room on Hand. His water skin had disappeared, replaced by a sword, and he had a thin black wand in his hand. There was a battle raging around him. The guards of the castle were fighting what appeared to be more barbarians. At the other end of the hall, by the throne, his father was fighting off one very large and determined attacker, Seamus' mother and brother behind him. His father was slowly being pushed backwards towards the wall. Very soon, he would have nowhere else to go, and Seamus could tell the man he faced was a much better and stronger swordsman.

There were too many men fighting between them for him to get to his father to help. He had a sword for sure, but he was about as much use with that as a newborn baby. He had magic also, but fire was the only thing he could really use, and his control of that was not very reliable. If he used it he could kill a lot of innocent people, and if he only saved his family, what about the others? The men in his father's guard? The people crammed up against the walls, trying to keep away from the weapons being swung in battle? Should he use magic to save them and confirm their fears about him? If he did, what would his father think?

The loud thuds of barbarian soldiers trying to get through the double doors came from behind him. For the moment, the Hand guards were still managing to keep them out. However, Seamus could see the doors bulging as the soldiers outside attempted to force entry. It was only a matter of time until the enemy burst through, and they would be overrun by foreign soldiers. When that happened, the battle would be lost.

Think, he told his brain. *There must be something you can do.* Fire was the only tool he felt confident using. Slowly a plan began to form in his mind. If he concentrated, it was almost like he could see things happening before they did. He could use that.

He ordered the guards away from the door behind him. They paused, but seeing who he was, soon responded. As they moved away from the door, he sealed it off with a wall of fire. Now knowing he could produce a lot of fire, he found it as easy as making a small flame, he just had to concentrate to keep it under control.

Next, he took a knife from the belt of one of the guards, and surrounded himself in a wall of flames. He easily moved to the centre of the room, as everyone moved away from the heat of the fire to let him through. Keeping in mind what had happened in the family rooms, he focused on keeping control of the flames, making doubly sure they did not expand to touch anyone.

Stopping when he had a clear aim, he took a deep breath and threw the knife at the sword arm of the man fighting his father, letting out his breath with relief as the man's sword clattered to the ground. Seamus' father moved quickly to hold his sword to the man's throat as the barbarian clutched at his injured arm, attempting to remove the knife.

'Who is next?' Seamus boomed in his loudest voice, and the

fighting around him stopped as all in the room took in his presence. Glimpsing a movement to his right he felt, rather than saw, a knife coming towards him. A sweep of his hand, and the knife fell uselessly to the floor before it reached the ring of defensive fire.

Scanning the room, he located the knife thrower. Seamus' eyes bored through the crowd, and caught sight of a barbarian trembling in fear. As Seamus raised his hand, he thought of pulling the air from his attacker's body, not stopping until the last moment, when the man slumped to the ground, not dead, merely winded.

'Anyone else?' No one moved. 'Those who do not belong here, drop your weapons and move to the middle of the room.' There were loud crashes as swords and other weapons hit the floor. The barbarians moved to the centre of the room and were soon encircled by Hand guards. Some of the court men busied themselves gathering the discarded weapons.

Behind him, Seamus heard guards from the town arriving outside to deal with the barbarians still trying to get into the Throne Room. Then, before he could decide what to do next, he found himself back in the cave, facing the seven gods.

The goddess moved forward from the group of seven. 'You have done well, young wizard. You showed you could use your minor gifts to manage a situation without having to resort to killing as your only option. Even though you had the wand to amplify your power, you showed restraint. You have earned the wand you now hold.' She stepped back.

Seamus glanced down to see that a plain, wooden wand had replaced the shiny black one he had held in the Throne Room. This one may not have been as impressive looking, but he could feel the energy throbbing through it.

'Although you have won the day today, you should not forget you still need much training in how to use your powers before you will be ready to face the god, young wizard. Also know this, although you have demonstrated restraint and shown you have a good heart, if you ever misuse what has been gifted you, you will find that what has been given, can also be taken.'

Surprised by that last comment Seamus wondered, *am I not really the wizard then*? But that thought was quickly lost as another filled his head.

'What about my family? Is Cara all right? Or did I burn her with the others?' He needed to know.

'Seamus, did you really not realise? This was a trial of our making, none of it was real.'

Seamus' shoulders sank in relief, then tensed in anger. 'You made me live through that just to test me?'

'We had to be sure you could make good decisions under extreme pressure.' The goddess did not apologise, merely explained.

Lost for words, Seamus did not know what to think.

'Remember, you are the Hand that will deal the blow in battle, but you cannot do that without the arm to support you. It is the combined power of the Wizard and the Warrior that will win the day. You will also need others for the coming fight. The man who is not what he seems will be needed, but it is the wolf who will be especially important to you.'

Shaking his head slowly from side to side, Seamus was even more confused than ever. But before he could form the questions he wished to ask, the gods faded. Left alone in the cave—which suddenly seemed much smaller in their absence—Seamus decided there would be time to ask those questions later.

As he walked out into the late afternoon sun, he thought, *that took longer than it felt*. Maybe time moved more slowly when you were in the presence of gods. His second thought was, *that was almost too easy*. Although he believed he had killed some men and lost his sister, it had only been for a short time until the gods had explained it was all an illusion. He had not been in any real danger. All he had done was show he could learn and be himself.

It made him wonder if the gods knew he was the only one stupid enough to take up the mantle of the wizard and face the danger ahead.

OUTSIDE THE CAVE, he found Caraig waiting. He had been joined by Dominic, Daniel, and Emer. To say they looked worried would have been an understatement.

'Ah, Seamus.' Caraig smiled. 'Congratulations on the success of your quest.'

Seamus looked at Dominic, who refused to meet his eyes. Daniel on the other hand, stepped forward and took him by the shoulders.

'Did you see Aliah in there?' he asked impatiently.

'Aliah?' Seamus was bemused. 'No. I thought you knew, our trials were to be separate.' Suddenly his mind focused. 'Daniel, what is happening here?'

Caraig stepped forward. 'Aliah began her quest at the fifth candle-mark this morning. We are now heading towards the sixth candle-mark in the afternoon.'

Looking at the worried faces, Seamus finally realised what had caused them 'Did she only have twelve candle-marks to complete her quest as well?'

Caraig nodded.

Seamus' stomach clenched with concern. 'What cave did she choose?' He looked around to see which one had the closed door. Their mouths all stood wide open.

He dashed into the middle cave, and then the one to the right. They appeared to be normal caves and they were empty. Turning to Caraig he asked again. 'Which cave did she choose?'

'The same cave as you,' Caraig answered 'But there is nothing we can do. The gods have closed the door back to this plane.'

'The hell they have,' Seamus said angrily, and pushed past the others to head back to the left hand cave.

When he entered, it looked just like the other two. Seamus sensed rather than saw Dominic join him, but he may as well not have been there at all, because it was not him Seamus wanted to speak with. Angrily he threw his wand on the ground.

'I will not do it,' he yelled. 'Without Aliah, I will not go forward.'

'You are the wizard,' came the words in his head.

'I might be the wizard, but I will do nothing without her, unless you tell me how I fulfil the prophecy without my warrior.'

The cave disappeared and he was once again standing alone facing the gods. This time he forced himself to look at all of them, even though it hurt his eyes and his head throbbed unbearably to do so.

'You cannot refuse to move forward. You made a promise. You have been chosen and tried, and you are the only one who can deal the fatal blow to the god.'

'I will not.' Seamus stood defiant. If they took his warrior, and they could take his powers if he misused them, then he really did not want to be the wizard.

'What do you want from us, mortal?'

'I want to know what happened to Aliah.' Seamus stood with his hands on his hips.

'Aliah passed her trial, but did not complete her quest within the time allotted. She was mere steps from the door when her time ran out.'

If anything, this answer made Seamus even more angry. 'You mean she is the warrior, but you are holding her because of some time limit you imposed?'

There was silence. The gods appeared to be deep in thought. Seamus watched as they looked at each other. Some shook their heads, some nodded. Finally he had his answer.

'That is one way to look at it. The other, is that we open the portal for a given length of time for a quest to occur. When it closes, the quest is at an end.'

'I have never heard anything so stupid in my life.' Seamus spluttered in astonishment. 'Hold on. You allowed me to come back after I had completed my quest. How could you do that?'

'You are still within your allotted trial time.'

Seamus bit his lip, trying to piece what he knew together. 'So, is Aliah with me on this plane still?'

'Yes, she is.'

An idea began to form in Seamus' mind. 'Can I see her?'

As one, the gods turned and looked to the left. Seamus saw a form lying on the ground behind them, clutching a sword.

'After the time of the quest, mortals left behind fall into the dreamless sleep. They can stay like that for months before fading away.'

'So, Aliah is here and cannot leave. I am here and I can leave, but only if I leave within the time allotted to my quest?'

The gods nodded as one. Seamus sat on the floor, his mind made up

'What are you doing?' Although the faces of the gods did not change, they sounded astonished.

'If she stays here, then I stay with her.' Seamus folded his arms to emphasise his point.

'What about the fact you agreed to save the world as the wizard?'

'I agreed to save the world as the Wizard along with the Warrior. You told me I could not deal the fatal blow to the god without the warrior. You have confirmed Aliah is the warrior. Or do you know of another warrior who can help me?'

There was more silence.

'If there is no other, then I cannot leave here without her because I will not be able to do what I need to without her.'

Seamus waited, the gods waited. A bell tolled.

'The time for your trial is running out. You must leave.'

'Not without Aliah,' Seamus responded.

'The world can not get through this crisis without you.'

'Without me and my warrior,' Seamus answered stubbornly.

The silence lasted longer, and another bell tolled. The changing expressions on the gods' faces were the only signs they were communicating.

'One more bell and the doors will close. You will be left here with the warrior and the world will have to weather this crisis without you.'

Seamus' resolve wavered a little. Did he really want to be stuck here? Then he thought about what he would be facing, and what would happen to his people if he lost this battle. They would only have half a chance of ending the threat they faced without Aliah. Although fear squirmed in his stomach, he really had no choice. He said nothing.

Finally the goddess stepped forward.

'Are you certain you can work as a team with the princess? After all, it was not so long ago you were angry with her for leaving you in Sunnydale without a word and abusing your trust.'

Seamus went to answer *of course,* but stopped himself. The goddess was right. Not that long ago he had sworn to himself he would never trust Aliah again. When had that changed? He was not sure when it had happened, just that it had. He could not, and would not, face the renegade god alone.

'I will not do it without her,' he answered determinedly.

Everything went black and suddenly he was in the cave entrance, sitting on the floor, wand in hand, with Aliah asleep in front of him. Before he could stand, Dominic had Aliah in his arms, hastily exiting the cave. Seamus moved quickly to follow him, before the gods changed their minds.

CHAPTER 26
A RIGHT BUN FIGHT

As she awoke, all Aliah could think about was how much she ached all over. There was not a single part of her that did not feel like she had been in the most horrendous fight. Her hands ached worst of all, almost like they were continuously cramping. She opened the fingers of one hand, and it closed back onto something cold and hard, clutching it as if her life depended on it. She half opened her eyes, surprised her hands were grasping a sword.

'Pleased you could join us again. I was actually starting to get worried.'

Slowly she turned her head. She was in the room she and Amelia had chosen in the guest quarter. Dominic lay back on one of the other beds attempting to appear relaxed. He might have pulled it off, had he not been tapping his foot and frowning.

The tapping stopped and he swung his legs over the edge of the bed. Leaning towards her, he frowned again. 'Are you ready to give up that sword now? No one has been able to get it out of your hands since you left the cave.'

Sheepishly, Aliah thought, *it is just a sword, why do I not want to let it go?* 'I have a feeling it does not like being touched by anyone but me,' she told Dominic, feeling rather foolish. 'Although for the life of me I do not know how I know that.'

'Odd.' Dominic responded. 'Swords do not normally care who holds them, although I have always suspected they prefer to be wielded by someone with at least a little skill.'

'It is odd,' Aliah admitted. 'Then again, it is a god given artefact, so I am not sure whether this is normal or not. What I am sure of is that I cannot carry it with me always. It will not be allowed at state functions.'

Dominic's frown deepened. 'Perhaps it is a touch thing. I want to try something.' He took the rug folded at the end of the bed he sat on, then opened it up, and placed it over the sword. Now able to pick it up, he lay the sword on the end of his bed.

'Mmm, interesting. Maybe it is a built-in defence against someone else using it,' he mused. 'We should see if the people here have a sheath we can purchase for it.'

Aliah smiled wanly. 'You are a very useful person to have around.' She tried to sit up and could not. Collapsing back on the pillows she groaned in frustration.

'You need to rest. You were unconscious and pretty beat up when Seamus brought you back.' Dominic sat on the edge of the bed.

'Seamus brought me back?' Aliah puzzled. 'Brought me back from where?'

Dominic's face showed more worry, if that were even possible. 'What is the last thing you remember?'

Aliah screwed up her face, trying to concentrate. Then it all came back to her. 'I failed the test. I remember getting to the door just as it closed.' She frowned. 'But if I failed, how do I still have the sword? How am I here, and not stuck in the cave?'

Dominic shrugged. 'I am not sure of the details, but Seamus would not accept that you had not come out. I followed him back into the cave. We were standing there, and he disappeared for the blink of an eye, then reappeared with you in his arms. He mumbled something about damn gods and extra tests as we were walking out. That is all I know, although I suspect he went and had a strong word with someone about their rules. Was it tough?'

'Harrowing, and one day I may tell you all about it. But not today.' She closed her eyes, even talking tired her.

'So? We all want to know. Are you the warrior? Caraig said the sword was proof you were.' Dominic's voice came from a great distance, and she opened her eyes.

'Yes, I am the warrior. Well, I think I still am, even though I got caught behind the door.' Aliah closed her eyes again. 'What I would not give for a nice hot bath to soak my aching muscles.'

'That has been arranged. There is a girl outside who can help you.'

Grateful Dominic had anticipated her needs, she was about to thank him when, *wait, a girl is outside?* 'I would prefer Amelia helped me. If she would not mind, and some food would be good. I am sure I will feel better soon.'

'Ah, Amelia is not here.' Dominic would not meet her eyes. Something was up.

'Who is here?' Aliah demanded.

'You and me.' Dominic seemed to find some spot on the blanket very interesting.

She raised an eyebrow. 'And the others are...?'

'In a Council Chamber,' Dominic said the words very quickly, almost as if he thought she would not hear them if he spoke fast.

Questions swirled through her mind. She chose one. 'Daniel went and left you here? That sounds unlikely.'

'Daniel was here until a candle-mark ago, when he was called away to help Liam organise meeting up with the muster of Malorian warriors.'

'Oh. And the others did not think to wait for me before they began their discussions?' Aliah's voice hardened.

'Yes, they did. Well, at least Seamus did. He kept saying something about the hand and the arm. Sounded bizarre to me, but it seemed important to him.

'He insisted on staying here with you, but you were sleeping so soundly, he decided it was better to go and make sure they did not set any plans in stone until you were awake.'

Dominic repeating the words the serpent had used was comforting in an odd sort of way. 'Right,' she said, forcing her body upright. 'I need a bath, a change of clothes, and some food. Oh, and some of that caffe.' And with that, she shuffled out of the room with as much dignity as her aching body would allow.

Stopping at the door, she looked down at her arms. The scratches from the bats were gone. And, although her body ached, her leg muscle did not seem to be strained. She was in much better shape than she should have been after her trial. Maybe it was not a case of the sword not wanting to be touched by others, maybe it needed to touch her so it could heal her wounds. Thinking of ways she might be able to test her theory, she went to bathe.

A CANDLE-MARK later Aliah entered the Council Chamber on Dominic's arm. The warm soak and food helped, but she had pushed her body to the limit. There was no doubt she would have been better off staying in bed. When the ruckus from the Council Chamber reached her ears, she wished she had done just that.

It was more like a bun fight in a bakery than a council meeting. The table had somehow been removed, and the room was packed full of people, some of whom Aliah had never seen before. Not much planning could be done when everyone was talking at once. She spotted Seamus sitting in the corner to the left, arms resting on his legs and looking at an odd shaped piece of wood. *Not wood, a wand.*

She and Dominic sidled over to him and took two other chairs leaning against the wall.

'We did it,' she whispered to Seamus, a grin plastered all over her face. He smiled wearily.

'I know. I cannot believe it. They gave me this.' He showed her the wand. 'It might not look like much, but I can feel the power in it.'

'I have a sword. But of course you have seen it. It also has some strange powers. I am not sure how to use it yet, but I think I am supposed to learn.' She frowned as voices rose in the chamber. 'What is going on here? I take it this is not a celebration of our being the ones to fulfil a great prophecy?'

'No, it is nothing like that. In fact, that seems to have been forgotten. They have been yelling and arguing for two full candle-marks.' Seamus grimaced as someone else shouted.

'About anything important?'

'Well... it seems Amelia has had what they call a "true seeing" to do with our great prophecy.'

'When did this happen?' Aliah frowned.

'From what I can tell, while we were returning to our rooms after our trials.'

'Why has it caused such a furore? I mean, we knew she could sense things. We knew there was a prophecy. Another seeing about the prophecy should not have been such a big deal.' Aliah yawned and shifted in her seat. She really would rather be back in bed.

'Do you want everything from start to finish?' Seamus sighed. Aliah raised a questioning eyebrow, and Dominic nodded.

'Just the summary version please,' Aliah spoke for them both, stifling yet another yawn.

'Thank goodness. It started with Daniel calling everyone together to let them know how unhappy he was your life had been placed in jeopardy. As you can imagine, that was not well received. The meeting was interrupted by Eon, who is Caraig's trainee or something, blabbering about Amelia. Apparently she had fainted

343

and they could not rouse her, and Caraig needed to come and hear what she was saying.

'We had a bit of a break while Caraig went to see Amelia. Amelia and Walter came back with Caraig, who promptly declared to all that Amelia had a true seeing, and they have been arguing and debating like this ever since.'

'Do you know what they are actually yelling about?' Dominic asked.

Shrugging, Seamus answered, 'No one thing, from what I can make out. Eon is apparently trying to gather support for his point of view that Amelia did *not* have a true seeing at all. Caraig wants Amelia to stay here as he says he finally has a successor. He insists they need to restudy the prophecy in light of Amelia's seeing. Daniel wants us to leave as soon as possible so we can get back to the fighting that will now be happening. That military looking man over there wants Daniel to stay so he can help organise the fighting men from Maloria. I do not know what Liam is doing. He has had his head down, talking to that man dressed like a protector the whole time, and they have not been loud enough for me to hear. I think that is about all of it.'

'Wow,' was all Aliah could think to say. 'So you have not been a part of any of this?'

'I am pretty sure none of this has anything to do with what we are supposed to do next, although much of it is important in the grand scheme of things.'

Aliah nodded. 'I feel the same. I am sure you and I are meant to head back to the coast and take part in defending against the invasion.'

It was Seamus' turn to nod. 'There is nothing further we can do here, and they might need what little help we can give them against Carsten.'

'And I will be accompanying you,' Dominic inserted.

'I think that is right too,' Seamus confirmed.

'Not that I need your permission, wizard boy.' Dominic smiled but his voice was serious, making a point to Seamus.

'No, I did not mean it like that.' Seamus frowned, and he paused, as if trying to find the right words. 'In the cave, I sort of came into my powers, or more like... I now understand what they are and how they work a little better. As part of that, I realised the feelings I get—the notion something is right or wrong—is a form of foresight. It has been stronger this afternoon since my trial, but maybe I am just paying more attention to it.

'As I have been sitting here, I have come to the realisation we are not all meant to go on to battle the Carstenites together. I believe it may be because the battle we need to face is still a way off.

'I think to fight that battle, we all have to prepare in different ways. But you and I must stick together no matter what. We are the hand...'

'...and the arm,' Aliah finished for him, not really feeling much like a unit as her stomach sank in recognition of the changes that had occurred between them. With Seamus having foresight, he would be best to take the lead. If he could foretell the right thing to do all the time, she was really only the hired muscle. She needed to concentrate on her role as warrior, even if only to prove to herself she really was the warrior in spite of Seamus having to save her.

Seamus smiled. 'Some of our individual trials must have had cross-overs, we should compare notes. In the meantime, I feel Dominic must come with us. I think he is the man who is not what he seems. I also have to find a wolf to come with us too.'

'A wolf? Are you sure?'

As she spoke, Aliah saw Emer stiffen on the other side of Seamus. She hesitated, frowned, then leaned down.

'Apologies, I could not help but overhear your conversation.'

Laughing, Aliah said, 'This is not the place for private discussions and we were not talking quietly. If you know something that might help us, we would be happy to hear it.'

Emer inclined her head. 'I have an idea about how to find your wolf. Here is not the place, but if you come with me after this meeting is over I will show you.'

Seamus was clearly relieved. 'Great, I really had no idea where to start looking, and I did not want to delay our departure trying to find a needle in a haystack.'

'So are we ready to contribute then? I think this one is yours to take the lead. I do not have the strength or the will to take part in this today,' Aliah spoke to Seamus.

'I guess so, although I am not sure what to say. I will have to trust this new foresight I have, I guess. Well, here goes.' He stood and offered Aliah his arm so they could make a united front. Pleased by the gesture, not just because they would appear as a team, but also because she could barely stand by herself, Aliah took her position beside Seamus. Dominic stood behind her, and Emer fell in behind Seamus. Something about this group had Aliah feeling she could face anything.

As all eyes turned to them, Aliah swore she witnessed the very moment Seamus got his foresight. He stood taller and radiated confidence.

'Aliah and I have had a long day and we need to get some sleep. Before we leave, we wanted to let you know what we will be doing next.'

Aliah could see the others stood poised mid-debate. Walter held out his hand and stepped forward. 'But we have not agreed to a course of action yet, so how can you know what you will be doing next?'

Seamus glanced around the room, ensuring he had everyone's attention before he spoke. 'Aliah, Dominic, and I are leaving tomorrow. That is not up for debate. The only thing that might delay us is the fact we need to find the wolf we are to travel with. Emer thinks we can sort that out tonight and, if that is the case, we will be heading back to the coast.'

Caraig's face froze and he looked towards Emer. Emer was staring back, almost like they were communicating, and Caraig frowned. Emer turned away and Caraig's attention returned to the meeting. *I wonder what that was about?* She had no time to think it through because Walter spoke, and she turned her attention back to the discussion taking place. Walter seemed to be telling Seamus they would need to wait because there were other things that needed to be agreed before they could all leave.

'No, Walter. If any of you had asked, we would have told you that Aliah and I know what we must do, and standing here, I came to realise what you all must do. Amelia, you need to stay here with Caraig for however long it takes to interpret your seeing. You are not needed to fight the invasion, but what you find out now will help us with resolving a bigger problem.'

Before anyone could argue this, Seamus plowed on. 'Walter, of course you must stay with her because it will require your combined knowledge, along with Caraig, to interpret the seeing in a timely manner.'

Aliah could see Caraig nodding, but Eon stood behind him, scowling and looking daggers at Amelia. *He is not happy about something. I must remember to warn Amelia and Walter to watch out for him.*

'Daniel, Dominic is well able to escort us back, your job is to ride out with the Sanctuary forces tonight. You are needed in battle.'

Liam stepped forward. 'Yes, Liam you are to go with him. You know the coast better than anyone else here and that knowledge will be invaluable in the battle we face.'

'Thank you, Seamus. I have been training in a new form of fighting with Dirk here, and I would like the opportunity to continue, and learn what he has to teach.'

'I am sure it has nothing at all to do with Dirk's daughter,' Emer whispered under her breath.

Seamus did not falter, in spite of his smile at Emer's observation. 'Liam, I sense your lot in life is about to change. I have a feeling you will be representing Hand's interests in the Sanctuary for many years to come, should we be successful in repelling the threat that heads towards us.' Liam's grin nearly split his face.

'Now, if you will excuse us.' Seamus made to leave, but Walter's voice stopped him.

'Seamus, how am I to train you for the coming battle if I am to remain with Amelia? I cannot just abandon you, no matter how much I personally want to stay.'

'Walter, we have not had much success with training to date, and a couple more days would not make much difference.' Seamus smiled. 'During my trial I found out why I have had such a problem learning to manage my powers with traditional methods. My gifts are unique, and I think we are safe to say if the best teacher in the human realm could not teach me, then no human could. I will be taught to control and channel my powers by new tutors, who understand how I must use them.'

Walter went to say something else, but Amelia placed her hand on his arm. 'It is as he said, Walter. His powers are god given, and he must be trained by the gods to use them.'

'You are not abandoning us, Walter, you will merely be helping in a different way,' Aliah reassured him. He relaxed a little, but the frown between his brow told Aliah his duty of care towards Seamus had him warring internally.

'Walter, we are the Wizard and Warrior. No one else can carry our burdens, no one else can do what we can do—or what we will be needed to do—to save Aria. You have got us this far, but now you need to let us go and concentrate on what your role is to be in the final battle. You will know when it is time to follow us.' Seamus softened his words with a smile.

As they made to leave, Daniel grasped Dominic's arm. 'We need to talk.' Aliah inclined her head in agreement and the two men left the room to find somewhere quiet. Seamus watched Emer, who had been detained by her father, as she looked regretfully back at him.

Aliah guessed that whatever she had to show him would have to wait until tomorrow.

As they slowly walked through the corridors, Aliah kept her arm through Seamus', partially because she was tired, but also because after the day's events she needed to know he was still there with her.

'Thank you for coming back for me,' she said as she leaned her head on his arm.

'There was not any chance I was going to do this alone.' Seamus laughed.

'Was it another test?' she asked. 'I nearly had my foot through the door as the last bell rang. I could not believe they were going to fail me for the sake of a footstep.'

Seamus stopped walking and turned to her. 'You had passed. I was still being tested. They wanted to test my resolve to work with you.'

'And you passed?' she asked, suddenly worried that he still did not trust her fully after she had deserted him in Sunnydale.

'We are both here, are we not?' Seamus turned and they carried on walking. As she leaned into Seamus for support, Aliah suddenly had a new spring in her step. They were here together, and that was what mattered most.

———

BY THE TIME they arrived back at the guest commune, Aliah was leaning more heavily on Seamus for support. Even so, she had insisted they share the details of their trials with each other to see if they could learn anything new by comparing their experiences.

Sitting down, they poured some caffe from the pot that had been left for them. Dominic arrived soon after. Seeing them deep in discussion, he yawned and retired to bed, tactfully giving them some privacy. After having shared their stories, Seamus thought Aliah's experience had been much tougher than his, and his guilt at the ease with which he had obtained his wand rose. The concerns nagging at the back of his mind all evening surfaced.

He had not yet told Aliah his power could be removed at any time if the gods judged he was not using them correctly. He had to force out the confession. The uncertainty of not knowing what would cause this to happen, made him feel the gods had not really endorsed him as the wizard, and he was going to be continuously on trial. Aliah was quiet for a moment after he spoke, so quiet he wondered if she had actually fallen asleep. Continuing to look into her cup of caffe, she finally responded.

'I believe you are looking at this the wrong way. Firstly, let me say, you must be the wizard. I do not believe they would have given you your wand if they had not thought you were, or that you were capable of fulfilling your destiny. In the same way, I believe I am the warrior even though I did not make it through the door before it closed. They would not have given me the sword if they did not believe in me. It is now up to us to live up to their faith in us.

'As far as your test being easier, well it is easy to design a test for strength, endurance, and ability to fight in unusual situations. It is probably not very easy to design a test to show how someone will deal with abilities beyond those any human before them has had. They showed you had a good heart, and you would not kill just because your family were threatened. Maybe all they needed to know was you could, and would, limit the power you use.'

Feeling a little more confident, he decided to risk telling Aliah about his first test, when the fire got out of control, and his concerns about being able to access something that could so easily kill others. He suspected this was the reason the gods decided to continue his trial. Aliah was silent for a moment, twirling her plait as she often did when she was thinking.

'I really do not know any more than you Seamus. They gave you the wand so they must trust you. Perhaps it is a warning for you to be careful with your magic, and to take care in your lessons.'

Seamus sighed inwardly. It was not that he had not already said that to himself, but more that it was good to hear it come from someone else. Aliah looked up from her caffe and her tired blue eyes captured his gaze.

'You *are* the wizard, and I believe in your ability to control your powers and fight the rogue god with me.'

'Thank you,' was all Seamus could think to say in response, but it seemed inadequate recompense for the comfort her words brought to him. Briefly, he wondered if the gods saying Aliah was the arm to his hand described their mental bond, rather than something physical. Unable to think of any words to explain his gratitude to Aliah, he changed the subject and asked about the battle focus she got when she held her sword.

Aliah attempted to describe it for him, and he concluded it worked in a very similar way to his foresight. Together, these tools would give them an immense advantage in the upcoming, if only they could learn to use them effectively in time.

As he mused, he noticed Aliah's head dropping, although she strongly denied needing sleep when he suggested they go to bed. So he helped her out by admitting he was quite weary himself, and if they wanted to start their return journey tomorrow, he would need a good night's sleep.

Once in his room, he found he was exhausted. Not long after lying down, he fell into a deep sleep. He half-woke at a light touch on his shoulder. Thinking it was Liam annoying him before going to bed, he shoved the hand off and told him grumpily to leave him alone.

'Will you sleep through the upcoming battle?' A voice vibrated through his entire body. He sat bolt upright to see one of the seven gods in his room. The female god stood before him, dressed as a Malorian protector.

'Come, we need to train.' She turned, expecting him to follow her. Liam was asleep in the bed beside him, but he did not even stir. 'None will see us except those who know how to look.'

What does that mean? Seamus mused as he followed the goddess out to the amphitheatre at the back of Sanctuary, which was now bathed in moonlight.

'We have seen that you already know how to use fire. I am here to begin your education on the other elements; how to control each one, and how to use them together to greater effect. In each area, you will never make a great wizard, but your ability to use all elements together will make you strong in a way no other wizard has been before you. We will start slowly, beginning with air.'

Seamus found the word "slowly" to be an understatement. The goddess would explain once, then expected him to follow exactly what she said without any mistakes. Every time he could not do what she said, he worried the goddess would strip his powers from him. She did nothing of the kind, however, and he spent the rest of the night learning how to master air and land, and then how to mix these elements along with fire defensively. He learnt to use the elements with a light touch, and with full force. Then, when he could barely stand, the goddess led him back to his room.

Before she left him, he found the courage to ask her the question that had been on his mind the entire lesson.

'Wait, please. I would like to know, if you can remove my power if I displease you, does that mean you do not trust me to be your Warrior?'

If a goddess could be said to smile, this one did just that. 'Seamus, you are our wizard. You have our wand and our support, but you need to understand no mortal has ever held the power you will when you are fully trained. We do not know how that power will affect someone even as pure hearted as you, so we need to have the ability to remove that power if it corrupts you, or it places the world in danger.

'You will make mistakes while you are learning, that is only to be expected, but it is the thoughts behind your decisions that will tell us whether or not the power is too much for you. Sleep now, you will need all your strength in the coming days.'

The goddess led him to his bed, touched his forehead, and Seamus was asleep before he even lay down.

CHAPTER 27

SURPRISES

Seamus awoke when Liam began moving about their room. 'Sorry Seamus, it is early, go back to sleep.'

'Where are you going?' Seamus asked, feeling strangely awake and invigorated in spite of his nocturnal activities.

'I am going to early training,' Liam said into his shirt as he pulled it over his head.

'They start training this early? Wow, the soldiers here are really dedicated.' A blush crept up his cousin's neck. 'Oh, special lessons. Perhaps with a girl?' He laughed, and received the pillow from Liam's bed in his face as payment.

Liam left, and he had no sooner shut the door than it opened again admitting Walter, his face a picture of worry and concern.

'It is funny, Walter, but I do not need my newly discovered foresight to know what you have come to say. It is written all over your face.' Seamus sat forward, hugging his knees.

'And just what is it I am going to say?' Walter asked dourly.

'That you cannot stay here with Amelia because your duty is to teach me all you know.'

Walter's eyes widened in surprise. 'Well, yes, I was going to say something along those lines.'

It took all of Seamus' control not to sigh, instead he said, 'Even if I did not know that Amelia will need you here with her more than we will need you with us, I still would not ask you to come along just to train me.'

As he spoke, Seamus picked up his wand from beside his pillow, pointed it at the chair, moving it from the wall to behind Walter. Then he concentrated really hard, envisioning Walter seated in the chair. Walter eventually sat down, a stunned look on his face. It would have been funny if Seamus had not been making an important point. For a wizard to make a person do something even as small as sitting, took a lot of power, and a lot of training. Yesterday Seamus had barely been able to move an object, let alone a person.

'I spent last night training with a goddess. She began teaching me how to use my powers,' Seamus explained. Then he continued to tell Walter what he had learnt during his training and how his powers worked by using thoughts alone, rather than the traditional way where wizards manipulated the elements using spells and gestures. By the time he was dressed and they were sitting down to breakfast, Seamus had managed to convince Walter his training was best left to those who had given him his gifts.

Walter was thoughtful as they served themselves food, then he shook his head. 'When I first met you, you were leaking magic all over the place. You were just like every other untrained wizard. Then, when I taught you to control your powers and I could no longer feel them, I thought to myself you were going to be very strong. I did not question anything when one of the strongest wizards could not sense your power. Even then, it must have been changing, becoming something else.

'When you could not learn to control your magic, I assumed it was because you were starting a little later than others. It is all so obvious when I think back.' Walter finished musing and began eating his food.

It was good to see Walter was no longer worried about abandoning him, and was at ease with his role supporting Amelia. Now Seamus could leave the older man behind, without feeling any guilt. Turning his attention to his breakfast, Emer walked in though the door behind Walter before he could manage to drink a mouthful of his caffe. She inclined her head, indicating he should come outside with her. Reluctantly, he asked Walter to excuse him, and leaving his meal behind, followed the Malorain outside.

Emer kept walking until she came to the edge of the forest, where she turned to make sure Seamus was still behind her. She disappeared into the shade of the trees followed by Seamus, who suddenly stopped short. Not only had he lost sight of Emer, but sitting there in front of him was a grey she-wolf, calmly licking her paws. He did not know what he had expected Emer to show him, but it certainly was not this. Something was tugging at the back of his mind, but he could not grasp it.

'Emer,' he called. 'This is not funny. Where are you?' The wolf appeared to shimmer and there, standing in its place, was Emer.

With everything that had gone on in the last couple of days, Seamus had thought himself beyond the ability to be surprised, but he was wrong. Emer shimmered again, and there was an eagle flying back towards the dwellings. Seamus could do nothing but trail after her, all the while wondering just how much more his poor, tired brain could take.

Although there was much he still had to do to save Aria, and potentially the world, a large part of him wished he could slink off somewhere quiet and have some time to himself. Some time to think about what he actually wanted to do with this life. Shrugging, he pushed those thoughts away, he had other things he needed to concentrate on now.

He found Emer alone in the guest commune, sitting in the seat Walter had vacated. Seamus sat back down with his breakfast in front of him. It had not even had time to get cold.

Emer helped herself to breakfast rolls and caffe. 'I have organised horses for you, Aliah, Dominic, and myself. We can leave after break-fast, if you think you can be ready.'

Seamus was still too stunned to speak, but the situation called for him to say something. 'You changed into a wolf.' It was the best he could manage.

Emer's deep brown eyes sparkled with laughter. 'Yes. And an eagle.'

Is it just coincidence I saw an eagle on Hand? Seamus wondered, but instead of voicing that thought, he came out with, 'How?' He was doing himself proud this morning.

'It is a unique form of magic,' Emer told him around mouthfuls of breakfast. 'Shape shifting is one of the oldest magics, but there is normally only one or two born each generation who have the gift. Most shape shifters can change to one other form, two is very rare.'

'I have so many questions. I want to know what it feels like? Do you think like the animal you turn into? How long can you stay changed for? What happens if you do not turn back?' He paused. 'But really what I want to know is... what makes you think you are the wolf that is supposed to come with us?'

'You mean apart from the obvious?' Emer raised an eyebrow in enquiry, and Seamus had the grace to blush.

'Yes. Apart from that.'

Emer put down her cup of caffe. 'Two things. One is the wolf was the first form I took, and still my preferred form. And two, my father had a true seeing when I was born. He told me the day would come when the wolf would be called to action in defence of Maloria. I have discussed this with him, and we both agree it must be that time.'

Seamus sat back, drinking his caffe and staring at Emer. Then it dawned on him. 'Emer, did you change into wolf form when you were on Hand?'

A smiled tugged at the edge of the girl's mouth. 'I may have.'

'And you came out riding with my brother and me?'

'Wolf form is the best way to move through a forest. I can cover great distances more easily.' She did not really answer his question, but Seamus was convinced she was the wolf he had seen.

He slowly shook his head. He still could not get over the fact this girl in front of him could become a wolf and a bird. There was little doubt she was the wolf he was told should travel with them, but how could he ask her to join their battle when her land was not yet under threat?

'Shall I break it to the others I am joining you, or would you like to do it?' she asked, and Seamus almost laughed out loud. She was so confident it was funny and maddening at the same time.

'You could at least pretend I had a say in this,' he grumbled, and it was Emer's turn to laugh.

'I want to come so much I do not want you to even consider the possibility I might not be your wolf,' she admitted, staring down into her caffe so she would not have to meet Seamus' eyes.

'But why do you want to come so much? You will be leaving your home and your family. Sanctuary is not even threatened, and we may not survive the upcoming battle, let alone the fight with the god.' Seamus could not understand her eagerness to leave her loved ones behind.

'It is hard to explain.' Emer's brow knitted together a little, nearly, but not quite, frowning. 'And it does not sound very noble. Since my father found I was destined for great things, I have not been allowed to do anything apart from training, least I not be ready when I am needed. I was surprised my father even let me become a protector until I realised he thought I would need military training if I was to meet my destiny.

'Then he let me escort you all here. That was the first time in my life I had been allowed to leave the Sanctuary. I hoped he was finally giving me some freedom, then I found I was likely destined to be a part of your group, which was the only reason he let me go.

'If this is not my time, then I will have to remain here doing nothing. I want this to be what I was born for so much, I cannot bear to think you might all leave without me.'

Emer's face was earnest, and he realised he had known for some time that Emer must be a part of their group. She must be the other person in the prophecy who was not what they seemed. Another piece of the puzzle had been found. Part of him wanted to leave her hanging for a while, but he could not do it.

'I think you are meant to come with us,' he admitted to her. 'I will tell the others you are joining us, but I will leave it up to you how you tell them about your unique abilities.'

Emer beamed. 'I will make sure the horses and supplies are ready, and meet you out front in two candle-marks.'

After Emer disappeared, Seamus walked towards the door of Dominic and Daniels' room. He could hear arguing from within. Deciding to forego normal courtesies, he opened the door to find the two older boys arguing over who was meant to be Aliah's guard and had the right to return to Hand with her.

Seamus sighed. 'I thought we dealt with this yesterday, boys.' They turned as one to the sound of his voice. 'If it were not enough that I know it is meant to be Dominic who comes with us, he is also mentioned in the prophecy. *Old and new blood will combine, With the two who are not what they seem...* Dominic is a spy and is clearly one of those who is not what he seems. I do not think you can say the same about yourself, Daniel?'

It was too much to ask they take his word for it, they had to battle it out themselves. Dominic smirked, clearly happy to have Seamus on his side. Daniel launched into the argument that his orders had come from the king himself, and no mere duke's son could alter them. Aliah was his responsibility, and he had better fighting skills with which to protect her should anything happen. Clearly he was the better guard, because it was what he had trained for. Dominic countered Aliah was more than able to fight off any direct attack, she was the warrior after all, and what she really needed were skills to compliment her own, such as his.

'What good is being able to gather information going to be in a fight?' Daniel argued.

'I did not mean that skill, although gathering information is always useful,' Dominic answered. 'I meant *this* skill.'

Seamus thought he could no longer be shocked, but this day was intent on proving otherwise. Dominic moved over towards the wall and then seemed to simply melt into it until he disappeared. Both he and Daniel stood there, mouths hanging open. They remained open even when Dominic re-emerged.

'Umm... Er... Well... I guess that is a useful skill...' Daniel started, then seemed to simply run out of words.

'What... How...' Seamus added to the conversation, wondering to himself what use foresight was if he was going to continue being surprised like this. It struck him that his foresight would not be able to tell him everything.

'I do not know exactly what, except that it is some form of magic. How? I concentrate on not wanting you to see me and blend into the background.' Dominic smiled sheepishly. 'I discovered it one day when I was in a certain duke's library and he entered with another man. I did not want to be found so I started thinking, "please do not see me, please let me blend into the background". I was sure I would be caught, but they came in, had their meeting, and left without even knowing I was there. Later, I used a mirror and trained myself to blend in with my surroundings at will. It has come in most useful in my line of work.'

'So does that make you a wizard?' Daniel asked.

'I am not sure,' Dominic admitted. 'No wizard has ever suggested they could sense magic in me, and none has ever noticed when I have been hiding in a room. Yet this is not something everyone can do.'

A thought occurred to Seamus. 'The other night when I left you all to meet my father in the library, I thought I heard someone on the stairs behind me—was that you?'

Dominic had the grace to look embarrassed. 'Umm... er... yes. Aliah asked me to follow you to see where you were heading...'

'...and that was how she knew where the library was.' Seamus finished for him. 'And when I nearly sat on you in the armchair by the fire...'

Dominic laughed. 'Sometimes blending in is useful to play jokes on people.'

'Well, I am sure it comes in more useful when you are spying, although it is kind of creepy to watch.'

'It is useful when looking after your friends as well,' Dominic interrupted. 'I followed you and Aliah to the Council Chambers the other night. I spent the night outside your rooms, and I escorted each of you to your trial.'

Seamus' eyes widened in amazement. 'I thought there was someone there, but I could not see anything.'

'It was a close thing,' Dominic admitted. 'When you came through the doorway to check, you nearly stood on my foot.'

'Really?' Seamus shook his head in wonderment, but then focused on the issue at hand. 'All this is irrelevant. Dominic comes because he is part of the prophecy, Daniel stays with Liam to marshal the Malorain forces. If you need more reason than that, Dominic is perfectly able to do as good a job as you protecting Aliah, Daniel, but I would not feel safe with him running a battle strategy for the Marlorians.'

The two looked at him with a new respect. 'Have you been taking lessons in statesmanship from Aliah?' Daniel asked smiling. 'I concede. I cannot fight your logic, and I certainly would not let Dominic loose on the battlefield.'

Pleased to have settled that long running argument, a sudden thought stopped Seamus from leaving. 'Daniel, I thought you were to ride out with the Sanctuary forces last night?'

'Do not panic. The main force left as planned. A few of the protectors who are coming did not get back to Sanctuary until last night. They rested and will head out today to catch the others up. I can leave with them.'

'Oh, all right then. We leave in two candle-marks,' Seamus informed Dominic.

'What about the wolf?' Dominic asked before Seamus could leave the room.

'I have found her, and she is the other who is not what she seems,' Seamus told him. 'Emer will be leaving with us.'

'She is quite fierce, but I would hardly describe her as a wolf,' Dominic joked.

'I am betting you will change your mind on that,' Seamus said as he left the room.

SEAMUS, Aliah, and Dominic walked out of the guest commune and into the clearing in front of the Sanctuary to find Walter, Amelia, and Caraig waiting to send them off. Standing nearby, Emer had four horses saddled and ready with supply bags. When she saw them emerge from the doorway, she walked over and asked Dominic and Aliah to please come with her. They looked at Seamus, who smiled and confirmed they had time. The others followed Emer into the woods, and Seamus turned to Amelia and Walter, who were deep in discussion with Caraig.

'I am happy to stay for a while,' Amelia said to Caraig. 'To look into my seeing and what it means. I believe I am meant to do that, but I cannot see how you think all of this means I am your successor.'

'You are the first seer in your generation to have a true seeing. I have had many apprentices, but none have done what you did,' Caraig responded. 'You are my best and last hope for someone to follow me.'

'It might be unusual to have a true seeing, but that does not make me a great seer.' Amelia stood her ground, looking to Walter for support.

Walter seemed reluctant to say anything until Amelia forced his hand and asked directly for his opinion.

'Well, I do not see that what Caraig suggests will hurt. If you underwent a trial, you would at least know one way or another.'

'I thought trials took place on a full moon?' Seamus interrupted. 'Does that mean Amelia would have to stay here until then?'

'I am not staying here a full moon turn.' Amelia was adamant.

Caraig held up his hand to forestall any further protests. 'In special cases we can petition the gods to hold a trial before the next full moon. If they agree then they will open a doorway to their realm.'

Amelia did not look pleased. 'And what if I did undertake this trial? What if it turned out I was a great seer. Would I then be able to go and help fight the god?'

Caraig answered. 'Of course you could, if that is what you are called by the gods to do.'

'Called by the gods? I am afraid I do not have much time for all that rubbish,' Amelia answered. 'Though, if a great seer does not need to remain in Sanctuary, I might consider undertaking the trial.' She frowned as she pondered this new information.

Seamus chuckled at an image of Amelia facing the gods; he was not sure who would come off worse.

Aliah and Dominic emerged from the edge of the forest, stunned looks on their faces, bringing Seamus back to reality. Emer followed a few paces behind. Was she actually grinning? As they got closer, Dominic said to Seamus, 'Makes my trick look kind of small, does it not?'

'Your trick?' Aliah asked. 'You mean there is more? I am not sure I can take any more surprises.' Aliah appeared overwhelmed, and Seamus knew exactly how she felt.

'One for later, fair princess,' Dominic said annoyingly, and Aliah gave him her most cutting look.

They began stowing their travel packs on their horses when they heard a flurry behind them. Eon stormed out of the main entrance, his face beetroot red and screwed up in anger. He had barely left the doorway when he began yelling,

'How could you? A stranger to be the new Great Seer. After all the work I have put in. After all I have done for you.' He rushed at Caraig and Seamus notice a knife in his hand. Before he could raise it to strike, Seamus used air to bind the apprentice in place, arms pinned firmly at his sides.

Eon's face turned an even darker red and he opened his mouth to speak again. Tired of his tirade, Seamus used air to fill his mouth as a sort of gag. Satisfied with his work, he went back to packing his horse, missing the look of shock that passed between Aliah and Dominic.

'Eon, I am sorry you had to hear this from someone else. I did try to find you so we could talk about it, but you were not in any of your usual haunts, and no one had seen you. I have always been honest with you, many have the minor gift of foresight as you do, but only those with the potential to be a great seer have a true seeing. You have not had such a vision, and you may never have one. Amelia has had a true seeing and has agreed to undergo the trial to find out if she is indeed worthy to become my successor.'

'I agreed to think about it,' Amelia interjected.

Caraig carried on as if Amelia had not spoken. 'It is time you thought about what you want your future to be.'

'Argh. Ahhh.' Eon struggled to speak.

'Seamus, if you would please let him speak?' Caraig asked, and Seamus released the air-gag.

'But she is an *outlander*! And she is a *woman*. She is not worthy,' Eon spluttered.

Caraig sighed. 'There is nothing to say the Great Seer must be Malorian, Eon, or that it cannot be a woman. And you know as well as I do the trial will decide whether or not she is worthy.'

'I will never accept her as Seer,' Eon spat out. 'I would kill her before I would see her take my place.' He struggled against the bonds that held him.

By this time two protectors emerged to take Eon back inside. Seamus loosened the bonds enough so the apprentice could walk, and he warned the protectors the magic constraining Eon would be totally gone by the time they were inside the Sanctuary. Caraig followed after them, turning to wish them a safe journey and good luck, assuring them Eon would be managed by the elders and Amelia would be safe.

'I wish we could come with you.' Amelia hugged both Seamus and Aliah. 'Do not let any harm come to them,' she warned Dominic. 'Or you will have me to deal with, young man.'

'Amelia, we are the Wizard and Warrior, we can take care of ourselves.' Aliah laughed.

'Have you changed that much since you tried to set off up the length of the country in no more than the clothes you stood in?'

Aliah blushed, remembering how Amelia had to provide provisions for her journey from Port Marden to Bannock.

'Come, Amelia, we have done what we can to prepare them. It is time to let them follow their own path.' Walter put his arm around Amelia's shoulders. 'I wish you luck, and will pray to the goddess we will see you again soon.'

Realising Amelia and Walters' relationship may be more than friendship, Seamus was pleased for his aunt. He hoped he and Aliah could ensure Amelia and Walter had time to find out what it was they felt for each other.

'Thank you, Walter, for all you have done. You have prepared me well for what I must face.' Tears stung Seamus' eyes at the thought of leaving his mentor. He shook them away and grasped the older man's hand. 'I could not have done this without you.'

'Oh my, what a thing to say.' Walter shook his head as if shaking off the compliment. 'You were already a fine young man, I only showed you a few things to keep your magic in check.'

'You did more than that,' Seamus said. 'You taught me to live with my magic. For someone from Hand, that is a great gift.'

Walter shuffled his feet in embarrassment, and Amelia saved his dignity by pulling Seamus into another hug. 'Look after yourself, and we will soon see you in Port Marden.'

Holding her tightly, he whispered in her ear, 'Do not let them force you into anything you do not want to do.'

'As if they could.' Amelia laughed, letting him go.

Farewells done, they turned their horses and headed for the coast, but were stopped in their tracks by a shout. They turned to see Liam and Daniel running out towards them.

'Did you think you were leaving without saying goodbye to us?' Liam panted as he caught up with them at the edge of the forest.

'With you having to catch up with the Sanctuary forces who left last night, we did not think you would still be here,' Aliah answered for them all.

Liam handed Seamus a letter. 'Please give this to the duke. It explains what I am doing here and why I am not following his orders.'

'You know I would have explained it to him, and he would understand,' Seamus said.

'I do, but things must be done properly.' Liam tapped Seamus on the leg. 'See you soon, cousin. We will have your back, never fear.'

Seamus clutched Liam's arm. 'I know you will. Be careful.'

'And these are for you,' Daniel said to Aliah as he handed her some documents. 'To take for your father or whoever is in charge when you reach Port Marden. They contain details of how the Sanctuary forces will offer support in the upcoming battle. Well, what we have managed to agree to so far. We have based them on details we were discussing in Hand. Safe travels, and try to keep out of trouble. *And* try not to give Dominic too hard a time. He really is only doing his job, you know.'

Aliah hugged Daniel. Seamus could see it was as hard for her to leave him behind as it was for him to stay, even though both agreed it was the right thing to do.

Aliah let go, and Daniel stood back. 'Caraig assures us all you need to do is make sure the battle is not lost before they identify the god we are to fight, and how to defeat him.'

'Well, if that is all, I am not sure what we are all so worried about.' Dominic laughed as Aliah remounted, and he turned his horse around.

'Hold on,' Seamus stopped them. 'Daniel and Liam are going with the others to catch up with your warriors. How will they make it to the battle in time if they are skirting around the forest?' he asked Emer.

'Some of those travelling with them have a special trick to help get there quicker. We will be taking a game track along the base of what you call the Ariel Mountains to save some time, and we should come out about a day's ride from Port Marden.'

'What trick?' Seamus was intrigued.

'Did you not notice we travelled to Sanctuary more quickly after meeting with Eon?' Emer asked, and Seamus shook his head.

'I will explain it to you as we ride, for we really must be leaving.' The four entered the forest and started their journey back towards the coast.

FOR TWO DAYS the four from the prophecy travelled through the forest towards Port Marden. Occasionally Emer took to the air, or ranged forward in wolf form, to ensure their path was safe. Each night, unbeknown to the others, a different god woke Seamus to teach him more about what he could do with his abilities. Before the god left him on the second night, he informed Seamus that soon the hand and the arm would need to train as one, as they would need to work closely together to defeat their enemy. When he turned to ask the god when he would start training with Aliah, Seamus was alone in the clearing.

Each morning when he awoke, Seamus felt as refreshed as if he had a full night's sleep—certainly more refreshed than his travelling companions. However, on the third morning, Seamus was as irritable as if he had not had any sleep at all. He was worried about training with Aliah. Did their training together mean they would have to physically fight the god? He was not sure how they would do that, especially as his skills were not that practical in close combat. It was so frustrating to have this gift of foresight and still know so little.

Emer made them some caffe for breakfast, and that helped calm him a little as they prepared for the last day of their journey. Because they were now close to the coast, Emer in wolf form, and Dominic on his horse, went ahead to make sure they were not going to fall into any traps.

The scenery was so monotonous, Seamus found his mind wandering, but he was jolted awake by a screech in his head. *Run. Danger.* He looked at Aliah, but she carried on riding, leading Emer's horse as if nothing was amiss.

He heard something crash through the undergrowth, and Dominic's horse bolted towards them, stopping abruptly just before he would have bowled Seamus over. Aliah was off her horse within seconds, sword drawn. Seamus followed her lead, and was soon by her side, knife in one hand, and wand in the other, their horses as protection behind them.

Seconds later, soldiers wearing uniforms unknown to them entered the clearing and surrounded the two fighters. Two men on horseback followed the soldiers. Aliah gasped as she recognised them; Millard, and his protégé Gaius.

Seamus' stomach sank. Millard had been King Terion's advisor, but Walter had found he was plotting the downfall of the royal family, believing wizards should rule Aria. Gaius plagued Seamus and Aliah in Duncameron, and if there was anyone who could make him nervous, it was this particular wizard. Gaius was a people sensor, he could track people by smell.

Inspire by the unease the wizards brought out, they were not the immediate threat. Seamus counted six soldiers between the wizards and them and their relaxed stance told him they believed they had

Aliah and himself at a disadvantage. That would give him the opening he needed.

We need.

What?

I said the opening we *need...*

Aliah?

This is weird, but it seems we can mind link when we hold the wand and sword.

Distracting.

Shhh.

'Little Princess.' Millard sneered as he edged his horse through the soldiers in front of him. 'I finally have you where I want you.'

Gaius stayed behind the soldiers, the smirk on his face showing he was clearly pleased to have Aliah at his mercy.

'I am sure you believe that.' Aliah sounded strangely calm. 'You need to be careful though, Millard. You have really shown your true colours, turning up with foreign soldiers.'

'I no longer need to hide my allegiance. My true master lies off the coast, and soon he will ensure I rule in Aria.' Millard stayed on his horse, towering over Seamus and Aliah. 'Now you will come with me. He has been looking forward to meeting you both.'

'I do not think so,' Seamus interrupted.

'You, boy, you think to say no to me, the most powerful wizard in all of Aria?' Millard straightened in his saddle, as if to make himself more imposing.

'I think you may need to rethink your definition of power,' was all Seamus said in response, in a voice that sounded much calmer than he felt. As he took a deep breath in preparation for the coming fight, Millard's power gathered.

Aliah, he is going to strike with magic.

Can you stop it?

Seamus had no time to answer as a bolt of pure power was released from Millard's hand. Without even thinking, Seamus used air to divert the attack upwards. He mentally thanked the gods for his training as he deflected another attack the same way, and then decided to conserve energy by erecting a wall of air.

Another volley of attacks were repelled by his blockade, and Millard's face contorted into a snarl. Gaius looked around, clearly trying to identify where the magical defence was coming from.

'What... what is happening? Gaius, can you feel where that magic is coming from?'

'I can feel no magic. I do not know what is happening.' Gaius frantically looked around. 'There is no wizard.'

'Arrrh,' Millard groaned as he tried another volley to break the shield.

'We are not so easy to beat,' Aliah told Millard as Gaius motioned for the soldiers to move in closer.

'Who is doing that?' Gaius asked, still trying to identify where the magic was coming from.

'My friend Seamus has powers you could never understand,' Aliah told him.

'He has no magic,' Millard snarled. 'I can not feel any around him.'

'Or I am stronger than you could possibly imagine,' Seamus said as he struggled to maintain his air shield against another attack.

Out of the corner of his eye, a soldier charged at Aliah, who moved to parry his blow and cut his horse's saddle strap. Her movements almost a blur as Aliah's skills were boosted by her god-gifted sword. The soldier fell to the ground, dazed.

'That cannot be. My power comes from a god,' Millard shouted. 'You cannot be more powerful, unless...' The realisation of who he faced was reflected in his eyes. 'The wizard...' he whispered.

At that moment, a wolf rushed from the cover of the trees, snarling and snapping at the hooves of the horses who, unsettled, broke formation. Dominic appeared out of nowhere behind Gaius. Jerking the wizard from his saddle, he pressed a knife to Gaius' throat before the wizard knew what was happening. The wolf turned and stalked the two men, then sat down in front of Gaius and snarled.

Seamus used the distraction to drop the wall and wrap the two wizards in air, preventing them from using all but minor magic that would not be strong enough to harm anyone. By the time the soldiers had their horses under control, the two wizards were out of commission. Aliah stepped forward, sword at the ready.

'You have a choice. You can continue with your attempt to capture us and risk getting yourselves and the wizards hurt, or you can let us leave peacefully.' Aliah spoke to the soldiers.

'We have our orders. We are to bring you back alive. We will do that with or without the help of the wizards.' The leader of the group urged his men forward to once again surround Seamus and Aliah.

'Dominic, I can handle the wizards. Aliah might need your help though.' Seamus moved back towards their horses, still maintaining the web of air around his charges.

Dominic disappeared from view and reappeared beside Aliah, sword in hand. One of the soldiers jabbed at Seamus, thinking him unarmed, and Emer growled and snapped at his horses hooves. As Emer forced the horse and rider away, she moved in to set herself between Seamus and the soldiers.

Somewhat protected, Seamus watched as Aliah and Dominic fought side by side, their swords moving so fast he could barely keep track of them. He had not realised the spy was such an accomplished swordsman. Soon they had soldiers moving back towards the trees. As their sword-work slowed, it appeared they were tiring more quickly than their attackers. In addition, Seamus could feel one of the magicians working to undo his air weave. He knew he could not hold it for much longer. Slowly he put all the pieces together, realising they could not win this battle. They had moments before the tide would turn against them. They needed another plan, and quickly.

Aliah, we need to run. When I say go, we need to head into the woods taking separate paths.

All right.

We can double back and meet up by the coast at sundown.

Dominic and I can stay behind and harry anyone who follows.

... Emer?

I can mind speak with people close to me when I am in animal form. How else would I be able to communicate?

I do not know? In fact, I did not really think about it.

I can tell Dominic the plan.

There was a pause. *We are ready. Can you double the air around the wizards so they are held for a time?*

I think so. It is sort of like weaving a basket. If I pull together a few more strands, I can tie off the end. Seamus concentrated for a moment. He had only succeeded doing this once before in training, and doing it while already holding a weave in place was even harder.

Seamus, can you hurry please?

This is not easy, Aliah. Ah, there. Done.

'Go.'

Aliah and Seamus took off in opposite directions, Emer ran directly at the soldier's horses, causing them to bolt and add to the confusion. Dominic moved to the tree-line and simply disappeared.

It only took a couple of heartbeats before the commander was directing his soldiers to split up; half to follow Aliah, the others to track Seamus. They deserted the two wizards, leaving them to concentrate on removing their invisible bonds.

CHAPTER 28
A BATTLE FINDS THEM

Seamus crashed through the forest, following the path Emer's wolf form set for him. Branches whipped around his face and roots grabbed for his ankles. Just when he thought he could go no further, Emer told him to hide—their pursuers were close.

Looking around, Seamus spied a fallen tree and managed to wriggle under it, pulling some forest debris in front of his face just as the thud of horses' hooves came up behind him. He glimpsed Emer moving to eagle form as he squeezed back as far as possible into his hiding place.

'I am sure I saw him through here.' The voice was not far away.

'Well, you can get off your horse and go and look,' another voice ordered.

Saddle leather creaked, followed by the crackling of someone walking through the dead leaves littering the forest floor. The tree above Seamus shifted as it took the weight of a man, and he held his breath.

'What do you see?' The question came from behind.

'Trees and more trees. No wolf. No boy. But I do see something not often seen this far into the forest. There is an eagle here.' The voice was so close to Seamus it was as if it were coming from right beside him.

'It is probably injured. Unless you are planning to catch it for dinner, we had best get moving.'

Seamus readied himself to attack in Emer's defence, until the tree shifted again and the sound of retreating footsteps were accompanied by a grumbling, 'Not enough meat on it for one, let alone three.'

Slowly letting out his breath, Seamus waited until he could no longer hear hoof beats before wriggling himself back out from under the tree. He brushed debris off his clothes as Emer walked up beside him. It was comforting to see her in human form.

'I followed them for a little bit, then went high to see a way forward. If we go in that direction.' She pointed almost at a right angle to the path the soldiers had taken. 'We should reach the edge of the forest near the road to Port Marden without encountering any further danger.'

Seamus looked where she pointed. 'You could not choose a way that included an actual path?' He sighed, resigning himself to fighting the forest. To his dismay, Emer burst out laughing.

'Seamus, you are a wizard with the power to command the elements. Do you not think you could make a path should you wish one.'

'But then everyone would know where we have gone,' Seamus said, and immediately regretted it as Emer laughed even louder. He realised how silly he sounded as he thought about it. Of course he could move the forest around them, then let it fall back into place as they passed. He could remove any sign of their passage the way Walter had taught him.

He concentrated and took a couple of steps, willing the forest to move. His first attempt was clumsy. He created a clearing around them, and he could actually feel the forest groaning with the effort. He stopped and thought again. What was the minimum they needed for comfortable travel, and how could they get it without disturbing the forest? An idea came to him. He imagined hard disks of air under his feet, and an air tunnel in front of him. He took a few steps and found himself forest-free, and no longer harried by the forest's disapproval.

'I am ready, but you will need to walk close to me.' Seamus turned to Emer. No longer laughing, she watched him thoughtfully.

'Inventive,' she responded. 'But you need to keep your use of magic small lest you tire yourself. I will fly for the moment and keep a look out.' Before Seamus could say anything, Emer changed form and flew up through the trees.

The rest of the day passed without incident, but by evening, Seamus was tiring. When he stopped for a break, Emer dropped down beside him and hopped over to a bush.

These are good to eat, and there is a stream twenty paces behind it. Eat til you can eat no more. Drink. Then we will rest until the moon is high enough to travel safely.

The berries were good, and Seamus had stripped the bush nearly bare before his stomach stopped groaning. After quenching his thirst, he waited for Emer to join him.

'Left you some berries,' he told her.

Emer smiled. 'I just had a rabbit. Eagles do not mind their meat raw.' Seamus shuddered at the thought and Emer laughed.

'It is a useful ability when you need to travel without a fire,' she lectured him.

'That is all very well Emer, but as you pointed out before, I am a wizard who can control the elements. I could cook you meat without needing a fire.'

'Really?'

'Well, I am pretty sure I can.'

In a flash, Emer again turned into an eagle and disappeared into the trees. A few moments later, she dropped a dead rabbit beside Seamus and changed back to human form, the challenge clearly written on her face.

Seamus studied the rabbit and thought about all the skills he had learnt. At last, an idea came to him. He warmed the air around the rabbit, increasing it slowly so as not to burn the flesh, then willed the hot air through the rabbit's body. He counted to one hundred, then used the knife in his belt to test the meat. Not quite ready. Trying again for a further count of fifty, he tested again. Perfect. He looked triumphantly at Emer.

'Well, I have never seen that done before.' She sat down beside him, and he apportioned the rabbit between them.

After eating a more satisfying meal, they settled down to rest and wait for the moon to rise.

Seamus awoke to the touch of Emer's hand on his arm. She had her finger to her lips, and beckoned for him to follow her. As he rose, hushed voices sounded close.

'There they are.'

In the bright moonlight, they had been easy to spot. Emer pulled him by the arm. 'Run.'

They took off into the trees at a sprint as Seamus wondered why foresight could not have warned him their pursuers were close. Learning what it could and could not tell him was frustrating.

At first they managed to keep ahead of their pursuers, and were even keeping to the course that would take them to the meeting place on the coast. As if the soldier knew where they were heading, they suddenly changed direction, cutting off the route to their destination. Each time they managed to make headway towards their destination, the soldiers changed their tactics. It was as if they were herding them back towards Sanctuary.

Lungs burning, Seamus could run no more. Looking around, he found a thicket of prickly bushes and started for them. 'We can hide in there.'

'Are you mad? We will be cut to shreds,' Emer whispered.

'That is exactly what the soldiers will think. That is why it is the perfect place to hide.' Seamus concentrated and used his magic to pull some of the branches apart.

'We cannot both fit in there.' Emer was unconvinced his idea would work.

'If you were in wolf form we would.' Seamus told her.

Sighing, Emer changed. *All right, we can give it a try.*

In spite of Seamus' magic parting the branches, they both received quite a few scratches as they crawled into the hiding space, and even more when Seamus closed the branches behind them. Then every time they tried to move thorns clutched at their clothes and tore at their skin.

Cold and sore, with limited ability to move, they stayed cramped in the bushes while the soldiers searched for them, then searched again. Every now and then, a soldier entered the clearing in front of their hiding place. Occasionally they would stand a hand's breadth away from where Seamus and Emer hid, but none even considered their thorny hiding place as somewhere to look.

Candle-marks passed, but still the soldiers did not give up their chase. Seamus's muscles began to cramp, but still he could not move for fear of giving their position away. At one stage, he half dozed, leaning his face on Emer's warm back.

Just before the sun began to rise, the soldiers called off their search, agreeing it would be easier to catch their quarry on the coast. When the forest was free of the sound of men and horses, Seamus let out his breath and had the bush release them from its midst. Seamus stretched out his muscles, and actually sighed with pleasure.

Those leaves over there—no, those ones, can be used on our scratches.

'Do I just rub them on?' Seamus asked.

Yes.

He dealt with Emer's cuts first, then was amazed at the relief the leaves brought to his own wounds.

'Do you know where we are?' Seamus asked looking around, not certain which way they needed to go to meet up with Aliah and Dominic.

Yes. We have a lot of time to make up. Have you been taught how to feed yourself energy so you can keep going for long periods of time?

'No.' Seamus knew it could be done, just not how.

Let us start at a slow jog then, and we will see how we go.

As they headed towards the coast, Seamus reviewed everything he had learnt about magic and how to use it, trying to devise a way to give himself energy.

SEAMUS' plan had worked better than Aliah expected. Used to being the one taking the lead, it had been strangely liberating concentrating on responding to orders, rather than giving them. Still, she had been surprised at how sound Seamus' decisions had been. *His foresight must give him great advantage,* she marvelled as she ran.

As she tired and started to think of her next move, she took control of the chase. The horses were not as mobile through the woods as a person. With her sword still in hand, she was also extremely sensitive to her surroundings.

Dominic was running behind her, using branches, stones, and knives to dissuade any pursuers who came too close. Eventually she found a dry riverbed and began following it towards the coast, stopping every now and then to hide as a pursuer came too close. Late into the afternoon, the woods began to quieten down and she could no longer hear anyone following her.

She stopped by a stream to get a drink, and was startled by Dominic appearing right in front of her. With her sword on the ground she had not sensed he was nearby.

'We seem to have outrun them.' Aliah smiled.

'Sorry, princess, but no. I overheard them when you started following the stream. They know where we are headed and have planned to ambush us when we reach the coast.' He bent down to scoop a drink of water. Aliah scowled and picked up her sword.

Seamus, they are waiting for us on the coast.

That is not good.

Do we risk a coastal trip?

I feel like we should avoid the coast and head straight for Port Marden. Stay separate. Come out at the edge of the mountains as Emer planned.

As Seamus' words entered her head, he transmitted his belief this was the right way to move. For that moment, she understood Seamus' foresight. Taking a straighter path to the coast now would result in certain capture, and she and Seamus were not yet ready to face a god.

We need to stop communicating this way. Because it uses magic I worry the wizards can use it to track us. No more mind-speak until we are near Port Marden.

All right.

Aliah turned to update Dominic, who was still drinking. He told her the plan sounded fine.

'Just how long have you been able move from one place to another like that?' Aliah asked out of the blue, hoping to shock Dominic into an answer.

But Dominic was better trained than that. He carried on as if nothing were amiss.

'I think if we go that way, we should be able to reach the base of the mountains again, and follow them to the coast.'

'Dominic, if we are to work together I need to know how you move like that,' Aliah said patiently.

Sighing, Dominic kept his gaze on the woods as he answered. 'It is not that I move, as such. I sort of blend in with the surroundings, which allows me to watch and move around without being seen.'

'Oh, that is a little creepy.' Aliah shivered.

Dominic continued looking away, not able to meet Aliah's eyes. 'That is what most people think. That is why I do not tell them.'

'Still, it must come in very handy in your kind of work,' Aliah joked. Realising this was quite a sensitive issue for Dominic she did not want to make him any more uncomfortable than he already was.

'I try not to use it too often, but it has saved my neck on more than one occasion.' Dominic still would not meet her eyes. Concerned, she was sure he thought she did not want him travelling with her because of her dislike of spies, and now the discussion of his gift had made the situation even more uncomfortable. This saddened her, because lately, she had begun to rely on his advice and the different perspective he had, and she really liked the way he always supported her.

'Well, I guess it is no less strange than getting strength and speed from a sword that only allows you to touch it. And at least you do not have to carry anything around to actually access your gift,' Aliah said, attempting to repair the damage. She leaned over to try and see Dominic's face, but he turned even further away.

'We need to get moving. It will take the rest of today, and almost all of tomorrow, to reach Port Marden, and we will still have to walk most of tonight.' Dominic turned and started walking. Aliah sheathed her sword and followed.

The silence hung between them as they walked through the forest. Any of Aliah's attempts at conversation were met with either silence or curt answers. Eventually she gave up trying. She did not understand why Dominic was so stand-offish after having talked about his gift, but if he did not want to talk to her, then she was fine with that.

As dusk fell, they continued walking through the forest. When it grew dark they stopped and rested for a while, drinking some water from a stream. They found a sheltered space and curled to catch some sleep. Aliah awoke some time later to find herself snuggled close to Dominic, drawn to the warmth of his body. Stretching the stiffness from her limbs, she allowed her eyes to become accustomed to the moonlight.

Disturbed by her movement, Dominic began to rise. 'Come on, sleepyhead.'

'No. Wait a moment.' Aliah grabbed his arm and pulled him back down. 'What is the problem with your gift? You seem embarrassed by it, when you should be pleased to have such a useful ability.'

Dominic turned away, before raising his eyes to look at her. 'I saw your reaction when we talked about my special skill. Everyone who knows I have it finds it difficult to deal with. No one likes to think someone can spy on their most private moments without being discovered. My father is so disgusted he will no longer speak to me. In fact, he will not let me back in the family home.' He turned away, as if he did not want her to see the hurt written on his face.

'Oh, Dominic. I did not know. I mean Daniel told me you were estranged from your family, but I thought it was because your father is, well... you know... he is quite a brute.'

'We never really got on. My brother and I are nothing like him, but I used to visit home occasionally to see my twin brother and his wife. My father wanted nothing more to do with me when he found out I used my gift to uncover one of his plots to bring a vassal in line. He was disgusted by me, although I am not sure whether my gift made him feel that way, or the fact I refused to use it to further his petty schemes. I do sometimes get letters from my brother, when he can sneak them out. That is all the contact I have with my family.'

Aliah stood and looked down at Dominic. 'Well, that is his loss, not yours. If he cannot see past something that makes him feel uncomfortable to the person you are inside, then he is not worth worrying about.'

Dominic laughed as he rose to his feet. 'That is one of your dukes there, princess, perhaps you should speak a little more respectfully of him.'

'Perhaps he should do something to actually earn my respect. As for your brother, will he not stand up to your father and be his own man?' Aliah retorted.

'Please, do not judge him harshly. Our father is not an easy man to live with, and it was hard enough to stand up to him when we were both there. Now he has no one on his side, and if my brother does not speak out against my father's excesses, then it is not because he supports him. He bides his time, knowing soon he will be able to do things differently.'

'You are more charitable than I. I believe if someone stands by and watches something bad happen and does nothing, then they are equally guilty.' Aliah tossed her plait over her shoulder and adjusted her sword.

'On that, we can agree to differ. Where you see black and white, I see shades of grey. Shall we get moving?'

'Lead on.' *And that is why your council is so valuable,* Aliah thought as she followed him. *Your views help me see things in a different light.*

'You know you came to my home when you were younger,' Dominic told her as they walked. 'Your father needed to sort out something between my father and a vassal.'

Aliah sorted back through her memories and came across one of a dark eyed boy who had left his home and travelled with them back to Bannock. Surely that boy could not have been Dominic—his eyes were blue. 'Did you leave home with us?' she asked.

'Yes,' Dominic answered in surprise. 'I cannot believe you remember me. It was an important day in my life, it was the day your father took me into his service, I did not think it would be something another child would remember.'

'I almost did not for a moment. How is it you have blue eyes now?'

Dominic stopped and stared at her. 'You really do remember? It happened slowly. At first, I barely noticed it. My eyes lightened and I thought it just my body changing as I grew up. Then I noticed the more often I used my gift, the quicker my eye colour changed, until they ended up the blue you see now. The colour has not altered for a while, so I am thinking they will either stay this colour, or the changes will be minimal.'

'Mmm, that is interesting. It is almost as if your magic is taking a toll from you. I wonder if that is the same for all magic users?'

'Much as I would love to stay here and discuss the impact of magic on individuals, we need to keep moving. We should keep quiet from here on in as we do not want to alert anyone to our presence.'

They walked in silence through the rest of the night, using the moon to light their way. Not long after sunrise, the forest started to thin. As they were about to emerge into the open, Dominic stopped them both. 'Let me go ahead to see what I can see.'

He disappeared, and Aliah strained her eyes, trying to track him. Frustrated with not knowing what he was doing, she put her hand on the sword hilt, closed her eyes, and tried to use her other senses to find Dominic. She opened her eyes with a start as she sensed something, then closed them again and concentrated.

With her eyes closed, she could see an image of the vista in front of her, and moving along that vista was a shimmer. Focusing, the shimmer turned to the clear form of a man. She gasped as he transformed into a brilliant light behind her closed eyes. His gift was as beautiful and god given as hers.

Aliah followed Dominic's progress as he crested the hill. Her gaze followed him as he lay down flat on the ground and looked around. For a moment, he released his gift and waved for her to come forward As she moved, he turned his hand palm down and patted it towards the ground, indicating she should keep low.

She joined him on the crest of the hill, overlooking the bay where Port Marden sat. There were no soldiers anywhere in sight, but the scene before her caused her to utter a strangled cry. A full blown sea battle waged in the strait between Hand and Port Marden, and the Arian ships were outnumbered by three to one. As they watched, an Arian ship listed and floundered, allowing an enemy ship to head for the beach to off-load soldiers.

'Oh no, we are two late.' Aliah collapsed on the ground. 'We can do nothing from here, and once they have a foothold, they will be almost impossible to remove with the numbers they have.'

'Is there nothing your gift can do?' Dominic asked equally dismayed, rolling over, and watching her as she surveyed the battle ahead.

'Not that I know of. Seamus had mentioned the two of us training for battle, but we have not yet had a chance. I am almost sure in this instance I would need his magic to have an effect on this.'

Dominic burst out laughing, and she hit him on the arm. 'This is not funny.'

'Well it is when you say you need Seamus to fight this battle, and as you speak he emerges from the trees.'

Aliah turned to see Dominic was telling the truth. Seamus jogged up the hill, followed by Emer in wolf form. She resisted the urge to call out to them in case there were foreign soldiers anywhere about.

'Were you followed?' Dominic asked as the two came within earshot.

'No,' Seamus gasped as he slowed to a fast walk. 'We are all safe now, the Sanctuary forces have already reached the coastal road, less than half a days march from here. Our wizard friend is about half a candle-mark in front of them. With any luck, the Malorians will catch him up and deal with him for us.' He grinned at them.

'I would not say we were all right,' Aliah interrupted. 'Come and see.'

AMELIA STARED in wonder at the sight before her. In the scene that had appeared on the sheet of ice covering the rock wall, she saw hundreds of ships fighting a battle. Amazed at the number of ships the Carstenites had brought to Aria's shores, she was still unconcerned about the outcome of the battle.

'You are not worried Aria might lose this battle and all you know will be lost?'

'No,' Amelia answered. 'I sense this is not the day our forces are overrun, this is the day we show the invaders what we are made of.'

'You are confident that Aria will win the war?'

Amelia turned from the scene in the ice in front of her and faced the assembled gods. She touched her lips with her forefinger and thought for a moment before answering. 'The outcome of this war is still in flux. I sense something will happen today that will change the balance a little in favour of Aria, but it will not be enough for a decisive outcome.'

'Good,' the gods answered in unison. 'You understand the limits of your gift. We have one more scene to show you. This is not from your present, but from the past.'

Turning to the cavern wall, it shimmered and Amelia was transported into another cave. There were priests of some order she could not identify, placing a casket on a stone altar. She sensed the words they chanted were powerful ones, perhaps a spell of protection? The vision wavered, then disappeared.

'Well?' the gods pressed her. Not to be rushed, Amelia thought through what she had been shown for a moment. She had no feeling for why it was important, so she used her common sense to interpret it instead.

'I believe you showed me this because it has something to do with the outcome of this war. It is unlikely to impact the battle between Aria and Carsten, so it must have something to do with the god to be defeated. Maybe we will need to find that casket if we are to be successful?'

The gods did not smile, but Amelia could sense their approval. 'Good, you do not just rely on your sight, you also have strong powers of reasoning.'

Amelia blushed like a young child being praised, then mentally shook herself. She had no need of praise from the gods, she had lived her life until now without their help. Besides, this trial may not be over yet, and she needed to concentrate if she wanted to come out in one piece. She waited for the next challenge, but the gods seemed to be having some sort of internal conversation. Finally they broke away and spoke to her.

'For the last step in this trial we will need to look into your very essence. If you are a true seer, you will be able to accommodate a godly consciousness entering your mind; if you are not, it can send you insane. You need to be warned there are only one of two outcomes if you proceed from here. Firstly, you are not the seer, and you leave here as if you were a child, never again to be an adult. Or, secondly, you leave here as a chosen seer, never to see the world through your own eyes again. You still have the choice to end this trial and leave as you are now.'

Amelia froze. What a choice to have to make. While she wanted to leave because she did not need to be anything more than she was now, something niggled in the back of her mind and stopped her. For a seer, everything that happened had a meaning. Why, after all of these years of waiting, had the successor to the seer finally been found when the Wizard and the Warrior had also been identified?

'If I choose not to go forward with this trial, will Caraig still be able to advise Seamus and Aliah on their quest to beat the god?'

There was a pause while the gods debated their answer. 'We are not sure if telling you this will upset the balance of forces, but we all agree you need to know only the seer chosen in the time of the Wizard and Warrior can be of direct help to them.'

Her stomach sunk. She really had no other option. 'I will proceed.'

Another short pause, and then a blinding light entered her head.

CHAPTER 29

THE BATTLE

E mer shimmered and changed back into human form. Aliah briefly wondered what happened to her clothes when she turned into a wolf or eagle, before following the two new arrivals to the top of the hill.

'Oh no.' Seamus' face dropped. 'They have nearly landed their first boat, and after that...'

'Is there anything you are able to do?' this time Dominic directed his question to Seamus.

Seamus quietly followed the scene below. 'Would you say the battle is being directed from that large ship at the back?' he eventually asked.

They all watched the battle unfold for a moment longer. 'It is hard to tell,' Dominic said. 'We would need to be closer to find out for sure.'

'I can help out with that,' Emer answered.

'No.' Seamus' tone was emphatic. 'It is too dangerous.'

'How can you help?' Aliah asked.

'When Emer is in her animal form she not only mind-speaks, she can also link with specific people and share what she sees. She showed me how when we were trying to find exactly where you were.'

'That is great. You can get a better view of the battle and we can see what we need to do,' Aliah said enthusiastically.

'No. It is too risky. A bird has no place in the middle of all that fighting. It would be too dangerous.' Seamus stared out at the sea, a determined look on his face. Emer put her hand on his arm.

'Seamus it is not your decision. I am a guard. It is my job to fight battles in whichever form is best suited. If I am able to do this, then I must help.' Emer stared at Seamus, waiting for his reaction.

Aliah stepped between the two of them. 'Seamus, we need her. She is here for a reason, and perhaps this is it. She is right, it is her decision.'

Seamus sighed. 'I cannot see any other way to stop the battle that does not kill most of the people out there. There is only one way forward, and that is to remove whoever is leading the battle. To do that, we need to know exactly where he is, and for that, we need Emer to fly above.'

'What exactly do you mean by "removing him"?' Aliah asked frowning.

Seamus turned to look at her. 'We may need to kill one to save many, but it may suffice to knock him out if we can control our magic to that degree.' Seamus held her gaze.

'Have you ever killed anyone before?'

'No,' he answered, not counting the men he burned in his trial because that was not real. 'And I am not sure I want to after the experience I had during my trial.'

'Me neither. Can we control the magic enough not to kill him?'

'We can only try.' Seamus did not sound confident, and that surprised Aliah. Surely his foresight would tell him if their plan would work.

'Are you sure the gods will allow this?' She needed to check it would not be considered misusing his powers. It would be a shame if he lost them just when they needed them most. This was magic directed against a person, with a high risk the person would be injured, making it very close to being battle magic.

'I do not know, but I can see no other way to stop the Carstenites from gaining a foothold in Aria. I hope that, because we aim to incapacitate not kill, the gods will understand.' Seamus sounded confident, but he chewed worriedly on his lower lip. 'I do not know what will happen if we kill him by mistake though.'

'And you are sure there is no other way?'

'When Emer offered to fly over the battle, I had this feeling the way to defeat the attack today is for us to remove the battle commander. To do that we must risk killing him.'

'Then that is what we must do.' Aliah said firmly before Seamus could voice any more doubts. They had to trust his foresight. 'Do you know how?'

'I think so. I think it has something to do with me providing the magic and the intent, and you using your strength to send the magic that little bit further.' A furrow formed between Seamus' brow. 'I wish we had trained for this, but we will just have to do the best we can.'

'Whatever we are going to do, we had better do it fast, before this battle is lost,' Dominic interrupted.

Emer immediately changed into her eagle form. *I will start with a sweep, and share images with you all. This will give you a big picture. When you know exactly what you want to do, I will link mind to mind with Aliah so she can use my eyes to direct the attack.* With a sweep of wings, she caught the breeze and rose to the air.

Within seconds, Aliah was looking at a bird's eye view of the fight below. From above, it was obvious which boat directed the battle. It hung at the back, and on the foredeck stood a figure pointing and moving ships as if moving pieces on a game board.

I can feel the power coming from him, can you? Emer asked.

Yes. Seamus and Aliah sent back. *He is the one we need to stop.*

Oops. The picture blurred as Emer plummeted.

'What was that?' Seamus broke off, looking around them. 'Oh, no.' He pointed along the coast towards Port Marden. On the trail just below them were the soldiers they had evaded, rejoined by Millard and Gaius. One of the soldiers had a crossbow out. He had nocked another arrow and was again aiming at Emer, who had righted herself and flown out of range. Millard and Gaius were arguing and gesturing. The soldier ignored them, concentrating on Emer.

'How did Millard get around us?' Seamus asked.

'We cannot worry about that now,' Dominic advised. 'Let me take care of them. You focus on turning the tide of this battle.' Dominic disappeared.

'How do we do this?' Aliah asked, looking to Seamus for direction.

'Hold your sword, we need to mind speak from now on. It will help if we can share thoughts.'

I am not sure what the gods would have taught us, but I think we need to meld our powers in some way. If I think about what I want, the way I normally work magic, then when the thought is formed in my mind, you point your sword at the figure on the deck, like a wizard uses a wand. Imagine pushing all your power through that sword. Once we are working together, we can use Emer's sight to show us whether or not the attack is hitting the target, who I am pretty sure is the King of Carsten. Do you understand?

Aliah nodded, taking a deep breath.

Before we start, we should give Dominic a little time to get down to the soldiers so he can disrupt their activity.

He is nearly there. He has just dipped behind a rock and has pulled out some knives. I think we are good to try this.

How can you see him?

I will show you later, Seamus. Now focus.

Emer?

I am here.

Are you all right? His heart was in his mouth as he waited for her answer.

The arrow just grazed past me, throwing me off track. I am good now. When you are ready, let me know. I will link and swoop down so you can see where to send your bolt of magic.

SEAMUS TOOK a deep breath and placed his hand on Aliah's shoulder. He closed his eyes and used his senses to find Aliah's life force, just as his teachers had shown him to find it within himself. Fortunately, he felt a strong pull as her force was boosted by the sword she carried. He could not believe this was working.

Then he lost the connection.

Aliah looked round at him with such belief in her eyes that the full force of her trust almost crushed him. *What have I done to earn that?* He took a deep breath, wondering when it was she had decided he was the one in charge. He was the one getting magical training, sure, but he knew no more about this than she did.

Then it dawned on him; because he could sometimes see which path they were to take, she expected him to also take the lead. Now was not the time to explain to her that even when he could see the best path, there were many ways it could be travelled, and it was too much to expect him to decide which way on his own.

Taking another deep breath, he connected with Aliah again. Once he was sure the connection was strong, he used the training Walter had given him in the basement in Duncameron. He thought of his magic as a life force flowing through his veins, and he sent it through his arm and out through his hand to mingle with Aliah's. As the two life forces met, Seamus felt something rather like a twang, then what he could only describe as an "Aliahness" infused his body. He waited a moment more allowing the life forces to entwine, like two strands of twine wrapped around each other, making a stronger rope.

That is so strange. I feel like you are a part of me.

We need to test this out before we actually use it on someone.

Are you sure that is wise Seamus? As soon as you use your power, the god's chosen will know you are here. Emer interrupted.

Aliah?

Emer is right. We have to trust ourselves. Go for the attack, and if we get the first one wrong, they will at least be on the back foot while we ready ourselves for a second attempt.

All right, we will go ahead then. Aliah, first we have to gather our strength. Imagine you are gathering your energy to deliver the hardest punch you can give, but hold it. At the same time, I will imagine pulling air from around our target—the man on the ship directing the battle, who is likely the king. When I say, put all your gathered strength into pulling backwards from where the sword is pointing.

So, I just point the sword like a wand at our target and imagine pulling backwards? That is it?

Yes and no. It is a little more complicated than that, but in its raw form, yes. Ready, Emer? You need to circle over the king so Aliah knows where to direct the attack.

Ready.

Aliah?

Ready.

Here we go.

Seamus felt Aliah's power building as he watched Emer fly towards the ship. She started circling, then slowly spiralled lower. As Emer connected with Aliah, sharing her vision of the deck of the ship, out of the corner of his eye he saw the soldier below raise his bow. Before he could release the arrow, the bow dropped to the ground and the soldier clutched at his arm as a red patch of blood spread under his hand. Aliah's body tensed and Seamus was drawn back to the task at hand, taking comfort in the fact Dominic had them well protected.

Once again looking through Emer's eyes, Seamus concentrated on pulling the air from around the king figure on the ship, in much the same way he had with the man in his father's court during his trial.

NOW, he commanded.

Aliah raised her arm and pointed. There was a rush of energy and Seamus threw his power through Aliah's sword, out towards the ship. When the distance was right, he commanded, *Pull!* Seamus imagined pulling back on a rope like in a tug-of-war and felt Aliah's strength join with his. Through Emer's eyes, he saw water surge up from the ocean near the command ship. They had missed their mark. He broke off the attack and the ship rocked as the water they drew up with their spell spilled back into the ocean.

Loud shouting penetrated his consciousness, and Seamus looked down to see Gaius and Millard had spotted them. Fortunately, the wizards were both pointing and gesticulating, obviously arguing over what to do next.

Quickly. We need to move before Gaius and Millard can coordinate a counter-attack. Seamus sent to the others.

In response to his thought, Aliah's power begin to build again. Without needing to be told, Emer began her downwards spiral. Unfortunately he could also feel Millard pulling energy into himself, preparing to attack.

Are you ready?

Just about.

Emer?

Yes.

Aliah tensed, preparing to release her power.

Emer?

At Aliah's query, the man who was his intended target came into focus. The picture was clearer this time. The man they believed to be King of Carsten was staring directly at him. His eyes bored through Seamus, like he was staring into his very soul.

Seamus? Aliah called him back to the task at hand.

He shook his head. *NOW!*

Aliah raised her arm and released her power, at the very last moment Seamus changed his intent. As Aliah's force stretched out towards their target, he sent his magic inside of her power-stream, imagining his force as something akin to an arrow inside a tunnel of air. Just as the point of his imaginary arrow touched the king, he pulled back with all his will, and Aliah pulled with him. Seamus kept pulling the air from the king's lungs, then, as the king struggled for breath and started to sway, Seamus cut off their attack.

Emer rose high above the Carsten command ship. Sailors gathered around a man who had fallen to the deck—the man they had attacked. With their commander out of commission for the moment, would it be enough to stop the attack for the day? They could only wait and see.

'Can you tell if they will stop now?' Aliah asked.

'Foresight does not work that way,' Seamus told her, his attention focused on the battle before them.

Suddenly his ears filled with the sound of screaming and his eyes burned with a bright explosion. Everything went blank, but before he could adjust to using his own eyes again, the ground moved beneath his feet and he sunk into darkness.

As she tried to disconnect her vision from Emer's, the ground crumbled beneath Aliah's feet, and everything went dark. Aliah struggled to breathe. Buried under a mound of dirt, Aliah struggled to stay calm and control her rising panic. She pushed with her arms and the earth overhead give way a little. Breathing became a little easier, but she would need fresh air soon or she would suffocate. Pressure built behind her eyes and her head throbbed, making it hard for her to think.

Do not think you have won. The battle may be over, but I will win the war!

'What is going on?' Seamus' voice came very close to her ear, and she realised she was lying on top of him in their dark prison.

'You have merely destroyed the body of my servant, I am still very much alive. Soon I will find another servant to do my bidding and bring me through to your plane of existence. Then beware, I will be truly unstoppable.'

'Are you hearing this?' Seamus whispered.

'Yes. Do you think it is...'

'Yes, I think so. He said we killed the king, but I am pretty sure I saw him breathing.' Aliah could almost see Seamus frowning in the darkness as he wondered what actually happened.

You know I am a god, I can hear your every word and thought if I choose to. I know you think to fight me and win. You are but children, still unsteady on your feet. You cannot defeat a god. At best, you can delay my plans like you have done today. But I will join you on your plane, and I will rule the land as I see fit. There is nothing you can do to stop me.

The rantings of this pompous god made Aliah's blood boil. *If we are such unworthy opponents then why are you wasting your time scaring us off?* The thought jumped into Aliah's head before she could stop it, and as soon as it finished, the god presence abruptly left.

'Ahhh,' Aliah spluttered. Dirt filled her mouth as she was pulled back by her feet.

'Aliah? Seamus?' Dominic's voice seemed to come from far away. Then, suddenly, fresh air filled her lungs and she gazed up at blue sky. The pressure on her ankles ceased, and she sat up to see Dominic pulling Seamus from a pile of dirt.

'What happened?' she asked, turning to Emer who was back in human form.

'You were attacked by magic and the ground you were standing on collapsed, burying you both.' Emer told her.

'No,' Aliah shook her head. 'I mean with the battle.'

'Oh. We knocked out the Carsten King with our last attack. Just after he fell to the deck, my head was filled with screams of rage, and the ship he was on exploded,' she replied and turned to look out to sea. 'It looks like their forces lost co-ordination when their command ship sunk. They have retreated back in line with the Isle of Hand, but they are still fighting.'

'Oh no,' Aliah cried in dismay as Seamus stumbled to his feet to take a look as the battle continued below.

'I may be able to help.' He tipped his head to the side as he considered his options.

'How?' Aliah asked. 'There is no other single target for us to fight at the moment.'

'I have an idea, and I think I can do this alone.' He closed his eyes and started moving his hands. Aliah placed a hand on Seamus' shoulder so he did not feel he was doing this alone. With the other hand resting on her sword hilt she found if she closed her eyes, she could follow what he was doing. He pulled air to him, then started to push it away, towards the sea. The water rose in between the two sets of ships as Seamus used the air to put pressure on the sea water to move the Carsten ships out a day's sail beyond Hand.

When the sails barely dotted the horizon, Seamus released the air. Turning back to them, he collapsed to the ground. Emer rushed to him and rolled him onto his back. 'He is all right. The magic has taken a bit out of him. We need to get him food soon or he will become very ill.'

'Food? Where are we going to find food out here?' Aliah swept her hand, taking in the barren countryside.

Aliah turned to Dominic, surprised to find him grinning from ear to ear. 'Funny enough, we may just be in luck.' He pointed to the coastal path below, and Aliah turned to see two horsemen in strange livery heading up the track towards them.

'What?' she asked, confused, not understanding why Dominic was so pleased to see complete strangers in the midst of battle.

'While you and Seamus were doing your magic thing, our friend Millard caught wind of it and directed a blast at you both. I managed to get a knife in his arm which threw him off, hence this.' He gestured to the debris that were once the ledge she and Seamus had been standing on. 'He was about to strike again when we all heard the thundering of hooves.

'From what I can make out, the Sanctuary troops spied a ship about to land soldiers on the shore below, and sent a party on ahead to ensure they did not reach the beach. Realising they did not want to be caught alone by our troops, Millard and his off sider thought better of finishing you off, deciding their interests were best served making their escape with the retreating longboats. Last I saw of them, they were swimming out to sea.' Dominic laughed.

'So, if I am not mistaken, those two riders should be...' he continued.

'Daniel and Liam,' Aliah exclaimed excitedly as two riders crested the hill heading towards them.

CHAPTER 30
PORT MARDEN

After a day of travelling through the forest on foot, it was a relief to once again be on the back of a horse, well fed and on her way to the relative safety of Port Marden. Although Aliah was more than capable of looking after herself, she really had not enjoyed being hunted. Seamus, looking wan but awake, shared a horse with Emer. Dominic and Daniel were riding on either side of her as the city walls came into sight.

Camped out along the base of the walls were guards, each gathered around the banner of the lord who had brought them, another large group of fighters under no banner camped nearby. Aliah voiced her surprise at the number of citizens who had flocked to Port Marden to fight for the freedom of their country.

Their party stopped well before the walls at a road block staffed by a mixture of guards and free fighters. As they waited to pass through, Aliah's eye caught one of the free fighters watching her. She glanced away, then glanced back as the man sauntered towards her.

'Hello again,' the fighter said, grinning. 'I did not think to find you at this battle. And I see you found our friend.' He nodded towards Seamus. 'You are both a long way from Duncameron.'

Aliah frowned and tugged at her plait, then managed to see through the grime to his face. 'Able.' Surprised, Aliah beamed down at him, pleased to again see one of the group of people who managed to smuggle her through to Bannock a moon or so ago. 'I am where I should be, but what are you doing here?'

'Boss and some of the others in our group, Megan included, have joined the fight to save Aria from invasion. We have not seen much of the real fighting.' He shrugged. 'We get mostly sentry duty, or drills for the moment. But every man and woman is freeing up a guard from duty for the real fight.'

'And what about Pauley? Did he manage to get back home?' Aliah asked about the young boy who had guided them through the sewers to escape Duncameron. They were so closely pursued he had been forced to join them as far as Bannock.

Able laughed. 'He was only home for a short time. He decided to join us and come and fight for Aria. He is a brave one, that lad.'

Aliah glanced towards Daniel, who was taking care of the formalities. They had all agreed they did not want anyone to know the Heir to the Throne was with them until they were safely in behind the walls of the town. She frowned and turned back to Able.

'Ah, I see, you are still incognito,' Able said. 'Do not fret, I will not give your secret away. There are still those who say they are on our side, but I would not trust them with my back turned.'

'Thank you, Able. Please say hello to Megan and the Boss for me. I am pleased to see you supporting us, but would not wish harm to come to any of you.'

'I will do that. And do not worry about us, we look after each other.' Able turned to retake his post, giving her a brief wave as a small part of their group moved forward. The guard commander had been reluctant to let such a large armed force pass into the city area, despite Daniel's assurances they were allies. Finally they agreed a small party would enter the city, and the rest of the troops would stay at the guard post until they received new orders.

At long last, they entered the city walls and Aliah relaxed a little, although she was strangely nervous about once again becoming Princess Aliahanna, and taking on all that position entailed. She stayed that way until they entered the courtyard of the local garrison, and Tomas, the Captain of the Palace Guard and Daniel's father, came out of the main doorway. Again, she tensed, waiting to see who she needed to be wary of here.

Dominic came up beside her and placed a hand on her arm. 'Remember, it is best we wait a little and see who is with your father before we announce your presence.'

Aliah turned to argue, then stopped. Of course that was sensible, given the circumstances. Daniel dismounted, saluted his father as a senior officer, then hugged him hello. Relief that his son had arrived back safely flickered over Tomas' face, to be quickly replaced by a formal demeanour.

He gestured for stable hands to come and take their horses and their small party dismounted, following Tomas into the commander's quarters. There, much to her surprise, they were greeted by her father and The Duke of Hand.

Duke Damon took one look at his son and wrapped him in a bear hug, leading him to a chair to sit down, with Emer trailing close behind. Aliah turned to find her father, arms opened, ready to give her a similar welcome.

'Father,' she whispered. 'We thought it best if no one knew I was here.'

King Terion laughed. 'Good thinking, but as you will soon find out, there is no need for that any more,' he said as he drew his daughter into his arms.

The king led her to one of the chairs around the council table that dominated the room. Duke Damon, Liam, Tomas, and Daniel were already seated. Dominic took up a position behind her chair. As they settled down, a wizard entered the room. He was wearing the gold lightening bolt sigil that showed he was a strong magician, and had risen to the highest ranks in the Wizard Isle. He was vaguely familiar, but Aliah could not immediately name him.

'Ah, Pieter, please join us.' King Terion gestured to a spare seat at the table, and the Gold Wizard took his place. 'You already know Tomas, and his son Daniel, and Duke Damon. This is Duke Damon's heir, Seamus and his squire, Liam. And this is obviously my Heir, Princess Aliahanna.'

Aliah noticed the look of surprise on the wizard's face, instantly telling her he could be trusted. Wizards from the rebellion had known where she was from the time she left Bannock on her mission to Hand, and this man clearly had no idea she would be likely to turn up in Port Marden.

'Aliah,' King Terion continued with the introductions. 'Tomas has been promoted as my new Chief Advisor after finding out Wizard Millard was a traitor. The Wizard Council has been in a bit of a flux as they try and weed out all the other traitors. In the meantime, they have sent Pieter to advise me on all matters magical. I asked him for a report on what happened today during the sea battle we appeared to be losing, then strangely won. In particular, I wanted to know if someone used battle magic to turn the tide in our favour.'

Aliah glanced at Seamus, who shook his head. Like her, he probably wanted to know what the wizard had to say before they apprised Terion of what really happened.

'As I have already told you, Your Highness, there was some strange magic in play. All wizards on your staff felt what can only be described as a draining of magic. Once before a spurt of water flew up, and once before our far-seer saw the King of Carsten collapse on the deck of his ship. As we sensed no loss of life, we believe the magic caused the king to fall, almost as if he had received a strong punch.

'Whether or not this is battle magic is not clear. It is a grey area as the attack did not appear to be aimed to injure or kill, but rather to disable the king. If there was no intent to injure, then this is something similar to how we hold people in bonds of air to prevent damage to themselves or others. Without knowing what the magic user intended, I would err on the side of this not being battle magic.

'Then there was a scream, and what we magic users can only

describe as a building of pressure in our heads. The ship exploded. The explosion was definitely magic used with the intention to kill, and so would be against the Wizard's Law. The power seemed to come from on board the ship itself, unlike the other attacks which we know came from somewhere along the coast.'

Aliah placed her hand on the hilt of her sword. *That is exactly as Emer described it. Did the god really destroy the ship in a fit of anger?*

I think so. I know the worst we might have done was to kill the king as we tried to disable him, and I do not believe we did that—we only made him collapse. I also know the type of magic we used would not blow up a ship. Besides, we were tumbling into a dirt prison when that ship exploded.

Relieved Seamus' opinion was similar to her own, Alain still had doubts. *I hate to say it, I am a little relieved we did not actually kill anyone. However, I still feel responsible for what happened to the crew on that ship. I mean, we caused the god's fit of anger because we disabled the man he was using.*

I understand what you are saying, but we can really only be responsible for our own actions; not what others do in response to them. Seamus' voice in her head was confident, but as she took her hand off her sword, she thought they would have to agree to disagree on this point. As her attention returned to the meeting, Aliah heard her father asking the wizard about the wave that pushed the ships out to sea.

'Creating the wave seemed to use the same type of magic as the initial attacks, and came from the same location. As far as we can tell, there were no ships or lives lost during that use of magic, which is a good thing. However, it is harder to determine whether this action was actually battle magic. Once again, much relies on the intent of the user. If they were sending ships away in a controlled manner with the intention of savings lives, it was not battle magic. If they were striking at the enemy without thought for what would happen, then that would indeed be against the law. Without being able to question the magic user, we will never know the answer to that question.

'However, whether or not battle magic was used is the least of our worries. What concerns us all is that if the intent in both of these attacks was to injure, and battle magic was used, we are in trouble. There is not a wizard here who would even know where to begin to counter magic such as this.'

'Sorry? I am unsure what you mean by that.' The king closed his eyes wearily as he tried to understand the implications of Pieter's words.

'We are concerned because this is a type of magic unlike our own, we have never seen anything like it before. This means we would not have anything prepared to counter the magic or disable the user.'

There was silence around the table as the elder members of the council took this in, and the younger members tried to look innocent of the knowledge of what went on. The king looked thoughtfully at them all, before turning his attention back to the wizard.

'Thank you, Pieter. We will need to consider all that you have told us, about the battle and the potential threat. I will call you if we need any further assistance, in the meantime, I suggest you all put your heads together and see if there is anything you can think of to counter such magic should it be directed against us.'

Dismissed, Pieter stood, bowed, and left the room. Pieter had barely shut the door when the king turned to his daughter with his eyebrows raised.

'All right, Aliahanna, what do you know about this?'

'I am not sure what you mean.' Aliah tried to stare her father down and failed. Her face flushed as she looked down at her hands.

Fortunately, Seamus came to her rescue. He placed his wand on the table in front of him. Aliah raised her head and glared at him. He shrugged his shoulders. Well, if Seamus believed this was the right course of action, she had best go along. She took out her sword to place it in front of her.

'Umm... it seems after some debates and trial by gods, we are the Wizard and the Warrior who were prophesied as the saviours of our people.' Seamus barely got the words out before they were inundated with questions, the disbelief of their elders apparent in every word.

The questioning continued as servants came in and lit the wall sconces. It continued as others came in to feed the large fire that warmed the room, and through the serving of the evening meal, and the clearing away of dishes. Some time later, it seemed all their questions had been asked and answered and the room was silent.

—

KING TERION LOOKED Seamus directly in the eye. 'All right. I can nearly believe you have been tested and you are the wizard and that my daughter is the warrior, but that still does not answer one question. Have you brought back battle magic?'

Seamus wanted to answer immediately, but he stopped himself and thought through what the king was actually asking.

'Well, Your Highness, I wish the answer was a simple yes or no, but the truth is more complex than that.'

The king stared at him, not letting him off the hook that easily. 'Young man, you had better come up with something better than that or I will be forced to have you stand trial before the Wizard Council.'

Seamus chewed on his lip, thinking carefully about his answer. Battle magic as he understood it was using magic to deliberately injure an enemy, and his problem was that he would very definitely have to try and hurt anyone the god attempted to use if he thought it would stop him. The question was, had he really used battle magic today?

'The wave I caused was no more than pushing the ships away to end the fighting, and was no different to a wizard binding a criminal in my mind. Although I have to be honest and say it was more a reaction to the continued fighting, rather than a well thought through plan.

'As for what I did to the King of Carsten? If you literally take battle magic to mean magic used against an enemy, then on the surface I guess the magic we used to stop him would fall into that category. Our intention was to wind him, but we knew what we were doing would not be very precise, and there was a chance we might kill him. We continued, even though we knew death was a potential outcome, because we felt it was the only way to prevent Carstonites from winning the sea battle and invading Aria.'

He stopped talking for a minute, not sure how best to say the next bit in a way the council would not automatically think he had lost his mind. He took a deep breath, feeling somewhat like he was jumping off a cliff.

'We took this dangerous action not just to save Aria, but also to prevent a god from achieving his aims of causing the devastation of our world.' Amidst gasps of surprise, Seamus pushed on. 'We believe Spearon was possessed by a god, and no ordinary attack from your guards would have affected him in any way. So, you could say we were not attacking a man but a god, and so we did not use battle magic as the law defines it.'

After the initial shock, there was silence in the room as the council digested his news. Seamus could not say exactly what he expected the reaction of the Arian War Council to be, but laughter was not exactly on the list—until he realised the laugher was because they did not believe him. When they stopped, the king directed his cold, calculating blue eyes at Seamus once again.

'You have imagination, I will say that. Unfortunately you will have to stand in front of the Wizard Council and answer one count of using battle magic.'

'Then I must stand trial with him.' Aliah rose and moved to stand beside Seamus. 'It was our combined magic that felled the god.'

'Aliah, you cannot be serious. You do not have magic.' King

Terion set off laughing again as Duke Damon stood to command the council's attention.

'Your Highness, you seem to be taking this all too lightly. I know it is hard to believe our children have been chosen as the Wizard and Warrior, and have come to rid us of the evil that plagues us, but stop and think for a moment.

'I have commissioned research into the prophecy, and I am slowly gaining some understanding of its importance as it has been woven through our history for hundreds of years in various forms. You knew your daughter had travelled with my son to be tested as the Wizard and Warrior of prophecy. On some level, you must have considered whether or not Aliah may actually be the warrior, and thought about the impact of that. Even I realised my son might return the wizard of legend.

'Add to that the fact your own advisor described the attacks made from the shore today as being like no other magic. That strange magic could have come from our children, whose gifts they say come from the gods themselves, and if so, would account for them being so different.

'If we can admit the possibility all this might be true, is it really such a stretch to believe these gifts and powers have been bestowed on our children because they will actually have to face a god?' There was stunned silence as the duke finished speaking and sat down.

King Terion was no longer laughing—in fact a frown settled on his face, while deep in thought as he processed Duke Damon's words. Tomas also looked puzzled, and he was the first to respond.

'I have never been one for blind faith, Damon, and you are asking us to put aside one of our most sacred laws to trust these children had only good intent when they used magic against a man. You, who have abhorred any use of magic all the years I have known you.'

'It is hard to believe, but if you had read the documents I have over the past few moons, you would recognise there is more going on here than a simple invasion.

'If you cannot believe the hand of the gods is involved, then think on this. Why would the King of Carsten be driven to invade Aria? They are a warrior-like people, but they must have stripped their country bare to mount a force the size that arrived on our shores.

'We must also consider, would a warrior-like people take the time to subvert the Wizard Council and offer up Aria to our traitors? When they invade other lands, they raise their army by promising land and plunder to their troops. That runs counter to offering Aria to Arians. So why are they spending such large resources to conquer a land they do not intend to hold?

'You also know the Carsonite soldiers we have captured were very keen to surrender. When questioned, they told us they had been forced to leave farms and shops and fishing boats to join the army. This is all very unusual, as we have discussed before today. Is the reason Seamus and Princess Aliahanna gave us any more far fetched than those we have already come up with?'

King Terion sighed. 'You do have a point. And as I think on what you have said, if the fate of our land does lie in the hands of our children, I would be very foolish to have them locked up. On the other hand, this is quite a leap of faith.'

There was silence as the King tugged at his beard, thinking things through. Dominic stepped forward. 'If I may, Your Highness...'

'Yes, young Dominic.'

'I am obviously one of those who has already made the leap of faith Duke Damon is asking you to make, but I have had more evidence of the existence of the gods than you, which made it easier for me. I could not ask you to make that same jump without more information, so may I suggest a compromise?'

The king nodded for him to continue.

'How about you let us leave and go about what we have to do to stop the invasion, and stop the god. Once we have won the battle, then you will be able to judge whether Seamus and Aliah have told you the truth. If you believe they have not, then they will undertake a trial in front of the Wizard Council. If we lose, well, there will be no need to make the decision.'

There was silence as the king considered Dominic's proposal. 'Once again, Dominic, you have shown me why I wish you were your father's heir. What say you, Seamus and Aliah? If we so deem, will you stand trial after the war is over?'

Seamus looked at Aliah. For once he was not chewing his lip in thought, he was resolved as he reached for his wand. She reached for her sword to put back in its sheath, and as she did so, she heard his words. *I know you want to argue this through until the bitter end, but this may be the only way we get out of here to do what needs to be done.*

Pausing, she considered her options. Seeing this was for the best, she nodded and turned to her father. 'Yes, father, we agree.'

As if he had been holding out just for this, Aliah had no sooner agreed to her father's terms than Seamus collapsed, slipping from his chair to thump on the floor. Aliah was rooted to the spot with shock. Emer pushed her out of the way, and she and Duke Damon helped the boy to his feet.

'He has been drained by today, he needs rest before we decide our next steps,' Emer declared.

'I will show you to your rooms.' Tomas stood. 'I am sure all of you could do with baths, a change of clothes and a good night's sleep.'

'Tomas, by all means take the others to their quarters. They should be ready by now. I need to talk to Liam and Daniel about the additional soldiers they brought with them today. They need to be properly housed and deployed.'

Aliah followed Tomas out of the room and through some corridors to a section of the building she assumed usually housed officers. 'You and the other young lady are in here.' Tomas indicated a door. 'We are short on space so you will have to share. There should be a bath in there ready for you to use, and someone hopefully has found you each a change of clothes close to your size.'

'You go ahead,' Emer said to Aliah. 'I will see Seamus settled, then return to see to myself.'

The others continued down the corridor as Aliah opened the door. She had to bite back her squeal of joy when she saw a full sized tub in the room, steam from the water rising above it. It was all very well being a warrior and saving the world, but nothing could beat the pleasure of soaking in a hot tub. In very little time at all, she removed her clothes and sunk into the delicious bath. Luxury, she sighed, closing her eyes. All too soon, the water began to cool and she hurried to wash off the dirt and wash her hair before it was completely cold. After towelling herself dry, she was weary to the core. Quickly pulling on a sleep gown, she slipped in between the sheets of one of the beds and was soon oblivious to everything around her.

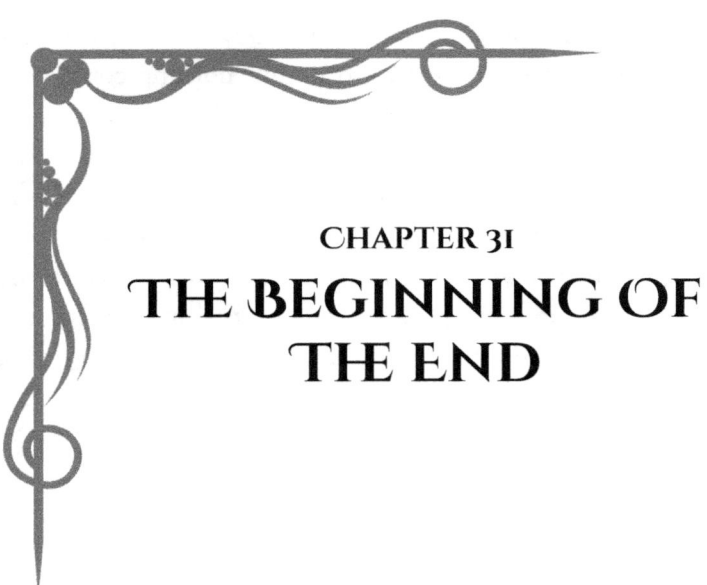

CHAPTER 31
THE BEGINNING OF THE END

Seamus could not remember a time when he had been so exhausted. As he attempted to roll over, his body would barely follow his commands. Shaking his head, he remembered how he had drawn energy from around him when travelling with Emer, and he reached into himself to find his magic. There was nothing there. He sat bolt upright in pain. Had he burned his magic out? *Oh no, the gods must have taken it. What did I do wrong?*

His thoughts were interrupted by a knock on the door. He opened it to a servant with orders to fetch him for an urgent meeting. Wishing he had had time to bathe and change his clothes, Seamus followed the servant through the dark stone corridors to the Council Room, all the while worrying about the loss of his magic. How would they defeat a god without it?

All except for the king and his advisor Tomas were there when Seamus arrived, still a little groggy headed from overuse of magic the day before. Everyone was deep in conversation, but his father broke away to welcome him.

'Ah, Seamus, I am pleased to see you have recovered from your activity yesterday. The king's advisor on magic tells me you must be more careful in the future as you came close to doing yourself some serious harm. I am told using magic can drain a person's energy, and it seemed you used a lot of yours during the battle.'

Seamus stopped dead in his tracks. He never thought he would hear his father talking so openly about the using magic, and especially not his own son's use of it. How ironic it happened now when the gods had taken it from him. He decided there and then, that he would tell no one what had happened. So he merely shrugged, and frowned. 'I am feeling better, thank you.'

'Good. Good. I was just showing the others where I believe you may find some information on early magic that might help you in your fight.' He showed Seamus a roughly drawn map of a library. It seemed familiar, but through the fog of his brain, Seamus could not place it.

'There are some very old papers your aunt knows of. We did not have a chance to go and get them when we evacuated to Port Marden, but from what she said, there should be a wealth of information there.'

'Ahh... Father?'

'Mmm...' Damon added some notations to his diagram.

'You know over the next few days I will have no choice but to practice and use magic if I am to learn how to defeat a god. And I cannot guarantee no one will see me use it. You know what I am saying.' Seamus watched his father carefully to gauge his reaction.

Duke Damon stopped writing, but did not look up. The others sheepishly searched around for something else to be busy doing. Eventually, he raised his head to look his son in the eye.

'I know what you are saying, Seamus. It is the only way forward. I am more convinced than ever having spoken with your friend Emer.'

'People will know what I am. There will be no going back. I will no longer be able to be your heir.' Seamus' stomach churned as he admitted out loud what he had known for some time.

'No, Seamus, you will not.' Duke Damon shook his head sadly. 'But we must do what is right for now, and worry about the future if

411

—when—we get through this.' Damon moved to face his son, and put his hand on his shoulder as he stared him in the eye. 'I want you to know this. I am proud of you, and I am proud of the courage you are showing. Whatever happens, I will not turn away from you.'

Seamus was embarrassed to find tears in his eyes as Duke Damon took him into a hug, and he was ashamed he had put his father through this, especially now when his powers had deserted him. His thoughts were interrupted as the door banged against the wall and King Terion entered.

'Oh, good. I worried I would be too late for the farewells. You have everything you need?' He waited for each of those assembled to agree before he moved on. Seamus merely stood there, dazed. *We are leaving? Where are we going?*

'Good. There is a small fishing boat waiting for you at the harbour. They will sneak you across and leave you at the docks. You will have to find your own way up to the town and to safety.

'Just so we are clear, because I understand there was some confusion on your recent mission, Daniel, you are in command. I know Aliah outranks you, a fact she may remind you of to make sure she gets her way, however I need her to concentrate on whatever she has to do, not to be worrying about everything else. Is that clear?'

Daniel stepped forward. 'Yes, Your Highness. And I have letters from the duke to his commander outlining my responsibilities.'

Aliah's face clouded over, and Seamus held his breath waiting for the explosion. When it came, it was small compared to some he had witnessed.

'When all this is over, Father, you and I are going to have a very long discussion about my future position, as heir *and* in general.' She forced out through gritted teeth.

'I would not have thought otherwise.' The King smiled at his daughter before turning back to the assembled group. Aliah's foot tapped her frustration, but she managed to contain her temper, something she would not have done when Seamus first met her.

'Dominic, Emer, and Liam you are responsible for ensuring our

Wizard and Warrior come to no harm. One of you must be with them at all times.' The three guards nodded their agreement. Aliah went to speak, but Terion held up his hand.

'Aliah, I am aware you are the Warrior, and I know that you are more than capable of looking after yourself, as is Seamus. I am also capable of defending myself, but I have guards who follow me everywhere at all times. It is only sensible to take precautions to ensure you are present when we need you to battle this god.'

Aliah sighed, and Seamus was pleased she was not going to argue with her father on this point. He agreed with King Terion. If they were to concentrate on what they needed to learn to defeat a god, they could not be forever looking over their shoulders, worrying about everyone else. Besides, the prophecy had said they would all need to work as a team to defeat their foe.

'Has anyone heard anything from Walter and Amelia?' he asked. 'We have a lot of research to do, and our two best minds are not even with us.'

'Nothing as yet...' the king responded, only to be interrupted by Emer.

'I had contact with my father last night, and he said they have set out from Sanctuary and should arrive here soon.'

'That is good. We will send them after you as soon as they get here. Now, are we ready?'

'We have a few more things to organise, and Seamus needs to bathe, change, and pack,' Daniel informed the king.

'I have to meet with the commander of the forces from your Sanctuary, so I will say my farewells now.' King Terion walked over to his daughter and wrapped his arms around her.

The good byes were quickly said, and a servant appeared to lead Seamus back through the corridors to his room. As he walked, he realised he had no idea where they were actually going, although there was a niggling thought at the back of his mind that he might just know after all, but he could not fully grasp it. Anyway, he had much more important things to worry about.

413

GAIUS STOOD COWERING behind Millard as the god figure in front of them drew up to twice the height of a human male. The thundering of his voice caused the waves to rise, which in turn caused the ship they were on to dip and swirl in the ocean. Millard seemed unconcerned by the god's wrath at their inability to stop that brat Aliahanna and her friend Seamus.

'It was not the right time to defeat them magically.' Millard spoke firmly to the god, as if he were placating a wilful child.

'Not the right time? NOT THE RIGHT TIME?' The god shouted so loudly Gaius' teeth chattered together from the shock. 'In your opinion, when exactly would be the right time? When they are about to kill you?'

'No, of course not. But we do need to be sure we know the full extent of the magical threat against us before we attack. We do not want to be caught out thinking we have won, only to find these two are mere annoyances and we still have our real foe to take on.'

The god shrank back to human size and moved forward until he was nose to nose with Millard. Even though his form was not solid, his ghost-like persona reeked of power and was more frightening than a human could ever be. Still, Millard did not flinch away.

'You do not understand the importance of the two you let escape.' The god was even more scary when his voice was so low. It resonated through every fibre of Gaius' body as he spoke. 'These are the only two who can stop me, and if I lose, so do you. How will you win over and rule your precious Aria without my support? *Bah*! I should never have trusted a mere human to help me.' He turned away and his form floated to the bow of the boat.

Millard tensed and Gaius sensed his fear that his plans to rule Aria were slipping though his fingers. He moved as if to follow the god, then stopped, thinking better of it. Gaius took a breath and whispered in his master's ear. 'He still needs us, master. He cannot act upon the real world in his present form. He needs us to act for him, and to bring him through to this plane of existence.'

Millard smiled, but before he said anything, the god whipped around and fixed his gaze on Gaius. Gaius, whose stomach did somersaults every time the god noticed him, again shrank behind Millard.

'You are right, boy. I cannot act in your world like this. Maybe the two of you can still be useful to me.'

A flash of light blinded Gaius, and he shuddered as something began rifling through his body and his mind.

'No,' Millard shouted close to his ear. 'Get out of my head.'

'I do not know why I did not do this sooner. My last body was definitely warrior-like. But, oh how good it is to taste powerful magic again. Now, I will be unstoppable.'

BACK IN HIS ROOM, Seamus knew he should prepare for wherever they were going, but instead, he sunk down on his bed and once again tried to reach for his powers. Still nothing. With a worried knot in his stomach, he lay back and closed his eyes. *Why are you punishing me? What did I do wrong?*

Seamus found himself back in the cave with the seven gods, who were seated on chairs as if sitting in judgement.

'You have had some training, and you have used your powers to help achieve your calling. But you have also used your power without thought. We are concerned about those times.'

Seamus thought hard. When had he used his power without thought, or without good reason? Thinking back over the last few days there was nothing, until he came to the farewell outside the Sanctuary.

'I gagged Eon with air because his whining, annoyed me,' Seamus responded.

'That is indeed one of the times. Magic used for your benefit alone is not magic used wisely.'

'But it was only a small incident,' Seamus argued.

'Small it may have been, but if we allow you to act thoughtlessly with small things, what is to stop you acting without thinking with bigger magical feats? Yesterday you did just that, and endangered thousands of lives.'

Seamus looked at the Gods, trying to think of what he had done that met that description. He stroked his chin. 'Do you mean when I moved the ships?'

'We do.'

'But I controlled my magic, I used only what was necessary to move the ships away. No one was hurt. I may even have saved lives by stopping the battle when I did.' Seamus could not see what was wrong with his actions.

'That is correct, and that is the only reason why you have been given the chance to explain yourself.'

'Then what did I do wrong?' Seamus was really perplexed.

'You saw what was happening and you reacted. You decided you were the solution without stopping and considering whether you should do anything, or whether there was another course of action.'

Opening his mouth to argue, Seamus stopped. He could not fault what the gods said. He had considered all possible courses of action, before deciding the best way was to cause King Spearon to collapse, removing the commander from the battle. He had not given the same consideration to his actions when he decided to move the ships to stop the fighting. He dropped his head in shame. This decision of his might have killed thousands.

'You are right, I am not ready to wield this power.' He took his wand from his pocket and held it out to the gods. No one moved forward to take it.

'We have taken into account no one died, and we had all agreed before bringing you here that if you understood the importance of the lesson, then this time we would be lenient. But remember, the most important learning from all of our training is not how you should act in any given situation, but whether you should act at all.'

'Seamus. *Seamus.* Seamus, wake up.'

'What?' he asked groggily.

'Seamus. Come On. We have to go.' Aliah stood over him, hands on hips, dressed in clean travelling clothes that included a divided skirt, sturdy boots, and a thick warm coat.

'What? Why? I only just got to sleep.' He wearily rubbed the sleep out of his eyes, swung his legs over the side of the bed, and sat up. *Thank goodness someone put sleeping clothes on me last night,* he thought to himself. *Aliah and I would be feeling pretty uncomfortable now if they had not.* He smiled at that thought, only to be jolted by Aliah shaking him by the shoulders.

'You are not listening to me. You were only meant to bathe and change, not to have a nap.' Her blue eyes were glaring at him.

'Sorry,' he mumbled. 'Still feeling a bit woolly headed after yesterday.' He shook his head to clear it, remembering it was not morning, and he was supposed to be getting ready to leave for somewhere, but had been distracted by... oh, yes... *the gods.*

'Seamus.'

'Sorry. You were saying?'

'Some of the witches working in the hospital tents came and met with father this morning. They overheard some of the wizards talking about our arrival, and were saying Gaius would need to hear about it. Those wizards cannot be found this morning.'

'Sorry? There are witches working in the hospital tents? Women have not been allowed to practice magic in any official capacity in Aria for generations.' Seamus dragged a hand through his hair.

'Gah! That is what you took from that story? You really are impossible sometimes.' Aliah turned on her heel and headed for the door, but stopped before she actually opened it.

'A local coven of witches came and offered their help healing the injured. Against the advice of the Wizard's Council, my father agreed. With half the wizards from the Wizard Isle defecting with Millard, we would have been severely short of people able to tend the wounded otherwise.'

Seamus stood. 'You learnt all of that in a short space of time.'

'What time do you think it is?'

'Late morning. Or possibly a little later. After all, I only had a short nap when I returned to my room.' He guessed.

'You slept through most of the day before we had our meeting, and you have just dozed again. It is early evening.' Aliah was clearly exasperated.

Seamus tried to pull himself together and think clearly. 'So, while I slept you all decided we have to go somewhere away from where the wizards expect to find us, to learn what we need to know? And you want to leave by cover of night?' Seamus nodded his head, appreciating the planning that had gone into this. 'That is smart. Where are we going?'

'Hand.'

'Are you out of your heads?' Seamus thundered as he leapt to his feet, suddenly realising why the plan he had seen in the Council Chambers had seemed so familiar. 'That is the closest place for the enemy fleet to land, given where I sent them.'

'Please do not yell at me like I am an imbecile,' Aliah clearly enunciated each word to make a point as she turned to face him again. 'While you were sleeping, Emer flew over the island. The enemy command is camped on the far side of the island. Port of Hand is still protected by the mountains between, and relatively safe. There is a garrison in Port Hand guarding the city walls, looking after those who were not able to evacuate, so we will not be alone and will be relatively safe.'

'Oh,' Seamus responded feeling a little silly, but he was still annoyed they had made such a big decision without him.

'So why Hand?' he asked, trying to be open minded as to why they would choose such a silly place to retreat to, and going though other options for a hiding place in his head. *Maybe Amelia's farmhouse?*

'Seamus, please pay attention.' Aliah sighed, he had been wool gathering again.

'Sorry, you were saying...'

'We had to consider three things. Firstly, we needed somewhere no one would expect us to go. Secondly, we needed somewhere where we can research what we need to do to defeat a god. And, lastly, it needed to be somewhere easy to defended from attack, where we can practice what we learn before we face the god.' Aliah stood in front of him, hands on hips, patiently waiting for Seamus to process everything.

'Oh. Right.' Seamus had to admit they had chosen the perfect place. 'I had best get ready then.'

'At last. Dominic left you some things on the end of the bed, along with a pack.' She indicated a pile poking out from the bedclothes.

'Thanks, Aliah, I will not be long.'

She turned to open the door. As she placed her hand on the door handle, he could not help himself. 'Aliah? So you do not think it is great they actually let female magic users work with the wounded?'

'Grrr.' Aliah slammed the door behind her.

Grinning, because he had managed to get Aliah to react, Seamus readied himself to leave. When he was nearly ready, he cautiously reached for his magic, and sighed with relief when he found it where it usually was.

A FEW MOMENTS LATER, he tightened the straps on his pack as he joined Aliah in the corridor. She started off without saying a word. He caught up with her and asked, 'Where are we going?'

'There are some tunnels underneath the city that lead to the docks. We will be able to leave unseen from there.' They walked along in silence, until Aliah touched his arm to stop him.

'So we are really going to do this? We are going to try and win this war together?'

Seamus laughed. 'No, there are soldiers to fight this war. Our job is to fight and defeat a god.'

'Oh well, when you put it that way, I have nothing at all to worry about.' Seamus caught the note of fear behind her levity.

'I am worried too.' He admitted. 'In fact, I am scared out of my wits, especially after yesterday.'

'Then why are we doing this?' Aliah asked the obvious question.

Seamus chewed on his lip for a moment before answering. 'Because no one else can.'

'I am not sure we can either,' Aliah whispered, almost as if she did not want to admit her fear.

'Nor am I. It seems so overwhelming even just saying we need to defeat a god.' Seamus' stomach did a somersault as he spoke the words out loud. 'I mean, we barely stopped him from overrunning Port Marden. He destroyed a ship full of men in anger because we challenged him. Then he laughed at us. I am not sure I even know where to begin.'

Aliah was quiet for a moment, then he heard the familiar swish of her plait being flung back over her shoulder, and he knew things were going to be fine.

Aliah the warrior was back, and she had an idea. 'We start at the beginning, we take it one step at a time, and we remember we are not in this alone.' Aliah slipped her arm through his.

Seamus grinned as he caught her mood of defiance. 'And if we do it right, they might even write an epic ballad about us.'

They managed a laugh as they continued through the tunnel towards the docks.

BATTLE

THE WIZARD AND THE WARRIOR
Book Three

PROLOGUE

After the decimation and the fall,
When the new power rises
And the Wizard and Warrior meet,
Old and new blood will combine
With the two who are not what they seem.
The key is the Ember Casket, to trap and calm the chaos,
Or send it beyond to save one and all.

Themhe petite woman stumbled out of the cave and fell face first onto hot sand. She struggled to stand, too exhausted to move any further. Shadows sheltered her body from the mid-afternoon sun as her two companions joined her.

'I see there is a new Seer in Sanctuary,' a friendly voice congratulated her.

'What did you learn?' a more demanding voice asked. 'Did you find out how to defeat the god?'

Gentle hands helped her sit, and cupped her fingers around a mug of water. She downed the cold liquid, and only after she quenched her thirst, did she answer.

'Our god can be bound or he can be banished whence he came. There is a scroll in the library at Hand containing the details we need to achieve this.'

'Obviously you must go there and ensure the document is found,' the second voice decided. 'I will make the preparations while you rest and recover from your ordeal.'

Hot sun scorched her again as the man departed. Before she could pull herself to her feet, a light touch on her arm halted her. The grip firmed as her friend assisted her to stand.

'I guess life is going to be a bit different from here on in,' he said as he tucked her hand through the crook of his arm and led her into the cool entrance of the Sanctuary.

CHAPTER 32
AN INAUSPICIOUS START

'W hen this is all over, I do not want to see another boat again. I am wet through, tired and ...'

'... exceedingly grumpy,' Aliah finished for him, and Seamus could not help but laugh.

'Yes, that too. Were we really not able to find somewhere better than the palace on Hand to plan this final battle?'

'Let me think ... No.' Dominic, Liam, Emer and Daniel laughed at Aliah's reply.

'There is nowhere else on the doorstep of our enemy with an extensive library for us to research how we might defeat him. Well, nowhere with a ready-made guard for our protection, and comfortable beds.' Aliah finished listing off the benefits of his home island as the fishing boat they were travelling in dipped quite heavily in the growing swell.

Seamus' stomach threatened to expel its contents and it took all his concentration to stop that from happening.

During the battle the day before, he had faced a god. The ensuing fight drained almost all the energy from his body. Even after sleeping most of the day, he still was not up to travelling through the night to the Isle of Hand.

'Could we not have travelled in something bigger than a fishing boat?' he continued, as much to take his mind off the churning in his gut as to voice yet another complaint.

'Was yesterday's battle not enough for you?' Emer asked. 'You know the enemy is probably camped on the other side of the island. Did you want to announce our presence to the entire Carsten Army so we can fight them again?' He had hoped Emer at least was on his side, but she was laughingly supporting Aliah.

'No, I guess not,' he admitted, finally running out of things to whinge about.

Liam decided to add his thoughts to the argument. 'Our enemy has a god on their side, so it would be prudent to assume they know what we are up to anyway.'

'Thank you, Liam,' Seamus commended his cousin for coming to his support.

The small fishing boat lurched again, throwing the two boys together, as if the vessel was reacting to Liam's comment. As their fisherman guide righted them, Seamus was pleased to find the outline of Hand Port appeared in the distance. He hoped they arrived soon, otherwise he would be forced to embarrass himself by throwing up over the side of the boat. A hand slid into his, and he turned to find Emer beside him, concern written on her face.

'Not long now,' she whispered. 'You will feel much better about this after some food and sleep.'

'Food? I am not sure my stomach could take it, but I like your optimism. And I also find it hard to see how I will ever feel better about having to fight a god and rid him from this world.' He forced a weary smile at his joke, appreciating his attempt at humour was pretty weak.

'Hey,' Aliah interrupted. 'You are not alone in this. We are the Wizard and the Warrior, remember? We are in this together.'

'And what are we? Extra baggage?' Dominic playfully shoved Aliah and she grinned.

'If the cap fits ...'

Seamus understood they were trying to lift his mood, but he continued to worry none-the-less. Relaxing was not an option while he attempted to figure out how a warrior princess, a disappearing spy, a shape-shifting girl, two soldiers and a trainee wizard, could hope to get rid of a god who seemed determined to set the people of this world on a chaotic path to war.

The boat dipped alarmingly again and the captain swore. Shouting over the noise of the sea he said, 'I do not like this at all. I have never seen a wind like this in the seas between Port Marden and Hand.'

Seamus looked questioningly at Aliah, who shrugged her shoulders. It was possible the god-enemy might have something to do with the odd weather. Certainly if he got rid of them here, there would be no one to stop him from taking over Aria, followed by the rest of the world.

Having hauled every able-bodied person from Carsten into this war, there was no reason to think he would not do the same with the people of Aria. Seamus and Aliah would fight with everything they had to prevent that from happening.

Hands gripping the seat, knuckles white with the strain, Seamus considered what actions he might take to ensure the fishing boat made it safely to the docks as they passed through the entrance to the harbour.

As though the sea recognised its quarry was almost beyond its grasp, the waves gave one final shudder and Seamus was flung through the air, before disappearing under the ice-cold, churning waves.

Icy wet fingers clutched at him as he started to sink through the midnight black water. Part of him thought how easy it would be to allow himself to carry on to the bottom. He would never have to worry about facing a superior foe with Aliah ...

Wait, Aliah.

Where was she? Forcing himself upwards, he broke the surface spluttering and gasping for air.

Treading water to stay afloat, he turned around and around, trying to find his friend. She could not swim and must be terrified. The fishing boat was on its side, the captain using all his skill to try and right it. Aliah must be in the water.

Swimming around the boat he found her, struggling for breath as Dominic tried to keep her head above the water line. He shouted something and Seamus assumed he was telling Aliah to stop struggling.

When this is over, that girl really needs to learn how to swim, he thought as he turned to check on the others.

Liam and Daniel were also on the opposite side of the boat, gathering belongings from the water. Where was Emer? His stomach lurched again as he frantically scoured the water for her. At a noise from above he raised his eyes, catching sight of an eagle overhead.

I am fine. I had time to change. Take care of yourself and I will meet you on the docks. I want to scan around and check if the weather is the only thing they sent to vex us.

With her words sent directly to his head via mind-speak, Emer flew off. Holding onto the side of the boat, he attempted to help the captain.

'Leave me,' the man bellowed. 'Make for land. If I cannot save her, I will follow behind you.'

Seamus nodded his understanding and as he turned to comply, something bumped into him. He let go of the boat to reach for the object and found it was his travel pack. He grabbed a hold and combed the waves for other salvage. As he searched, his body started to shake uncontrollably, and he realised if he did not head to land soon, cold would overtake him and he would not make it at all.

Leaning his chin on the pack, he set out swimming for the port, heading for the docks. Alternating swimming on his side using his left arm, then his right arm was slow going. At one stage he even considered leaving the pack and making a dash for the shore. The only thing stopping him was the thought of losing his wand, which he was sure was in the bag.

Gifted to him by the gods when they named him the Wizard, it was irreplaceable. Besides, he might need it if he survived today, if only to assist him while he learnt to control his magic.

The distance to the dock was longer than he first thought, and he was not in the best condition to be swimming in the freezing night water. He pushed on. His vision grew fuzzy, and he resisted the urge to close his eyes. Soon his arms and legs were moving automatically and he drifted into a half-sleep that was much more inviting than the freezing water.

'My sword!' Aliah yelled again, certain Dominic had not heard her the other three times.

'I got you the first time. The sword is no use if you drown or die of the creeping cold. Calm down so I can support you and get you to safety.'

Listening to the tone of his voice, she realised if she did not do as he instructed, she would be putting both their lives in danger. She willed herself to relax and let Dominic support her.

'Better. Listen, Liam and Daniel grabbed most of the packs, and I think I saw Seamus swim away with one. Was your sword in your pack?'

Aliah's panic levels rose again. 'No, beside it.'

Without any further conversation, Dominic pulled her towards the half-overturned boat. There in the bottom she spied the scabbard containing the weapon the gods gifted her when she proved herself to be the Warrior of Prophecy.

'Grab a hold of the side.'

Aliah forced her freezing fingers to grip the wood as Dominic leaned forward to free her sword from whatever prevented it from falling into the ocean. As far as she could tell, there was nothing holding the sword in place. Her weapon had magical powers, maybe it waited for her to come to the rescue. She laughed out loud at her fanciful thoughts.

'Hold this,' Dominic said, before rolling her on to her back and starting the slow journey to the dock.

They had not gone far when she felt the cold creeping into her lower limbs, she realised if she did not move, the cold would soon kill her. Yet she was unable swim to keep herself warm. Panic began to swell in the pit of her stomach.

She shouted, 'Dominic, my feet are going numb.'

Her rescuer's initial response was one best suited to a guard's barracks.

'All right, you need to start kicking your legs. No, wait until I finish,' he told her as she writhed in his arms. 'They need to be large, slow kicks. You need to keep your legs straight and not bend your knees. Keep your body as still as possible. When you kick that way, I can still support your head.'

After a couple of attempts, she was kicking evenly and they were moving much more quickly towards the wharf. Her feet were still a little numb, but at least the cold had stopped moving up her body. In what seemed like no time at all, Dominic placed her hand on the wooden strut of a ladder and she was able to climb up onto one of the wharves.

As she stamped her feet to return circulation, she saw Liam and Daniel yelling to Dominic, whose head had just popped above the timber of the jetty. A moment later, he let go and dove back into the water with a resounding splash.

'What is happening?' she asked a worried looking Liam.

'Seamus. He was swimming towards us, then he just stopped. I do not know what is keeping him afloat, it must be something in his pack. He is drifting back out to sea and I cannot attract his attention.'

Aliah peered into the dawn light, and was just able to detect Dominic dragging Seamus towards the dock. Only the fact the younger boy clutched the bag he used to keep himself afloat showed he still clung to life.

Liam pushed her aside and climbed part-way down the ladder to help bring Seamus up. Just as Liam pulled the younger boy's body out of the water, Emer appeared beside her. In human form, the girl carried a pile of blankets.

'When I persuaded the Harbour Master we needed these, I did not realise how much.' Emer offered one to Aliah. 'He has more if we need them. He said to help ourselves as he and his men are going out to assist our captain to right his boat before it crashes into the rocks.'

Aliah took a blanket and wrapped herself up, grateful for the added warmth. Leaving her side, Emer went to assist with Seamus.

'Take his clothes off and wrap him in these blankets,' she ordered the others, who worked fast to oblige. Even with her limited knowledge, Aliah could tell it was not enough. Seamus' mouth was turning blue, and he was so still she could barely see the rise and fall of his chest.

Emer frowned in thought. 'With the creeping sickness you need to be warmed slowly from within. There is no healer to help us, and I do not know what else to do.'

'I might be able to do something,' Aliah volunteered tentatively. 'My sword is working to warm me and refuel my body. I shared energy with Seamus in battle yesterday, and I think I remember how to do it without his guidance. Perhaps I could use the same process to share some of my sword's healing powers.'

Emer looked at her thoughtfully and nodded her head. 'I believe you should try.'

The others moved to give Aliah room. With one hand on her sword, she placed the other one underneath the rough woolen blanket, on Seamus' chest. Turning her thoughts inwards, she searched for the strand of magic coming from her weapon. When she found it, she imagined taking a hold of it and pushing out towards Seamus.

The magic leaked through the skin of her hand and then dispersed, as though it did not know where to go.

'It is not working.' Her voice shook with frustration. 'Why not? What is different?' She closed her eyes, blocking out everything else, and went through the steps she and Seamus had taken to share their power when they defeated the King of Carsten. An idea came to her. 'Hurry, find Seamus' wand.'

There was rustling behind her as they searched their belongings. 'I cannot find it,' Liam muttered. 'No, wait, his head is still lying on the pack he carried to shore.'

Gently, Liam placed his cousin's head on the wooden planking, and hurriedly undid the straps. The wand fell out, almost as though it were trying to reach Seamus by itself. Liam grabbed it, unfolded the blanket, placed the wand in Seamus's hand, then replaced his coverings.

Aliah took a deep breath. Finding the magical strand was easier this time, and at the edge of her hand it jumped forward, almost as though it sensed the wand and reached out towards it. The sword gifted to her by the gods warmed them both. Lying down beside her friend, she wrapped her blanket over both of them and concentrated on keeping the energy flowing.

'Come on Seamus, do not leave me now. I cannot do this without you,' she whispered, blinking the tears from her eyes as she snuggled under the covers.

Some part of her was aware Emer organised the others to arrange transport to the palace, but that was her last conscious thought as the sword lulled her to sleep.

'NOOOOOO.' The god's anger reverberated through Gaius' body as he cowered in the safe place he had made for himself in the corner of the invader's mind. 'They escaped again. This vessel is worse than useless.'

Give it back to me if you do not want it, Gaius thought before turning his attention back to the activity outside his self-imposed prison.

'You chose to take a human body so you could act in this world,' Millard explained in patient tones, as if he were explaining a complex idea to a child. 'You took it knowing your powers would be limited to those of the body you occupied. Gaius did not have an aptitude for weather magic when he was alive, you cannot expect him to have one now just because you took over his body. Only your guidance and knowledge allowed his limited skill to raise enough wind to overturn the boat.

'What is more, I explained all this to you when you told me of your plan to kill Aliah and Seamus. I said Gaius' weather magic would not be able to cause a big enough swell to ensure the party travelling to Hand would drown.'

'Your human bodies are too limiting. Perhaps I should get rid of this one like I did the last,' the god growled, and Gaius froze in fear.

During the battle to invade Aria, the divine entity had possessed the body of the King of Carsten. When that brat Aliah and the boy Seamus caused the king to faint, the angry god blew up the king's entire ship, not only destroying the body he inhabited but killing hundreds of innocent men. With their commander gone, the Carsten invasion faltered. Before they could regroup, a magical force had driven them out to sea, beyond the island of Hand.

With his body gone, the god was released back to the only shape he was able to take on this plane of existence, a spirit form. Unhappy with his inability to act without a physical presence, he decided he once again needed a body to use.

The god had forced his way into his and Mallard's heads. Gaius had retreated to the smallest corner possible and imagined himself walled within a box, using a similar technique taught to novice magicians to manage their magical flow. Taking this for submission,

the god decided Gaius' body was a better option, and took possession with no thought for the man who already owned it.

Please do not blow up my body, Gaius pleaded to himself. *I would
like it back when you have no more use for it.*

Millard too seemed to have plans to keep his apprentice's body in
one piece. 'Yes, you could do that, but then you would be totally
reliant on me to work magic for you. The form you inhabit is strong
in different magics, and is still useful in helping us bring you fully
into this world.'

Gaius sensed the being who controlled his body retreat into his
thoughts, and he wondered if the god knew he was privy to all that
went through his mind. Did the divinity even know he still existed?

Although he might have appeared weaker willed, Gaius had a
strong desire to live. With little to do, he waited and planed for a
future that did not include his body being used by a higher entity.

Once the god established himself and felt comfortable in his new
skin, Gaius had allowed a small hole in his box and taught himself to
walk around in his own mind without being noticed. So far, the
divine being gave no indication he realised the body's original owner
was still there. Terrified every waking moment he would be found
out, Gaius knew this great risk might bring great reward.

Looking out from his safe place, Gaius quietened his thoughts to
lessen his chance of detection, content for the moment to observe
and learn and plot. When the god left him to take his true form,
Gaius would have leant much and would be a stronger wizard than
Millard. He would over-power his old master, then it would be he
who ruled Aria.

'Might I make a suggestion?' Millard asked the thoughtful god,
who stirred and once again looked outwards at one of Aria's
strongest magicians. Gaius wondered if Millard realised the god
thought of him as little more than an intelligent animal to do his
bidding.

'Instead of trying to find ways to beat the Wizard and Warrior in
your current form, formidable though it might be, perhaps we

should concentrate on the plan to bring you through to this place. Everything we need is here on the Island of Hand. We can set the army to harry the Arian forces and keep them occupied while we search unhindered for the solution.'

The god turned the idea over in his head, but was yet to be convinced. 'The Wizard and the Warrior still live, and are looking for the solution too. The casket is a double edged sword, it can be used to contain my essence before I return to my natural form, or free me by bringing my body here from where it slumbers.'

'Then we must use all the resources at our disposal and be the first to find its location,' Millard pressed. 'We have the advantage in that we at least know what we are looking for, and we can keep an eye on our friends to ensure they are not ahead of us in the search for the chest.'

Retreating into his own thoughts again, the powerful entity gloated, *When I take my true form in this world no one will be able to stop me from doing what I came here to do.*

'All right, magician, we will do it your way, for the moment. Bring me the man who now calls himself leader of the Carsten invaders, and let us set this plan in motion.'

CHAPTER 33

SCROLLS AND MORE SCROLLS

S eamus dropped another scroll on the table, toppling the pile of discarded documents already there, causing the whole lot to tumble to the ground.

'Goddess!' he muttered as he bent down to pick them up, placing them on the shelf cleared yesterday to store the completed works. 'How many more of these are in the area my father told us about?' He directed his question at Liam, who carried another armful of ancient writings from the lower library.

'I estimate we are about half way through once we read these.' Liam dumped his load on the far end of the table, where they joined another twenty or so unread tomes.

Emer groaned and fell across the table, her head cradled in her arms. 'I cannot go on. It has been two days, and there is not even a hint of anything to tell us how to stop a god from taking over Aria.'

'What are you complaining about? At least you get to sleep at night. Seamus' god friends insist on us training together every evening, linking our gifts, fighting and using magic at the same time, providing energy to each other.

'Their gift of sleep recharges my body, but I am mentally

exhausted before I start here.' Aliah stood and stretched out her stiff back.

'I thought you said the gods made sure you woke up refreshed after your classes.' Daniel peeked worriedly over the document he had been immersed in.

Aliah continued stretching her back and legs. 'They do. It is hardly their fault the lessons are still running around in my head when I wake up. I come here and I spend all day cramming more information into my tired mind. Sometimes my head feels like a squishy melon about to explode.' She slumped in her chair to add emphasis to her words. 'Besides, even without sleep I look better than you. Are you sure you are not coming down with something?'

'Just a bit of a tummy upset,' Daniel mumbled, ducking back behind his scroll before Aliah could find something else to complain about.

'The problem is ...' Seamus began, and stopped mid sentence.

All eyes in the room swung to him. So many people looking to him for leadership was disconcerting. Especially as only two days ago he almost killed himself while escaping the overturned fishing boat. If Aliah had not warmed him, he would have died from the creeping cold, and then where would Aria be?

Since almost drowning, Seamus had been berating himself. When he took air from the King of Carsten, causing his collapse and throwing the invaders into disarray, he used up much of his magical reserves. To make everything worse, he followed up by sending the fleet from Carsten out beyond Hand, over-using his energy, and he collapsed. Not looking after himself then meant he almost died when he was thrown into the water of Hand Harbour.

At his next lesson a taciturn god reluctantly finished healing him, grumbling under his breath as he did so. Once Seamus was back to full strength, the god warned him using magic was like over-exercising; use too much and it drains your body, which adversely affects your health and can even kill you.

The god then continued to lecture Seamus to practice using his magic more, because the more he trained, the less toll it would take on his body when he used it. This became the subject of their class, as their god-instructor drilled them in sharing energy in a way to enable them to both remain strong.

Still, Seamus felt a little foolish. Walter's first session on magic included instructions to think about using it like you would intense physical activity. You would tire quickly unless you trained, and you needed to eat more to replace the lost energy.

In the heat of battle that first very simple guideline slipped his mind. Now everyone turned to him to lead the group, and he was not even able to take care of himself. Shaking off the negative thoughts, he remembered the others were still waiting for him to continue.

'Er, umm, what I was saying is we are not scholars. We have no idea what we are looking for. We scan scrolls for mention of anything religious or magical, and that may not be helpful at all. What we seek may be less obvious than that. We need Walter and Amelia. Emer, do you ...'

The door swung open, interrupting Seamus. Dominic entered, a grin plastered over his face. 'They are here. Walter and Amelia, I mean. A ship just docked, it must be them.'

'Are you sure they are on it? Did someone confirm it or see them?' Aliah frowned at the king's spy.

'Well, no.' Dominic's smile faded. 'But who else would come to Hand with an army of occupation just over the mountains? Come to think of it, who else would your father allow to come here when we are supposed to be in hiding?'

'My father may be the king, but he does not personally oversee the actions of every single subject in the realm,' Aliah countered.

Seamus sighed, sometimes Aliah and Dominics' bickering wearied him. Today it particularly grated on his nerves. Time was running out and they were still no closer to understanding how to stop a god-driven army from overrunning their homeland. They had more important things to focus their energies on than petty squabbles.

'It is them,' Emer said.

'How can you be sure?' Liam asked.

'My father travelled to Port Marden with them. He and some of the other magic users from Sanctuary have volunteered to help repel the Carsten invaders. They arrived last night. Walter and Amelia left with a small, personal guard this morning.'

'When were you going to tell us this?' Seamus' anger burned bright, but it left him as quickly as it came when Emer's face crumpled at his harsh tone.

'We have had so little good news, I thought the surprise of their arrival would cheer us all up. I was just waiting for the right time to announce it,' she said through gritted teeth as her spine stiffened.

Seamus regretted his tone as soon as the words left his lips. He could do nothing right at the moment. He had not meant to snap at Emer, who had been nothing but supportive of him. Part of him had been waiting for Walter and Amelia, perhaps as he hoped they might shoulder some of the burden currently weighing him down. Still, that was no excuse for being rude.

'I am sorry, Emer.' He reached out and touched her shoulder. 'I am such a grump at the moment. Please forgive me.'

Emer's dark eyes bored silently into his own. 'We all understand, Seamus, but you need to learn to control your fears, not take them out on those who are here to help you. You are forgiven ... this time.'

Seamus broke contact first and found everyone still watching him. 'I guess I owe you all apologies as well.' The silence in the room confirmed his fears.

'I am sorry. I am not handling this at all well,' he acknowledged. 'I know you are all here to help me, but in the end, it will come down to whether my magic can defeat this threat to our people.'

'And what am I? Just someone to hang off your arm?' Aliah growled at him. 'I will be there at the end as well. We will all face this together. Remember the prophecy, the gods said we cannot do this alone.'

Taking a deep breath, Seamus attempted to let go of his worry. He knew Aliah's words to be true, but they did not change how he felt. Since he and Aliah fought the god to fend off the attack on Port Marden, the enormity of what they needed to do consumed his every waking moment. His fears crowded out everything else, even his common sense, to the extent he often wondered why he was risking everything to do this.

'I am overwhelmed by everything at the moment,' Seamus admitted. 'I do not see how we can win, and I do not want to lead my friends to their deaths.'

'Silly, you are not leading us.' Aliah walked over to him and placed a hand on his shoulder. 'We are walking beside you to our doom.'

He had to laugh at the absurdity of the six of them facing a powerful other-worldly figure. At least if he ever managed to pluck up the courage to confront their foe, he would do so in good company.

'What shall we do while we wait for Walter and Amelia to arrive?' Liam broke the silence.

'Scrolls.' Seamus laughed as the others groaned.

WITH WALTER LEADING, Amelia walked the familiar corridors of her childhood home towards the library. Stopping abruptly, she expanded her senses. Something was not quite right.

'Walter, I think someone might be observing the palace. Can you sense anything?'

Walter did not answer straight away, but the air tingled as he sent his magic out to test her theory. The warm glow slowly expanded, then suddenly disappeared.

'You are right. Someone is using scrying to keep an eye on what is going on in the palace,' Walter answered before releasing her arm.

Again she sensed the warmth of his magic, but this time it extended outwards, like a bubble. The sensation of being watched disappeared.

'You are a clever man. How long will that hold for? And will it keep out ...'

'... a god?' he finished for her. 'The scrying was carried out by a human. Well, at least I think it was a person. I imagine magic from the deities looks different from ours. When Seamus returned from his trial his magic felt different, I could not sense it at all. As his abilities are god-given, it is therefore reasonable to assume the magic they use is also different.

'Anyway, I think we should be safe from prying eyes for a little while. We are lucky you are here to sense if things change.' Walter said as he took her hand and placed it back on his arm, continuing to the library.

As she and Walter entered, the room fell quiet. Strong arms enveloped Amelia, hugging her close, wrenching her hand from Walter's arm and nearly pulling her off her feet.

'Seamus.' She hugged him back. 'I take it you are pleased we are here?' His enthusiastic welcome warmed her heart.

'We are. Not only did we miss you, but we could definitely use your help sorting through these scrolls,' Seamus said into her shoulder before letting her go.

Amelia experienced a momentary panic as she lost all sense of where she was in the room. Only for the blink of an eye though, because Walter soon tucked her hand back through his arm.

'Seamus, we are pleased to be here too, and not just because we bring information to share with you all. But first things first, let us find Amelia a chair before we get started.' Walter took control.

A gentle hand on her elbow propelled her forward. The person thoughtfully guided her hand to the back of the chair, enabling her to seat herself.

'Thank you, Emer.' She correctly guessed the daughter of the seer from Sanctuary was her helper. Living with a sightless father, she instinctively knew how best to assist Amelia.

'You are welcome, Seer,' the girl responded.

'No, I do not deserve that title yet,' Amelia said as she sat down. 'My training will not start until after we sort out this mess we have on Hand.'

'Will someone explain what is wrong with my aunt?' Seamus' impatient tones cut through their conversation.

'Amelia has undergone her trial to be a seer, obviously successfully,' Emer said.

'I got that. But why is everyone treating her as though she is breakable?'

'Oh, of course you would not know. If a person is successful at a seer trial, they lose the use of their eyes to increase the power of their inner sight,' the girl informed him.

'What?' Seamus gasped, and a set of large hands enveloped her smaller ones as her nephew asked, 'Amelia, is this what you wanted? To walk through the world unseeing?'

Concern was evident in his voice. She could almost see the frown that must be furrowing his brow. Grasping his hands in hers, she took a deep breath before responding.

'If given a choice, I would not give up my vision for foresight. Then again you did not choose to be the Wizard either. From what the gods told me during my trial, my seer sight will be needed to help in your battle against the rogue god. Like you, I would never refuse to serve our people.'

Seamus' body stiffened, and anger laced his voice as he responded. 'Amelia, the people of Hand expelled you from their island because of your magic. You, of all people, do not owe them anything.'

'Oh, Seamus, I know you do not truly mean that. You too will face exile once this is over, and yet you choose to continue on regardless. Our family and friends should not be left to fend for themselves when we can help. That is why we do this, even though it is not in our best interests.'

'I, for one, am not sure we should be doing anything. I mean, no one asked us if we wanted our lives to be taken over in this way.'

'Seamus, I hope you do not truly mean that. We are who we are, and we help when we can. In time, I will be able to move more freely. The Great Seer, Caraig, told me as my skill in foresight develops, I will be able to sense things in the world again.'

She untangled Seamus' hands from her own and turned to where she knew the others in the room were seated before she continued. 'I am blind, not useless, and I am here to help. So will one of you please tell us what we missed?'

'Are you sure you would not like some refreshments first?' Emer asked. 'I know from my father your journey here was swift, with little time for rest.'

'Thank you, Emer, but I will not be able to relax until I find out what has been happening and how you all are.'

'Amelia, it is nice to know your newfound sight has not changed you one bit. I am so pleased you are back with us.'

Grateful to hear Aliah's voice, Amelia was happy the young woman had taken her at her word and decided to continue as if nothing had changed. As much as Amelia attempted to behave as she had before, she was still a little lost without her sight, and more than a little concerned she would no longer be useful. The princess' support meant more than she could say.

'Seamus and I, with Emer and Dominic's help, managed to stop the Carsten ships reaching the mainland, at least for the moment. It appears the god possessed the body of Carsten's king. When Seamus and I worked magic to cause him to collapse during battle, he had a tantrum and blew the ship up. But I guess you already know that, having journeyed through Port Marden.'

'We heard,' Amelia interrupted. 'Lucky for you we managed to persuade the king and his advisors we are indeed battling a god here. He has reconsidered his stance on having you both face the Wizard's

Council for misusing magic once the threat to Aria has been repelled.'

When Amelia and Walter first met with the King's Council, the members had been highly concerned about Seamus and Aliah's potential use of battle magic during the Carsten invasion. Battle magic, defined as magic used against a person, was illegal and punishable by having your magic removed.

When questioned by the king and his advisors, Aliah and Seamus argued they fought a god, not a man. They maintained in this instance, using their magic on whatever form the god took was not only justified, but essential, if they were to defeat him. In principle the council agreed, magic used on a god was legal under the current laws. However, they were unable to believe Aria faced a non-human enemy.

In order to find a solution agreeable to them all, Dominic suggested they wait until after repelling the invasion before making a decision on whether or not Seamus and Aliah had used battle magic. A relieved king agreed.

Together Amelia, Walter and Caraig persuaded the council their foe was indeed a god and, after a long discussion, they decided Aliah and Seamus were justified in their actions against the being leading the invasion fleet.

'Well, that is a relief, not that I believed they would follow through on their threats. Seamus and I have been most careful about how we use our gifts,' Aliah continued. 'The fleet is now off the far side of Hand and has been harrying our ships night and day.'

'I believe the king can manage to deal with them.' Amelia again stopped Aliah mid-flow, trying to move her on to more relevant topics. 'In fact, Caraig travelled with us and remained with the Port Marden garrison to assist your father with keeping the Carstenites from landing. We need to focus on dealing with the larger threat. Do you know where our enemy is now?'

'No.' Seamus was once again all business.

Although he and Amelia only met a few moons ago, when his

aunt stumbled on him leaving Port Marden, heading to the Wizard Isle in the hope they would accept him for training, he gained a great fondness for her. Their familial bond strengthened on the journey from Hand to Sanctuary when Seamus and Aliah travelled there to find out if they were the Wizard and Warrior from prophecy. Amelia had gone to support them, and also partly because she wanted to meet the legendary Great Seer.

Having grown close, she did not want her loss of sight to affect their budding relationship.

'We believe the wizards from the Wizard Isles who took part in the invasion conspiracy are now with the forces from Carsten.'

'What makes you say that?' Walter sat forward in his chair, eager to hear the answer.

'We saw Millard and Gaius leave with the departing Carsten fleet, and while we were in Port Marden, a number of wizards absconded and could not be found. We assume they joined Gaius and Millard, and are on the other side of the island with the Carsten army,' Seamus advised them.

'I heard my old friend Millard finally displayed his true colours and came out openly in support of the Carsten invasion,' Walter said dryly.

'Yes, their plot to remove the royal family and rule Aria them-selves was uncovered in advance of the Carsten fleet turning up on our shores. Thanks in part to the information Seamus and Aliah jour-neyed from Port Marden to Bannock to bring to the King, and thanks also to you, Walter.' Daniel now added to the conversation. 'As luck would have it, support amongst their fellow wizards was not as high as they believed, and the Wizard Congress expelled them all.'

The guard seemed pleased at the removal of a threat to their nation. Not least because his father, previously Captain of the King's Guard, was now the King's Chief Advisor, the role having been left vacant by Millard's departure.

'Although I am pleased the plot was exposed, now the invader's magical strength has been added to by wizards who are happy to break the age old laws against battle magic,' Walter said. 'I cannot help wondering if I might have stopped Millard and Gaius had I been with you. That would have been a blow to our enemy. Instead, they are back with their god, and we have no idea where to find them.'

Not wanting to indulge Walter's fear about having made the wrong decision when letting the others travel back to Port Marden without him, Amelia moved the conversation in a different direction.

'Seamus, have you found anything of interest here?'

Groans of exasperation filled the room, and Amelia suppressed a smile as Seamus grumbled, 'Nothing. So many scrolls, so little information.'

Amelia shifted in her chair and patted Walter's hand. 'Now, Walter, I understand why you wanted to travel here with the others, and what you gave up to remain behind with me. Surely now you realise our discoveries while remaining in Sanctuary more than make up for that.' Turning around so she faced the table, Amelia grinned. 'We found some very interesting information, which I am sure you are all waiting to hear. But first, perhaps you would give us an idea of what scrolls you have read and how you approached your task.'

FROM HIS SAFE PLACE, Gaius learnt he could once again use his own eyes if he left his thoughts quiet, and was satisfied with observing the world rather than controlling and commenting on what he saw. At the moment, he looked through his eyes, watching events unfold in the palace on Hand through Millard's bronze mirror.

His body fidgeted as the god inhabiting him became more agitated, his anger barely kept in check. The mirror went dark and he lost control, giving a roar that shook the ground. Gaius momentarily lost the link to his eyes.

'What is this? Why can we no longer see what they are doing? I thought you said your strongest far-sight wizard set the scrying spell.'

'He did, and he is very good at what he does. Something must have changed in Port Hand. There is a new power there, one able to block our vision. I will task our best wizards with finding out what happened and who caused this. If that fails, we can contact our eyes and ears in the ducal palace to find out what the Wizard and Warrior are doing. It is a momentary set back, that is all.'

Millard steered him away from the other wizards, who were clearly unsettled around their old friend whose body now housed a god.

'There is some positive news. One of the wizards back in Carsten located a scroll that might help us find what we seek. I am just heading out to their ship now so we can link with him to find out the details.'

'I will come with you.'

'Perhaps you should stay here. You tend to make everyone nervous, and that affects their ability to work.'

The god stopped and stared at Millard, contemplating the thin, greying man who always appeared to be looking down his nose at people, even those taller than himself. He wondered at the power this nondescript being held over others of his kind.

'They do right to fear me. However, mind speak is difficult over long distances, even for one as strong as I. In this instance I will listen to your advice. Mark me though, there are only two people in this world I wish to know of the chest's location: me and you. You, because you need to bring me the item, and me, because I do not completely trust you.'

The god stared directly at Millard, ensuring the wizard heard his next words. 'If the others have found it, you know what you have to do.'

'I am not sure killing them is necessary.' Millard blanched at the thought. 'We may need all the magical help we can get in this battle.'

The Gold Wizard had always shown a distaste towards killing

people. Well, at least with his own hands. To Gaius' surprise, the god laughed, the sound coming from deep within his belly.

'Your own twisted mind provided that particular solution, wizard. It may surprise you to know, I appreciate too many deaths unsettle those who serve my goals. A little mind wiping will suffice in this instance. Wait, I perceive this is not a skill you possess. Perhaps I had best join you after all.'

The god strode off towards the transport boats dotting the shore-line, and Millard had no choice but to follow.

CHAPTER 34

OLD FRIENDS RETURN

While Seamus outlined their approach to working through the scrolls in Hand's oldest library, Aliah took the opportunity to observe Amelia. Although she met the other woman only recently, she respected her as a strong, independent soul. Now, her dark hair was peppered with a little more grey, and her once brown eyes were more opaque. Tension around those eyes told Aliah maintaining the facade she was still in control was not completely effortless.

Of course she had lost her sight, and so many of her movements showed a hesitancy not previously there, although she did seem to be able to easily identify who spoke. Her questions were insightful, and kept them all focused on the subject at hand when they drifted off onto more interesting topics.

What concerned Aliah was the way she kept hold of Walter's hand throughout the entire conversation, as though he anchored her to the world. As if she sensed someone watching her, Amelia's head lifted and she turned her sightless gaze in Aliah's direction.

Do not worry so, Aliah. Although I miss seeing things, in its place I am developing other gifts. In time I will not need to rely on Walter quite so much, but I am thankful he is with me now.

How did you read my thoughts?

I did not, well not exactly. I have found I am more aware of other people's feelings than before, which is perhaps a byproduct of losing my sight. I sensed your unease, and it was easy enough to guess the reason why because on the way here Caraig, Walter and I spent time discussing how the changes to me would affect you all. We knew you in particular would be concerned about how all of this affected me mentally. And Seamus, he will worry I am not physically able to help now until I am used to being without my sight.

I am a little disappointed, I think. I really thought you could read minds. Aliah caught herself before her laughter bubbled up and out.

Amelia's own amusement at the comment coloured her thoughts. *Thank the Goddess, no. I do not think I would be able to work with you all if I could do that. With my heightened senses your tension and angst are tangible, and that is more than enough for me to guess the rest. I want you to understand that while I regret losing some of my independence, it is only for a short time, and the closeness I now have with Walter more than makes up for that loss. All the years I lived alone, I forgot the warmth and comfort of a like minded companion can provide.*

Why, Amelia, you are not going soft on us and falling in love are you? Aliah joked, and was met with a silence she did not expect. *Oh, Amelia, how thoughtless of me to be so brash.*

Amelia paused before she responded, trying to gather her jumbled thoughts. *With everything going on I had not considered my feelings for Walter in that way. You bringing up the idea merely threw me off balance.*

Do not mind me. Whatever you and Walter feel for each other, it is no one else's business but your own, Aliah reassured her friend.

'Excuse me, Amelia? Aliah? Have we bored you both to sleep?' Seamus' impatient voice caused her to lose eye contact with Amelia as she turned to face him. 'Did you hear any of what we said?'

Amelia saved her from answering. 'I am sorry, Seamus, I became lost in my own thoughts. Your approach was thorough, but quite broad. With the information we brought with us, I fear you may have wasted much time as you could have targeted your search a little better.'

Seamus' face turned beetroot as he worked up to an explosion. Aliah held her breath, waiting for the outburst. Instead, Seamus walked away from the table and left the library, the only sign of his anger was the door slamming behind him. The room was quiet. Before the silence became awkward, Emer spoke for them all.

'Responsibility has been weighing Seamus down. In his head, he understands we all share the burden of fighting this god, but his heart is yet to accept this,' she told the new arrivals.

'Duty always lay heavily on the shoulders of my family,' Amelia said. 'Let him walk off his frustration. In the meantime, perhaps we might organise some refreshments. I believe a break away from the library would do you all some good. Aliah, would you be so kind as to ask the cook to send up some food to your rooms, and we can all meet up there?'

The request surprised Aliah. Although as a princess she held a higher status than the others, she worked hard to be treated like everyone else. Even so, it was unusual for anyone to ask her to fetch and carry for them.

As Amelia asked her politely, and she owed this woman a debt of gratitude for her help in leaving Port Marden, and for seeing her ready for the journey north to warn her father of the coming invasion, she did as she was bid. Closing the door gently behind her, she turned and was sure she glimpsed self-satisfied smirks on Amelia and Walters' faces.

Although she had only been back in the palace a few days, she had made sure to learn the way to the kitchens early on. With so few servants left on the island, the group ate their meals at the large table usually used by serving staff. Closer to the kitchen, the smell of roast lamb filled the air. She hoped it was being prepared for their evening meal as the delicious scent had her stomach rumbling already. Aliah opened the door to her destination only to be nearly bowled off her feet by a whirlwind with red hair. Her jaw dropped in shock.

'Aliah, you are safe. Walter said you were, but I would not believe it until I saw you with my own eyes.'

Aliah returned the hug of the younger boy who a moon or so ago led Walter, Seamus and herself out of Duncameron through the sewers below the streets. Pauley had been forced to share Aliah's horse all the way to Bannock to avoid capture. They parted ways abruptly, leaving him at the markets with the farmer who had smuggled them in to town, while they went to report news of the pending invasion to her father.

She always regretted not being able to say a proper farewell to the boy, and only found out Pauley had made it safely home from his adventures a couple of days ago. He then left a short time later when some mutual friends came south to help fight against the Carsten invasion.

'Pauley, it is good to see you too. What are you doing here?' Aliah untangled herself and found the man everyone called Boss sitting at the table with a mug of steaming tea in front of him.

'Princess, it is a relief to find you alive and well. Pauley, let the girl catch her breath. Go and fetch her a tea.'

Pauley paused briefly. Thinking better of disobeying the older man, he disappeared into the kitchen to find her something to drink. Aliah took a seat at the table.

'Boss, you are the last person I expected to meet here.'

The man in front of her smiled a slow smile and took a sip of his tea, and Aliah wondered if Amelia sending her for refreshments was as spontaneous an action as it first appeared.

'When I ran in to Walter in Port Marden and he mentioned he needed a guard, I volunteered. Better than manning the gates at the port.'

'And Pauley?'

Boss barked out a laugh.

'That lad pretty much does what he wants. His parents were against him coming with us when we left for the war, but we found him stowed away. Much like someone else here.'

Boss referred to his finding Aliah in his wagon in Duncameron, having secretly journeyed with them from Sunnydale. When they found her, instead of handing her over to the authorities, they introduced her to Walter. They also helped her get back to Bannock when they learnt of her mission to tell the king about the invasion from Carsten.

'When he heard about my journey, knowing you were here as well, let me just say we found him when it was too far for him to swim back to Port. Very determined is that young boy.'

'As Walter is safe here with the garrison left behind to defend the palace, he no longer requires your services.' Aliah probed a little more.

'He is indeed safer here, but Amelia asked us to stay. She said there is still work for us to do.' Boss frowned into his tea. 'Odd, it felt almost like a prediction.'

'Maybe it was,' Aliah agreed.

Pauley returned with a fresh mug of tea for her. Handing it over, he slipped into the chair beside Boss.

'Amelia is a seer,' he informed her proudly.

'I know, Pauley, but not everything she says is a foretelling,' Aliah said as she took a sip from the mug.

'She did say we needed to stay because our part was not yet complete. That means we have important work to do to help you.' Pauley puffed out his chest, proud of the responsibility.

'Or it may merely mean Walter wants another pair of hands he can trust.' Boss added wryly.

'Pauley, I need you to do something for me, if you do not mind?' Aliah solemnly asked the boy, who beamed at the possibility of helping her. 'I need cook to gather some refreshments for my friends so I can take them upstairs. Do you think you might help her do that for me?'

'I certainly can,' Pauley affirmed. 'I used to help in the inn kitchen at meal times. Leave it to me.' He scampered back into the kitchen.

'I think you have found an admirer,' Boss chuckled.

Ignoring the remark, Aliah said, 'He is a good boy. Am I right in thinking Amelia sent me down here specifically to meet with you?'

'She did,' boss nodded as that slow smile returned to his face.

'Do you know why?'

'Mostly because she thought you would want some time with us before we meet the others, but also because she thinks we are to be a part of whatever is going on. She is telling the others about us now, and I think she wanted to make sure you and Seamus are happy about ...'

'... about what?'

Aliah turned in surprise at the voice from the hallway.

'Seamus, good to see you again boy, or should I call you My Lord?'

Aliah had the pleasure of seeing her friend smile for the first time in days.

'Boss, you need never call me anything other than Seamus. You gave me work and you protected me from that wizard, even though it placed you and your family in danger. It is good to see you.'

A couple of moon-turns ago Seamus drove a wagon from Sunny-dale to Duncameron for Boss Allum, unaware Aliah had stowed away in the back of one of them.

On that journey he first encountered one of the rogue wizards from the Wizard Council looking for Aliah. After he threatened Seamus, Boss arranged for Pauley to take him to Walter. After teaching Seamus to control his magic, the wizard then escorted him to the sewers, where they met up with Aliah, and they all escaped to Banrock.

Pauley returned carrying a tray loaded with savouries and cakes, dishes clattering together as he placed them on the table.

'Cook will not let me carry the drinks,' he complained as he raised his head and caught sight of Seamus. A smile replaced the annoyed look on his face. 'Seamus, hello. I am about to go and ask cook to give me the tea to bring at least this far.' With that he disappeared back into the kitchen.

'And there is a little bit of hero worship there too I see.' Boss laughed. 'Ever since Amelia told us you two are now our Wizard and Warrior, Pauley had been busting his gut to meet with the you two again. He finds it amusing when you first met, he assumed you were the ones from the legend. He says you denied it, but he knew all along.

'Anyway, Amelia wanted me to make sure you two were happy about Pauley and I joining your group before introducing us to the others.'

Seamus' smile left his face. 'I am not sure we can ask any more people to put themselves in danger.'

Aliah did not need magic to appreciate the more people who joined their endeavour, the heavier the responsibility on Seamus to keep them all safe.

'Seamus, Amelia thinks it is important they stay, otherwise she would not have asked them to be here.'

For a moment she thought he was still going to refuse, but instead he shook his head and settled into the seat beside her.

'I do not know whether more people lessen the danger, or it means more people I care for are placed in harm's way. Unfortunately what I think does not really matter in this instance. Amelia is right. Boss and Pauley need to be here, for the moment at least.'

Aliah placed her hand on Seamus' arm in a gesture of solidarity.

'While we are here in the palace, we are all relatively safe, and there is nothing suggesting they are meant to carry on with us when we leave. If they do, we can worry about that later.'

'Well, I would not count on our being too safe here.' Boss Allum folded his arms in front of his chest and refused to say anything else, no matter how much they cajoled, merely repeating, 'I promised Walter and Amelia I would share that information with everyone at once.'

Seamus held the door for Aliah and Pauley as they carried trays into the sitting room of the guest suite he and Aliah once again occupied. Without his parents in the palace, the family quarters seemed empty, so he joined the others in the guest wing.

Having arrived before them, the company were comfortably settled into the chairs around the fireplace. The chairs from the table by the window were squeezed in between the more comfortable ones. Pauley flopped down on the floor, back against the wall, as the others seated themselves.

Seamus waited until everyone loaded plates and helped themselves to tea before he introduced the newcomers. Formalities out of the way, Seamus started.

'Boss, you said you learnt something we all needed to hear?'

Before Boss answered, there was a knock at the door. Dominic opened it and found the duke's steward, Robin, outside. He had no option but to step aside as the man pushed passed him and entered the room.

'Excuse me, Your Highness, Seamus, but I wanted to ensure you had everything you need. Do you want someone to tidy away the scrolls in the library if they are no longer required?'

Seamus frowned, he ordered the library off limits when they first arrived. No one was to enter, not even for cleaning. He even went to the trouble of placing a guard outside the door when they were not in there so no prying eyes could work out what they searched for.

He shook his head, deciding he was jumping at shadows. Robin arrived at the castle as a young boy and had worked closely with his father since then. The duke trusted him, that was enough for Seamus.

'Thank you, Robin. We have everything we need here, and our

work continues in the library, so my orders to leave things as they are still stand.'

'As you wish.' The man lingered by the door, seemingly reluctant to leave.

'Is there something else?' Seamus asked.

'Well.' Robin looked sheepish. 'From time to time I research things for your father, and I wondered if you might not find what you are looking for sooner if I assisted you.'

Seamus relaxed, the man was only trying to be his normal, over-helpful self.

'Thank you, Robin, that is very thoughtful of you, but we are fine. Perhaps, though, you could ready some guest quarters for our new arrivals. They will all be staying a few days.'

'Consider it done.' He bowed and walked backwards out of the room.

Dominic watched him retreat down the corridor before shutting the door behind. 'We may need to watch him,' he said as he retook his seat.

'He is perhaps a little over-zealous,' Seamus reassured them. 'My father trusts him, so we should too. Boss, you were going to tell us some important news.'

'I am not sure how important it is for you, given I know very little of what you are doing here.' Boss sat up straighter in his chair as everyone directed their attention to him. 'I recently received a report from the underground, from one of the wizards currently with the Carstenites on the other side of the island.'

'Wait a minute,' Dominic and Daniel said at the same time. Daniel nodded for Dominic to continue.

'You mean to say you placed a spy in the Carsten camp? How did you manage that? Not even the king's Spymaster was able to get someone close enough to the traitors for them to be taken into the inner circle.'

As one of Aria's most accomplished spies, Dominic was aware of the difficulties involved in inserting someone into a foreign enemy's camp. Also, his daily briefings from Port Marden had not mentioned any information sources close to the Carsten leaders.

'Many of you know my group closely watched some wizards on the isle, having realised for some time they were plotting against Aria and the king. That was one of the reasons we assisted Aliah and Seamus to get a message to King Terion about their activities.

'Earlier on our concerns led us to place a man with the traitors, and he has been feeding information to us since. This was way before the wizards were cast from the isle. As part of the inner-circle of conspirators, he left with the others when the king expelled the traitor, Millard. He has been risking his life for his country since then,' Boss responded.

'Have I met him?' Walter asked. The older wizard had been exiled from the Wizard Isle when he stumbled on the conspiracy Boss spoke of, and there was a real possibility the man on the inside worked with Walter in the past.

'You have,' Boss confirmed. 'I was unable to tell you this before because I needed to ensure his safety, but in fact he was one of your students. I remember you sharing your disappointment when he began spending time with Millard.

'You always thought his change of heart odd, as he had previously despised the man and his methods. His brother served with me for years, and when the wizard voiced his fears about what Millard and his friends were up to, he was able to persuade his brother to spy for us.'

'So you are telling me ...' Walter started, before Boss rushed in.

'I do not like to say his name out loud, anyone might be listening. If we have spies in their camp, we must assume there are spies in ours.'

Seamus sat upright and stared pointedly at Dominic, who shrugged his shoulders.

'We are aware of at least one person here who is passing messages on to our enemy. We made sure the information they have access to is misleading. However, it is only smart to conclude where there is one, there may be others. I am keeping an eye out, and so is Daniel.'

Seamus was silent for a moment, unable to understand why someone on Hand would want to help the invading force. It made him uneasy, but he could do little about it. What he could do something about was the fact no one had discussed this with him.

'You did not think to talk about this with Aliah and me? Or does she know already?' He glared at Dominic, but it was Daniel who answered him.

'No, Seamus, we have not talked to her about this. Emer, Liam, Dominic and I have been making sure the two of you are safe and secure, and able to concentrate on what you need to do.

'Of course if that situation changes we will include you in future plans.'

Seamus did not know what annoyed him more, Daniel's calm manner as he offered his explanation, or the fact he was right. The king had placed the guardsman in charge of the group's security so he and Aliah would not be worried by such details, then requested the others work with Daniel to keep them from harm.

Although he raged inside, he knew there was no point in pursuing this any further, they had more important things to discuss. Taking a deep breath, he pushed his frustrations down, and carried on.

'So, Boss, what news did your spy send?'

'I am sure this first bit of information will come as no surprise to you,' Boss started. 'But the wizard, Millard, is with the Carsten Army.'

'We saw him escape Aria with one of their landing forces, so we guessed that was where he would go.' Seamus spoke for them all. 'We are also aware if he is there, he is ensuring our enemy succeeds so his own plans to rule Aria come fruition.'

'I see you have his measure then,' Boss continued. 'However, I am sure this next piece of news is going to sound unbelievable. My informant told me we are not just fighting an invading army. He believes some magical force inhabited they body of our enemy's king, controlling his actions. The report stated whoever controlled the king blew up the Carsten command ship.'

Boss held up his hand, expecting objections to this bizarre news. 'Before you tell me this is all madness, hear me out. This wizard believes the magical entity now resides inside that slimy wizard, Gaius. The one who followed us to Duncameron, Seamus.'

No one spoke for a moment after Boss finished. Then, as if on some secret queue, most of the room burst out laughing. The perplexed look on Boss' face soon turned to anger at not being taken seriously. Before he did something he would regret later, Aliah pulled herself together and shushed the rest of them.

'Oh, Boss, we are not laughing at you. In fact, we believe you. We know the king was indeed possessed when he died, although it was not by a magical entity, as such, but by one of the gods.'

Now it was Boss' turn to let out a full belly laugh of his own. 'You are teasing me. A god? They are things the churches make up to keep us all in line.'

'I wish that were so. It may surprise you, but only last night I talked to a god. Seamus has spoken directly to them all, except the one who is trying to take over the world. The gods of old tried us and named us the Wizard and the Warrior.'

Pauley stared at Aliah, a look of wonder on his face. He was still young enough to believe in magic and fairy tales. Boss was another matter. The ex-guard had seen much in his life, and was a skeptic by nature. He took some convincing.

Eventually Walter, whom he had trusted for years, managed to persuade him they were not joking. They were actually preparing to face a god and stop him from turning their world into a battlefield for his own amusement.

'Our laughter was partially from relief,' Aliah explained. 'We all dreaded revealing who our real enemy was to anyone outside our group. Most people find it difficult to believe.'

'The god will be hard enough to face, but it will be harder if we cannot find him. Now we know he resides in another human body we will at least know what he looks like. And we also confirmed he is back with the invading army, which is helpful as well,' Seamus continued.

Although he was giving them the benefit of the doubt, Boss still appeared a little unsure of himself as he asked, 'So what does it mean, you being the Wizard, and Aliah being the Warrior? How does that help us in all of this?'

Everyone turned to Seamus, waiting for him to answer, but he said nothing. It was not only that he was still learning about being the Wizard, nor even that he was not sure he wanted to be the Wizard at all, it was deciding what to tell Boss.

He trusted the man, but learning there could be a spy in their midst made him a little more cautious. Looking at Walter for guidance, the older man shifted his weight in his chair then stood and moved to stand in front of the fire.

'I have known you for a long time, Boss, and I have trusted you with my life. You fought for Aria as a guard for years, and after your service you set up a network to fight against a danger you saw coming but few others believed in.

'Your loyalty is to your network, and that is as it should be. The people here, well, our loyalty is to each other, to see the Wizard and Warriors' task through to the bitter end.

'If we share our secrets with you, we need to know you will put us first until the god is vanquished. No one will think any less of you if you decide this is not the fight you signed up for. But if you stay, we must have your full commitment.'

Boss thoughtfully tapped his fingers on his leg, then spoke slowly, as if he were still thinking things through. 'Before I make my decision, I need to ask you a question. Do you personally believe the plot we fought to foil, to stop the wizards from ruling Aria, was a smaller part of this bigger threat?'

'I do, Boss. That is why I am here now.'

The room was silent, as if everyone was holding their breath.

'I cannot speak for all of my network, but I personally will stay and support you all for as long as you need me.'

Walter glanced back to Seamus. 'If he is with us then he deserves to know everything.'

Nodding his agreement, Seamus waited until Walter had retaken his seat before starting off. 'Your daughter found out about my magical abilities when I travelled with you. They turn out to be quite unique. I am being trained to use them so I will be ready when we face the god. Aliah has been given skills to balance mine so we have a chance when we eventually battle our foe. At the moment we are researching ways to fight him.' Seamus stopped short.

There was little more he could tell Boss about what they would do with those powers because they still had not found the scroll telling them how to defeat their enemy.

Amelia started to rise, but before she did, Emer stood and moved to stand in front of the fire.

'If you are to join with us, I think it best you know Seamus and Aliah are not in this alone. Nor are they the only ones with unique skills. Dominic?' Emer looked to the spy, who blushed, but did not move. 'If we are to be a team we all need to know what the others can do.'

Again Dominic did not move, but simply faded away. For a moment he disappeared, then he was back.

'Goddess, I have never seen anything like it.' The words escaped from Walter's mouth before he turned and whispered to Amelia.

'I heard tales of the old ones from the north who could melt into the shadows, but I always thought it a myth,' Amelia said after hearing Walter's explanation.

'Wait, there is more, is there not Emer?' Dominic smirked.

With everyone's attention on her, Emer changed into her wolf form, then back to human. The amazement he felt when Emer first showed Seamus her skill appeared on Boss, Pauley and Walters' faces. Walter leaned over and spoke to Amelia, her mouth forming an 'o' of surprise.

Liam gave a nervous laugh. 'With two wizards, a magical warrior, a seer, a shape shifter and an invisible man, I consider it somewhat of an honour to be one of the non-gifted people in the room. I cannot help thinking though, surely we cannot fail with so much talent on our side.'

'You, Daniel, Boss and Pauley are as important in all of this as we are. You all have unique skills even if you do not possess magical abilities,' Seamus told them.

'Umm.' Pauley shifted uncomfortably on the floor. 'Umm, me mam says I have a gift, so I guess I should tell you.' He waited for Boss to give his permission before proceeding. 'I can see in dark rooms or places where there are no lights. I can also find my way around streets and places I have never been to before. It was my skill that guided you through the sewers.'

It was Seamus' turn to be surprised. He thought the boy's ability to lead them out of the sewers under Duncameron came from studying the paths.

'I had no idea,' Walter said. 'Your parents kept that secret well hidden.'

'They did not want Pauley to go to The Wizard Isle for training, so they kept quiet about it. Only a few of us know,' Boss informed them.

'How is it Dominic, Emer and Pauley have these gifts, yet I cannot sense magic in them, nor can I sense anything when they use their skills?' Seamus asked his old teacher.

'I am not sure,' Walter answered. 'Just as I cannot explain why I could sense your magic once, but when you do something magical now, I sense something is happening but it does not feel the same. But these are perhaps questions for another day.'

Seamus nodded in agreement, and continued, 'Pauley, thank you for sharing with us. Who knows when your skills might become useful? As for those without magical gifts, your skills are equally as important. We need strong arms to defend us against non-gifted enemies. This is more than my opinion. Since we gathered here today I have a feeling of ... well, the best way to describe it is rightness.'

Amelia nodded her head. 'I believe all those we need to complete our quest are here. Now, moving on, Walter and I brought back with us another piece of the puzzle; we found what we need to do to defeat the god.'

GAIUS SPENT most of the afternoon in his safe space as the restless god rifled through his memories, searching for information to help him find the casket he needed. It was called the Casket of Ember and, so far, he had not uncovered anything useful. On the other hand, Gaius found out about the casket, its importance to the god, and a little something about the being who now lived in his body.

He now knew that since the god's brothers and sisters refuse to help him escape to the world of humans, the being took matters into his own hands. He designed a wooden box, about the size of a small travel pack, for the express purpose of storing enough magical energy to transport himself to this world without their help. Forged in a river of embers to increase its strength, and filled with magic from their home world, the casket was discovered and confiscated by his family.

In a fit of anger, the god drew a large amount of magical energy and attempted to escape his siblings. Although taking in so much power had almost killed him, the magic had not been enough to bring him all the way through. He ended up trapped in between worlds.

While he recovered his strength, his siblings expended a great deal of energy and sent the casket to this world for safe keeping. They believed it to be secure and, if by some chance, the god ever managed to break through there, it might be used to assist the people against the god's havoc.

Knowing he might eventually try to reach his original destination, they planned and prepared for the coming of a wizard and guardian warrior to balance his power in the world of humans. If they could get to the casket, they would have the means to send their brother home.

For millennia, a lack of magical energy imprisoned the errant god on the in-between-world. Frustrated, he lashed out. Causing a volcano in a far land to erupt, destroying villages and killing many.

The event caused chaos, giving him an energy surge, just enough to enable him to move his spirit to this world. Chancing on the leader of the people of Carsten, he pushed the weak willed man aside, then took control of his body and the country he ruled.

Now everything hinged on the casket. It was an object of great power, but could equally be used for or against him. Its construction meant it could imprison his spirit and prevent him from acting in this world again.

However, the casket still contained the power he harnessed a millennia ago. Destroying it would release a burst of magical energy, enough to allow his body to be brought through to this plane of existence if he incited the right spells while releasing the power.

Until the god began sifting through the memories Gaius allowed him access to, he had never heard of a magical chest. Nor had he been aware the old gods still kept an eye on their world.

In the distant past the country now called Aria worshipped many gods, but in recent years, The Goddess held sway on the continent. Although she was a popular figure, no one used her actual name in worship as they did in the past. In fact, as far as Gaius knew, no one even remembered what it was.

When he stumbled on memories of the forgotten gods, his oppressor was initially angry he and his brethren were now so little thought of. Then his mood changed and he laughed out loud.

These heathens have forgotten everything about my family. The fact they are no longer known by name means their power here has diminished, which in turn means they have little more influence than I do. I am unlikely to find anything else from this source of information, as the wizard who had this body before is unfamiliar with the old ways. I need to find worshippers of the old religions. Where is Millard?

Gaius shrunk further back into his safe place, away from the invader's mind. Going through what he learnt, he started planning what he might do should he manage to gain control of the magical artefact first.

CHAPTER 35
HOW TO KILL A GOD

Amelia turned towards the fire. Enjoying the heat on her face, she also appreciated the break from the assault on her senses. With so many people in the room and so much going on, the constant input was overwhelming. She thought about how best to approach the knowledge she needed to share before she started speaking.

'I spent a large part of my trial talking with the gods, and sharing revelations around the prophecy of the Wizard and the Warrior. The gods are careful not to upset the balance of powers governing our world, but at the same time, they are unable to stand by and let one of their own roam free causing havoc. To allow him freedom to do as he pleased would cause such disharmony we might never recover.

'Many years ago, a special relic was sent to Aria, and the reason we currently face invasion is because the god wants to retrieve it. When I shared my vision with Caraig, he remembered a scroll from the Sanctuary library. Its contents had been deemed so obscure no one had been able to interpret its message. Caraig allowed us to study it in light of my vision.

'When translated, it told of the making of a magical item called

The Casket of Ember, and about the people here in Aria who the gods appointed to protect it. The chest, which we think is about two handspans wide and about one and half handspans across, was brought here to use against the god should he make his way here. The primary function of this chest is to contain the essence of the god should he appear in Aria.'

She did not need her sight to know how restless her news made everyone. Sensing the array of questions flowing through their minds, Amelia held up her hand for silence before they escaped their lips. 'Please, let me tell you everything first, and I will answer all your questions later.'

No one spoke, and although the room stilled, she had no way of knowing what was happening until Walter gently touched her arm, signalling for her to continue. Facing the others, she found she had a strong sense of those she shared a close bond with: Liam, Seamus and Aliah. The others appeared as background noise to her newly honed senses.

However, if she stilled her mind, she found vibrations through which the others transmitted their worries and their fears. Although this was all new and interesting, it was distracting her from her task.

She continued. 'Obviously we need to find the casket as this is our best and easiest way to control the enemy we must defeat. We will talk more on how we might do that in a moment. Before moving on, we need to consider something Walter found in a related scroll.'

Sitting forward in his seat, Walter continued, almost as though they rehearsed their presentation beforehand. 'The ancient relic is a source of unimaginable power as it is strong enough to contain the essence of a god. We must also remember the god himself is searching for it. The scroll I read hinted the chest is a double edged sword. If the god manages to retrieve it first, he might be able to use it to his advantage.'

'How?' The voice sounded like Daniel.

'Well, as best I can make out, he might be able use the power to draw his physical form into this world.'

Gasps escaped.

'He did warn us he was coming,' Aliah said. 'Why else are we focusing on stopping him from getting here before that happens?'

'I know he did, but I hoped the boast he made when we fought him was an empty threat, meant to scare us off.' Seamus shared his thoughts out loud. 'It never occurred to me what would bring him here would also be what we would need to control him. In my mind I had it all planned; we find a magical object to help us, then face him, and hopefully defeat him.'

'I thought that too. Now we will have to plan carefully, and gather everything we need to vanquish him in either form before we retrieve our final weapon. While doing this we also need to ensure he does not get to the magical object before us.'

'Wait, there is more,' Amelia interrupted. 'Imprisoning him in the casket is the easiest way for us to prevent the god from tearing our world apart, but I also found another, more difficult, way to deal with him.

'As best as I can understand, the god is not truly here. Nor is he on the same plane as the other gods themselves, but rather stuck somewhere in between. In my vision, when the god ran away from his siblings, he used a huge amount of magical energy to pull himself from his home towards our world. Unfortunately he did not gather enough, and he was unable to complete his journey.

'Now, he either needs to come here, or return to the world where his body lies. If we could find a way to send him back home, the gods might then be able to restore the balance in their world and ours.'

The room filled with unasked questions, but no one wanted to speak first.

Boss broke the silence, summing up the situation in true military fashion. 'It seems the obvious course of action is to contain the god in the ember casket, but the best solution is for him to return home.'

Walter agreed. 'Yes, except at the moment the only option available is sending him back, unless we can find the casket, that is.'

'And where do we start looking?' Aliah asked.

'All the scroll said is the casket has been looked after by an ancient, secret order. I got a glimpse of one of their ceremonies during my vision, but I was not shown who they were or where they might be located.'

'How ancient would this order be, Amelia?' Seamus asked.

'Quite old, I would guess.'

'Hold on, wait here,' Seamus said, and she heard the click of the door closing.

SHUTTING THE DOOR BEHIND HIMSELF, Seamus turned and almost fell over Robin.

'What are you doing lurking in the corridor?' Seamus gasped in surprise.

'Lurking, sir? I never lurk.' Robin managed to look both superior and a little guilty. 'I came to see if you required more refreshments.'

Seamus frowned. 'I thought we agreed my friends and I would serve ourselves as most of the palace staff left for Port Marden with my father and mother.'

The man in front of him shifted uneasily. Small in stature, dark haired and with darting dark eyes, Robin often appeared shifty. Seamus remembered being told off by his mother when he told her his father's chancellor was the image of a sneak thief in one of his story books. He quickly brushed the thought away as Robin answered him.

'We did, Sir, but I noticed you were all hard at work so I took it upon myself to make sure you were being looked after.'

He should be grateful, but Seamus was annoyed. Robin ignored orders coming from both his duke's son and the king's heir. Seamus always felt uneasy in the man's presence, but deciding it was not the time to dwell on personal animosities, he attempted to smooth things over.

'Thank you for thinking of us, Robin. As we explained when we arrived, we are more than capable of looking after ourselves.' Seamus went to pass the chamberlain, but found himself blocked.

'I am not sure your father would approve of the Heir of the Realm looking after herself. He would expect me to see to her comfort.'

Keeping a firm grip on his rising temper, Seamus ground out a terse response. 'I think, as the eldest son of the duke, the hospitality is mine to extend. At this moment I can assure you Princess Alia-hanna is more than happy with the level of comfort we are providing. If anything changes, I will inform you.'

He swept past Robin and continued down the corridor, fists clenching as he imagined wiping the smug smile from the man's face. By the time he reached the stairway to the lower floor, he realised Robin had remained outside the guest room door.

'Robin, I am sure what the princess would most like at the moment is privacy.' His voice rang through the corridor. He hoped the others would hear his warning and realise someone might be listening.

This time he waited until Robin passed him and was half-way down stairs before he continued through the entrance hall, past the state rooms, and down the narrow corridor to the old part of the palace housing the library. Looking round the room, he confirmed someone had tidied up since they had left, just as suspected from things Robin had said. *Goddess, how will I find that scroll now?*

When he had been listening to Amelia talk about the secret sect who might be looking after the chest, something niggled at the back of his mind. One of the documents he read yesterday contained an account of a group on Hand similar to the one Amelia described, a report to the then king from one of his men. Initially he discounted the document because it did not speak directly of magic, or gods, and was old. Now, he was having second thoughts.

Scanning the documents, he resisted the urge to delve into the scrolls and tried to identify when he had read it. Early the previous morning perhaps? He picked up a scroll. No, he had read it this morning. He chose another; late yesterday. He moved again. No, those were from the first day. Picking up a few scrolls in between, he soon found the one he searched for. Rolling it back up, he returned to the guest room.

On the stairs he met Emer carrying a tray with fresh tea and some cups. His automatic response was to offer to carry it for her, but he stopped himself. Like Aliah, Emer would see the gesture not as good manners, but as a comment on her ability to carry out a simple task. Instead he walked ahead of her, opening the door to ease her way.

Waiting until she placed the tray down, he held up his find and announced, 'I read something I think will help.'

'What?' Walter asked, an excited twinkle in his eye.

'Early yesterday, I read this report from one of my ancestor's Guard Captain. He tells of a vassal on the southern coast who set up a monastery in tribute to one of the minor gods, the God of the Sea. Two things stood out when I read it. The first being the rise of religious houses worshipping the Goddess around the same time. Many of the monasteries and churches for the other gods were being abandoned, or converting to her.

'The second was the secrecy surrounding the order. Neither the guard nor his men had been admitted to the area dedicated to the monastery. In fact, they were turned away by force of arms.' Seamus laid out the scroll on the table, and all but Amelia, Pauley and Boss gathered round to read it.

'This is pretty flimsy to base our next moves on,' Daniel said, and Dominic nodded his agreement.

'Except,' Liam interrupted. 'The current Baron Wexler, like most of his forefathers, refused his place in the Ducal Court, preferring to stay close to home. Few people visit him, and he is almost a recluse.

'There have also been rumours about the monastery he has on his lands. There are enough men there to make up two guard units, or more, and those who have been seen in the village are said to carry themselves more like soldiers than monks.'

'My father sent emissaries inviting Lord Wexler to court to attend councils, but most of them were turned back at the gates to his lands. The only one who was let through was allowed to stay the night because he arrived in the midst of a horrendous storm. He dined with the staff and, as soon as the storm cleared the next morning, he was sent on his way.

'When he reported back, he told my father he had not even met with the baron, and the staff he ate with barely spoke to him,' Seamus added. 'I think there is a very good possibility this may be what we are looking for.'

'Amelia, what do you think?' Walter asked.

'I have had no vision about this, if that is what you want to know. But if it is my opinion you want, then my seeing led me to believe we needed to be on Hand, there are things for us to do here. It would therefore be reasonable to assume what we are looking for must be here.

'I also agree with Liam and Seamus about the Wexler's. For generations they have held themselves apart from others on this island. Add that to the rumours the lands they gifted to the monastery included some ancient caves and dwellings believed to be magical.

'The long held belief is that particular parcel of land was given to the order because the Wexler's wanted to rid their lands of the taint of magic. It is just as likely the land was used because its magic was needed to protect something of importance. I cannot think of a better place on the island to start our search.'

'I am not totally convinced, but at least if we follow this lead then we will be doing something other than reading in a library. So, shall we prepare to leave in the morning?' Aliah asked.

'Wait a moment,' Daniel interrupted. 'Let us not get ahead of ourselves. Firstly, we need to find out a little more about what is happening with the soldiers camped on the other side of the island before we leave the safety of the palace.

'Those ships off our coast contain rather a lot of men, and they must be running low on supplies. As they have not yet made landfall on the mainland, they must now be thinking about taking control of this island. Hand provides the perfect foothold to launch their next attack, while also giving them access to food and water.'

'I did not think of that.' Aliah frowned.

'Nor did I. I really must discuss this possibility with the captain of the guard to ensure we are prepared to defend the island, and provide refuge to those left behind should they need it,' Seamus added.

Daniel placed a hand on the younger boy's shoulder. 'Seamus, that is why I am here. Your only job is to learn how to vanquish a god.'

'But I cannot leave the people of Hand at the mercies of an invading force.' Seamus seemed to shrink as the weight of this new problem settled on his shoulders.

'There is little we can do about it tonight.' Emer moved to stand beside Seamus, as if by physically being near him, she was able to shoulder some of his burden. 'I suggest tomorrow I take a flight over the island so we know exactly what is happening. After, we can make plans to take care of the people of Hand, and to find what we need to do to beat this rogue deity.'

As always, Seamus was calmed by Emer's pragmatic approach. Every time he found himself caught up in the enormity of the task they faced, it was she who came up with something practical to do to move forward.

'I agree, further planning can wait until tomorrow. We have come a long way today, perhaps it is time to take a break and enjoy the dinner cook prepared for us.' Seamus stood and stretched.

'Just so long as we do not spend tomorrow in the library, I can agree to that,' Aliah said.

'I for one vote we go and find what cook has prepared for us, I am sure I smelled lamb before. I mean we cannot be expected to fight a God on and empty stomach, can we?' Liam's own stomach rumbled, emphasising his point.

Laughing, Dominic opened the door. 'Lead the way, Squire Liam, I think we could all do with some of cook's fine fare, especially if we are soon to be dining on travel rations again.'

A GENTLE TOUCH on her shoulder awoke Aliah.

'Warrior, it is time for training.'

Seamus, already dressed, stood waiting by the door. He turned and led the male god out of Aliah's room so she had some privacy to throw on some outdoor clothes.

Since she had been included in the night time training sessions, Aliah had taken to sleeping in trousers and a shirt. All she had to do was pull on some boots and a warm jacket and she was ready to join the others.

Moments later, they were all down in the back courtyard. The space was enclosed by the palace on one side, the garrison quarters on another, the stables opposite, and a high wall adjacent to the stables closed the square. Sheltered from the elements and prying eyes, it was the perfect place for their nightly lessons.

Aliah began limbering up, then she and Seamus went through the forms of unarmed combat they were developing. Based loosely on sword forms, running through the attack and defence positions helped focus their minds for the coming lesson. Before they completed the attack forms, Seamus stopped and turned to the watching god.

'Before we begin tonight, I have some questions for you. May I ask them?'

'You know I cannot give you information about the forthcoming battle.'

'Yes, but I understand you are still able to provide me with some general information.'

'I am not sure what you mean by that question,' the god said, regarding Seamus quizzically.

'Can you tell me things about the gods as a group? Or your world as opposed to the world where we live?'

'I do not believe answering such questions will affect the balance. So yes, you may ask.'

Seamus winked at Aliah, and she wondered what he was up to.

'We found a scroll suggesting we must find the Casket of Ember.'

'I am unable to talk to you about that.'

'I do not want to talk about it either. While I was reading the scroll, it occurred to me we call you all gods, yet here in Aria we worship only one of you, and we simply call her Goddess. When meeting with you all together, I met four female and three male gods, and the one we are looking to banish would make four males.

'You told me each of you have different abilities, and I think this has something to do with the balance you speak of. Balance in numbers, balance of the sexes and balance in powers.'

Intrigued, Aliah stopped her warm up to listen.

'So, here is my question: were you once worshiped as individuals by the people of this world who knew and used those names?'

After thinking for a moment, the god answered. 'Yes, in the past people used our names to pay homage to us and the individual gifts we bestow on the earth.'

'And when we worshiped all of you, there was balance and unity in our world, and yours?'

'That is correct.'

'Is there a power in knowing your names, or using your names?' Aliah chipped in.

'I am not sure you would call it power in the way you understand the word. Using a god's name calls their attention, creating a direct, mutually beneficial link between a worshipper and their chosen god.'

'That is almost as I thought. If one god was worshipped more than another then there would be disharmony?' Aliah continued.

The god considered this for a moment before responding. 'That depends. When we are all worshipped equally, there is complete balance, but we are also paired. For instance, you worship the Goddess here, in the southern realms they worship her male opposite, so the world stays in balance.'

Aliah was pleased she figured the direction Seamus' enquiries were heading. Though his next question caught her by surprise, and made her realise how much thought Seamus had been putting into defeating their foe.

'So, if I know the god's name, and I use enough force behind my command, he will have his focus drawn to me. In effect, binding him to me in some way?'

'I guess that is one way of looking at it.'

If the last question had been a surprise, the next totally confused her.

'This un-named god is not on your plane of existence, and he is not on ours, is there a place where he actually exists?'

The god thought for a moment. 'Yes and no. My brother is between worlds. He is alone with some stray souls also trapped there. It is not a place where life grows, so magic is sparse, and his existence is limited.'

'As I understand it, he wants to move here for some reason and you want him back, thus restoring the balance on both worlds. What stops you from just getting him yourselves? No, wait, you cannot because you would be pitted against each other, causing destruction on a level we can only imagine.

'May I ask another question? Can we deal with him while he is where he is now, or must we wait until he is here?'

'Of course you can fight him if he reunites with his body, and in some ways this would be the best course of action for all as he would be returned to us in one piece. However, there are also ways to defeat him before he fully manifests.'

Aliah's jaw dropped. She could not believe the gods thought they should let their brother fully enter their world before confronting him because that was best for them. Angry, she forced her next words out through gritted teeth. 'If you wanted us to fight him in person you could have warned us earlier, or at least trained us specifically for that eventuality?'

'We are not able to tell you the best way to fight our brother as that would have the same effect as fighting him ourselves. However, we can confirm whether or not you are on the right path as that is within the balance.'

Blindsided by the notion they might truly have to face the god in his physical form, Aliah lashed out in anger.

'Damn your balance. You gods had a fight amongst yourself and one of your number decided to take off on his own and wreak havoc on our world. You failed to stop him, and now you are expecting us to clean up your mess. Yet you say you cannot give us even the most basic of information to help. If he is not playing by the rules, why should you?'

'Because that would make them as bad as the god they are trying to stop. If they break the rules to capture him, then what is to stop them breaking the rules for other things?' Seamus answered for the god.

Aliah paused, unsure why her friend was standing up for them. As his words sunk in, she grinned. 'A good point, two wrongs do not make it right.'

'But still frustrating?' Seamus raised a quizzical eyebrow.

She laughed out loud. 'Very. Have you finished your questions, or is there something else we need to ask about?'

Seamus sucked thoughtfully on his bottom lip. 'I do have more things to ask about, but I need to think a little on what we learnt tonight, move the pieces around and see how it changes things.'

'Do you want to share?'

'Yes, soon, but not yet.'

'Do not leave it too long. Now, I need some physical activity to work off this frustration.'

Side by side they started at the beginning of their forms to refocus for the night's training.

CHAPTER 36
WE NEED A PLAN

Amelia awoke in darkness, shaking, her body drenched in sweat. The door opened and she tensed under the bedclothes.

'Amelia, are you all right? You shouted out again. Are you having another bad dream?'

She relaxed as the welcome voice of Walter filled the blackness. 'Thank you, Walter, I am fine now.'

'Do you want to talk?'

She felt the weight of the bed shift as he sat beside her, then took her hand in his. 'No, really, I am fine.' The mattress moved as he made to stand. Changing her mind, she gripped him tightly. 'No, please do not go. I think maybe we should talk. You might be able to help me understand what is going on inside my head.'

Waiting until he settled back down, she continued. 'The last two nights the same dream haunted me, and I cannot let it go, not even during the day. I am unsure whether my dream is a seeing, or just my imagination creating nightmares.'

Amelia hated relying on someone else, but losing her ability to see, on top of the changes in her gift had shaken her usual confidence. Over the last few days she had begun to wonder if her loss of sight was not to improve her foreseeing, but to teach her a lesson on not being so aloof and arrogant. The need to rely on others simply to move around was teaching her a large dose of humility. An unfortunate side effect was she now questioned other decisions, and even her visions.

'I am not sure I can be of much help. I never studied foretelling and prophecy in any great detail. Caraig would be of more assistance, perhaps we can ask Emer to help us contact him.' Walter's voice sounded uncharacteristically uncertain.

'Caraig has other more pressing duties, like helping to prevent the Carsten army gaining a foothold on the mainland. Besides, all I require is a good old dose of common sense, and you have that in abundance.'

'If you say so.' Walter chuckled. 'Let me get a chair from the other room so I can make myself comfortable.'

Walter and she occupied the suite of rooms across from Seamus and Aliah in the guest wing of the palace. Although the rooms were not as spacious or ornate, the layout mirrored the suite across the hall in that it contained two bedrooms joined by a common lounge.

Normally Amelia would have preferred a single room to herself, but in the few days since being named seer and her sight being taken, she found having someone close by helped her relax. It may just have been that the sounds of someone else moving filled the silence, but she was self-aware enough to know she also appreciated having help at hand should the darkness overwhelm her.

When they first arrived, Emer offered to share with her. Even though she was busy with other duties, she thought herself best qualified to help Amelia as her own father had not been able to see for most of her life. Travelling from Sanctuary to Hand, Amelia had grown used to Walter's strength, and his ability to assist without suggesting she was unable to do things herself, so she turned the girl down.

Walter returned and placed a chair by the bed. She waited a few moments while he made himself comfortable before speaking.

'Remember the night before last, in Port Marden, you woke me from a horrendous dream?'

'You sounded in such torment, everyone within earshot worried for your safety.' Walter took her hand, which she found reassuring.

'That dream was similar to the one I had tonight. I was somewhere dark and confined and I think physically I could get out, but I was trapped none-the-less. An overwhelming sense of dread filled me every time I thought about leaving. I believe perhaps something dangerous waited there for me.

'Every now and then, I caught a glimpse of things on the outside, and as I watched I gathered information. Perhaps to plan an escape, or for something else. Or maybe I was preparing to fight my captors —no, maybe not that.

'My captor frightened me. In fact, I have never been so scared of anything in my life. He had the power to extinguish my very existence, and he would do it without a second thought.

'Yesterday and tonight's nightmares were similar, only it is growing more intense.' Amelia finished speaking. Walter said nothing. 'What do you think?' she asked, unable to bare the silence any longer.

'Before I answer, I would like to hear what you think.'

She took a moment to gather her jumbled thoughts and calm her nerves before answering. 'After the first night I thought such a vivid and disturbing nightmare might be a reaction to losing my sight. Without being able to see, I do feel somewhat trapped. Although I am sometimes able to make out shadows and shapes, I am saddened to think I will no longer experience the beautiful colours of the world around me. My improved foresight is no where near compensation for losing so much, but it would be a stretch to say I am terrified by the experience.

'Then tonight's dream differed slightly. I was able to glimpse some of my surroundings, and the land was not familiar, which I thought to be strange. Also, I could swear I saw guards in Carsten livery sitting around a fire. I am now wondering if I am having a different type of foreseeing.'

With no immediate response from Walter, the silence in the room made her uneasy. 'Walter?'

'Sorry, I am thinking, trying to remember something I read once when I was teaching on The Wizard Isles.'

Amelia attempted to quieten her unease, taking calming breaths while she waited for Walter to continue.

'I am not sure what I am going to share is one hundred percent accurate, and I am not in a position to double check my facts. Some time ago, I had a student with the gift of foresight. While teaching him I did some research as he developed some strange abilities. Not only was he able to predict the future, he also experienced what I can only describe as extreme empathy.

'My research into the subject found some of those gifted with foresight are also able to pick up other people's emotional turmoil. Sometimes it assists them in seeing into the future, other times it merely alerts them to someone's distress. Is it possible you are sensing what is happening to someone on the other side of the island?'

'It is definitely possible, except I was not trapped in a cave or prison, or anything else so mundane. If you are pressing for a more accurate description, I would describe myself as being mentally or emotionally trapped.'

'There is more than one way to be held prisoner. Perhaps some of the people over there are being forced to work with the army, or are too scared to leave. Perhaps the person whose emotions you have linked with came into contact with our god friend in Gaius' body. Their reaction to meeting a god might generate enough fear for you to make a connection.'

Amelia considered his words before responding, struggling to capture the essence of her experience to see if Walter might be right. 'If I am honest, the fear was completely overwhelming, almost paralysing, I do not believe an encounter of that type would generate the crushing fear in my dream. Any other ideas?'

As another frustrating gap in the conversation lengthened, Amelia realised how much she once relied on visual clues to tell her what a person was doing. Had Walter's attention drifted from the conversation? Was he thinking, or had he fallen asleep?

As she waited, she tried to use her other senses to find out what was going on. If she closed her eyes—she did not know why she still did that when she needed to concentrate, but she did—she envisioned someone shuffling through scrolls or books.

'Walter, are you trying to remember something else you read?'

'Yes,' his tone was quizzical. 'Why do you ask?'

Amelia laughed at her discovery and explained it to Walter. This was one way her other senses were developing to help her make up for not being able to see. It appeared once she tuned into a person's thought waves, it was much easier to read their actions, or inactions in this instance.

'That confirms my suspicions. Your abilities definitely lean towards the empathetic side. I think that makes it all the more likely you picked up someone else's feelings while you slept and your mind was more receptive. The question we need to answer now is who might be having intense enough feelings for you to tune into them from so far away?

'Mmm, someone who is trapped? Someone in mortal fear for their life?' he mused.

The image of a lamp being lit and illuminating a room flooded into Amelia's mind. 'Walter, you have worked out who it might be.'

'I believe I may have. Think Amelia. Who do we know of who would consider themselves psychologically trapped, scared to make themselves known in their own body?'

'Oh. Oh, Walter, you clever man. Of course. If a god took over my body I might feel just like I did in the dream. We should tell the others. This might be useful to know.'

'Amelia, it is not yet dawn. Perhaps waking everyone up now is not such a good idea. Shall I go and get us some tea while we wait?'

'Yes please,' Amelia said, and she waited for Walter to leave so she could ready herself for the day.

***

SITTING BY THE FIRE, Aliah sipped her tea and let her mind wander back over Seamus' conversation with the god the night before. The depth of the questions Seamus asked surprised her, and annoyed her as well. They were a team. They should be working together. So why did he not discuss his ideas with her first?

As her tea cooled, her anger bubbled. Seamus had been taking the lead in almost everything since they passed their trials. It was almost as though fighting the god was his personal crusade, and she had been relegated to supporter and ego booster.

The more she dwelled on it, the angrier she became. How dare he slot her into the traditional role of a woman, being supportive rather than active? Besides, Emer already filled that role, he did not need her hanging round cheering him on as well.

Oh, she stopped herself. That was unfair. Emer was not only a guard by profession, but she had taken on the dangerous role of scouting for the group. Aliah was ashamed she used the girl's growing fondness for Seamus against her, even if only in her mind.

Gazing into the flames of the fire, she went back through the past few days and considered her actions. Soon her anger was as cold as her tea. It struck her Seamus was not responsible for her background role, she had relegated herself to supporter.

When she failed to leave the trial area by the allotted time, the gods took her away. She was only here because Seamus came and rescued her. From that moment she had been proving to herself, and to the others, that she deserved the title of Warrior. While she concentrated on showing her worthiness, she had forgotten who she was, and what she could contribute outside of the gifts the gods bestowed on her.

This ends now.

Having given herself a wakeup call, she decided it was Seamus' turn. Thinking they had much to discuss before they met with the others, she walked over to his room. She knocked and flung open the door in one movement, only to gasp in embarrassment and walk straight back out.

'Well, that is a sight I can never un-see,' she said when Seamus entered the room a few moments later, clothed and ready to face the day. Her attempt at lightening the situation failed dismally.

'It is traditional to knock and wait to be invited into someone's sleeping quarters, especially when they are from the opposite sex,' Seamus commented dryly as he poured himself some tea, still unable to look her in the face. 'Perhaps if you did, you would not walk in on people when they are not fully dressed.'

Or not clothed at all. 'Sorry.'

Blushing with embarrassment, the one word apology was all she was able to manage.

'So, what have you made your mind up about?' he asked as he sat down in the chair opposite.

'How do you know I have decided anything?' she countered, playing for time as she attempted to compose herself.

'You always get impatient when you make a decision, as though you think you will change your mind if you do not immediately act on it.'

Aliah sighed. She disliked it when people guessed her thoughts. Then again, if she and Seamus were to work closely together, maybe it was not such a bad thing. Still, it would not do their relationship any good if he learnt he could read her so easily.

'Well, you are wrong. I only wanted to talk about what happened last night, and agree how we move forward from here so we can present a united front.'

'Thank the Goddess.' Seamus' response was unexpected, and momentarily stopped her in her tracks.

'What do you mean by that?'

The temper she calmed earlier flared again. Seamus looked like an animal caught in a trap as he lowered his eyes and flicked an imaginary fleck of something off his trousers.

'I am not sure I should say, given your tone.'

'No, tell me what is on your mind,' Aliah insisted, sitting forward on the edge of her chair.

Working really hard, she managed to push her anger down so she could focus on what Seamus had to say, and not react straight away.

'All right.' Seamus sounded skeptical but ploughed on in spite of his fears. 'Recently you seemed more interested in your warrior training than actually thinking about how we are going to defeat our enemy. You have pretty much left all the planning to me.'

'I have not.' The words escaped from Aliah's lips before she could stop them. 'Sorry, maybe you are right. It is just hard to listen to someone else say that.'

Seamus took a deep breath. 'At the risk of you snapping my head off again ... over the last couple of six-days you have been working on being more like a leader, and part of that is allowing people to work to their strengths and you taking more of a behind the scenes role but ...'

Seamus stopped and looked at her, as if deciding whether or not it was safe for him to continue. She forced herself to calmly meet his gaze, hiding the hurt his words caused. It was one thing telling yourself off, but someone else doing it, however much the criticism was justified, was difficult to take.

'Well, I do not think you were chosen as the Warrior for your measured thinking and ability to let others take the lead. I think we need your spark and, dare I say it, the way you sometimes just act on instinct. No one can predict when you might do that, and I believe it is a weapon we will need when we face our final battle.'

'Oh.' No one had ever praised her impetuous actions before.

'It is bad enough I must dither and think things through until I understand it from every angle. If you are doing that too or, even worse, not making any decisions at all, then I am worried we will not be able to act decisively when the time comes.' Seamus sunk back into the chair, as if a great weight had been lifted from his shoulders.

'Oh,' Aliah said again. It was more of a placeholder while she organised her thoughts, than her actual response. 'So you think I have not been pulling my weight?' It sounded like an accusation, although she did not mean it to.

'Well ... I would not have put it so bluntly.'

'Sorry, Seamus, I did not mean to say that out loud, or to attack you. In fact, I was sitting here thinking something very similar before I came and got you. I admit I concentrated so much on proving myself the Warrior and a leader, I forgot so much of warfare is not about the battle, but about the preparation and planning. A good leader should concentrate on both. And a good partner should be more supportive.'

Seamus sat forward to speak.

'No, please wait a minute, I need to get this all out. While we are being honest, I must confess I am a little intimidated by your fore-sight. If you are already certain about what we should do, what more can I contribute?'

Now everything was out in the open, relief surged through Aliah and she felt a renewed sense of vigour.

In contrast, Seamus' earlier energy seemed to leave his body, and he slumped even further in the chair. Only then did Aliah realise the mistake she and the others had been making. They always stated they were working as a team, but in reality, they had been relying on Seamus to move them in the right direction. So rather than supporting him, their actions increased the pressure.

'Seamus, how reliable is your gift at predicting our best course of action?'

Seamus stared at the floor.

'When I know something for certain it is as though a piece of a puzzle has finally fallen into place. I can almost hear the click. Like yesterday when I sensed all the people we needed to defeat the god were here.

'Almost everything else is far less reliable. For instance, when we talked about how to stop the Carsten invasion I believed we needed to remove the king or the battle would continue until many died. What I did not know was how to do that, or whether or not we would succeed.'

'So ...' Aliah strung the word out while she sifted through the information in her head. 'How much are you certain of? Are you sure of what we need to do to defeat the god? And by sure, I mean what do you know for a certainty from your gifts?'

Seamus raised his head, displaying the worry in his eyes. 'Just what I told you, all the people we need are gathered here.'

'What about retrieving the casket?'

'That is an odd one. I cannot tell if it is important for us to find it, or if it is enough that we stop the god from getting his hands on it.'

'So, the casket and anything else is speculation? Even the questions you asked last night?'

'Yes. Everything has been spinning around in my head since we arrived. Yesterday was helpful in that some ideas began to form. Until then, it was like looking at thousands of puzzle pieces, not knowing which ones were important, and which were not. Last night helped clarify the relevant pieces, and I feel a little more confident of the direction we should be looking in.'

'Not to mention having it confirmed from on high we might not get to fight the god until he is here in Aria.'

Seamus smiled a wry smile. 'Yes, that was a bit of a worry. Still, better to find out now than later. I have been forming a plan to fight him in person, but I view it more as a worst case scenario option.'

'Well, at least we agree on that. He is scary enough when he speaks into our minds, I shudder to think what it would be like facing him at his most powerful.

'So. What does this plan look like so far?' Aliah asked.

Seamus found the imaginary piece of lint on his trousers again.

'Seamus?'

'It does not look like much really. I believe we need to isolate him so we are not distracted when we face him. Which means the other's role must be to protect us while we deal with the god.

'We need the casket, although I am not sure whether we need the power it contains or the casket itself, and we need to send him back to his home.'

'Mm, not really a detailed plan, is it?'

'I guess not,' Seamus admitted. 'I have been focusing more on ways to control him, or be rid of him before he gains his full strength. I believe we have a better chance of success if we face him when he has not gained enough energy to be fully here.'

'Have you considered he might be weakened by reuniting with his, like you were after the battle the other day?'

Seamus' head jerked up. Clearly this had not occurred to him. 'No. So if he does make it here, we need to attack him quickly, before he recovers. That means we cannot let him get too far away from Hand.'

'So, you sure you want to fight him before he has his body? He has Gaius' power at the moment and he is quite a strong wizard.' Aliah just wanted to be certain Seamus had thought everything through.

'Yes, I am. Gaius' power is from here and we know how it works, as well as its limitations. I would rather face his magic than the power I sensed in the gods.'

Aliah sighed with relief. 'Me too. You also asked about the god's name last night. I appreciate you think it might be able to be used against him, but have you figured out who he is, or are you still working that out?'

'I am not certain of his name, but I think there is something in the library that might help me figure it out. If I find it, I do not want to say it out loud, or write it down, in case his attention is drawn to us before we are ready. The element of surprise might come in useful.'

Aliah thought for a while, and weighed her need to know against the usefulness of knowing now. Realising there were more important things to discuss before the others arrived, she decided to let it go.

'Back to our main problem,' she started, not sure how Seamus would take the next bit. 'You need to stop taking so much on yourself, and perhaps tell us if you are worried about something. If we had all understood your gift a little better, we would not have relied on you to set our course quite so much. You would have felt less pressure, and would have behaved less like a spoilt brat.'

'Oh.' Lost for words, Seamus traced his finger thoughtfully over his lips. 'So while you should have been acting like more of a leader, I should have been acting less like a dictator?'

Aliah laughed out loud. 'That is one way of looking at it, but I am serious. You need to accept a little more help.'

'All right, you made your point. We should have more talks like this,' Seamus said dryly.

Not sure whether or not he was being sarcastic, Aliah decided to take him at face value. 'Yes, we should, because if we cannot be open with each other, how can we even consider taking on a god together?'

'I am not sure we should,' Seamus responded.

Aliah laughed, but when Seamus did not join in, she stopped dead. He was serious.

'Seamus, what do you mean?' Aliah said the words slowly, suddenly fearful of where this conversation was leading, but deep down knowing it was important she understood what was going on in Seamus' head.

'Aliah, we can plan all we want, research all we want, and train all we want, but I have to say I have serious doubts about whether we can actually take on this god and win.' The words were wooden, and Seamus would not raise his eyes to meet hers.

'Well, it is a bit late for this,' Aliah responded, a shiver of fear running through her. How could they save Aria if Seamus was not fully committed? 'If you were not prepared to do this, we should never have gone to Sanctuary to be tested.'

Slowly Seamus raised his head and reluctantly met her gaze. 'I will follow through what we started, Aliah, because there is no one else to do it. But our last fight with the god showed me how woefully unprepared we are, and I cannot help thinking maybe there is someone out there better able to win this battle than me.'

'Than us, Seamus. Than *us*.'

'Us then. But this is not some training exercise, Aliah. This is perhaps the biggest battle in the history of our land, and our chances of success are not good.'

'Well, Seamus, we will not be letting you stand before the troops to rally them for battle, will we?'

When Seamus' head dropped again, Aliah realised her attempt to inject some humour into the situation had fallen flat. This called for a more heartfelt approach. Moving from her chair, and crouching so Seamus could see her face, she tried again.

'Seamus, if you think we do not all know the odds are against us in this fight, then you are wrong. Just because we do not dwell on it does not mean we forget the stakes are high, for us as well as for Aria.' Holding his gaze so he would know the truth of her words, she saw the moment they sunk in.

'So, we can sit here and wallow in our worry, or we can get out there and do the best we can with what we have—which is quite a lot by the way.' She stood up and looked down at the top of his head. 'I know what I choose to do.'

SEAMUS FINISHED DRESSING QUICKLY and slipped out of the suite he shared with Aliah. There was something he wanted to do before he met with everyone else.

Walking briskly to the library, he experienced a confidence he had not felt in days. This he was good at. Searching through scrolls, finding information, putting together a plan. If this was all the Wizard was expected to do then he was fine.

It was not though. At some stage he was expected to battle a god and win. This was the bit he was not so sure about. He still felt sick at the thought of what he had done to turn back the Carsten ships from Port Marden.

His actions caused a whole ship of people to be blown up. Oh, Aliah could talk all she wanted about not being responsible for how people responded to something they did, and part of him believed that. Still, the guilt weighed heavy.

Then he had pushed those ships out to sea. It had seemed a good idea at the time, but he had not considered whether or not he was able to move the fleet without killing the thousands of souls on those vessels.

It was those decisions that needed to be made in the heat of battle that scared him. He had not trained to be a guard or a soldier. He had been educated to be a duke, someone who had time to think through all the options and consult with others before making a decision.

Mentally shaking himself, he remembered Aliah's words. *"We can sit here and wallow in our worry, or we can get out there and do the best we can with what we have."*

She was always so confident, or at least she appeared so on the outside. Maybe that was her secret, if you act as though you can do something, perhaps you eventually believe you actually can. There and then he decided he would hide his fears and do his best. And then maybe he too would come to believe in their eventual success.

Nodding a greeting to the guard on duty, he opened the door to the library and slipped inside. Searching through the documents they had read through, he found what he was looking for; a scroll of the creation myth.

Yesterday he had cast it aside, today he was not so sure. Now he knew names were important when dealing with gods, he thought he should learn more about them. Opening the scroll, he skipped the first stanzas about how the creator of all built the physical worlds, looking for the bit where he created his children to tend his creation. Then he stopped.

Wait a moment, yesterday Amelia had said they could send the god back to his own world. This might actually be important as it appeared many a truth had been hidden in myths and legends.

"In the void of before The Great Creator used all that was around to build a home, populating it with plants and animals. The Creator was happy. With nothing left to do, he again entered the void and built a new world, and then another, and another, until he used up all that was around him.

Returning home, the Creator was too tired to continue tending to the numerous worlds he had made so, in one final burst of creativity, he birthed children to help tend to his creations."

Before reading on, Seamus stopped to consider how this information might help. It confirmed the idea there were a number of worlds out there other than their own, one of which was the home world of the gods. He read on.

The next section told him the Creator birthed four boys and four girls, something he already knew. Running quickly through the females: Zoia, Goddess of Life; Xira, Goddess of Land; Armonia, Goddess of Harmony; Polema, Goddess of War; he moved onto the male gods.

In opposition to the females, the male gods represented death, water, chaos and peace. Logically he thought it unlikely Erinos, the God of Peace, would start a war. Given the Wexler monastery was dedicated to the oceans, the God of Water could likely be ruled out as well.

Death? Or chaos? It could be either. He would need to do some more digging. Rolling up the scroll, he had just returned it to the shelf when the door opened behind him and the others began wandering in.

EVERYONE except for Boss sat around the table in the library. Given the recent discussions about someone in the household spying on them, the retired soldier elected to stand guard to ensure their privacy. So far Robin had been the only one to venture down the corridor, and only then to ask if they needed any refreshments. When Boss explained they would be happy to go to the kitchens themselves, he left. Pauley slipped in behind him, declaring he was too young to spend the day sitting around in a library.

After Amelia told them of her dream the night before, there had been a brief discussion. Prompted by Aliah, Seamus then told them what he found during their nightly training session, after which they sat quietly, waiting for Emer to return.

I can sense your impatience, Seamus, but I am truly flying as fast as I can. I can see my bedroom window and will be with you soon.

I am not impatient, Seamus sent.

Hah.

All right, a little, but I was worried as well.

I have done this before. No one saw me. Patience now.

Emer's presence left his mind and Seamus turned his attention back to the map of Hand in front of him. The Isle of Hand was divided by a mountain range; giving the island the fertile ground around Hand Harbour, a high plateau where most of the island's cattle and sheep grazed, and the coastal flats on the other side of the island which was the primary source of seafood for the locals.

Without the mountains, it would take two days to ride coast to coast. With them, it usually took three or more, depending on how well you knew your way through twisting alpine paths.

The mountains were bisected by four passes, two from this side of the island; the Low Pass which led from Port Hand to the village of Wexon, and the High Pass which was more northerly and led to the village of High Hand. The other two passes connected the fishing villages of North Piscine and South Piscine with the rest of the island.

Lord Wexler's lands were almost directly due south of Port Hand, on the southern end of the high plateau. Close by as the crow flies, the mountain range added time, making the journey take the best part of a day. Not far from the manor was the small village of Wexon, which serviced the farms in the region. The land given to the Brotherhood of the Elm was closer to the coast, between the village and Baron Wexler's holdings.

Aware the Carsten fleet waited off the North West Coast, and were likely using North Piscine as their base, they would not be able to confirm any further details until Emer returned. Almost as though his thoughts had called her to him, the door opened, admitting the shapeshifting girl.

All eyes turned expectantly to Emer as her report on enemy activity would largely dictate their next moves. Gathering round the map, they all watched while Emer described her fly over the enemy position.

'Given they have now been anchored off the coast of Hand for a full six-day, it was surprising how many soldiers are still living onboard ships. Row boats were moving between them and the land, dropping soldiers, then coming back in. From the sky it looked as though they are giving groups shore leave, rather than disembarking the entire army.

'Some of the ships sailed off towards Port Marden, I assume for their daily attack. Apart from that, activity on the other vessels was limited to a few watchmen.

'The leadership is in North Piscine as we expected, but the village is not fortified in any way. They removed people from their homes and commandeered fishing boats to transport soldiers, but little else. It is almost as though they are not planning to stay. There are patrols around the village, and it did look as though a garrison was building a camp near the High Pass.'

Having completed her report Emer stepped back and waited for questions.

'Are there any other signs of what they might be doing militarily?' Daniel asked.

'Apart from the gathering of soldiers near the High Pass, as best as I can tell, they seem to be waiting.'

'For what?' Liam pondered out loud, and started pacing around the map as though looking at it from a different angle might give him some new ideas.

'What about the people from North Piscine?' Seamus asked, frowning.

'There were some heading through the High Pass towards High Hand. Still others were making their way towards the Lower Pass. A tent town has sprung up on the outskirts of South Piscine. Also, I saw people packing things into fishing boats there, I believe some may be preparing to leave.'

'Surely they would not brave the treacherous waters around the southern coast? They would be risking their lives at this time of year,' Seamus worried.

'I think we should be more concerned about the men on those warships. There are a lot of them, and their provisions must be nearly gone after such a long sea voyage. There is little in the way of food on the coastal flats, meaning soon they will have no option but to head to the High Plateau. I believe the garrison is securing access to the main route to the rest of Hand. From there, they will be able to raid the farms on the High Plateau.'

Seamus looked at his cousin in surprise.

'What? Do you think all I do around here is fetch and carry for your father? I listen and learn as well,' Liam scolded.

'I think you are right, Liam,' Daniel chipped in. 'I would do the same thing in their position. Manage the passes and you control all the farm land on the island. Once they are secure, you can move your army around at will.'

'I thought you preferred to be just a soldier,' Aliah joked with Daniel, who ignored her, turning back to the duke's squire.

'Liam, how many of the barons left with your uncle to join the fight from Port Marden?'

'None,' the squire answered. 'They all remained with at least half of their guards just in case the invaders tried to use Hand as a base to invade the mainland.'

'So, as I understand it, we need to make sure the Carstenites stay on the coastal side of the North and South Passes otherwise we will lose the island's entire source of food, and most of its defence force. Not only will their presence on the plateau place us in danger, but we will not be able to search for the casket as easily if they control the island. If they are setting up a base camp then they intend to move in the next few days.'

'That is exactly what I thought,' Liam said, and the two turned to the rest of the group who had been silently watching in wonder as the two military minds worked their own special magic.

'So my plan is ...' Daniel started.

'Hold on there,' Aliah interrupted. 'We need to consider every-thing together. Seamus' information from last night, Amelia's dream of Gaius, all we learnt yesterday, and of course Emer's report. We have to fit in a lot of things over the next few days.'

'Or we need to split up to cover them all,' Dominic suggested.

The frown on Aliah's face told them she was trying hard not to contradict the spy, causing Seamus to smile in pleasure at the old Aliah's return.

'We can certainly consider that option,' Aliah finally forced out. 'Although I had assumed we would stay together from here on in. After all, both Seamus and Amelia said we were all together for a reason.'

Before the two began an argument, Seamus decided it was time to speak up. 'As I explained before, Aliah, I know it is right we are here now, but I cannot tell you if we are all meant to stay together until our confrontation with the god. Do you have any ideas Amelia?'

His aunt frowned, then shook her head. 'If only foreseeing provided all the answers ... in truth, I am unable to tell one way or the other.'

'In the absence of any "feelings" to the contrary we can consider all our options. As I see it, we need to motivate the barons left on the island to defend the passes. We also need to make sure we read all the documents we can about the Wexlers and the Brotherhood of the Elm before we approach them. Having done our research, we have to retrieve the casket and use it to imprison the god's essence.' Seamus finished summarising and waited for ideas. He did not have to wait long.

'If we must split up, then I think we should leave Walter and Amelia here to research, Liam and Daniel should go and talk to the barons, and you and I should go and speak with Baron Wexler and retrieve the chest.' Aliah outlined her plan and as soon as she finished a massive argument erupted.

Seamus dropped his arms to the table and placed his head on top. This was not one of the times when his foresight would help him dictate a path, and he had no idea of how to begin to moderate the strong personalities voicing their opinions around him.

CHAPTER 37

WE HAVE A PLAN

How could one comment cause so much dissent? Unable to hear herself think over the raised voices, let alone call everyone to order for a reasoned discussion, Aliah placed her hands over her ears. Dominic touched her arm to get her attention.

'You need to manage this.' He leaned in close to speak, so close his warm breath brushed against her cheek.

She closed her eyes, wishing the scene away. Dominic was right, someone needed to take control and keep everyone focused on the task at hand, and it may as well be her.

'Quiet,' she yelled, and to her surprise, the room fell silent. Seamus even took his head off his arms and reengaged.

'Maybe I picked the wrong people for the wrong jobs, but the idea itself is sound. Let us talk this through rationally, each having our say and listening to the others.'

Now she appreciated how the tutors in Bannock felt when faced with a bunch of unruly children. When she returned home, she owed them an apology.

'Firstly, let us talk about the research we need to do. Does anyone doubt Walter is the best scholar among us?'

She took their silence as agreement and was about to move on to her next point when Seamus raised his hand. She nodded for him to speak.

'While I agree Walter is the better scholar, I might need to use the knowledge he finds out, and so might you.'

'Yes, I would guess so, but surely he can keep us updated on anything he learns.'

'What if there is a problem and he cannot pass something critical to our success on to us? Something that might be the difference between winning and ... well, you know.'

'That is a good point.' Aliah twirled her plait before answering. 'Am I right in thinking it is only one day to Wexon from here?'

Seamus nodded.

'And at least two days if you were coming via the northern routes?'

'More like three and a bit,' he said.

'All right, we can stay behind for two days and gather as much information as we can, then head to Wexon.'

Seamus agreed and she was relieved to have passed her first hurdle.

'Right. Amelia needs to stay with Walter to help with interpreting anything he finds.' There was no further dissent.

'As I said before, Liam and Daniel can go talk to the barons and ask them to move their guards to the passes.'

Up until then she had been doing so well, but an eruption of voices followed her last comment as they all tried to shout over each other.

Aliah held up her hand and raised her voice so she could be heard above the noise. 'One at a time, please. Daniel, you go first.'

'I am an Arian Guard. What makes you think the barons will listen to me?'

'Why do you think I am sending Liam with you?'

Liam burst out laughing. 'You think they will listen to me, the son of a minor noble, squire to the duke? Sending me is an insult.'

Aliah frowned. 'I had not thought of that. As Seamus' cousin I always assumed you were as high born as him, especially as no one in the family treats you differently.'

'My father is Duchess Elise's brother. As nephew to a baron he is a minor noble, who manages the duchy business out of Port Marden. While we do not make distinctions of rank within our family, other nobles certainly do.'

'How annoying!' Aliah tugged on her plait again. Liam and Daniel were tasked with keeping them safe while they learnt how to battle the god, and now it seemed like they would not be able to do their job because they were not suitably high enough in rank. 'We cannot send Seamus ...'

'They would not listen to Seamus either,' Liam interrupted. 'The island is small, and by now everyone will have heard about Seamus' magic. They would not allow him in their homes, not even if he carried the Ducal Seal, and not even as the King's Ambassador.'

'But they would let you in, Aliah.' Daniel realised where Liam was heading, and provided the solution.

Silence. No one else spoke. Seamus sat there with a wry smile on his face as though he was enjoying this, and the rest of the group were looking expectantly at her.

'You cannot be serious. It is common knowledge Arians are not well liked on the island, and I know nothing about Hand Protocol. I might single handedly set Hand-Arian relations back centuries without even realising I was doing it.'

'Take Robin with you,' Seamus suggested, his eyes twinkling with amusement. 'He has been desperate to help, and this would give him something practical to do.'

'But I will need to be with you when we face the god.'

How would she and Seamus train if they were not together? And what would happen if the god attacked either of them while there were apart?

'Half a day to Baron Tappit, on this side of the High Pass. One day to Baron George on the other side, and a little over half a day to Baron Rassmussen near the Northern Pass. If you stay overnight with Rassmussen, that gives you time to meet with Seamus near the South Pass after we have searched through the scrolls,' Amelia informed them.

The older woman had been silent since she told them all about her adventure into Gaius' mind the previous night, but it appeared she continued to listen to the discussion.

'But what about our training?' Aliah looked to Seamus for support.

He chewed his lip. 'Last night we were repeating the same exercises together. We can check with our trainer tonight, but maybe there is no more they are able to teach us. Or perhaps we can practice on our own.' He did not look convinced or happy about the thought of them being parted.

Aliah frowned back. 'But what if it is not enough?'

Seamus shrugged. 'I do not know, Aliah. We can only ask.'

'What if something happens while we are apart?' She was unable to shake the feeling it was a bad idea for them to split up.

'I will be here with Seamus, and I can fly to where ever you are in a very short time.' Emer told them.

Although she looked uncomfortable, with all her arguments countered Aliah had nowhere else to go. Tossing her plait over her shoulder she said, 'Right, Daniel, Dominic and I leave tomorrow with Robin to tackle the barons, unless our nocturnal trainer vetoes our plan. We meet with Seamus, Emer, Walter, Amelia and Liam at the South Pass at around midday in four days.

'In the meantime, they spend two days gathering all the information they can, travel to Wexon to get the casket and wait for us near the pass. Emer will carry messages between the groups as needed. Simple.'

'I think you should take Boss and Pauley with you, as you might need the extra protection in case the Carsten soldiers send out some scouting parties,' Seamus offered.

'What about you? You might need support as well.'

'With two magicians and two soldiers in our party I think we will be fine.'

About to argue, Aliah stopped herself. Boss would be a welcome set of hands on this journey, and she always enjoyed Pauley's company. Although part of her wished to command the boy to stay behind, safe in the palace, experience taught her he would just follow them anyway.

Before turning back to the group to sort out the finer details of their travel arrangements, she wondered what Pauley was doing now. With no one to keep an eye on him, he would no doubt be up to all sorts of mischief.

KEEPING TO THE SHADOWS, the young boy crept around the stables and stopped at the end of the block. Risking a quick peek, he pulled his head back as the man he followed turned to check he was alone. Counting to ten, Pauley attempted another look.

Robin had moved to the shelter of a large oak tree and stared down at something in his hands, glancing furtively over his shoulder every few seconds to ensure no one crept up behind him.

Unfortunately the Chamberlain's body was between Pauley and the object, hiding it from view. When the older man turned again to check his surroundings, the boy managed a fleeting glimpse.

His eyes must be playing tricks because it appeared the object in Robin's hands was a common tin mirror. Surely all this creeping around and hiding was not to provide him with opportunities to gaze adoringly at himself.

Having assured once again he was alone, Robin fixed his attention on the mirror. Sensing this might be his only opportunity to find out more, Pauley slipped from the edge of the stables, running swiftly to a tree. If he timed it right, and was quiet enough, he should be able to loop round through the underbrush until he was in line with Robin. From there he would be able to get a better view of what the man was up to.

As he prepared to move to the next tree, a loud crack pierced the crisp morning air. In his haste he had stepped on a rotting branch.

Ducking back behind the tree, he held his breath and closed his eyes. Shutting out the world would not help him hide, but it helped calm his nerves. This time he counted to fifty before risking a quick look. He was rewarded with a view of Robin's back as he disappeared behind the other side of the stables, returning to the palace.

'Goddess,' Pauley cursed as he left his hiding place, almost able to see his mother's frown as he spoke the curse. He felt justified though. Robin was up to something, and if he had been a little more careful, he would have found out what it was. Well, he would find out eventually, just not today.

For a moment he considered whether or not he should tell Boss about his concerns. The older man was far more experienced in this type of thing, and he might be able to give him some ideas on what to do next.

Shaking his head, he decided to wait a little. He had no evidence Robin was doing anything wrong, just a gut feeling and a description of some unusual activity which might be easily explained away. He would keep an eye on him. No doubt there would be another chance to catch the creep out.

***

ALTHOUGH THE EVENING air was cool, Seamus and Aliah removed their jackets in preparation for the training session. Normally they waited for the god to call for them, but tonight they had much they needed to cover, and so decided to wait for their tutor in the courtyard. Rushing through his warm-up, Seamus went over different ways to ask for what he wanted in his head.

'Seamus, slow down. In such a confined space we need to move together if we are not to get in each other's way.' Aliah interrupted his thoughts.

'Oh, all right.'

Seamus stopped, watched until he knew where Aliah was in the sequence of moves they used to loosen up, then joined her. Once back into the rhythm, his mind again focused on his problem.

We need to be able to work as one over long distances. That would not work. What if the gods did not want them to be apart in the first place, he would be handing them an opportunity to forbid it. *Do we need to be together ...*

His arm hit something solid and Seamus looked up to find Aliah rubbing her own arm and glaring accusingly at him.

'Seamus, be careful.' Aliah's voice was grumpy.

Shaking his head, he asked, 'What?'

'You just flung out your arm and punched me. Keep your mind on what you are doing, can you?'

'Sorry, I was just ...'

'Tonight we will work on linking without touching. This will require you to work together in harmony.' The god with the face of the Arian Goddess appeared in front of them, a ghost of a smile hovering around her lips. Either she had been watching them warm up and was amused, or there was another reason for her smile.

'Were you reading my mind?' Seamus demanded.

'Seamus, we are gods. If we want to find out what is happening anywhere with anyone we only need to think on it. We learnt of your plans and, although we do not approve, we can think of no better way for you to proceed. So we will assist in this small way.'

Aliah's laugh cut through the night air as Seamus blushed. Sometimes he felt so in charge of everything, other times things like this occurred, reminding him control was merely an illusion.

'Right, let us start. Seamus stand where you are. Aliah take two steps back. Excellent. Now, this works exactly the same as when you are touching. Seamus, you first. Reach down into your body, find your magic, then push it out slowly towards Aliah until you can feel her.'

Seamus took a deep breath, closed his eyes and began the process Walter taught him some time ago to touch his magic. As he slowly pushed his magical essence out towards Aliah, he hit a wall.

'You can sense this is different already. When you touch a person, you breach the natural barrier surrounding their body, so linking minds is easier.

'Try again, and at the same time, Aliah, you need to gently reach out and find Seamus' essence then guide it to you.'

Seamus reached out again and soon touched Aliah's barrier. A moment later there was a tentative pull of what he could only describe as "Aliahness". He grabbed for her and she disappeared. He opened his eyes to a frowning goddess.

'Patience, young man. Combining magical essences is not like a handshake between soldiers, more like a kiss between lovers.'

Seamus grimaced at the image the goddess created, and tried again. This time he was gentler. Instead of grasping for Aliah, he imagined passing a knife through butter and managed to link minds with his warrior.

The goddess had them repeat the exercise to ensure Seamus' technique was perfect. Then she asked Aliah to take a step back, and then another. At each point Seamus managed to connect minds with her, until they were five steps apart. By then his energy was flagging, and he could no longer join with her.

The goddess bid them rest, and when they restarted, it was Aliah's turn.

'We know you managed to share energy with Seamus once before, but it was clumsy, as have been all your attempts since. You need to learn how to make the connection faultlessly with Seamus while touching, before you can move to making the link when you are apart.'

Aliah scowled, but she did not voice her objections. Instead her face became a mask of concentration as she attempted to do as she was bid.

Seamus' skin tingled as Aliah reached out, tentatively at first, then her "Aliahness" surged through, and they were connected.

'Now, do it without the sword.'

'What? Are you crazy?' Aliah turned on the goddess. 'I can only do this because I have the sword.'

'That is where you are wrong. You only connect with the sword because you have the ability to link with magic. It is not an active magical talent, but it is an important one.'

'Like Boss' daughter,' Seamus said under his breath.

'Sorry?' Aliah looked confused.

'Boss' daughter, Megan, could not perform magic, but she sensed when others used it, or had magical abilities.'

'You are correct, Seamus. There are many people with passive magical talents. They are generally no use to them except in the presence of other magic. Now, Aliah, put your sword down and try again. Reach inside yourself until you find the essence that is you, bring it up along your arm and push it towards Seamus.'

Aliah concentrated, trying again and again to connect. Each time she tried, she grew more irritated, until her frustrations finally bubbled over.

'I cannot do it.'

'Yes, you can.' The goddess was not moved by Aliah's anger.

'Remember it took me a while to do this, and I had been training to use my magic for some time.' Seamus' attempt at support fell flat as Aliah glared at him.

'Try again,' the goddess ordered, not prepared to give in to Aliah's show of temper.

Seamus was pleased she said that because he was sure if the

words had come from his mouth, Aliah would have snapped his head off. Not that she would not do the same to a god, it was just a little less likely. For a moment, he thought she was actually going to refuse, then she sighed with resignation and closed her eyes.

This time Seamus could feel a slight warmth on his skin.

'Nearly there,' he said in encouragement, and the warmth disappeared.

Aliah uttered a curse more suited to a soldier's barracks than a princess and shot him a look full of daggers, before taking a deep breath and trying again. This time the warmth was a little stronger, and Seamus sent a little of his energy to greet it. As if sensing him, Aliah crashed through the barrier and joined him. Her face lit up with a fleeting look of triumph, before it was replaced with dismay as her presence abruptly disappeared.

'I am barely able to link with Seamus when I am touching him, and he cannot connect with me if he is further than four steps away.' Defeat sounded in her words as her shoulders slumped.

'And you leave tomorrow.' Seamus understood why she was so upset.

'Did you not hear me before? You have the ability to link to anything magical. Your sword, other people with magic ...' The goddess stopped as if waiting for Aliah to catch up with her line of thought.

'I know I cannot practice with my sword so that means I need to find someone to work with?'

She looked to the goddess to see if she was correct.

'And ...'

A frown appeared between Aliah's brows. Seamus himself could not see where this was leading. 'But Walter is staying with Seamus. I cannot practice with him.'

'Dominic.' The name fell out of Seamus' mouth before the thought was fully formed in his brain. 'Dominic's ability to blend in with his surroundings is a form of magic.'

Aliah's frown deepened. 'You are suggesting I train with him?'

The goddess looked at Aliah, head tilted to the side. 'I see, no, that would not work. The young boy who travels with you. You could train with him.'

Having considered the options, Aliah slowly nodded her head. 'Yes, that would be acceptable.'

'And you, Seamus, should train with Walter. Now be aware, you do not need to make a full connection with these people, you just need to practice making the link.

'There are rules to this. You must first get their permission, and you must promise not to share with others anything you find while linked. You also need to be aware your connection will not be as strong with your training partners as it is between the two of you. Your magics complement each other, like two halves of a whole, and nothing will ever be as strong as your bond together.

'Although your training is not as complete as we would like, we will not come to you both again unbidden. It is moving close to the time when you will confront our brother, and we cannot be seen to be helping you in your confrontation with him in any direct way. Seamus, if you have any questions on how to use your magic in general, we can still help you, but that is about all.

'I can see little of your path ahead from here, and what I see leads to sadness. Then again, all possible paths from this point lead to sorrow. All that is left is for me to wish you god speed and good luck.'

The goddess blinked out of sight and, suddenly exhausted, Seamus bent over, placing his hands on his knees, drawing in deep breaths, attempting to control his panic.

'Sadness,' he whispered. 'Our way ahead is paved with sadness. Maybe we should not do this?' He looked up to see Aliah shaking her head.

'She said we might find sorrow down which ever path we take. She also said there is not a better option. We went over this time and time again. We should proceed as planned.'

Seamus' body sagged a little with relief, and the heaviness in his heart eased. It was great to have the Aliah of old back to share the burden.

'She forgot to send us to sleep,' Aliah gasped.

Realising she was right, and that they would not wake rested tomorrow, Seamus groaned. 'Of all the nights for one of them to forget, it had to be the night before a busy few days. Best we try and get what little sleep we can then.' He sighed as he picked up Aliah's sword and handed it to her.

As they headed back inside the palace, they glimpsed movement in the shadows. Stopping, Aliah drew her sword and it glowed at her command, dispelling some of the darkness around them. Going first, Aliah checked the courtyard and found nothing there.

'We must be tired,' she said as she sheathed her sword and carried on inside.

Glancing behind him as he entered the doorway, Seamus caught another movement out of the corner of his eye. Unease flowed through him as he closed the door and rammed the bolt home behind them, and it did not leave until they were safely back in their quarters.

DARKNESS PRESSED in on her as the sweat on her brow began to cool, making her shiver. Sitting up, she took deep breaths, trying to calm her frantically beating heart. While she was no closer to finding out what danger her dream foretold, she now knew what she had to do.

'Amelia?' Walter's voice came from the doorway. 'Are you all right?'

'Did I scream out again?' A frown creased her brow, this was happening far too often. Her decision to leave Sanctuary to support Seamus and Aliah meant she postponed her training as a seer.

Perhaps once she returned, she would be better able to control her visions.

'No,' Walter reassured her. 'I was reading by the fire when I heard you muttering.'

'It was another dream,' Amelia told him.

'A foretelling?'

Amelia closed her eyes. 'Yes and no. I sensed great danger, but that is nothing new given the circumstances we find ourselves in. There was nothing specific, but ... now I am awake, I realise something is telling me my path is not to stay here with you and Seamus, I must travel to visit the barons with Aliah.'

She did not need her eyes to sense the growing tension in the room.

'Amelia, are you sure that is wise?'

Walter's voice was filled with concern. Of course he would not come straight out and say he thought her travelling without him to guide her was foolish. He understood her well enough to appreciate it would play to her stubborn streak, and she would go regardless of what he thought.

No, he would share his worry with her, the very same worries she herself had, and his concern would make her pause and think. If only she had known how difficult it was to make a decision when you cared for someone, she might have let her heart remain in the box she had kept it in for most of her adult life.

Taking a deep breath, she opened her eyes and turned to face Walter. 'No, I am not sure it is wise. I am also not sure how I will cope without you there to guide me. What I am sure of is this is what I am meant to do.'

Walter was beside her in a heartbeat, clasping her hand in his. 'Then I will come with you and help with whatever it is you need.'

Unable to help the grin that appeared on her face any more than she was able to stop the blush from rising up her neck, Amelia gripped Walter's fingers. Goddess! She was behaving like a girl with her first crush. Amazed at how tempted she was to take Walter up on his offer, she knew she should not. Letting go of Walter's hand, she told him so.

'Seamus needs you. He needs your guidance and your support, and your wealth of magical knowledge. Although he is putting on a good show, he is scared and worried, and he needs someone to be there for him; someone he respects. Also, I do not believe anyone else will be able to find the answers you will in those last few scrolls.'

The bed sagged as Walter sat down, still holding her hand. 'I know, but I will worry less if I am there to protect you should something happen before you are comfortable and confident with the changes in your life.'

'Pauley will be there. I will ask him to act as my guide. It will do the boy good to have something to do rather than running free. Goodness only knows what mischief he caused the castle staff these last few days.' Amelia laughed out loud as a thought occurred to her. 'The boy who can see in darkness will lead the woman who cannot see in the light.'

Appreciating the irony, Walter's laughter joined her's, easing the tension between them. Then he was suddenly silent.

'Amelia, there are things I would like to talk of before you leave,' Walter started, and she squeezed his hand before she interrupted him.

'Walter, we can talk of these things later, when this is over.'

'But there is a chance ...'

'Yes, and if that does happen, we will not be any better off for having had this conversation. We are no spring chickens, and I think our feelings for each other are quite clear. Let us leave it at that for now. If we have a future after this is all over, we can talk then.'

Silence hung in the room, and not for the first time since she lost her vision Amelia wished for it back. If only for a moment to see Walter's thoughts written on his face. The bed shifted and lips lightly touched her cheek.

'We will have this conversation, I promise you that.' Walter's breath warmed her face as he spoke. Then he was all action. 'Right, I had best find what I can pull together for your travels, if anyone is up to help me. And you had best get some rest as you will not sleep in a bed as welcoming as this for a while.'

And that is how he managed to wriggle his way through defences it took me years to build, she thought as she snuggled back down under the blankets.

CHAPTER 38

DIPLOMACY DIES

As Daniel led their horses over Aliah sighed, her breath creating a mist in the chilly just-before-dawn air. Missing her god-given sleep the night before meant she woke up tired and grumpy. The hard ride in front of them to reach Baron Tappit's holding before midday filled her with dread.

'I have a thought. If the baron's stayed behind with enough guards to block the passes and prevent the Carsten Army from taking over Hand, why are we riding like mad things to get them to do what they should already be doing?' she asked Daniel as he drew up beside her.

'I see someone woke up on the wrong side of the bed this morning,' he started in a cheery voice that did absolutely nothing to lighten her mood. Taking one look at her face, he was all business as he continued, 'We are doing this because we do not want them to protect their own areas, we want them to work together to contain the army in one place. Not only so we can do what we need to, but also because it is the best way to protect Hand and Aria.'

'Humph,' Aliah grunted, taking the lead rein from Daniel.

As she readied herself to mount, she was distracted by the sight of Boss leading out another three horses. Looking around the court-yard she found Robin checking the saddle on his horse. Dominic was holding the bridle of a bay gelding as he talked to Seamus, no doubt giving some last minute instructions. She frowned. A horse for Pauley, one for Boss and one for ...

Before the question formed, Pauley emerged from the palace leading Amelia. They were followed out by Walter carrying a travel pack. She relaxed. Walter would be a great asset to their group, although she thought it strange he elected to leave Seamus to finish going through the scrolls, let alone trust him to face Baron Wexler with only Liam and Emer. Still, it would be useful to have a wizard with them.

She mounted her horse, glancing over to see Amelia settling herself into a saddle. Her surprise must have been written over her face because a chuckling Dominic walked over, leading his gelding.

'It appears loss of sight does not stop a person from riding,' he said as he pulled himself into his own saddle.

'Amelia is coming with us.'

Aliah realised she was stating the obvious, but she could not help herself.

'It would appear so. She had a dream last night, and in is sure her path lies in the same direction as ours.'

'Is that wise, given how fast and hard we need to move to have any chance of achieving this mission and meeting up with Seamus?'

She knew Amelia would be more than a little annoyed her ability to keep up was being questioned based solely on her loss of sight, but Aliah's concerns were real. They could not slow down for Amelia, nor could they simply leave her somewhere if she started lagging behind. As if he sensed her discomfort, Dominic's answer was uncharacteristically tactful.

'I asked the same thing, but Walter arranged everything early this morning. Amelia is a confident horsewoman. The mount is her own, and is used to her commands. Boss is happy to keep a lead rein so the horse does not wander off, and Pauley will act as Amelia's guide when she dismounts. Everything is organised to ensure she will not place our mission at risk.'

Aliah considered the information and, although the plan had more holes than a leaky bucket, she would not be the one to forbid Amelia from doing something just because she no longer had her sight. Shrugging her shoulders, she turned her horse.

'Besides,' Dominic added. 'With Amelia in our group, Emer will be freed up to help Seamus and Walter.'

'Oh? How come?'

'She and Amelia can mind speak more easily than I can over long distances, so it is likely she will not need to fly to us at all unless there is an emergency.'

'Well, I guess that is something. All right, are we ready to leave?' she asked, her voice carrying in the morning air.

'Daniel has the maps and, should you manage to get lost, Robin will guide you to safety,' Seamus was saying as they joined the others.

'All right, then let us proceed,' Aliah instructed with more confidence than she was actually feeling.

Seamus nodded wearily, telling her he was just as unsure about splitting the group as she was. Daniel and Robin took the lead, with Boss, Pauley and Amelia falling in behind. Aliah moved her horse beside Dominic at the rear and followed them through the gate.

Turning in her saddle, Aliah caught sight of Walter and Seamus heading inside. No doubt they were eager to cram as much time as they could in the library before they left on their own journey in a couple of days.

Realising she had fallen a little behind, she nudged her horse to catch the others up. Daniel was setting a quick pace. As they rode, Aliah studied Amelia, relieved to find she seemed surer of herself on horseback than she had been walking. If the look on her face was anything to go by, she enjoyed the sense of independence riding was giving her. A rare experience since losing her sight.

Pauley. She groaned. If Pauley was busy helping Amelia, he would not be able to help her practice her magical connections.

'Is everything all right?' Dominic asked, and she realised she must have groaned out loud.

Without stopping to think, she found herself telling Dominic her problem. 'I was supposed to be practicing making a magical connection with Pauley while we travelled. I am not very good at it, and I need all the practice I can get before Seamus and I face this god.'

It was hard for Aliah to admit she was less than perfect at the best of times, so she was surprised she had been so open with Dominic. Bracing herself for a sarcastic comment, Aliah almost missed his response.

'I can practice with you.'

'What? Really? I knew you could talk with Emer, but I thought that was all led by her.'

'Yes, I have done this before. Wizards and other spies connected with me when I went places they could not go.' Aliah stared at the boy. Would he ever cease amazing her?

'Did you not find it a little, umm, invasive?' she asked, remembering her initial worry about practicing with Dominic last night.

When she joined with Seamus, the moment they connected his emotions swamped her. With him, they had shared so much already it made little difference to how they treated each other. Pauley would have been too young to be bothered with such things, but what if it happened with Dominic? Surely he would be able to pick up on the jumble of emotions threatening to overwhelm her whenever they were together.

'No.' Dominic appeared blissfully ignorant of her concerns. 'I was taught to erect a barrier in my mind so wizards used my eyes only. If I had not, the noise from having another mind inside of mine would have been quite distracting, and might have placed me in danger. I assume one of the first things you were taught was erecting a barrier?'

Aliah considered his words for a moment. 'No, I think Seamus and I are supposed to be able to blend and act as one, a barrier would be counter-productive.'

Dominic fell silent for a moment. 'I am not comfortable letting you link minds with me without having a barrier in place,' he finally admitted. He paused before continuing. 'If you promise to practice making a connection and not the blending, I think my barrier should be sufficient to maintain both of our privacy.'

'You do?' Relief washed through Aliah. 'I know it is asking a lot, but I appreciate it.'

'I am at your service.' Dominic's mocking tone returned. 'Now we are dropping a little behind. If we do not want to lose the others, we had best catch them up.'

Without realising it, their pace slowed during their conversation, and Aliah raised her eyes to find their companions about to drop out of sight as they crested a hill. Urging her horse forward, she and Dominic rode to catch them.

As the afternoon sun began to wane, Aliah glimpsed the outline of a large country house in the distance. It had taken far longer than anticipated to reach their destination. A fallen tree forced them to detour via a more coastal track, extending their journey, which not only lost them valuable time, but also made them tired and cranky.

Groaning with relief at the sight of Baron Tappit's house in the distance, she regretted not spending more time on a horse the last few moons. Every movement of her mount sent a jolt of agony through the tender flesh of her rear end.

A candle mark later, the sun was blocked completely as they rode up the tree lined driveway to the baron's manor. Aliah's daydream of a cool bath was rudely interrupted as a group of armed men challenged them, their stern faces not showing the smallest glimmer of welcome.

'Halt. Identify yourselves!' their leader ordered, sword at the ready should he not like the answer.

Robin eased his horse forward. 'I am Robin Gadfell, Chancellor of the Duchy, and I am here with some very important guests who wish to speak with Baron Tappit about the defence of Hand.'

The chancellor stood tall in his saddle, his voice haughty and full of entitlement, but the man in front of them appeared unimpressed by his show.

'We are not receiving guests at the moment. These are dangerous times. We look to our own safety, the rest of Hand can take care of itself.'

Unmoving, the guards continued to block their path. Appreciating they were at a disadvantage should it come to a fight, Aliah urged her mount forward.

'I am Princess Aliahanna, and I am here on behalf of your king and your duke, I suggest you allow us by, unless you want to answer directly to either of them.'

Behind her Daniel muttered, 'Always use a sledgehammer to crack a nut, that is our Aliah.'

Aliah bit back a smile as she faced down the guard captain. Now was not the time to let her imperious manner slip.

'With all due respect ... er ... Princess?'

Aliah gritted her teeth. Any statement starting that way was highly unlikely to be respectful at all.

'Our duke ran to the safety of the mainland, joining the king in a well guarded town. I do not fear his retribution at this time.'

Clenching the reigns until her knuckles showed white, Aliah's self-control was near breaking. Robin moved forward to take charge again before she said something they would be unable to repair, ending their mission before it had even begun.

'Duke Damon went to Port Marden to co-ordinate our forces with those of Aria, and to lead our guard in battle. He left his son and heir, Seamus, to organise defences here. At present he is detained organising the forces left at the palace. We have been sent to rally the rest of the island. With me are King Terion's own daughter and heir, Princess Aliahanna, Guard Captain Daniel, the son of Aria's military commander, and Lord Dominic, the son of one of the northern dukes, sent to aid us. Please do not embarrass our people and your lord by being so discourteous to those sent to assist us in these trying times.'

Ignoring Dominic's scowl at being recognised and presented using his actual position, Aliah lent some force to Robin's introduction.

'We are here to help, and just wish a word with the baron.' Aliah simpered, hating the fact she could not appear as strong as a man and still be taken seriously, but knowing she had to play the game if she wanted to get anywhere.

'You have proof ...' the leader started.

'Guard Daniel has a letter signed by Duke Damon himself giving us authority to do what we need to protect Aria and Hand.'

The guard's gaze slipped from Robin to Daniel.

'I will present it only to the baron.'

The guard confirmed the letter's existence, but Daniel was not going to show it to someone of so low a rank.

Although he appeared to want to question them further, the imperious set to Aliah's face must have convinced him against continued questioning of the princess.

'... umm ... if you are happy to surrender your weapons, you may continue on to the manor.'

Pondering her options, especially with regards to her own sword, Aliah responded. 'As you just admitted, danger is close by and I would be foolish to agree to my party being unable to defend themselves. You have my word we will not draw arms against your people, and that will have to be enough.' Her direct stare challenged the captain to disagree.

For a brief moment, he looked as though he might object, but changed his mind as Daniel and Dominic drew alongside Aliah. Admitting defeat, the man turned to the guard closest to him.

'Escort them to the house and see their mounts are cared for. I will go and warn the baron of their arrival.'

Aliah watched him depart before riding past the weary gaze of Baron Tappit's guards. As she drew level, Aliah was sure she heard one of the guards mutter, 'At least they did not send that wizard spawn of a son.' Anger rose in her stomach but, given the hostility of the situation, she chose to ignore the comment and carried on up to the manor house

Although her blood boiled at their treatment, she schooled her face to calm serenity. She did not want word of her unease to find its way back to the baron, least he use it to his advantage. Only the set of her jaw alerted those who knew her to the fact her control was near to breaking.

Drawing up at the front of the manor, Aliah waited for one of the grooms to take her horse's bridle before dismounting. Brushing dust from her riding clothes, she glanced up the stairs to take a quick peek at her host, only to find the door remained closed, and he was no where in sight.

'If you would allow me, Your Highness?'

Stifling a frustrated groan, Aliah admitted it would not do for a princess to request permission to enter a mere baron's home. Not only would it be a breach of protocol, it would also place her on the back foot when she came to bargain with the man for troops. She agreed to Robin's suggestion he seek admittance for them.

The door creaked open just as he reached the top step, saving Robin the indignity of knocking, and allowing a tall, gaunt man to emerge. With his nose pointed skywards, he could not have looked more haughty if he tried. Her immediate thought that the baron had seen sense and come out to meet them was crushed as the man spoke.

'If you will follow me, Baron Tappit will meet with you in his study.'

For a mere baron not to greet a princess in person and welcome her into his home, was extremely bad manners. Robin turned to take direction from Aliah. Biting back her instinct to march herself into the manor and demand Baron Tappit tell her what he thought he was playing at, Aliah straightened her back and led her party indoors, as though the idea to enter without waiting for the baron had been her own.

The baron's minion followed the group in, closing the door with a loud thud behind them.

'This way,' he instructed.

Aliah did not move. She had met the baron half-way, and that was as far as she was prepared to go. She would not attend him in his study like a supplicant. He would have to come to her as he should have done in the first place. Now she was physically inside the man's home, he no longer had the option of ignoring their presence on his lands.

'Please, the baron awaits you. If you will just follow me.' The man indicated the way with a sweep of his hand. His voice wavered a little as he realised he had lost his advantage and did not quite know what to do next.

'And I await the baron here. You can tell the baron Princess Alia-hanna, his future Queen, awaits him in the hall. If he wishes to still have a study in this manor after I take the crown, he had better make haste and get himself out here.' Aliah raised her chin and showed she could beat the best of them at being stubborn and haughty.

Wringing his hands in front of him, the man appeared uncertain of his next move. Aliah glared at him, but before she could say anything else and ruin the moment, Robin stepped forward.

'I suggest you do as the lady asks, we would not want to insult the princess anymore than we already have, would we?'

Scuttling away, the man shot a nervous glance back over his shoulder before opening a door to the right and disappearing. Even though the door was made of the stoutest wood, they all heard the baron's voice as he berated his servant for not carrying out his orders.

Waiting for the tirade to finish, Aliah glanced around the entrance hall. Ornately furnished, with thick carpet and heavy dark wooden furniture, displayed around a grand staircase that swept upwards to a second level, it announced loud and clear the Tappits were moneyed and not afraid to show it. The display was obviously intended to intimidate visitors, but the ostentatious decor only served to annoy Aliah more.

A few moments later the door opened, and the servant returned. 'My Lord, Baron Tappit,' he announced as he moved aside to admit a rotund man in his mid-twenties, his face and bald head flushed with barely concealed anger. The waxed moustache sitting atop his sneering lip did nothing to dispel the image of a child playing in the world of grown ups. He stopped just in front of the party and waited. Ever the diplomat, Robin stepped forward.

'Your Royal Highness, Princess Aliahanna, may I present Baron Micheal of Tappit.'

Aliah inclined her head in what she hoped was a regal manner, and held out her hand for the baron to press his lips to it in a gesture of fealty. The baron's obvious reluctance as he followed protocol made up a little for the clammy coldness she endured as his lips met her flesh.

The minimum of formalities complete, Aliah wasted no time getting to the point. 'Baron we are here to request a complement of your men to assist in defending Hand. Is there somewhere a little more comfortable we can talk?'

'YOU MUST UNDERSTAND, Princess Aliahanna, Baron Tappit is a second son. His brother died in an unfortunate riding accident, thrusting him into a role he had no desire, and no training for.'

Robin explained this in the privacy of the manner's guest suite. Baron Tappit reluctantly made the rooms available to them, but only after he realised his unexpected visitors were not leaving his manor that night, whether he offered hospitality or not.

Aliah stopped her pacing while she considered the chamberlain's words, then responded tersely, 'That does not excuse his rudeness. All children in noble households are brought up to respect common courtesy. Nor does it excuse his stupidity. His advisor immediately saw the sense in our plan, yet he could not be persuaded to it.'

'The problem is,' Dominic interrupted. 'He is so scared of making the wrong move, he cannot make any move at all.'

Aliah stopped to stare out the window, enjoying the colours of the sun as it set behind the trees surrounding the manor. Unable to comprehend anyone's inability to take action when necessary, none-the-less she agreed with Dominic. The man was clearly paralysed with fear.

'I think you should be happy he agreed to provide men should Baron George send word he will be joining with us.' Dominic's face joined her reflection in the glass as he moved behind her. 'Sometimes you just have to be happy with what you have, and move on.'

Sighing, she moved away from the window and took a seat beside the fire. 'You are right, Dominic, and we only got that concession due to some quick talking. Thank you, Robin, we could not have done this without you.'

'I was just doing my job, looking out for Hand's best interests.' Robin bowed. 'Now, if you will excuse me, I will go and make sure the others are settled into their rooms and see if I can arrange for some food to be brought up.' Robin bowed again as he left.

'I am not unhappy the baron's hospitality did not extend to a formal evening meal,' Aliah said as she stretched catlike, absorbing the heat from the blaze. 'If I had to spend another moment with that spoilt child I swear I would have strangled him.'

Dominic's laughter erupted, filling the room. 'I am pretty sure he felt the same way about you. It seems our baron is not used to having strong women boss him around.'

The room fell into silence and Aliah mulled over whether or not now was the right time to ask Dominic something that had been on her mind for a while. Taking the plunge, she asked, 'Dominic, why do you not like Robin?'

The boy tensed at her question. 'Umm … it is not that I dislike him, more that I do not trust him.'

'Why?'

'It is hard to place my finger on. All the times I attended the court on Hand I could never get a sense of who he was as a person. His only interest is serving Hand. Everyone else I meet in this line of work has a life outside of their official duties—except him.'

'That is hardly a reason for you to bristle every time he is in the same room.' Aliah turned so she could better read his reactions.

'Not normally, no. But you should note I said he serves Hand, not Duke Damon. I have long since believed Robin works towards his own vision of what Hand should be. While this aligns with Duke Damon he is a valuable asset, but what happens if the duke wants something for Hand Robin disagrees with?'

Head cocked to the side, Aliah considered Dominic's words. 'And you think something happened?'

Dominic shrugged. 'I am not sure, but Robin is acting strangely of late, and he has turned up in places I would not expect him to be. Coupled with the fact he always seems to be hanging around closed doors, well, let us just say I am concerned.'

Aliah turned back to the flames. 'And you would like to use your special talents to check up on him?'

'Mmm, yes. But I do not think you should be left alone in this house. You shamed the baron today, and I do not completely trust him either.'

'I do not think he would do us any physical harm, not least because that would require him to decide to take action. Still, you could send Daniel in to keep me company, and you go and do what you need to do.'

The door latch clicked as Dominic let himself out, and Aliah relaxed back in her chair, letting the warmth of the flames lick her tired muscles. She must have dozed, because the next thing she knew a hand on her arm caused her to tense. With her sword on the bed on the other side of the room, she ran through possible means of escape.

'You are lucky I am not an assassin.'

Her eyes flew open to find Daniel standing over her, his face grey and dotted with beads of sweat.

'With the way you look at the moment you assaulting me would be beyond you, you would be lucky to best a new-born kitten. What is a matter?'

Her friend slumped into a chair. 'I ate something off at dinner. I am sure I will be better by morning.'

'No, I do not believe you will.' Aliah's brow creased with concern. 'Come on, we will go and get Amelia to take a look at you.'

Aliah stood and grabbed Daniel's arm, half-dragging him next door to the healer's room.

———————————

'Here you go. This is a little stronger than the tonic I made you in Sanctuary, so it should last a little longer.' Amelia handed two bottles of liquid over to Daniel. 'One finger width twice a day.'

'Thank you, Amelia.' Daniel took the medicine. 'I do not know what I would do without this, or you for that matter.'

'Humph. Perhaps if I were not here to make your tonic the others would notice you were ill, and you would be forced to tell them the truth.'

The guard shifted from foot to foot, uncomfortable under Amelia's gaze, which was no less cutting for her lack of sight.

'I am fine with them thinking I have had a few stomach aches from eating different food and the like.'

'They will soon start to notice those tummy upsets are becoming more frequent. Anyway, this is as strong as I can make it without people noticing the side effects. Any stronger and you will start to appear drunk or confused to others. Are you sure it is not time to tell them?'

When no response was forthcoming, Amelia tried another tactic. 'You could return to the palace, say you need to oversee defences there. You could rest up, allow your body time to heal and gather some energy to fight this.'

'Amelia, I told you what I want. I need to support Aliah through whatever this is, and do my duty for Aria. You promised ...'

'I know exactly what I promised, young man, and even if I had not promised I would not say a word to anyone. It is a healer's oath.' Amelia's voice was tart, but she softened it before continuing. 'That does not stop you from saying something to them though. They are already starting to notice something is amiss. Perhaps it is time.'

'Soon, Amelia, soon. I must return to Aliah now, but I do not want to leave you alone. Where is Pauley?'

'Off doing the things young boys do, I suspect.' Amelia chuckled. 'Boss is in the corridor outside looking out for both Aliah and myself. If you are going to be with our princess, you can send him in to stay with me until Pauley returns.'

The air cooled as the young guard opened the door, and moments later she heard the familiar footsteps of Boss as he entered her room.

'Where is Pauley, he said he was just nipping out for some air?' Boss's stern voice announced his entrance.

'You know exactly where he is, Boss Allum. I know what you and he have been cooking up. So there is no need to put on a show for me.'

'Oh, he told you about his concerns?' Having closed the door Boss still felt the need to whisper his question.

'Not in so many words,' Amelia responded. 'My hearing is much improved since I lost my sight, and I overheard snippets of your conversation on the journey today. So take a seat and perhaps you can fill me in on the details as we wait for our young friend's return.'

KEEPING TO THE SHADOWS, Dominic followed the elusive Robin through the manor's back corridor. Before opening the door to the courtyard, the older man turned around to check behind him. Satisfied he was alone, he slipped outside.

Unable to leave the house without being noticed, Dominic slid through another open door into what appeared to be the servant's dining room. Through the window, he could make out Robin standing nearby, staring intently at something in his hand while his lips moved.

Someone had left the window partially open, so the spy crouched to get his ear as close to the gap as he could, hoping some of what his quarry said would drift through.

'I cannot do that, not without people suspecting ...' Robin paused, as though listening to someone, but all Dominic heard was an almost undetectable hum. 'Can you guarantee ... all right, if you put it like that. I will need to wait until we are closer though. I will contact you again in a day's time.' More low humming, then. 'About my ... Goddess!, you always break off before I get to ask.' Robin shook whatever he held in his hand, and stomped in frustration. He placed the object in a pocket on the inside of his coat and glanced around to make sure he was still alone before heading back into the house.

As Duke Damon's closest advisor drew close to the door, Dominic thought he saw a movement in the shadows by the hedge. Deciding he had all he would get tonight from the chancellor, he allowed Robin to pass by and continued to watch the greenery by the house.

The sun soon finished its descent and as the courtyard fell into darkness, Dominic's keen eyes spotted a slight movement, followed by soft footsteps heading towards the back door. A faint snick told him the door had been opened, and a fainter thud informed him the new object of his interest had entered the manor.

Waiting behind the door, he timed his attack perfectly, and soon held the intruder by the collar, his other hand over his mouth as he dragged the boy into the room, pushing the door closed behind them with his foot. In the light from the dying fire, Dominic lifted his captive close to get a good look at him, then nearly dropped him to the floor.

'Pauley, what on earth are you doing?'

The boy shrugged as Dominic realised he could not speak with a hand still firmly placed over his mouth. Lowering the boy to the ground, Pauley adjusted his clothing before answering.

'I guess I am doing the same as you, trying to figure out what that slimy eel Robin is up to?'

Dominic wanted to laugh at the young boy's daring, but his first thought was one of worry. 'Do you realise you could get hurt if you are found out? Robin may not be much of a fighter, but I think you would be hard pressed to fend him off if he decided to do you some harm.'

Pauley squared his shoulders and stared disdainfully at Dominic. 'He would not be able to get close enough to touch me. More dangerous men than him have tried to catch me and failed.'

Initially Pauley's bravado took Dominic by surprise, then he laughed and took a closer look at the boy. He had guts, and he could see well in the dark, but did he know what he was looking for?

'So, tell me what you found out?' Dominic gestured to the table, and he and the boy sat.

'Well, Robin has this mirror type thing he keeps in his coat pocket. Every day or so he finds somewhere quiet and talks to someone through it.'

'Do you know who he speaks to?'

'No,' he shook his head emphatically. 'I can make out what he is saying, but all I hear from the mirror is a buzzing sound. I am pretty sure you must be holding on to it to pick up what the other person is saying.'

Dominic stroked his chin. He knew what he thought, but he wanted to see how the boy had pieced this together. 'What do you think he is doing?'

'I am sure he is not talking to the duke.' Pauley started cautiously.

'Because?'

'Because if he was, he would not mind others seeing what he is up to.'

Dominic nodded for the boy to continue, impressed with what he had heard so far. More confident now, Pauley told Dominic what he had seen, and what worried him so much.

'He is reporting everything we are doing to the person on the other end of the mirror. It worries me because last night, he told them Aliah was leaving the palace to visit the barons. Even though I do not know who he is talking to, I cannot imagine anything good will come from the information he passed on.'

'You have done well, Pauley.'

Dominic did not give his praise easily. This boy had found out more than he had and, although he did not like placing the boy in danger, he had not been much older than Pauley when he was sent on his first assignment. People often over-looked the young, thinking they could not possibly comprehend what was going on around them.

'I also believe you are correct. Robin does not mean us well. Although my special talent helps me follow him, he is aware of what I do for the king. That is why I think perhaps it is better if you continue to spy on him, and report back to both myself and Boss Allum.'

'How did you ...'

'Come now, Pauley, I would not be such a great spy if I was unable to work out you are too smart to be doing this alone. It is then not such a great leap to work out Boss Allum knows about this too.'

Smiling, Dominic was pleased he had at least managed to show the boy he had some skills of his own. Truth be told, he was a little put out Pauley managed to discover more than him about Robin's comings and goings, and he had not noticed him doing it.

Making up his mind, the spy decided he would talk to the king about Pauley's future employment in his next dispatch. His monarch was always on the look out for people to act as eyes and ears, and for Pauley, this would be a great opportunity to rise up in the world.

'So, I think I might try to get a look at his mirror.'

'Pauley, I do not think that is such a good idea. In fact, you should not try it under any circumstances.' Dominic was shocked back into focusing on the boy in front of him. 'You would run the risk of whoever Robin is talking to finding out you know about them. Not only would that place you in great danger, but it would blow your cover. At the moment no one knows what you are up to and you are relatively safe, but if they learnt what you were doing ...'

He let the boy draw his own conclusions as he searched his face for compliance, but the stubborn set to his mouth told Dominic he had not convinced Pauley of the danger. It was time to try something different.

'Please, Pauley, I am asking you as a favour to me. I do not want to be the one to tell Aliah something dreadful has happened to you. At the moment it is enough we know we need to watch Robin, and I believe from hearing his side of the conversations we will be fore-warned of any danger to us.'

Pleading and using Aliah had the desired effect. 'All right. I will not go looking for the mirror; for the moment.'

'That is all I can ask. Now you had best get back to Amelia. She will be wondering where you are.'

The boy pulled the door behind him, leaving Dominic staring into the fire, assessing the new information in light of what he already knew. Robin was definitely working for someone, but what was he getting in return? If they could find that out, they might be able to work out who his other master was.

Knocking on the door to Aliah's room, he waited for her command to enter, then let himself in. He had been surprised no one was guarding her door, but understood why when he saw Daniel seated opposite the princess drinking tea.

'Good, with both of you here I need only say this once.' Dominic sat on the edge of the bed and relayed everything he learnt that evening.

As he recounted his tale, Aliah stood and started pacing the room. 'I do not understand this at all. Robin was so helpful today. Baron Tappit only made the small concession he did because of Robin's intervention. He has Hand's best interests at heart. I do not believe he is doing this for money.' She tugged at her plait.

'He was working for the good of Hand when he negotiated with the baron,' Dominic pointed out. 'I am thinking maybe it is not Hand he is betraying, but us—we Arians.'

Aliah stopped and gazed into the flames, pondering Dominic's comment.

'You may be right. Duke Damon is no fool. I am sure if Robin had been up to something before now, he would have been found out. I wonder what he has against us?'

'What if it is not that he has something against us, but rather that someone had something against him?'

Daniel had been so quiet, Dominic had almost forgotten he was still in the room.

As Aliah turned round to face her friend, her plait swung back over her shoulder. 'What do you mean, Daniel?'

'Well, you both are assuming Robin is in this for some sort of personal gain, or because he dislikes Arians. But you have not considered the alternatives. What if someone is blackmailing him, or worse still, holding one of his family members for ransom. There are many reasons why someone would betray their countrymen.'

'We need to find out. I cannot bear to think of the man being held to ransom.' Aliah looked at Dominic.

'Hold on a moment there, we have no idea what Robin's motivation is, and with an invasion and a god to fight, do you not think there is enough for us to worry about?'

'But would it not help us if we helped Robin? If we could find out what is going on, perhaps we can do something about it. Then he would be able to stop spying, and we would have one less thing to worry about.'

Aliah's plan was logical, and Dominic hated to squash her idea, but it was in her best interests that he did so, and quickly before the idea took root.

'We know he is up to something and we are keeping an eye on him. Our resources are stretched as it is. We cannot risk failure against our errant god to try and save one man, and that is if he even needs saving. My advice would be to continue with our current plan.'

'I agree with Dominic,' Daniel said. 'We have no idea who he is working for and why. To make any sort of move we would need more information, and we do not have the time or resources to focus on that task as well as everything else. So if we are all happy, I shall be off to bed and leave the first watch tonight to you, Dominic.'

Assuming Aliah's agreement, Daniel rose from his seat, picked up some bottles from the side table, and let himself out of the room.

Before Aliah realised she had not agreed to anything, Dominic distracted her by asking, 'What is wrong with Daniel?'

'Mmm ... umm ... he has some sort of stomach upset. Amelia made him a tonic.' Wearily massaging her brow, Aliah dragged her thoughts back into the room.

'He has had a lot of stomach problems lately,' Dominic commented, and Aliah was suddenly alert.

'Do you know something?'

Startled by her intensity, Dominic stuttered. 'Umm ... no ... I was just saying ... Hold on, do you think there is something more to it than traveller's tummy?'

'I am not sure,' Aliah sank into the nearest chair, despondency overtaking her.

'You should ask him.'

'I did. I also asked Amelia.'

'I bet that was a fun conversation,' he chuckled.

'They were both very tight-lipped.' Aliah was unable to see the funny side. 'And that makes me all the more worried.'

Dominic moved over to the now vacant chair by the fire. 'When he is ready, he will tell you. Until then, you just need to keep an eye on him.'

When Aliah did not respond, Dominic decided she needed a change of focus, something to divert her from her worries.

'Are you ready to try linking minds?'

The look on her face would have been comical, if it had not shown him how worried she was about this aspect of her warrior training. 'What? Now?'

'There is no time like the present. Get your sword and we can start.'

Aliah looked as though she wanted to argue, but stood and went and retrieved her sword from where it rested on the bed. Sitting back down she stared at Dominic, waiting for him to begin.

'Right. I think the first thing we should do is figure out if we can make a link.' When Aliah nodded, he continued. 'What do you do when you make a link with Seamus?'

'I place my hand on the sword, and I touch him. Then I push my mind out towards him.'

'Then that is what we will start with. Go ahead.'

Dominic held out his hand and Aliah took a hold of it. With her face a mask of concentration, he observed her until a whisper of a touch stroked his senses. Letting down his natural barrier a little, Aliah tentatively entered his thoughts.

Hello.

The link broke.

'Why did you do that?' Aliah snapped.

'I was letting you know you had succeeded.'

'Oh.' Bewildered, she admitted, 'I did not even know I had joined with you. When Seamus and I link minds, I can pick up his thoughts right away.'

'You are both new to this. When you are a little more practiced you can let someone into your mind and share only what you choose to. If you imagine your mind as being a house, you can let someone into an entry hall, then choose which rooms you allow them access to.'

'Oh. How come you are so good at this?'

Dominic could not tell if she truly wanted to know, or was just putting off any further lessons.

'My spymaster was able to mind link, it was one of the reasons he was so skilled at his job. When he found I had a talent for it, he taught me as well. It made reporting easier as he could see everything I experienced on a mission as if he were there.'

'Oh.'

'Shall we try again?'

'If we must.'

This time when Dominic felt the gentle brush of Aliah's mind, he let her inside the part of him in the room at this moment, sealing off all other feelings and memories.

'I did it?'

'Yes, you did.' Her pleasure rushed through him, almost over-whelming him.

'All right, now do it again.'

The connection came more easily this time. She was ready to try this without touching.

Excellent. Now let go of my arm, Dominic instructed.

Are you sure?

Yes.

Again her presence faded, then returned. Not as strong as before, but she was still there.

Now walk to the door. Slowly. Making sure each step you take the link is maintained.

He studied her as she did as he asked, feeling her struggling to maintain contact. About half-way across the room she disappeared from his head.

'Goddess!'

'No, that was very good. Let us do it again.'

They repeated the process until Aliah was able to keep the link up all the way to the door.

'Well done. Now try linking to me without touching the sword.'

'I do not think I can.'

'It should be easy, given the last two times you linked with me you did not touch it at all.' Aliah's eyes widened in surprise. 'Now, see if you can do it consciously.'

Aliah took his hand and closed her eyes, concentrating. Frown-ing, she let go of his hand.

'I cannot do it!'

'Yes, you can. Try again.'

He felt her tentative brush against his mind, then she was gone. Her head dropped down and she stared at the floor.

I cannot do it, no matter what he says. He is so infuriating.

Not so much infuriating, as right.

'What?'

'See, you did it without touching me. Try again.'

You know you are a right royal pain in the ...

Princess Aliahanna, that is no way for a lady to speak.

Aliah's blue eyes sparkled with pleasure as she looked at him. 'Do I try walking away and keeping the link again?'

Dominic shook his head. 'We are both tired, and I cannot send you into a healing sleep. It is a long ride tomorrow, so I think it best we finish for now. Besides, I am meant to be guarding the corridor.'

Aliah stood and stretched, and the stretch turned into a yawn. 'I guess you are right.'

Dominic rose to leave, but was stopped by Aliah's hand on his arm.

'Thank you. I feel so much more confident after tonight. You are a way better teacher than the gods.'

Hiding his embarrassment the only way he knew how, Dominic made light of the situation. 'So, you are saying I am godlike? Or I am more than godlike?'

'Ahhh...boys. Go.'

Dominic departed before Aliah decided to throw something at him, the warm glow growing in the pit of his stomach giving him a surprising sense of happiness.

CHAPTER 39
A GLIMMER OF LIGHT

The palace was quiet, almost too quiet. Seamus' footsteps echoed as he made his way to the library. Sighing, he opened the door and steeled himself for another day going through dusty scrolls. He found Walter already at work, in fact the magician was so engrossed he did not notice Seamus enter the room, grab an armful of scrolls, and dump them on the table. Even noisily pulling the wooden chair out and slumping down onto it could not pull Walter from his study.

Unfurling the scroll closest to him, Seamus let out a groan, predicting today would be much like yesterday. After the others left, he, Walter, Liam and Emer went straight to the library. Around lunchtime, Liam suggested an afternoon of outdoor training, and Emer leapt at the chance of leaving the dusty documents for a while. Seamus watched them go, longing to join them.

Although sword training did not really interest him, the release of physical exercise appealed to him more than an afternoon of study. However, his sense of duty forced him to stay with Walter, and he had left the library later that day as frustrated with their progress as when he entered.

Now they only had the remaining day to go through the last few documents to try and find something to give them a little edge over the god they were to fight. Frustrated, he called on the gods for an additional training session, hoping to salvage at least something from the day.

While he waited, he managed to work off some steam. His intention was to work with the god to contact Aliah. Although he wanted to find out how her mission was going, he also wanted to see if they were able to communicate over long distance. The god's response to his request further added to his frustrations.

'No.'

'Because we might be overheard?'

'No.'

'Why can I not try a mind-link with her?'

'Because the Warrior is busy with her own training. I do not want to interrupt her and her instructor.'

'She is working with a god tonight as well?'

'I did not say that.'

Once again, the god's inability to answer a question directly annoyed Seamus.

'So what are you saying? Or is this one of the times when you are unable to say anything? Will contacting her upset the balance or something?'

The god looked at him in confusion. 'I answered your questions.'

Seamus replayed their conversation in his mind and he realised the god had, in fact, given the information he asked for, and not one shred more. Thinking for a moment about the essence of what he wanted to find out, he reframed his question.

'Who is Aliah training with and what is she learning?'

'She is training with the one you call Dominic. He is teaching her mind-linking.'

Seamus could not hold back his snort of laughter. He would love to be a fly on the wall in that training session.

'Is there anything else, young Wizard?'

Seamus paused before answering, not quite sure how to word what was on his mind. 'I am worried. Aliah is so far away, and I think we should be working together to plan how to deal with your brother. I believe I should be with her, or at least talking with her.'

'You know as well as I there is nothing to indicate whether you and Aliah being together or apart leading up to your confrontation will change the outcome.'

'I know, but I would feel better if we were together.' Even as he said the words out loud, Seamus heard how childish they sounded, but it was how he felt.

'You will know when the time for your warrior to rejoin you has arrived, until then, you should concentrate on the tasks assigned to you.'

The god's words were practical, but did nothing to calm his fears. Still, he knew there was nothing he could do about anything there and then.

His lesson that night was to practice his magic with and without his wand. If taken by surprise, he might not have time to draw it, the god explained, but if their enemy managed to bring his own body here, Seamus would need the wand's power to increase and focus his magic.

When he could barely stand, the god led him to his room, wished him luck, then gifted him a deep sleep before leaving. This morning he had awoken refreshed, if not completely enthused about another day leafing through dusty documents.

At breakfast, Liam and Emer offered to organise the horses and food needed for their journey. Liam had even said he would sort out Seamus' pack for him—anything to get out of more reading. Reluctantly he left them to their preparations and headed to the library alone, still not unable to shake his unease about Aliah not being by his side.

A little while later, he was seated and began scanning his first scroll, a lengthy tome on breeding cattle, that he quickly assessed as useless. Before starting on the next text, he made sure he rolled the first one up and re-tied it, putting it to the side so he did not end up reading it again.

He learnt that lesson yesterday when he thought the library contained duplicates of some scrolls, then realised for a candle mark or so he had been picking his reading material from the completed pile. When he complained, Walter treated him to a long and detailed explanation of why being orderly and methodical was the linchpin of any scholarly endeavour. Today he was not just attempting to avoid duplicating his efforts, he also wanted to avoid another lecture.

As he unrolled the second scroll, his heart leapt into his mouth. This document contained a drawing of a casket, similar to the one Amelia described to them the other day. Not wanting to get his hopes up, he sped through the first two paragraphs of the document. It was a letter from a previous Baron Wexler to a captain of the Ducal Guard, the same captain who produced the report he shared with everyone when Amelia told them of the casket's existence.

The first paragraph explained Baron Wexler appreciated the duke's concern about a new brotherhood devoted to the god of the ocean, especially one with a military arm. He wanted to reassure everyone his new brotherhood would not be used against anyone in Hand. It would only be used to protect an important religious artefact.

The second paragraph was quite apologetic in tone, and while reading it Seamus thought the baron sounded like he could not quite believe what he was writing. Apparently he had been visited in the dead of night by a god, who gave him a casket. He instructed the baron that he and his descendants now had the sacred task of guarding the chest, ensuring its delivery to the Wizard and Warrior sometime in the future. Until then, the very existence of the casket was to be kept secret.

When the captain and his men arrived at the Wexler estate, the baron was flummoxed. He did not want to commit treason, but nor could he tell anyone about the casket. So he refused entry to the duke's men. This act left him uneasy so he prayed on the matter and received divine guidance.

The god informed him the Wizard and Warrior would come to the duke's library in Hand for answers on their quest, so writing a document explaining everything to the captain would serve two purposes; to reassure the duke Lord Wexler was no threat, and provide valuable information to the Wizard and the Warrior in the future. To this end, once he and the duke read this document, they were instructed to leave it in the palace library.

After his signature, Baron Wexler had added a coda.

'Goddess, I think this is it.' The words escaped Seamus' lips before he could stop them. He looked up, but Walter was so engrossed in his own work he had not heard a thing. Seamus read the coda under his breath.

'A good thing I did not forward this to you yesterday as I had another visit from a godly form last night. I was instructed to add the following, word for word, in my letter to the duke. "When attempting to capture a being without a body, containing them in something like a casket is desirable. Traditional spells will not work, you need to find someone who works magic using images not words. To truly be rid of a god from your realm, you need to send them back from whence they came. This is the only way to restore the true balance."

'When I asked the god what this meant, I was assured a wizard would understand. At first, I thought he said *the* Wizard, but I must have misheard him. I have done as I was asked, and I beseech you to leave this in your library for future generations.

'Well, I am the Wizard and I am not sure I understand. How is it no god will tell me exactly what I need to do, but they are happy to leave instructions in a scroll for anyone to find?'

'Sorry, Seamus, did you say something?' Walter distractedly ran a hand through his hair as he looked up. 'I understand this work is boring for you, but there are only a few more scrolls to go. We must find something soon.'

'I found it, at least, I think I did. If I understand this hint correctly, if we face the god before he is here in his own form, we are to place the god's essence in the casket and send him home. We had already guessed that, but there is still nothing on the how.'

Seamus shoved the scroll towards Walter, venting his frustration. He paced the room while Walter read through the document, mouthing the words and running his finger along under each sentence as he went. Re-reading a particular section, the furrow in his brow deepened before he continued until the end.

'You know this may not be the document we were directed here to find. There might still be a scroll in this lot with some more explicit instructions.'

Walter's attempt to buoy his flagging spirits fell on deaf ears.

'Great. But if this *is* the document, we are little better off. If it is not, there is only a little time left to find the real one.'

Walter stood and placed the scroll at the far end of the table, not wanting to risk losing it. He calmly sat down and picked up the document he had been working on previously.

'Well, we will not know for sure until we complete our search, will we? Besides, look at it this way, we might also find something unexpected in these last few scrolls to help us out.' Walter returned to his study.

Seamus half-heartedly kicked a chair, thought about letting the rant in his head out, before making do with muttered curses as he sat back down. In is heart of hearts, he knew that scroll was the one they were sent to find. However, Walter was right. Before they spent any more time studying the document, they needed to be sure none of the remaining items from the archive section of the library contained anything useful.

Seamus added more wood to the fire, warming the servants dining room, before taking as seat at the large wooden table just as Liam placed down a loaf of bread. His cousin took the chair next to him, and started helping himself to food. The room was quiet except for the clanking of cutlery as they finished filling their plates with the collection of cold meats, cheeses, vegetables and fruit in front of them.

'Why so glum?' Emer asked, staring pointedly at Seamus once everyone was eating.

He silently cursed the growing closeness between them. It seemed not only to enhance her ability to read his moods, but also gave her the confidence to voice her thoughts.

'Do not tell me. You are going to work through the night to find the scroll, and you are not happy.'

'No, we found it.' His tone sounded flat, even to his own ears.

'So, I ask again, why so glum?'

'Surely we should be celebrating?' Liam asked as he stood. 'Shall I find out if cook can rustle up some ale?'

Seamus reached out and grabbed a handful of tunic, pulling his cousin back into his seat. 'Apart from the fact I do not fancy a full day's ride with a fuzzy head tomorrow, the scroll tells us nothing more than we already knew. The god needs to be trapped in the casket. It does not tell us how. There are no spells or magic words to help. I feel like we wasted days looking for something that was no help at all.'

Although he tried to keep his frustration to himself, he gripped his fork so hard his knuckles turned white.

Walter paused, carefully placing his knife and fork on his plate, and said, 'To be fair, we only read the scroll once before double checking the last few documents to make sure we had the correct one. We did not have time to do more than scan the contents. Maybe there is more to it than the initial reading let on.'

Walter's ability to focus on the positive had never grated on Seamus' nerves as much as it did at that moment. He wanted to shout and yell and rail against the unfairness of spending days searching for a scroll that turned out to be no help at all. He could not understand how Walter did not.

Gripping his fork more tightly, he stabbed violently at the meat on the plate in front of him. As he brought a forkful of food to his mouth, he caught Emer's worried look before she attempted to hide it by turning her attention to Walter.

'Do you truly think the document might contain more? Maybe some secret message? Did you bring it with you? Can we look?'

Even Emer was hopeful. So why was he so despondent? Walter was right, they had only scanned the document. A second reading might actually reveal more information. Yet he could not bring himself to raise his hopes.

'I would not go as far as to say it might be hiding a secret message,' Walter said. 'But if you study things from a different angle, sometimes more is revealed. And yes, I did bring the scroll with me. I thought we might go over it after dinner.' His contribution finished, Walter continued methodically eating his meal.

I am full.' Emer started clearing away amidst Liam helping himself to more as the dishes passed him by. 'I will make us some tea, and we can go over the scroll together. Liam?'

'Give me a minute, I have not finished dinner yet.'

The girl's hard stare must have convinced him otherwise, because he stuffed the rest of the food on his plate into his mouth, and stood to help clear the table as he attempted to chew and swallow a few last morsels.

Seamus pushed his plate away. His hunger disappeared when the subject of the scroll's contents came up. There was nothing he wanted to do less than review the words he had read this afternoon, but nor could he leave this up to the others. After all, the scroll had been left for him and Aliah.

Closing his eyes to give himself a moment's peace, they immediately flew open. Hold on, how did he know the scroll was meant for him? Was it just because it said the Wizard and Warrior needed to find it, or was there another reason?

With his eyes again closed he went over the words in his mind, and he kept sticking on the phrase, "thoughts not words". Of course there had not been a spell or a method for him to capture the god in the casket. During his trial, the gods explained how different his magical gifts were. He did not need gestures or words like other wizards, he only needed to imagine what he wanted and use the elements to make it happen.

He allowed a little relief to trickle through, then tensed again. His training enabled him to move objects, but how did you move a non-corporeal being like a spirit? He needed to concentrate on that, not re-reading the scroll.

Turning to Walter, who was still busy with his meal, he asked, 'Walter, have you ever heard of someone's spirit being bound?'

The older man paused, fork half-way to his mouth, and stayed stock still for a moment. Slowly he returned the fork to his plate and turned to Seamus. 'That is an odd question, and the answer should be no, no person should bind another person's soul. In reality though, binding is done relatively regularly.'

Seamus' face froze in surprise. 'Are you able to restrain someone like that?'

'In theory, yes, in practice, no. Although most wizards are able to bind a spirit, it is best performed by someone with healing gifts because so many things might go wrong.'

'So ...' Seamus encouraged Walter to go on.

'Umm, I am not really sure I should be passing this on, but I assume you are asking for a good reason and not just idle curiosity.

'Binding is often used by senior healers when someone has serious mental problems that place them, or those close to them, in physical danger. If the healer can isolate the source of the problem, they bind that part of a person's mind—or soul, if you prefer.'

'That sounds exactly like what I need.'

Walter chewed thoughtfully for a moment, swallowed, then

continued. 'I am not sure I should be doing this, but, given our unique circumstances, I trust you to only apply this learning to our enemy.'

He placed his cutlery down again, giving Seamus his full attention.

'I assume your teachers showed you how to mind-link?'

'Yes.'

'Good. Now try and link minds with me. Excellent. Now, what can you tell me about the link you just made?'

'Umm.' Seamus frowned, trying to find the words to describe what was happening. 'Connecting with you is different to when I link with Aliah. You feel, well, it feels like a "Walterness" is surrounding me.'

'You are experiencing a full mind link. When most wizards connect, it is more like this.'

Seamus' sense of Walter changed, almost as though the wizard closed a part of himself off. Now he appeared more as a ghost than a complete person in his thoughts.

'Generally a link is agreed to, and the two wizards will create a space in their consciousness to allow another person in. This does two things, it stops the person linking from being overwhelmed by the other person, and allows each wizard to maintain some control over what they share.

'When a wizard needs to apply healing to a tortured soul, the interaction is much more intense than what you felt when you first joined with me, because the emotions the person is experiencing are so much more intense.'

Walter dropped his walls, once again appearing to Seamus as a full person.

'Now I want you to expand your presence in my mind, see if you can surround everything you perceive as my "Walterness".'

'You mean like when I first learnt to control magic and you taught me to move my magic in and out of my body?' Seamus attempted to put Walter's words into a context he could understand.

'Yes, although then you thought of your magic as a stream, this time I want you to flatten out your gift, like you are casting out a blanket and wrapping me up in it.'

Seamus imagined himself in Walter's mind, standing in front of what he perceived as Walter. He closed his eyes so he would not be distracted. He imagined himself walking around his projection of the wizard. Where he could not sense Walter's person, he saw a deep blackness and changed his direction. Once he completed the circumference, he floated over top to ensure he had an idea of the full height of the "Walterness". Satisfied with his survey, he imagined throwing a blanket over everything he saw as his friend.

'Walter? Walter? What is wrong?'

Seamus' eyes flew open and he found himself staring into Emer's worried face. His gaze followed hers, and he saw Walter sitting quite still, eyes wide open, staring blankly at the wall in front of him. The only sign he was alive was the gentle rise and fall of his chest. As Seamus rose to check on the older man, he released his magic. The light returned to Walter's eyes and the wizard returned to himself.

Collapsing back into his chair, Seamus worked hard to stop his dinner from making another appearance. 'Walter, what did I do?'

'It is all right, boy, you went a little further than I thought you would be able to for your first attempt. None-the-less, you learnt the lesson I wanted you to learn.'

Walter serenely took the cup of tea Emer had poured for him, and waited for her and Liam to sit at the table.

'You expected me to do that? Or something like that?' Seamus was astonished.

'Well, yes, of course. Otherwise why would I have you do what you did? I must say though, those gods have been teaching you well because your skill is far in advance of where I estimated it would be.' Walter continued the conversation as if nothing much had happened.

Seamus was unable to let things go that easily. 'When I looked at you, it was as if you were no longer in your body.' Seamus' hand shook as he took a cup of tea from Emer.

'In many ways I was not. The blanket you threw over me hid my essence, or soul. I was not in any danger. I could have thrown the blanket off at any time as you had not secured it. I wanted to show you a way to identify my soul, and, as I found out when I taught you magic, you learn better by doing than by hearing.' Walter took a sip of his tea while Seamus fought to get his hands under control.

'Why ever would you want to do that?' Emer admonished them both. 'That is an awfully dangerous lesson. Seamus might have made a mistake and extinguished your light, or cut you off from your magic.'

'What?' Seamus stood and started pacing around the room, still fighting to keep his dinner inside. 'Emer, please explain.'

'If you had closed the "blanket" you placed around him and spelled it, Walter would have been like a zombie until you undid the binding. If you pulled the blanket tight and crushed him, his light would be gone and his body would continue on as a shell without a soul until it withered away.'

Seamus' hands clenched tightly around his mug. He had always feared the process of quietening, believing taking someone's magic was removing a little of what made a person who they were. Now he had almost done something worse to Walter. His stomach roiled at the very thought.

'Excuse me.' Seamus dashed into the kitchen, and through to the scullery. Reaching the stone sink just in time for it to catch his dinner.

Moments later, feeling wretched but a little more settled, he joined the others. 'Please explain to me the details of the process to cut someone off from their magic.'

He did not actually want to find out as just the thought of cutting someone off from their magic al essence made him sick to the stomach, but realised he must know details if he was to fight the god.

550

Liam passed him a cup of water, his eyes sparkling with mischief. At least someone appeared to be enjoying Seamus' discomfort.

'You realise what you just did is one of the ways they take away magic. You know, to quieten people?'

The shock of having his fears confirmed caused Seamus to knock the cup in front of him, spilling water across the table. His stomach clenched again, but he fought to control his emotions as he answered.

'No, well, sort of. After listening to you I thought it might be.'

Realising all this was truly new to him, Emer carried on a little more gently.

'To quieten a person with magic, you cut the link from their soul, or essence, to their magic. You get the same result if you hide the soul for any length of time. The connection weakens and eventually withers. Cut it off for too long, and the bond cannot reform.'

'Humph, a soul needs to be hidden for days, even moon-turns before that happens. And as I said, I was in control all the time. While he followed my instructions Seamus would not have been able to extinguish or damage my light. Now quit making the boy ill and let me finish my lesson,' Walter grumbled.

Emer made to say something else, then thought better of it. Concentrating on her tea, she allowed Walter to go on.

'When a person has a sickness of the soul or mind their essence becomes fractured. A healer will find the core of the person and repair or remove any of the fractures. The process is a difficult one, and always leaves the person less than whole. So it is only used in extreme cases.'

'Why was Seamus trying to find your essence anyway?' Liam asked.

'I believe because he is attempting to find some way to control a god who does not have a body. Am I right?' Walter asked.

Seamus nodded reluctantly. Although he now had an idea as to how he might isolate the god's essence, he was not sure he actually had the heart to do it.

'How do you know a god has an essence like a person?' Liam turned to his cousin.

'I do not,' Seamus admitted. 'But I have to start somewhere.'

'Perhaps you can ask one of your god instructors,' Liam suggested.

Raising his eyebrows, Seamus turned towards Liam, 'That is a surprisingly good idea.'

Seamus now felt in control enough to drink a mouthful of tea. When he finished, he stood and asked, 'Shall we take another look at this scroll?'

———

WHILE LIAM and Emer leaned over the kitchen table, pouring over the scroll's contents, Walter finished his meal and Seamus allowed his stomach to settle while sipping another mug of tea.

'Ahh.' Emer pointed something out to Liam.

'So that is why he wanted to know.' His cousin glanced up at Seamus, then back down at the document in front of him. Emer elbowed him in the ribs and pointed at something else. Liam shrugged and carried on reading.

'Did you translate the writing in the drawing?' Emer looked up at Walter and Seamus.

'What?' Walter had been daydreaming.

Seamus leaned forward to get a better look. 'The picture of the casket has writing? I thought it was just an elaborate sketch.'

'I would have been surprised if you recognised the words, but I thought Walter might. It is an extremely old form of our language, but most libraries still contain at least some scrolls written in it.'

Turning the paper to give Walter a better view, Emer moved to stand behind him. Running her finger along, she showed him where the writing was.

'Oh my, how did I miss that? Many of the documents I studied while at the Wizard Isle were written in the same language. Here, let me see if I still have my touch. It has been a while.' The room was silent as he concentrated.

'If I am not mistaken this is another version of the Wizard and Warrior Prophecy. Let me see...

"After the decimation and the fall,

When the new power rises

And the Wizard and Warrior meet,

Old and new blood will combine

With the two who are not what they seem.

The key is the Ember Casket, to trap and calm the chaos,

Or send it beyond to save one and all."

Emer stared at Seamus. 'Even if you missed the prophecy, this scroll is more useful than you give it credit for.'

'Really?'

'Yes, really. It confirms you need the casket. Obviously you now realise you need to put the god's essence inside, otherwise you would not have been fooling around with Walter and his soul. That lesson has also given you the bare bones of a plan to transfer his soul to the box.'

Seamus admitted to himself she was right, but did she have to sound so much like a tutor when she pointed things out? Elbows on the table, he cradled his chin in his hands.

'And ...' Liam chimed in. 'It tells you placing the god in the casket is only part of what you need to do.'

Sitting upright, Seamus swung his head to look at his cousin. 'What do you mean?'

'Well, this bit here.' Liam indicated the coda at the bottom of the scroll. 'If I read it correctly, it says once the god is safely in the casket you need to find a way to get him and the chest he is imprisoned in back to the gods so balance can be restored.'

Surprise did not truly describe Seamus' reaction at that precise moment. Although his cousin was by no means stupid, he preferred

553

physical activities to book learning. Still, how did Liam figure that out when his own brain skipped over it?

'He is right, Seamus. It is stated in the new version of the prophecy as well.' Walter leaned back. 'I wish we had taken the time to read the complete prophecy in the Sanctuary before we left. Knowing the thing in its entirety would be useful about now.'

'I had forgotten about that,' Seamus shook his head. 'Aliah and I asked to see it before our trials, but we were told we could not read it until the gods confirmed us in our roles. Afterwards, everything moved so fast I never thought to ask again.'

'Amelia and I were so caught up in the idea we needed to be back with you as soon as possible, we never thought to go through it either.' Walter's shoulder sagged.

'I think you are wandering off track.' Still in tutor mode, Emer moved so they could all see her. 'If you needed something else from the prophecy the gods would have found a way to let you know.'

Seamus chewed this idea over. The gods made sure Amelia found out about the casket and the scroll, so possibly Emer was correct.

'Besides, if there was anything else obvious in the prophecy documents my father would have told us. He knows that particular prophecy backwards and forwards.'

'All right, I believe you.' Seamus held up his hands for her to stop bombarding him with logic. 'There is only one more thing to worry about. I have a plan for moving the god to the casket, but how do I move him from this plane. Any ideas?' He waited for the others to speak. 'Anyone?'

The hush that fell over the room was so complete Seamus heard the plop of a dripping tap in the scullery.

'Nothing? Nothing at all? Not even a spark of an idea? Walter, maybe something in the library that might help? We still have a few hours before we need to leave.'

The older wizard shook his head. 'Sorry, although I understand the general principles, large scale transportational magic is beyond me. There are not many wizards able to move items beyond their line of sight, and even then, the objects are small like, umm, this cup of tea.'

'This gets better and ...'

Seamus stopped mid-sentence as something caught his eye.

'Seamus? What is it?' Liam asked.

'I thought I just saw ...'

It was as though he could see Dominic sitting in front of the fire, but there were no chairs there. As he tried to focus on the form of his Warrior, the room in front of Seamus disappeared and he was staring into a crackling blaze.

Seamus? Is that you?

Aliah?

Yeah! I did it.

Seamus found himself back in the kitchen looking intently at the grain of the wooden table in front of him.

'How odd,' he mused

Swiftly sitting bolt upright, Liam had his hand on the knife at his belt and wearily searched the room.

'What is happening?'

'Nothing, I am just tired.' Shaking his head clear, Seamus returned to the matter at hand. 'If we are not going to find anything further here, we may as well all get a good night's sleep. We have a long way to go tomorrow.'

Not waiting for anyone else, Seamus rose and left the room. Had Aliah really managed to contact him from so far away? If she had, then something good had come from today.

He was so engrossed in his thoughts he did not notice the guard in front of him until the man put out a hand to prevent Seamus from bowling him over.

'Pardon me, sir, but there is a man at the door asking for Boss Allum. I explained Mr Allum left this morning, but he is insisting on seeing someone.'

Seamus stopped in his tracks, waiting for his brain to catch up with what the guard had said.

'Umm, do we know this man?'

'Hardly, sir. He has an Arian accent, and he looks like he has not seen a bath in weeks. However, he is wearing wizard robes.' The guard's lip curled with distaste.

'Perhaps you can go and ask him what his business is, then I can decide whether or not to see him. I will wait in my father's office.'

It felt odd opening the door to the room his father ran the duchy from and not see his father seated behind the desk. Sighing, he plopped down in the nearest chair, then immediately stood. If he wanted to be taken seriously as the person in charge he could not sit there, but it felt odd to sit in his father's seat.

Wandering round behind the desk, he paused at a knock.

'Enter.'

The young guard opened the door and slipped in, closing it behind. Seamus nodded for him to speak.

'Sir, the man says he has come from the Carsten camp on the other side of the island. He says he was there as a spy for our side, and that he needs to speak to someone here to pass on some news before he leaves for the Wizard Isle.'

When Seamus said nothing, the guard continued, 'I can send him away, sir. I mean to try and gain entry with such a preposterous story ...' The guard trailed off mid-sentence when Seamus sat down in the duke's chair.

'No, no, bring him in. I want you to stand watch outside the door here, and send one of the other guards to fetch Walter, we will need him to verify this man is actually who he says he is.'

'Sir, I am not sure I should do that. He could be someone sent to spy on us, and I would be placing you in danger. The duke would never forgive me.'

Sitting as tall as he could in the chair, Seamus did what his father would in the same situation. 'You have your orders,' he said, and stared at the guard, challenging the man to defy him.

The ploy may not have worked with a more seasoned soldier, but the guard was new enough to the ranks that he did not yet feel confident to defy the duke's son. Moments later, he returned leading a balding, round faced man dressed in wizard black, who started when he saw Seamus sitting behind the desk.

'Oh, I am sorry, I thought I was being taken to whomever is in charge.' He moved as if to leave the room, but was forestalled by the guard shutting the door firmly behind him.

'That would be me,' Seamus assured the wizard. 'Please take a seat.'

The man remained standing.

'I have important information those defending Aria must hear, I need to talk to the person who is leading Hand's defence against Carsten, or at the very least, someone who can get a message to that person.'

An amused smile played around Seamus' lips as he answered. 'Once again that would be me. Perhaps if you would take a seat, we can introduce ourselves and that might clear things up a little.'

He waited patiently while his guest considered his options, sighed, and took the seat opposite Seamus.

'You are?' Seamus asked.

In a tone clearly telling Seamus the man would play his game, but only for the moment, the wizard answered. 'Braxton, Wizard of the Gold.'

Before Seamus could introduce himself, the door opened and Walter barged in. Glancing quickly at Seamus, his eyes moved to the man in the chair, and his face split into a wide grin. Braxton stood and embraced the older man, a look of relief clearly written on his face.

'Ah, Walter, I am so pleased to see you.'

'As am I to see you,' Walter answered. 'I have to say when Boss

Allum told me you were working as a spy I had mixed feelings. The first was relief, because you had not gone over to the enemy as I suspected, but it was followed by concern, because your life was clearly in danger. Now I am pleased to see you back safe and sound.'

'Walter, I knew what I was getting into when I started this. Besides, you know me, as soon as things became sticky, I left. One of the Carsten truth sayers was showing an awful lot of interest in me, and I knew it was only a matter of time before I was found out. Besides, I have some interesting news I need to pass on. Perhaps you can take me to whoever is in charge. My boat leaves just before midnight and I do not have much time.'

Walter frowned, 'Person in charge? But ... Ah, Braxton, let me introduce you to Lord Seamus, Duke Damon's eldest son.'

Braxton at least had the grace to blush when he realised who Seamus was, but he was still not convinced.

'Walter, I am sure this young man is the highest ranking noble here, but I need to talk with someone who is actually going to be fighting in this battle and understands a little more about the real enemy we face.'

Seamus stood to protest, but Walter's laughter stopped him, and he sank back into the chair, realising the wizard had this all in hand. 'Why, Braxton, this boy is not only going to be fighting in this battle, but he is one of the two most important combatants for our side.'

Walter sat down, and Braxton joined him, still looking skeptical. 'I will have to take your word for that, Walter.' The wizard turned to Seamus. 'No offence, lad, but you are just so young, and this news is important for the safety of our realm.'

'I understand your concern. Perhaps it will help if I tell you I am in contact with both the king's forces in Port Marden, and the guard captain put in charge of defences here in Hand. At the very least I can pass on your message, at best your information might also help us with a plan we are cooking up to deal with the being pulling the Carsten Army's strings.'

Braxton considered Seamus' words, but still looked to Walter for confirmation before answering. Seamus suppressed a frustrated sigh, realising to assert who he was and his role in this war to a complete stranger was not the best course of action. If Walter had introduced him as the duke's son, then he had a reason to not name him as the Wizard.'

'All right, I guess this is the best I can do for the moment given I have not got much time. I and two other wizards fled the enemy camp two nights ago, after Wizard Millard sent two battle ships to destroy the Wizard Isles. He was so incensed so many of our brothers had not joined him in his attempted coup, he decided they did not deserve to live.'

'Are there many wizards left on the isle?' Walter asked. 'I thought most were with the king's forces.'

'From what I can tell, there are maybe twenty wizards there, but I suspect the attack is against the wizards in training, the next generation,' Braxton answered.

Walter's eyes widened. 'Oh, no.'

'That is why we left. We could not get a message to them while we were still in camp as we would have been detected and our lives forfeit. We got through, and the school is being evacuated as we speak.

'We have a boat in the harbour. I am travelling with a weather magician, and another magician who can do some travel magic. Combined with my skills, we should be able to arrive at the isle before the Carsten ships. We will meet with the remaining wizards and rescue as much of the library as we can.'

'Even with your skills, they have had two days start on you. Are you sure you can make it there first?' Seamus asked.

'It will be close, but they have had to travel some way out to sea so as not to be detected by Arian forces. We can take a more direct route. Still, I must be on my way as soon as possible.'

'Wait.' Walter placed a restraining hand on the wizard's arm. 'I think good fortune brought you here today of all days. Am I right in remembering you had some skill in transporting magics?'

'Umm, yes. It is not my primary area, but I have some aptitude.'

'Before you go, could you please describe for us the process of moving an object from one place to another?'

Braxton appeared confused.

'I would not ask, but it is really important, perhaps more important in the long run than saving the library at the Wizard Isle.'

'Umm, all right. My primary skill is in elemental control; manipulating fire, water, earth and air. I can spell the elements to do more or less of what they do naturally, depending on the situation. While studying, I found if I spelled air to cocoon an object, I could then use the air to move something from one place to another.

'I know that is not strictly transportational magic as others with a true gift would describe it, but it works for me. Now, I really must be going.'

'Ah, Wizard Braxton, while the attack on the Wizard Isle is important news, I find it hard to believe that is the important news our military strategists cannot do without,' Seamus interrupted.

'Oh dear, you are quite right, I almost forgot. Millard and his goon Gaius have been searching for something, and they have had the magic users from Carsten helping them. I believe they are close to finding out where that something is, and once they have it, there will be full scale war. From the intelligence I picked up, I believe the main battle will begin in less than a six-day.'

'Thank you, Braxton, that is most useful. I will be sure to pass the message on.' Seamus stood and shook the wizard's hand, then slumped back into his chair as Walter escorted his former pupil out of the palace.

His mind was buzzing with all he had learnt that day, attempting to fit all the pieces together. A bare bones plan was forming in his mind, and he was confident he knew what to do even though there were areas he needed to tease out.

However, there were two things that worried him. The first was he knew what he had to do, but what role was Aliah to play when the final battle came? He knew enough to know it would not be as simple as standing there guarding him while he fought the god, but he had no idea what else she would do instead. Nor did she, he suspected.

Then there was the news they had less than a six-day to stop the god before the final battle for Aria. This was all getting very real, and the desire to flee somewhere far from the war was growing stronger. The only thing stopping him was the knowledge that if the god came through to this world, nowhere would be safe.

CHAPTER 40
A BUSY NIGHT

Heat scorched through her divided riding skirt, bringing Aliah back into Baron George's finest guest room. During her contact with Seamus, she had inadvertently wandered too close to the roaring fire warming the room.

'You did it.' Dominic's grin spread from ear to ear.

Absentmindedly moving back from the flames, Aliah sat down, still lost in her own thoughts.

'Hey, Aliah, you should be celebrating.'

Coming from afar, her tutor's words scarcely pierced her consciousness. Something disturbed her about the way she joined with Seamus, and she needed to figure out why.

'I could feel Seamus, and I was drawing towards him, but something prevented be from getting through. Perhaps a lack of magical power? Then ... it was like a sort of bump ... and we connected, and he flooded my mind. I was so surprised I dropped the connection.'

Angrily she turned to face Dominic. 'You helped me?'

Although framed as a question, her tone suggested she already knew the answer. Before Aliah wound herself into full-blown anger, Dominic held his hands up in surrender.

'I understand you wanted to do it all by yourself, and you almost did.'

'Almost. Why did you not just let me fail? I am no shrinking violet to be put off by failure. I would have tried again.'

Weary from her magical training, she slumped in the chair, glaring at Dominic.

'There was more thought behind my actions than merely assisting you to join with Seamus. In my experience, it is easier to connect to someone you have joined with before. Remember when we started tonight, I asked if you could see or visualise a link to Seamus?'

'Yes,' she answered, unsure where this was going.

'When I connect with someone I have linked with before, I can see a faint trail to their mind, no matter how far away they are. Each time I connect with them the link to them becomes clearer. At first, I thought you might be able to see a path to Seamus, when I realised you could not, I decided to give you a helping hand to create one.'

'Oh.' Somewhat deflated, Aliah let the tension and anger drain from her body. 'I did not see anything leading me to Seamus when I was searching for him. Should I try again and see if I can find it now?'

'Maybe, but why not recharge your energy first? We can attempt another connection tomorrow. Perhaps it would be more beneficial to discuss what happened and see if we need to make some adjustments when you try next time.'

Skeptical about his motives, Aliah gave Dominic what she hoped was a piercing stare. 'Are you handling me?'

A chuckle escaped, and soon the boy in front of her was laughing out loud. 'Sorry, yes. You must appreciate sometimes it is easier to work around you than take you on directly.'

If she had had any energy left Aliah would have feigned annoyance, but in truth she was too tired to bother.

'I know. I sometimes react when I should think first. I am working on it.'

Dominic took some time to calm himself, and while she waited, Aliah replayed the process of making her link with Seamus.

First, she formed a clear picture of her Wizard in her mind. That was the easy part. Then she reached out and search for what felt like Seamus' energy. When a person stood near to you, it was easy to sense them. When contacting someone far away, your consciousness needed to keep expanding until you found the person you were looking for.

In theory it sounded simple, in practice it was not so easy. Between her and Seamus lived hundreds upon hundreds of conscious minds—animals as well as people—not to mention the tiny pinpricks of light she assumed were insects. Some of the larger lights were dull and uninteresting, but others were bright and shiny. The difficulty was not to be drawn off track by the more interesting glowing balls.

Finally she found a luminous presence, pulling her towards it like a magnet. Drawing closer, the "Seamusness" of the light washed over her. Excited at having found her destination, she rushed forward only to find she could not penetrate his mind.

Almost overcome with frustration she thought about with-drawing when, suddenly, they were linked. Instead of the gentle contact she planned, Seamus said her name and had blundered into her head.

Now she realised Dominic had given her a nudge, there was no longer a mystery about how she connected. All she needed to work out was how Seamus managed to overwhelm her by simply acknowledging her presence. Dominic's laughter was back under control and he was ready to answer her questions.

'Much as I hate to say it, you are right, I need to understand what happened. When I linked with Seamus, I caught a brief glimpse of where he was, I am sure he was at the table in the palace kitchens. There were some people with him, I guess Emer and Liam, but I cannot be certain. What worries me is when I join with you it is like entering a house. You allow me to come in and the space is welcoming.

'The moment Seamus was aware of me he filled my head with his presence, and I lost control. I spoke to him but he seemed unaware of anything I said, so I shut down the connection.'

She closely watched Dominic for his reaction, but he continued staring into the fire.

'Did you hear me?' Aliah attempted to keep her temper under control, but it was not easy when being ignored.

'Yes, I am thinking.'

'Oh, you could have said.'

The moment the words escaped her lips she realised she sounded like a petulant child, and wished to take them back. This new closeness with Dominic unsettled her. Should she treat him as a friend, a tutor, or a guard? None of the traditional roles seemed quite right to describe their new relationship.

'Aliah, are you there?'

Goddess! Her face warmed with a blush. Had he guessed she was thinking about him? Did he see her blush, or would he assume heat from the fire caused her to turn red?

'Yes, carry on.' *Argh, how formal.* Now he would know something was up. *Just calm down and stay focused,* she commanded herself.

'Normally the person who initiates contact stays in control of the process. Perhaps Seamus took over because his magic is really strong, or maybe it is because your sword and his wand support the link?

'We need to work on your defences before we try again, otherwise you will never be able to communicate clearly with him. In the normal course of things that would not be a problem, but if you need to pass on a brief message you might run into trouble.'

'Oh. So I did not do anything wrong.' Relief flooded through her, giving hope she might actually be able to do this, eventually.

'I am sure your linking will improve with practice. Now, I believe rest is what you need as we are meeting early with Baron George again tomorrow to finalise details before heading to Rasmussen's.'

With Dominic's departure, Aliah found herself feeling more alone than she had in a while. Without Seamus who would talk through the days' events with her and figure out what it all meant. Without Daniel, who was still not recovered from his stomach problem, and was in bed resting for tomorrow's ride. Amelia and Boss had their heads together over something and she thought maybe Dominic would stay after their lesson. Even his know-it-all comments would be preferable to this loneliness.

Something had definitely altered between the two of them, and she was not sure she liked it. Yet, things could not return to the way they were either. Annoyingly, she should be concentrating on their more pressing problems, but thoughts of Dominic and the changes between them filled her head.

A yawn escaped as she stood and picked up her travel pack. Exhausted, she decided to take Dominic's advice and get some sleep. There would be plenty of time for her to worry this through while they travelled tomorrow.

Mulling over things in his head, Seamus realised he was in for a busy evening as he urgently needed to speak to two people and a god. First things first, he sent out a prayer to the gods, asking for another extra training session. That done, he searched for Emer and asked her to pass on the information he gathered from Braxton to her father, ensuring the king would remain informed.

He did not ask her to pass anything on to Amelia for Daniel yet, he believed he had that message covered. All he had to do now was wait, and he had to wait for quite a while for a god to appear.

'You have need of us again?' the god asked. 'Are you still worried about not being able to train with Aliah?

Instead of answering, Seamus launched into a series of questions coming from his discussion with Walter over dinner, starting with whether or not it was possible to link with a god's mind in the same way you could with a human one.

Not really knowing what to expect, he was taken by surprise when crystalline tears streamed down the warrior god's face as she tried to hold the laughter in and answer Seamus' question.

'Young Wizard, you are indeed strong for a human, but you are not strong enough to enter a god-mind. Here, let me show you.'

Feather-light, the god reached out and touched his cheek with her hand, gently drawing him towards her mind. Before he was anywhere near the core of the god, light over-whelmed him and Seamus mentally pulled back with such a force his consciousness snapped back into his own head with an almost audible thud.

'What did you see?' asked the god.

'Colours so bright I could hardly bring myself to look at them. I was not even totally in your mind and I felt like I was standing on the edge of an abyss. I knew if I went any closer, I might never be able to return to myself.'

Settled safely back into his own mind, worry overtook the awe. How would he ever be able to force the god into the Ember Casket if he was not even able to look at him?

'There is more you wish to ask?'

'I fear the task you have set me is insurmountable. I know you cannot discuss any details with me, or tell me what to do, but how am I to control an entity such as you for long enough to force them into a chest, presuming you have not spelled it so he will enter himself when he is close by?'

The god tapped an index finger on her lips as she thought how to answer, or perhaps she was communicating with the other gods.

'You are correct, I am unable to instruct you in what you have to do, and no we have not set a trap for our brother. However, what I can do is tell you a little about we gods in general, which may assist you in your preparations.

'For one of us to come and teach you each night in corporeal form it takes the combined will of all seven of us. We are hundreds of times stronger in this form than in any other, therefore our lights shine brighter.

'The trial you undertook was on a mid-plane. When the veil is thin, we can appear there in ethereal form, and communicate using our minds with those of you on this world with very little effort.

'Once every hundred years or so, the veil between the worlds thins enough so we can project an ethereal form onto your plane of existence using only a little of our energy. In that form, we are able to communicate with your kind, if invited in we can even share a physical body. With an especially weak mind, we might even take over a body if the mind occupying it is weak of will.

'What we cannot do is move our physical selves from our world to your world, or even to the mid-world, without an exceptional amount of magical power.'

The god was silent while Seamus mulled over what she said. Knowing the god could not confirm or deny anything specifically to do with her brother, Seamus noticed when she spoke there were often micro reactions indicating whether or not he was on the correct path. A small tightening of the lips when he was wrong, or a twitch at the corner of her mouth that was almost a smile when he headed in the right direction. Speaking his thoughts out loud, he watched his teacher's reactions.

'Mmm, if I understand what I heard correctly, you are here in physical form so your light is very bright. If I had attempted the same exercise during my trial, I would not have found your essence to be so all-encompassing.'

Was that an almost smile?

'Continue,' the warrior god commanded.

'If I came across you in ghost form on this world you would be even duller in appearance, perhaps much closer to the essence of a human.'

'How dare you even suggest my essence could ever be close to a human's. I would still be brighter by far.'

Although the god appeared to be boasting, Seamus took note of the information she was passing on.

'If it takes seven gods to send one of you to train me for even a few candle-marks, it stands to reason it will take an equal amount of power to send a god back to where they came from.'

Click, click, click. Pieces fell into place. 'I am looking for an artefact to contain a god-mind. I am thinking perhaps the chest contains a magical boost, enough to send the god back to where he came from.'

Perhaps a slight surprised rise of the eyebrows there?

'Oh no.' Seamus' stomach lurched as more puzzle pieces fitted together. 'If the chest holds enough magic to send the god away, it also holds enough to bring the god into this world. Whoever gets to the chest first is likely to win at least the first round of our battle.'

Sadness swept so swiftly across the face of the god, he almost did not see it. Defeat seeped through him as he realised the full extent of the task before them. They had to beat the god in a race to an object of power, then use that object to send him out of this realm of existence. A small misstep and he could actually end up helping the god to come here in all his glory.

No matter the gods said they would be able to fight their brother even if he was physically on this world, with the Ember Casket in his hands, where would they find enough power to send him home?

Sinking to the ground, he held his head in his hands, going through everything he had learnt again to see if he could find any glimmer of hope. There it was, a dull light flickered in the recesses of his mind. *I know his name.*

As if she read his thoughts the god asked, 'Have you another question for me, or shall we train?'

'Wait a moment, I need to think this through. When we worshipped you all, and called you by your given names, a link must have been created between you and the people who prayed to you. Perhaps it not only kept balance between the worlds, but did it also make it easier for you to move between the them?'

'It was a very long time ago, but yes, that is correct. When we were worshiped in all the lands equally, the veil between the worlds was thin enough for us to have full contact with your kind.

'Now few of us are worshipped in your world, and some not at all. The balance is not as strong as it once was, and it is more difficult for us to contact you.'

Slowly the small light was growing brighter.

'So ... if a god was no longer worshipped here and people had forgotten their name, there would be no link. If one person was to own the name and be the only person to call it, there would be a strong link, perhaps almost tethering the god to that person?'

The god in front of him was completely motionless, as if she dared not give anything away at all. Seamus knew he must be onto something, but he was not quite sure what. He needed to think through how to use the small advantage he unearthed.

While his mind whirred with all these new thoughts, he asked the final question he had for the god.

'Can you help me connect with Aliah?'

The god considered his request. 'I could, but I think your mind is too distracted to communicate effectively. When you have settled down, and your mind is quiet, you can look for your link to Aliah. When people have linked before it leaves a trail to that person. The more you connect, the clearer the trail. If you can follow that link and find your Warrior you can try connecting like you did here.

'If there is nothing else, I need to return. We have preparations of our own to make. Would you like me to send you to sleep before I depart?'

'I have things to do, so I am fine, and I cannot think of anything else to ask,' Seamus responded distractedly. 'Thank you for coming.'

'You are welcome,' the god said as she winked away.

EXHAUSTED, Seamus flopped down on the bed and thought through what the god said to him about people and energy. At first, he cast his mind out around the palace and found little balls of light. From their positions in relation to each other he could work out who each of them belonged to.

Leaving the confines of the building, he was overwhelmed by the sheer number of lights in the half-deserted town of Port Hand, and he retreated back to his room in frustration. When Emer spoke of connecting with her father she made it seem easy, almost as easy as he and Aliah connecting when they were together. He knew if there was a way to filter out the other lights and just concentrate on Aliah, he would be able to recognise her.

Clearing his mind again, he thought only of Aliah and let his consciousness leave his body. As he disconnected, he glimpsed a gossamer thread of light. Wondering if this was the connection to Aliah the god described, he followed it.

Racing along the thread, he soared above all the other consciousnesses until he spotted a glow he recognised. Relief filled him, and he rushed towards her, slamming into her mind.

ALIAH.

Seamus? She was groggy, telling him he had probably woken her up.

His elation at finding her was soon superseded by surprise as he felt himself violently pushed out of her presence.

Back in his room, frustrated, he tried again. He was able to find Aliah more easily this time. Rather than rushing in, he imagined himself whispering her name.

He watched a small opening appear and he rushed forward, only for it to close before he could enter.

Aliah?

The opening appeared again, and this time he moved forward at a gentler pace.

Hello, Seamus.

Aliah? What was that all about?

If you remember, the gods told us there are rules for entering people's minds. In fact ...

Rules? Seamus asked.

Yes, remember, you ask first if you can make a connection. Then you do not just barge in, you enter respectfully.

Oh. Right. You were making a point.

Ignoring him, Aliah continued. *And, when you enter, you hold some of yourself back so you do not overwhelm the other person.*

That seems sensible. But am I really linked with you? This feels different somehow?

It is. We are not fully linked, but we are communicating.

You seem to have learnt a lot from Dominic, Seamus commented.

How did you ... the gods.

Yes. Anyway, I am pleased I have made it here. Did you just yawn?

I am exhausted. Why are you here? I hope it is not only to see if you can? Travelling for days on end is tiring and I really need to get some sleep, Aliah answered dozily.

No. Well, yes, but also to pass on news. How did you go today?

Not so good. Baron George is lovely, and we have his full support. On the other hand, Baron Tappit was, well, let us just say he is not very nice. We did not manage to secure his troops yet, but we have a plan.

I met Baron Tappit once, not long after his brother died, and I know what you mean about him. We do need his troops though.

As I said, we are working on it. Fortunately, Baron George has been most helpful. He is such a dear man. What is your news? Aliah asked sleepily.

We had an unexpected visitor today. Boss' spy friend.

What? Why? Aliah's mind was now fully alert.

He is heading back to the Wizard Isle, it seems they are soon to be under attack. Apparently Millard wants to be rid of all opposition, both present and future, Seamus updated her.

Will he be able to get back to the other wizards in time?

He has ways of getting there. Although that news is important, he had more. Now Aliah was more fully awake, he decided it was time to tell her the worst of it. *From what he said, I believe the god and Millard are looking for the same chest we are, and once they have it, they intend to launch the final attack. He said they know where it is and we will be fully at war before the end of this six-day.*

He paused and waited for Aliah to process the news before continuing.

I am thinking in light of this new information, you should head directly to Baron Wexler's and meet me there. Leave the others to finish rallying the troops.

Whoa, Seamus, slow down. What has changed so dramatically to make you think we should alter our plans?

Aliah appeared much calmer than Seamus expected her to be. Did she not see how important it was for them to be together now?

The time for our battle is drawing close, we should be together, Seamus said.

Do you feel that is important? You know what I mean by feel? Is this a premonition sort of thing?

The question made Seamus stop and think.

Seamus? Is this something we have to do, or are you worried about us being apart?

It is more something I would feel better about, if I am honest, Seamus eventually admitted.

When I left, you were all right with my going. What has changed? Do you need my help planning for the final battle?

Again Seamus paused before he answered, trying to be clear about his concerns.

I think I know what needs to be done. We need to find the chest, bind the god and send him home using the power the chest contains. I also have an idea on how I might do that.

Then what is the problem? Aliah interrupted.

The prophecy and the gods have always said we need both a Wizard and a Warrior to defeat the god. I cannot see what your role is meant to be in all of this.

573

Ah, and you think if we are together my role might just suddenly appear? Aliah's voice seemed amused.

Well, I suppose that is one way to put it. I was thinking perhaps by talking with you I would more clearly understand what you will be doing while I am taking care of all the magic stuff.

Seamus, sometimes you do make me laugh. Firstly, have you considered my role might actually be what I am doing now, making sure the island is not over-run by Carstenite soldiers so we can access the chest and prepare for the battle? Aliah did not wait for him to answer before continuing. *Secondly, what are we doing right now? Talking. We can go over things any time you want now we know we can contact each other. And, finally, you know any battle plan only holds up for the initial engagement, after that you are merely reacting.*

There was silence as Aliah waited for Seamus to respond. While he thought about what his friend said, he hoped this new sort of link did not let her know how stupid he felt.

Seamus? Are you all right? You may be wondering if you overreacted a little, and I think you are probably kicking yourself right now. Well, stop. You take your role seriously, I know, and it is good for us to talk like this. It will give you perspective.

Seamus sighed. It seemed Aliah did not need a mind link to know what he was thinking.

Thanks, Aliah, I do feel a little better. Now, if I think about it a little more clearly, we are going to meet up in two days and that should still give us time to finalise our plan before we face our enemy.

It will, now stop worrying and get some sleep.

Good night.

Good night, sleep well.

As Aliah pushed him from her mind, Seamus cursed, he had meant to tease her a little about training with Dominic. The thought made him laugh out loud as he realised just this small contact with Aliah had lifted a weight from his shoulders, and now he might actually get some sleep.

Cowering behind the solid oak door he had imagined in his mind, Gaius looked out through the tiny knot-hole in the wood, the only view of the world he allowed himself at the moment.

'I found it.'

Millard stood triumphantly in front of the form of his former pupil.

'The casket is not far from here,' the wizard informed the god.

'We must go and collect it immediately.'

Reverberating through his body, the god's response emanated pleasure and anticipation.

'I am not sure that is the best plan,' Millard advised.

If the god had not been so intent on crushing Gaius as he took over his body, he might have retained access to his memories. Gaius knew the look on his old master's face. Millard was up to something, something likely only to benefit himself.

The young man drew away from the door, surrounding himself with the darkness of his hiding place. For a moment, he allowed the hurt inside to take over. His former tutor had not so much as tried to find out if he were still alive inside the body he once owned. In fact, Gaius finally admitted to himself the wizard's reaction to losing his apprentice was not sadness, but clearly relief at not having been chosen to host the god himself.

As he drew further inside, Gaius wallowed in self-pity, bemoaning how he had ended up in this position. He spent so much energy on his own bitter quest for power, it had blinkered him to Millard's manipulation of his life. The man encouraged his isolation from children his own age, and helped him build his cloak of superiority. He had been flattered someone holding so prestigious a position had shown an interest in him, and he allowed that to blind him to all the signs the older man used him only to further his own ends.

Mentally he pulled himself back from the path of remorse, and forced himself to return to the tiny opening. The past was just that, in the past. He needed to focus on the present, which meant gathering as much information as possible if he was to take advantage of any opportunities to gain his freedom.

'Let me go and retrieve the chest for you as I promised I would. I will be able to sneak in and out before anyone realises I am there. In the meantime, you will be able to focus on your main problem, the Wizard and Warrior.

'As you pointed out on numerous occasions, I am no match for them. If you decide to act on the intelligence we received from our friend in their camp, you would clearly be best placed to take one of them on.'

While Gaius realised Millard was up to something, the god preened as the wizard flattered him into agreeing to his plan.

Fool. The thought leapt into Gaius' mind before he could stop it.

The god's focus turned inwards, searching for the origin of the word that popped into his head. Moving swiftly, Gaius pushed the plug into the hole just before the god's inner eye swept across his barrier.

You are the fool, he chided himself as he trembled in fear. *He must never find out you are still alive, or you will never escape.*

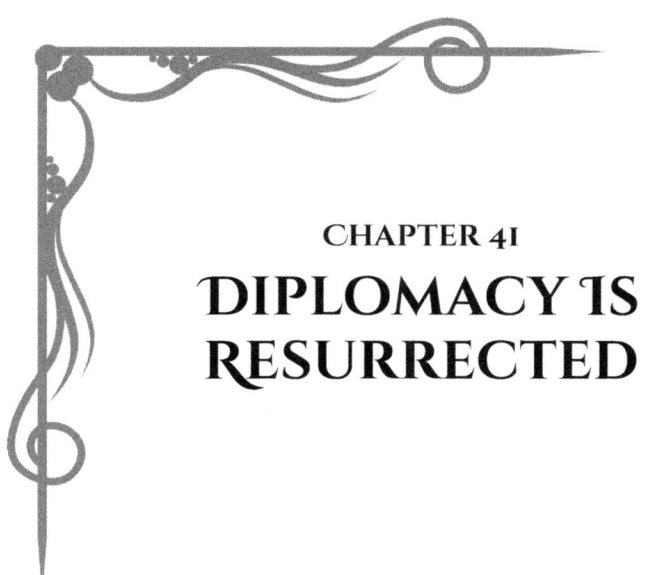

CHAPTER 41

DIPLOMACY IS RESURRECTED

Dappled sunshine draped itself across the bed like a quilt. Stretching cat-like, Aliah allowed herself the luxury of a moment more of blissful relaxation before forcing her weary body out from under the covers. She hardly remembered the last time she stayed in bed until she woke naturally, rested and able to face the day. No use complaining though, there was work to be done.

When the maid appeared to open the curtains, she left some warm water for washing, and a pot of tea. Most civilised, Aliah thought, as she washed and dressed herself quickly so she was able to take a moment to sit and enjoy the refreshing beverage.

With almost perfect timing, just as she finished the last of her drink, there was a knock at the door. Daniel entered, looking much better this morning. The dark smudges under his eyes were barely noticeable. Aliah attempted to hide her relief with a cheerful, 'Good morning.'

'Shall I gather the others for the meeting?'

'Yes, it is time. Are the horses ready?'

'Boss and Pauley are in the stables as we speak, making sure everything is set for our departure. Would you rather I took your belongings down, or would you like me to come to the meeting?'

His tone suggested he would prefer not to attend the breakfast arranged by Baron George last night. Using the pretext of needing to finalise everything they agreed to, it was more an opportunity for the lonely baron to spend time with his guests than to rubber stamp everything.

'You can take my things down, and anything the others need as well. Although I should make you have breakfast with us, you know. The baron is a lovely man, he just wants some company. It is not his fault he recently lost his wife, and his two sons are off fighting with Duke Damon. With the help he is giving us with Baron Tappit, a quick breakfast is the least we can do.' Aliah spoke as she followed Daniel out of the room and down the stairs.

'I am a soldier, Aliah. I only ever wanted to be a soldier. I wish you would stop trying to mould me into something else.'

Daniel's words were sad and heavy, causing Aliah to pause and remember Dominic's words from the night before.

'Daniel, is everything all right?'

'Of course, silly. I just want you to realise I am happy doing exactly what I am doing. So stop meddling and trying to change me.'

'If you so order, captain, it shall be done.'

Parting company at the door to the dining room, Aliah's eyes pierced her friend's back as he carried her travel pack out to the stables, almost as though she wished she could see into his very soul. Something niggled her about Daniel's behaviour lately. Try as she might, she could not place her finger on what it was. Shrugging with defeat, she plastered a bright smile on her face and opened the door.

'Ah, Princess, we were just wondering when you would turn up.'

A middle aged man, still in his prime with a homely face, beamed as she entered the dining room. Dominic turned in his chair to say good morning, then promptly turned back to his meal and attacked it as though he would not see another for all eternity. Sitting down beside Amelia, a servant brought her a full cooked breakfast, the size of which she would not be able to eat even if she sat at the table all day.

'Dig in, my dear. Do not feel you have to eat it all. The servants are used to catering for my boys, who eat every meal as though it is their last,' the baron joked. 'I was in the middle of recapping what we talked about yesterday when you entered, so I shall start again.

'This morning I dispatched a rider to Baron Tappit with a message directing him to get off his butt and send some men to this fight. I worded it in terms he will find very difficult to ignore. He is not a bad lad, but he has a tendency to only stir himself if everything is guaranteed to turn out in his favour.

'Half of my men are preparing to ride out today, and will meet with you at Rasmussen's. They will give you enough time to talk to the baron and gain his agreement first, but in good time to add a little pressure if he is being indecisive. Although, given his holdings are closer to the enemy camp, I doubt he will need the extra incentive.'

'Why, Baron George, you have been busy this morning, and here I am just out of bed.'

Aliah overdid the compliments, but the baron's blush of pleasure made it well worth the extra effort.

'Is there anything left for us to do?'

Baron George's face clouded over and his tone became serious. 'My dear, you are already doing more than we could ever ask of you. You are all going to face our enemies and put your life on the line for Hand, and Aria. The little I am doing pales in comparison.'

'Bet that took the wind out of your sails,' Amelia said under her breath.

'Wow, Aliah, great way to change the mood of a celebration meal.' In contrast, Dominic's teasing comment was loud enough for all to hear.

'Please show some manners, young man. It was I who changed the tone, because I cannot believe you all, and my own sons, are being forced to fight for our way of life. I never thought I would see the like in my lifetime. My poor Clarissa will be turning in her grave.'

A chastened Dominic returned to his meal. However, finding she no longer had much of an appetite, Aliah laid down her cutlery. 'Baron George, we will do our best to make sure you and your people remain safe.'

'I know you will, my dear. What I worry about though is you placing yourself in such grave danger.'

Amelia took Aliah's hand, as if she sensed the worry churning in her stomach. Daniel was not well, something had changed with Dominic, and now this dear man expressed heartfelt concern for her safety. The morning started so full of promise, and now she felt as though everything was slipping through her fingers. A knock on the door prevented her from completely falling into melancholy.

Daniel popped his head around and grinned. 'Everything is ready when you are, Princess.'

'I wish you had more time to spend here, but I appreciate you must be on your way.' Baron George was the perfect host as he stood and accompanied them to the door, easing their departure with a practiced hand.

Aliah was not just being polite when she spoke of her sorrow at leaving so soon. In the baron's warm, capable presence, she could let someone else take care of the details, and the impending battle seemed so very far away.

ACHING muscles in her bottom creaked, forcing a groan from her lips as she hauled herself into the saddle. Unaccustomed to two days hard riding, her body protested at the thought of more of the same. Glancing at Amelia, she found her friend sitting straight backed and relaxed on her mount. Moving her horse closer to the older woman, she touched her gently on the arm to gain her attention.

'You are looking sprightly this morning, Amelia, it would not be a result of some practices forbidden on Hand, would it?' she joked conspiratorially.

Inclining her head towards Aliah, the woman also spoke in hushed tones. 'You mean to say you are not using that sword of yours to give you energy and soothe your aching muscles?'

Bewildered, Aliah stammered. 'I ... I never thought to. Would that not be cheating a little? I mean, using the sword for my own benefit seems against the god's intentions when they gave it to me, you know, to save Aria.'

'Sometimes I forget you are a child, then you make silly comments like that and I remember how young you still are. Aliah, you are gathering defences to fight Aria's enemies. At any moment they might appear and you need to be fighting fit to face them and survive. Under the circumstances, I would say using your sword to maintain your strength and agility is your duty, not some sort of a short cut.'

Amelia's words hit her like a slap, and she cringed at her own stupidity. She had been gifted the sword to aid her on her journey, of course the sensible thing to do would be to use its powers. Reaching forward, she undid the soft leather covering the hilt and placed her hand around it. Immediately a healing warmth spread through her body. By the time they were ready to leave, she felt revitalised and her aches had almost disappeared. Now ready to face the day, she rode until she drew up beside Dominic.

'Are we to work some more today while we ride?'

'How can you be so cheerful? We worked late into the night, and with our early start ...' His words trailed off.

Aliah took a close look at her friend and realised he too had been burning the candle at both ends. Sure he continued working once she took to her bed, she regarded the dark bruises under his eyes and his grey pallor. Her friend was exhausted.

Once again, she placed her hand on the sword, then reached out with her mind to find Dominic, just like she did when they practiced mind to mind communication. Sensing his barrier, she pulled a trickle of healing magic from her weapon and guided it towards that barrier.

'Hey, what are you doing?'

Concentrating only on the task at hand, she ignored his question and kept feeding him the healing strength until he no longer looked grey and the weariness around his eyes was almost gone. Releasing the sword, she found herself face to face with a very angry Dominic.

'What do you think you are doing?'

'Giving you energy. From the look of you, you needed a boost.'

'I do not need your energy,' the spy forced out through gritted teeth.

Annoyed at his reaction, and not understanding why he turned this into a big issue, Aliah's own temper flashed.

'Do not be such a baby. I did not deplete my own resources to assist you, it came from the sword. And rest assured, it would not have allowed me to continue if I was doing anything wrong.'

'You think that is why I am upset?' Her companion stopped his horse and she followed suit.

'If you are not worried about me, why are you so grumpy?'

'You broke through my personal barriers without my consent.'

'I did not.' Indignation fuelled her anger to new heights. 'You told me that was incredibly intrusive, so I have been careful to respect your boundaries and not enter your space unless invited.'

Confusion clouded Dominic's face. 'How did you feed me energy then?'

'I fed the energy to your actual barrier, your body absorbed it and did the rest.'

Smirking, Dominic said, 'I might have known you could not get through my barrier by yourself.'

Kicking his horse, Dominic headed off after the others. Resentment and rage warred inside of Aliah. All he thought to say was a

582

smart comment. No word of thanks. No apology for falsely accusing her. How dare he treat her gift like that! And how dare he underestimate her abilities! She would show him exactly what she was capable of.

Without thinking, she sent her thoughts after Dominic, quickly found his barrier, slipped through and into his mind. Instead of the normal bland room he allowed her into previously, she found herself in a rainbow coloured cloud. Before finding herself booted out, she learnt why entering someone's mind unasked was such a mistake. His mind was filled with an overwhelming sense of loneliness and anger. Then, behind his fury at her actions she found admiration, exasperation and ... love.

Thoughts in disarray, she found herself frozen in place, not quite knowing what to do next. When she came to her senses Dominic was in front of her, his face carefully schooled to give nothing of his emotions away.

'Oh, Dominic ... I ...'

Before she completed her thought, the boy who was in love with her cut in.

'Do not say a word. Those were my private feelings. It was my decision whether to share them with you, or to keep them to myself. You have taken that choice from me and that makes me beyond angry. I am also saddened because I can no longer trust you enough to carry on with your training.

'As we need to focus on making sure Aria is not overrun by a god, I do not have the luxury of walking away from you, which is what my gut is telling me I should do. So, for now, we will pretend this moment never happened.'

Before Dominic could steer his mount away, Aliah did something she did not know was even possible to do. Reaching out with her mind, she grabbed what she could of Dominic, and drew him back into her, laying herself bare.

Apologising the only way she knew how, she allowed him to experience her shame at her own actions. She let him know of her own confusion, of her desire for his good opinion, and how she thought she was a better person with him around. She allowed him full access to all the other confusing emotions and feelings swirling in her mind. More importantly though, she showed him how devastated she was knowing she had lost their friendship because of one act of pique.

Loneliness overtook her as he withdrew from her head and met her gaze with his own.

'I am still angry with you,' he said, and paused for a moment as if carefully considering his next words. 'In time, I might forgive your intrusion into my thoughts, but it is clear we have much more to consider, and perhaps even more to talk about. This is such bad timing.'

Oh no, Aliah thought. *I have lost him before I found out if we have a future together. I am such a fool.*

The silence drew out to an uncomfortable length, before Dominic finally said, 'We should forget this ever happened,'

Embarrassment and confusion raced through her. She was not sure she heard him correctly. 'You want us to forget everything?'

Dominic placed a hand on her arm. 'I mean to say, we need to move beyond your thoughtless breach of protocol, and mark it up to a learning experience. If you promise never to do such a thing again, I promise to try and move past it. But, if you really want us to forget everything, we can do that too. We can agree to never speak of today, and what we have found out about each other, again.'

'No,' Aliah gasped as he finished speaking.

'Good, because it is not what I want either.'

Hope fluttered in the pit of her stomach, but she pushed it back down.

'What do you want?'

'I want to be back in Bannock courting a girl I rather like, finding out if she is the one who will cause me to set aside my wandering ways and settle down.'

The words were tinged with sadness, and Aliah understood why.

'That would be perfect, but it is not going to happen any time soon, if ever,' she said.

'So, what I want and what I must do are two different things. What I must do is make sure my Princess Warrior is as prepared as she is able to be to face and defeat a god. If I do that, then I may one day get my wish.'

'I can see it is in my best interests to make your wish come true.'

'Hurry up, you two.' Daniel, who had been riding rear guard, dropped back to join them. 'Quit mooning about, Baron George's men have nearly caught us up. If you do not pick up the pace, they will beat us to the Rasmussen place.'

Dominic was first to break eye contact, before he fell in beside the guardsman he said under his breath, 'If you ever enter my mind without permission again though ...' He left her own imagination to fill in the blanks.

Although his tone was playful, Aliah heard the steel beneath the words and her stomach churned as shame at her actions arose anew. Although now a hopeful butterfly also fluttered in there as well. Pushing both feelings aside, Aliah nudged her mount and rejoined the others, ready to focus on the task ahead.

ALIAH SHIFTED UNCOMFORTABLY in her saddle, happy to see the end of the day's journey in sight. They had kept a steady pace all day so as to maintain a reasonable distance between themselves and Baron George's men, barely even stopping for lunch. Her body was so weary, she had resorted more than once to drawing some energy using her sword, but refrained from offering a magical boost to anyone else.

As their party clattered into the stone courtyard in front of the baronial manor, they found Baron Rasmussen already there, seemingly mustering his men. It reminded Aliah of Robin's quick rundown of the baron, who had recently been awarded the vacant property for services to the duchy. It had only been a few moons since he left his post as Guard Captain, and brought his wife to this remote spot.

The tall, well built man flicked his blond hair out of the way and looked about in surprise as they entered. However, gratitude soon filled his blue eyes as he heard they were followed by a guard contingent from his neighbour.

'Your arrival could not have been more timely. One of my patrols arrived back a short while ago to report unusual activity by the pass to the costal lands. They believe some men may have passed through last evening, or perhaps early this morning.

'I am about to send these men out to begin securing the top of the track, while the bulk of my men prepare to leave in the morning to begin fortifying in earnest. I would welcome the assistance of the guards you say are coming from Baron George, as my men alone would not be able to hold the pass from a serious attack for long.'

'Perhaps we might ride along with you and be of some assistance ourselves,' Aliah offered as the baron helped her down from her mount.

From the look on the baron's face, Aliah understood he was struggling with something, and waited more patiently than she was used to for his response. When it was not forthcoming, she said, 'You can be direct with me, if you think we will be more of a hinderance than a help then I am prepared to hear your reasoning.'

Smiling with relief, the baron took her arm and escorted her towards the hall.

'I do not know how many men slipped through the pass, and I am only sending out a small force tonight. I would rather they concentrated on the job at hand than being worried about the safety of such an important person as yourself, Your Highness.'

Aliah laughed at his forthrightness. 'Baron, while I can look after myself, I appreciate your concern, and will abide by your direction.'

A slight blush rose to the baron's cheeks, but he surprised her with his next comment. 'I am sure Baron George's men would welcome the opportunity of a night's rest before engaging the enemy, and you yourself might like to enjoy the luxury of a bath before eating tonight. Then you can all ride out with the rest of my men in the morning, feeling refreshed and ready to face anything.'

Laughing out loud, Aliah could see why Duke Damon had raised this man to his current position, and she responded, 'Baron I think you have missed your calling. You would fit in well with the diplomats at my father's court.'

Embolden by her response, the baron pushed his hand a little. 'I hope you will forgive me, Princess, but with your leave I would like to ride out with my men to see what is going on for myself.'

Aliah smiled. 'Baron, in times of war the people's safety must be placed before social niceties. I am sure your wife will see us well looked after, and you no doubt would not be such good company worrying about what is going on elsewhere.'

Bowing, and thanking the princess, the baron quickly excused himself as the baroness deftly took charge and saw them to their quarters.

She chatted non-stop to Aliah as she escorted her to her rooms. Born in Port Hand, she was not yet used to life on the quiet plateau, so took great pleasure from their company. By the time Aliah arrived at her room she found there was already a wooden tub inside, and a maid had begun the process of filling it with hot water.

Sighing out loud, she thanked the young woman for her thoughtfulness. Closing the door behind her, Aliah intended to make the most of this little luxury. So relaxed was she, she was still in the tub herself when the dinner going sounded.

Having rushed to meet with the others, Aliah was able to relax during the meal as Daniel and Dominic plied the young woman with stories, each trying to capture the pretty girl's attention. She and Amelia politely answered questions, and made the occasional comment when required, but both were clearly exhausted.

Aliah excused herself early saying she was tired from the constant travel. She had not found the opportunity to tell anyone she had been in contact with Seamus, and that was really why she was going, because she wanted to talk with him tonight before she was too tired. Amelia had looked at her with concern, but said nothing, and Aliah promised herself she would explain everything tomorrow.

Back in her room, she stilled her mind and reached out for Seamus.

CHAPTER 42

MAGIC IS ALIVE ON HAND

After his nocturnal activities, Seamus spent sleepless hours pondering how to place the god in the casket and send him back at least to the mid-plane so the other gods could deal with him. He almost had it worked out, except he did not yet know how the name fitted into it all, nor had he had any inspiration as to what Aliah would be doing while he fought the god.

Forcing himself to rise as sunlight crept through a gap in the curtains, he hurried to join the others in the stables preparing for the journey ahead. Once on the road, instead of enjoying his first opportunity to be outside in days, Seamus sunk deep into his own thoughts, determined to work out how to use the last piece of the puzzle. He also still needed to formulate a Plan B for defeating the god, if they failed with the casket and he made it to Aria.

Would it be possible to somehow use worshippers of the goddess if the god managed to reunite with his physical form? Then an idea hit him, worshipping a god made a connection and thinned the veil between worlds. Seamus realised it was no mistake Aria was the site chosen to battle the god. Worship of the goddess was strong here, so perhaps the veil was thinner. Was there some way he could use that to their advantage?

'Seamus? Seamus? Are you all right? You are not really with us this morning.' Emer had pulled her horse up alongside his.

'I am sorry. I have just been imagining my meagre magical abilities coming up against the enormous power of a god in all his glory. Every time I think about us facing down such a formidable foe, all I imagine are mice nibbling at the feet of a giant. At any time, he might decide to simply blast us with a fireball, and it is all over. I cannot see myself coming out of this alive.'

Shoulders slumped, Seamus avoided looking at Emer, not wanting to face her disappointment in him reflected on her face. A gentle hand was placed on his arm. Understanding—that was even worse. The hand gripped his arm tightly, almost painfully.

'I loathe self-pity, pull yourself together. If the gods thought an all out battle was needed to defeat our enemy do you not think they would have the sense to ensure you were given enough power to fight him head on. They are seven of the most powerful beings in the universe, yet they were unable to stop him.

'This suggests something different is needed to defeat him. Your magic is different, something never given to another human, and you yourself are different. You and Aliah have unique powers, and unique ways of approaching things. Perhaps you should spend less time worrying about what you cannot do, and more time thinking about how you can use what you have to your advantage.

'A single rumour can bring down a leader more effectively than an army. So we mice can definitely bring down a giant.'

Seamus found the courage to look up into Emer's face and saw, not anger, but determination written there. Straightening his shoulders and sitting more erect in his saddle, he decided there and then to stop feeling sorry for himself and start believing there might be a way for them to win this battle.

Sometime later, as grey clouds threatened rain, they arrived at the entrance to Baron Wexler's estate. The tall wrought iron gate was locked closed, guarded from inside by four burly men who did not look welcoming at all. With his new found confidence, Seamus urged his horse forward and took control of the situation.

'I am Lord Seamus, and I wish to speak to your master on behalf of the Duke of Hand.'

Under any other circumstances his words would have caused the gates to be swept open and he would be beside a fire, drink in hand, in less than a candle-mark. In this instance, the men did not move a muscle.

'Did you not hear Lord Seamus?' Liam moved his mount alongside.

'We heard, but we have our orders. No one is to enter the estate until morning.' The man who spoke left the group and approached the fence. 'You are welcome to make camp where you are, and tomorrow I will escort you to the baron myself.'

Flummoxed by the response, Seamus was unsure what to do next. 'Why? Why can he not meet with me now?'

'That is his business.'

In the face of such obstinacy there was no obvious path to take. Turning around, Seamus rejoined his companions.

'What now?' Emer asked

Unsure whether to be annoyed at being denied entrance, or relieved he had not needed to face the baron today after a sleepless night, Seamus considered options as he surveyed their surroundings. The forest they had ridden through for the last candle mark or so thinned out near the gates, and the wrought iron fence surrounded the baron's land for as far as they could see. Beyond the boundary, tussocky hills led down towards the coast.

'How much do you want to bet the baron could not afford to put such a high fence around the entire boundary of his property?'

'You are thinking of sneaking in and finding out what he is up to?' Liam's eyes glimmered with excitement in the fading light.

'Are you sure that is wise? It is a very confrontational thing to do.'

Walter, as ever counselled caution, but Seamus was not ready to listen. Although part of him wanted to delay the meeting and get some sleep, he knew their cause would be better served by confronting the baron tonight. Besides, after days stuck in a library his body longed for some action. Then there was this nagging feeling he had had for the last candle mark or so, a feeling he really needed to meet with the baron today.

'Come on.' Turning his horse to the left, he headed off along the boundary line. For the benefit of the guards he threw back over his shoulder, 'We should find a more secluded spot and set up camp for the night.'

SKIRTING the tree-line near the barrier, they rode for another candle mark without finding a break in the fence line. As the sun began to set, colouring the sky with crimsons and purples, they came to the end of the enclosure.

Groaning, Seamus halted his weary horse and slid from the saddle. Leaving the animal to nibble on some grass, he walked towards the edge of the cliff and looked down. Iron spikes continued more than a body length down the face of the cliff. Below was a sheer drop into the swirling rocky depths of the sea.

'Who would have thought the baron would fence his entire property?' he said the words mostly for his own benefit. 'What a waste of time. We may as well make camp for the night and go and meet with Wexler tomorrow as the guard suggested.'

As he said the words, Seamus still searched for another way in. He could not shake the feeling it was important he reach the baron tonight. Walter joined him, staring out to sea.

'If you are intent on finding out what the baron is up to, I believe I can help.'

Unwilling to raise his hopes, Seamus cautiously asked, 'How?'

'I can bring a tree from the forest down on top of the fence and we can use it to climb over.'

'Could you not have suggested that before we rode all this way.' Unable to keep the frustration from entering his voice, the hurt in his friend's eyes made him instantly sorry for snapping.

'I was not sure breaking in was our best course of action. Also I did not really want to use magic in broad daylight on Hand.'

'I am sorry, Walter. I spoke thoughtlessly,' Seamus apologised. 'Your suggestion is a good one. Let us set up camp and eat something. When it is dark, we can bring down your tree and take a look at what the baron is going to such pains to hide. You can remain behind if you do not approve.'

Leaning back against the trunk of a tree, Seamus gazed into the fire. His belly full, he no longer felt such a burning need to enter Wexler's domain. It would be so easy to curl up in a blanket by the fire and get a good night's sleep. Still, a niggling thought pestered him, compelling him to move.

Just as he was about to stir himself to action, he felt a tugging at the edge of his thoughts. Something had been nagging him all day, but this was different. Almost as though someone was knocking to get in.

Aliah?

As soon as he thought her name, there she was, inside his head.

What is it, is there something wrong? Seamus asked, sensing Aliah was not her usual self.

No. Well, yes, but nothing you can help with. Nothing to do with our upcoming battle, she was quick to reassure him.

Seamus was not so easily put off. *Anything that has you so worried I can sense it, needs to be dealt with before we face the god. If we are distracted when we fight him, it will lessen our chance of success.*

It is ... well, it is personal.

I can help with personal.

Umm ...

593

Aliah, what did you do to Dominic? I knew it would not be easy, you two mind linking, especially given the way you feel about each other.

What do you mean? Aliah was immediately defensive.

Laughing, Seamus answered. *Well, given the fact you like each other, it cannot have been easy.*

You knew?

Aliah, we all know. I think you were the only people who had not acknowledged the fact. At least now it is out in the open.

Oh, Seamus, I broke into his mind and that is how I found about his feelings for me.

Although Seamus felt her shame at the action, he could not stop himself. *You did that after lecturing me about over-taking a mind.*

Waves of shame rolled of Aliah, and Seamus regretted his words.

We are all entitled to one mistake, and I can tell from how you are now you are unlikely to make the same one again. Dominic will forgive you given time. You need to stop beating yourself up and forgive yourself.

Rather than continuing the conversation, Aliah changed the subject, clearly not yet ready to let herself off the hook.

Are you with Baron Wexler?

No, we have not been let onto the baron's lands. Something is up here.

Oh? Are you going to do something about it? Aliah asked. *It is kind of urgent we find out whether or not the chest we need is there.*

Thank you for stating the obvious. As it happens, we are planning to break in soon and find out what he is hiding.

Aliah chuckled. *I bet Walter is ecstatic about that.*

Not really, he would like us to wait until tomorrow.

I bet he would. Are you totally sure you should not wait? I mean, much as we are on a strict timeline here, we do not want to get off on the wrong foot with the baron.

Seamus considered his response, he found it hard to put into words the need he had to find out what was going on tonight. *Maybe it is premonition, or maybe it is just a gut feeling, but I think I need to find out what is happening today. I will be careful though, and try not to do anything to upset the baron too much.*

If we carry on talking there will not be much of the night left for you to break in. I should let you go, Aliah said.

Yes, I guess so.

Seamus was reluctant to break contact. Everything always seemed so much clearer in his mind when Aliah was near.

Seamus, thank you. Aliah's voice broke into his reverie.

Huh?

Thank you for listening, I feel so much better now. Let me know how you get on tonight if you have a chance, otherwise I will see you at the rendezvous the day after tomorrow.

With that she was gone and he was left alone again, wondering what on earth he was doing. Reluctantly, he drew his gaze back to the fire. As he did, the nagging feeling he had been experiencing returned, and he sighed as if he carried the weight of the world on his shoulders.

Turing to the man seated beside him, he said, 'Walter, it is time. Can you please bring down the tree for us?'

'I am sure with your magical training you are able to do it yourself now I have given you the idea.'

About to agree, Seamus stopped himself. When he attempted to clear a path in a forest to escape pursuers once before, he had been flooded with the pain the vegetation endured as he forced it to do something against its nature.

'I think it best you do it. My magic connects me to the earth in some way, and I suffer the consequences of any such magical actions,' Seamus explained.

'Interesting, yet you suffered no backlash when you used magic on a living being when you struck down the King of Carsten.' Walter stroked his beard as he considered the implications.

'This is not the time to discuss magical theory.' Emer pulled Walter's attention back to the task at hand as she stood and picked up her sword and knife. 'If we are to survey the lay of the land and still get some sleep tonight, we need to get moving.'

Liam joined her, and Seamus unwillingly rose and reached for his own weapons. Having placed a knife in the sheath at his side, one in each of his boots, and a fourth in a special sheath on his forearm under his shirt, he was ready to go.

'I will take you up on your offer to stay behind,' Walter informed them as he motioned for the three youngsters to stand behind him. 'I am too old for daytime rides followed by night-time adventuring. Besides, I am still not sure this is the best way to get the baron on our side.'

Lowering a sturdy tree onto the fence, Walter held it in place while Liam led them upwards. Tying a rope to one of the branches hanging over the other side, Liam shimmied down, followed by Emer.

Before he climbed up, Seamus turned to Walter. 'I know you do not approve of what we are doing, but I cannot help thinking we need to be here tonight. I am sure something important is going to happen. Keep your eyes and mind open, we may need your help.'

'I will try not to fall asleep, but these old bones are weary after travelling today, so I cannot promise anything.'

Chuckling to himself, Seamus hurried up the tree and dropped down over the other side. Before catching up with the others, he heard the earth groan as the older wizard placed the tree back in its original position.

THE ESTATE on this side of the wall was similar to the untended countryside on the other side. Near the costal cliffs the grass was short and scrubby, changing to pasture moving more inland. There were small copses of trees dotted around, intermingled with groups of hardy shrubs. A quick scan of the area showed nothing was moving in between the trees, and Seamus was confident they were alone for the moment.

'Do you smell that?' Emer asked as Seamus joined them.

Sniffing the air, he caught a whiff of something, but could not make out what it was. 'Sort of.'

'A large fire has been lit close by, or a number of small ones. Somewhere over that way.' She pointed along the coast. 'Should we head over there, or sneak up to the house?'

Seamus did not hesitate. 'We head for the fires. All day I have had a niggling sensation. When I try to reach out, the energy around me feels strange. Something is up. I aim to find out what, and it is more likely to be at the beach than in the manor.'

'What makes you say that?' Emer asked.

'Well, I think we would be able to see lights on in the manor from here, and yet it is dark. Besides, I just have this feeling,' Seamus responded.

Beside him Liam tensed, then shrugged as if trying to loosen his limbs. 'I always thought I was all right with magic. When I thought about people having it, I felt no fear like some on Hand.

'In practice though, I find it gives me the heebie jeebies. All this talk about feeling and sensing energies around us unsettles me.'

'Why did you not say anything Liam? I had not realised it made you uncomfortable to be around me. I would have sent you with Aliah, and asked Boss to come with us if I had known.'

Seamus' concern for his cousin's wellbeing overrode his disappointment at Liam not being able to accept magic as a part of him. Pausing briefly to punch Seamus on the arm, Liam laughed.

'You dolt, if I had grown up with magic around me, I would find it as normal as swinging a sword. It is only fear of the unknown, and I will not allow it to control my life. Besides, my place is by your side, and being jittery about something so silly will not stop me from being with you.'

'If you boys have finished having your moment, I think it would be a good idea for me to change and range ahead,' Emer interrupted them. 'With my improved night vision in wolf form I should be able to scout out any problems.'

'Oh, yes, of course. Sorry, I should have planned this better instead of focusing on the fact I wanted to find out what we were being excluded from.'

'It is not up to you to think of everything, we are a team, remember?' Emer changed as she spoke, then, with a flick of her tail, her wolf form strode off into the night.

'That is so amazing. Why is your magic not as incredible as Emer's?'

'So sensing things is creepy, but totally changing form is not? How is it I never noticed how weird you are?'

Continuing their whispered banter as they walked, calmed Seamus' nerves, making their outing seem more like an amble along the coastal cliffs than a midnight mission to find the cause of a disturbance in magical forces. So engrossed were they in trading insults, they started and banged into each other when Emer-wolf appeared in front of them. She changed back before reporting.

'A little further ahead is a path winding down to a cove. On the beach are about four or five fires, with a handful of guards sitting around each one. At first glance, it looks like they are having a relaxing meal, but they are all fully armed, and they search about as if expecting an attack.'

'Could you see anything to tell you why they are gathered?' Recovering from the collision first, Liam was also quicker to begin assessing the situation.

'I could not. A wolf atop a cliff face observing activity would be considered quite normal. One walking on a sandy beach, not so much.'

Not to be outdone by his cousin's recovery speed, Seamus felt the need to contribute his wisdom. 'We will not be able to see anything from the top, one of us needs to go down and find out what is going on.'

'I can quietly slip down and look around.' Liam made as if to go.

'I am not sure you are our best option,' Seamus placed a hand on his cousin's arm before he moved too far away. 'With so many fires in a confined space, I assume the cove is well lit with no shadows for even the most agile of boys to hide in.'

'That is correct. They are strategically placed to ensure the guards can see anyone approaching from land or sea.'

'So a wolf on the beach would be remarked upon, as would an eagle flying at night?'

'Yes, Seamus, this is one time when my animal forms will not be of any help.'

'I would not say that. As a wolf, your improved vision will be useful helping Liam guard the top of the cliff while I go down and find out what is happening on the beach.'

A snort escaped from Liam, and he placed a hand over his mouth to stop any more getting out. When he regained his composure, he removed his hand and spoke. 'If I cannot sneak in there, Seamus, how do you expect to? When it comes to stealth, you are like a stampeding horse compared to my mouse.'

Although he would like to deny the charge, Liam was correct. In normal circumstances, the shorter, slighter boy was far better at moving undetected. In this instance though, he believed he might have an added advantage.

When he found out Dominic was able to blend into the background, he had tried to mimic the ability using his own magic. Unable to disappear like the spy, he asked for a lesson. No matter how hard he tried he could not do it. Not even when Dominic let him in on the secret words he used when he first found out he had the ability to become invisible. Saying, "you cannot see me" had no effect at all for Seamus.

Since then, he had been trying to find a way to make himself invisible at will using his own magic. If he could not blend into the background, he wondered if his ability to connect to people might be used to influence their minds, convincing them they could not see him.

Having moved stealthily to the edge of the cliff overlooking the cove, Seamus pondered some more how he might influence the thoughts of others as Emer changed back into a wolf. Shrugging his shoulders, he decided there was no time like the present to try. In his mind he formulated an idea; "Seamus just disappeared before my very eyes". Once the thought emerged crystal clear in his mind, he took hold of it and gently pushed it out towards Liam and Emer in much the same way he pushed his mind out to connect with Aliah.

Liam looked at him quizzically, but it was clear he could still see Seamus. Pushing a little harder he was rewarded with a look of complete shock on the other boy's face. As Liam searched around, Seamus turned to find Emer's head cocked to the side.

What are you doing to Liam?

I told you both I disappeared. Seamus mind spoke to her so as to remain silent.

You did? I can still see you, but your body is shimmering, like my eyes cannot quite focus on you. Perhaps your trick does not work as well on animals? Or maybe on magic users. It is risky to assume there will be no magic users below.

I think it will be worth the risk, unless you have a better idea.

'Seamus?' Liam hissed loudly, 'Where are you? This is not the time to play tricks.'

Releasing the thought, Liam stumbled in shock as Seamus appeared before him. Reacting quickly, he grabbed Liam's arm before he fell back over the edge of the cliff.

'What the goddess are you playing at?' If they had not been trying to stay undetected, Liam would have yelled the words. As it was, he hissed them loud enough to startle Seamus.

'Calm down, would you? I needed to find out whether I was able to creep through the guards without them seeing me. This is new, and I thought it would not be such a great idea to find I could not do it in the middle of hostile guardsmen.'

'Well, you might have warned a soul rather than scaring them half to death.' Grumbling, Liam attempted to regain his composure. 'I guess you are the best to find out what is going on, after all.'

Will you be able to influence so many minds? Emer-wolf asked.

'Emer just asked if I would be able to convince a number of people I am not there. It is a good question, and the truthful answer is I am not sure. Perhaps for a short time—time enough to find what I need to, I hope.'

'Most days I am a little sad for you,' Liam mused. 'You have to stay away from your family because of your magic, you have this great destiny to fulfil and your life is constantly in danger. Then you do something incredible like you just did, and I come down with a huge case of envy.'

'I would gladly switch places. Just say the word and I will ask if the gods would agree.'

Holding his hands up in front, Liam shook his head. 'No, I am good.'

Once again, Seamus, while this bonding is all well and good, can we please do what we need to and get out of here? I sense a change in the air, and I think the sooner we are on the other side of the fence with Walter, the better.

Emer's anxiety caused Seamus to pause, maybe Walter was right. In light of their larger goals was it sensible to go rushing into danger tonight? Emer flicked her tail and headed off into the night. Liam followed after.

'I guess we are doing this,' Liam said as he departed.

'I guess we are,' Seamus affirmed, realising the decision had been made for him.

A warm orange glow from the fires below lit the pathway down to the cove. Emer led them to a clump of scrub large enough for them to hide behind while they surveyed the scene below.

'Look,' Liam pointed. 'The fires are arranged in a semi-circle around that particular part of the cliff. That formation is common in military training books. I would say they are guarding something along the wall.'

Nodding his head in agreement, Seamus plotted the shortest way through the groups of men to the point in the centre of the arc of fires.

'All right, wish me luck.'

Do not cast your thoughts until the absolute last minute. Bending so many minds to your vision will quickly drain you, so you need to limit the amount of time you send them.

Emer sent her warning as he reached the beginning of the path. Trusting her experience with magic, instead of walking down, he dropped to his bottom and slid towards the beach.

The trip down took longer than walking, but it was worth it to conserve his magic. At the last bend before the cove, he stopped. In his head he started forming a thought; "I cannot see anyone walking through the fires".

Screwing up his face, he scrubbed that idea. Surely it would suggest they should be looking for someone, and they might look all the more closely. This was going to be harder than he thought. Perhaps he should have planned this better before starting out, maybe even tested it on Liam some more.

Running through ideas in his mind, he eventually found one he believed might work. Closing his eyes to concentrate, he began forming an idea; "What is that noise? Is it oars? Someone is coming to attack us from the sea". He lay on his stomach and popped his head around a tussock, looking towards the first couple of groups of men.

He let the thought go. Gently at first, then with more force as he saw a few of the men turn and peer out to sea. When all the guards in his line of sight were looking away, he rose to his feet. Fortunately, he was greeted with the sight of everyone on the beach searching the ocean for something. Not knowing how long the illusion of an invasion from the sea would last, he rushed towards the area Liam previously pointed out.

As he drew closer, he spotted a cave entrance. Not much taller than him, and very narrow, he turned sideways to enter. The flickering glow from inside told him whatever he searched for was likely to be in there.

Once through the opening, the tunnel widened a little and

natural steps in the rocks led upwards. Torches were spaced at regular intervals, illuminating the pathway. Steadily climbing, he slipped on seaweed and sea slime left by the tides, sometimes losing his footing. The steps rose until he passed the high tide line and the path cleared of debris.

Turning a corner, the path widened out into a cave so enormous he could not make out the roof, let alone the other side. In the centre stood an altar, and before the altar, with his back to Seamus, knelt a man dressed in plain brown robes. On hearing his footsteps, the man rose to his feet and turned.

SQUINTING INTO THE SHADOWS, the man by the altar asked, 'Are you real, or an apparition?'

'Oh, sorry.'

So engrossed was he in reaching his goal, Seamus had forgotten to release his mind cast. A mistake he fixed immediately.

'Definitely real,' the stocky grey haired man acknowledged moments later. 'Seamus, I believe, I am Gareth Wexler. You certainly took your time getting here.'

'You knew I would come?'

'I have been calling out to you all day, asking you to come. I was unsure whether you could hear me. All I could do was hope you would respond in time.'

'How?' A flash of inspiration. 'Your family has the gift of calling. You used magic to draw me here. That explains the feeling I have had most of today.'

Sheepishly the man shrugged his response. 'Guilty as charged. If you felt the pull, what took you so long?'

'Your ... your guards turned me away at the gates.'

'What?' The baron was genuinely surprised.

'When we arrived earlier this evening, the guards at your gates informed us you were not available until tomorrow. I am only here because I had a strong urge to find out what was going on.'

Baron Wexler's amiable countenance changed to concern, then outright fear as he glanced around the cavern, nervously checking the shadows.

'Come. I suspect we shall soon have visitors, so we had best get this over with.'

'You can just give me the casket and I will go.'

'You must know by now nothing to do with the gods is that easy. There are two sets of instructions I am to pass on before I hand you the casket.

'If you have chosen to fight the god before he appears and cast him from this world, the first thing you must do is bind him securely, making him as small as possible, before placing him in the casket.'

'I guessed that. Can I please just take it and go?' A deep sense of foreboding ran through Seamus, causing him to forget his usual good manners.

'The next is the most important piece of information you need so, no, I will not hand over the chest my family has guarded for generations until I have completed the task I have been set.'

With little grace, and more than a little impatience, Seamus offered, 'Go on.'

'After you capture him, the god must leave this plane. One of the gods took me between the planes a few nights ago so I could describe the experience to you.'

The baron shivered from head to toe as he remembered.

'The god appeared in my room, sat on my bed and began explaining the universe is like an onion, made up of many layers. We live on an outer layer, the gods inhabit the innermost one. In between each layer is a skin shielding it from the others. As you move towards the middle, the protecting membrane gets thicker.

'Having told me this, he pushed me from this plane to the next and pulled me back. He asked me to describe my experience. I did, and after that he instructed me to call you today and repeat what I told him word for word. I will do that now.

'As I was pushed from our world, I hit what appeared to be incredibly dense water. I sort of squelched through it like when you pull your foot out of mud. For a brief moment I was encased in the substance, then there was a popping sound, and I was on the other side. When he pulled me back through, the whole thing happened in reverse.'

Closing his eyes, Seamus tried to imagine the journey. 'Was your body transported?'

'Oh, that is an interesting question. Let me think. It did not feel like I was moving, it felt more like I was dreaming or imagining what was going on. Does that help?'

'Yes, you have no idea how much. You have given me the final piece of the puzzle I need to rid the world of the god presence.'

'I told you the second part was the most important. Now, although there is much I wish to ask you, I appreciate time is short ...'

'Wait, wait a minute.' Seamus stopped the baron. 'All your instructions are about dealing with the god if he has not joined with his body. Have you nothing to offer should the god arrive in his full form?'

Pausing before he answered, the baron said, 'My family have guarded the casket and we have kept the law of how the Wizard and Warrior are to use it. I guess the gods assumed if we gave it to you, you would know what you needed to do.'

Seamus nodded. 'That makes sense. I am sorry this meeting has been so short, but I must really go now.'

'Perhaps once this is over, we can compare—who are you?'

Seamus turned, following the baron's gaze and audibly gasped when he saw who stood behind him.

'I hoped to be a little quieter, but it does not matter. The chest will still be mine, regardless of who guards it.'

With a flick of his hand, Millard sent a wave of power. Without thinking, Seamus threw up a defensive wall of air around himself and Wexler. He was not quick enough to save the baron. Millard's attack flung the older man against the wall. Crashing to the floor, the old man lay motionless. Running to his side, Seamus was pleased to see him still breathing.

In the moment he looked to the older man's safety, Millard made it to the chest and reached out to pick it up.

'I would not do that if I were you. You know what happened last time we met,' Seamus threatened as he wondered what he would actually do if Millard ignored him. Almost as if he sensed Seamus was not prepared for this confrontation, the wizard scooped the chest up in one arm as he flung a fire bolt from his other hand. Seamus managed to roll away just in time. Jumping to his feet, he paused, glancing down at the injured man beside him.

'Ah ... what?'

Baron Wexler attempted to raise himself up on one elbow in time to see Millard slip through the opening. 'What ... what are you waiting for, boy? Get after him. Send one of the guards of the brotherhood to me if you get a chance.'

As the baron lay back down, Seamus took off after the man who had stolen the one thing he really needed to dispel a god.

CLOSE ON THE wizard's heels, Seamus urged his legs to pump faster. His body was slow to respond, appearing sluggish, almost as if he were running through water or very thick air. Of course, Millard had learnt from their last encounter. To avoid a confrontation, he must have cast a spell to slow Seamus down.

Pausing, Seamus called air to himself and created a defensive shell around his body. He imagined it moving outwards, giving him enough room to take a long stride. Walking forward, he practiced moving the bubble as he walked, then ran. Freed from the wizard's constraints, he now used his youthful speed to return to the cave opening.

As he approached the exit, the ring of metal striking metal filled the night moments before something bounced him back, off his feet and onto his butt. Standing, he checked for injuries and wondered how to bypass Millard's new spell.

Shaking his head, he laughed at his own foolishness. This was not the wizard's doing, it was his own. His shield would not fit through the narrow gap. Dropping it for a moment, he turned and wedged himself through, hurriedly raising it again while he surveyed the mayhem in front of him.

Emer? Can you tell me what is going on?

Phew, we wondered if we had lost you. I watched you enter the cave. Then, from out of nowhere, soldiers appeared and rushed down to the cove. We stayed hidden, waiting to see if you needed us.

Did you see Millard enter the cave?

Millard? Are you sure?

Did you see him? Seamus asked impatiently,

I saw another shimmer after you disappeared into the wall, but then the fighting distracted me.

Seamus had no time to soothe her regrets. *Do you see him now?*

No. Seamus did you get the chest? Emer asked.

He has it, I need to find him.

Wait, Liam has just seen you. He says the only way out of the cove is up the path. Head that way and we will cut him off up here.

Heeding his friends' advice, Seamus ran towards his escape route, strengthening the shell around him to ensure any arrows or stray sword jabs slid away, leaving him to concentrate on weaving through the battle zone.

By the time he reached the pathway, a handful of Wexler's guards were in front of him, chasing a couple of fleeing intruders. Allowing his hand through the protective barrier, Seamus tapped one of them on the shoulder. Startled, the man turned and raised his sword ready to strike.

'Stop. I am Lord Seamus. The baron sent me. He is in the cave, injured. You need to send him help.'

'How do I know you are who you say you are? This could be a trick.' The guard turned as if to follow the others to the top of the cliff.

'I do not have time for this.' Seamus grumbled as he sent an image of the baron asking Seamus to get help to the guard.

The man paused, looked back towards the cave, then up the path, undecided on whether to help stop the intruders or help his lord.

'My friends are at the top of the path. They will help stop the thieves. Go to your master.'

Although his face wore his doubt like a beacon, the guard decided to help his baron. 'Thanks for the warning, I will go to our brother.'

Seamus wasted no more time, dodging around the guardsmen he began his ascent. As he reached the top, he found Liam and Emer, returned to human form, fighting beside the baron's men.

'Millard slipped by us, he headed back the way we came.' Liam managed to get out before turning to block a blow to the head.

Leaving them to their task, Seamus sped off along the coastal path, keeping his shield up just in case. About a quarter of a candle mark later, he saw a shadowy figure in front. He put on a burst of speed but, seeing his pursuer gaining, Millard did the same.

Unable to make any ground, Seamus would have sighed with relief if he had any breath to spare as he made out the dark shadows of the fence line.

Walter, can you hear me?

No need to shout, boy.

Walter, no time I need ...

It is all right, I see what is happening. Wait a moment. Done.

A she watched, Millard's feet lifted from the ground and in the blink of an eye he was flat on his back, almost as though someone had tackled him round the ankles.

Standing, still clutching the stolen chest, he rounded on Seamus, teeth bared, snarling. So strong was the hatred rolling off him, Seamus could almost see it.

'Still on your crusade, boy? You will never win. You cannot win against a god. I was sure you would have figured that out by now and run away, tail between your legs.'

'Then you do not know me or Aliah well. Can you not see if we stand by and do nothing the world as we know it will disappear into despair? You must realise the god has no intention of sharing power with you. Once he is in his own body and in this world, he will no longer need you as his minion.'

A look of cunning crossed the magician's face. It was so quickly replaced by his usual superior demeanour, Seamus was unsure of whether it had been there in the first place. 'You could join me, and together we could make sure the god never controls our land,' Millard offered. 'Together we can send him back to Carsten. They deserve him for trying to invade Aria.'

While they were talking, Seamus dropped a knife from its sheath into his hand while he worked out how to wrest the chest from Millard before he found a way to escape and deliver it to the god. Then it dawned on him, Millard had no intention of handing the chest over to anyone.

This changed everything. Now he needed to get the artefact back before Millard decided to use it for his own ends.

Seamus, do you realise he is quite mad?

Yes, I know. Let me concentrate. Protect yourself any way you know how, just in case.

'Millard, you and I both know our god friend will not give up that easily. He would hunt us for the rest of our days. How about you help Aliah and I rid the world of his presence, and we can talk to her father about reinstating you to your position on the Wizard Isle? Or perhaps he can find you a barony if you prefer.'

A glimmer of hope flickered in Millard's eye. Appealing to his need for recognition seemed to be working. Regrettably, the look left as swiftly as it appeared, replaced by a shining mania.

Walter, he is really unhinged. This is not going to end well.

'I am worth more, boy. I set out to be ruler of this great nation, and I shall settle for nothing less. Watch and learn.'

Swinging the casket round in front of his body, he rested his other hand on the top.

'Wait, Millard. You do not know what you are doing.'

'In here is enough power to turn me into a god. I will be the most powerful being in all of Aria.'

Jerking the lid up, a golden glow spilled from the box, covering Millard. Dropping the chest to the ground, he swung his arms out wide, and looked up at the sky as he opened himself to absorb the power released from the magical artefact.

'Ahhh ...' a sound of pure bliss escaped from his lips.

Seamus, frozen in place, watching his chance of dispatching a god drawn into the mad magician. At the same time, he reached out with his own gift, attempting to close the lid of the chest before Millard released all the stored energy. Neither air nor earth were able to help him as the power being released from its centuries old prison was too strong, thwarting every attempt. Mesmerised and unable to prevent what happened next, Seamus stood by, hopelessly watching his chance of saving Aria slip away.

'Ahhhhhhh ...' The noise was no longer one of joy, but a rising screech of pain as the wizard's face contorted to reflect his inner battle.

Millard's body was not capable of taking in the torrent of energy it called forth, and had begun to expand and bloat. The wizard's eyes widened in fear as he realised the inevitable conclusion to his action only moments before his body blew apart.

Blinded by the explosion, Seamus belatedly threw up a protective shield. Ringing in his ears blocked out any noise, and as his eyes adjusted to the darkness, he realised he now stood at the edge of a gaping crater.

Walter? he urgently sent out.

You are yelling again.

Walters grumbling tones were drowned out by the buzzing in his ears as it became a roar, and he tingled all over from the top of his head to the tips of his toes. The world tilted, then went black as he slipped into unconsciousness.

CHAPTER 43

DISASTER STRIKES

'No ...'

The god released the word with such force, Gaius was hauled from his prison and into his mind. Cringing and making himself small so as not to be seen, he slunk back into his cell and shut the door. He need not have worried, the god was clearly in too much of a state to notice his presence.

'You fool, Millard, what did you do?' he shouted to the moon. 'I knew you could not resist looking inside and stealing some of the magic for yourself. You released so much I can feel it from here. Will there be enough left for me to come through?'

What had Millard done? Opening the door a little and peeking out, he allowed his senses loose for the first time in a while. He was bombarded with a multitude of magical pin-pricks, the like of which he had never experienced before.

Basking in the essence, he pulled some into himself, and squirrelled even more away in his prison. He needed to be prepared for any eventuality, and this magical energy might come in handy.

Time passed and the energy levels dwindled. Aware the god had stopped his wailing, Gaius closed the door and hunkered down, trying to piece together what happened.

The god's sense of loss overwhelmed him. What might cause such intense feelings? The casket? Then it hit him.

Millard, the sly old dog, had opened the casket and used some of the power for himself. What he felt must have been the dregs of magic the wizard had been unable to absorb. How much had the wizard released? It must have been a lot to have reached them from so far away. How big a setback was this?

Apparently the god thought it was a major one. He muttered something about having to gather additional magic to refill the casket, and how this might delay his plans.

Finally he calmed down, and turned to the small force he had been travelling with. They had spent the night hidden not far from the top of the pass. The god informed them today's operation would go ahead as planned. It was critical to their ultimate success, especially now.

As they busied themselves, the god continued to mutter under his breath about how he would punish Millard for being so wasteful when they met up tomorrow. Still, this was a minor set back, he told himself. Things would just take a little longer. He would need to gather a little more magic before he was able to be reunited with his own body.

Gaius smiled, he had more time now. Time to plot for the return of *his* body.

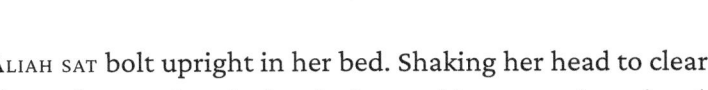

ALIAH SAT bolt upright in her bed. Shaking her head to clear away the sleep, she wondered what had scared her enough to drag her from a deep slumber. There was nothing obvious in the room, but she could not shake the feeling something was different with the world.

After tossing and turning for around half a candle mark, she could stand it no longer. Rising quickly, she dressed, packed and took her gear downstairs only to find the others waiting for her in the half light.

'You felt it too?' Amelia asked.

'Yes, what was it?'

'I do not know. I felt a huge shift in the future. Everything is now poised on a knife edge. I can see thousands of possible futures, but none clearer than any other. Every action from here on in decides Aria's future one way or the other.'

'To me it sounds as if nothing has changed.' Daniel grunted as he dropped his pack to the ground.

'Oh, there was a massive change. Before there were one of two futures; the god won, or we won. It is now as if those futures have been shattered into a thousand pieces and anything might happen.'

A frown creased Aliah's brow. 'What might cause such a change? What do we do now?'

Amelia shrugged her shoulders. 'Perhaps in one way Daniel is correct, we go on as before.'

'Breakfast is served.' A maid interrupted their discussion.

The baron met them in the dining room, and briefed them while they ate. Blockade building had started, but footprints in the area indicated a large force left the pass sometime the day before, heading around the coastal path towards Port Hand and Wexon. He suggested they stay with his guards until the pass, and that they pick up some tents for the next part of their journey.

With their party re-provisioned, they headed to the stables to find only six horses waiting for them and Robin standing, head down, looking decidedly sheepish. At their arrival he straightened up and told them his news.

'I am not continuing with you. By introducing you to the barons and working with you to ensure the pass cannot be used to invade Hand, I fulfilled my duty to the duke. Now I wish to return home.'

Aliah's initial reaction had been to let Robin go, but Dominic placed a hand on her arm, preventing her from speaking.

'Robin, we still have much to do, and we may need your skills with Baron Wexler.'

Pauley and I are sure he is up to something, and at least if he is close by, we can keep an eye on him.

'I appreciate your having so much faith in me, but my relationship with that particular baron is not good. I fear I would be more of a hinderance than a help. Besides, my mother has been unwell. I left her in the care of others while I travelled with you. It is now time I returned home and saw to her myself.'

We cannot force him to come, Dominic, especially not if he has a mother to care for. That would make him suspicious and, if his story is true, it would be downright mean.

'Of course you must go to her, Robin. We really appreciate all you did for us. I hope your mother is better soon.'

As Aliah shook the man's hand she thought she caught a look of fear in his eyes, and perhaps a little sorrow. She had no time to follow up though as Rasmussen's guards were already mounted and filing out of the courtyard.

During the first part of their journey Dominic made his displeasure known. He and Pauley had been unable to find out what the man had been up to, and the spy grumbled most of the first candle mark about how now they would never know. When Aliah remarked they should be pleased he was no longer with them as it was one less thing for them to worry about, he gave her such a withering look she decided to ride with Amelia.

At various times during the day, Aliah let her mind spread out to find Seamus, wanting to ask if he had met with the baron, and wondering if he knew what had happened overnight. She was unable to find the link to him.

With Dominic in such a bad mood she did not want to ask him what might cause this to happen, and she certainly did not want to worry Amelia about her nephew. Besides, everything was strange today, and they had only ever made contact at night before. She would try again after dinner before she raised any alarms.

As the sun slipped lower in the sky and the air began to cool, Aliah sighed with happiness as Captain Williams called a halt to their journey. The young guard rode to the back of the column, to where Aliah and her party had been travelling that day, and stopped.

'The pass is up ahead. I sent the first watch forward, and we will make our camp here. You are welcome to stay with us tonight.'

Aliah did not even wait to ask the others before giving her answer. 'Thank you, we will be happy to join you.'

'Aliah,' Daniel stopped her from continuing. 'We are close to the meeting place, perhaps we should press on and make camp there.'

Trying hard not to glare at him, she forced her body to half turn in the saddle. 'We have been riding since sun-up. I think breaking now and starting fresh tomorrow would be best for those of us unused to spending days in the saddle.'

Admitting defeat, the Arian guard drew his horse alongside his counterpart from Hand.

'If you could direct us to a camp site out of your way, we will make use of the tents your lord kindly sent for us.'

Captain Williams showed Daniel to a space at the edge of the camp, close to the path they followed that day. As they dismounted, Aliah was not the only one groaning with relief at having their feet back on the ground.

Boss and Pauley helped her set up one of the tents Baron Rassmussen loaned them, before attending to one for themselves. She would share the middle tent with Amelia, while Daniel and Dominic would sleep in the tent on the other side. One of the guards brought over some stretchers for her and Amelia, saying they did not mind the ground for one night. Grateful for their thoughtfulness, Aliah thanked the man.

With the others having tent erection in hand, Aliah offered to take their mounts to be cared for while the others finished setting up camp. When no one objected, largely because they were all so busy and had likely not heard her, she removed the saddle bags and piled them in a heap. Still no one noticed her, so she gathered the reigns and led the horses round the edge of camp towards the picket line.

'Where would you like these?' she asked the soldier tying up the last of the guards' mounts.

'Just at the end there would be fine.' He pointed down the end of the line, under some trees. 'If you tie them up, I will remove their saddles later, once I have seen to the feed and water.'

Thanking the man, she led the horses to their assigned place, and began tying them up. Halfway through her task, she heard a noise behind and turned, expecting to find the soldier had returned, but she was wrong.

Swinging around to greet him, she came face to face with the one person she had not expected to see. 'What are you doing here?' she asked a little surprised, but more annoyed at finding him here.

PAULEY PICKED up the last of the bags from the pile Aliah left for them when she took the horses. As he did, a package fell out of one of the travel packs. Picking it up to return it to its owner, it partially opened and a note fluttered to the ground.

Although his reading was not the best, the boy could not help himself. Labouring through the words, his eyes widened in astonishment as their importance sunk in.

Checking he understood, he opened the parcel and found something he had been trying to get his hands on for the last couple of days—a tin mirror. Suspicions confirmed, he ripped open the pack the mirror had fallen from. His hands trembled as he placed everything back inside and took the bag and two items to Boss.

'I think you need to see this,' he told the older man.

Taking the letter, the old soldier read it under his breath.

"I have done all you asked, even this last thing, placing the mirror in her pack. I kept up my end of the bargain, I hope you kept up yours and my mother is alive and well, and back in her cottage."

'Where did you find this?'

'It escaped from Aliah's backpack.'

'And where is ...'

Boss did not get to finish as the call to arms was issued. They were being attacked from behind.

THE CALL to arms came as Daniel and Dominic were almost finished erecting their tent. Pauley had tossed their gear just inside, and they fell over each other trying to gather their swords and escape through the tent flap. Leaving their half-collapsed accommodation, they stood side-by-side to assess the situation and identify where they could best help.

The attack had come from the back. It must have been the force who slipped through the pass the day before. Joining the lines on the far edge of the encampment, they fought side-by-side, both boys keeping an eye out for Aliah. Dominic could not believe she would miss the chance for some battle experience, and began to worry.

'You need to go find her,' Daniel shouted over the noise of the battle.

'I cannot leave you to fight alone.'

'I will join the group over there, the one holding the pass ensuring we do not get caught between two forces.'

Daniel started edging towards the soldiers in the midst of the fighting.

'Are you sure that is wise? If anything happens to you, I will never hear the end of it from Aliah.'

'I will be fine. I trained my whole life for this,' Daniel answered confidently as he began inching towards Rasmussen's men.

Dominic was not sure the guard would be fine at all, he still looked a little grey after his stomach upset, and his movements were a little sloppy, not up to Daniel's usual standards of perfection. Preparing to argue, he almost dropped his own defences when Aliah burst into his mind.

Dominic, I need your help. Come find me. I am by the horses with—

Without a further thought for Daniel, Dominic extricated himself from the battle, dodged bodies from both sides, until he arrived at the edge of camp where the horses had once been kept. Cut ropes littered the ground. There were no animals to be found and, more importantly, no Aliah.

He stopped and calmed his breathing, allowing his training to take over. Slowly he let his mind out. Grateful for their time spent practicing mind linking, he searched for the fine thread of consciousness that would guide him to her. There it was. The connection was faint, but still there. He could make her out at the edge of the battle, heading towards tomorrow's meeting place.

Sheathing his sword, he ran back to their tents. Reaching into the middle one, he grabbed the object he came for from beside Aliah's pack, and took off after the princess.

I am coming for you, he sent, but he could no longer find her.

AMELIA SAT on the fallen tree branch, her back against a boulder. Pauley stood to one side, and Boss to the other. Unbeknown to them, she cast a shield over the group so any stray arrows would fall harmlessly away. More than capable of looking after herself, she took the opportunity to keep them away from the battle by allowing them to believe she needed their protection.

Looking towards the sound of the melee she made out the shapes of the men fighting. She guessed under normal circumstances she would not be able to tell one side from the other. But as she observed without eyes, it seemed to her some of the men fought with real vigour, as if they had something to fight for. Others fought mechanically, as if they fought because they had no choice.

With her newfound insights, Amelia could also identify her close friends from the others. Two figures glowed more brightly, they fought side by side, like brothers. A dark cloud grew inside of one of them, and she knew that to be Daniel. The other figure suddenly broke away from the fighting and headed towards the edge of camp. It was then Amelia realised she had not accounted for Aliah.

'Boss, where is the princess?'

'We are not sure. Pauley and I were going to look for her when the fighting broke out.'

'Why were you looking for her?'

'Pauley found Robin's mirror in her pack, along with a letter. I think he placed the mirror there to lead someone to her.'

Amelia cast her thoughts out, searching for the Warrior. She found Dominic, but no Aliah.

'They have her,' she said.

'I thought as much. There is nothing we can do about that at the moment. If we go after her now, we will be making ourselves targets, and that will not do anyone any good.'

'Agreed,' Amelia said out loud, while thinking to herself that did not mean she had to sit back and do nothing.

Leaving her protection up, she closed her eyes and reached out to search further afield for Aliah. She knew the girl had been practicing mind talking, so would not be surprised if Amelia spoke to her. Unable to find her, she opened her eyes in time to sense Dominic running around the edge of the camp, enter a tent, then run out clutching something. He barely paused before skirting the edge of the battle and disappearing. When he did not come back into her line of sight, she reached out for him.

Dominic?

Amelia?

Yes. Where are you?

I am going after Aliah.

Do you need help?

I am not sure. Let me catch up with her and I will let you know.

Stay in touch.

Once Dominic had broken off contact, Amelia again concentrated on the fight. Enemy soldiers were being rounded up and placed under guard, the main battle was over. Searching, she tried to find Daniel. Panic welled up, she could not sense him anywhere.

No, there he was ...

On the ground.

'Boss, I need you to help me. I want to get over there to Daniel.'

A firm hand grasped her elbow and assisted her to her feet. The same hand clasped hers, and tucked it through an arm. Boss Allum led her through the debris of the camp to where she pointed. Dropping to her knees, Amelia searched for Daniel's arm, and found his wrist. Taking his pulse, she found it weak and thready.

'Daniel? Daniel? Can you hear me?'

'Amelia,' his response was almost at the level of a whisper.

'Hold still and I will try to heal you. This is not really my skill, but I might be able to do enough to stabilise you.'

As she sent her awareness into Daniel, his other hand weakly grabbed at her arm.

'Do not waste your energy.' His voice gained a little strength. 'You and I both know you would only be delaying the inevitable.'

Amelia found the cause of Daniel's pain, a wound just under the ribs, a sword had nicked his lung on the way through. The lung had collapsed, causing air to escape, and the wound bled profusely into his chest. Unless she healed the lung and stopped the bleeding, the boy would not survive.

'Daniel, I can help with this, please let me. You might live for another year or so before your disease overtakes you, or we may even find a cure in the meantime. Perhaps even Aliah's sword might be able to help,' Amelia said, attempting to convince him to fight for his life.

'I am a soldier. This is all I ever wanted. Please let me die in battle rather than waste away, being a drain on my friends and family. I do not want to see the pity in their eyes every time they look at me. I am a coward, I know. But if I die fighting for something I believe in, if I die fighting to save Aria, then my death will at least mean something.'

'But ...'

A hand dropped on to her shoulder as Boss crouched down beside her. 'These gents here say Daniel fought off three men who pinned them down. They thought they were done for. They say Daniel fought like a hero of the old tales. He saved those boys, to be sure. Let the lad die a hero if that is his wish.'

Wiping the tears from her cheek, Amelia turned back to the young guard. 'What can I do to help? Can I take away your pain?'

'I feel so light headed, the pain seems so far away.'

'That is because your body is not getting enough air.'

'If it is not too much to ask, could you hold my hand? I am not as brave as I thought.'

The tears flowed freely now as Amelia settled beside Daniel. 'I will stay with you, you are not alone.'

'Tell Aliah I am sorry I could not be there to help her at the end. I would not be much use like this ...'

'You have done so much Daniel, I think she will let you off this once.'

'And tell Dominic ... tell him he is the only one to look after her now ... he best not let me down ...'

'Do not worry, I believe that boy will spend most of his life near Aliah.'

'Seamus ... tell him ... world needs good ... men as well as ... fighters ... take care of him.'

'I will.'

'... and ...'

Amelia leaned close to Daniel to hear these last words.

'... tell father ... died fighting for Aria ... not that ... I was ... sick ... or scared.'

'Oh, my lovely boy, your father loves you and will feel your loss no matter how you die.' A squeeze on her shoulder reminded her. 'Of course I will tell him, and he will be all the more proud of you for it.'

'Thank ... you ...'

The grip on her hand loosened as Daniel passed on his last message.

'Just rest now.' She brushed the hair back from the young boy's forehead. Amelia held the guard's hand as his breathing slowed, then stopped. She held it a while longer, until the hand in hers grew cold and loss tugged at her heart.

Although the soldiers were ferrying away the dead and wounded from around her, Amelia could not let go of Daniel, not wanting the boy to be left alone in this place so far from his home. She wondered how she would break the news of the brave soldier's fate to Aliah, as tears fell freely down her cheeks and soaked into the blood soaked ground beside her. Finally, Boss gently released her grip and helped Amelia to her feet. Leading her back to the tent Pauley had fixed up for her, he led her inside.

'I will let you know when we are ready to bury him. Until then, perhaps you should rest.'

The words jolted her from her grief and she drew a long, shuddering breath then squared her shoulders. 'No, please bring my bag of herbs, there are others here who need my help while we wait for Dominic to return.'

CHAPTER 44
AN INTERVIEW WITH A GOD

Something sharp dug into Aliah's arm. Rolling to ease the pressure, she found herself unable to move. The pain intensified, cutting through the fuzz inside her head. Gaius had knocked her out. Where was she? Why was she unable to move?

Forcing her eyes open, all she saw was green. All right, she was lying on grass. Wriggling her body, she found her arms tied behind her back, and her feet bound together and pulled up behind her. Hog tied? Someone had hog tied her.

'Ah, you are awake. What fragile bodies you people have.'

'Mmm ... mmmm.' Aliah struggled to speak through the gag.

'Oh, I forgot. I guess we are far enough away now that no one will hear you scream.' He wrenched the cloth from her mouth, banging her head on the ground and grazing her cheek.

'What was that you were saying?'

Ignoring the sting of the graze, she answered, 'I said your body is breakable too, Gaius, and once I am free, I will show you just how easy it is to break.'

'Yes, yes, this body will break, but by the time you are free I will have no care for this vessel. You can do what you will with it, if you yourself are still alive that is.'

The voice was Gaius', but the words did not sound at all like him. Through the fog in her brain, she tried to remember something important someone said about Gaius. No, it would not come.

'You are a disappointment, Warrior. You are nothing without your sword.'

That tone was familiar. Where had she heard it before? Ah, now it came to her.

'What have you done with Gaius?'

'Mmm, what? You worry about the weak wizard who left this body for my use?'

'He cannot have been that weak, otherwise you would not have desired his body.'

'There are many different kinds of weakness. He was weak of will, he did not even fight me when I decided to use him. Still, he is no more.'

'You killed him for his body? You treat us like we are worthless.'

'Oh no, little Warrior, you all have value. Your worth is measured by what you are able to do for me.'

'So, if I am still here, you must think I am able to do something for you.' Aliah shivered as she spoke the words. The god could have killed her any time he liked having caught her unawares, but he kept her alive. Why? It would not be for anything good.

'Of course,' the god responded to her question. 'I want you to witness your failure before you die. I want you to witness my coming to this world in my true form, then I want you and the wizard boy to fight me. I want to show you how weak you really are, and what nonsense it was for you to ever dream of taking me on. You are to be an example for others who think to thwart me.'

He kept her alive simply to preen and show off in front of her. To ensure an admiring audience as he took over the world. He would not discard her until he had proven to her how strong he was. For all that he spoke of other's weaknesses, could he really be so blind to his own? Her only thought now was to keep him talking so she could think of a way out of this. She would not let this be the end of her battle.

Dominic? Seamus?

'Do not bother calling for your friends. I wrapped you in a bubble. You cannot send thoughts out, and no one can find you.'

She could not contact Dominic to tell him where she was, and she could not let Seamus know either. A little snake of despair wormed its way into her heart, but she crushed it before it could take hold. There had to be something she could do. The sword had been given to her because of her courage, she did not have strength only because she held it.

'If you are so keen to bring your physical form here, why are you wasting time with me?'

Gaius-god laughed, a hollow sounding laugh with no real mirth, and it grated on her nerves.

'You think I wait here because of you. No, no. You are simply a diversion to fill in time. My servant Millard is bringing me the casket of power so I may make my transformation and be here in all my true glory.'

Now it was Aliah's turn to laugh, and hers came from deep in her belly. 'Perhaps you should not have been so quick to get rid of Gaius. He would have warned you; Millard is no one's servant. The only person he serves is himself. If you wait here for him, you wait in vain.'

'You lie. You would say anything to keep me from the casket. With my help he searched for the vessel, and then offered to go and fetch it for me. He knows I will reward him once we have Aria under our control. Until then, he is my loyal servant.'

'Can you even hear what you are saying? You helped him find something containing great magical power, then he asked you to stay behind while he went to fetch it. What has Millard ever done that would lead you to believe he would give up such an important magical artefact?'

The god glared at her but said nothing. A frown slowly worried its way onto his face. As she thought of something, anything else that might needle the god, an idea flashed into her mind.

'You must have felt the disturbance in the air last night, and how odd the world is today. Can you be sure that Millard has not already accessed the power of the casket?'

The god paused his pacing. 'I am sure he has, but the little he could hold will not diminish the power by any great amount, there will still be plenty left for me.'

Aliah almost lost her focus. *Millard has the chest, how will we defeat the god now?* Again, she would not let herself sink into despair. They needed to fight until the very end. 'That is if he intends to give the casket to you and not keep it for himself.'

The god's face turned to thunder and Aliah tensed her body for the attack that would inevitably follow. Instead, Gaius-god walked over to her and stuffed the gag back in her mouth. 'We are finished talking.'

Aliah's eyes followed him as he returned to the fire and sat down, then stood, then paced, then sat again.

As she watched the restless figure, her mind conjured an image of Gaius from her childhood. He had been a nasty boy. Always putting everyone down, pointing out their failings and getting them into trouble, making enemies at every turn. As he grew into manhood, he became even more unpleasant.

Once she had tried to befriend him, after her mother admonished her for her uncharitable utterances one day when she wished the boy dead. Her mother's lecture on tolerance made her feel guilty. As did her recount of Gaius' early life.

His own family abandoned him on the Wizard Isle when he was found to have magic. They wanted nothing to do with such an abomination. Compassion rose up inside Aliah, and when she next organised a riding party to escape lessons, she invited Gaius to join them. Instead of his gratitude, she earned his condemnation, and he told her father of the plan.

From that day on, they had been enemies, something she was now grateful for as it made it much easier to hate the god who wore his form. As she glared at her foe, he stood, walked over and began saddling a horse. Leading the animal back over to the fire, the men looked up as he approached.

'I go to meet with Millard and assist him with retrieving the casket. Stay here with the girl until I return. If any harm comes to her, it will be done to you, tenfold.'

With his instructions delivered, he hauled himself into the saddle. Looking down at Aliah he said, 'Do not think this has anything to do with your words. I will return, and you will witness my arrival in your world, and you will be in awe of me as you should be.'

So many responses bounced around Aliah's mind, but all she was able to do was shake her head in frustration, unable to give voice to any of them.

With the god gone, the camp relaxed. Aliah rolled around to find a more comfortable position and her hands touched something cold. Wriggling and stretching her fingers, she grabbed a hold of it. Strength flowed through her.

Her sword? How was it here? She had left it behind with her gear when she went to tether the horses. It was then she realised Dominic was close by; all would be well now.

Fingers still on the sword, Aliah used the artefact's magic to push away the bubble encasing her. Much calmer now, she attempted to sleep until the opportunity came for rescue. She would need all her strength to get away and make it to the rendezvous on time.

The guards glanced over at her, checking to see she was all right. Not wanting any of them to return her to her prison, she wondered how she might hide herself so the wizards amongst them could not sense her. Reversing the process Dominic taught her for casting out her senses, she drew herself back in and imagined herself locked behind a door in her mind. The guards settled back down. She waited for them to sleep, and for Dominic to signal the time for her escape.

An exhausted Amelia paused to take a breath and surveyed the scene around her. Many of the injured guards were sleeping peacefully, having taken a sleeping drought after their wounds had been tended to. Just as many again lay waiting for herself and Baron Rasmussen's surgeon to attend to them.

Sighing, she picked up her bag and moved to the next poor boy, aware she brought this on herself when she insisted they treat the injured soldiers from Carsten as well. As Captain William's objected, the baron himself rode up and she found a surprising supporter when he insisted they treat their enemy as they would wish to be treated should the tables be turned.

Now she paid for her folly, but still, it was good to be busy. It stopped her thinking about poor Daniel, and the other boys who had not survived to be treated by her. She was so engrossed in her work, Boss had to touch her on the shoulder to alert her to his presence.

'We are ready to bury Daniel now, if you want to join us.'

The ceremony was short, and Amelia struggled to keep her tears inside as she said goodbye to the brave guardsman and friend. Even though his illness may have taken him soon, she mourned his life cut short by senseless fighting.

Once the brief funeral was over, Amelia stayed behind to say a private goodbye.

You are free of the constraints of your body now, Daniel, but we will honour your courage and loyalty by doing all we can to make sure we win this battle. And never fear, we will make sure Aliah is well looked after.

As she spoke to Daniel another voice brushed her mind.

Amelia?

Dominic?

Yes. I have found Aliah.

Good. Are you on your way back here, or will you head directly to the meeting place?

I said I had found her, not that I had rescued her, Dominic corrected Amelia.

I assume you have a plan?

Well, rescuing Aliah is my plan.

I take that as a no then, Amelia was tired and her words were tart.

Amelia, is something wrong?

She though about telling the boy, but then changed her mind. He had enough to worry about.

Nothing that cannot wait until later. Do you need any help?

Thank you, but I think this is a stealth mission and so I am better off on my own.

All right. Let me know if that changes.

How did we fare in the fight?

We are mostly all right, I am off to tend to the wounded now.

Be well, Amelia, I will be in contact.

Rising from her knees, Pauley and Boss flanked her as she left the graveside. The young boy slipped his hand into hers and gave a small squeeze of understanding.

'What do we do now? Should we go to the meeting place and help Seamus? Or are we to help Dominic search for Aliah?' Boss asked. 'The baron is gathering a party to head out this evening to try and find the princess and chase down any stragglers. He would be more than happy for us to join with him.'

Pausing to see if the future was any clearer, she eventually said, 'Dominic has found Aliah, and I believe our part is done for the moment. We three can do nothing to influence events now. I believe our efforts are best spent staying here and helping with the wounded.

'If things in the coming battle come out in our favour, what we do here will go a long way towards healing the wounds between our two nations.'

Unsure whether or not Boss' grunt signalled his agreement, Amelia had made her decision and turned towards the make-shift hospital. She intended making herself very busy so she had no chance to worry about the fate of her beloved Walter, and Seamus, and Aliah.

WITH STIFF FINGERS, Aliah grasped her sword and followed Dominic through the surrounding undergrowth. The sun was just beginning to peek above the horizon, and the sleeping guard would no doubt awaken when it fully rose. They wanted to be well away before that happened.

When she realised they were heading towards the rendezvous point rather than back to the pass, she placed a hand on Dominic's arm to stop him.

'Are we not going to pick up the others and get our horses?' she whispered, careful not to use mind speak as she did not want any of the magicians they left behind to be able to trace her.

Dominic shook his head. 'We can make good time on foot, and it is likely the Carstenite guards will assume that is where we have headed, so this might give us a slight advantage.'

Nodding her head in agreement, they continued on, staying within the trees until the sun was high in the sky and no obvious sounds of pursuit disrupted the quiet of the forest. Leading them back to the trail, Dominic explained they needed to move a bit faster if they were going to meet the others as arranged, but it was important they kept an ear out for the sound of horses following.

As they jogged side by side along the path through the forest, Aliah used the sword to revive her energy. Dominic even allowed her to give him a boost, reasoning they both needed to be in their best fighting form should they be found.

Although they were heading towards Seamus, Aliah could not dispel the unease growing in the pit of her stomach. She had not been in touch with her Wizard since the day before yesterday, and she just knew that was not good.

When they stopped by a stream for a breather and to quench their thirst, Aliah voiced her fears to Dominic.

'So you managed to mind speak with Seamus by yourself?' Dominic was amazed.

Hands on hips, Aliah glared at the boy who rescued her, for the moment her gratitude swamped by anger.

'Did you not hear me? I said I could not find him at all yesterday. I think something is wrong, and I do not want to be walking in to a trap.'

With a patience that irritated her even more, Dominic responded, 'These things are not predictable. Sometimes you can contact someone easily, other times it takes a little longer dependent on what they are doing. I would not be too worried just yet. If he is not at the meeting place when we arrive, then perhaps we should risk a little mind linking.'

Aliah humphed, but could not think of anything to counter his argument.

'If you are ready, the meeting point is about a candle mark along here,' he said.

The speed at which they travelled prevented any further speech, but that did not stop Aliah from re-imagining how the last conversation could have gone if she had only thought of her come backs earlier. She was so engrossed in her one-sided re-enactment, she did not notice Dominic coming to an abrupt halt. Slamming into his back, she muttered, 'What ...' Only to be silenced by Dominic placing a hand over her mouth, and pulling her roughly back into the bushes surrounding the clearing in front of them.

Once Aliah had regained her dignity, she surveyed the scene.

'Oh, no, that is not good,' she said under her breath.

On the far side of the clearing, was a group of Carsten soldiers readying themselves for battle. The only good thing about the situation was they were so caught up in their preparations, they had not noticed their two visitors.

'How did they know we were meeting here?' Dominic asked.

'They may not have, this may be a coincidence,' Aliah answered. 'It does not look like an ambush, if it was, they would be hidden. It looks more like they camped here last night and are waiting for orders, which I assume they expect to come soon given their activity.'

Dominic watched a little longer, 'I think you are right, even so, Seamus and the others will be walking right into them any time soon.'

'Not if we can circle round and warn them.'

Dominic nodded his head once, then started moving around the clearing towards the path opposite. They had just made it round the other side, and were creeping through the undergrowth by the track when it happened. Aliah froze at Seamus' call. She took one look at Dominic, broke cover, and ran faster than she had ever run in her life.

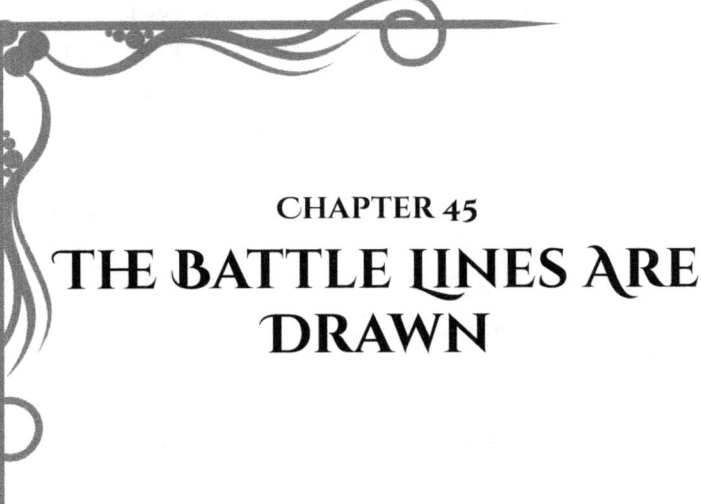

CHAPTER 45
THE BATTLE LINES ARE DRAWN

'He really is making a habit of fainting.'

'I know, Emer. Do you think we should point it out to him when he wakes?'

'Probably not a good idea. He is glowing after the explosion. There is no telling how that much energy might affect his mind ... I would hate for him to blow up.'

'I can hear you.'

'Oh good, you are awake. Walter, he has come to.'

'No need to shout, Emer, I am right here.'

'Oh, sorry.'

Forcing his eyes open, Seamus found himself back by the fire. Someone had tucked him into a bedroll and he had snuggled down inside. The morning sun was just peeking through the trees, telling him he had been out for a few candle marks.

'How did I get back here? Did someone carry me up the tree?'

'Sometimes I wonder if you have the sense you were born with. After the explosion, there was no need to find a way over the fence. Millard's stupidity blasted a hole straight through it,' Emer responded.

'I feel like I have been run over by a horse,' he groaned as he stretched out. 'It is a good thing we are not due to meet up with the others until tomorrow, I think I need to take it a bit easy today.'

'What are you talking about?' Walter joined them by the fire. 'You slept through a day and a night, we have to get moving soon if we are to be at the meeting place on time.'

Lifting his hand to push the hair back out of his eyes, Seamus stopped and stared. His hand glowed with a golden light. Slowly, his mind grasped onto the fact this must have been what Emer and Liam were joking about.

'Ah, so you found our little problem.'

'Little problem? Walter, I am glowing.' Panic began to worm its way up from the pit of his stomach.

'While you rested, I have been thinking how we might deal with this, and I have a plan.'

'Good, but perhaps you can first explain what this is before we decide what to do about it.'

As Walter settled beside him, Emer and Liam drifted away to get the horses ready to move. As he settled down, Seamus suddenly sat bolt upright.

'Walter, the casket! Did it survive?'

'I am sorry, nothing in the area survived the explosion.'

Abruptly Seamus rose to his feet and started pacing, trailing a fine golden light behind.

'What am I going to do now? The box was the only thing able to hold a god, and it contained the power we needed to send him from this world.'

As suddenly as he stood, Seamus dropped to the ground. 'We are defeated before we even begin.'

'Seamus, if you were not glowing a strange colour I would shake you senseless.' Emer's voice carried from where she tended the horses. 'If all it took to dispel the god was a simple box, any one of us could have done it.'

Turning away from her, Seamus stared sulkily into the fire. 'So what is this then? A minor set back?'

'If you are going to be such a baby about this, I am not going to talk to you anymore. If you want to listen to what I have to say, come and find me when you have grown up.'

'Seamus, although you may not want to hear it, Emer is right. The other night was not a complete loss. Your glow tells me that,' Walter advised.

'My glow? Yes, you were going to tell me about it.'

'I believe your shields were not fully in place when Millard opened the casket, releasing the power inside, and I think you retained some of the stored magic.'

Eyes widening in surprise, Seamus asked, 'How is that a good thing? Correct me if I am wrong, but Millard exploded when he tried to take magic from the casket. Now you are saying that same magic is in me.'

Walter's fingers gripped his arm. 'Stop looking on the bad side of everything. If you were going to experience adverse effects from this magic they would have shown up by now. Quit brooding and think for a moment.'

Tired, scared and worried, the last thing Seamus wanted to do was lift himself from the darkness of his thoughts. Fortunately, he was his father's son and he realised he had a duty to perform, and he could not do that while he was feeling sorry for himself. Keeping his gaze firmly focused on the fire's dancing flames, he shuffled the puzzle pieces in his head until they formed a different pattern.

'If the casket is gone the god no longer has enough energy to bring his body though, so we have that in our favour.'

'And?' Walter prompted him.

'I had to bind the god in some way to force him into the casket, so maybe I can think of some way to strengthen those bindings so we can hold him long enough to send him away.'

Pulling his eyes away from the fire he found Walter nodding his encouragement. The silence from behind told him Emer and Liam also stopped to listen.

'I have lost most of the magic intended to send the god away, but there is still some, quite a bit in fact, within me. Walter, are you able to help me store it until I need it?'

'I can, it is a simple task.'

'Then all I need to do is find more magic to replace the power Millard squandered. I do not suppose it is still around?'

'Funny you should ask that.' Walter grinned. 'Unused magic is all around us all the time, including the magic that foolish man released. We may be able to add to our store of magic as we travel.'

'Excellent, so we are not completely helpless.'

'Before you get your hopes up, I need to caution you each person can only hold so much magical energy. The amount differs between wizards, but you have already seen the effects of trying to store too much. Between the two of us we will not be able to hold nearly as much as the destroyed artefact did. So we will be limited in what we can do.'

'Still, we are not defeated yet. All I need to do is figure out how to bind a reluctant god, and identify enough energy to push him through to another plane. Oh, and of course we have to meet up with Aliah, then find the god.'

'I am pleased you are in a better frame of mind.' Emer joined them beside the fire, with Liam close on her heels. 'Maybe, though, before we do anything, we should eat something. You have had a day without food, and you need to keep your strength up.'

'We should also store my excess magic then find out how Baron Wexler is.' In response to their perplexed looks he said, 'I will update you all on my time in the cave as we eat, but I need food before anything else, that is if my glow does not need to be dealt with first.'

Walter laughed. 'It has waited a day, it can wait until you have eaten.'

STOMACH NOW FULL, all Seamus wanted to do was go back to sleep, however he was aware he needed to start building his magical reserves as rapidly as possible. Liam pushed for them to be on their way to the meeting place, but Seamus had other ideas.

'Liam, the fight will be here soon enough, whether we run to it or it comes to us. I need some learning time with Walter. Perhaps you and Emer should go back down to the bay and make sure the baron is all right for me.'

'Come on, Liam, the two of them are best left alone. And I for one would like to make sure none of those Carstenite soldiers are still hanging around. The last thing we need when we are in the midst of confronting a god is for them to spring up from behind.'

'Surely we would have seen them by now if there were any still around.'

Liam was reluctant to move. Emer grabbed the boy's arm and hauled him to his feet anyway.

'You know something,' he said to Seamus as the girl released his arm. 'You know it is going to be today.'

Reluctant to say the words out loud, Seamus did anyway, because his cousin deserved to hear them. 'Yes, it will be today. So we have to prepare as best we can. Emer is right, we need to make sure there are no surprises. This battle will be difficult enough as it is, we need to give ourselves the best possible chance of seeing it through to the end.'

With his fears confirmed, Liam was now happy to be doing something, anything, rather than sitting around waiting. Although he did throw a concerned look over his shoulder, to check on his cousin one last time, before mounting and heading off through Millard's devastation.

'So, shall we begin?' Seamus asked. 'Walter, I asked if you were ready.'

The older man was silent.

'Walter, what is it?'

'Huh. Oh, sorry. There is something not quite right this morning. I cannot quite place it, but the world feels, um, slightly out of alignment.'

'I know what you mean. It is strange, but now is not the time to be distracted. Today is the day, we need to stay focused.'

'Um, yes, of course. Let us begin. I want you to find your magic.'

Seamus confirmed he had it.

'Good. I know you see it as a glow, now imagine it is in the centre of a container.'

'I think I have,' Seamus told him.

'Good, now can you see the magic gathered around your body?'

Seamus nodded.

'Excellent, now imagine drawing that into your container.'

Seamus concentrated on doing as Walter instructed.

Around the time he could no longer feel any more magic being stored, Walter said, 'Well done.'

Seamus opened his eyes and, to his relief, he found he no longer glowed. 'That was surprisingly easy.' Seamus congratulated himself.

'Well, you sound very pleased with yourself. All we have to do is expand this process so you can collect magic from the world around you. We have to be a little more careful with this because it can be very dangerous.'

'What, and storing all that magic was not?' Seamus barked out a nervous laugh.

'I guessed you would be able to store the magic clinging to you from the casket because it had not torn you apart already.'

'Oh, all right, and now?'

'Now you are taking on more, and we do not know where your limits are. Do not worry though, I will take you slowly through the process, that should lessen the risk. First, can you tell me about your container?'

'Huh?' Seamus was remembering Millard exploding the night before last, and was now feeling a little more cautious about this whole process. 'I imagined I stored it in a water skin, to allow it to expand as I added more magic.'

'Yes, um, yes I guess that does help. In fact, it is perfect because you already have the idea a water skin can only be filled so far before it bursts. You need to understand you cannot fill your magical water skin beyond its capacity.

'Now, collecting magic is similar to sending out your consciousness to find a person, or maybe even how you can sense the energy of everything living in the forests. I want you to reach out and feel the air around us.'

Seamus closed his eyes, as he always did when concentrating, and allowed his consciousness to flow out of him. He could sense Walter and the living beings of the forest, but nothing else.

'I can only feel living things, Walter.'

'Ah, you are reaching out in a clump. How do I explain how to do this? When I taught this before, my students were boys who had studied for years to be able to draw in magic, and showed an aptitude for this sort of thing.

'Let me see, imagine you are casting a net, not like a fisherman, one with no holes. No, no, this is better. Imagine you are throwing a sheet over a bed. Cast yourself out like that, only suspend the sheet in midair.'

'Ah, like when I wrapped your essence the other day, I imagined casting a blanket over you.'

'Yes, exactly.'

Seamus tried again, this time imagining himself as very thin and very large, like a blanket. He held himself midair and waited. Tiny pinpricks of something clung to him. Letting himself come back, he explained the sensation to Walter.

'Yes, boy, that is the magical energy of our world.'

'How do I harness it?'

'Yes ... mmm, well of course you do that every day. Those with magical abilities absorb magic without even knowing they are doing it, and it settles in their bodies, waiting to be used. When they use their magic, their bodies replace it, like it replaces air in your lungs.

'If you use too much, more than you stored, your body starts to convert your own energy to magic to finish what you are doing. If you do not have sufficient control of your magic and you cannot stop the process, you can steal so much from your body it withers away and shuts down.

'Alternatively, if you take in too much energy, your magical store keeps increasing, much like a pig's bladder when it is blown up to use as a ball for games. If you take in too much ...'

'... you explode, like Millard did the other night.'

'Yes, yes. I know you are impatient to get started, but if you interrupt me this will take much longer. I need to be sure you understand the dangers before we begin.'

'Sorry. Continue.'

'There is no way of knowing how much magic is too much until it is almost too late. So, the way to manage harvesting extra is to take a little at a time. Check your body, then check again.

'So what I want you to do is find your magic.'

'I have it.'

'Wait, wait a moment. I missed a step. Do you know what colour your magic is normally?' Walter asked.

'Yes, a deep yellow.'

'All right, check your magic now.'

'That is interesting, it is a bright yellow, almost orange.'

'Good. Now we know the colour, we need to continue to check in between harvests to monitor the changes. As soon as you see any tinge of red, you need to stop,' Walter instructed.

'Does the size I imagined my water skin to be matter? It is only small.'

'I am not sure of the mechanics, perhaps a healing wizard would know more. All I know is your container adjusts to be able to hold your magic, however large a storage container you imagine. It is only when your energy turns red your storage stops growing. If you continue, the container is compromised, spilling out the excess energy.'

'Right, let us do this then.'

'This time I need you to imagine yourself to be as thin as a sheet, but only about the size of a pillow case. Limiting your size will limit the magic you harvest to a manageable amount. Are you ready?'

Seamus followed Walter's instructions to the letter. He waited until the magical pricks covered him. Holding himself there he said, 'I have some, how do I bring it in?'

'This is when the net analogy worked. You need to imagine closing it and hauling in your catch.'

It sounded simple, but doing it was harder. The first attempt Seamus lost almost all of his haul. With the second, he drew in a little.

Walter then made him stop and check the colour of his internal store. Disappointed, he found it unchanged.

'Interesting. Maybe you are doing it wrong.'

'Or maybe what I am bringing in is such a drop in the ocean, compared to the energy from the casket, I am not noticing any change?'

'That is another possibility. Try again.'

Concentrating, Seamus attempted another harvest, sure he took in much more magic this time. There was still no change in colour. The fourth time, his colour deepened a little and Seamus heaved a sigh of relief. He was doing it right. With his fifth cast he could not sense as much magic, it was more of a tingle than a prick. When he told Walter, the wizard explained,

'Living things generate magic, but it is a slow process. Once it is gone from an area you either cast wider, or move.'

Seamus tried turning his pillow case into a sheet again, and was surprised to find more energy. While Seamus was checking his colour, which was now a dull orange, the sound of hoof beats filled the morning air.

A re-energised Seamus opened his eyes just as a group of men rode into sight. Reaching for his knives, he relaxed a little when he made out the colours of the baron's men. As they drew closer, he saw Baron Wexler riding with them.

'A FINE MESS you made of my lands,' the baron said as he dismounted with some difficulty, the stiffness of his movements indicating he was not entirely recovered from his encounter with Millard.

'Not me, I am afraid. It was the thief. He thought the casket's magic was better used to boost his own powers, than passed on to the god.'

'That was a little foolish of him, and not so good for you.'

'No. Now I have to find a way to hold the god until I can figure out how to send him back.'

'So, I may be able to assist you in two ways again today.'

'Two ways? I am sorry, but I do not understand.'

The baron held out his hand. In the palm rested an amber glass vial, which he offered to Seamus.

'This is not the casket, but it may help. In addition to the minor skill of calling, my family's magical ability leans towards protection and wards, which is why we were given the casket to look after.

'However, my mother's family had a different skill. They were healers. In the past, their skills were used in battle. With so many magic users stripping an area clean of energy, they took to storing magic. They became rather good at it, and there is more magical energy in there than you would expect from so small a container.

'When I heard the explosion the night before last, I sent one of my men back to retrieve this. My last one I am afraid as I did not inherit the skill to make more. It may be of some help.'

Seamus was touched by the man's gift. 'Thank you, I am sure this will be most useful.'

'Not as useful as the other gift I have for you: advice.'

'Advice?'

'I am aware the plan was for you to bind the god in the casket. With its loss, I feared you might now fail. As I slept last night I dreamed of my great-grandfather, and of a story he used to tell about the wars.

'When he was on the battlefield and they ran out of cloth bandages, he used to create a magical bandage to bind wounds.'

Seamus had been so busy looking at the vial of magic he had not really been paying attention to the man. Slowly his last sentence penetrated and he immediately realised its importance.

'Really? I do not suppose he told you how he did it?'

'That is the thing, he did. He said he would send out a thread of magical energy and wrap it around the wound. It was more effective in containing that which should remain inside the body than actual bandages, but it took a lot of energy, so it was only used when absolutely necessary.'

Mulling this information over in his head, Seamus realised this was the solution he had been looking for. He was so overwhelmed with gratitude, he hugged the man.

'Well, well, there is no need for that, young man,' the baron said gruffly, but his face told a different story. He beamed with pleasure at having been able to help the young wizard again.

'Remember, when you need some energy, just break the vial. I must return home now. The events of the last couple of days took a little out of me and I really could do with some rest. I have much to do this afternoon.'

'Baron, I think you have done enough. You should take the time to get over the injuries Millard gave you.'

'No, no, my task is not yet finished. The brotherhood and I will spend the afternoon in prayer to our god in support of the coming battle. We also organised the people of the village to attend church and pray to the goddess to lend her support as well.'

Seamus was about to ask what good that would do, then he remembered in the training session when the god explained the power of prayer and how it affected the physical world.

'I will also pray that when I wake up tomorrow you have solved our little problem and our world is safe once again.'

'Once again, baron, I am at a loss at how to thank you for all your support.'

'Am I sensing a but?'

'Yes, I have a question. If your family has been practicing magic for all these years, how is it you do not support the open use of magic on Hand?'

Baron Wexler looked thoughtful, as though he was deciding whether or not to answer. Finally he turned back and placed a hand on Seamus' shoulder.

'Lad, I know after this you will want nothing more than to go home and live out the rest of your life with your family, perhaps even become duke someday as was planned.

'Sadly, although there are some here who would be happy for you to do just that, more than you might even imagine, we are still not the majority. There are many people on Hand who are vehemently opposed to any magic in all its forms.

'You might even be forgiven for thinking some of those people will be so happy you saved them from the god, that they will embrace the use of magic. However, in my experience, people are more likely to take a stronger stance against magical users in these circumstances, claiming if there were no magic at all, none of this would have happened.

'Things are changing, but slowly. I would suggest if you come through this in one piece you think about what else you might do with your life, away from Hand.'

As Seamus watched the baron's party ride away and sensed Walter beside him.

'I fear the baron is right, Hand will not be able to be your home after this. While I know you have been focused on the battle you must face, it is only natural for you to wonder what you will do after.

'Amelia and I have been considering our own futures. After this we will be returning to Sanctuary. She, to take up her training as a seer, and I would like to spend time in their libraries, learning about their use of magic. We also thought of starting our own school to develop the use and understanding of magic. One open to both boys and girls.

'If that interests you, I know Amelia and I would both love to have you return with us. I also suspect there is one other person who may be pleased if you choose to live in Sanctuary.'

With a blush rising from his collar, Seamus chose to ignore the last remark.

'Thank you, Walter, I will think on it should we make it through today.'

'Do that. Sometimes having a future to fight for makes us fight all the harder. Now, we should ready our horses, I see Emer and Liam are nearly here.'

WITH NO SIGN of the soldiers from Carsten, Emer suggested they head on to the rendezvous point. While they rode, Seamus sunk further and further inside of himself.

He was not worried about the up coming battle. In fact, he felt strangely fatalistic about facing the god. He had worked out what to do, he just did not know whether he and Aliah had the strength to do it.

What he dwelled on was his conversation with Baron Wexler.

Although he would not admit it to the others, he always believed he would die fighting the god, because to defeat him would require the ultimate sacrifice. It was only when the baron raised the possibility of him surviving, he considered his life after the battle—a life without needing to save the world.

All his anxiety about his future and what to do if he was not going to be Duke of Hand was back, and he was again mulling over the options. So caught up was he in his own thoughts, he did not notice Emer ride up beside him.

'You are unusually quiet. Anything you want to share?'

'Um, no.'

'Are you worried about today?'

'No ... yes, a little of course. I know what I need to do, and I will feel a little better when Aliah is with us again.'

'So you are not thinking about the battle?'

'No.'

Emer was quiet for a while as she continued to ride alongside him. Her company was soothing. With her near, wallowing in his worries seemed impolite and indulgent. After a while Emer broke the silence.

'You know worrying about anything else is a waste of time.'

'Sorry?'

'If you are worrying about what happens after your battle with the god today, it is a waste of your energy. If you do not win, the future will be the least of your worries. If you do win, there will be time enough to consider what happens after.'

'That is an interesting philosophy. Walter says I will fight better if I have something to fight for.'

'Silly, you already do; your friends and family and loved ones. It is them you are fighting for.

'I am talking about the details of what happens after. We can worry about those later.'

Seamus marvelled at how Emer worked out his inner-most thoughts and found a way to pull him out of his own head without making him feel stupid. Well, she did make him feel a little stupid. Although he did not totally agree with her, he was now much calmer and began to enjoy the ride, until Liam joined them.

'There is something going on behind us. I caught a glimpse of men through the trees. They saw us ride by and have been keeping pace. I think they are the remnants of the Carsten soldiers from last night.'

'What do you want to do?' Emer asked before Seamus was able to even process the news.

'The way I see it, we have two options; we can try and out run them and meet up with the others, or we can stand and fight.'

'Or we can do both,' the girl said. 'I do not like the idea of fighting here. There are too many trees, and it would be easy enough for them to surround us. We should ride on and find somewhere more defensible.'

'Good idea. Seamus? Walter? Ready to ride?'

Their response was to urge their horses to a canter along the tree lined path in single file, Walter at the front and Liam bringing up the rear. For some time, they fled the enemy soldiers, and it took all Seamus' concentration to keep his mount on the track. Finally, they broke into a clearing and Emer called for them to halt.

Surveying the area, she nodded to Liam, who shrugged in agreement. Unsure just what they were agreeing on, Seamus dismounted and walked around, cooling his horse down and stretching his muscles.

'This will do. It is defensible and close enough to where we were going to meet the others. We will wait here,' Liam declared.

Emer led her horse to the edge of the clearing at the farthest point from where they entered. Tying her mount to a tree, she had a drink of water, then drew her sword. 'Ready, Liam?'

'Yes.'

He handed the reigns of his horse to Seamus, grabbed his own weapon, and followed Emer back the way they had come.

Seamus overheard him saying, 'We should wait either side of the road about two hundred paces back. That should give us enough room to fight.'

'And what should we do?' Seamus asked, annoyed at being left out of the discussion. He may not be the world's best swordsman, but he was still pretty handy in a fight.

His cousin and his friend turned as one, perplexed at his question.

'I can fight with you, you know.'

'Are you mad?' Liam asked. 'If you die here fighting some poxy soldiers, who will fight the god for us?'

Astounded he had not thought of that himself, Seamus dropped his head in shame.

'Besides, we need you to deal with any who manage to get past us, of course,' Emer told him, a little more sympathetic to his feelings than his cousin. 'And maybe you should cast your mind out and see if you can find the others. Let them know we are here rather than where we said we would be. We could certainly use their help if there are any more stray Carstenite soldiers heading our way.'

Leaving Walter and Seamus standing in the middle of the glade, she joined Liam. Unsure of what to do, Seamus took the two horses over and tied them up. The older wizard joined him and helped him unsaddle the animals.

As they stowed their gear, the horses became restless. Seamus attempted to calm them, but one broke away as something crashed through the undergrowth behind. Thinking it was one of the stray soldiers, Seamus drew a couple of knives and turned to face him.

'You think you can stop me with puny knives boy?'

Seamus started at the familiar voice.

'Gaius, I did not expect to find you here. Have you come to fight your master's battles for him?'

Caught on the back foot, Seamus needed time, and his first thought was to play dumb, and have the god believe he did not know he inhabited Gaius' body while he thought about his next moves.

'Gaius is no more, and I need no one to fight my battles.'

'You must be Gaius, because I see you in front of me. If you are not Gaius, who are you then?' Seamus looked around and cast his mind out to see if anyone else was close by to help.

'Feel my presence, child. I am a god.'

Seamus laughed, 'So you are stuck as Gaius now. That must be really frustrating.'

'It is temporary, until I am brought through to your world.'

Gaius' face clouded over. Seamus' jibes were clearly hitting the mark, but he still had no idea of how he was going to do what he needed to do to defeat this being. So he kept going, hoping for some divine inspiration.

'Perhaps not so temporary a residence. I assume you thought to use the power of the casket to bring your physical form through the veil?'

'Correct. I sent my faithful servant Millard to fetch it. We were to meet up around here. He should arrive soon, and then you can witness me in my full glory.'

Seamus laughed out loud, surprised he could find something funny about this whole situation.

'Tell me, when is the last time you could sense Millard?'

The god looked perplexed. 'Not for a day or so. I assumed he had come into contact with you and was masking his trail so you could not find him.'

'Well, that may have been your second mistake, your first being not to realise Millard works for no one's cause but his own. He opened the casket almost as soon as he had hold of it, and let loose the magic it contained. Surely you felt it?'

'Yes, I felt it. But what you do not realise is I knew the fool would not be able to resist opening the it, allowing a little magic to escape into the world. But I knew he would be unable to hold even a fraction of what was contained inside. Now, after I deal with you, I will find him and release the rest of the magic.'

Again, Seamus found this hilarious. 'How could you be so blind?

Millard attempted to take all the energy into himself. He managed to blow both himself and the casket up.'

'You lie. There must be something left. Perhaps even the casket itself.'

'I assure you, I never lie.'

Gaius the god stood unmoving, only the twitching of his face betrayed the battle going on inside of him.

'No, not even the casket? I could have at least used that to build up enough magic over time to return my body to me. I will not be trapped in this body. There must be another way. What about a sacrifice of wizards? Might that release enough power? Mmm, how many would I need?'

As the god pondered his dilemma, still not confident in his eventual success, Seamus heard the sound of metal striking metal nearby.

'Ah, the battle has begun, your end is near,' the god crowed. He turned his face skyward, and literally glowed.

Seamus slowly let his awareness reach out to touch the edge of the god, trying to find out what he was doing. From this slight touch, he could tell the god was talking to someone—the other gods. Seamus pushed a little harder, attempting to find out what they were saying, and found himself faced with a bright light that almost blinded him. In his attempt to eavesdrop, he had entered this god's mind.

His appearance had clearly caused some disruption as the god pulled away from his communication with his siblings, just as Seamus took a deep breath and decided to make his first move in the final battle.

Imagining his power reaching out like an arm, at the same time he called out a name not used in hundreds of years, 'Xanthos'. Unable to resist the pull of his own name, the form was drawn to Seamus, and, as it came close, Seamus grabbed hold of the god's essence with a magical hand. Pulling with all his might, the god attempted to free himself.

Seamus had the god, now he needed his Warrior. Reaching out, he tried to find out how far away she was. As he did, he realised he had not been able to sense her since last night, and in his panic, he almost let go of his enemy.

Perhaps the explosion severed whatever it was that tied them together. No, whatever happened occurred before that, he had not sensed Aliah since before he went into the cave. Something was wrong. How was he to defeat a god without her? She was his arm. He could not go into battle without an essential part of himself.

Trying to damp down the panic, a presence brushed gently against his mind and Walter asked, *She is not here yet, what can I do to help?*

Can you help me hold him so I can bind his light?

With all his attention focused on holding the god in place, Seamus was unable to follow what Walter was doing. However, he knew when the wizard's force joined with his own as the god's tension against his hand lessen. With that small amount of assistance, Seamus was able to release a little of his power and begin the binding process.

Imagining a thread like a bandage, he forced it away from himself and around the god, at the same time he occasionally uttered the god's name, hoping it would cement the hold he had on him. It was a slow process, especially with his enemy fighting him all the way, and he worried this would not be enough.

Aliah, where are you?

CHAPTER 46

FIGHTING A GOD

CHAPTER 46

FIGHTING A GOD

Bursting into the clearing, Aliah pulled up short as she spotted Seamus on his knees in front of Gaius. Beside Seamus, hand on his shoulder, stood Walter. Her sudden appearance went unnoticed because they were so focused on their enemy.

This was not what she expected their final battle to look like; Seamus locked in a fight with the god, who wore the face of the person she disliked most in the world. She had also expected the sounds of armies fighting to fill the air, but this was eerily quiet, and very intense. Then again, maybe the real battle had not yet started.

Dominic appeared at her side. 'I did not know you could run so fast, or was that sword assisted speed?'

When she did not reply, he surveyed the scene in front of them to identify the cause of her concern. 'Where are Emer and Liam?'

Aliah had not even noticed their absence until that moment. Now she looked around, searching for the missing members of their team. As she focused, the clash of metal against metal reached her ears and she turned to Dominic.

'I will go and see if they need a hand, that is if you think you will be able to manage here without me,' her companion said.

'Go. I am not sure what you would be able to do if you stayed.'

As Dominic left to find his battle, Aliah turned her attention back to the tableau in front of her. Nothing had changed, no one had moved, and they had yet to acknowledge her presence.

Calming herself the way Dominic taught her, she tentatively let her consciousness flow outwards. Initially it was difficult, but she resisted the urge to grab her sword to boost her link, appreciating subtlety was the best approach here.

Poking around the edges of Walter's mind, he showed her a small opening, and she joined her consciousness with his. As she entered, she felt warm and cocooned, like sinking into a comfy armchair.

Walter?

Now is not a good time. I am lending all my power to Seamus and it is difficult to hold the link. Our friend here is trying to sever it and isolate him.

As she stood patiently by, Walter shared information in small pieces.

... casket ... exploded ... killed Millard ...

Walter's thoughts drifted away.

All right, just say yes if I am correct. Millard had the casket, it blew up in some way, killing him. The god cannot use the power, but nor can we. And we have nothing to contain his essence in.

Yes.

Walter's relief at her understanding his message was clear. He and Seamus obviously needed her help, but Aliah had to find out more before she did anything. If she did the wrong thing, she was more likely to hinder them than help. How could she get more information?

Allowing her consciousness to expand into the space Walter created for her, she could almost feel the link he held with Seamus. Closing her eyes, she attempted to visualise the connection.

There it was. With a calming breath, she stretched out along it until she met resistance. Then, with a gentle push, she left the welcoming comfort of Walter into, well it could only be described as chaos.

She lost her hold on Walter, but quickly regained it. Expecting the man to have created a full link with Seamus, she was surprised to find herself inside the battle field of Gaius' mind.

Now she had her bearings, she let go of Walter and looked around. What she saw worried her. In the centre of complete darkness was a fiery ball of light so bright it hurt to look at it. Attached to the light were two pure silver strands, thick and strong.

Nothing moved. It was as though the two silver ropes were in a tug of war with the orange-yellow light. Both sides were evenly matched. This could go either way.

Unsure what to do, but knowing she had to do something to tip the balance in their favour, Aliah placed her hand on her sword. Immediately the battle became clearer.

Walter's silver light had a hook on the end, and it was sunk deeply into the ball, as if anchoring it in place. Yellow fingers of fire were trying to prise the hook out as it attempted to sink deeper inside.

Seamus' strand of light was split in two. One part held onto the fire like a hand holding a ball, the other part was snaking around again and again, reminding Aliah of winding wool into a ball. Orange fire pushed against the hand, attempting to loosen the grip, while squirming to free itself from the wrapping.

She watched for a moment more to ensure she understood what was happening. It looked as though Seamus was trying to bind the god. Understanding the situation did not immediately give her any ideas on how to help.

He is weakening them. Unless you do something, he will win.
What ... who?

Aliah looked around. She must have been imagining things.

Why are you just standing there? You are the Warrior. Do something.

The sneer in that voice was familiar.

Gaius?

Yes, you dolt. We need to help them.

Why should I trust you?

Because I want out of this prison and you are the only people who can help me.

I thought you were working with the god, Aliah said.

I was, until he took over my body and tried to obliterate my soul. I have hidden in a small corner of my own mind for endless days, shielded, waiting for my revenge. Now quit talking and start acting, or neither of us will ever be free from this nightmare.

I would love to help, but I do not know what to do.

Perhaps if you had spent more time on your studies and less time trying to get out of them, you would be able to think this through rationally. The sneer in Gaius' voice was back.

Hello, Gaius, I missed you.

Concentrate. Seamus is trying to bind the god's essence into as small a ball as possible.

Ah, that is what the thread is.

Yes, of course. You need to help with that.

How? Aliah asked.

He cannot let go of the god to take the power thread around fast enough to contain and weaken him.

Mmm, if I can grab the thread and somehow run it round would it help?

Yes. Gaius' answer was as swift as it was short.

I do not suppose you have any tips on how to do that?

Honestly, I cannot believe you were chosen to save us all. Have you not learnt anything about your powers that might help?

There is no need to be snippy about it. You have trained all your life to use your gifts, we have had less than a moon turn to prepare for this.

Watching Seamus laboriously wind his luminous silver thread around the god fireball, Aliah thought about all she and Seamus had done together, all the training sessions, and all the conversations. Surely she could use something from there.

Then she remembered back to their trials. Although they were the Wizard and Warrior, and they shared a single prophecy, they were tested separately. Seamus was tested on his ability to control magic, and her test had been around her physical abilities and endurance.

If you are going to help, you need to do it soon, Gaius interrupted her thoughts.

All right, do not rush me. I may only get one chance at this.

She did not need Gaius to remind her time was running out and she needed to hurry. *Ah, hurry.* The sword lent her speed when she needed to get here quickly. It could lend her speed now.

Imagining herself in her physical form, her body instantaneously appeared. She walked over to Walter's now pewter-grey light. It was taking all his energy to simply hold the god in position. She placed her hand on him. Drawing energy from the sword, she passed it on until his light once again shone a pure silver.

As she pushed energy through Walter, the god pushed some of it back. Unlike the pure clean feel of Walter's energy flow, the power she fought was swirling and chaotic, and when she broke off, she nearly stumbled from dizziness.

Ignoring the nausea, she walked over to Seamus. His light had dulled so much she was surprised he still held onto the god. As she stepped closer, she thought she heard him whispering something, perhaps a prayer. No, it was the same word over and over again, like a mantra.

Blocking everything else out, she repeated the process to brighten his light, feeding him energy. This took a little longer as the god was concentrating more of his attacks on Seamus, seeing him as the major threat. When Seamus was sufficiently bright again, she reached out her hand and took the end of his silver thread. Then, she ran like she had never run before, round and round the massive ball of power.

Of course it was not quite that easy. As she wound the thread, the god presence pushed back, wriggling so the thread slipped and she would have to backtrack and tighten it up. Every time she touched him, she became dizzy and had to force herself to push through the sensation and keep going.

Exhausted, she paused when she estimated the god was two-thirds covered in the magical binding. As she drew some energy from her sword, she was dismayed to find binding him did nothing to diminish his strength. Inside he still glowed as brilliantly as when she arrived. On the other hand, Walter and Seamus had used so much magic they were now storm-cloud grey.

Holding the magical thread, she fed energy via her sword through to the wizards so they could hold the god in place while she finished wrapping him.

One last push. If she had run fast before, it was nothing to how she ran now. Knowing if she did not finish this soon the god would break the hold they had on him, and all their good work would be for nothing, lent her extra speed. Everything became a blur, and all that remained was running and binding.

You can stop now, it is done.

ABSOLUTELY SPENT, Aliah stopped running in time to see Walter's light wink out. Without thinking, she followed him out of Gaius' mind only to find herself in the middle of total chaos.

While they had been intent on binding the god, a battle had found them. They were in the centre of a group of Hand guards who seemed intent on defending them from a greater number of Carsten soldiers. Seeing they were safe for the moment, she knelt to check on Walter.

The older wizard looked pale and drawn, and there was a sheen of sweat on his brow. She let out a sigh of relief as she saw his chest rise and fall. Placing one hand on him and the other on her sword, she channeled a little healing energy, and was relieved when Walter opened his eyes. He managed a weak smile before falling back into unconsciousness.

Knowing it would take all she had to fully heal the man, she gave him energy until she saw his chest rise and fall with a good rhythm, then stood. Finding Baron Rasmussen in the ring of defenders, she made ready to join him.

The defensive circle was two men deep, the men fighting in pairs. When one man tired, he dropped back and his partner took his place. Likewise, if a man was injured, he was soon replaced.

Aliah took position in the inner-circle, and when a man took a strike to the arm, she quickly replaced him on the Baron's right. The fighting was fierce, and Aliah had never faced anything this intense.

The knot of fear in her stomach soon disappeared as her training took over and she cut and thrust with her sword. Never tiring as her weapon fed her energy, she was pulled back for a break by the panting baron. He slipped between two men, dragging her behind him. The look of anger on his face drawing her to a stop.

'What do you think you are doing?' he yelled at her over the sound of fighting around them.

'I am doing what I am meant to do, fighting to win this battle.' Aliah was perplexed. Surely as the Warrior this was what she had trained for, keeping Seamus safe while he dealt with the god.

The baron removed his helmet and ran a weary hand through hair that was darkened with sweat. 'Princess, I may only be a soldier raised to rule by a benevolent duke, but even I know the gods did not give you that sword to fight men. Your job is to stand beside the Wizard and fight whatever is behind this invasion.'

Aliah blinked, and shook her head. All this time she had seen the sword as a sign her role was to fight their physical enemies while Seamus took care of anything magical. Was the sword symbolic? Were its magical abilities more important than its physical ones?

'Princess? Aliah? You need to go and fight your own battle. We have this covered.'

The baron replaced his helmet and joined his men holding the circle. Left alone in the middle of the chaos, Aliah remembered Seamus' words about her acting rather than thinking being the thing that might actually help them win against the god. Without wasting another moment, she returned to her Wizard.

GAIUS?

Concentrating on making his link with the god smaller and smaller until it melted away, Seamus opened his eyes. Well, mentally opened his eyes inside Gaius' body.

Gaius, Amelia thought you were still alive but I thought the god of chaos killed you when he took your body.

So did he.

Walter? Seamus asked.

His light faded out moments ago.

Aliah?

She went after Walter, I guess to make sure he is all right. She will be ... ah here she is.

How is Walter? Seamus queried her.

He is weak but breathing easily, Aliah answered. *What do we do now?*

Well, the plan was to make the god smaller, then push him through to the next realm, Seamus informed her.

I am sensing a but.

Mm, it took more energy than we planned to bind him. I knew he would be strong, but I never imagined ... Seamus simply ran out of words, unable to describe what he experienced when he touched the god's essence.

I can feed you through the sword.

I am not sure that will be enough. I believe the sword channels magical energy from the natural environment. It will take a huge burst of power to make him smaller, then another much larger one to push him through the veil. Wexler gave me a magical boost in case I needed it. Perhaps it will be enough to make him smaller.

And we cannot use that to push him through as he is now?

Not from what we know, no. It would be too difficult, even with the veil as thin as it is at the moment.

All right, one step at a time. Use your boost and we will make him small, Aliah took control.

Unsure whether or not this was the best approach, Seamus knew they had to do something because he could sense inside his bindings the god was already working his way free.

His physical hand grasped the glass vial Wexler had given him, and crushed it. Pain lanced through his hand as the glass cut his palm, but it was minor compared to the pain his body experienced as the great store of magic pushed its way through his very being.

Just when he thought he might explode from excess power, it stopped. Before he could think too much about it, he began the process of reducing the god. He imagined his hands growing until the bound god was like a ball held between them. Then he pushed and pushed and made his hands smaller, until the god was a tiny ball inside tiny baby hands.

Dropping to his knees, he was spent.

ALIAH STOOD by as Seamus grew to an enormous silver light, encompassing the god. The light became so blinding, she closed her eyes. When she dared to open them again, Seamus' body had turned a dull grey, and in his hand was a bright silver pea.

Seamus, you did it.

I ... I made him small, but I do not think there is much time. He is fighting back.

As Seamus spoke the pea rolled out of his hand to the ground.

I can fix him.

The two of them had been so engrossed in their work they had forgotten Gaius was there. Aliah swung around to find him in his human form, even if only in his mind. Walking over to them, he raised his foot to stamp on the pea sized god.

Seamus moved to create a protective barrier as he shouted, *NO.*

Gaius reluctantly returned his foot to the ground. *Why not? He has tortured me for long enough. I deserve to be the one who kills him.*

You would not be killing him. You will only break the shell, releasing him again, Seamus explained.

Oh. We cannot do that. What do we need to do with him then? I am not having him live in my body forever. You mentioned something about pushing him through a veil.

Yes, there are different planes of existence, and they are separated by protective layers. I need to push him back through the way he came. Baron Wexler and his people are praying in an attempt to thin the barrier around here, but I will still need a great boost of power to push him through, and I am out.

So let me summarise; he is fighting his way out of his wrappings, and the only way to be rid of him is to send him back where he came from, and to do that you need a great deal of magical power. If we do not do this soon, he will be back in my body and very angry, Gaius paced as he outlined their situation.

Yes.

The wizard stopped and looked directly at Seamus. *I think I may be able to help.*

How? Aliah and Seamus asked together.

I have been stealing bits and pieces of the god's magic and storing it in my prison. Millard breaking the casket gave my stockpile an unexpected boost. I held it against the day I found an opportunity to free myself. I guess this is that day.

Aliah watched as Seamus brightened a little in colour, and it gave her an idea. Walking over to him, she placed her hand on his back and fed him energy through the sword until his body brightened. As she did so, she found she was having to reach further and further away to find energy. The area around them was stripped bare. This was the last time she would be able to help boost their power, which was all right, as this really was their one and only chance to rid themselves of the god who plagued her home.

Standing tall, Seamus picked up the god-pea, placed him in the palm of his hand, and looked at Gaius.

I have not done this before, so before we waste your energy store let me find out if I can find the veil between the realms. If I can sense it, I will say now, and you give me all the energy you can.

I understand.

Gaius had a sly smile on his face as he answered, causing Aliah's stomach to knot. Was he up to something?

Seamus picked up the god between two fingers, raised his arm, then seemed to push upwards.

I can feel it, it is like trying to push a pea through cloth. I need your magic now.

Not trusting her former enemy, Aliah began searching as far as she could for additional magic. The countryside around them had been bled dry. There was nothing.

Wait a minute …

There were two bright lights. Sending her senses closer she found Emer and Dominic. Their stores of magic were a beacon in a magical wasteland. With no time for niceties, she reached in, tapped into their energy, then sent the boost to Seamus.

Sorry, it was necessary, she sent before she broke off.

The veil is stretching, but the more I push the more it expands. This is not enough. Seamus' voice was laced with effort and worry.

It is time, Gaius said, and he pointed to the sword. *You know what you have to do.*

What? Aliah started. *Are you joking? Just share your power with Seamus.*

You and I both know that will not be enough. However, when a wizard dies, all the power in his body is released in a massive surge. That should work.

Before she had a chance to object, Gaius pushed her from his mind.

ALIAH GRASPED the sword in her hand, aware it was the only thing preventing her collapse. As she regained her balance, she found herself staring into Gaius' eyes.

Panic momentarily clouded her vision. Calming her breathing, she settled her nerves, and looked around. Still safe in the defensive circle, she was worried by the number of Baron Rasmussen's men who were now contained inside, injured and unable to re-join the battle.

There was only one layer of men desperately fighting to keep them safe while they dealt with the real threat to Aria. They needed to finish this soon or all would be lost. She turned back to Gaius.

'Gaius, no, there must be another way.'

'There is not, it is too late for me. I had hoped, but now I realise I was dead as soon as that monster took over my body. Maybe this is the true reason why I managed to stay alive? You have to do this. Either you do it and we win, or he wins and will kill me when he gets the chance to leave my body.'

Many times in the past Aliah had wanted to kill Gaius. But now, faced with the very real possibility, she could not do it. All she could think of was the poor child abandoned by his parents because of his magic.

'Before you do this, I just wanted to say I have had time to think over the last few days. I gave my life to Millard, trusting in him completely. I see now how he used me, and how desperate I was for his approval that I did everything he asked of me regardless of who it hurt. In that desperation, there are many things I did that I perhaps should have done differently.'

'Why, Gaius, do not go all soft on me now. You will have plenty of time to make amends.'

'No, Aliah, you have to do this. My stored power combined with the extra energy when I die, along with the boost from your magic sword will end this. You must do it, do it now! Or I will haunt you forever for leaving me to his mercy.' Gaius beseeched her as he stared into her eyes. 'Do it, quickly, please, before I lose my nerve.'

As he pleaded with her, Aliah knew in her heart what he was saying was true, she had no option if they were to win. Slowly raising her sword, a tear escaped and made its way down her cheek. 'You die a hero, and I will see to it you are remembered that way.'

One swift swing of the sword and it was over. Tears flowed unhindered now as she stared at the body on the ground in front of her. Although part of her registered Seamus also collapsing beside her, she fell to her knees and emptied her stomach in the grass.

Sometime later she stood on unsteady legs and turned slowly, realising the fighting around her had simply stopped. The baron was busy rounding up the Carstenites, who seemed to have surrendered just when they were on the verge of winning.

Dazed, she searched for Seamus and Walter. Walter had dragged Seamus over to the shade of a tree and was busy making the boy comfortable. Standing beside them was Liam, supported between Emer and Dominic, his face grey and pinched with pain.

Stumbling over to them, she did not know where to start. The shame she felt at stealing magic from her friends, combined with her grief at having to kill Gaius, warred inside.

'I am sorry ...'

She did not get a chance to finish. Dominic bundled her into his arms and whispered into her hair, 'You did what you had to do in the heat of battle. It will be all right. I promise.'

Sinking into his embrace she could almost believe it would be.

⁂

EVERY OUNCE of his energy and concentration was taken over by the need to push the tiny god form through the veil. As he pushed, the veil stretched and stretched. Every fibre of his being ached as he exhausted his store of energy.

Despair overwhelmed him, and at the very moment he thought I can do no more, a massive surge of power infused him.

All through this journey, he believed he and Aliah would finish the final battle together, but he could not sense her presence. Never had he imagined the final act of banishing the god would be done alone.

Seamus coiled for one last, massive push. The veil expanded some more, and then a little more. Then, with the smallest of pops that was altogether unsatisfying after so much effort, he broke through. Letting go of the pea, the god essence drifted from his hand.

Just as he was about to withdraw his fingers, something grabbed hold of them, and pulled him through into another realm.

The sensation of moving between worlds was somewhat like being dragged through mud, and was most uncomfortable. That discomfort was nothing compared to the churning in his stomach.

Surveying his new surroundings, he found to his surprise, the landscape was similar to where his body was on Hand. There were minor differences; flowers he had never seen before bloomed, the grass was an unusual shade of green and the sky had a purple hue. As he looked around, he realised he could no longer see the god, and he had no idea who so clumsily requested his presence.

Unsure of his next move, he collapsed on the ground, suddenly aware of how weary he was. Reaching out, he searched for magical energy. It was there, but it felt very different. He attempted to produce a small flame, but either his magical reserves were depleted beyond his expectations, or the magic behaved in a different manner here. Either way, it meant he was not going anywhere anytime soon.

Closing his eyes, he rested his back against a tree and tried to rest. He had plenty of time to worry about getting home when he regained his energy.

He could not say what made him open his eyes when he did, maybe it was a slight change in the air around him, but whatever the reason, he found himself watching six gods appear on the other side of the clearing.

As he wondered why only six of them had journeyed here, the seventh god walked from behind Seamus to join his siblings, answering the unasked question of how he had arrived.

One of the gods bent and picked up the now very dull looking god-pea between two fingers. Squeezing the tiny ball, there was an audible 'snap' and the gods were joined by their errant brother.

At first, the god faced his siblings defiantly. Then, as they surrounded him in a group hug, he almost seemed to crumple. The group joined together and pushed upwards, returning home.

No matter how many times Seamus imagined the end to the invasion of his homeland, it was not this. The god forgiven by his siblings and he, the supposed hero, left alone on another plane of existence; one with no sounds of life.

Oh well, at least he was comfortable, and he could congratulate himself as being part of the team who saved the world.

'Seamus.'

He had not sensed the gods appear this time, but six of the seven who named him Wizard stood in front of him.

'We brought you here so you might see you were successful, and remove any doubt about whether or not you banished our brother. Aria is now free from his meddling.

'Unfortunately, your victory came at a cost, but not so great a cost as there would have been if our brother succeeded.

'Thank you for returning him to us. It is now time for you to return home.'

Before he could open his mouth to ask some of the many questions he still had, Seamus was squished back through the barrier.

CHAPTER 47

ENDS

For a moment Seamus thought about disobeying orders and getting up, that was until his sister poked her head around the door.

'Mother said to make sure you are still in bed. Are you still in bed?'

Slipping his feet back under the covers, he lay against the pillows.

'Yes, I am still here.'

'Good, because she said if I found you up and about, I was not allowed to let your visitor in.'

'Visitor? What visitor? Is it Amelia?'

Since awaking the day before in his old bed, in his old room in the palace, Seamus' mother had been a strict nurse. Having rushed back from Port Marden to take care of him, she was allowing no visitors, and no talking about anything that happened until Amelia could check him over and pass him as fit.

At first Amelia had been on her way back from the plateau. She stayed a day or two with Baron Rasmussen, caring for the injured soldiers, arriving back a few candle marks after Seamus and Aliah.

Then she had been visiting and caring for Walter, who had been more seriously affected by fighting the god than Seamus. Now, hopefully, it was his turn.

'Of course, silly, and she has brought someone with her.'

'Off you go now, Cara, I want to spend some time with your brother. Perhaps you could go to the kitchen and fetch him some soup.'

'Soup? I am sick of soup. I want some real food.'

Seamus' wishes were ignored as Cara said, 'Yes, Aunt Amelia.'

Before he could argue, Cara launched herself out the door and ran off on her mission.

'I would ask how you are, but I can see for myself,' his aunt said as she led Walter to the chair beside his bed.

Once the older man settled in, she herself sat on the edge of the bed and took Seamus' hand in her own.

'There is a lot to talk about, and I want to make sure you are strong enough for this conversation.'

Seamus groaned. 'Please do not tell me the god is back.'

'What? No? Is there reason to suspect he might be?' Amelia gripped his hand tightly and Walter sat forward in his chair.

'No. Sorry. I just thought from the tone of your voice you had bad news, and that was the first thing that popped into my head.'

'We do have news, and it is not the best.' Walter sat back again. 'Before we go into that, I am interested to find out why you worried about the god returning. Are you certain he is gone?'

'Yes, I saw the other gods take him home. They expended a lot of energy to show me where he had gone, I think so I would be certain and we could all move forward.'

'Good.' Walter relaxed back into his chair. 'I do have another question for you. Before I joined you in battle, I heard you call a name. It was a name I had not heard spoken aloud in my lifetime. You then repeated that name over and over as we held the god in place. How did you find out his name?'

Seamus laughed. 'I guessed. There were eight gods, I met seven.

Of those seven four were women, so I knew our god was male. He also seemed to cause massive upheavals wherever he went, so I took a leap and called out the name of the god of chaos.'

Walter seemed impressed. 'Seamus, there is hope for you to become a scholar yet.'

Amelia had not moved a muscle during their conversation, and Seamus remembered they had come to give him bad news.

'Amelia, if you did not come to talk to me about the god, then what did you come about?'

He looked at his aunt. She appeared the same as before, in fact she was more confident than she had been when he saw her last. She had entered the room leading Walter, not the other way around. He turned his gaze to the wizard. The older man's skin appeared waxy and grey, his face wore a few more wrinkles, and some of his hair had turned white in the few days since the battle.

'Walter, are you all right?'

'This stupid, brave man is fine, but lucky to be alive. He gave more of himself than he should to rid this world of a great evil.'

Seamus reached out for Walter and found his magical energy barely there.

'Oh, Walter, please tell me you did not burn your magic away when you helped me?' The worry was a crushing weight on Seamus' chest.

The wizard took both Amelia and Seamus' hands in his own. 'There is still a little magic left, but I will never be able to weave great workings again.'

'I am so sorry, I ...'

'Please, Seamus, it was my choice to do what I did. Do not take that away from me. My life will be no less rich for the loss. I will still be able to teach and study as I planned, and I will always be proud of the contribution I made during the battle. Perhaps the history books might even make slight mention of me.'

Biting back his sorrow at his friend's loss, Seamus said, 'I will make sure they do. We could not have done any of this without you. And if that is all we lost in this battle then we came off lightly.'

He looked from Amelia to Walter.

'All right, I see there is more. I am well enough for you to tell me it all.'

Amelia took a deep breath before responding, as if stealing herself to his reactions. 'I am unsure if you realise, Gaius also gave more than he should when helping you. He sacrificed his life to send the god away.'

'I was surprised when he offered to helped me. I am even more surprised to hear this, but it does explain where that last lot of energy came from, the one allowing me to push through the barrier. I will not sully his memory with a lie and say I will miss him, but I appreciate his sacrifice and I am saddened by his loss. Is there anything else?'

'Emer and Liam were pretty beaten up by the Carstenite soldiers. Emer is healing well, but the wound in Liam's leg is very deep. If he gets to keep his leg, he will carry a limp for the rest of his life. I am afraid his fighting days are over.'

Pausing to let the information settle, she took another breath before rushing on. 'And Daniel died bravely fighting for Aria.'

'I must go and see them. Hold on. What did you say? Daniel? No? No!' Seamus clutched at his chest as the loss of his friend nearly broke his heart.

'How is Aliah taking it? Are you certain? Goddess, I must go to her.'

Before anyone could stop him, he leapt from his bed, rushed out of the family rooms and down the corridor to the guest quarters. Bursting through the door, he found Aliah staring forlornly into a raging fire. Dominic sat in a chair across from her. He rose when Seamus entered.

'It is good you are finally here, I think she needs to talk with you. But, um, wait a minute.' Dominic ducked into the bedroom beside them, returning with a blanket. 'You might need this.'

Looking down, Seamus realised he had fled through the palace in only his underclothes. Grateful, he took the offered blanket and wrapped it around himself.

'I shall leave you two alone. Call me when you are done, I do not want her left by herself at the moment.'

Seamus hesitantly walked over to the chair beside Aliah, and placed a comforting hand on her arm. The girl looked up, her eyes red rimed and her face pale, and one cheek marred by an angry red graze.

'I thought we would all make it, or none of us would,' she said. 'I was not prepared for this loss.'

Unable to put into words his own sorrow at the death of someone who had become his friend, he sat down beside her and held her hand.

'He was ill, did you know?' she asked.

'No, I had no idea,' Seamus admitted, wondering how he had missed the signs.

'I suspected, but Amelia confirmed it this morning. Something was growing in his stomach and Amelia did not know how to deal with it. He would not wait until we returned home to see if the wizard physicians could help. No, he went out and sacrificed himself saving a group of fellow guards.'

'So it was serious? His illness, I mean. Was it life-threatening?'

Aliah nodded, still too angry at her childhood friend to speak.

'He chose to die on his own terms. You cannot be upset at a person for that.'

Turning towards him, her face a picture of fury, something about his own sadness took the wind from her sails. 'I want to agree with you, I do. But I am so annoyed with him for not coming back, I cannot see past it.'

'We shall all miss him, but I cannot help thinking he died as he would have wished, in battle. No doubt a hero as well. For me, that makes my grief a little easier to bear.'

They were silent for a time, lost in their own thoughts. Sighing heavily, it was Aliah who broke it by taking his hand.

'I killed him, Seamus.'

'Killed who? Daniel?'

There was another deep sigh before Aliah answered. 'No, Gaius. He knew it was the only way to get enough energy to send the god away, and he asked me to do it.'

'Oh, Aliah,' Seamus wrapped her in an awkward hug. 'I thought my task was hard, but in the end, it was you who had to do the most difficult thing of all. I have no words.'

She allowed him to hold her for a little longer, before pulling herself together. She shrugged off his embrace and stood.

'I bet you have not even been to see Emer and Liam yet. Come on, we can mourn the dead later, it is the living who need us now.'

Before he joined her, Seamus stared thoughtfully into the fire, then asked, 'Do you think we should talk about it some more, what happened, I mean? I thought I would come here, see you, mourn Daniel, then say some miraculous words that would put all of this behind us.'

'Oh, Seamus, this will never be behind us. It is too much a part of who we are now. No doubt there will be celebrations once the Carsten fleet return home, then we will be relegated to the annals of history as having helped defeat a foreign invasion.

'Only we will know the truth of it, and how it changed us all. And maybe, someday, we will want to talk about it—but not now.'

Smiling at how her words reflected his own feelings, he stood and followed her to find their friends. Pausing at the door, Aliah turned and raised an eyebrow.

'Are you forgetting something?'

Following her gaze, he realised he was still dressed only in a blanket. 'I suppose there must be some of my clothes left in the bedroom here,' he said as he ducked inside, only to return moments later, dressed and ready to face the world.

'Do you know what this is all about?' Aliah asked as she and Dominic joined the group assembled in the main reception room.

Seamus shook his head. 'No, no one does. All we know is that Amelia asked for us all to gather here, dressed for a celebration. We think she is throwing a farewell party.'

'Where are your father, and Amelia and Walter then?'

'What, are you surprised someone is later than you?' Dominic asked, and earned a glare from the princess.

Ignoring the dig, Aliah turned her back on him, focusing her attention on Seamus.

'I do not know about Walter and Amelia, but my father is in his office talking to Robin, who showed up earlier today.' Seamus braced himself for an outburst from Aliah, but he was more than surprised with her answer.

'I hope your father goes easy on him. I know he betrayed us, but it was for a good reason. They were holding his mother captive, after all.'

'Father and I talked about it before they met, he asked my opinion on whether or not the punishment he planned was suitable.'

'Oh, no, he cannot punish Robin for protecting his family.' Aliah had tears in her eyes as she spoke. 'That poor man must have been under so much pressure.'

'I am afraid there must be some consequence to his actions, after all he did set up your kidnapping. From what father said, I think he is going to release Robin from his duties, but he will be given a small holding in recognition for his years of service.'

Aliah was prevented from commenting by the clattering of a chair falling to the ground. Tired of waiting, Cara and Pauley had commenced a game of tag, much to Jonas' obvious dismay. Seamus' brother was at the age, no longer a child he was not yet an adult, although he was trying hard to be.

Before Duchess Elise had a chance to sort them out, the library door opened, admitting Duke Damon, Walter, Amelia and a cloaked figure. The duke took his place on the dais and called them to attention.

'I would like to welcome you to a very special event, not as special as I would like to make it, but it is what Walter and Amelia wanted, and I guess that is all that matters.'

'Damon,' Duchess Elise's tone threatened censure, and the duke sighed.

'Anyway, without further ado I would like you to welcome Father Christopher, who has agreed to perform a marriage ceremony for my sister and her chosen husband, Walter.'

There were audible gasps of surprise as the father led the happy couple up to the dais, to be joined there by the duchess.

It was a short, but moving ceremony, and throughout Seamus could not help but notice the glances between Dominic and Aliah. He thought to himself they would not be long in following his aunt's example.

After the formalities and congratulations were over, they all retired to the banquet hall, where the cook had managed to put on a grand feast, even given the short notice. As they sat, Seamus felt happy and relaxed for the first time in ages. All the people he cared about were here. They were safe, and he just wanted to enjoy the moment.

Dominic spent most of the meal trying to convince Pauley to take up a position at court with the king's spy-master. He had already turned the job down once, when King Terion himself had asked before departing the previous day, and he was unlikely to change his mind now. It seemed he had found his niche as Amelia's apprentice and was not interested in anything else.

Relieved of his role as heir to the duchy, Seamus smiled to see Jonas taking his new duties so seriously as he sat next to their father.

'Any regrets?' Emer leaned over to ask.

He smiled at her. 'None. I have just fought the battle of my life, I do not want to spend the next few years battling to have magic accepted on Hand. I want to go where I will be welcomed.'

Emer blushed. 'You will certainly be welcomed in Sanctuary.'

A warm glow spread through him as he thought how pretty Emer looked in the finery she had borrowed from Aliah, but if he was honest, he thought she was far more beautiful in her travelling clothes.

'What is that stupid grin about?' Aliah interrupted.

'What?'

'Never mind. I just asked your father what happened with Robin. He said he was so ashamed of his behaviour he would not accept the holding. But Duke Damon is going to put it aside for him anyway.'

'Aliah, this is a celebration. Leave Seamus alone and let him enjoy the, um, company,' Dominic interrupted, nodding his head towards Emer. 'There is plenty of time for business tomorrow.'

Seamus felt a blush rising, but none-the-less was grateful when Aliah sat back down and he could return his attention to Emer.

STANDING by the ship leaving for Port Marden, Aliah waited for Seamus to say goodbye to his parents and brother. Cara had been so upset at Seamus' leaving again, she refused to come out of her room. Understanding how much her rejection hurt Seamus, Aliah had persuaded the young girl to at least say goodbye to her brother, but Cara drew the line at coming to the docks.

The new heir to the Duchy of Hand wandered over to stand beside Emer, who appeared very uncomfortable at being included in the family farewells. Jonas gave her a rough hug goodbye, and she seemed to relax a little.

Maybe Seamus and Emer were not quite there yet, but everyone else knew these two were much better together than they were apart. Perhaps once Seamus was settled in his new home, he would feel confident enough to start courting the girl from Sanctuary.

'Matchmaking, I see.' Dominic's voice came from close by her ear.

'I really wish you would make some sort of noise when you approach.'

Laughing, he answered. 'Sorry, occupational hazard.'

'Have you forgotten already? You are now Ambassador to Hand. You need no longer skulk in the shadows. And I do not think those two will need any assistance finding they are made for each other.'

She leaned back into the arms Dominic wrapped around her. 'Besides, is it wrong to want everyone to be as happy as I am?'

'I guess not, I was merely stating my surprise at your not having managed Seamus and Emer's lives as well as you organised our own.'

The lightness in his tone told Aliah he was teasing. In fact, Dominic knew just how abysmal she had been at sorting out their future. She had consulted with Dominic before meeting with her father after his arrival on Hand a few days ago. They had discussed what they both wanted, but she feared she did not have the skills to enable her to persuade King Terion.

Flushed with the success of their campaign, and relieved Aliah survived unhurt, King Terion wanted nothing more than to wrap his daughter up and return her home to Bannock. Part of Aliah wanted that too, but mostly, she knew she could not return to her old life. She had proven to herself she was more than an adornment, and she wanted a real role governing Aria.

She also wanted Dominic, and there in lay the problem. The second son of a duke was not going to be accepted as the next King of Aria, which meant they would not be able to marry, something Aliah planned for their future together. Aliah even had a solution to that problem. When her father was ready to step down from the throne, they would become joint rulers of Aria.

Now all she needed to do was convince her father. Arming herself with as many arguments as she was able to cram into her head, she met with the king in private. After their reunion, he sensed she was anxious about something.

'Father, we need to discuss my future.' She raised the subject in a non-threatening way, just as Dominic schooled her.

'We do indeed. I asked Duke Damon if you can stay here with him a while longer. Although most of the Carsten Army decided to return home and rebuild their country, there are some who lost everything and wish to remain here in Aria. I would like you to work to find them all suitable homes and employment. Of course, you will also have to help overcome some resentment from many Arian's who do not wish to have the enemy stay on. Are you up to that?'

Taken by surprise, Aliah was unsure of what to say. 'I can only try,' was the best she could come up with.

'That is all I can ask for in such a difficult role. I instructed the leaders of each town and village to come up with a list of skills they lost with the deaths of our soldiers during the war. I would like you to work with the people left here. Make sure they are housed, clothed and fed, and start matching them to the gaps. Then there will be plenty of work helping the two communities accept each other.'

This was more than she hoped for; a real position helping real people. Her delight in her new role was tempered as she remembered the other side of her problem.

'I would be happy to do that father, but it is too big a job for one person. Perhaps Dominic could aid me.'

Her heart sank at her father's answer. 'I am afraid that will not be possible. I arranged a very important job for him, if he will take it.'

'And that would be?'

'Between him and me, my love. Are you interested in helping the refugees, or shall I find someone else for the job?'

'No, I am interested, it is just I wanted to talk to you about Dominic too.'

'I felt certain you would, but I need to talk with him first, and there are a number of other people I have to meet with. Maybe we can talk again later.' Kissing her on top of the head, he practically bundled her out of the room.

Unable to speak to Dominic until later that evening, she spent a very fruitful day with Martha sorting out long term living arrangements. Since Robin's disappearance, the housekeeper had taken on more of the household management, and was thriving with her new duties.

Before dinner that evening, Dominic slipped into her room, excited to tell her what he had agreed with her father.

'You agreed to something without talking with me first?' she demanded, hands on hips.

'So are you telling me you did not accept your father's offer already?' Dominic did not back down. 'I at least got your father to reassure me we would be together, or close by, over the next few moon turns. Did you even do that?'

Scrunching her face in annoyance, Aliah admitted she had not thought to check where Dominic would be before saying yes. 'All right, I am sorry. Clearly I am not as good at this as you are.'

Dominic drew her into his arms. 'You are forgiven. Now, do you want to hear my news?'

'Yes, I do. Please tell me you are not to be sent off spying somewhere. Or that my father has appointed you Chief Spymaster.'

'No, I am not going anywhere. I am to stay in Hand as Ambassador from the Court of Aria. There has been no posting here, ever, but the duke has agreed to my staying. In return, I am to assist with moving Hand towards accepting more of the laws of Aria, including the use of magic.'

'Wow, Dominic, that is fantastic news. If you can bring Hand into the Arian fold, well ...'

'... people will begin to look to me as someone who might be able to rule at your side someday?'

'Exactly, and as I am ...'

'... staying here on Hand, we can still be together. Although the duke has provided a house for me, and you will be residing here, in the palace.'

'You found out about what father asked me to do? That is so annoying.'

'No, what is really annoying is your father planned this all before he even arrived. I am not sure whether to be upset he organised us in this way, or grateful for his forethought.'

Dominic moved into his residence, and Aliah moved into Seamus' old room in the family quarters. As the Heir Apparent, Jonas had been given his own suite in the palace, and Cara had been moved into his old room. Duchess Elise thought Aliah would be more comfortable living with the family, adding Cara would benefit from having the older girl for company. Aliah also thought Duke Damon was more relaxed with her being close by until she and Dominic were formally betrothed.

'What are you thinking now?' Dominic's words brought her back to the present.

'I am thinking how lucky we all are.'

She pointed to Liam making his way up the gangplank on crutches. It seemed he would get to keep his leg, but he would never become the Guard Captain he had hoped to be. Still, his future looked bright.

'Liam has a new position as Ambassador to Sanctuary on behalf of Aria and Hand. Also, from what Emer tells me, there is a certain young lady waiting for his return.'

Gesturing to Walter, who was overseeing the correct storage of some special trunks, she added, 'Walter has raided the library here and cannot wait to ensconce himself in Sanctuary, comparing histories and starting a magic school. I have no doubt he and Amelia will settle in well together.'

Dominic and Aliah laughed as Amelia headed towards her new husband. Although unable to see as such, she could now confidently move around using her "new sight" as she called it.

'I am going to help Walter with those trunks. He will not be happy until they are stored to his satisfaction.' Dominic kissed the top of her head before leaving her to her thoughts.

Although pleased to have survived their recent ordeal, and she was happy she and her friends were embarking on new phases of their lives, she was somewhat reluctant to say goodbye to Seamus.

They met only a few moon turns ago, yet their experiences together had drawn them closer than most brothers and sisters, and for him to be heading away felt like losing an arm.

Oh, no, he was coming over. What was she going to say? What could she say as a suitable farewell to someone who had become such an important part of her life; to the boy who helped her grow from a disenchanted princess to a potential queen.

As HE WALKED TOWARDS HER, Aliah looked like an animal caught in a trap. If he had not known better, he would have thought she did not want to say goodbye to him at all. Pausing for a moment, he thought, I do not really want to part from her either.

'Stay here with us,' Aliah said as he stopped in front of her. 'Well, at least in Port Marden, until your father fixes things here.'

'You know that would not work. Jonas needs to be seen as the heir now, and that will never happen while I am still around. Also, I cannot spend my life waiting for something that might never be.'

She sighed as he hugged her. 'I know.' Her voice was muffled by his chest. 'You might still take father up on his offer of a position as one of his advisors. We could see each other more often if you did.'

'I could, that is true. And believe me I gave it deep consideration. But I think it is time for me to figure out what I want to do with my life on my own. I have put it off for too long now.'

Seamus stopped, trying to put into words the turmoil he experienced the last few days as he attempted to plan his future.

'When I rescued you and left home, I knew I was never going to be Duke of Hand, but I did not know who I was other than Heir to the Duchy. Nor did I know what to do with my life. I thought my only option was going to train on the Wizard Isles, but even then, it was just to be doing something.

'I guess back then neither of us were happy with our futures, but you know you want to rule Aria. You always have. Now you are openly working towards that goal, and it obviously makes you happy. Well, that and Dominic.

'I am a work in progress. I am not a duke, nor will I ever be. I am a wizard with unusual skills. Not good at one thing in particular, except fighting gods, and I hope there will not be much call for that sort of thing in the future.

'I need more. I need to know what I can contribute. So, I am escorting everyone back to Sanctuary and I agreed to stay on and help Amelia and Walter set up their school. I will also work with Walter, showing him how my magic is different.

'While I am in Sanctuary, perhaps I can find out who I am and what I am meant to do with my life.'

Aliah pushed herself out of his embrace. 'Seamus, that is plain self-indulgent. Not everyone in life needs a grand plan, nor will they play a pivotal role in history and have ballads sung in their honour.

'Most people are happy to have enough food in their bellies, a roof over their heads and to be around people they love. While you have family and friends, you are someone—someone special, to them.

'We have been lucky—is that the right word? We were involved in some of the greatest events in our lifetime. Nothing else will be able to compare to that. All we can do now is what is right for us. Why did you decide to go to Sanctuary, given all the other options on the table?'

Seamus thought for a moment before answering. 'The people. If I cannot be with my parents and siblings on Hand, I want to be with the rest of my family; my family, and Emer. And I will be doing more with my gifts than fighting, I will be adding to our understanding of magic and the gods' influences on the world.'

In the whole time he had known Aliah, he had never really felt comfortable in his own skin, but at that moment, she had given him something greater than any other gift he had received; she had given him his identity. He finally realised he was no longer running without direction, but was headed right where he needed to be.

Hugging her to him again, he whispered, 'Thank you,' into her hair.

EPILOGUE

X anthos glared belligerently at his brothers and sisters.

'You think you have won, but deep down you know the real threat is still out there. Only one of us had the guts to go and attempt to stop it from destroying all the lands of the furthest world.

'It has been waiting a long time, and you know once it is finished there, it will turn inwards, to us.'

'We know. We also know you still believe you might have stopped it, but at what cost? Would any life have been left on that world once you were done? Or on any of the others it must travel through to reach us? Would there have been balance in the universe?'

Oh how it made his blood boil when they spoke to him in one voice.

'What is your solution? Another prophecy? More human heroes? The darkness will not be obliterated that way.'

'Our role is not to destroy, but to maintain the balance.'

'Do you believe keeping things in balance will be enough? I think not. But what can I do now I am trapped back here with you all? You won, and now we are forced to do things your way.

'When the great evil stirs, as it inevitably will, we will find out whether or not your way is enough.'

Xanthos turned his back on the gathering, and waited for them to leave his home. Suddenly weary, he sank into a chair and closed his eyes.

As the God of Chaos, he had drawn power from the turmoil he created in his time on the far world. He had not done it for his own glory, but to fight their greatest foe. If he had managed to send the whole world into chaos, he may still not have generated enough power to defeat the evil presence lurking in the darkness below.

However, his brothers and sisters had ensured he would never know.

THE END

About the Author

Vivienne has been writing books since she was fifteen years old, but only friends and family were allowed to read them. Forced to give up work because of family commitments she was encouraged by friends and family to finally put some of her writing out there for others to read.

In the real world after leaving university with a BA in History and Politics she worked as a Personnel Officer, an Office Manager, a Project Manager, a DBA and IT Manager then as a Business and Data Analyst, adding an MSC in Information Systems along the way. In her world she continued to write.

Born in Invercargill (New Zealand), she has lived in; Dunedin (New Zealand), London (England), Petersfield (England) and currently lives with her husband and son and their dog Trouble and kitten Lola in Sydney (Australia).

For future releases and current news you can find Vivienne at www.viviennelfraser.com.au

ACKNOWLEDGMENTS

This series was years in the making and and I have had so much help and support along the way it has been almost unbelievable.

I had proof-readers and pre-readers galore; Sandra Korres, Marj Fox, Avis Williamson, Gary Halder and Amanda Harle. Thank you all for your input, support and comments.

Heather Bosevski, an amazing author in her own right, edited this series. Heather, you challenged me to write better and to improve my story and characters, and I shall miss your little comments as you edited. This series was all the better for your input and guidance, as am I.

The publishing of this series would not have been so easy (haha) without the help of K. A. Last. The fantastic original covers and the cover for this series are due to her amazing skills under the guise of Kila Designs. However, her biggest influence was sharing her self publishing knowledge and experience, and really this book would not be what it is without her—in fact it probably would not have been here at all. You can find her amazing stories at www. kalastbooks.com.au.

Thank you also to Anna Basel who did all the original illustrations. You patience working through ideas with me helped bring my tale to life, and added that little bit extra to help reluctant readers with my books. Unfortunately not all the images made it into this version, I only picked the best of the best.

I have to acknowledge my constant writing companion, Trouble. When everyone else is out and I am alone in my fictional world

Trouble is always there forcing me to break with his need for ball throwing. I should also thank Lola, but her contribution is more in the way of standing in front of my screen demanding attention.

Thank you also to Sam, the reason I started writing YA fiction. Your comments, both the brutal and the supportive ones, have influenced this series, but have also inspired series two; which is almost planned and ready to write.

And lastly, but never least, I thank my lovely husband Jim who supports all of this and respects my writing as the hard job it. He picks up the cooking and cleaning duties when I have a deadline, reads all my books and even takes time to produce the maps of Aria. You are indeed my lobster.

As always I want to thank you for reading my book. I feel humbled that you took time out of your busy life to read my flights of fancy. I hope I managed to transport you to another world for a short time, and I hope you will carry on this journey with me and read Admina's Argument, which is due for release early 2021.

www.ingramcontent.com/pod-product-compliance
Lightning Source LLC
Chambersburg PA
CBHW070341030726
47504CB00001B/32